King's Dragon

King's Dragon

VOLUME ONE

OF

CROWN OF STARS

Kate Elliott

DAW BOOKS, INC.

DONALD A. WOLLHEIM, FOUNDER

375 Hudson Street, New York, NY 10014

ELIZABETH R. WOLLHEIM
SHEILA E. GILBERT
PUBLISHERS

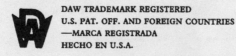

This book is lovingly dedicated to my sister,
Ann Marie Rasmussen.

AUTHOR'S NOTE

My thanks to Katharine Kerr for supplying me with a title when all seemed lost;

to my husband, Jay Silverstein, for his continued support while he has himself been engaged in a great enterprise;

to the Reverend Jeanne Reames Zimmerman, O.S.L., for her immense aid with matters classical and linguistic;

to my sister, Dr. Ann Marie Rasmussen, whose knowledge of the medieval milieu was invaluable;

to Dr. John W. Bernhardt, whose lecture on itinerant kingship in Ottonian Germany inspired the setting;

and to Widukind of Corvey, monk and historian, whose History of the Saxons—made accessible to me through a 1949 translation into English by Raymund F. Wood—spoke to me across a thousand years.

Since this is a fantasy, many details borrowed from our Middle Ages—large and small—have been altered, but all mistakes are mine alone.

RECENT RULERS OF WENDAR AND VARRE

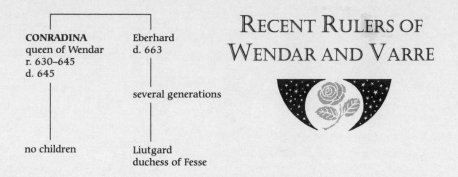

CONRADINA
queen of Wendar
r. 630–645
d. 645

Eberhard
d. 663

several generations

no children

Liutgard
duchess of Fesse

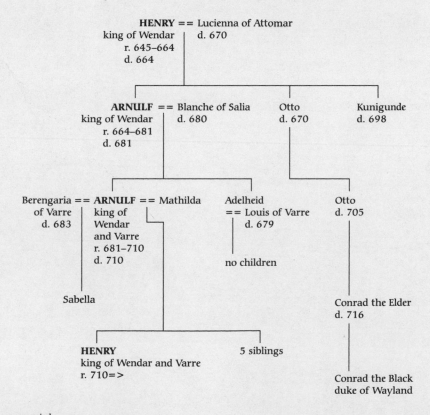

HENRY == Lucienna of Attomar
king of Wendar | d. 670
r. 645–664
d. 664

ARNULF == Blanche of Salia
king of Wendar | d. 680
r. 664–681
d. 681

Otto
d. 670

Kunigunde
d. 698

Berengaria == **ARNULF** == Mathilda
of Varre | king of
d. 683 | Wendar
and Varre
r. 681–710
d. 710

Adelheid
== Louis of Varre
d. 679

no children

Otto
d. 705

Sabella

HENRY
king of Wendar and Varre
r. 710=>

5 siblings

Conrad the Elder
d. 716

Conrad the Black
duke of Wayland

== married
r. reigned
d. died

CONTENTS

PROLOGUE   *1*

PART ONE

🌹

THE MOTHERLESS CHILD

I   A Storm from the Sea   *11*

II   The Book of Secrets   *33*

III   Shadows from the Past   *57*

IV   The Treasure-House   *89*

V   The Inner Heart   *131*

VI   The City of Memory   *177*

VII   Leavetaking   *209*

PART TWO

🌹

THE DEEDS OF THE GREAT PRINCES

VIII   On the King's Progress   *233*

IX   The Dragons   *247*

X   The Sin of Pride   *289*

XI A Mouse's Hunger   323

XII Bloodheart   363

XIII The Shadow of the *Guivre*   431

XIV The Promise of Power   471

EPILOGUE   523

PROLOGUE

ON a hill surrounded on three sides by forest and on the fourth by the ruins of a fortress stood a ring of stones. They crowned the hill with stark beauty, like the bones of a castle buried so deeply in the soil that only the battlements of the tallest tower rose above the earth. It was said by some that chambers lay beneath the standing stones, rooms filled with treasure, with haunts, with creatures not of human form. It was said that passageways led out from these chambers like rivers stretching from a landlocked lake, leading from this hill across the land, even to the cold sea in the north, even to the great mountains far to the south.

On the third day of the month of Avril, as afternoon faded into twilight and the full moon shone low in the darkening sky, a lone traveler made her way up through the tumbled stones of the old fortress. She wore leggings, a plain linen tunic, and sandals laced up to her knees, human clothing which she had become accustomed to here in this foreign land but not what she felt comfortable in. With a staff gripped in one hand and a small pouch tied to her belt, she negotiated the maze of walls as if she knew it by heart.

The ruins lay on a gentle incline, stretching from the banks of a narrow river up to where the last wall, no taller than a year-old child, lay crumbling into the dirt and grass. The forest rose beyond. A single watch fire burned on the other side of the river, past the stumps of felled trees and fields newly burned for a spring planting of barley, marking the only village that lay within sight of the hill crowned by stones.

The traveler paused before she stepped over the last wall of the fortress. She threw back her hood. Her hair was so pale it seemed to shine with a light of its own. She reached into the pouch and drew out a scrap of torn cloth, stained with red. With a grimace, she made to cast it to the ground, as if by throwing it away she would free herself from its binding power before she passed into the wild majesty of the stones.

But she paused, cocking her head to one side, listening. And she cursed. She hesitated, and that moment was enough for the lead horseman to spot her.

It was dusk, but her hair was bright and his eyes were young and keen, and he was looking for her.

"Alia!" he cried. "Beloved!" Recklessly, he urged his horse forward, picking his way up through the fort. More riders appeared behind him. He paused, reining his mount aside, so men on foot, carrying torches, could catch up and guide him forward. He used only one hand on the reins. In his other arm he carried a bundle of cloth tucked against his chest.

She winced away from the sight of that small burden. The vow she had made years ago, as humans measured time, seemed rash and ugly now. She had stood up in front of the assembled council and spoken boldly, but she had not known then what she would suffer in the world of men.

Then her gaze caught on a banner. A battle-scarred man in a gold and black surcoat closed the gap between himself and the young prince. Upright and arrogant in the saddle, he held in one hand the dragon banner, symbol of the elite guards who protected the heir and by extension the kingdom itself: a black dragon coiled on a gold background; a cluster of seven brilliant stars studded the gold field above the dragon's figure. She traced this constellation with her gaze to remind herself of what it stood for, the Crown of Stars worn by the ruler of the ancient Empire, half-forgotten now in the world of humankind but destined to return. It was for this she had made the sacrifice.

By this time, aided by her hesitation, the young prince had pulled his horse up beside her. Torches threw wings of light over the ruins, and their heat surrounded her like a prison built with walls of fire.

"Why did you follow me?" she asked. "You knew I intended to leave."

"How can you leave?" he demanded, like a child wailing against being abandoned. But he was so young, barely a man, only eighteen years old according to the calendars of this world. With an effort he schooled his expression to one of haughty disdain and tried a different path. "Surely you will stay until the child is a year or two old, so you might know that it lives and thrives."

"No disease known to you will touch him, nor will any wound

inflicted by any creature male or female cause his death." She spoke without thinking.

A murmur, like the breath of wind through a forest, passed through the assembled soldiers, those close enough to hear her prophesy whispering her words to those who stood farther away. The old soldier urged his horse forward to halt beside the young prince. The dragon banner lapped over the saddle, brushing the young man's arm.

At that moment, the bundle stirred. The baby woke, batting aside the swaddling with blind infant groping. She saw the black shock of hair that crowned the baby's head, the tiny face and its open, staring eyes, as vivid as fine green jade, its skin that marked it as flesh of her flesh, a fine burnished bronze nothing like the northern pallor of the young prince's complexion even where it was roughened by exposure to sun and wind. The tiny hand closed on a corner of the dragon banner, gripping it with infant strength. The men-at-arms pointed and exclaimed over this omen: The bastard child born of no human woman sensed its fate already, though it was not yet two months old.

The prince turned his face away, not wanting to look. Instead, he carefully—so carefully!—handed the baby over to the old soldier, who gave the banner into another man's hands in order to hold the infant. Then he dismounted, gestured to his men to move away, and faced her.

"You care nothing for the child?"

She did not look after the old soldier as he guided his horse to a patch of ground less racked with loose stone and sudden sharp drop-offs that might catch a horse unawares.

"He is no longer mine."

"How can you say so? He is the most beautiful child I have ever seen!"

"Only because he is yours!"

"Yours as well!"

"Not mine! I carried it inside me, gave birth to it, bled enough blood to cover the fields that surround the village we just passed through! Never mine, and never meant to be. Leave me, Henri." She had never learned the eastern accent and still spoke his name as a Salian would. "I never promised you anything but the child. Let me go in peace."

The young man said nothing for a long time, or at least, not in words. He had an expressive face, but he was learning to control it. She wondered, watching him, what he wanted to say, and what he would say. When she had first met him a year ago, he'd always blurted out the first words that came to his tongue. Now, made heir by right of fertility, he was learning to think before he spoke.

"I do not want to let you go," he said at last. "By the invocation of your name, Alia, I beg you to stay with me."

"Alia is not my name, Henri. It is only what you call me."

"You aren't well enough to go. You were so ill after the birth."

"I am well enough now."

"Then why did you come to me? Don't you love me at all?" His voice broke on the last words and a moment later he caught himself and tensed, his face freezing into a mask of stone.

That mask, she thought, *will be the one he wears most often when he becomes king.*

She thought of telling him the truth, because she did not dislike him. He was still young, a little callow, but he had strength in him, and he was ambitious, and clever, and handsome in a human way, elegant and proud.

But the truth was not hers to tell, nor his to know. King he might become, but he was only a pawn in hands whose power was greater than his would ever be as regnant of two kingdoms. She and he were both pawns, and this gave her some sympathy for him.

She leaned forward and kissed him on the mouth. "I am not immune to human charms," she lied. "But my duty lies elsewhere." That at least was true.

She could not bear to hear more from him. She could stay in this world no longer. It weighed too heavily on her; it had stolen so much of her precious blood. She fingered the scrap of bloody cloth, torn from the sheets in which she had given birth; it—and what it signified, her link to the child—was the last thing that bound her here. She let go of the bloody rag, and it fluttered to the ground.

As he knelt to pick it up, she stepped across the last crumbling wall. He rose, calling after her, but he did not try to follow. Nor could she really hear his voice any longer as the stones rose up before her and she heard at last the faint music of their alignment singing to her.

With her inner sight she touched the wind stone, the stone of light, the stone of blood, of water, of fire, the other stones, each according to its properties. Here, in the human world, in order to touch the heart of any object, to find and manipulate its essence, she had to trace winding paths around the walls and barriers built by human magi, for they chose to constrain and then master what they could not understand. But as she entered the precinct of stone, those walls fell away. She lifted a hand. Mist arises from the commingling of water and air, and so mist rose around her, at her suggestion, hiding her from view as she entered the ring of stones.

Above her, unobscured by the mist that surrounded her, stars shone. She read their alignment and called down the power that sang from them and melded it to the alignment of the stones, each to each, a choir raising its voice to heaven. She called to the heart of her own land, and at the altar of fire and blood a portal opened.

Neither a door nor a wispy shimmering of air, it looked like an arbor, a lush flowering vine grown over an arch. She smelled snow and felt the cold sting of a winter wind beyond. Without hesitation she stepped through and left the world of humankind behind.

Prince Henry, heir to the kingdoms of Wendar and Varre, watched Alia walk away from him, up into the ring of stones. He steeled his face, his heart, his whole body, and when the mist rose and covered her, he simply tightened his hand on the scrap of cloth she had left behind that contained all he had left of her: her blood.

Three of his men stood beside him, holding up torches to drive back the mist that had swollen suddenly from the ground, a night-crawling fog that surrounded the stones. Light flashed within the stone ring. A chill wind stung his lips. A perfect crystal flake of snow spiraled down on the last of the wind and dissolved on his boot. Mist still clung about the stones.

"Shall we go up, my lord, and look for her?" asked one of his men.

"No. She is gone."

He tucked the cloth into his belt and called for his horse. Mounted, he took the baby back into the crook of his arm and, with his entourage around him, began the slow descent of the hill. The baby did not cry, but its eyes were open, and it stared at the heavens, or at its father, or at the dragon banner. Who could tell?

A breeze swelled out from the stones, and mist rolled down over the ruins from the height of the hill, swathing the crumbling buildings in a sudden thick fog and hiding the moon. The men picked their way carefully, men on foot grabbing hold of horses' harnesses, the rest calling out to each other, marking distance by the sound of their voices.

"You are better off without a woman like that," said the old soldier suddenly to the prince in the tone of a man who has the right to give advice. "The church would never have accepted her. And she has power over the ways of nature which it were better not to meddle with." The dragon banner hung limp, sodden with the weight of the fog, as if this unnatural mist was trying to drag the banner down.

But the prince did not reply. He kept his gaze on the torches surrounding him, like watch fires, light thrown against the gloom.

A ring of seven candles, light thrown against the gloom.

Watchers stared into a mist that rose from a huge block of obsidian set in their midst. Their faces were hidden by darkness.

In the mist they saw tiny figures, a young nobleman carrying an infant, ringed by his faithful followers. Slowly these figures descended through a fortress, seen half as ruins, half as the ghost of the fortress that was once whole. The tiny figures walked through walls as if they were air, for they *were* air, and it was only the memory of what was once there, in the minds of some few of the watchers, that created the ghostly walls, the suggestion of the past built anew.

"We must kill the child," said one of the watchers as the mist faded, sinking into the black stone. With it faded the image of the prince and his retinue.

"The child is too well protected," said a second.

"We must attempt it, for they intend to shatter the world itself."

The first among the watchers shifted, and the others, who had been whispering among themselves, stilled into an uncanny silence.

"It is never wise to seek only to destroy," said she who sat first among them. Her voice was rich and deep. "That way lies ruin only. That way lies darkness."

"Then what?" demanded the first speaker. He shrugged impatiently. Candlelight glinted off his white hair.

"Just as the Enemy turns the faithful from the Path of Light toward the Abyss, so can unbelievers be turned away from their error to see the promise of the Chamber of Light. We must counter the power given into the hands of this unwitting child with power of our own."

"There is this difference," said the second speaker, "that while we know our opponents exist, they do not know of us."

"Or so we believe," said the first man. He sat stiffly, a man of action unaccustomed to long stillnesses.

"We must trust to Our Lord and Lady," said the woman, and the rest nodded and murmured agreement.

The only light given to their circle was that flickering from the candles, bright flames throwing sharp glints on the surface of the obsidian altar, and that from the stars above and the round, still globe of the moon. Great blocks of shadow surrounded them, an entourage of giants.

Beyond, wind muttered through the open shells of buildings, unseen but felt, the last relics of a great empire lost long ago to fire and sword and blood and magic. The ruins ended at a shoreline as abruptly as if a knife had sheared them off. Surf hissed and swelled at the verge. Sand got caught up on the wind and swirled up from the shore into the circle, catching on tongues and in the folds of cloaks.

One of the watchers shivered and tugged a hood hard down over her hair. "It's a fool's errand," this one said. "They are stronger than we are, here and in their own country."

"Then we must reach for powers that are greater still," said she who sat first among them.

They responded to her words with expectant silence.

"I will make the sacrifice," she continued. "I alone. They wish to sunder the world while we desire only to bring it closer to the Chamber of Light toward which all our souls strive. If they bring one agent into the world, then we must bring another. Of ourselves we cannot defeat them."

One by one they bowed their heads, acquiescing to her judgment, until only one man remained, head unbowed. He rested a hand on the woman's shoulder and spoke. "You will not be alone."

In this way they considered in silence. The great ruins lay around them, echoing their silence, the skeleton of a city unattended by ghost walls or visions of past grandeur. Sand skirled up the streets, spattering against stone, grain by grain erasing the vast murals that adorned the long walls. But where the walls marched out to the sea, where the knife-edge cut them clean, the shadow form of the old city mingled with the waves, the memory of what once had been—not drowned by the sea but utterly *gone*.

Stars wheeled above on their endless round.

The candles illuminated the gleaming surface of the obsidian altar. In its black depths an image of the distant ring of stones, far to the north, still stood, and the last torches borne by the prince's retinue flickered and faded into nothing as they passed beyond view.

PART ONE

THE
MOTHERLESS
CHILD

I
A STORM FROM THE SEA

1

WHEN winter turned to spring and the village deacon sang the mass in honor of St. Thecla's witnessing of the Ekstasis of the blessed Daisan, it came time to prepare the boats for the sailing season and the summer's journeying to other ports.

Alain had tarred his father's boat in the autumn; now he examined the hull, crawling beneath the boat where it had wintered on the beach on a bed of logs. The old boat had weathered the winter well, but one plank was loose. He fastened the plank with a willow treenail, stuffing sheep's wool greased with tar into the gap and driving the nail home onto a grommet also made of wool. Otherwise the boat was sound. After Holy Week his father would load the boat with casks of oil and with quernstones brought in from nearby quarries and finished in workshops in the village.

But Alain would not be going with him, though he had begged to be given the chance, just this one season.

He turned, hearing laughter from up the strand where the road ran in to the village. He wiped his hands on a rag and waited for his father to finish speaking with the other Osna merchants who had come down to examine their boats, to make ready for the voyage out now that Holy Week had ended.

"Come, son," said Henri after he had looked over the boat. "Your aunt has prepared a fine feast and then we'll pray for good weather at the midnight bell."

They walked back to Osna village in silence. Henri was a broad-shouldered man, not very tall, his brown hair shot through with silver. Henri spent most of the year away, visiting ports all up and down the coast, and during the winter he sat in his quiet way in his sister Bel's workshop and built chairs and benches and tables. He spoke little, and when he did speak did so in a soft voice quite unlike his sister's, who, everyone joked, could intimidate a wolf with her sharp tongue.

Alain had darker hair and was certainly taller, lanky enough that he was likely to grow more just as certain spring days are likely to bring squalls and sudden bursts of rain. As usual, Alain did not quite know what to say to his father, but this day as they walked along the sandy path he tried, one more time, to change his father's mind.

"Julien sailed with you the year he turned sixteen, even *before* he spent his year in the count's service! Why can't I go this year?"

"It can't be. I swore to the deacon at Lavas Holding when you were just a new babe come into the world that I would give you to the church. That is the only reason she let me foster you."

"If I must take vows and spend the rest of my life within the monastery walls, then why can't I have just one season with you to see the world? I don't want to be like Brother Gilles—"

"Brother Gilles is a good man," said Henri sharply.

"Yes, he is, but he hasn't set foot off monastery lands since the day he entered as a child of seven! It isn't right you condemn me to that. At least one season with you would give me something to remember."

"Brother Gilles and his fellow monks are content enough."

"I'm not Brother Gilles!"

"We have spoken of this before, Alain. You are of age now and promised to the church. All will pass as Our Lord and Lady have decreed. It is not for you or me to question their judgment."

By the way Henri set his mouth, Alain knew that his father would not reply to any further argument. Furious, he strode ahead, his longer strides taking him out in front of his father, though it was rude. Just one season! One season to see something of the world, to see distant ports and unfamiliar coastlines, to speak with men from other towns, from other lands, to see something of the strange lands the deacon spoke of when she read the lessons and saints' lives of fraters—the wandering priests—who brought the Holy Word of the Unities to barbarous lands. Why was that so much to ask? He crossed through the livestock palisade and by the time he reached Aunt Bel's longhouse, his mood was thoroughly foul.

Aunt Bel stood in the garden examining her newly planted parsley and horseradish. She straightened, measuring him, and shook her head. "There's water to fetch before feasting," she said.

"That's Julien's job today."

"Julien is mending sail, and I'll ask you not to question me, child. Do as you're told. Don't argue with your father, Alain. You know he's the stubbornest man in the village."

"He's not my father!" shouted Alain.

For that he got a sharp slap in the face, delivered with all the force of thirty years of kneading bread and chopping wood behind it. It brought a red stain to his cheek and silence to his lips.

"Never speak so again of the man who raised you. Now, go on."

He went, because no one dared argue with Bel, elder sister of Henri the merchant and mother of eight children, of whom five still lived.

He sat at the evening's feast in silence and went in silence to the church. The moon was full, and its pale light filtered in through the new glass window which the merchants and householders of Osna had bought for the village church. But with moonlight and candlelight there was illumination enough to see the walls, whitewashing over timber, painted with the huge murals depicting the life of the blessed Daisan and the deeds of the glorious saints and martyrs.

The deacon raised her hands in the blessing and began to sing the liturgy.

"Blessed is the Country of the Mother and Father of Life, and of the Holy Word revealed within the Circle of Unity, now and ever and unto ages of ages."

"Amen," he murmured with the congregation.

"In peace let us pray to Our Lord and Lady."

"Kyrie eleison." *Lord have mercy.* He clasped his hands and tried to pay attention as the deacon circled the church, pacing out the stations marking the blessed Daisan's life and ministry, bringing to the faithful the Holy Word granted him by the grace of the Lord and Lady. "Kyria eleison." *Lady have mercy.*

On the walls stark pictures stood out brightly in the light cast by torches. There, the blessed Daisan at the fire where first he encountered the vision of the Circle of Unity. And again, the blessed Daisan with his followers refusing to kneel and worship before the Dariyan Empress Thaissania, she of the mask. The seven miracles, each one depicted with loving detail. And last, the blessed Daisan dead at the Hearth from which his spirit was lifted up through the seven spheres to the Chamber of Light, while his great disciple St. Thecla wept below, her tears feeding the sanctified cup.

But to Alain's eyes, there in the midnight church, other more shadowy forms lay as if hidden beneath the bright murals, their outlines embellished with fine gold, their eyes like jewels, their presence like fire on his soul.

The fall of the ancient city of Dariya to savage horsemen, its last defenders clothed in gleaming bronze armor, spears and shields raised as they fought a hopeless fight but with the honor of men who will not bow down before an honorless enemy.

Not images from the church at all, but the stories of brilliant lives of old warriors. They haunted him.

The fateful Battle of Auxelles, where Taillefer's nephew and his men lost their lives but saved Taillefer's fledgling empire from invasion by heathens.

"For healthful seasons, for the abundance of the fruits of the earth, and for peaceful times, let us pray."

The glorious victory of the first King Henry of Wendar against Quman invaders along the River Eldar, where his bastard grandson Conrad the Dragon charged his troop of cavalry straight into the midst of the terrible host of Quman riders, breaking their line and sending them scattering back to their own lands, hunting them down like animals as they fled.

"Blessed are they that mourn, for they shall be comforted. Blessed are the merciful, for they shall obtain mercy. Blessed are the pure in heart, for they shall speak with the Holy Word upon their tongues."

The last ride of King Louis of Varre, just fifteen years old but undaunted by the approach of raider ships on the northern coast of his kingdom, killed at the Battle of the Nysa though no man knew whose hand had struck the final blow. Had it been that of a raider prince, or that of a traitor serving the schemes of the new king of Wendar who would, because of Louis' death, become king of Varre as well?

Instead of the voice of the deacon, reading the lesson, Alain heard the ring of harness, the clash of swords, the snap of banners in the wind, the sweet strength of the gathered warriors singing a Kyrie eleison as they rode into battle.

"For Thou art our sanctification, and unto Thee we ascribe glory, to the Mother, to the Father, and to the Holy Word spoken in the heavens, now, and ever, and unto ages of ages."

"Amen," he said, stumbling into the response as the congregation raised its voice as one in the final exclamation. "Let us depart in peace, in the Name of Our Lord and Lady. Have mercy upon us."

"Have mercy upon us," echoed his father, his voice as soft as the whisper of leaves on the roof.

He put an arm around Alain as they left the church and made their way by torchlight back to the longhouse.

"It is as it must be," he said, and Alain sensed that this was the last word Henri would ever speak on the matter. The choice had been made long ago, one to the sea, one to the heart of God.

"What was my mother like?" Alain asked suddenly.

"She was beautiful," said Henri. Alain heard the raw scrape of grief in his father's voice. He dared not ask more, for fear of breaking the wound wide open.

So they went inside and drank a last cup of warmed mulled wine. At dawn, Alain went down to the strand and saw them off, rolling the boat down the logs and onto the beach, shoving it into the waves. They loaded it with the cargo. Cousin Julien was white with excitement; he had gone once before but only to a nearby Varren port. He had never gone south for an entire season.

"Do honor to your kin," said Henri to Alain. He kissed Aunt Bel and then got in the boat last of all. The oarsmen began to row, and Julien fussed with the square sail.

Alain stood on the beach long after the others had gone back up the road to the village. He stood until he could no longer see any trace of sail on the gray-blue waters. At last he turned away from the sea, knowing Aunt Bel had work for him to do. With a heavy heart, he walked back to the village.

2

IN the distant haze where the sky met the sea, the islands that dotted Osna Sound rose as dark peaks of earth marking the horizon. When Alain stood, shading his eyes with a hand, and stared out across the bay toward the islands, the water gleamed like metal. It lay still and smooth, and from the height of the Dragonback Ridge the swells were lost under the glare of the sun. Up here, he could not feel a breath of wind. Out beyond the islands he saw a veil of low clouds pushing in toward land. Rain was coming.

For an instant, caught by a trick of the light, a white sheet of sail stood out, the merest speck that vanished into the horizon of cloud and iron-gray water as he watched. Perhaps it was his father, making his way out through the islands.

Alain sighed and turned away from the sea. He tugged on the rope, pulling the donkey away from a tuft of grass. It moved reluctantly, but it did move. Together they walked on, kicking sand up from the path that ran along the spine of the ridge, leading from the town to the monastery. The surf muttered far below.

The path began to slope down toward the Dragon's Tail, where the monastery lay. Soon Alain caught a glimpse of buildings spaced out around the church with its single tower. He lost sight of them again as the path cut down through tumbled boulders along the landward side of the ridge and, farther down still, turning to loam, wound through quiet forest.

He came out of the forest into cleared fields and soon enough trudged through the open gates and into the monastery that, on St. Eusebē's Day, would be his home for the rest of his life. Ai, Lord and Lady! Surely his guilt stained him red for all to see: The boy who loved the Father and Mother of Life and who yet rebelled in his heart against entering Their service. Ashamed, he stared at his feet as he skirted the outbuildings and arrived, finally, at the scriptorium.

Brother Gilles was waiting for him, patient as always, leaning on a walking stick.

"You have brought the tithe of candles from the village," the old monk said approvingly. "Ah, and I see a jar of oil as well."

Alain carefully unloaded the baskets slung by a rope harness on either side of the donkey. He set the bundle of candles, rolled up in heavy cloth, down on the tile floor of the scriptorium. Brother Gilles propped the door open. The few small windows were open as well, shutters tied back against the wall, but even so at the central lecterns it was dim work for the monks copying missals and lectionaries.

"The catch was poor last week," Alain said as he lifted out the jar of oil. "Aunt Bel promises that she will send two more jars after Ladysday."

"She is truly generous. The Lord and Lady will reward her for her service to Them. You may take the oil to the sacristy."

"Yes, Brother."

"I will go with you."

They walked outside, circling the church, passing the walled enclosure of the novitiate where Alain would soon be spending his days and nights.

"You are troubled, child," said Brother Gilles gently as he hobbled along beside Alain.

Alain flushed, fearing to tell him the truth, fearing to dishonor the covenant already agreed upon between the monastery and his father and aunt.

Brother Gilles grunted softly. "You are destined for the church, child, whether you wish it or not. I suppose you have heard too many stories of the great deeds of the Emperor Taillefer's warriors?"

Alain flushed more deeply but did not reply. He could not bear to lie to Brother Gilles, who had always treated him as kindly as if they were kin. Was it too much to ask to go only one time to Medemelacha or to ports farther south, even into the kingdom of Salia? To see with his own eyes the strange and wonderful things told of by the merchants who sailed out of Osna Sound each season? Such stories were told by all the merchants, except his father, of course, who was as talkative as a rock.

Imagine! He might pass men-at-arms bearing the standard of the Salian king. He might watch Hessi merchants, men from a foreign land so distant that none of the Osna merchants had ever visited their towns, men who had unusually dark skin and hair, who wore round pointed caps on their heads even when they were indoors, and who were said to pray to a god different than the Lord and Lady of Unities. He might speak with traders from the island of Alba, where, it was said, the Lost Ones still walked abroad in the deep forests, hidden to the sight of men. He might even hear the adventures of the fraters, wandering priests ready to venture out again to barbarous lands to bring the word of the blessed Daisan and the Church of Unities to people who lived outside the Light of the Holy Circle of Unity.

Once a year, during the summer, there was a great fair at Mede-melacha where any possible thing known to men might be bought or sold. Slaves from lands far to the south, where the sun, as fierce as a blacksmith's furnace (or so said the merchants), burned their skin black, and others from the ice lands who were so pale you could see right through them. Infant basilisks chained in shrouded cages. Goblin children from the Harenz Mountains, trained as rat-catchers. Bolts of silk from Arethousa. Cloisonné clasps in the shape of wolf heads, gold and green and blue, to ornament the belts and fasten the cloaks of noblemen. Finely wrought swords. Pitchers molded of white clay, painted with roundels and chevrons. Amber. Angel tears like beads of glass. Slivers of dragon's fire ossified into obsidian.

"You have left me, Alain."

He started back to himself, aware that he was standing like a lackwit ten paces from the door that led into the vestibule and thence to the sacristy, where the sacred vessels and vestments for the church were kept.

Smiling, Brother Gilles patted him on the arm. "You must accept what Our Lord and Lady have chosen for you, my child. For They *have* chosen. It remains only for you to understand what They ask of you, and to obey Them."

Alain hung his head. "I will, Brother."

He took the jar of oil inside and left it with one of sacrist brother's mute assistants. Coming back outside to an afternoon dimmed by the approach of clouds, he heard horses and the cheerful noise of riders unfettered by the vows of silence that most monks took.

Circling to the front of the church, he saw Father Richander, Brother Gilles, and the cellarer speaking with a group of visitors. The strangers were brightly dressed in tunics and capes trimmed with borders of red leaves and blue diamonds. There was a deacon and her attendant frater in drab brown robes, a woman with a fur-trimmed cloak, two well-dressed men, and a half dozen foot soldiers in boiled leather tunics. Imagine what it would be like to ride free of here, of the monastery, of the village, to ride outside the great Dragonback Ridge that bounded his world and venture into the world beyond!

He edged closer to listen.

"The usual tithe includes the service for a year of five young persons of sound body, does it not, Mistress Dhuoda?" Father Richander asked of the woman in the fur-trimmed cloak. "If you ask for more, then the townspeople may be forced to send some of the young persons we employ as servants here, and that would create hardship for us, especially now, in the planting season."

She had a haughty face, tempered by a grave expression. "That is true, Father, but there have been more raids along the coast this year, and Count Lavastine must increase his levy."

Count Lavastine! Mistress Dhuoda was his chatelaine; Alain recognized her now, as she turned toward him to gesture to the soldiers accompanying her. If he could not sail with his father then he had hoped that at least he might be called to service in Count Lavastine's levy, even if only for one year. But it was not to be. Alain knew why. Everyone knew why. The church was the suitable place for the child Merchant Henri had acknowledged and raised as his own but whom everyone knew was really the bastard child of a whore.

"God speed you on your journey, Mistress," said Father Richander as chatelaine and deacon mounted their horses. The soldiers readied themselves to walk.

Brother Gilles limped over to Alain. "If you wish for company on your path, you could walk with them," he said. "You will return to us soon enough."

"I will."

He fell in behind the foot soldiers. Chatelaine Dhuoda, leaning to talk with the deacon, did not even appear to know he was there, trailing along after the others. No one paid him any mind.

They passed out through the monastery gates and began the long climb up the hill. From behind, rising out of the church, Alain heard the cantors begin the chant for the office of Nones. The voices of the choir drifted after him as they marched up into the trees. Then they were engulfed by forest.

He was used to the walk, but Count Lavastine's soldiers grumbled among themselves.

"*King's* monastery, that's what they are," said the youngest of the men.

"King of Wendar, you mean. No king of ours, even if he claims the throne."

"Ha! Selfish bastards, too, fearin' count's levy will take their servants away. Don't want to sully their hands with commoner's work, do they?"

"Hush, Heric. Don't speak ill of the holy brothers."

Young Heric grunted irritably. "Do you think the abbot wonders, though, if the levy is being raised to fight raiders or to join Lady Sabella's revolt?"

"Quiet, you idiot," snapped the older man, glancing back.

Alain tucked his chin down, trying to look harmless. Of course they had noticed him. They just didn't think he was worth acknowledging. But no man, even in Varre, would talk rebellion against King Henry in front of a man whose loyalties he did not know.

They trudged the rest of the long walk in silence. Alain measured it reflexively by the offices which would soon circumscribe his day. It took from Nones to Vespers to walk up and over Dragonback Ridge, down the long slope to the dragon's head where lay the prosperous village of Osna. Fittingly it began to rain, a dreary mist that settled in around them. By the time the little party reached the longhouse of his Aunt Bel, he was soaked.

Chatelaine Dhuoda was expected, of course. She arrived once a year to exact the portion due to Count Lavastine from the village. Usually the young people who had spent the previous year in the count's service returned with her. Over time St. Eusebē's Day had become the traditional day for a young person to embark on an apprenticeship or to bring a fosterling home. But this year Dhuoda was alone except for her retinue.

Alain stood by the hearth, drying his clothes by the heat of the fire, and watched the greeting ceremony at one end of the hall. At the other end of the hall, his siblings and cousins and the servants of his aunt's household laid the table on which they would serve a feast. Under the shadowed eaves on either side of the long hall the youngest children sat on chests or huddled on beds, keeping out from underfoot.

The baby began to cry. He walked over to the cradle and picked it up, and it stilled at once, sucking a finger and staring with now perfect equanimity at the scene. Motherless, this child, as he was; its mother had died birthing it, but there was no doubt that his cousin Julien was the father since Julien and the young woman had declared before the village deacon their intention to wed. Because Aunt Bel's daughter Stancy was nursing a child and had milk to spare, Bel had fostered the baby in her house.

When it came time to serve, Alain handed the baby over to one of his young cousins to hold. It was a mark of Chatelaine Dhuoda's importance that Aunt Bel, one of the richest persons in the village, had her own kin rather than her servants serve the table at which Dhuoda now sat. Alain poured ale and so he was able to hear much of the conversation that went on between the chatelaine and the merchants and householders who were important enough to be seated at table with Count Lavastine's representative.

"Count Lavastine has been forced to keep for an extra year of service all of your young people whom you sent to us last year," Dhuoda explained calmly, although most of the townsfolk regarded her with ill-disguised annoyance.

"I expect my son's help in the harvest this year!" protested one; and another: "My daughter's skill at weaving is sorely missed in *my* household, mark you, and we are well into negotiations for her betrothal."

"These are troubled times. There have been raids along the coast. We need everyone who is already at Lavas Holding. More men-at-arms are needed. The cloister at Comeng was burned—" Here the chatelaine paused to survey the various expressions of distress on her listeners' faces. "Yes, alas, the raiders grow more bold. They are a terrible threat to all of us who live near the sea." She beckoned to Alain. "More ale." As he poured, she turned to Aunt Bel. "A likely-looking lad. Is he one of yours?"

"He is my nephew," said Aunt Bel coolly. "His father promised him to the monastery. He enters the novitiate on St. Eusebē's Day."

"I am surprised that you would enrich the King's monastery with such a well-grown lad."

"The church serves Our Lord and Lady. What goes on in the world concerns them not at all," retorted Aunt Bel.

Dhuoda smiled gently, but Alain, backing away, thought her expression haughty. "What goes on in the world concerns them as much as it concerns any of us, Mistress. But never mind. That oath, once taken, I will not attempt to break.''

The conversation traveled on to kinder subjects, last fall's harvest, the newly minted sceattas bearing the impression of the hated King Henry, trade from the southern port of Medemelacha, rumors of tempestari—weather sorcerers—causing hail and ice storms along the border between Wendar and Varre.

Alain stood in the shadows and listened as the evening wore on, coming out into the light of the lanterns posted around the long table only to pour ale into empty cups. Dhuoda's deacon was, by chance, a woman of great learning and had a particular interest in old tales. To Alain's surprise she agreed to recite a poem.

In those days　　　　　　　*when the Lost Ones held sway*
When these lands　　　　　*lay under the hand*
Of the people　　　　　　 *born of angels and human women,*
Out of their people　　　　*came one who ruled*
As emperor　　　　　　　 *of men and elvish kind both.*

These skills he had,　　　　*that he could bind*
And he could weave,　　　 *and out of the stars*
draw down to him　　　　　*the song of power.*
These arts we call　　　　　*by the name of sorcery.*
He was taught them　　　　*by his mother.*

In those days　　　　　　　*out of the north*
In the bright spring　　　　*there came a dragon.*
To all the lands　　　　　　*bordering the sea*
it laid waste.

But the emperor came himself to fight it, and though it wounded him unto death, in the end with his last strength he cast a great spell and turned the creature into stone. And here it lay, the ridge that bounded Osna Sound, known to all as the Dragonback.

Alain watched them: the arrogant chatelaine, her attendants, the learned deacon and the young frater, who, a man, was sworn to the order of wandering priests rather than to a monastery where a man would be interred for his entire life within the walls of a single cloister. If only *he* could travel, even if just once, to Lavas Holding, as his father had before him. If only he could pledge service for a single year to the count. His father had gone there seventeen years ago and served the elder Count Lavastine for one year, as was customary, but he had returned home with an infant in his arms and a sorrow in his heart. He had never married, to his elder sister's dismay, but had turned his heart to the sea and now was gone more than he was home.

Bel had raised the child, since hers was a generous heart and the child was healthy and strong.

What was it like, the place where he had been born? His mother had died three days after bearing him, or so his father had always claimed, but perhaps someone there remembered her.

Alain blinked back tears. He would never know. Tomorrow, on St. Eusebē's Eve, he would leave to pass the night in vigil outside the gates of the monastery, as was customary for conversi, those who wished to convert to the service of Our Lord and Lady as adults or young persons just come to adulthood.

The next day he would swear his oath and be lost inside the monastery walls. Forever.

"What is it, Alain?" asked his cousin Stancy, coming to stand beside him. She touched his cheek with her fingers. "Weep if you must, but go with a good heart. Think of what great good your prayers will bring to your kin. Think even that you will learn to write and read, and perhaps you will come to be as learned as the deacon there. Then you can travel to many far places—"

"But only in my mind," he said bitterly.

"Ai, my little one, I know your heart. But this is the burden that has been given to you to bear. You may as well bear it gladly." She was right, of course. She kissed him affectionately and went off to the back of the hall to fetch more oil for the lanterns.

3

ST. Eusebē's Eve dawned clear and fine. The netting shed doors creaked lazily all morning in a soft spring breeze. Red streamers painted with the Circle of Unity snapped and fluttered from every eave in the houses set around the village common.

Every person in the village came to the common to watch Chatelaine Dhuoda collect taxes. Vats of honey. Ambers of ale, both clear and dark. A cow or five wethers. Geese. Cheese. Fodder. Smoked salmon and eels. Aunt Bel had fine brooches brought from the south by Alain's father to pay in lieu of oil and ale. One farmer signed his son into service to the count for five years so that he would not have to turn over his two best milking cows. Another couple had a slave, a young girl brought north from Salia, whom they could no longer feed. Dhuoda looked her over, pronounced her fit enough, and took her as payment. Old Mistress Garia, who had five adult daughters who were all as accomplished at weaving as she was, presented, as usual, lengths of finely-woven cloth which Dhuoda received with evident pleasure. A few paid in coin, and only a very few were marked delinquent since Osna was a wealthy place and the townsfolk here were, Alain knew by his father's reports, prosperous.

This went on all morning and past midday, when folk from outlying farms arrived to pay their respects and deliver their rents or taxes.

In the late afternoon Alain took his leave. He knelt before his aunt and said the traditional words: "It is customary for a conversus to stand vigil at the gates, Aunt, to prove his desire to enter into the service of Our Lord and Lady."

"Go with my blessing, child, and with the blessing of your father." She kissed him on the head.

He rose and made his good-byes to the rest of the family. Three of Aunt Bel's children were now adults with children of their own, so there were many farewells. Last of all, he gave the baby a kiss, hugged his aunt a final time and, with a shake of his shoulders, set off.

By now the wind had picked up. The netting shed doors banged restlessly against the hex poles. A misting rain began to fall. Glancing behind, he saw Chatelaine Dhuoda hastily moving her table into one of the houses that bordered the common, to do the rest of her business under shelter.

The rain began to fall in earnest as he passed through the livestock fence that bordered the village and set a steady pace for the three hours' walk back to the monastery.

The wind increased as he climbed the path that led up the ridge. Dirt churned into mud and stuck to his soft leather shoes, seeping through the stitches. His small pack scarcely gave him enough ballast as he reached the dragon's back height and headed out into the full force of the wind. Now he was alone, only the wide swell of the bay, choppy and white-frothed, below him. The high forest hills stretched out behind. Both the village and the monastery were hidden by the ridge's convoluted path along the middle rim of the bay.

Alain had to lean forward into the wind to make headway. He wondered briefly about the ship he had seen yesterday. Was it caught outside the shelter of the bay, or had it put into one of the many island coves to wait out the storm? He turned his face into the wind and looked seaward. He gasped. Amazement stopped him in his tracks.

The storm was coming in, fast. He had never seen such a storm as this.

Half the bay was gone, obliterated from view. A flat bank of mist scudded toward him, pursued by a dense curtain of dark cloud that engulfed everything in its path. In moments he was surrounded, fogged in. He could not see three strides before or behind himself. He hunkered down before the first fierce gusts hit, turned his back on the bay, and bent his head.

The wind roared as if the dragon beneath this petrified dragon's back had come to life. Even crouched, he fell forward to his knees from the force of it. Roiling black clouds girdled him. Bitter, hard rain drenched him, hammering in sheets. Between one breath and the next he was soaked to the skin.

This was not natural rain.

Even as he thought it, the pounding rain ceased entirely, although the wind did not slacken. Surely this was the punishment sent on him for betraying, in his heart, the pledge given in his name to the service of Our Lord and Lady. Or else it was a trial.

He struggled to his feet and turned again into the gale. Despite everything, despite his own desire, he *would* reach the monastery. He would not shame his father and aunt. The wind tore at his hair, stinging his eyes. His lips, wet half with salt spray and half with cold rain, parched in the harsh current of air that whirlpooled around him.

The fog lightened. An eerie light glowed down the straight road that led along the dragon's back height. An unearthly presence, it grew closer, and broader, dispelling the fog as it went . . . but only around itself. He saw with a strange kind of distant tunneling sight that the storm closed back around once the light passed. He smelled spring blossoms and the fresh blood of slaughter.

A rider approached. Armed in bright mail, it guided its horse forward at a sedate walk, untroubled by the raging wind. Alain thought about running, but it was so brief a thought that it was ripped away on the air almost as quickly as it formed. Because he had to stare.

The horse was beautiful, as white as untouched snow, almost blinding, and the woman—

He could not have moved even if he had tried. She reined her warhorse in beside him. She was a woman of middle age, scarred on the face and hands, her boots muddied and scuffed, her coat of mail patched here and there with gleaming new rings of iron. Her long sword, sheathed in leather, swayed in front of him. A battered, round shield hung by her knee, tied to the saddle. She shifted in the saddle to examine him. They stood in dead calm. Three strides beyond the storm raged around them.

Her gaze was at once distant and utterly piercing. If her eyes had color, he could not make it out. They seemed as black as a curse to him. He stared up at her, and a cold fear gripped his heart.

"What must I pay you, to ride to war?" she asked. Her lips moved with the words, but her voice, low and deep as the church bell, rang in his head with echoes scattering off it.

Not knowing what else to do, he knelt. He did not let his gaze falter from hers; to blink might well prove fatal. "Lady." His voice was as hoarse as hers was resonant. He tried again. "I am sworn to the church."

"Not in your heart," she said. She drew her sword. Whatever he expected, no light flamed off the blade; it did not gleam or spark. It was dull metal, hard, good metal, made for killing. She swung it over his head in a high arc and pointed back the way she had come.

The air seemed sucked away from the height on which they stood. As down a long tunnel, seen with the sight of eagles, he saw the monastery, though he could not possibly see it from here. The orderly pattern of buildings, the retaining wall: Seen from so high, he thought for an instant he could discern a second pattern underlying the monastery buildings, something ancient and troubling.

But his view tumbled, down and down and down, until he saw two boats drawn up on the strand and the creatures pouring forth from them. They could not be called men, with their strange, sharp faces and inhuman coloring. Naked to the waist, their torsos and faces were patterned with white scars and garish painted colors. They carried axes and spears and bows with stone-tipped arrows, and their skin bore a scaly, metallic sheen. Some had claws bursting from their knuckles, a horrible, white growth. Dogs ran with them, packs of huge, ugly dogs that had less mercy than their masters.

They burned as they went, setting fire to the thatched roofs of the outlying buildings. They slaughtered the monks without mercy. Somehow he could see inside the chapel. He could see Brother Gilles, where he knelt praying at the altar, silver-haired and frail, clutching his beloved gold-leafed *Book of Unities*, the treasure of the monastery. A white-haired barbarian stuck the old man through from behind and wrenched the precious book from his dying grasp, then ripped the gold, jewel-encrusted cover off the binding, tossing the parchment leaves like so much offal onto Brother Gilles' bloody corpse.

"You are not yet sworn by your own oath," said the woman. With a wrench Alain stood again on the ridge, hemmed in by storm.

"I must go!" he cried. He started up, impelled forward by some wild notion of saving Brother Gilles.

She stopped him with the flat of her sword. "It is too late for them. But see."

And pointed with her sword toward the village.

A haze of lights. Red streamers flapped damply against eaves. Most of the houses were well shut, except for Aunt Bel's. She stood huddled in the doorway, staring forlornly, with bitter concern, up the road in the direction he had gone. Behind her, Stancy played chess at the table with her youngest sister, little Agnes; she moved, white Dragon takes red Castle. The other children cast circle-sticks by the hearth, and the baby slept in its cradle. The fire blazed and cracked, hot, smoking.

Alain's eyes watered from it, such heat, and then he was yanked outside into the sharp cold and the stinging wind. On the strand below the village, a long, narrow boat beached. Ai, Lord and Lady! There were more of them! They flooded out of the boat, clawed, painted, readying their weapons.

Fog boiled past his eyes. He swatted it away. Tears streaked his face. "It's too late." He turned to her where she sat as serene as death on her white horse. "Why are you showing me this?"

She smiled. She had a terrible beauty, seared by hardship and agony and the wild madness of battle. "Serve me," she said. "Serve me, Alain Henrisson, and I will spare the village."

"How can you?" he gasped, remembering Brother Gilles impaled, the monastery in flames, seeing the wild, savage creatures who charged up the strand toward the houses of his kin and neighbors.

"Serve me," she said.

Alain collapsed to his knees. Was that the baby's scream on the wind? "I swear it."

"Stand."

He stood. The cold steel of her sword came to rest on his right shoulder, then his left, then, last, achingly cold, so that it seemed to suck all heat from him and yet burn him at the same time, she rested the flat of the blade on his head.

"Who are you?" he whispered.

The sword, like death by pain, was lifted. Her reply rang out and yet was muted by the howl of the wind. "I am the Lady of Battles. Keep this, my token."

And she was gone. A blinding light pierced his eyes, and pain stabbed through his heart. The dark clouds blew up and enveloped him. Far away, he heard a hoarse, gleeful battle cry, and then he fainted.

He woke suddenly. Sat up in fear. It was morning, St. Eusebe's Day, a bright, fine, clear spring dawning without a trace of cloud. A day of good omens. The bay ran in smooth ripples below. The rich old green of trees rimmed the blue bowl of the sky. He swore, shaking off his stupor, and stood up.

And saw, on the path, a tiny blood-red rose. It glittered like a jewel, but when he reached to pick it up, its petals were as soft as the first flower of spring. He shifted his grip, and a thorn pricked his skin, drawing a welling bulb of blood.

"Aunt Bel," he murmured. "Stancy." The baby. He thrust the rose stem under his belt and ran all the way back to Osna.

A few people stared when he halted, gasping for breath, at the edge of the village common. Aunt Bel saw him, and her face went from white to red in one instant. She rushed across to him and pinned him in her arms.

"Alain! Oh, my child, I thought you were lost to us."

"You're all here? All well? Where is Stancy—?"

"In the workshop. My poor lad, come in, come in." She led him unprotesting into the longhouse and sat him at the table, setting a mug of warm goat's milk in front of him. "Lord and Lady." She wiped a tear from her weathered face. "I was sure you must have been there. Lord and Lady, thank Them, thank Them." She drew the Circle of Unity, throat to heart and back again. "How did you escape? When old Gilles brought the news—"

He felt a surge of hope and relief. "Brother Gilles?"

"No, lad. Gilles Fisher. He never saw the ships, they came so fast, in with that cursed storm and gone again as quickly. The whole monastery they burned, and every monk they slaughtered where he stood. All dead. But somehow, Their blessings on us, we were spared. Never a sound or a sight of them here. We're all safe. I'm sure Henri is well south by now. They came from out of the north."

"I never got as far as the monastery," he whispered, but all he could see was that distant, unnatural sight of the painted men, burning, killing . . . beaching their ship on the strand below the village. He could not bring himself to speak of his vision, if vision it was.

"But I'm fair willing to believe," continued Aunt Bel in a low voice, "that it was the Lord and Lady's judgment on them in the monastery, for turning against her as ought to be Queen Regnant. Still, no use speaking ill of the dead. Some of the village men have gone over to give them a decent burial."

"There's something I must see." Alain rose. Aunt Bel looked at him questioningly but he did not stay for questions, he was out the door so fast. He ran down to the strand where the fishers and merchants pulled up their boats, coming in to trade or shelter at Osna.

It took him a bit of a walk, down along the foot of the ridge, to find the long deep scar where the low-bellied ship had beached and been dragged up onto the sand. Where the tide had not obliterated them, some of the footsteps were still left, racing upward, and then stopping, milling about. There was even one thin stain of blood, coloring the dun sand, and a single shod hoofprint.

The morning stayed clear and fine as he climbed the ridge. From the dragon's back he could see no sign of ships at all on the flat opacity of the bay or on the farther blue-gray horizon of the sea. He walked farther yet and came to an overlook where he could stand off from the path, which now wound down away from the ridge into the forest, and see down from the height to the monastery far below. It lay in smoking ruins. A few vultures circled. To the north of the church tower a pit had been dug; he saw it from here as a dark mouth. Men moved, dragging bodies into the grave. He ran, now, but by the time he reached the remains of the monastery, Chatelaine Dhuoda's deacon was reading the mass for the dead over the grave as men from the village pitched dirt in to cover the bodies of the slain monks.

"You, boy," said Chatelaine Dhuoda, startling him. He had not seen her. "You are the boy who was to be sworn into the novitiate today, are you not? You're of good age? Sixteen? Yes, and you're a fit, tall lad, I see."

The way she looked him over made him feel like a horse or a slave from beyond the northern sea brought to the auction block.

"There's nothing for you here now, and Count Lavastine has need of many more strong arms, as you can see yourself. These are bad times. I'll speak with your aunt, but in any case, it is my right to mark you out for service to the count. You will come with us when we leave tomorrow."

He did not know what to say. Overjoyed for the chance to go, he feared that it was his own desire to be free of his duty to the monks that had brought death on them. But that, as his father would say, was pride of self, to think his selfish, trivial wishes could affect the world as God's will does. It was the godless barbarians who had brought death so cruelly; it was nothing to do with him.

Dhuoda regarded him impatiently, waiting for his reply. He nodded his head, and she turned away, dismissing him. Her fur-lined cloak swayed as she walked briskly toward the deacon, who had finished the hasty mass.

Alain's hand caught on his belt, and suddenly he remembered the rose. It was not crushed. It had not wilted. It was as perfect as a budding rose just plucked from the bush. He held it in his hand all the long walk back to Osna, and still it did not change.

In the morning, he carefully bound the rose to a thin leather string and hung it around his neck, tucked between shirt and tunic where no one could see. A thicker string held the wooden Circle of Unity Aunt Bel gave him to wear as a reminder of his father's promise to the church.

After bittersweet farewells, he slung his pack over his back and followed Chatelaine Dhuoda and her retinue out of the village, into the world beyond.

II
THE BOOK OF
SECRETS

1

IN the northernmost reaches of the North Mark of Wendar lay a cluster of hamlets and villages known as Heart's Rest. The people here spoke a peculiar dialect of Wendish flavored with odd words and unconventional pronunciations.

Traveling fraters noted with distress that an alarmingly pagan-looking Tree figured as prominently in the wood-frame churches of Our Lord and Lady as did the Circle of Unity. The biscop of Heart's Rest turned her gaze the other way, concerned more with the yearly increase in raids along the coast. But she did not prohibit the most punctilious of the fraters from sending reports south of this hea-thenish practice.

Nothing ever came of these reports. Heart's Rest was too far north, too sparsely populated, and by no means wealthy enough to attract the attention of either king or skopos. It was a quiet penin-sula, set apart from Wendar proper. People spoke softly and kept to their own business. They remained as tolerant toward the occa-sional outsider who washed up on their shores as their biscop remained to the lingering taint of pagan rites in the handful of churches under her watch.

Let well enough alone. People said it often, and firmly. Those outsiders who came to rest there might find peace, for a while.

It depended, really, on who they were running from, and how far their enemies were willing to track them.

"See, there," said Da. "Setting below the trees in the west. The Rose Star, known by the ancient Babaharshan magicians as Zuhia, sun of the night, mage and scholar. What can you tell me about him?"

"The Dariyan astronomers called the Rose Star by the name Aturna, the Red Mage. It is a lesser light than the Blood Star but of a truer cast. Aturna is one of the traveling stars, also known as the erratica, or planets. It rules the seventh sphere, whose upper surface is tangent to the orb of the fixed stars beyond which lies the Chamber of Light. Its lower surface is tangent to the sixth sphere, that ruled by the planet Mok. Aturna takes twenty-eight years to travel along the path of the twelve Houses of Night."

They stood in the clearing, trees below, the rocky verge of the hill above. The grass, growing hard now that spring had come, reached their knees. Behind, on a level terrace of ground, the cottage sat dark but for a faint red glow, the hearth fire glimpsed through the open door and window. It was a perfect night for viewing: There was not a trace of cloud in the sky.

"Name the seven spheres and their order," said Da.

"The sphere closest to the Earth is that of the Moon. The second is that of the planet Erekes, and the third is that of the planet Somorhas, also known as the Lady of Light. Fourth is the sphere of the Sun. Then comes the fifth sphere, which is ruled by the planet Jedu, the Angel of War. The sixth sphere is ruled by Mok, and the seventh—and last—by Aturna. Beyond Aturna lies the field of stars each of which is a fire burning bright before the Chamber of Light."

"And the seven ladders known to the mages, by which the learned can ascend as if through the seven spheres to the place of wisdom and mastery?" He turned over the book he held in his hands but did not open it. Three partridges, shot by Liath, hung on a line from his shoulder. They had been out hunting and came back late, but since they always—*always*—carried book and astrolabe with them, they could observe the heavens anywhere.

Liath hesitated, shifting bow and quiver on her back. This knowledge was new. She and Da had traced out the stars, fixed and traveling, since she was old enough to point at the heavens. But only last month had he suddenly begun to teach her the secret lore of mages. Last month, on the feast day of St. Oya, saint of mysteries and secrets, he had remembered—as if the turning wheel of the stars in the heavens and the progress of days on the Earth had taken a sudden, unexpected forward leap—that she would turn sixteen on the spring equinox, first day of the new year. St. Oya's Day was indeed an auspicious day for a girl to have her first woman's bleeding, and Da had taken her down to the inn for the traditional celebration.

Liath had enjoyed the feast and the songs, but she had felt no different except for the changes in her body. But ever since St. Oya's Day Da treated her differently: He made her read and recite and memorize at a furious pace, like heaping wood on a fire and expecting it to blaze brighter and hotter.

Yesterday, by the reckoning of days and years she had learned at Da's knee, had been the first day of the new year. She had turned sixteen. And this year when she and Da had gone to the village church for the celebration of Mariansmass—the name the church gave to the day of the spring equinox—she had sung in the congregation as a young woman, no longer as a girl at the children's benches.

"Liath?" Da waited.

She bit at her lip, wanting to get it perfect because she hated to disappoint him. She took a breath and spoke in the singsong voice she always used when she first memorized the words and sequences her father taught her.

> "By this ladder the mage ascends:
> First to the rose, whose touch is healing.
> Then to the sword, which grants us strength.
> Third is the cup of boundless waters.
> Fourth is the blacksmith's ring of fire.
> The throne of virtue follows fifth.
> Wisdom's scepter marks the sixth.
> At the highest rung seek the crown of stars,
> The song of power revealed."

"Very good, Liath. Tonight we'll continue our measurements of the ecliptic. Where is the astrolabe?"

The instrument dangled by its ring from her thumb. She lifted her arm out straight before her and sighted on the delicate cluster of stars called "the Crown," now descending into the west. It was so clear this night that perhaps she could see the seventh "jewel" in the crown of stars; usually only six were visible, but she had keen enough sight that she could sometimes make out the seventh. She was about to calculate the altitude and rotate the brass rete when a movement caught her eye. An owl took flight from a tree on the edge of the clearing. She followed the bird with her gaze, up, its wings pale against the night lit only by stars and a crescent moon. And there, low in the east—

"Look, Da! No, *there.* In the Dragon. I've never seen that star before, and it's not one of the planets. All the other stars are in their rightful places."

He peered into the sky. His eyes were no longer as keen as hers, but after a moment he saw it: a star out of place in the constellation of the Dragon, Sixth House in the Great Circle, the world dragon that bound the heavens. It was of middling brightness, although even as Liath stared she thought it grew brighter; the light it cast wavered as if it were throwing off sparks.

"Lady's Blood," Da swore. He shivered, although it was warm for a spring night. A white shape swooped past them. The owl struck not ten paces from them, and when it rose, it bore aloft a small, struggling shape in its claws. "So descends the greater upon the smaller. Let's go inside, daughter."

"But, Da, shouldn't we measure its position? Shouldn't we observe it? It must be a sign from the heavens. Perhaps it's an angel come down into the lower spheres!"

"No, child!" He pulled his cloak tight and turned his face deliberately away from the sky. His shoulders shook. "We must go in."

Clutching the astrolabe, she bit back a retort and followed him meekly inside their cottage. It was really too warm inside, with a fire still roaring in the hearth. But the fire always roared, and Da was often cold. She remembered being a little girl, when he could with a single gesture call butterflies of rainbow light into being for her to chase through the herb garden. All that—if they were true memories and not illusions brought into being by her own desire— had died with her mother. All she had left were memories clouded by the years and by the endless miles they had journeyed, across the sea, over mountains, through new lands and strange towns. That, and a fire always burning in the hearth.

He barred the door behind them and suddenly bent over, racked by coughs. Recovering, he placed the book on the table and threw his cloak onto the bench. Went at once and poured himself ale.

"Da," she said, hating to see him this way, but he only took another draught. To her horror, his hands shook. "Da, sit down."

He sat. She set the astrolabe on the shelf, rested bow and quiver in the corner, and hung the partridges from the rafters. Placing a log on the fire, she turned to watch her father. As she shifted, the plank floor creaked under her feet. It was such a bare room. She remembered richer, but that was long ago. Tapestries, carved benches, a real chair, a long hall, and wine served from a pitcher of glass. They had built this little cottage themselves, dug out the ground, driven posts in, sawed planks from felled logs and set that planking over the cellar, caulked the log walls with mud and straw. It was rough but serviceable. Besides the table and bench that doubled as their clothes chest, there was only her father's bed in the darkest corner and their one luxury—a walnut shelf, the wood polished until it shone, its surface carved with a pattern of gripping beasts curling down the sides, their eyes painted red.

Da coughed again and fumbled to open the book, searching for something in the dense text written within. Moving to help him, she passed by the window. The shutters were still open, and through the thin skin tacked over the opening, rubbed so fine that it was translucent, she saw a dim light. It bobbed closer, following the well-worn path that descended to the village.

"Someone is coming," she said, going to the door.

"Don't open it!"

His voice cut her, and she flinched. "What is it? What's wrong?" She stared at him, frightened by his abrupt and manifest terror. "Was that new star an omen? Have you read of its coming? Does the book speak of it?" They never called it by its title. Some words, spoken aloud, called attention to themselves.

He slapped the book shut and clutched it against his chest. Jumping up, he grabbed his bow out of the corner, then, with book and bow, walked across to the window. Suddenly he relaxed, his expression clearing. "It's only Frater Hugh."

Now it was her turn to shudder. "Don't let him in, Da."

"Do not speak so harshly, child. Frater Hugh is a good man, sworn to Our Lady and Lord."

"Sworn to himself, you mean."

"Liath! How can you speak so? He only wants instruction. He is no less curious than are you yourself. Can you fault him for that?"

"Just give me the book, Da," she said more gently, to coax it from him. What she now knew of Hugh was too dangerous to tell Da.

But Da hesitated. Four other books sat on the shelf in the corner, each one precious: Polyxene's encyclopedic *History of Dariya*, *The Acts of St. Thecla*, Theophrastos of Eresos' *Inquiry into Plants*, the *Dreams* of Artemisia. But they did not contain forbidden knowledge, condemned by the church at the Council of Narvone one hundred years ago.

"But he might be one who could help us, Liath," he said, abruptly serious. "We have been running for so long. We need an ally, someone who could understand the great powers that weave their trap around us. Someone who could help us against them—"

She snatched the book out of his hands and scrambled up the ladder that led to the loft. From her shelter under the peaked roof she could see down into half the room and easily hear anything that went on below. She threw herself down on her straw mattress and pulled a blanket up over her. "Tell him I'm asleep."

Da muttered an inaudible reply, but she knew once she had made a decision, he would not gainsay it. He closed the shutters, replaced the bow in the corner, then opened the door and stood there, waiting for Frater Hugh.

"Greetings, friend!" he called. His voice was almost cheerful, for he liked Hugh. "Have you come to watch this night with me?"

"Alas, no, friend Bernard. I was passing this way—"

I was passing this way. All lies, delivered in that honey-sweet voice.

"—on my way to old Johannes' steading. I'm to perform last rites over his wife, may her soul rise in peace to the Chamber above. Mistress Birta asked if I would deliver this letter to you."

"A *letter!*" Da's voice almost broke on the word. For eight years they had wandered. Never once had they met anyone Da knew from their former life. Never once had he received a letter or any other kind of communication. "Ai, Blessed Lady," he murmured hoarsely. "I have stayed too long in this place."

"I beg your pardon?" asked Frater Hugh. The light of his lamp streamed in through the window, illuminating her father's figure in the threshold. "You look ill, my friend. May I help you?"

Da hesitated again, and she held her breath, but he glanced up toward the loft and then, slowly, shook his head. "There is nothing you can do. But I thank you." He reached out for the letter. Liath ran her fingers along the spine of the book, feeling the thick letters painted onto the leather binding. *The Book of Secrets.* Would Da invite Frater Hugh inside? Da was so lonely, and he was afraid. "Will you sit with me for a while? It's a quiet night, and I fear it will prove to be a long one."

She eased backward into the deepest shadows of the loft. There was a long pause while Hugh considered. She could almost feel, like the presence of fire, his *desire*—his wish to enter, to coax Da into trusting him more and yet more until at last Da would trust him with everything. And then they would be lost.

"Alas, I have other duties this night," Hugh said at last. But he did not leave. Lamplight shifted, spilling in turn into each of the four corners of the room below, searching. "Your daughter is well, I trust?" How sweet his voice was.

"Well enough. I trust the Lady and Lord will watch over her, should anything happen to me.

Hugh gave a soft laugh under his breath, and Liath curled farther into the shadows, as if hiding could protect her. "I assure you They will, friend Bernard. I give you my word. You should rest. You look pale."

"Your concern heartens me, friend." Liath could see Da's little smile, the one he placated with. She knew it was not sincere—not because of Hugh, but because of the letter, and the owl, and the *athar*, the strange new star shining in the heavens.

"Then a blessed evening to you, Bernard. I bid you farewell."

"Fare well."

So they parted. The lamp bobbed away, descending the path back toward the village, toward, perhaps, old Johannes' steading. Surely Frater Hugh would have no reason to lie about such a serious thing. But he was hardly "passing by."

"He is a kind man," said Da. "Come down, Liath."

"I won't," she said. "What if he's lurking out there?"

"Child!"

It had to be said, sooner or later, if not the whole truth. "He *looks* at me, Da. In such a way."

He hissed in a breath in anger. "Is my daughter so vain that she imagines a man heartsworn to the church desires her more than Our Lady?"

Ashamed, she hid her face in shadow although he could not see her. Was she so vain? No, she knew this was not vanity. Eight years of running had honed her instincts.

I was passing this way.

Hugh stopped by the cottage often to sit and visit with Da; the two men discussed theology and the writings of the ancients and now, six months into their acquaintance, they had begun tentatively to discuss the hidden arts of sorcery—purely as an intellectual exercise, of course.

Of course.

"Don't you see, Da?" she said, struggling to find words, to find a way to make him understand without telling him the thing that would ruin them, as it had in the city of Autun two years ago. "Hugh only wants your knowledge of sorcery. He doesn't want your friendship."

Hugh stopped by often, but now, since St. Oya's Day, he had also begun "passing by" when he *knew* Da was out on an errand or on a laboring job, though Da's health had taken a turn for the worse and he wasn't really strong enough for day labor. Liath would have gone, but as Da always said: *"Someone must stay with the book."* And he didn't want her out alone.

"I was passing this way, Liath. Has anyone ever told you how beautiful you are? You're a woman now. Your father must be thinking of what will become of you—and of all that he has taught you, and everything that you know of him and his travels and his past. I can protect you . . . and the book." And he had touched her on the lips as if to awaken the breath of life in her.

For a pious brother of the church to proposition an innocent girl not yet sixteen was obscene, of course. Only an idiot would have mistaken his tone and his expression; Liath had never much liked Hugh, but this had shocked and horrified her because Hugh had by this action betrayed Da's trust in him in a way Liath could never ever reveal.

If she told Da, and Da believed her, he would accuse Frater Hugh, might even attempt to strike him. Two years ago in Autun something like had happened; Da in his impetuous way had attacked the merchant who proposed a concubine's contract for Liath but only managed to get himself a beating by the city guards and the two of them thrown out of the city. But if Da accused Hugh, if he attacked Hugh, he would make a powerful enemy. Hugh's mother was a margrave, one of the great princes of the land, as Hugh himself made sure everyone knew. She and Da had no kin to protect them.

And if she told Da, and Da did not believe her, then . . . Ai, Lady. Da was everything to her, he was all she had. She could not take such a risk.

"Da?" In all her long silence, he had not replied. "Da?"

When she heard a pained grunt from below, the faint crackling of parchment, she half slid and half jumped down the ladder. Da crumpled the letter and threw it into the fire. Flames leaped, flaring. She jumped forward, grabbed—and Da slapped her hand.

"Leave it be!" He was pale and sweating. "If you touch anything their hands have touched, they have a further link to you." He sank down onto the bench, resting his forehead on a hand. "We must leave tomorrow, Liath."

"*Leave?*"

"They will not let us rest."

"Who, Da? Who are we running from? Why won't you tell me?"

"Because your ignorance is all that protects you. They have the power of seeking and finding, but I have sealed you away from them." So he always said. *In time. When you are stronger.* "If we go in the morning, we'll have several days' start at least. We should not have stayed here so long."

They had stayed here so long because she had begged him to. Because for the first time in her life she had made friends. Standing in the center of the little cottage, her head almost brushed the rough planking of the loft. Da was a shadow in firelight, half formed, half sunk in gloom, but she could see him clearly despite the dimness. It was a joke between them: salamander eyes, named for the salamanders, the tiny spirits who inhabited the element of fire. Liath remembered seeing them, many years ago before her mother died, their forms as liquid as water, their eyes sparks of blue fire.

No longer. No matter how closely she peered, no matter how long, she saw only flames leaping and sparking in the hearth, consuming the wood until it burned as red coal, ashes sifting down to make a dark blanket beneath.

"She is not strong enough yet," he said into his hand.

"I'm strong, Da. You know that."

"Go to bed, child. Keep the book with you. We'll take what we need in the morning and go."

She swallowed tears. They would go, and leave behind two years of contentment. This was a fine place, this village, or had been at least until Frater Hugh had arrived last autumn. She could not bear the thought of leaving her friends behind: two friends— imagine!—as close as if they were her own kin, of which she had none. Only her father.

But they would go. Whatever drove Da drove her along with him. She would never abandon him.

"I'm sorry, Liath. I'm a poor excuse for a father. I haven't done well by you. I should have—" He shook his head. "I was made weak by blindness."

"Never say so, Da!" She knelt beside the bench and hugged him. He had aged so fast in the past two years, since that beating in Autun. His hair was now gray, that had once been a rich brown. He walked bent over, as if under an invisible burden, who had once strode hale and straight. He drank enough ale for four men, as if to drown himself, despite that they could not pay for so much. There was little enough work to be had in such an isolated spot for a man who was no longer strong enough for field labor, whose only skills were drawing hex signs against foxes around hen coops and setting down on parchment or strips of bark the words of women and men wishing to make contracts with colleagues many leagues away or send letters to relatives. But they had managed.

"Go to bed, daughter," he repeated. "We must leave early."

Because she did not know what else to say, she did what he had asked of her. She kissed his cheek. She let go of him and stood. Pausing by the fire, she searched in the flames but the parchment was burned to nothing. To ashes. Her father sighed heavily. She left him to his thoughts, for certainly she could not fathom what they were or where they led him.

In the loft, she stripped to her shift and lay down under the blankets, tucking the book against her chest. The fire's shadow danced on the eaves, and its soft pop and roar soothed her. She heard Da pouring more ale for himself, heard him drink, it was so quiet.

So quiet.

"Trust no one," he murmured, and then her mother's name, on a dying breath: "Anne."

Many nights she heard him speak her mother's name, just so. After eight years his sorrow still sounded fresh, as raw as a new knife cut. *Will I ever be bound to someone so tightly?* She wondered.

But the dance of shadows, the rustling movements of her father below, the shush of wind over the steep roof, the distant whisper of trees, all together these weighed on her, bearing her down and down. She was so tired. *What was that strange star that came to life in the Dragon? Was it an angel? A daimone of the upper air?*

She fell into sleep.

And sleeping, dreamed.

Fire. She often dreamed of fire, cleansing, welcoming. *There are spirits burning in the air with wings of flame and eyes as brilliant as knives. At their backs a wall of fire roars up into black night, but there is nothing to fear. Pass through, and a new world lies beyond. In the distance a drum sounds like a heartbeat and the whistle of a flute, borne up on the wind like a bird, takes wing.*

Wings, settling on the eaves. A sudden gust of white snow blew down through the smoke hole, although it was not winter.

Asleep and aware, bound to silence. Awake but unable to move, and so therefore still asleep. The darkness held her down as if it was a weight draped over her.

Bells, heard as if on the wind.

Had old Johannes' wife passed on into the other life? Did the bells ring her soul's ascension to the Chamber of Light? One bell to toll her past each sphere and the last three for the *Alleluia* of the voices of the angels raised to greet their new kinswoman.

But the bells were a voice shuddering in the air. Two sharp thunks sounded, something hard striking wood. If she could only look, she could see, but she could not move, she dared not move. She had to stay hidden. Da said so.

"Your weak arrows avail you nothing," said the voice of bells, whether a man or a woman she could not tell. "Where is she?" Liath felt that voice against her like the touch of something old and corrupt dragged over her skin.

"Nowhere you can find her," said Da, panting, out of breath as if he'd been running.

Sweat started up on her forehead as she strained to move. But it was only a dream, wasn't it?

The fire flared suddenly until it flashed, brilliant, and sparks glinted in sudden bursts and then all was dark and quiet.

She slept.

And woke. It was the hour before dawn, the light more a suggestion of gray. She stirred, caught herself with the book pressed against her arm, fingers tingling, half asleep.

Something was not right.

Da had fallen asleep draped over the bench, arms thrown over the table, head lolling at an odd angle. His bow, strung, lay on the floor beside him. Cold all over, she scrambled down the ladder.

Da was not asleep.

The shutters were closed and barred. The door was barred. For eight years, wherever they stayed, there was always a fire in the hearth. Now the hearth lay stone cold.

And there, as if tracked out of the hearth itself, a slender footprint dusted with gray ash. Two of Da's arrows stuck out from the log wall beside the hearth.

And on the table, next to Da's right hand, lay a white feather of a kind she had never seen before, so pale it shone.

Wind whistled down through the smoke hole, stirring the feather, smoothing the ash footprint and scattering its lines until no trace remained. She reached for the feather. . . .

Leave it be!

She jerked her hand back as if Da had slapped it. *If you touch anything their hands have touched—*

"Where is she?" the voice had said. And Da refused to answer.

She stared at his body. He looked so old, as if his mortal frame would crumble into dust at the slightest touch of wind.

Trust no one.

The first thing she did was to hide the book.

2

THE slow drip of water nagged Liath out of her restless sleep.

"Da?" she asked, thinking the trough behind the cottage had sprung a leak again. Then, opening her eyes into the gloom of the cell, she remembered.

Da was dead. Murdered.

The thin slit of a window, set high into the earthen wall, admitted only a dim streak of light that the stone floor absorbed like a dry plant soaks in water. The drip still sounded. Liath curled up to sit. Dirt clung to her tunic, but she was too filthy and too tired to brush it off. Her face still hurt from Frater Hugh's blows. She lifted fingers to her right cheek. Winced. Yes, it had bruised. Her left arm ached, but she did not think it was broken. She allowed herself the barest of smiles: small favors.

She sat forward onto her knees. The movement brought with it a lancing pain in her head, and for an instant she was back in the cottage. She was kneeling on the bench next to Da's body. It seemed to stiffen as she watched. The door banged open and the draft pushed the white feather against her bare skin.

Pain, like a knife driven into her temple. A voice, so far distant that it was no more articulate than the surf on a rocky shore. . . .

She pressed her palms to her head and shut her eyes, as if that could shut out the vision. Slowly the pain, and the memory, ebbed. She set a hand on the wall and got up on her feet. Stood a moment, testing her strength.

The drip came from the opposite corner, steady and remarkably even. A dirty pool of water covered the earth there. She didn't really remember coming in here, but she was sure this must be the Common House root cellar. Even Hugh could not have persuaded Marshal Liudolf to confine her in the church crypt. Which meant, by the drip, that she must be below the pig troughs and therefore just five strides from the edge of the wood. If only the window were not so narrow and the four iron rods barring it so very thick.

A hissed whisper sounded, sharp and anxious, next to the slit. "Liath? Are you there?"

"Hanna?" Her heart raced with sudden hope. "Did you find the book?"

A gusting sigh, of anxiety lifted, answered her. After a moment Hanna spoke again. "Yes. Under the floorboards, just where you said it would be. And buried it where you said to."

"Thank the Lady," Liath murmured.

Hanna went on, not hearing this brief prayer. "But we haven't enough coin for the debt price. Or . . ." She hesitated. "Not even the bond price. It'll be the auction tomorrow. I'm sorry."

Liath went to the window and grasped an iron bar in each grimy hand. Peering up into the sunlight, she could not quite make out Hanna's face. "But Da's four books. Surely they brought a good price. Those four books alone are worth two horses."

"Didn't Marshal Liudolf tell you? Frater Hugh said those books were church property and he confiscated them. They're not to be sold at all."

"Lady's Blood," swore Liath, but the bitter anger, filling her, made her hurt everywhere. Why had Da trusted Hugh?

"I'm sorry—" Hanna began again.

"Don't be sorry. What could you have done?"

"If Inga hadn't been so selfish about her wedding feast, we might have been able to at least pay the bond price—"

"It isn't Inga's fault. Frater Hugh means to pay the debt price, so it wouldn't have mattered."

"Even so, Liath, how did your Da run up such debts in two years? You never said anything. All this time . . ." Her voice dropped even lower. A shadow colored the ground and Hanna's chin and mouth appeared to Liath's view. A moment later, a strong hand gripped hers. "My mother says it isn't from *natural pursuits.*"

Hanna's hand felt warm in hers. Liath held it tightly. *My father is a sorcerer. Of course it isn't from natural pursuits.* But she could not say it aloud, not even to her dear friend. In the village they all had thought Master Bernard was a defrocked monk, a man who had dishonored his vow to Our Lady and Lord and been forced to leave the cloister because he had confessed to getting a woman with child. A churchman knew how to write. A churchman understood the power of herbs and hexes to ward off pests and sickness and worse evils. Da had never disabused them of this notion. It made it possible for the villagers to accept him without fear. A fallen monastic was a shamed man but not a dangerous one.

Only Frater Hugh had suspected. Only he had wormed himself into Da's confidence. Footsteps sounded in the corridor behind. She heard muffled voices.

"Hanna. Go."

"But, Liath—"

"Someone's coming."

"Mother is going to bring you food. I'll come tonight."

A key scraped in the lock. Chains met and rang softly.

Liath turned as the shadow vanished from the lip of the window. With a slow grind of wood against stone, the door opened. Liath retreated until her back was against the wall. She lifted her chin defiantly.

Three figures stood at the door. Two entered: Frater Hugh and the marshal. Hugh carried a candle. *The better*, thought Liath coldly, *to illuminate his handsome face.*

"The book," Hugh said immediately in his clipped, arrogant voice, so unlike the honeyed tones he used to cozen her father. "After a night here, have you thought better of telling me where the book is?"

"Frater," interposed the marshal in a calm voice. "You have finished with the child's testimony, I believe. I am satisfied that she had nothing to do with her father's death." Marshal Liudolf had an accounts book clasped under one elbow. "Now, child," he said, turning to Liath, "I have tallied the whole of your father's debts and possessions, and Frater Hugh has copied them here, in these pages. I will list them to you now."

Hugh was staring at her. Even when she kept her eyes focused on the old marshal, she could feel Hugh's gaze. Four books he had found in the cottage; four books he had stolen, whatever he might say about the church. He knew there was a fifth book, one she had hidden.

Marshal Liudolf stated the tally aloud, not referring to the parchment, since he could not read. But his memory was good. The tally of debts was impressive, and the tally of possessions short in comparison: one bow, a quiver, and fourteen arrows; quills and scraping knife and parchment; a silver sceatta minted during the reign of the Emperor Taillefer; one cooking pot, one bowl, two spoons, and one knife; a honestone; two shirts and one wool tunic; a wool cloak lined with rabbit's fur; a bronze brooch; leggings, boots; a bed, a table, a bench, a shelf, and a copper basin; two wool blankets; half a barrel of ale, honey, smoked meat, and three soapstone vessels, one filled with salt and two with ground wheat; two hens; two pigs; and one daughter.

"Aged fifteen," Liudolf finished.

"I turned sixteen four days ago, on Mariansmass."

"Did you?" Liudolf asked with interest. "That changes the auction, then. There can be no question of a bond price. As a legal adult, you assume all of your father's debts. Unless there is some other living relative?"

"None that I know of."

He sighed and nodded. "Then whoever assumes your debt will buy your freedom with it."

"There were books," she said quickly, not looking at Hugh. "My Da had four books and a . . ." Here she must be circumspect. "And a brass instrument for telling the time."

"Those items have been confiscated by the church."

"But they would bring enough to pay Da's debts!"

"I'm sorry, child." He said it firmly. She knew at once there was no point in arguing. Why should he listen to her, a kinless girl with no possessions and no one to protect her? "Here, you must mark the page where this is all written, to show that I've tallied it out correctly, so far as you know."

She took the pen and balanced the open book in her left hand. Hugh watched her avidly, but she carefully drew an awkward 'X' below the last bit of writing. She handed the book back to the marshal, and he clucked under his breath, looking truly sorry for her plight, sighed again, and scratched at his hair.

"It will be the auction tomorrow, child." Liudolf glanced at Hugh, knowing as well as Liath did that the frater was the only person able to buy off the entire price—especially now that he had also taken the books. Or at least, Hugh was the only person who might want to buy her. Old Count Harl had the wherewithal, and he even had a few slaves, but he had never interested himself in the affairs of the village except to hire Hanna's mother as a wet nurse for his children.

"Begging your pardon, Frater, Marshal," said a woman from behind them. "May I come in now?"

"Of course, of course. We're finished here." Liudolf retreated.

Hugh glared at Liath, not moving. "Frater," said Liudolf mildly. "We've business to finish before tomorrow, have we not?"

"I'll have that book," muttered Hugh. He left, taking the candle with him.

Mistress Birta came forward out of the gloom, holding a pitcher and a small package wrapped in cloth. "Here, Liath. I heard you had no food nor drink at all yesterday."

"I had a little wine." Liath took the pitcher. Her hands shook as she set it down on the floor, and she unwrapped the cloth to find a loaf of bread and a square of goat's cheese. "Oh, bless you, Mistress Birta. I'm so hungry. I didn't know it until now."

Mistress Birta glanced behind. The two men stood in the dank corridor, waiting for her. "I'll see that you've food in the morning, too." She raised her voice slightly. Daringly, Liath thought. "It isn't right to keep you hungry, no matter your circumstances." Taking a step closer to Liath, she dropped her voice to a whisper. "If we could have, child, we would have made the bond price at least, and treated you well. But custom has been off this year, and with Inga's wedding feast last autumn . . ."

"No, please, Mistress," Liath said hastily, embarrassed. "I know you did all you could. But Da never had any head for what it cost him—" She broke off, aware of the silence from the corridor, of Hugh listening avidly to every least word she said. "To live as he wished. He loved it here and had many a good evening at the inn gossiping with your husband."

"Yes, child," said Birta briskly, taking Liath's cue. "I'll leave you now. They wouldn't let me bring a blanket, but I trust to the Lady and Lord that it will stay warm tonight." She kissed Liath on the forehead and left her.

The door was shut behind her, scraping along the stone. Liath was alone. She ate first, all the food, but drank the ale sparingly. Then she paced.

Walking helped her think, even if it was only five paces and a turn, five paces and a turn. But though she might pace the cell a hundred times, she could not escape what Da had left her. Da was dead. Tomorrow his possessions would be sold to pay the debts he had left, and then she would be sold to cover what remained of those debts. Tomorrow she would lose her freedom. But she possessed Da's treasure, *The Book of Secrets*, and as long as she had that, she still possessed a measure of freedom in her heart.

She curled up in one corner, hugging her knees to her chest. Small comfort. She tucked her chin down onto her knees and closed her eyes. Liath started once, thinking she heard a soft voice calling her name. It did not call again. She rubbed at her eyes and curled tighter for warmth, shivering, and fell into a fitful sleep.

Murdered. Whoever had been hunting him had caught up with him at last. When had he lost his power? Or had it been her mother's gift he had used to call butterflies from empty air to charm a small child's lonely days?

"They've killed her, Liath," he had said to her that day eight years ago. "They've killed Anne and taken her gift to use as their own. We must flee. They must never find us."

Her mother. Her face rose from the remembered dream, her hair as pale as straw, her skin as light as if sun never touched it even when she sat for hours under the sun in the garden, eyes seeing elsewhere. Liath would sit and watch her and, sometimes, scrub her own skin, hoping to make the dirt come off, only the dirt never came off because it was baked there as if she had been formed in an oven and her skin baked to a golden brown before she was brought into this world.

Once they began their long, their endless, trail leading away from the little cottage and the garden where her mother had been killed, she had come to appreciate her skin, for even in the deepest heat of the summer's sun, she never burned or blistered. At first she thought it was Da's magic that spared her, for he burned and he blistered. Then, when she understood that Da had no real magic, no sorcery beyond tricks and homely remedies, beyond his encyclopedic knowledge, she thought it might be her own magic that protected her, waiting, quiescent, to be born when she grew old enough. Strong enough.

But Da told her over and over that she must never hope to have the gift. What little frail sorceries he conjured had not the slightest effect on her. If he called fire, it did not burn her hands. If he spelled a door shut, she could open it as if the spell had not worked at all, and then Hanna would come by and wonder how their door had gotten stuck.

She was dumb to it, Da said, like a mute who cannot speak. Like a deaf man who can see others speaking but not hear them. Once Da had caught her reading aloud a fire spell out of the book. Nothing had happened, but he had been so mad at her that he had made her sleep in the pig shed for the night, to teach her a lesson. But she had never minded the pigs.

"Liath."

She jerked awake, rose, and found her way by touch to the window. But there was no one outside. Wind whispered in the trees. Nothing else stirred. She shivered, rubbing her hands along her arms. She was not cold, really; she was scared.

However much they had roamed, however much they had lived from one day to the next, picking up and moving at the strangest signs, to the tune of mysterious portents that only Da recognized, she had always had Da. Whatever else he might be or failed to be, he had always taken care of her. Loved her. She wiped a tear from her cheek, and another.

"I love you, Da," she whispered to the cool night air, but there was no answer.

In the morning Marshal Liudolf escorted her to the common. The entire village had turned out, and quite a few farmers from farther out had heard the news that an auction was to be held and had come in for the occasion. The inn had set up tables out front. Liath could not bring herself to blame Mistress Birta and Master Hansal for taking advantage of this windfall to increase their custom. She refused the marshal's offer of a seat. Frater Hugh stood to one side, silent, while the marshal sold off each item from the list. However eccentric Da had been, he had been a man willing to help any woman or man who came to his door and no doubt Liath was the poorer now for Da having spent much of his substance trying to help others for no return. But even with the bidding running high, for Da had been well-liked, when all his worldly goods were sold, the debt was not yet covered.

Liudolf nodded and sighed his great, gusting sigh, and looked at her. The crowd looked at her. By the inn door, Hanna stared, face caught between anger and grief. But not crying, not Hanna. A sudden commotion stirred at the far edge of the common, and a horseman appeared.

Hugh flung up his head, starting 'round, his fine profile set off by his angry expression.

"Ivar!" cried Hanna. She ran to hold the horse's reins while Ivar dismounted.

They were too far away for Liath to be able to hear what they said, but Hanna spoke quickly, gesticulating wildly. Ivar shook his head. Hanna said something more, impassioned, but Ivar simply shook his head again. He led the horse across the common, Hanna walking and still talking beside him, and halted before the marshal.

Liudolf raised his eyebrows. "My lord Ivar," he said politely. "Have you come at your father's bidding?"

Ivar glanced once, swiftly, toward Liath, then away. Where she and Hanna, at sixteen, looked more like women now than the girls they had been two years ago when the three of them had formed their bond of friendship, Ivar still carried much of the coltish boy in his limbs and in the awkward grace that he would soon grow out of.

"No," he said in so low a voice she barely heard it.

Hugh smiled contentedly.

"I just heard of Master Bernard's death," Ivar went on. He turned to face Hugh. "I came to see that . . . that Liath is treated well." He said it sturdily, but as a threat or promise, thrown up against Hugh's overweening confidence, it had little impact. Hugh had at least eight years on Ivar and the kind of natural grace that comes from a tyrant's soul melded with a handsome man's conceit. And though Hugh's father might be baseborn—or so at least Birta gossiped—his mother was a margrave, by several degrees Count Harl's superior. Bastard or not, Hugh was destined for greater things, starting with the vast church holdings endowed by his mother and mother's mother. While it was rare for a man to act as an administrator of church property—as the Lord tends the wandering sheep so the Lady tends to the hearth—it was not unknown, especially where monasteries controlled vast estates. Or so Mistress Birta had said when Frater Hugh came as wandering priest to Heart's Rest last year to minister to the folk hereabouts. Mistress Birta was the most reliable source of news, gossip, and lore in all of Heart's Rest.

"Marshal," said Hugh quietly, looking bored, "may we finish? I haven't the leisure to stand here all day."

Ivar grimaced, blushing, and made a fist with his right hand, but Hanna grabbed him by the wrist and led him back to the inn. That he went unresistingly was marked by the crowd, which had gotten an extra bit of drama out of the morning. Liudolf sighed again and made a great show of tallying up the coin and barter gained from the sale of Da's possessions.

"How much remains?" demanded Hugh.

"Two gold *nomias*, or sceattas of equal worth."

"It's a shame," muttered someone in the crowd.

"The price of the books," whispered Liath.

Without blinking, Hugh handed two coins to the marshal. She stared, trying to get a look at them, but Liudolf closed his hand over the coins quickly, a startled expression on his face which made Liath wonder if *he* had ever seen a nomia either. Hugh turned to Liath. "Will you come? Or must I drag you?"

Da always said to let them think you knew something they did not. Liath spared a glance for Hanna and Ivar, who were standing together under the eaves of the inn, watching her. Hanna was pale, Ivar flushed. Liath nodded toward them, hoping her expression was calm. She began to walk toward the church, which lay down the road from the common. Hugh was caught off guard by her abrupt acquiescence, and he had to hurry to catch up. That gave her some small satisfaction.

He grabbed her arm at the elbow and with that grip walked out of the village and to the chapel, going inside and all the way along the nave and past it into the little warren of chambers behind. All the way to the small chamber where his bed stood.

"Here." He held onto her tightly. This room was rather more luxurious than Liath expected. Frater Robert, who had ministered here before Hugh, had slept on a cot in the nave. The chamber held a finely carved table and chair and a wooden chest inlaid with bright gems and enameling. On the table sat parchment, three quills, and a stoppered bottle of ink. A thick rug covered the floor, an expensive carpet woven with eight-pointed stars. Liath knew better than to let Hugh realize she recognized the pattern as an Arethousan design. A featherbed and a feather quilt lay heaped on the bed. "Here is where you sleep," he said.

"Never."

"Then with the pigs."

"Gladly, as long as it spares me from you."

He slapped her. Then, while her skin still stung from the blow, he pulled her hard against him and kissed her on the mouth. She got a hand in between them and shoved him away.

He laughed, wild and a little breathlessly. "You fool. My mother has promised me the abbacy of Firsebarg as soon as the old abbot dies. With the abbacy I will have entry into King Henry's progress, if I wish it. And in a year or five more, there will be a presbyter's crosier in my hands and I will walk among those who advise the skopos herself. Only give me the book and show me what your father taught you, and there is nothing you and I could not accomplish.''

"You took his books already. You *stole* them. They would have matched the debt. I would have been free."

His expression chilled her. "You will never be free, Liath. Where is the other book?"

"You murdered Da."

He laughed. "Of course I didn't. Died of a bad heart, that's what Marshal Liudolf said. If you think otherwise, my beauty, then perhaps you ought to confide in me. Another season and your father would have taken me into his confidence. You know it's true."

It was true. Da was lonely, and Hugh, whatever else he might be, could be charming. Da had liked him, had liked his quick mind, his curiosity, even his arrogance, since Hugh had the odd habit of treating Da as if he were his equal in social standing. But Da seemed to expect that.

"Da never had any sense in his friends," she said recklessly, to shake off these distracting thoughts.

"I know you've never liked me, Liath, although I can't imagine why. I've never offered you any insult." He placed two fingers under her chin and tilted her face up, forcing her to look at him. "Indeed, there isn't another woman in this village, in this whole frozen wasteland, that I'd ever think of offering my bed, and I've slept with a duchess and refused a queen. Once I'm abbot of Firsebarg you'll have your own house, servants, whatever you wish. A horse. And I don't intend to stop my whole life at Firsebarg. I have plans."

"If you have plans, then they must be treasonous." She twisted out of his grasp. "King Henry and the skopos have never tolerated sorcery. Only the Lady Sabella welcomes heretics into her company."

"How little you know of the church, my beauty. Sorcery is not a heresy. Indeed, the skopos is usually harsher toward heretics than toward sorcerers. Sorcery is only forbidden by the church when it is practiced outside the supervision of the skopos. I wonder what teacher your Da had. And in any case, you would be surprised how tolerant King Henry and the noble princes can be, if only the means further their aims. Where did you hide the book?"

She retreated to the door and did not answer.

He smiled. "I'm patient, Liath. Lady and Lord, what were your parents thinking, to call their child by an old Arethousan name? *Liathano.* An ancient name, linked to sorcery. Your Da admitted as much to me once."

"When he had drunk too much."

"Does that make it less true?" She said nothing. "Where is the book, Liath?" When still she did not speak he shook his head, but the smile remained on his lips. "I'm patient. Which will it be? My bed, or the pigs?"

"The pigs."

With a lightning strike he grabbed her wrist with one hand and slapped her hard once again with the other. Then he embraced her and ran a hand up her back. His breath was hot on her neck. She stood rigid, but when he began to move her toward the bed she fought against him. Got a heel behind his ankle and tripped him. They fell in a heap on the floor, and she pushed away and scrambled to her feet. He laughed and caught her by one knee, jerked her down so hard her knees bruised on the stone and the breath was jarred out of her. Then he let her go and stood, breathing hard. He bowed in the most formal, court manner, offered her his hand to help her to her feet.

"You'll come to my bed willingly or not at all." He pulled a scrap of white linen from his belt, wiped her right hand clean, then bent to kiss her fingers. "My lady," he said, perhaps mockingly. She was too dazed to interpret his tone. His golden hair brushed her hand, and he straightened. " 'She is dark and lovely, this daughter of Saïs, touched by the sun's breath. Turn your eyes away from me; they are as bright as the star of morning.' "

She shoved her hand behind her back and wiped it against her tunic.

"Now. You will feed the pigs and the hens, sweep this room, get me a bath, and then tell Mistress Birta that she no longer need send a meal over twice a day. You can cook, I suppose?"

"I can cook. May I go?"

He stood aside so she could leave, but she had only gotten as far as the narrow passageway when he called her name.

"Liath." She turned back to see him leaning in the doorway. Even in the semigloom of the little warren of cells, his golden hair and his combed linen robe and his fine, clean skin made him seem to shine as he watched her. "You may even last out the summer with the pigs, but I don't think you'll like it so well when winter comes."

How far she would get if she tried to run away? A useless thought. She would not get far, nor would she have any means to live if she did escape from him. She had seen herself in eight years of running that there were far worse circumstances than these.

Hugh chuckled, mistaking her silence for a reply. "Tell Mistress Birta that she may tally up any food or goods you buy from her, and I'll pay her each Ladysday. I expect a good table. And you will dine with me. Go on."

She went. Going outside to feed the animals that were stabled in the shed alongside the storage rooms, she saw a horseman sitting astride his mount, out in the trees. It was Ivar. Seeing her, he began to ride forward. She waved him away, quickly, desperately. For there was another thing she had seen in Frater Hugh's chamber, resting on the feather quilt. A fine, gold-hilted long sword, sheathed in red leather. A nobleman's sword. She had no doubt that Hugh knew how to use it and would not hesitate to, even against a son of the local count.

Ivar reined his horse in and sat, watching her, while she worked. After a while she went inside. When she came out again, carrying two buckets yoked on a staff across her shoulders to fill for Hugh's bath, Ivar was gone.

III
SHADOWS FROM
THE PAST

1

IT took five days to walk from Osna village to Lavas Holding, the sergeant in charge told Alain. The journey this spring, however, took fifteen days because the chatelaine and her company stopped at every village and steading to accept taxes or rents or a young person in service for the upcoming year. They came to Lavas Holding on St. Marcia's Day, and Alain stared at the high timber palisade that enclosed the count's fortress, the timber great hall built on a rise with a stone bailey behind it, these two central buildings surrounded by a smaller palisade. The village spilled out below the outer palisade, down to the banks of a slow-flowing river.

He had little chance to gape. He and the others were promptly herded into the fort, where they waited in an untidy line in the huge dirt yard—the outer court—as Chatelaine Dhuoda and her retinue set up a table and began to call the company forward one by one. Alain found himself in a group of young men, and soon it was his turn to stand before Sergeant Fell.

"Can you ride a horse? Ever handled a spear? Worked with

horses, perchance? No, of course not." The burly sergeant motioned for the next man in line to step forward.

"But, sir—" Alain began desperately. Had it not been promised him, to learn the arts of war?

"Go on, go on! We haven't time to train new recruits into men-at-arms, not now. Count Lavastine is already gone out to hunt the Eika and we're marching out with a second force in twenty days. Get into the other group and don't waste my time, lad."

Chastened, Alain retreated to the other line, this one composed of women as well as men, lads his age, and girls not quite women, folk of varying degrees and ages and stations. He came in time and in his turn before Chatelaine Dhuoda. She asked him a few questions. He did not truly hear himself answer. Though her hair was veiled by a clean linen cloth, it showed a tendency to come free of its confines, wisps of reddish, coarse hair curling at her ears and on her forehead.

"What an accent!" she said to the young cleric in the plain brown robe of a frater who sat next to her, marking out the list for Count Lavastine. "Well, boy, Master Rodlin can use you in the stables. Who is next?"

"But Brother Gilles taught me the letters. I can write all of them in a neat hand."

At this, the frater looked up with interest. He had a fierce gaze, like a hawk. "Can you read?" he demanded.

"No . . . no, I can't read yet, but I'm sure I could assist with the clerics. I can count—" The frater had already looked away dismissively, toward the next candidate. Alain turned desperately back to Chatelaine Dhuoda. None of this was going as he had dreamed it would. "Surely you remember my Aunt Bel telling you I was meant to be confirmed as a—"

"Move on!" said Dhuoda. A young woman stepped forward to take Alain's place, so Alain had no choice but to do as he was told.

He found the stables and was at once put to work at a job any idiot could manage: filling a cart with manure and hauling it out to the fields. His only companion at this task was a halfwit called Lackling, a boy of about his age who was as thin as a stick, with bandy legs and a misshapen jaw through which he could not form true words. He was skittish and as likely to stare at the clouds or stroke the donkey as to keep to his work, but Alain did not have the heart to be angry at him, poor creature.

"I see you get along well enough with our Lackling," said Master Rodlin that evening after the two boys had been given a hasty supper of cheese and bread and an onion. "You can share the loft with him. Make sure the new lads don't tease him too much. He's a harmless creature and the animals trust him, for I suppose they know he's as dumb-witted as they are."

Lackling made an odd snuffling noise and picked up the crumbs of bread from the dirt floor of the stables. With his treasure in his hands he went just outside and stood, hand out and open, staring at the sky and shuffling nervously back and forth.

Master Rodlin grunted, not without pity. "Thinks the birds will come and feed from his hand," he said. "But Deacon Waldrada says it is our duty as good Daisanites to shelter the weak. And the lad was born here, in the shadow of the fort. His mother died birthing him, for it was a hard birth and perhaps it would have been best had the child died as well, poor dumb creature."

"I was born here," said Alain. "In Lavas Holding, I mean."

Rodlin looked at him with a keener interest. "Who was your mother?"

Now Alain flushed. "I don't know."

"Ah," said Rodlin knowingly. "Fostered out, were you? In a town like this there's always a woman or two who can't admit whose child she bore and so gives it away."

"She didn't give me away. She died birthing me."

"Had she no kin? What about your father?"

Alain hung his head, seeing the expression on Master Rodlin's face change from curiosity to a thin incurious smile: identified and dismissed as some whore's unwanted bastard.

"Go on, then," continued the stable master. "You'll do well enough in the stables. Just don't go into the kennels."

"There're no hounds in the kennels."

"But there will be when Count Lavastine returns. They'd as soon kill you as pass you by, lad. Don't forget it and don't get in the habit of going by there, for your own good. See this scar." He pointed to a ragged white scar that ran from ear to shoulder. "They gave me that, and more besides. Stay well away and you'll be safe."

"Why would the count keep such vicious hounds?" asked Alain, but Rodlin was already walking away, intent on more important duties than chatting with a motherless stableboy.

Lackling, crumbs still in hand, came back inside, looking disconsolate. Alain sneezed and wiped the dust of hay from his lips. "I don't suppose you know about the hounds," said Alain.

"Moewr," said Lackling. "Hroensgueh lakalig."

Alain smiled sadly at the halfwit. Wasn't it only self-pity to feel sorry for himself when faced with this half-grown manboy no longer a child and yet incapable of becoming a true man? In Osna village he had been Bel's nephew, and that counted for a great deal. Here he was just a village boy from the outlying lands who didn't know swordcraft and had nothing further to recommend him and no kin to come to his aid. So they made him a stableboy and ordered him to shovel manure. But he had his wits and his strength and a whole body.

"Come," he said to Lackling. He took the halfwit by the elbow and led him outside where dusk shaded the stone tower in a wreath of shadow and the last glint of sun sparked off the banner riding above the palisade gate: two black hounds on a silver field, the badge of the counts of Lavas. "Open your hand. Here, I'll cup your hands in mine. Now we must just stand still enough. . . ."

So they stood as dusk lowered down and the beasts thumped and rustled in the stables and the outer court quieted as day passed. A sparrow came, flitting out of the twilight, and perched on Alain's forefingers where they peeped out from underneath Lackling's smaller hands. It took a crumb. Lackling crowed with delight and the bird fluttered away.

"Hush," said Alain. "You must remain quiet." They waited again, and soon another sparrow came, and a third, and ate all the crumbs off Lackling's hands while the halfwit wept silently with joy.

Master Rodlin proved indifferent to Alain as long as the boy did as he was told. In fact, that first month while Sergeant Fell prepared his new soldiers to march out, everyone proved indifferent to Alain. He watched while the other boys got into feuds that escalated to fistfights and once to a knifing. He stared, shamed and yet shamefully curious, while the young men-at-arms flirted with the servant girls and slipped away with them to a dark corner of the loft. He studied the more experienced men as they readied their weapons and honed their fighting skills.

On St. Kristine's Day, she who was the holy martyr of the city of Gent, a woman cloaked and badged as a King's Eagle rode in to deliver a message to the count. That night at supper in the hall, sitting at the lower tables, Alain watched in astonishment as the Eagle's conversation with Chatelaine Dhuoda, at the upper table, degenerated into an argument.

"This is not a *request*," said the Eagle with obvious indignation. "King Henry expects Count Lavastine to attend his progress. Are you telling me that the count refuses?"

"I am telling you," said Dhuoda calmly, "that I will send a message to the count with Sergeant Fell and his company when they march out in two days' time. When Count Lavastine returns at the end of the summer, I am sure he will act as soon as he is able."

"If you send this sergeant and his company back with me, it would go a good way toward convincing King Henry of the count's loyalty."

"Only the count can make that decision." Dhuoda gestured for more ale to be brought. Alain recognized by now that wine was reserved for the most favored visitors, which this King's Eagle clearly was not. "The Eika burned a monastery and two villages already this spring. The count needs every able man in his county to strike back and protect his lands. But of course I will include all that you have said in the message my clerics write to him."

But it was clear to everyone present, and especially to the Eagle, that although Dhuoda's answers were perfectly legitimate, they were also evasive.

The Eagle left the next day, still looking angry. And the day after that Sergeant Fell and his company marched out. The remaining horses and cattle—except for a few workhorses, the donkeys, one old warhorse, and a lame cow who still gave milk—were taken out to the summer pastures. Most of the village worked out in the fields, labored in their vegetable gardens, or gathered fruit in the forest beyond the cultivated land. The few servants left in the holding went about their business with an efficiency that left them plenty of time to drink and dice in the long pleasant evenings.

No one bothered Alain; no one noticed him to make sure he did his work. Every night, lying beside Lackling in the loft above the stables, he would touch the wooden Circle of Unity Aunt Bel had given him and then draw out the string from which hung the rose and finger the soft petals. The vision he had seen from Dragonback Ridge above Osna Sound seemed so distant now. He would have thought it an illusion, born of storm and sorrow, except that the blood-red rose he wore as a necklace beneath his shirt had not withered or died.

In the holding, a quiet month passed. Trained by a navigator, Alain watched the skies when it was clear; the moon waned and waxed to full and began to wane again. Lackling showed him where all the best berry bushes ripened, in bright clearings hidden away in the forest. He found a path leading farther up into the hills, but the boy became frightened and dragged him away from it.

Alain asked Master Rodlin if he knew of any old trails in the forest, and the stable master merely said that an old ruin lay up in the hills beyond and that more than one foolish boy had broken leg or arm climbing on crumbling walls. Like the kennels, it was something even a halfwit avoided.

Now that most of the stable animals were gone, Alain was given whatever odds and ends of the worst work were left, whatever task no one else wanted to do. He spent more and more time leaning on a shovel inside the empty stables and staring at nothing. That moment up on Dragonback Ridge when the Lady of Battles had invested him with her terrible sword seemed like wishful dreaming now. How could he have been chosen for a special trial? Unless digging out the latrines was one.

"Oooo. There he is," said a female voice. This declaration was followed by a giggling.

Alain whirled around. Two of the kitchen girls stood at the stable doors, thrown open to admit more air. Light streamed in around them, showering their disheveled hair in dust motes. Hay drifted down from the loft to settle in the empty buckets they carried. One of the girls sneezed. The other giggled again.

Alain blushed, but he marched forward resolutely nonetheless, heading out through the door. He refused to be cowed by a pair of serving girls no older than he was, girls who would never have looked at him twice if there had been more single men than old Raimond and witless Lackling about.

The blue-eyed girl dipped her shoulders as he passed, enough that her shift slipped down to reveal a tantalizing expanse of flesh.

He stumbled on even ground.

"Isn't your name Alain?" asked Blue-Eyes.

They only meant to tease him. He knew that. And yet, he could not help but stop. "Yes." He knew he was still blushing.

"Have you heard about the ruins up behind on the hill?" asked

Blue-Eyes as she straightened up. Her friend, whose eyes were a nondescript hazel, giggled again, then covered her mouth with a hand to hide her crooked teeth.

"I've heard of it," said Alain cautiously.

"Withi, you daren't do it," said the friend in a choked voice.

Blue-Eyes cast her a scornful glance. "I'm not the one who won't dare." She looked back at Alain. "Where do you come from?"

"Osna village," he said proudly, but they looked blankly at him, never having heard of such a place. "It's called Dragonback, too, for the great ridge—"

For some reason this sent both girls into wild laughter, as if he had said something indecent.

"Dragonback, is it now?" asked Blue-Eyes finally. She was the prettier of the two, although she had an open sore on one lip and her hair was more grime than color. "I'll be walking up to the ruins at sunset, this evening. They say at Midsummer's Eve the ghosts of daimones walk abroad!" She blinked those blue eyes at Alain and put her hands on her hips, thrusting them provocatively forward. He knew he was flushing again, however hard he tried not to. Withi was one of the girls the men-at-arms took up into the hayloft. She had never had time for *him* before today.

He took in a breath. "Deacon Waldrada at last week's sermon said it wasn't devils or daimones who built those ruins. She said it was the people of the old Dariyan Empire built them, long ago, even before Taillefer was emperor over all these lands. That it was men, like us. Or maybe elves."

"Oooo. What a fine learned young man we have here. What was your father? The abbot of "Dragonback" Abbey, making dragon-back with a sweet innocent village lass?" She laughed, and Crooked Teeth laughed, too.

"My father's a merchant, and a good, decent man! He served the old count in his time. And the brothers of Dragon's Tail Monastery are dead, killed in an Eika raid this spring. The Lady scorns those who laugh at the misfortune of others!"

"Huh!" said Crooked Teeth disdainfully. "You sound like a cleric yourself. Think you're too good for us, don't you? I'm leaving, Withi." She swung her buckets out with a flourish and departed in the direction of the well.

Withi lingered. "I'm still going up there." She followed her companion but paused and looked back over her shoulder with a grin.

"If you're not too scared, you could meet me there. I might just show you something you haven't seen before." Then, to Crooked Teeth: "Wait for me!"

Digging out the latrines was such filthy work that he was relieved when Master Rodlin called him in. Sergeant Fell had brought a company of soldiers back to the fortress and Alain helped unload their wagon. Then he washed his face and hands and rinsed down his boots before going to supper.

Chatelaine Dhuoda had ridden east to escort Lavastine's cousin's wife to Lavas Holding for the remainder of her pregnancy. Because of the summer heat and the absence of lord and lady in the hall, Cook had set up two trestle tables out behind the kitchens. The party of young soldiers took up all of one table, where they boasted of their great exploits and ate their supper of wheat bread and pease porridge and roasted fish and berries with equal gusto. Sergeant Fell sat at their head, tolerant of their high spirits.

Lackling sat alone at the end of the other table, which was set beside the first. If the soldiers hadn't been too busy flirting with Withi and Crooked Teeth and a black-haired woman, they would likely have chased him off. Alain sat down beside the halfwit and was rewarded with a smile and one of the boy's incomprehensible phrases as greeting.

"So," said Sergeant Fell, continuing his news. He had a dramatic facial scar on his left cheek that had not been there when he and the others marched out. "Then the count tells us we're to be riding east to join up with the king's progress—"

"Nay," exclaimed Cook. "Say it's not so! Count Lavastine has decided to swear loyalty to Henry?"

Alain caught in his breath. He set his spoon down, porridge only half eaten, to listen more closely.

"I think not," said the sergeant. "I think he only wanted to beg aid from Henry, because these raids have been so bad. But it never came to that. For then a lad rode in from the west, saying the Eika have raided *again*."

Cook rubbed her chin. "But they've burned both monasteries along the coast, we heard. There's nothing else rich enough along there to tempt them, I'd thought."

"Not out along the coast, but if they was to sail in along the River Mese, they'd come up past St. Synodios' Monastery which was richly endowed by the count's grandfather and indeed all the way to this very holding."

"When I was a lad," said old Raimond in his querulous voice, "we followed the laws set down by the church. Our faith was enough to keep those barbarians away from Varre." He clapped his tin mug down on the table for emphasis. "Before Henry took the throne as wasn't his to take. When *I* was a boy, Eika raided all the way west and south to Salia, and laid it waste, we heard. We even got Salians come up hereabouts, running from them." Raimond was so old that he was bald and his beard was mostly stray wisps of curling hair. "That was when Taillefer's last daughter was still alive. Biscop she might be, but neither her prayers nor the Salian king's soldiers would drive the Eika off. Had to pay them, in the end." He clucked, pleased at this manifestation of the Lord and Lady's dislike of the Salians. "Those were hard times, I don't mind saying."

One of the young soldiers laughed. "How would you have known about goings-on in Salia when you've never set foot outside of Lavas Holding?" He snorted, pleased with his retort, and called for more ale.

Sergeant Fell swatted him in the head. "None of your impudence, Heric! You give the old man respect, you hear? If you live so long, I'll be amazed!" The other soldiers chuckled. "My old uncle said the same thing, that the Salian king had to pay the Eika to leave and that they left only after they'd plundered the countryside. Well, then, Cook, I don't know what is meant to be done about Lady Sabella and her banner, or the king's progress. I do know that we've been sent by the count's order to ask Biscop Thierra to offer up church's gold, for we've need of more weapons and more supplies. There are too many Eika and too many raids this year. Count Lavastine must have aid."

Withi paused beside the sergeant and leaned close enough that her clothing brushed his. "Is it true that Eika are dragon's get? That they have skin scaled like a snake's? And claws?"

Alain shuddered. Withi's interest seemed uncouth.

"I've heard a worse story," said the sergeant, settling a hand on her hip. "If you're brave enough to hear it."

"I am!"

He grinned. "Well, then. It was once told me that Eika came about by foul magic, and a curse. That a great dragon was killed and as it lay dying it cursed any who might dare profane its corpse. But all the women of the village had heard stories of the great power of the dragon's heart—power they could use to charm any man they wished, so they had been told. They cut open the dragon's body and pulled out the heart all bloody and steaming hot. They cut it into many pieces and shared it out between them."

"They *ate* it?" Withi made a face, pulling away from the sergeant's casual embrace.

"Ate it, every bit. And soon enough all those women were pregnant, and when they gave birth, they gave birth to *monsters!*"

His audience was hushed, and every person in the hall jumped when he spoke the word "*monsters.*" The sergeant chuckled, pleased with the success of his tale. "So these monstrous children, it is said, ran away into the north and were never seen again. Until the creatures we call the Eika came raiding."

"I saw one dead," said Raimond, undaunted by this story. "Saw no claws, but his skin was as tough as leather, and it shone like polished gold."

Young Heric snickered again. "Like polished gold! More like it was armor stolen off a Salian body. I heard they steal women, and what would they need women for . . ." Here he paused to measure Withi up and down with a grin. ". . . if they were dragon's get? They're men just like you and me."

"Oooh," said Withi in her most scornful tone, "and I suppose that you think the old ruins back up the hill were built by men just like you and me, and not by daimones and devils and other ungodly creatures?"

"Hush, Withi," said Cook in a brisk voice.

Heric laughed, as did some of his comrades. But the sergeant did not. "You've not seen the Eika yet, Heric," said the sergeant, "or you'd not laugh. Nor is it ever wise to laugh at the things left on this earth by creatures we do not know."

An indefinable hush settled over the older men and women, a taut attention, that the young soldiers seemed unaware of.

"I hear," continued Withi defiantly, "that if a person goes up to the ruins on Midsummer's Eve, you can see the ghosts of them who did build it."

"I'll go with you," said Heric, winking and nudging his fellows, "just to see what I might see." They snickered and coughed.

"You'd not joke," said Raimond, echoing the sergeant's grim words, "if you'd been there yourself. Ai, I recall it clearly. There was a girl, back these many years, who went up to those ruins on Midsummer's Eve. On a dare, it was." His gaze was sharp suddenly as he looked right at Withi. "She came back at dawn half crazy, and pregnant, too, or so we found out in due time. And she died bearing the child she'd taken from whatever haunts up there!" Hands shaking, he gripped the handle of his cup and banged it on the table for emphasis.

"What?" scoffed Heric. "She gave birth to Lackling here?"

"Nay, and you'd not laugh, boy. One of the men from the country took the child away."

"Now you listen to me, young Heric," said Cook in the assured voice of one who rules her domain completely. "It's true enough, what Raimond says. It happened not so many years back either, for I knew her when we were both girls. She was a pretty, black-haired slip of a thing. Her parents were Salian, fled from the Eika raids. She did go up to the ruins, though everyone said she shouldn't, and she told me—" Here Cook's husky voice dropped to a whisper and every stray conversation at the two tables vanished as does a snowflake in fire. Everyone strained forward to listen. "She told me that the shade of an elf prince come to her, one of the Lost Ones, and lay with her, right there in the altar house, and that it was his child she bore." No one, not even Heric, made a noise. "But the Lord and Lady grant it not to those of mortal frame to have concourse with the Lost Ones, for they are not believers. So she paid the price. She died three days after birthing the child."

Alain stared at Cook. Sergeant Fell had told a tale to frighten and amaze Withi. Cook's story was different. Certainly she was telling the truth. She was of an age to be his mother. He had black hair, and his features were sharper and a little foreign, or so everyone in Osna always said. What if this black-haired Salian girl *was* his mother, and the shade in the ruins truly his father? A Lost One! Wouldn't that explain why the Lady of Battles had come to him? He had always felt different—and it was often said that elvish kind were daimones in truth because unlike mortal men they did not die in the natural course of years, and if killed by accident or violent death, they were not succored into the Chamber of Light but damned to wander this world forever as dark shades.

"I'm going anyway," said Withi stubbornly.

"I'll go, too," said Heric with a leer.

"You'll not!" said the sergeant, "and that by my order. We've no time to waste. We ride to Biscop Thierra at dawn."

"None of you are brave enough to go," declared Withi with a contemptuous toss of her head.

"I'll go," said Alain, and then started, surprised to hear his voice so loud in summer's drowsing endless afternoon that melded into the long bright evening.

Everyone stared at him. Most of the men-at-arms laughed, eyeing him where he sat, the only person among them to keep Lackling company. He was nearly as filthy as Lackling.

Old Raimond snorted but said nothing.

"Who's this stripling?" demanded Heric. "Enough of a chickling to grow some down on his cheek but not more of a man than that! Or hoping to become one!" He chuckled at his own joke, although no one else did.

"He's the stableboy," said Cook, not unkindly.

Alain found that, once noticed, he did not like the attention. He had grown comfortable with anonymity. He lowered his gaze and stared fixedly at the table.

"He's the only one brave enough to go!" said Withi.

"Heric!" The sergeant looked annoyed. "If you've a mind to act like a fool, I'll see you're whipped in the morning. Here, girl. I've a better idea for your entertainment tonight."

Alain looked up to see the sergeant draw the girl closer against him, but Withi had a mulish look on her face now, and she shoved him away. "You may all laugh, but I'm going."

Heric stood up. "I won't let any stableboy—"

"Heric, sit down or I'll whip you right here!"

Heric vacillated between drunken pride and the fear of immediate humiliation. Finally he sat.

Lackling burped loudly and, when everyone laughed, blinked good-naturedly into their attention. Sergeant Fell went back to talking of the Eika raids and of the count's plans to protect his lands and villages along the coast.

It was easy enough for Alain to slip away, once the sergeant had gotten into full flood about the latest devastated village and the rumors that a convent much farther east—over the border into Wendar—had been set upon by the Eika. He had heard that all the nuns and laywomen had been raped and murdered except for the ancient abbess, who had been set free with her feet mutilated to walk the long, painful road to the nearest village.

It was finally twilight, a handful of stars coming to life against the darkening sky. It had to be true! Only by visiting the ruins on a night when the shades of the old builders might return could he learn the truth.

He changed into his clean shirt—for Aunt Bel was too proud to send him away with only one—and pulled his old linen tunic on over it. After some hesitation, he borrowed a lantern. Then, taking a stout stick from the stables, he set off on the track that wound around the earthen walls and four wooden towers of Count Lavastine's fortress and up into the wooded hills behind. Of Withi he caught neither sight nor sound. He walked alone except for the night animals: an owl's hoot, the flap of wings, a shriek, then a sudden frantic rustling in the undergrowth.

It was terribly dark and there was no moon, though the stars were uncannily bright. Eventually his eyes adjusted. He dared not use the lantern yet; oil was too precious. It was a fair long walk up along the hill and curving back into the wilder wood beyond. By the time the path led him up to where the tree line ended abruptly at the edge of the ruins, the bright red star—the Serpent's Eye—rising in the east had moved well up into the sky.

Alain paused at the edge of the trees. The forest ended abruptly here, thick, ancient trees in an oddly straight line at the clearing's edge. No saplings encroached on the meadow beyond. Though it had taken uncounted years for the old buildings to fall into such complete ruin—many generations back, long before the Emperor Taillefer's time, even back to the time when the blessed Daisan first walked on the Earth and brought his message to the faithful—still the forest had never overtaken the stones. There was something unnatural here.

He felt all at once that the stones were aware of him.

An outer wall of stone—still almost as tall as he was—circled the inner ruins. The craggy height of hill rose above it, trees straggling along its slopes. It was far quieter here than it had been in the woods. As he stared, a shadow flitted above and vanished into the trees. He gripped the stick more tightly in his left hand and picked his way carefully across the uneven ground to a gap in the wall. It looked like a sally port or servant's entrance, or something more arcane, unknowable to men. Now stone had fallen from the wall to partially block it. If the gap had once been shuttered by a door, that door was gone. He climbed carefully over the tumbled stone and paused at the top, staring into the ruin.

The stone itself gave off light, a pale gleam like the phosphorescence of foam and weed on the waters of Osna Sound. And the stars shone unnaturally bright. Indeed, some few of the constellations he knew—taught to him by his father who, as a merchant, needed to also be a navigator—glittered with an eerie brilliance, as if some unseen power called brighter fires up from their depths.

More shadows played among the ruins than ought to. Distinct shadows covered the ground at strange angles impossible to trace to any of the fallen walls. The air stirred, shivering, a faint noise. . . .

He froze, terrified. A silent shape winged across the ruins, and he relaxed. It was only an owl.

He stood there for a long time, balanced precariously on a block of fallen stone, just looking. It was not a good night to walk inside these ruins. He knew that now. And yet, he *had* to see the altar house, to see if he felt a link there, a calling of blood to blood. He lit the lantern, and as its light flared, he had to blink and look away. With its glow the shadows along the ground and walls shifted as he took a step forward.

He realized what he was seeing.

He was seeing the shadows of *what had been*, not the shadows of the ruins lying there now. The lantern's pale light and the gleam of stone illuminated the shadows of the buildings as if they still stood, complete, unfallen. This filigree of arches and columns and proud walls stretching out as impossible shadows along the ground was the shade of the old fort, come alive on Midsummer's Eve. There were four buildings: one at the west, one at the south, one at the east, and one at the north, and a circular building in the center; arcaded avenues linked them.

A branch snapped in the woods behind him. He flattened himself against the stone and looked back. Nothing, no one, appeared at the clearing's edge. But something stranger still: The shadow of the outer wall, next to the trees, was the shadow of the wall in its ruined state—its shadow as it stood now, this night, worn down by time and the Lord's and Lady's Hands. The enchantment, if enchantment it was, only lived within the ruin itself.

He slipped down and slowly walked forward into the ancient fort. Stepping around shadows of stones that did not exist, he saw at once that the stonework in here was as far superior to the stonework on the outer wall as the count's fine charger was to the old donkey he and Lackling hitched to the pony cart to haul manure out to the fields.

Grass grew from between cracks in the paving. He knelt and ran his fingers over a stone surface too smooth to be man's work, even old and broken as it was now. The wall of the nearest building stood only as high as his waist. It was built of black stone, as black as pitch. He held the lantern close to it and by this light examined it. Faint pictures had been carved into the stone, stiff figures of creatures with the bodies of women and the heads of hawks and snakes and wolves; their eyes glowed like lit jewels. Beyond, at the end of the avenue, the central building gleamed with a startling iridescence. Its white stone seemed to reach into the heavens, touching the sovereign constellations—the Sword, the Staff, the Cup, and the Queen herself, whose Bow was aimed at the Dragon—and drawing their light by invisible threads down into itself, casting it back as luminescence.

Round and white. That building was the altar house.

A shadow moved, detaching itself from a far wall. Alain jumped to his feet, then shuddered, suddenly unable to move. It was not Withi.

It walked with a man's form, moving toward the altar house.

Yet it was not a *man's* form. Tall and slender he was, yes, but indefinably different in the subtle grace with which he walked and in the strange cut of his garments. The figure halted at the shaded entrance to the altar house and slowly turned, surveying the ruins. At first pass his gaze traveled right over Alain, as if he could not perceive him at all.

He had a wonderful, disturbing consistency to him, partly shade and partly real. He was very dark, but Alain could still see his features clearly. A thin face, more bronze than northern pale, and deep, old eyes under a shock of black hair.

Black hair. Like Alain's black hair. The *man* was clean-shaven or else beardless, although how any man could truly be called a man unless he wore a beard Alain did not know. Unless he was no true *man*. He wore a fine metal cuirass decorated with intertwined beasts whose twining points led down onto the leather fringe that ended halfway to his knees. Under it he wore a plain linen tunic, and he held a white cloak draped over his left arm. He was looking for someone. Or meeting someone.

Alain heard the whisper of a tentative footstep. Over to his right, through a gap in the stone, he saw the opaque shape of a girl appear. But she had a leaden, earthy heaviness to her that marked her instantly in Alain's eyes as a mortal, like himself. She stared around, looking straight at the shade without appearing to see it, and then caught sight of Alain. Or at least, of his lantern.

"Alain?" she said, her tone low and uneasy. "Is that you?"

Alain took one step forward. The shade took a step forward, mirroring him, and their gazes met.

Dizziness swept him. The distant roar of flames sounded in his ears. He smelled smoke thick and oily in his nostrils.

"Where has Liathano gone?" The shade now held in his hand a lance, pointed and deadly, but it was held upright, not threatening Alain.

"I—I don't know," Alain stammered. He could not break his gaze away from the shade's eyes. They gleamed, like the altar house, like the fine outline of the shade's entire body, more gold than white. He heard the pound of horses galloping past, a haze of distant shouting, a faint horn caught on the wind.

"You are not of the blood," said the shade abruptly, lifting the lance like a challenge. "And yet, how else could you be here? What is your name? Who is your mother? How have you come here?"

Though he could not look away from the shade, Alain saw with his peripheral vision the shapes of the buildings. They stood tall, beautiful, and surprisingly delicate for such massive stone structures, but even now the dull red of flame cast its color across them. Burning. Burning. Smoke swelled from the burning and wind swept the thick oily stench across his face. He coughed.

A lost prince, truly. For now Alain understood what was happening, what he saw: The final destruction of this fort. The sounds of fighting came inexorably closer, the terrible music of fate.

"My name is Alain," he said, wanting desperately to help, yet knowing that this fort was already doomed. What could he possibly do? Who was Liathano? Was this shade his true father? "I don't know how I came here. I don't know who my mother is."

"You are a *man*," said the prince, and his eyes widened with elegant astonishment, "and yet marked. If only we had time to un-

ravel this enigma." But his chin lifted. He broke his gaze away from
Alain as if he had heard his name called.

A voice shrieked in terror. Alain staggered and flung a hand up to
press against his pounding temples.

"It *is* you, Alain!"

Through the pain in his head he heard her stumble toward him
across the cracked paving. "Did you see it? Did you hear it?" She
threw herself on him. He staggered back under the force of her fear
and dropped the lantern. It sputtered out. "All black, they were,
running through the sky like the count's own hounds but screaming with hunger! If they had caught us, they would have devoured
us."

The heat of her body pressed against him drained the fog from
his mind. He pushed her away though she was still babbling about
red eyes and six-legged dogs, grabbed the lantern, and ran to the
altar house. But the shade was gone.

"Don't go in there!" she screamed as Alain crossed the empty
threshold.

But there was nothing inside, nothing except the gleam of the
ruined stone walls and an ovoid stone of pale marble—what those
like Cook would call an altar—embedded in the earth at the center
of the chamber. Nothing else except for grass and one scraggly bush
whose waxy leaves left a trail of sticky ooze on his fingers. From
outside he heard sobbing and then the sound of Withi running
away down the broken avenue.

He sat down on the altar stone.

This place, this outpost of the old Dariyan Empire, had stood here
in all its glory so very long ago, for how many years he could not
imagine, knowing only that the Lost Ones lived many more years
than did men. Only in the end it had died, in its way, burning, while
the lost prince searched for his Liathano and horses galloped away
into a night drawn red with fire.

The gleaming stone faded to dull shadows. The stars lost their
miraculous glamour and moved onward, ever westward on their
endless round. He lifted a hand to his face and discovered his eyes
were wet with tears. A shadow raced overhead, but it was only the
owl, hunting in the night.

2

SUMMER passed. Alain did not have the heart to go back to the old ruins, knowing he would only find them empty. There was no answer for him there. Withi no longer spoke to him, and when he watched her, remembering her embrace, how she had clasped him close against her, he knew she was whispering of him to the others. Bitter, he kept to himself.

No other strange incidents disturbed the quiet of long summer days. Spelt was harvested. The oats were almost ripe. Chatelaine Dhuoda returned to the fortress with Lady Aldegund, wife of Lavastine's cousin Geoffrey. A girl of about fifteen, she arrived at Lavas faint from exhaustion and from her advanced pregnancy. A wandering laborer, come to Lavas for the harvest work, had been one month ago in Osna village; he reported that Aunt Bel and her family were all well and had given him three days' work hauling stone for quernstones from the quarry to Bel's workshop.

On the feast day of St. Tiana the Joyous, holy martyr of the town of Bens, a messenger rode in. Alain looked up from the shed where he had been stacking bundled hay from the second crop cut on the south quarter.

The man had a dirty white rag tied around his head, covering his right eye and ear. Old blood stained it brown. His clothes were worn out, patched with the remains of other hose and tunics. When he dismounted next to the hall, he walked with a limp. It took Alain that long to recognize him as Heric, the brash young soldier of midsummer. His entire aspect was muted now.

Alain leaned against the low fence that hemmed in the open side of the shed and listened as Heric delivered his message in a vivid, penetrating voice to Chatelaine Dhuoda and her shadow cleric, the frater. People gathered to hear the news.

"The campaign is done for the season. The winds are changing. The Eika have sailed north back to their own ports for the winter. All along the coast they attacked. But here at the end three Eika ships bottled themselves up the Vennu after the tide had gone out.

They built themselves a stockade, but the count begged for the Grace of Our Lord and Lady and led the attack. We stormed it!" He slapped a fist onto his other, open hand, grinning for the first time where he had been grim before. "Even their dogs gave way before us, and they more ferocious than their masters, for they would gladly eat any person who fell within reach of their teeth." His audience murmured appreciatively at this gruesome detail. He went on. "But this time we slaughtered them Eika like sheep. Though it's true they have tough hides. Hard as leather and gleaming like they was forged in a blacksmith's furnace, not born from a decent mam like the rest of us. Those that ran out onto the flats got caught as the tide come in, and their ugly dogs with them!"

"I heard they was shapechangers," said Cook, who had status enough that she might press to the front. "Half fish."

Heric shrugged. The brief note of triumph died in his eyes; now he only looked weary. "They drown as well as we do. If any swam away, well then, I never saw them go. We took a captive, a prince of their kind. Lord Geoffrey wanted to kill him, but the count in his wisdom said we'd do better to give his kin someone to ransom than someone to avenge. They're bringing the barbarian back, in a cage, with the count's hounds tied to the bars, so no one can get in nor the barbarian out." He shuddered and drew the Circle of Unity at his breast.

Chatelaine Dhuoda glanced about the fortress yard, marking each listener who loitered to hear the messenger's tale. "How soon will his lordship arrive?"

"Within a fiveday. They were marching hard behind me. It was a long summer, and too much fighting. We're all anxious to be home."

"Go with Cook, then, and she'll feed you." Dhuoda nodded briskly at Cook, who took the hint and hurried back into the kitchens. "Then you'll come back to me—what is your name again? You will give me a more detailed report." Her gaze raked the loiterers again. Alain, half hidden, watched as the others moved quickly away. He stayed where he was.

When the yard was clear, Dhuoda signaled to the messenger to wait for a moment. "Did the count give any direction as to where he wants this Eika prince confined? Below? Or in one of the tower chambers?"

"I can't be certain, Mistress," said Heric with a bowed head. Alain marveled at how much the young man-at-arms had changed since midsummer. "I believe he means to kennel him with those black hounds. I heard him say with my own ears that he can't be sure by any other means that the Eika will not find some *unnatural* way to escape."

The chatelaine's expression remained placid, although the frater drew the circle as against a bad omen. "That is all," said Dhuoda. "You may go."

Heric inclined his head obediently and limped off to the kitchens.

Dhuoda and the frater walked back toward the gate. Alain, shifting back against a shadowed wall, heard their voices as they passed.

"Is it true," the frater asked, "that it was those black hounds that killed Count Lavastine's own wife and daughter? That the count only keeps them because of a pact made by his grandfather with unholy devils, of which those black hounds are the living representatives?"

"I will only tell you once," said Dhuoda. Alain had to strain to hear her voice. "To talk of such things here, Frater Agius, will give you as good a reception as if you were to argue your heretical views in front of the skopos."

"But do *you* believe it to be true?" asked Agius.

"It is true that the original hounds, and the descendants born ever after of those first black hounds, obey only the trueborn counts of Lavas. Where they came from, no one knows, only that they were a gift from a Salian biscop—"

They walked on, and Alain could no longer hear them. Everyone said the black hounds traveled only and everywhere with Count Lavastine. No man otherwise could handle them, and they were known to have ravaged more than one servingman in the holding. Not even Master Rodlin, master over the stables and kennels, could control them.

"Horses," said Lackling.

Or at least, he made a noise which Alain knew he meant to signify horses because the boy then threw his head back and scraped the ground with one foot, remarkably like a horse. He sniffed the air, as if he could smell their approach. And perhaps he could. Cook sometimes called him a changeling, and it was true he had an affinity for animals, just as a child born of a goblin mother would have, though he looked human enough. The others, of course, said that animals—God's innocents—were said to recognize the halfwitted as innocents like themselves.

Impatient, Lackling dashed outside.

Alain finished oiling the harness he had in his hands. Eight days had passed since Heric had come to the holding and warned them to expect the count's return. Alain could wait a bit longer to look. It was an oddly auspicious day for the count and his forces to arrive back home: At the morning service the deacon had reminded them all that this was the saint's day of St. Lavrentius, the very saint venerated with relics and a chapel in Lavas Church, which stood just outside town. Lavas Holding rested under the protection of St. Lavrentius' hand. There was an ivory reliquary in the church that contained some of the holy martyr's bones and a scrap of the leather belt that had bound him to the wheel on which he had died his martyr's death in the last years of the Dariyan Empire. But thinking of the wheel made Alain think of the stars that wheeled in the heavens on their ceaseless round. It made him think of Midsummer's Eve and the vision he had seen, and of Withi's rejection of him after.

He sighed. Well, Aunt Bel would tell him that a serving maid like Withi wasn't worth pining over in any case. And she would bluntly remind him that he was sworn to the church and, thus, to celibacy. But he couldn't help thinking of Withi, even if he knew Aunt Bel was right.

By the time he hung the harness back on a peg and went to the stable door, he saw the guard waving one arm at a distant sight and then, in a loud voice, calling out to those below.

"They have come! The count arrives!"

The yard dissolved into a wild frenzy of activity.

Alain and Lackling found shelter at the corner of the stables, out of the way. From there they watched as the militia marched in through the gates, a lord who was obviously Count Lavastine at their head. The count rode a chestnut gelding. His kinsman Lord Geoffrey rode beside him on a roan, his fine armor betraying his status as a lord, and with them at the fore rode a young man wrapped in a cloak bearing the badge of the King's Eagles. With them also rode the count's captain, two clerics, and a dozen mounted soldiers Alain did not recognize. Behind these riders marched the militia, led by Sergeant Fell, and after them rolled the wagons and pack mules, kicking up dust.

The count pulled up his gelding in front of the steps that led into the hall. There waited Chatelaine Dhuoda, together with her retinue and Lord Geoffrey's young bride, Aldegund, now hugely pregnant. As soon as the count dismounted, Lackling ran recklessly forward and stood shifting from one foot to the next while the count handed his reins over to his captain and then walked forward to greet his kinswomen. The captain glanced at Lackling and, with the barest nod, allowed the boy to walk beside him as he led the chestnut toward the stables.

Suddenly all the horses in the yard flung their heads back and shied. One of the clerics was thrown from his mount, and Lord Geoffrey cursed and fought his mare to a standstill. Only the chestnut, under Lackling's hands, remained calm. Howling pierced the air, accompanied by a chorus of barks and ugly growls. Count Lavastine broke away from the women and hurried down the steps.

A wagon trundled through the gate, pulled by four oxen. A stocky man walked at the head of the lead ox, a good long way away from the bed of the wagon. Six black hounds lunged, snapping, toward the soldiers and onlookers, who shouted in alarm, or cried out, or scuttled back. But with yips and angry barks the hounds were, again and again, brought up short by thick chains fastened to the undercarriage. From the bed rose a cross built of heavy wood spars. To this cross was chained . . .

Not a man.

Like everyone else, Alain drew back, but more from the sight of the prisoner than from the savage hounds.

An Eika prince. Sergeant Fell's tale of a dragon's heart and its curse suddenly seemed more believable.

Alain had seen creatures like this before: the painted beasts, worse for looking so much like men, who had murdered frail, gentle Brother Gilles and the other monks at Dragon's Tail Monastery. Garish painted swirls faded from this one's face and chest. Hard white claws thrust out from the backs of his bony hands. The creature wore an armband of beaten gold around his right arm and two of bronze, curled like snakes, around his left. He wore as well stiff trousers caked with mud and a girdle of surpassing beauty, tiny links of woven gold chain and delicate faience, belted at his narrow waist and hanging down past his hips. He was naked above the waist, and his skin, under the paint, looked more like scaled copper than flesh. Despite his savage aspect, he looked every bit an arrogant prince, with black slit eyes and coarse white hair bound into a thick braid that ended past his waist. His thin lips were pulled back in an expression that resembled the hounds' baring of teeth more than a smile. Tiny jewels studded his teeth, giving his snarl an unexpected brilliance.

Chains bound his ankles to the base of the cross, and chains shackled his wrists against the crossbeam. As the wagon lurched to a halt, he deftly balanced himself against its rocking. The hounds yelped furiously, surging around the wagon, nipping and snapping at each other in their frenzy. No one dared approach. The Eika prince stared about the yard defiantly. Certainly all of those from the town and the fortress shrank away from him. Even many of the soldiers took a few steps back, now that he stood so boldly, though chained, among them.

Lavastine turned back to speak with Dhuoda. The Eika prince threw back his head and howled.

The hounds went wild.

They scrabbled madly against their chains, drowning out even the Eika's awful howl with their own cacophonous barking. As black as a moonless night, they were frightful creatures to behold.

With a splintering snap, part of the side board of the wagon broke off. Two hounds lunged forward. One of them pulled entirely free of the wagon and charged, leaping onto the nearest soldier. Bowling the man over, the hound went for his throat. At first, like an indrawn breath, no one moved. Then came screams. The crowd scattered as the hound, leaving a welter of blood and a still-twitching body behind him, raced on toward the count. The yard erupted with panic and at once dissolved into chaos.

But the other hound had not broken free. He yelped madly after his fellow, then, after straining forward to the limit of his new freedom, broke into a vicious growl, spun, and leaped up into the wagon to attack the captive.

To Alain it seemed an endless space during which no one apparently noticed that the Eika prince, helpless to defend himself, was being savaged. Other soldiers moved impossibly slowly toward their fallen comrade; the burly man at the head of the oxen yanked hard on the head of the lead ox, but to what end? Alain pushed himself away from the wall. He felt as if he were running in a world separate from the rest of the frantic activity in the yard: just himself, alone with the Eika prince and the savage dog.

He reached the side of the wagon. He grabbed the hind legs of the hound, bent his own knees, and tugged backward with all his might.

A new scream, shivering through him. He tumbled backward and fell. The hound landed heavily on top of him. For an instant Alain lay stunned. The hound scrabbled around, claws digging into Alain's tunic to tear at his skin. It growled deep in its throat.

Alain stared up at the maddened eyes, like dark amber, depthless. Another snarl sounded. He realized then that he had fallen within reach of one of the still-chained hounds. Saliva dripped onto his face, and he saw teeth.

His face was going to be ripped clean off by those powerful jaws.

Far away, like an echo, a man laughed.

Because he was about to die, he said, firmly, but calmly, the first thing that came to mind.

"Sit."

The hound sat, panting, on his hips. Its weight pressed his flesh into the hard ground, bruising on small stones. Saliva dripped down its incisors and wet Alain's tunic. The other hound, moving in, nuzzled him, licking his face, smothering his cheek with its wet tongue.

Abruptly, both hounds looked up and growled menacingly at the soldiers who had approached and lowered their spears but who still hesitated to come any closer, even with their weapons. Behind them, a man was alternately moaning and shrieking in pain. Another man issued orders in a curt voice, but Alain for some reason could not distinguish the words. His gaze tracked up and up and past the broad black back of the hound sitting on him and caught on the face of the Eika prince. The savage's eyes were as black as obsidian. The prince was, oddly enough, grinning down at him. His teeth had much the look of the hound's: sharp and white. The hound had ripped one trouser leg clean through, and blood seeped out through the torn cloth. A great deal of blood, as thick as a man's but with a greenish tint. If the wound pained him, he did not show it on his face.

The hound sitting on Alain lunged forward suddenly, plunging through the ring of lowered spears, and closed his jaw around the arm of a soldier. The formation vanished as the soldiers broke backward to escape. With a yelp of pain the poor soldier wrenched his arm free and staggered away. Brought up by his chain, the hound jerked back and growled. Then, content, he padded back and settled his weight on Alain's legs.

"Move back! Take those men to the infirmary. Get this wagon to the kennels. Go on, man, get those oxen moving. Hold one moment. Let the boy rise."

Count Lavastine appeared, a black hound panting beside him, his muzzle thrust into the man's palm. The Eika prince shifted his gaze to glare at his captor.

"Sorrow! Up, boy!"

The hound remained draped comfortably over Alain's legs.

"Up!" There was a tone to the count's voice that suggested he did not tolerate disobedience from his vassals. Sorrow heaved himself up and with a cursory tug at the chain tried to reach his master, then gave up.

"Get up!" said the count.

Alain suddenly realized that Count Lavastine was addressing *him*. He scrambled to his feet and barely had time to jump out of the way as the driver tugged the oxen forward and the wagon jolted on across the yard.

Alain found himself staring straight at Count Lavastine. The count was a slight man, not as tall as Alain. But he was no one to be trifled with. He examined Alain for a moment and then his gaze flicked away, seeking more important sights. The two mauled soldiers were carried away. Lord Geoffrey and the two clerics approached, pausing at a respectable distance. The hound, ears brushing Lavastine's fingertips, growled at them, but it seemed to Alain the growl now sounded more dutiful than heartfelt.

"Take Rage to the kennels as well," said the count, grasping the hound's broken chain and handing it without further ado to Alain. The broken links felt cold, their iron seaming rough, in Alain's hands. Lavastine turned away and walked over to Lord Geoffrey, and then, as if nothing untoward had happened, he returned to his chatelaine and they vanished into the hall.

Alain stared down at Rage. Rage snuffled at Alain's feet, then at his knees. Then the hound took Alain's hand between her teeth and held it there, and whined.

By this time, those few people who had not fled from the yard stared at him, safe in doorways or behind fencing, or protected by weapons, even if only a pitchfork. Rage wagged her whipcord tail, thumping it hard against Alain's thigh. Gingerly, Alain pulled his hand out of the hound's mouth. Red marks showed where Rage's teeth had pressed into but not broken the skin. Alain grasped the chain a little more tightly and took in a deep breath.

"Come, girl," he said and began to walk even as he braced for the hound's resistance. But Rage padded alongside obediently enough, pausing only to snarl and bare her teeth at anyone who moved toward them. On the steps, Frater Agius stared somberly at them, hand poised to draw a Circle at his breast. Alain shuddered. It was like that first moment in the old ruins, on Midsummer's Eve, when he had realized he had somehow stepped outside the world as he knew it. It was bad enough to have everyone staring at him, to know that everyone would be talking of this incident for days, but to have Agius mark him . . .

Alain had never cared for the militant gleam in Frater Agius' eyes, one so at odds with the peaceful serenity that had invested Brother Gilles' expression and, indeed, his entire being.

He passed around the corner of the hall, leading the hound past a knot of soldiers, who stepped away from him although they were not particularly close by. They drew the Circle at their breasts as though to avert evil. He heard them muttering.

"It's uncanny, it is."

"Not even Master Rodlin can handle them hounds. None but his lordship can, or his heir, if he had one."

"I thought he'd kill them all after what they did to his child—"

"Hush. Don't go speaking of that."

"It's unholy. Devil's blood, it is. My papa told me that those hounds will only tolerate the count or his heir, or those in whom they can smell devil's blood. Them hounds were bred by elvish kind."

Alain fixed his gaze on the ground and pretended not to hear. A furious chorus of barking splintered his thoughts. He passed through a palisade and came to the low stockade that enclosed the kennels.

Dirt swirled under the feet of the hounds chained to the wagon. They yanked at their chains and nipped at Master Rodlin and his two assistants, who wore padding bound around their arms and legs. The Eika prince, blood still weeping from his torn thigh, watched the spectacle with cool scorn.

"Go," said Alain in what he hoped was an authoritative voice, shoving the hound toward the gate that led into the enclosure. But the wagon had not yet gone in, though the oxen had been unharnessed and led away, and Rage dragged against Alain, pulling the wrong way, eager to fling herself into the fray. The knot of soldiers had drifted after Alain. Evidently they were the Eika prince's ostensible guards, although they were clearly more interested in watching the efforts of Rodlin and his dog-handlers as they attempted to unchain the hounds and get them into the kennel without being torn to bits.

Alain sighed and tugged the ungrateful Rage to the gate. "Go! Go in!" Rage went, whimpering an apology. Alain hurried back to the wagon. Sorrow had gotten hold of the leg of one of the handlers and was worrying at the padding, trying to rip through it to the tender flesh beneath.

"Stop that! Sit!" Alain grabbed the hound by his collar. Sorrow whined and then, sitting abruptly, released the man's leg. The man limped back, out of reach, and sat down heavily. Master Rodlin and the other handler backed out of range swiftly enough. They eyed Alain and the hounds uneasily.

They were as afraid of him as they were of the hounds. Ai, Lord and Lady, what had he ever done to deserve *this*?

"Come on, boy," he said to Sorrow. "In you go." One by one he led Sorrow and then the other four hounds into the stockade. Four other hounds, brought in a separate cage, had already been chained inside. He sat with them to one side, holding them back by word and once by main force as the soldiers skittishly rolled the wagon in and installed the Eika prince in an open-sided, barred shed that had been built by Chatelaine Dhuoda's order in the very center of the kennel. If the Eika prince somehow broke free of his chains, and then his cage, he would have the hounds to contend with.

"He'll need that wound looked at," said Master Rodlin, eyeing the prince from a watch platform built on stilts against the stockade, "but I daresay he'll be as likely to bite the healer as the hounds would."

The prince watched them. Blood still leaked from the wound although he seemed oblivious to it.

A cleric appeared, peering first nervously in at the kennel gate, first at the hounds, then at the Eika. "Master Rodlin. Begging your pardon, Master," he cried, finally finding the man above him. "His lordship wishes to see you and the boy."

"Which boy?" asked Master Rodlin. At once everyone else, and belatedly Rodlin himself, looked toward Alain. A moment later even the Eika prince turned his stare on Alain. Alain fidgeted. Rage and Sorrow, sitting at his feet, growled.

"Everyone out," said Rodlin. The haste with which the soldiers and handlers retreated brought a contemptuous grin to the Eika's lips, a savage baring of his sharp teeth. "Come with me, Alain." Rodlin disappeared down the stairs that led from the platform to the ground. Alain let go of the hounds. They bolted away and began to race around the kennel, barking. Rage and Sorrow followed him to the gate, but he rubbed their great heads roughly and promised them he would be back. Then he slipped outside and shut the gate. The handlers chained it tightly closed.

"Follow me," said Rodlin curtly. They walked together in silence, the cleric padding before them, into the hall.

Alain had never been permitted past the great hall where everyone ate. Rodlin led him out through a door that opened onto a tiny courtyard alive with color and fragrant with herbs and flowers, then up a curving staircase that led to a circular chamber in the stone tower. The chamber had been whitewashed, and a magnificent painted glass window depicting St. Lavrentius' martyrdom let light stream into the room. There was, amazingly, a second window in the chamber, though this one had no glass; its shutters were open wide to admit light and air. Count Lavastine sat behind a table, attended by Chatelaine Dhuoda, Lord Geoffrey, Frater Agius, and the captain of the Lavas guard.

Count Lavastine glanced up from some documents as Rodlin and Alain entered the room. The cleric crossed the chamber to take his station beside Lord Geoffrey. Rodlin bent one knee in a brief but clear obeisance, and Alain copied him, shaking in the knees.

But Lavastine looked away and returned to his other business. "I believe we are free of the threat for this season," he said to Lord Geoffrey. "I have no further need for you and your men-at-arms. You may return to your wife's estates when you are ready."

"Yes, cousin." Lord Geoffrey nodded. Though a good head taller and quite a bit heavier than his kinsman, Geoffrey seemed hopelessly overawed by his elder cousin, Lavastine. "But we hope you will suffer our presence a month or two more. My precious Aldegund is young and this her first confinement. It would be well—"

"Yes, yes!" Lavastine tapped his fingers impatiently on the table. "Of course you must not leave until Lady Aldegund has given birth

and she and the child gained strength for the fiveday's journey."
His lips thinned as he gave Lord Geoffrey what might have been
intended as a smile. "It is this child, is it not, if it is granted life and
health by God's hand, who will be named heir to my lands."

"Unless you marry again," said Geoffrey gravely. But even Alain
knew that as kindly and evidently unambitious a man as Lord Geoffrey
might harbor ambitions for his children. The Lavas lands were
considerable.

Count Lavastine made a sudden sign as if against the evil eye or
a bad omen.

"I beg your pardon," said Geoffrey quickly. "I did not—"

"Never mind it," said Lavastine.

Alain's knee, crushed into the carpet, was beginning to hurt. He
attempted to shift—

Like lightning, Lavastine's gaze jumped to him. "Master Rodlin.
This is the boy? What is his name?"

"Alain, my lord."

Lavastine looked Alain over. Seen so close and without his mail,
the count was slighter than he had first appeared. He had a narrow
face and hair of a nondescript brown, but his eyes were a keen blue.
"Your parents?" he asked. "What village are you come from?"

"Son of Henri, my lord," Alain choked out. He could scarcely
believe that he was talking to a great lord. "I never knew my
mother. I'm from Osna village, on the Dragonback—"

"Yes. The monastery there burned down early spring. A royal
benefice." He paused for long enough that Alain wondered if he was
pleased or displeased that a monastery which had received its grant
of land and rents from King Henry had burned down. "And it's a
port, too, one of the emporia. Do you know aught of that?"

"My father is a merchant, my lord. My aunt is a successful
householder in the town and she manages what he brings home
and manufactures goods for him to trade, finishing quernstones,
mostly, in the workshop."

"Have you handled hounds before?"

"No, my lord."

"You went up to the old ruins on Midsummer's Eve. Did you see
anything there?"

A casual question, seemingly. Alain dared not look anywhere but
at the count, and yet hardly dared look *at* the count. He struggled,
trying to sort out his thoughts and decide what to say.

"Well?" demanded Lavastine, who clearly had little patience for waiting on others.

Should he admit to his vision? What might they accuse him of? He felt Frater Agius' gaze on him, searching, probing. Witchcraft? Forbidden sorcery? The taint of devil's blood? Or ought he to deny the vision altogether and imperil his soul for the lie?

Lavastine stood up. "So you did see something." He paced to the open window and stared out onto the forest and hills beyond. "Master Rodlin, you will take this young man on as your deputy. He will assist you in caring for the hounds."

Disappointed, Alain began to bend his knee again, since Rodlin, too, was backing up, readying himself to leave. At least it was a step up from digging out latrines.

The count turned back from the window and for an instant stopped Alain short, measuring him. "You will report as well to Sergeant Fell, who will begin training you as a man-at-arms."

While Alain gaped, too stunned to respond as he ought, the count strode back to the table and sat down. "Frater Agius, tell Deacon Waldrada I would speak with her before supper." The frater nodded and with a piercing glance toward Alain, left the chamber. "Captain." Lavastine turned his attention away from Alain as thoroughly as if he was no longer in the chamber. "We will set stockades all along the Vennu shore this autumn. I will call out an extra levy for this work. If we set them up in these patterns—"

Rodlin touched Alain on the elbow. "Come."

Alain started and, turning, walked with Rodlin toward the door. But his eye caught on the two tapestries that hung on either side of the door. One depicted the Lavas badge: two black hounds on a silver field. But the other depicted a scene, and it was this he stared at.

A prince rides with his retinue through a dark forest. A mountain rises in the distance, touched at its height by the smoky gray of the mountain's breath eking into the twilit sky. A shield hangs from the prince's saddle: a red rose against a sable background.

Rodlin took him by the arm and tugged him out of the chamber while behind Count Lavastine discussed with his captain and kin and retainers his plans for the autumn and winter building and for the introduction of a new, heavier plough for breaking new fields in forest country.

A red rose on a shield. Of course the vision had been a true one. He had only to be patient.

In the castle yard, waiting while Rodlin spoke with Sergeant Fell, Alain brushed his fingers over his tunic. The younger soldiers lounged at their ease around the yard. Having nothing better to do, they stared at him and whispered among themselves.

Even through the cloth the rose felt warm to his touch, as if *she*, knowing somehow that he was to train as a soldier, was pleased. He shivered, though the day was warm. He felt blessed, indeed, to be granted his heart's wish. But he wondered now how *safe* it was to have come to the notice of such a power, whether she had been a dead saint walking abroad on Earth or the angel of war descended from the realm of the stars to mark out her champion . . . or her next victim.

IV
THE TREASURE-HOUSE

1

WHAT she hated most about Hugh was the way he watched her constantly. He was waiting. The effort of simply guarding her tongue, her every action, for every moment in the day was exhausting. He was waiting. Sooner or later she would betray herself.

She hated it most in the evenings after she had finished her work, when she ought to have been free of him at least for the hour between Nones and Vespers, before she settled down on her bed of straw in the pig shed for the night's sleep. Had he left her alone, she could have observed the heavens, held onto the memory of her old life with Da. But usually Hugh sat up until late on a chair placed out back, watching her, waiting for her to do *something* that would betray her to him.

Her only defense was to pretend she knew nothing: Da had taught her no secrets, of the heavens or otherwise; she said nothing when Hugh sat outside with the astrolabe in his hands, turning it over, spinning the alidade, tracing the lines on the plates with his fingers, and obviously having no idea how to use it even to tell time.

That Hugh, an educated churchman, did not recognize the athar, the spectacle that shone now so brightly in the Dragon that it cast as much light as the quarter moon, appalled her. And frightened her. She had never before realized how forbidden the knowledge of the heavens must be, which she had begun to learn at her Da's knee as effortlessly as a duck takes to water.

"*Sorcerers and navigators,*" Da always said, "*study the heavens because they must.*"

Now and again, when she judged she was alone, she observed as well as she could. Da always wrote down his observations in the margins of *The Book of Secrets* in a tiny, precise hand. She had perforce to write them in her mind.

"*For as it is written in the* Memoria *of Alisa of Jarrow, 'Knowledge is a treasure-house and the heart is its strongbox.' Make of your memory a great city, Liath, and map its streets as if you walked them in your own body. This is your own, your secret city, and in this city place all that you wish to remember, giving each thing a seal or a portrait by which you can recognize it. Each thing shall be set in its rightful place, in its rightful order, and by this means you shall be as wealthy as any king. Knowledge is an incorruptible treasure which can never lose its brightness.*"

So over the years and with much concentration, she had made her memory into an imaginary city she pictured in her mind, so complete that with her eyes shut she could walk through it as though it really existed:

On a great lake rests an island, perfectly round, its sides sloping gently to a small circular plateau. The city rises upon the island, seven levels ringed by seven walls, each wall painted a different color. Within the uppermost walls, on the plateau, lies a plaza bounded by four buildings, one at each compass point; in the center stands a tower of stone. The observatory, a circular building built of marble, sits on the north-south axis, on the point of north, its eye toward the north star, Kokab, and the constellation known as the Guardian.

When she stood outside on those summer nights, in the yard between the chapel and the pig shed, and looked up at the heavens, she made a picture in her mind of this observatory, its curved walls, the sighting stones and gaps, the central pillar. She imagined the twelve arches that represented the twelve houses of the zodiac, also known as the Houses of Night, the world dragon that binds the heavens.

In the house of the Dragon she placed, in her memory, a seastar such as she had once seen in tide pools along the Andallan coast. This seastar with its six arms glowed with a bright white light, like the spectacle. She placed it within the curved archway of the Dragon at fifteen degrees, so that she would always remember at what degree it had resided in the constellation. Around it she affixed imagined seals so she would remember where the Sun and Moon and other planets were, to what degree in which Houses; then in five or twenty years, if she were even alive then, she could show to another mathematicus—another sorcerer trained in the knowledge of the stars—precisely where and when the spectacle had first shone forth.

But summer passed and, three and a half months after it first appeared, the star faded, its sparking brightness diminishing. She could still see it, a star blended in among the others that made up the constellation of the Dragon, but it was now an ordinary star. Perhaps this was how angels were birthed: a brilliance to announce their nativity followed by the long steady glow of Our Lady's and Lord's work. Perhaps it was merely a comet, as mathematici called those stars which had tails and sometimes moved across the sphere of the Sun.

She had not known until then that she had hoped, somehow, that Da would return, that he was not truly dead, that he would miraculously rescue her. The strange star had shone forth on the night Da died as if it were a harbinger of death; certainly, she realized now, Da had thought of it that way. As the athar faded, so her hope faded. He was dead, gone, passed up through the seven spheres to the Chamber of Light. He wasn't coming back. She was alone.

2

LIATH was turning leaves and manure into the damp ground for next year's garden when Hugh appeared from the stable, leading his piebald mare. She glanced up at him, but he said nothing and seemed content to watch her work. When she had finished the row, she stopped, leaning on her shovel, and regarded him evenly.

He smiled, looking pleased with himself. "I'll be gone for twelve days, north to Freelas to get news from the biscop and to minister to the holdings between here and the town. You may take your meals at the inn while I'm gone. But you will dine with me on Ladysday after next."

Liath ducked her chin, in assent. He had ridden to Freelas six weeks ago and been gone eight glorious days. Something in her expression must have given away her feelings. He dropped the mare's reins and walked forward. Stopping before her, he lifted a very clean, very white hand and brushed her tangled hair, that which had escaped from her braid, back out of her eyes while she held herself stiff.

"There," he said, and went back to the mare. He swung on with the leisurely grace of much practice and studied Liath a moment longer from this high seat. "Take a bath. There's an underdress and a fine long gown in the chest. I want you to wear those when we dine." He reined the piebald around and rode off to the road and away, north, into the forest. Oddly, for a man wearing a frater's plain brown robe, split for riding and thrown over a nobleman's dress of tunic and hose, he wore his long sword strapped to his back.

Liath finished five more rows before she went to the kitchen to wash her face and hands. The water from the well was cold and getting colder as summer passed into autumn. Oh, yes, the summer had passed easily enough. But it was getting chilly at night. Last night she had been grateful when Trotter had rolled up against the wood rail set between her dry bed of straw and the pigs' pen, to give her warmth at her back.

She sighed and dried her hands on her tunic, then stoked up the fire to keep the great copper pot of porridge simmering. It was a little too hot in the cookhouse, a small building set a few strides away from the sprawling haphazard warren of chambers that had grown out over many years from the chapel. The central core of this warren of rooms had been built, it was said, by a frater from the kingdom of Aosta. Unaccustomed to the cold winters, he had sealed and insulated the timber frame so the building kept in warmth too well. She had probably been more comfortable out in the pig shed this summer than Hugh had been in his cell.

She sneezed, wiped a scrap of straw from her face, and went outside. Sun shone down on the autumn trees, turned gold and fire-red, and on their taller, evergreen companions. Hugh rode out frequently to make his rounds of the sick and dying and those isolates who simply wanted the comfort of a holy man's sermons and prayers, but those rounds lasted an afternoon or, at best, a single night. She had not dared, when he rode before to Freelas, to go anywhere or to attempt anything, she had been so sure for all eight of those days that he was simply lurking out of her sight waiting to catch her out. But Hugh *did* have his duties, and he did carry them out faithfully. This time, perhaps, she could risk the hike up to where Hanna had buried the book.

She thought of the book constantly. Could hardly fail to, because though Hugh had not spoken of it once this long summer, she knew it was always in his thoughts. She knew it by the way he looked at her, by the way he fingered the other books in front of her, as if to remind her of what she had hidden from him.

There are degrees of freedom among the unfree. Hugh owned her body. He did not own her mind or her soul. *The Book of Secrets* still belonged to her.

She rummaged through the storage rooms until she found a piece of oilcloth and the hand trowel. With a last glance up the north road, she set off west into the rolling wooded hills.

It was fine early autumn weather. As she left behind church and chapel, pig shed and stables, kitchen and garden, she felt a weight lift from her. Hugh's oppressive presence, everything that reminded her of her loss of freedom—all these, for this short walk, were gone. For this hour, she was no longer chained in the ranks of the unfree. Da would have wept to see her so, knowing that it was his own folly that had forced her into slavery. Poor Da. She wiped away a tear. She was so lonely.

A bird trilled. A squirrel chirruped and scampered out along a branch. Fallen leaves and summer's debris cushioned her strides. She sang. It came out husky and low at first, hesitant, then with more confidence; she sang an old song her mother had taught her, words whose meaning she did not know although they had a mellifluous flow that joined with the exotic melody to make beauty. She knew Dariyan well enough that she could guess these words were related to the language of that long-dead empire, for they wore some of the same cadences.

"Liath."

She stopped dead. "Hanna?"

Behind, an animal rustled in the trees. But when she whirled to look, there was nothing there. A trick of the breeze or the wish of her mind. The faint memory of her mother's voice. That was all. She went on.

When she came to the clearing where the ancient oak stood, she paused at the edge of the trees and listened for a long time and intently. A bird sang, the same repeated five-note whistle. In the distance she heard a steady, rhythmic chopping, someone out getting wood. Nothing else. She was alone.

After so long, she was amazed how vividly the book came to mind, how she could feel the texture of its pages against her skin, changing as the reader leafed through the book. For *The Book of Secrets* was truly three books, bound together.

The first book was written on parchment in Dariyan, the language of the church and of the old empire which had been born in the city of Darre, far to the south where now the skopos reigned at the great Hearth of Our Lady. Except for the first three pages it was all written in her father's hand or, toward the end, in her own, a long and rather confused compilation of the knowledge gleaned over the years by a mathematicus, thrown together as though Da had copied every reference he could remember or find in whatever library had been at hand during his travels. Although she had not memorized the entire florilegia, scraps of it emerged, quotations like fish swimming to the surface.

"Astronomy concerns itself with the revolutions of the heavens, the rising and setting of the constellations, their movements and

names, the motions of the stars and planets, Sun and Moon, and the laws governing these motions and all their variations. . . .

"The mathematici seek the secrets of the heavens even beyond these laws, for such movements invoke the powers and such powers can be used for sorcery. . . .

"So also the sea wonderfully agrees with the Moon's circuit. They are always companions in growing and waning. . . .

"If in the month of Novarian you ring the bell for Vigils when you see Arktos rise, then thirty psalms may be sung without difficulty. . . .

"Do not shave when the Moon is in the sign of the Falcon. . . .

"In this manner, when Aturna and Erekes are in opposition, the daimones of the seventh sphere may be drawn down through the second sphere and if the Moon is full her influence will pull them into the bonds of your invocation. . . ."

The third book was written in the infidel way—on paper—and in the infidel's language, its curling loops and swirls like fanciful bird tracks. This was the great Jinna astronomical tract, *On the Configuration of the World*, written by the infidel scholar al-Hasan ibn al-Haithan al-Tulaytilah. This copy came from the great scholar's own scribes, for they had met him when they resided for over two years at the court of the Kalif of Qurtubah in the infidel kingdom of Andalla.

The oldest and most frail of the books, written on yellowed and brittle papyrus, was bound into the middle. The hand that had painstakingly written out each word and page had done so in an alphabet she did not know, but the ancient text was glossed with notes in Arethousan. Its contents remained a mystery, for Da could not read the old text either, and though he knew Arethousan, there was simply no time to teach her a new and difficult language. What time they did have for learning he used to hone the skills she had: her memory city, her knowledge of the stars, her understanding of Wendish and Dariyan and Jinna. According to Da, she had spoken Salian and Aostan as a child, but she had long since forgotten them.

"Better to know three languages well than half a dozen badly," he would say to her.

The bird whistled again. Nothing moved except wind through the branches. She took in a breath for courage and walked across the clearing to kneel beside the old oak. Low, among roots bursting up through the ground, a little den lay, half filled in with leaves and debris. She worked quickly with the trowel, digging it out.

A branch snapped behind her. Birds shrieked, wings beating as they lifted out of the trees toward the safety of the sky. Silence fell. She started up, but it was too late.

Fool, and a greater fool yet. There stood Hugh at the clearing's edge, smiling. He walked forward slowly, savoring his victory. Liath planted her feet on either side of the gaping hole, even raised the trowel in useless protection. But what good would a garden trowel do against a man trained at arms and carrying a sword?

"Dig it out," he said, halting before her. He was too fine a man to get his hands dirty or to sully the hem of his fine azure tunic—where had his frater's robe gone?—by kneeling in the dirt.

She threw the trowel down. "No. Do it yourself."

He hit her so hard backhanded that she fell stunned to the ground. She could not make her hands move, or her legs, but she heard the soft noise the trowel made, stabbing into the dirt and debris and spilling it to one side, a shower of earth, like water.

Hugh gave a satisfied grunt. "There," he murmured.

She pulled in a deep breath, sucking in a cloud of fine dirt, and choked, coughing. But she could move again. She could not let him get the book. It was all that was left to her. She shoved herself up, trembling, only to see Hugh shake out an empty roll of cloth.

He stared. Streaked with dirt and damp from earth and leaves, the cloth stirred sluggishly in the breeze. Horrified, she scrambled forward on her hands and knees and dug frantically into the den. But the den was empty.

"It's gone!" She slumped forward and leaned her head against the oak. *Gone.* Some animal had rooted it out and torn it to bits. A child, digging for eggs, had found it and taken it home for fuel for the fire. Ai, Lady and Lord! Such a precious thing, to be lost so stupidly. If she had only thought of a better place to hide it, but she had only had one brief chance, begging Hanna before she was dragged off by Marshal Liudolf to her jail; the old oak was their favorite meeting place. What if Hanna had not hidden the book at all, but had only said she had? What if Hanna had taken it for herself—?

But this was Hugh's influence. If she could not trust Hanna, then nothing and no one, ever again.

"Damn you," said Hugh. "A pretty charade. But I'll have the book, Liath. I am more patient than you can imagine."

She ducked her head, waiting for the blow, but it never came. She heard his footsteps and turned to see him walking away. He vanished into the forest. A moment later she caught a glimpse of his mare; the sound of their passage through the undergrowth receded into the afternoon.

She began to cry, then squeezed her eyes shut. She would not give in to despair. All summer she had held out. If she gave in now, she might as well give herself entirely to Hugh.

"Never that," she said in a low voice. She wiped hard at her eyes to let the pain still the tears and, finally, went back to the chapel. First, she must talk to Hanna. As Da always said: *Take one step at a time so you may know where to place the next one.*

This time, wise to Hugh, she waited an entire day before she went to the inn. Master Hansal stood outside, daubing chinks in the timber walls. He laid off working when he saw her. "Greetings, child," he said in his slow, gruff voice. He looked to see her. "Frater Hugh came by yesterday to say he's off to Freelas for these twelve days to visit the biscop. You're to eat with us. Very generous, to my mind."

Very generous. Liath touched a hand to her left temple, where Hugh had hit her. It still hurt. "Good day, Master Hansal. Is Hanna in?"

"Yes. She's inside, helping the Mistress. I'm sure she can visit a moment, if you've time."

"Thank you." She hurried inside, relieved to get away from him.

Mistress Birta leaned over the great hearth, placing scrubbed turnips one by one into a bank of coals set off from the blazing fire. Finishing, she straightened. "Liath! It gladdens my heart to see you, child. Frater Hugh was by."

Liath stopped short. Where was Hanna? "Mistress Birta. I give you greetings in return."

Birta shook out her apron. She smelled of scallions. "I am well, truly, by the blessing of Our Lady and Lord. And you, lass? I was sore worried, I confess, after your father died. But the frater has been generous, more than generous, that I can say. There's many a freeholder works harder 'an you and lives not so well nor eats meat four times a week. I don't say you don't deserve it, mind. He's not a bad man, is Frater Hugh. A bastard he might be, and proud, but he's of noble blood, so we must expect that. I've never heard it said that he's stinted in his duties. Never afraid of the sick or too high to visit the humblest. Why, old Martha by River's Bank, dying of the pox, asked him to lay hands on her for his blessing and he was not afraid to do so."

"Martha died."

"Now, lass. It may not be to your liking, and I have no doubt that Hugh may ask of you what you may not wish to give him." Here Birta hesitated. "He's noble, and we can't argue with his kind. When old Count Harl, as was younger then, brought little Ivar down and told me to suckle the boy with my Hanna, I might have worried there wasn't milk enough for both, but I did as I was told. You must do the same. There's far worse you could be doing."

Liath flushed, heat like a slap stinging her cheeks. "He swore a vow to the church. Like all brothers he has shaven off his beard as an offering to the Lady together with his vow to serve only Her."

Birta snorted. "I'm sure he'll never marry, not wanting to risk Their displeasure or, to more point, that of the skopos. What has that to do with you? There's those who say a man's not a true man without his beard, and that the churchmen are but men pretending to be women, but it's a rare man, even sworn to the church, whose feet do not tread on the earth. Are we to expect them all to lack the appetites of men?" Then her expression changed, as if she had at that instant come upon a new thought. "Or were you thinking that he might forsake his vows to marry *you*?"

"I wasn't! I never said that!"

"Listen you to me, girl. You and your father came from far parts into these lands, and you with that coloring and accent and he with his fine educated ways. Anyone can see that you're not like us, landbred and freeborn, but of another place entirely, though I know not what that place might be. I've heard no talk of kin coming to rescue you, and you told Marshal Liudolf yourself that you have none. You're too handsome a girl to be on your own with no family to protect you. Frater Hugh will take care of you, if he's a mind to, and he comes from a powerful family with a noble mother. Ai, lass! Think before you cry out against injustice. You'll not do better than him."

Goaded beyond bearing, Liath lost her temper. "He *beats* me!"

"With that temper, I'm not surprised. He *bought* you. Whatever you may have been before, wherever you have come from, whatever kin you left behind, if there is any, you're a slave now. Hugh's slave. If you're smart, you'll see that he comes to value you. Perhaps in time, if you are obedient and useful, he'll write a manumission and free you from his hand, but until that time comes, you are lower than the least poor freeholder who farms in these hills. You're a proud girl, and I think you do not realize that yet."

Liath fought down several savage retorts. Ai, Lady, but weren't Birta's words the simple truth? At last, her voice strangled by anger and grief and a real fear of losing Hanna by antagonizing her mother, she choked out a reply. "Forgive me, my wretched tongue. You've been nothing but kind to me, Mistress, and I'm sorry if I've been rash and impolite."

Birta laughed uneasily. "You're a good girl, Liath. You must learn to make the best of what Our Lady and Lord have given to you. There's many a girl in this village who's looked longingly at our handsome frater. For all that the church teaches us that men sworn to the church have forsaken congress with women, it's a rare churchman who can say he's done so with a clean heart."

Liath could not stand to think that people already spoke of her as Hugh's mistress. "I've never—!" She stumbled over her own words, furious and flustered. "And I never will!"

Mistress Birta sighed and smiled sadly. Then, to Liath's immense relief, Hanna entered from the stable yard.

"Liath!" Hanna ran to hug her, then pushed away. "You smell like the pigs, Liath. The frater was by, to say he'll be gone for— What's wrong?"

"Perhaps you should take Liath outside and sit a moment, the both of you, drink a bit of warm milk."

Hanna looked startled. "Why, yes, Mama." She grabbed Liath by the wrist and dragged her quickly out of the front room. "Before she changes her mind." In the pantry she got down mugs and filled them from a pitcher, talking all the while. "She's never so generous when it doesn't bring coin with it. What's happened?"

"She's just told me that the whole village knows that I'm to be Hugh's mistress, and that the whole village approves it, and she's just discovered that I don't, and I'm not, and I won't be."

"Ah. Come outside. We'll sit on the bench." Hanna led Liath outside to the stable yard. The broom and rake leaned against the side of the house and a large swathe was raked clean, parallel stripes marking the beaten-down earth. The two girls sat on a bench in the sun. "You've never had time just to sit with me, not since the auction—except that week he was gone to Freelas and I came to visit you. I've seen how he never lets you out of his sight.'' She glanced toward the inn and lowered her voice. ''Do you really mean he hasn't bedded you yet? Everyone knows he intended—''

''Hanna!'' Liath laid a hand on Hanna's arm to silence her. ''What happened to the book?''

''The book?'' Then her face lit. ''I thought you'd come mad. Don't tell me you went looking for it?''

Liath grabbed both of Hanna's hands. Her heart pounded wildly. ''You have it?''

''Ow! Let me go! Yes! I buried it where you said, but then I thought that wild animals or young Johan's pigs, or even one of the children out looking for eggs might get to it, so I moved it. When were you up there?''

''Yesterday. I thought Hugh had gone.''

''You went up there the same day he left? I thought he looked angry when he came by. You idiot. *I* could have told you to wait a day or two, to make sure he'd gone. If he wants that book so much—''

''I know. I know. I didn't think. But he'd gone before. I thought it was safe. I just *have* to see it, Hanna.''

Hanna looked furtively around the stable yard. She got up, ran over to the cookhouse door, and peered inside, then looked into the back room of the inn. Finally, with a wordless sign, she led Liath into the stables.

All the way back, past the stalls and the sheep pen and the pig trough, back where straw and hay drifted lazily down from the loft above, spinning in sunlight streaming through the windows where the shutters had been thrown back. Up in the loft her younger brother was kicking at nothing, legs dangling.

''Karl. Out. You're to finish raking the yard.''

''That's your job!''

''It's yours now. Go!''

He made a face, grunted a ''hello'' to Liath, and clambered out by a side ladder. Hanna waited until he was gone and then knelt and pulled boards out from below the pig's feed trough. From underneath the trough she drew out a package wrapped in old, stained wool.

Liath grabbed it out of Hanna's hands. Her hands shook as she unwrapped it. Her fingers brushed the long metal clasps that held the book together and beneath it the leather binding, thick and graying with age, fine cracks like veins of hair revealed to the light as she pulled off the last of the cloth. She ran a finger down the spine, traced the brass roses that adorned the metal clasps, read with her fingers the embossed Dariyan letters: *The Book of Secrets*. A masking name, Da called it, to hide the true name of the books within.

Liath clutched the book against her chest. For a long while she simply gulped in breath, half panting, eyes shut. She opened her eyes at last to see Hanna watching her with a bemused expression.

"I thought it was gone." Liath's voice caught, then steadied. "Oh, thank you, Hanna. I knew you wouldn't fail me." She embraced her, the book crushed between them, then stepped back. "He thinks if he beds me that I'll give him the book. But I never will."

"Liath." Hanna regarded her with a frown. "That isn't a church book. I've seen the psalter Frater Hugh uses on Lordsday, and that once when the deacon came and read a mass here, she had the Holy Verses with her." She hesitated, looking troubled. With her pale hair plaited back and her blue eyes as bright as the clear autumn sky, Hanna looked as guileless as any ignorant freeholder's daughter ought to. But Liath knew she was deeper, and thought more, and understood much, though no one might suspect it of her. Hanna had inherited as well her mother's ruthless practical streak. And she never told secrets.

"Liath. I know very well you can read and write. Not just because you used to correct Mama's tallying, but—well—I would see you writing in that book you're holding, sometimes when I'd come up the path to your Da's cottage before you saw me coming. If you don't trust me, who will you trust?"

"It's true enough. I've no one but you now, Hanna."

"Ivar."

"Ivar is still a boy, with five elder siblings and that old bear for a father."

"He's the same age we are—"

"He never looks past his nose. He acts before he thinks, and then doesn't think anyway."

"How can you say so? He has a good heart, and he's not too proud to think of himself as my kinsman, though he's a count's son. He's never been ashamed to be my milk sibling. It's all very well for you, Liath. Even old Frater Robert, strict though he was, kept a mistress for a while. Old Martha, it was, and he was probably the one who gave her the pox. For all that the monks and fraters talk about giving themselves up entirely to Our Lady and Lord, there's always those who bind their hair or shave their beards and yet don't keep faith in every article. But Hugh's never noticed a woman in this village or any of the holdings hereabouts. Not even to be angry with, nothing except to order them to water his horse and fetch his bread. We're too far beneath his notice to even care for, except that he must minister to all. There's many who still think he's truly heartsworn to Our Lady and Lord, as Deacon Fortensia is, or the flock of brothers at Sheep's Head. Except for the way he looks at *you*, Liath. If it was just the book he wanted, he'd find another way to get it. He'd never sully himself with anything he didn't want."

Liath stood stunned by Hanna's tirade.

"Hanna—" Words did not come. "Hanna, I—" Hanna waited, and at last Liath collected herself. "You don't actually wish that Hugh would . . . that he wanted to—that—" She faltered. The gap was too great to leap. "But you and Ivar—"

"Ivar is my milk brother. Of course I'm fond of him. But Ivar is a boy. Hugh is a man. Haven't you ever noticed how clean his hands are? The fine weave of his clothing? The way he smells different, sweeter? How blue his eyes are? He even smiles sometimes. But he doesn't know that people like me exist."

Liath was so shocked by Hanna's confession that she did not know what to say, or how to say it. "I didn't want this. I didn't want him to notice me."

Hanna sighed. "Of course you didn't. You never do. Ivar loves you, Liath, but you never notice that either. I hope you never fall in love with a man you can't have. Now." She reverted to her usual practical self. "What do you mean to do with the book?"

From the yard, they heard Mistress Birta calling. "Hanna! You girls have spoken long enough. There's work to be done."

Liath clung to the book. It was all she had left of Da. Yet was it truly the only thing he had left to her? There remained a secret to be unlocked, her birthright, kept hidden all these years. But she could not imagine where to start looking.

"Liath," said Hanna, exasperated, "you'd be a fool to take it to the church if you don't want the frater to get it."

Reluctantly, Liath handed back book and oilcloth. She had to wring her hands together, biting her lips, as she watched Hanna wrap up the book and shove it into the gap below the trough and cover it, otherwise she would have snatched it out of Hanna's hands. But she did not. They walked together back through the stables.

"Hanna," she said softly as they crossed the inn yard where Karl raked away fallen leaves and sticks blown by last night's winds, "he may be handsome, I know he is, but you would never want him if you really knew what he was like."

"You're my friend first. That's all that counts."

Mistress Birta met them at the door. "Will you have supper in with us, then, Liath?" Her face was streaked with sweat and soot from standing so close to the hearth.

"Gladly. I'll return in the afternoon." She took her leave.

The walk back to the church seemed short enough, with her mind so confused. How could Hanna think of Hugh in that way? Da had always claimed that it did no good to take vows unless you meant to keep them. She had disliked Hugh the instant she first set eyes on him, that day over a year past when he had appeared at their cottage. He had said he was making his rounds, meeting his new charges, gathering his flock, but she felt instinctively that he had heard something in the village to make him investigate Da.

He had courted Da assiduously but carefully, and Da was so very lonely for another educated man to talk to. Da had never been the same since his beloved Anne had died; he had never really been able to take care of himself. For the two years in Andalla they had lived decently, but that had ended one terrible night. They had lived poorly and precariously in the four years since then, and while Liath never minded the extra work she sorely missed the sense of simple well-being. Or as Da sometimes said, when he drank too much: *What man can call himself a lord who has no retinue?*

She wiped away a tear. It had done no good to cry when Mother had died, and they had thrown what they could carry in packs and fled their house in the middle of the night. It would do no good to cry now.

There was a new animal stabled next to Hugh's bay gelding: a small gray mare. Liath found Ivar in the kitchen.

"Liath!" He hugged her. "You smell like the stables," he said, laughing self-consciously, and he pulled away from her, as if he was embarrassed to have taken such a liberty with her.

Liath smiled despite herself. Ivar had a sunny smile and he was very glad to see her. She kissed him on the cheek, and then they both blushed.

"I didn't expect to see you here," she said quickly, to cover the awkwardness.

Deliberately he put a log on the fire. "I saw Frater Hugh riding north yesterday. I thought you might be alone."

"I am. I went down to the inn."

He stayed by the fire, but his gaze lifted to her. The flames lit his reddish-blond hair and gave color to his pale, freckled cheeks. When he spoke, his voice was low and serious. "Come away with me. Now. Today. You can't stay here. I know he must—" He faltered. "He must mistreat you. I've never liked him. Thinking that he's better than my father and him just a bastard."

Here it came. Poor Ivar; he had always been one to shoot the deer before he had the bow in his hand. "Where would we go?"

"I heard the Dragons rode through Freelas, with the prince himself leading them. They say there've been Eika raids this spring and summer all along the northern coast. The biscop sent word to King Henry there'd been a sighting out at Sheep's Head."

"Do you truly suppose the Dragons would take me? You're a count's son, and you have fighting skills. If your father petitioned King Henry, he would take you. But I've nothing more than what my Da taught me to defend ourselves while traveling. I don't have kin to speak for me. And I can't imagine why I would want to join the Dragons, when everyone knows they get all the worst fighting and will most likely die before their first year of service is up."

Stung by her words, he flushed. "I suppose Hugh's bed is comfortable enough, is it?"

"Take it back! How dare you say that to me? I sleep with the pigs rather than with him!" All of her anger flooded out. She was shaking.

Ivar went so pale, even standing next to the fire, that his freckles stood out even more. "Forgive me," he said finally in a whisper. "It's just that I—" He broke off. She was still too angry to apologize for her outburst. "But what will you do? You may sleep with the pigs now. You can't think he'll let matters stay that way?"

"He's a brother of the church. You know what they swear when they are invested into orders." It sounded lame even to her.

"Perhaps you don't understand how this works. Hugh was invested into the church *because* he's a bastard. My own father had a girl child by—well, never mind by who—and she's now a deacon down south at Wisslaren. He has yet to decide which one of us younger boys he's going to give to the church. Before I was born, my sister Rosvita took orders first as a nun and then as a cleric in King Henry's schola. That was never by her choice, though she accepted it gratefully enough. So what makes you think Hugh ever chose to be in the church or ever meant to give up his . . . pleasures?''

She thought of ten answers, but there was no point in speaking words that were meaningless or, worse, lies. She could not lie to Ivar in order to try to lie to herself. She said nothing.

"Listen." Carefully, like a man approaching a wounded dog, he crossed to her and, gently, took her hand. "It's a fool's notion about the Dragons. I know that. But Father must send a levy next spring to King Henry, and if he does, he's sure to send me. Perhaps . . . well, if the Dragons really have ridden north, there must be some Eagles with them, to carry messages back to the King. I've heard it said that the Eagles will take any strong-minded person into their ranks as long as they're freeborn. And you *are* freeborn. Gero is riding up to Freelas tomorrow. I'll see what he can find out.''

"But you won't tell him what you plan?'' It was an idea made more horrible because she began to hope again.

"He guesses enough. We can trust Gero. He hates Hugh worse than you do. Here Gero is my father's heir and Hugh insulted him to his face last spring, treated him no better than a common pot-boy.'' Clearly the insult still stung. Ivar flushed and his tone grew quite heated. "My father is a count of the land, and just because we're so far north that the king's progress never comes here nor has any child of our line served the king except my sister as a cleric and a great uncle who died as a Dragon at the Battle of Lenzen. But no matter what Frater Hugh said, there was nothing Gero could do unless he wanted to raise his hand against a brother of the church.''

She scarcely heard him. "I always wanted to be a King's messenger.''

"But the Eagles ride alone. It's very dangerous, even with the King's seal to protect you.''

"It wouldn't be so different from the life Da and I lived. And I'd be free, Ivar. Not bound. The Eagles are beholden to no one but the king.'' She choked down a heartsick laugh. "Freeborn or not, they couldn't take me anyway. I'm not free. Hugh bought me for two nomias. I'd never seen nomias in my life before the auction."

Ivar released her hand and began to pace. "Your father had four books. They must have been worth a nomia at least."

"Hugh took them and never paid for them. He said they belonged to the church now. He *stole* them."

For once Ivar did not share her indignation. "Deacon Fortensia says all books pass to the church. Anyway, they're no good to you if you can't read. Liath." He stopped in front of her. "Promise me that if I can find a way to take you out of here, you'll come with me."

He looked so young, a boy pretending to be a man. He hadn't even begun to grow a beard yet. Liath felt infinitely older, wiser, felt so very tired, struggling against Hugh. Still, Hanna had gotten the book safely away. Ivar might yet discover an escape. "I promise. Thank you."

He flushed. Leaning forward, he kissed her, but he was inept and their lips did not meet squarely. He flushed more deeply yet, excused himself, and fled, leaving Liath alone in the kitchen.

Unexpectedly she felt heartened. She had touched the book. If there had been Eika raids in the west, then perhaps the Eagles would even take someone like her to fill their ranks. Perhaps Count Harl would need volunteers for his levy, to support King Henry against the Eika raiders. Perhaps the winter would be mild. She could outface Hugh. She *would*.

Five days passed too quickly. She was nervous, afraid Hugh would return at any moment, that every sound was the track of his boots. But he didn't come back. She slept in the kitchen, lingered at the inn and helped Hanna with her chores, and even, once, terrified and shaking for fear Hugh would appear out of thin air beside her, crept to the inn stables and leafed through her precious book. Hugh remained blessedly absent.

On the first Ladysday Eve, she stared up at the lowering sky and let herself embrace a brief contentment. Though it was cool and cloudy, so she could not observe the heavens while she had solitude to do so, still she had seven days until he returned. She poured a bath for herself, hauling the water, heating the water. As from down a long distance she recalled the old Dariyan baths in the villa where she had lived with Da and her mother. Remembering those times she luxuriated in the hot water, head back, hair floating on the ripples made by her body as she shifted in the great copper tub. The roaring hearth poured warmth over her. She heard the light patter of rain from outside. After she had soaked to her heart's content, she washed every piece of her clothing—something she dared not do when Hugh was around—and hung it to dry on chairs in front of the hearth. Wrapping herself in a blanket, she hesitated, then with a determined grimace walked to Hugh's cell.

The chamber was cold and empty. *Empty.* She poured a bucket of hot coals into the brazier and while it warmed the little room she knelt on the soft carpet and opened the chest. A rich emerald robe lay folded on top. Underneath it lay three fine linen undershifts. She lifted one out and pulled it on. The cloth felt so very soft against her skin. She sighed with pleasure and dug farther down to find cool silk beneath. There was a man's fine tunic and a woman's overdress of pale gold silk. She admired it for a long time. Had it been a gift to him from his mother? What was he keeping it for? She folded it up again and placed it back in the chest. Dug farther down yet . . .

And found books.

The first four she knew at once: Da's books. She felt down, seeking the astrolabe, but it was gone. Hugh must have taken it with him. At last she lifted out the fifth book. It had a frayed binding, but it was stamped in gold, and the spine was encrusted with pearls, some of them missing. She opened it.

The Acts of the Magicians. For the longest time her hand could not move, even to touch the words. Da had spoken to her of this book.

"Chaldeos was a minister to the Empress Thaissania, she of the mask. At her order he wrote a lesson for her three children, so that they might learn the magics by which the Aoi ruled their empire."

At last she managed to turn the first page. A neat scribal hand had written in three narrow columns on each page. The first was Dariyan, the second the graceful bird tracks of Jinna, and the third was Arethousan. Glancing at the Dariyan and Jinna, she saw that each column reproduced—translated—the others. If she could puzzle out the letters of Arethousan, comparing them to the other two languages, she could learn how to read it as one unraveled a code.

A spray of hard rain pounded on the shutters. A storm was blowing in. It had become much chillier and the coals had burned away. Her hands were numb with cold. Setting the book on the bed, she wrapped herself in the blanket and hurried back to the kitchen to stoke the fire, light a lamp, and bring more coals for the brazier. Back in the chamber she looked at the chair and then at the feather-bed. Surely, just this one afternoon, she could allow herself this lux-ury: to read until dark in this soft and gloriously warm bed. She could not decide. It seemed indecent somehow, and yet, the book, lying open to the first page of text, beckoned her. *The Acts of the Magicians.* Secrets her father had only begun to teach her the month before he died.

Why not? Why not be reckless this once? She settled herself in the marvelous soft bed and propped herself up on one elbow to read.

And lost herself.

Book One. The Courses of the Stars and the Spheres of the Heavens, how they may be divined according to the ancient Babaharshan magi-cians to lend strength to the Art.

Dariyan she knew so well that she could read it mostly with her eyes, her lips shaping the words but not speaking them aloud. To read the Jinna was a more laborious process, though she had once spoken it easily. She must sound out each letter and, melding them together, create the words.

But at least much of this material was familiar to her. The stars follow a fixed course, and the pole star, Kokab, is the axle around which the great wheel of the stars spins on its infinite round. The lesser wheel is known as the zodiac, the world dragon that binds the heavens. It is a circle of constellations, each representing one of the Houses of Night, and through these houses move the Sun and the Moon and the wandering stars known as planets. The ancient Babaharshan magicians gleaned this knowledge from a thousand years of observation and mastered sorcery by drawing on the pow-ers of the stars and the planets as they waxed and waned.

A scuffing sound. Then a low laugh. Utterly startled, Liath gasped and jerked her gaze up from the book. Froze, terrified. She had no idea how long she had been reading or how long he had been standing there, watching her scan the pages and turn them, watching her form the difficult Jinna words and speak them out loud. Thus did she betray herself to him.

Hugh walked into the cell. He was travel-worn and damp, his riding cloak slung over one shoulder and his frater's robe spotted with rain. His golden hair was wild in disarray, there was a smudge of dirt on his pale cheek, and he looked completely satisfied.

"What's this?" he asked. She could not move. He took the book from her nerveless fingers and scanned the pages that lay open. "Not only can you read, but you can read this edifying work. I am impressed, but not entirely surprised, that you know Dariyan, even in this antique form. Surely you do not know Jinna as well? Even I, with my court education, do not know Jinna, although of course I can read the Arethousan as well as I can read Dariyan."

"You know Arethousan?" she demanded, torn by such an acute desire to *know* that she forgot herself. Then she broke off, grabbed her own worn blanket, and wrapped it tightly around her torso. The linen undershift was far too light to wear alone, in front of *him*.

He smiled. He set the book down on the table, casually, loosened each finger of his gloves and drew them off slowly. He rested his hands on the bed, close to her, bending down right next to her, his face a hand's breadth away from hers. "I like your hair unbound." He lifted a hand and ran it up along her neck, then drew his fingers back down through her hair. "And so clean. Have you changed your mind, my beauty?" His voice changed timbre, taking on an odd, hoarse note.

"No." She turned her head away, out of his touch, and waited for him to hit her.

He straightened. "It *is* a comfortable bed. You'll share it with me soon enough. I want a bath. You may keep the undershift, as long as you promise me you will care for it properly. Fine cloth is too precious to be treated carelessly. And dinner will be tonight, instead of Ladysday next. You'll wear the gold overdress for dinner." He glanced down at the open chest. "Which you've already found." He smiled again. Liath could not imagine what had transpired to put him in such good humor.

"There will be much finer things than these, Liath. The abbot of Firsebarg has died at last. My mother has duly overseen the election of his successor. When shall we ride south? You'll like Firsebarg. I think you'll even like my mother. She was convent educated, so she can read, though not, I think, as well as you or I. And certainly she can't read Jinna, which is never taught in the church schools."

Ride south. Liath stared up at him. She had not really considered before that she might be torn away from the last people she knew and trusted, from her last link with Da. How could she possibly carry the book on such a journey without Hugh finding it? He must know she would take it with her. In Firsebarg, knowing no one, she would be entirely within his power.

Hugh watched her, enjoying her discomfiture. "Not until spring, I think. There's no hurry. I do hate traveling this late in the year."

She said nothing, only held tight to the blanket, gripping it around her as if it could protect her.

"Must we keep up this pretense? I know you are educated. You betray yourself constantly, with words, with the way you speak, with knowledge you ought not to have. I am bored, Liath. I have never been so bored as these last two years, wandering here in these northern wilds tending to my blessed sheep. Ai, Liath, we might at least call a truce so we can converse like the educated people we are. I will even offer you a trade."

He paused, to let her consider his generosity. "I will teach you Arethousan. *If* you will teach me Jinna. Queen Sophia, while she lived, was very firm that all of us in the king's schola be taught Arethousan. She was the Arethousan Emperor's niece, as I'm sure you know, a marriage prize brought to these benighted lands by the younger Arnulf for his heir. And although our praeceptor, Cleric Monica, thought it acceptable that those few of us chosen for her special tutoring should indeed learn Arethousan, should any of us ever be called upon to lead an embassy to that distant land, she cuffed me hard and well the one time I asked if she might teach us Jinna as well. 'A language fit only for infidels and sorcerers,' she said, which only made me wish to learn it the more, although I never said so to her again. But I never met anyone who knew it until I met your father. And now you, my treasure. What do you say?"

There was something very wrong with all this, and Liath knew it. As long as she gave him nothing, she was safe from him. But a small doubt had arisen. Perhaps he *was* owed some sympathy, flung from the bright center of the king's progress into these hinterlands, where there was no one like him. No wonder he had gravitated toward Da.

And if she could learn Arethousan, she could translate the glosses in the oldest text of *The Book of Secrets*. Perhaps she could even puzzle out the unknown language, written in that ancient hand. . . .

"I don't know," she said in a low voice.

He smiled. She understood at once that she had lost something important, that he had won this battle and was on his way to winning the war. She slid off the bed, pressing herself against the wall to keep as much distance between herself and him as possible, and ran out of the cell and down to the kitchen, to the safety of rougher work.

Behind, incongruously, she heard him begin to sing.

> "The Lady is glorious in Her beauty.
> The Lord is mighty with His sword.
> Blessed are we, Their children.
> Glory, glory, rests where Their eyes linger.
> Glory sleeps on Their hearth."

He had a beautiful voice.

3

ON the morning of the first hard freeze, Liath woke from a fitful sleep at dawn. It hurt to stand up. With her blanket pulled tight around her, she shuffled to the woodpile. It hurt to uncurl her fingers and touch any surface. A thin shell of ice covered the wood, and she bit at her dry lips to cover the pain of wrenching the logs free. She had to struggle with the latch before she could get it open and make her way into the kitchen. In here the change in temperature was abrupt. It hurt almost more than the cold did.

She stoked up the fire and simply stood before it, shuddering and coughing. After a while she bent to ladle warm water into her mouth. The water slid down her throat, warming her. She looked around, although certainly there was no one else here, then plunged her hands into the kettle of water and just stood there, letting her hands thaw. The fire snapped and burned so close her face felt seared, but she did not care. She heard something, a voice, a footstep, and she jerked her hands guiltily from the kettle and bent to scoop out rye flour for flatcakes.

Hugh appeared in the doorway. "It's cold. It's damned cold and I *hate* cold. I hate this frozen wasteland, and I damned well don't want to winter here. We should have ridden south last month when I got the news, but it's too late now." He strode across the room and gripped her chin, wrenching her face around so she had to look up at him. "You look like hell. You look like a damned land girl burned brown from doing a man's work in the fields all day long, with a chapped face and a running nose. Go make my chamber warm. Make me breakfast. Then get out of here. I can't stand to look at you."

He cuffed her on the cheek. It stung the worse because her skin was still chilled. She shrank away, trying not to cry. In his cell it was warmer even than in the kitchen. She heaped glowing coals into the brazier and crouched next to it, soaking in the heat. On the table rested a single neatly-trimmed piece of parchment with fresh writing in a graceful hand damp across the top. She craned her neck to read the words.

"Out! Out!" Hugh came up behind her and slapped her casually on the back of the head. "You're filthy. Get out!"

She fled back to the kitchen. She dawdled as long as possible, making porridge and flatcakes and then serving them to him. But she could only draw out the work for so long; soon he emerged from his cell and drove her outdoors. She tucked her hands into her armpits and set off briskly for the inn. She had to fetch meat, after all, from Mistress Birta. It was excuse enough. But she had scarcely gotten there, had only two heartbeats lingering in front of the hearth, surreptitiously watching a lone traveler eat his solitary meal at a table a few paces from her, when Hugh burst in through the front door.

He did not even have to say anything. She would have died rather than cause a scene. Mistress Birta emerged from the kitchen with the meat, dressed and wrapped since it was the frater's portion. She greeted Hugh but he replied with a monosyllable. Hanna appeared from the back room and watched as Liath took the meat from Birta and then retreated toward the door. Hugh walked two paces behind her, as if he was driving her. The traveler looked up. He was a grizzled, weather-beaten man wearing a fur-lined riding coat. He studied the scene with interest. Liath felt his gaze on her back as she left.

Outside, Hugh hit her. At least he was wearing his gloves, so the blow did not sting quite so badly. "Did I give you leave to come down here?"

"I had to fetch the meat—"

He slapped her again. Unable to help herself, she covered her cheek with a hand. Lady, it hurt. From the shadowed eaves of the inn came a movement, stifled; someone was watching them.

"You will ask my permission. Any time you go anywhere. Wait here." Hugh went back inside. Liath waited.

Hanna crept out from the side of the inn: "Liath—"

The door opened and Hugh came out, Mistress Birta following behind him as if she were his bonded servant. "Of course, Frater," she was saying with her hands placed just so and her expression as fixed with good cheer as any image carved into wood, "I'll have my boy Karl deliver everything from now on." She cast a piercing glance toward Hanna, and Hanna retreated hastily back around the corner of the inn.

"Come, Liath." Hugh grabbed her by the arm, his fingers as sharp as talons, and dragged her forward. She shook his arm off and kept up on her own. He said nothing more, the whole walk back. Nothing more the entire day, but he dogged her movements everywhere, and he hit her any time he thought she might be getting the least rest or respite from the cold.

She slept fitfully that night. The next day, and the day after, passed the same. And the next, and the next, until the days blended together into one seamless blur of cold misery and she lost track of time passing. The weather remained cold, but it was not yet bitterly cold. She settled her dirty heap of straw well in among the pigs. Trotter liked her best and allowed her to sleep huddled up against his rough back.

Once, brushing down the horses, she heard Hanna's voice outside. She ran to the door. There stood Hugh surveying Hanna with coldest contempt.

"Your young brother is to deliver goods, no one else," he said. "So I arranged it with your mother."

"I beg you, Frater, if you would only let me speak with—"

"I told you to go."

Hanna turned and saw Liath.

"Do you intend to challenge me, girl?" Hugh demanded.

There was nothing Hanna could do but leave.

"Get back to your work," Hugh snapped to Liath.

She slunk back inside the stable, denied even the solace of watching Hanna walk away.

One early morning Ivar appeared on his mare. He was bundled in a bulky fur-lined cape, his face white with cold and distress.

She was chopping wood. She stopped, staring; she had not seen a familiar face for so long that at first she thought she was dreaming.

"Liath." He spoke low and fast. "Come with me. I've got a plan. Gero will help to hide you, and then we'll—" He flung up his head, listening. From inside, Hugh called out to her.

She ran to Ivar, clutched his hand, jumped to get her belly awkwardly on the horse's back and swung her leg all the way over. Ivar turned the mare and kicked it forward. It was a sturdy creature, broad of beam, and it seemed able to carry both of them though it could not manage any gait except a jarring trot.

They made it most of the way to his father's holding before Hugh caught up to them on his bay gelding. He rode past the struggling mare and pulled around in front before drawing his sword.

"Are you armed, boy, or are you smarter than I thought?"

Ivar was alarmed only with a dagger. He stopped.

"Liath, dismount," said Hugh.

Liath dismounted.

"Liath," protested Ivar, "you can't just—"

"I have not done with you yet," said Hugh to Ivar. "You can come with me and present your case to Count Harl or I can simply present your folly to him by myself. I don't care. Liath. Walk beside my horse."

She walked, head down. At least walking had the benefit of keeping her almost warm. She stumbled once, not from fatigue but from sheer despair.

She could not look up as they crossed over the ditch and through the palisade and into the great open yard of Count Harl's castle. She stared at her feet, at Hugh's feet, which she followed up the broad path that led to the lord's hall, up a stone stairway, into the count's chambers. She heard voices, speaking her name, speaking Ivar's name. She could not bear to see their staring faces.

A chatelaine ushered them into Harl's private chamber. The old count was still in bed, covers heaped around him. A tonsured and clean-shaven cleric wrote to his dictation onto parchment. Ai, the room was so very warm. Liath inched toward the hearth. Hugh grabbed her and jerked her back to stand beside him in a cold eddy of air.

"Count Harl," he said curtly. He offered Harl only a stiff nod. It was a remarkable piece of arrogance, and if Liath hadn't hated him so much she would have admired his astounding vanity: that he, a mere bastard, considered a legitimate count his social inferior. But his mother was a margrave, a prince of the realm, and his family far more powerful than Harl's. "This stripling of yours has just attempted to steal my slave."

Liath risked a glance toward Ivar, who stood by the door. His face was bright red, and a few tears streaked his face. It wasn't fair that he be humbled so for trying to help her. Yet she dared not speak.

Harl rubbed at his grizzled beard and considered Hugh with obvious dislike. In the silence, a man marked on the cheek with the brand of the unfree came in to pour fresh coals into the brazier.

Liath's gaze flinched away from him. Harl ignored the slave and turned his gaze to his son. "Is it true, Ivar?"

"I've some silver saved, not enough yet, but . . . but *others* have offered to help me make the price. To buy out her debt price."

"She is not for sale," said Hugh smoothly. "Nor will there be any manumission but the one written by my own hand."

"You have not answered my question, Ivar."

Ivar glanced, searingly, toward Liath, then bowed his head. "Yes, my lord."

Harl sighed and looked back at Hugh. "What do you want?"

"I want nothing except your promise it will not happen again."

Hope flared. Could it be possible that Hugh actually feared that Ivar might find a way to free her? Everyone knew Count Harl disliked the frater.

"Very well," said Harl. He looked as if he were contemplating maggots in his meat. "It will not happen again."

"How can you assure me?" demanded Hugh.

Count Harl had much the same coloring as his son: Liath watched a flush spread across his lined skin. "Are you doubting my *word?*" he asked softly. The tone in his voice made her shiver. To gain this man's dislike was one thing; to gain his enmity, something else.

Hugh smiled, his ugliest, most insincere smile, made the worse because it affected his beauty not at all. "Certainly not, Count Harl. I would never question your honor. But your son is young and impulsive. And my property is quite valuable to me."

For the first time, Harl looked straight at Liath, so hard a gaze that she had no choice but to meet his eyes. He was appraising her— teeth, face, build, youth, strength—and whether he thought her worth unlikely or obvious she could not tell from his expression. At last he looked back at Hugh.

"You may rest easy, Frater. Your *property* will remain safe from my son. There is a monastery in Quedlinhame where my first wife gave birth safely in a storm, many years ago now. I have wished for these many years to endow them with some manner of thanksgiving. I intend to send Ivar south to be invested as a monk there. He will trouble you no longer."

Liath gasped. Ivar went white. Hugh's lips moved, not into a smile but into an expression so deeply satisfied it was almost obscene.

"Now get out," said Harl brusquely. "*If* you please. I've work to do. Ivar! You will remain with me."

Ivar cast her a last, despairing glance as Hugh shepherded her out in front of him. A man-at-arms escorted them down the hill to the palisade wall, where Hugh's gelding waited, tended by a stable boy.

"You'll ride with me," said Hugh.

"I'd rather walk."

He struck her, hard, and only by instinct did she duck away quickly enough that the blow glanced off the side of her head.

"You will ride." He mounted and waited there, the reins of his gelding tight in his hands, until she at last lifted a hand and he pulled her up behind him.

The ride back was long, and it was silent.

But he was warm.

That night winter blew in in earnest. It was cold, bitter cold. She could not sleep. She shuddered, there with the pigs, and rose in the middle of the night and stamped her feet, up and down, up and down, until daylight. She was so tired while she did her work that day that once he came upon her dozing on her feet. Or perhaps twice. Her shoulders and head were so bruised from his beatings that one more made no difference.

Clouds came the next night and with them snow. That eased things a little, for though it was damper it was slightly warmer. But all the next week, with snow still blanketing the ground, it was clear. So cold it was, all day. With every scrap of clothing she possessed, still she shivered all day. By evening she was numb with cold. She ached with it. She tried to move constantly, though she was exhausted, even when she was in the kitchen, shifting, stamping, trying to get warmth past the surface and down into her bones. She would never be warm again. It was a constant pain consuming her, the coldness.

He ordered her out of the warm kitchen at dusk. She shuffled out to the shed—she no longer had the energy to lift her feet—and sat next to Trotter. Even with the pigs it was still cold. She rocked back and forth, back and forth, back and forth, until the rhythm of her rocking lulled her into stupefaction. It was so cold.

She realized that she was going to die if she stayed out here. Not this night, but another one, tomorrow perhaps, or the next night, or the one after that. She wondered if she cared. Ai, Lady, and at once she knew, was horrified to know, that she did care. It was like a tiny, hated fire burning deep inside, that will to live.

"I don't want to die," she whispered. Her lips were too dry, too cracked with cold, too stiff, to form the words. She shuddered convulsively. Ai, Lady, she had not even the energy for that; there were not even tears left her. She was going to die, and she did not want to.

At first, seeing the light, she could not imagine what it might be. The athar, the spectacle, come down from the heavens? It staggered, swayed, bobbing up and down until she thought she was dreaming, seeing visions. But the light brought a breath of warmth, halting before her clouded gaze. It was the lamp.

"Liath." His voice was soft. "Come in now, Liath." He might have been coaxing a hurt child, or a wounded dog. "Come in now."

She shuddered, rocking. He placed a hand on her shoulder, gently, to stop her. "Liath," he said in the same quiet, soothing voice, "come in now." Then he removed his hand. And waited.

For the space of ten breaths, fought in, fought out, she just sat there. She was numb with cold. She ached with it, down to her heart. Anything was better than this.

She struggled, trying to get to her feet, and once he saw that she was trying to get up, he helped her. Only helped her, never pushed her, just guided, once her feet set off of her own choice for the kitchen.

It was gloriously, marvelously warm. Steam rose, or so it seemed to her, until she saw that he had made a bath, hauled the water and heated the water by himself. The tub sat in front of the roaring fire in the hearth. She just stood there while he unwrapped her filthy blanket, while he helped her out of her filthy clothing, carefully removing each piece. He handled these things fastidiously, with his gloves on, but once she was naked he stripped the gloves from his hands and rolled up his sleeves and helped her into the warm water.

The warmth hurt, like a hundred pricking tiny needles, elf-shot, stabbing her all at once. She wept dry tears. He scrubbed her with a stiff brush, chafing her skin, and that hurt even more, but she did not have the energy to protest.

With the pain came warmth, flooding down through her skin. Heat streaked off the fire. The hot water seeped into her flesh, into her bones. Periodically he would rise and fetch more hot water from the kettle for the bath; twice he disappeared outside with the buckets and filled up the huge kettle with water so cold it hissed as he poured it in.

He took a clean, soft cloth and washed her, her hair, her face, her hands and chest and abdomen, her hips and her thighs, her calves and her feet. While he washed her he sang, low, in his beautiful voice, a sinuous line of chant, only notes, no words. She was sinking with lassitude, with warmth. But she was still numb.

He took her by the hands and lifted her from the water. With a soft cloth he dried her. He wrapped her in a blanket of a fine plush weave and stood back from her.

He said nothing. He simply watched her. He did not smile, or frown. He had almost no expression, or at least no expression she could understand, on his face. But she had long since passed the point where she might have gone back out with the pigs. Da always said, *"There's no use swearing vows if you don't mean to keep them."*

She turned and walked down the narrow corridor to his cell. Two lamps burned, their light twin fires. The brazier glowed red with heat. The Dariyan lesson book of magic lay open on the table. She did not even glance at it but went to the bed and sat on its edge.

He followed her. Now he closed the door behind him and stood, leaning against it, to stare at her. His sleeves were still rolled up, revealing his pale, muscled forearms and their fine down of light hair.

"Will you teach me Jinna?" he asked. His voice was still soft, and his words sounded more like a question asked out of curiosity than like a charge driven to win the battle. Indeed, he almost sounded surprised.

She nodded. That was all. That was everything.

"Ah," he said. Then he was silent.

She finally looked up, because his silence was so odd. He was studying her. His expression was disturbing the more because he looked nakedly hungry.

"You don't even know what you are, do you?" he asked. "A treasure-house, as it says in the holy book. 'My bride is a garden locked, a treasure-house barred. I have come to the garden, my bride, and I have eaten my honey. I have drunk my wine. Eat, friends, and drink until you are drunk with love.'"

Unbidden, the next stanza rose in her mind as clearly as if she heard the words spoken aloud: *I sleep, but my heart is awake. Come, beloved, I will open the door.*

But she sat, as still as the bitter cold air outside, and watched while he undressed in front of her. Her flesh might be warm, now, might even be awake, but her heart had frozen straight through. She simply watched, unable to feel anything, until at last he was naked. Then she blushed and looked modestly away. That made him laugh.

In an instant he was beside her. He held her with one hand supporting her back and lowered her onto the luxurious softness of the featherbed. Stripping the blanket from her, he covered them both with the feather quilt.

"You're still cold," he whispered, running his hands down her arms and up her abdomen to her breasts. "Liath, say something to me."

This close, he was overpowering. She gathered up enough courage to meet his gaze. What she saw there cracked some of the ice off her numbness. Tears stung at her eyes. She turned her head away and shut her eyes and lay rigid in his arms. But she did not otherwise move or try to escape.

"I know what you want," she said softly. "But it's locked away. It's locked away, and you'll never get it."

"We aren't speaking of the book anymore, are we, my beauty?" He was a little amused, a little angry, but he shifted, embracing her, and he sighed, and suddenly his skin, against hers, went from cool to warm to hot. He said, under his breath, so quiet she barely heard him, " 'You who sit in my garden, my bride, let me also hear your voice.' "

His voice trembled, he was so overwhelmed by feeling, not just passion, what others called lust, but something stronger, something more frightening. He wanted not just her body, not just the book. He wanted *her*. There were deeper things still, things she only now realized might exist, the child of two sorcerers, deaf to magic but hiding something so far inside herself that even she could not see it.

But he could. If Liath had feared him before, it was nothing to the fear she felt now. He had enough training, enough knowledge, to see. He had sight, that allowed him to see past the *seeming*. For now, right now, as Hugh shifted against her, caressing her, she saw what the truth must be.

Da had been running all those years to protect *her*. To hide *her*.

Whoever—or whatever—had killed her mother now wanted *her*. She was the prize, the treasure. Only she did not know why.

Hugh sighed, his breath warm and sweet against her cheek. She kept her eyes clenched shut.

"Don't be afraid," he said softly. "I'll not be rough with you, not here. Not ever, here."

He knew what he was doing.

She found the city, standing fast in her memory. She set foot on the white shore against which lake water lapped in slow ripples as even as her heartbeat, and she ascended the spiraling avenue paved with marble, its seams so perfectly joined that it appeared as one smooth flat endless surface, twisting ever tighter as it approached the height. And as she climbed, as she passed through each higher gate, seven in all, she locked them each one behind her until she came to the summit.

She found the frozen tower of her heart and barred it with vines and thorns and spears of iron. Inside she went by the single door and up a ladder to the highest room, to the chamber of doors that Da had given her; this chamber only he had envisioned for her, four doors, north, south, east, and west, and a fifth door, set impossibly in the center of the room, which was locked even to her. Each door she locked with a brass key, locking herself in. Only in the door that opened to the north did she limn the shade of a door, a secret door that led into wilderness. There she laid a little path through trials great and small, through forests trackless and ways mysterious, to obscure it from view, so that only one who truly knew her heart might find this way in. Into that wilderness, into the trackless, tangled wild lands, she threw the key. If any man sought that key, let him look at his own peril.

She clung to that, to that vision, to save herself.

Hugh was gentle. He was warm. He spoke sweet words to her. At last, he slept.

She lay awake, sealing the city of memory shut, each wall seamless and strong, until she was safe within it. Until she was alone and unreachable but for the little path where Hanna might enter, undisturbed. At last she allowed herself to relax, although Hugh still circled her with a heavy arm. At last, in the marvelously soft, the gloriously warm bed, she slept.

4

THE next day Hugh hired a woman and man from the hamlet down near Count Harl's holding to come in daily and do all the work about the church.

They dutifully cleaned out the cell next to his while he rummaged around in the storage rooms and found a serviceable table and one broken chair, soon mended. The hired man, Lars, killed a goose, and while Dorit cooked it, Liath made quills. Hugh opened two locked chests from the storage room, and they revealed unexpected treasures: parchment and ink, a wax writing tablet and stylus, and other necessaries of a church schoolroom as well as two more rugs (neither as fine as the Arethousan carpet in his cell) and other comforts.

Liath studied. If she studied, she could forget everything else, push it away as if it didn't exist. For part of the day they spoke only Dariyan together. For the second part he taught her, letter by letter, word by word, the language of Arethousan, and she taught him Jinna with its curling letters she herself could only write awkwardly. For the last part she read aloud to him from the books her father had left. She read about healing herbs and the pharmacology of flowering plants in the *Inquiry into Plants*. She read about omens and portents and visions seen while sleeping in Artemisia's *Dreams*. She read history, of the trials and blessed acts of St. Thecla, founder of the Church of Unities in Darre, first and greatest disciple of the blessed Daisan and the first martyr to the faith when she stood firm against the persecutions of the pagan emperor. And she read of the early days of the Dariyan Empire, during its greatest triumphs, as written by Polyxene, an Arethousan scholar in the imperial Dariyan court whose stated intent in writing her history was to discover ''by what means the Dariyans, who are known to us as being not of human kin, succeeded in less than fifty-three years in bringing almost the whole of the inhabited world under their rule.''

Together, as well, they proceeded slowly through the lessons in *The Acts of the Magicians*. Once he made a candle light without touching flame to it. Once he predicted a storm. She remained deaf and mute to all but the sense of the words. She translated the Jinna for him and began to puzzle out letters and words in the column written in Arethousan. On this she concentrated her being. All else passed in a haze, especially the time they were together in the night. She felt so utterly detached from herself that it was as if she were two people, one to whom all this was happening, one watching from her safehouse within the frozen tower.

Sometimes he was called away to give last rites, to bless a newborn child or perform a healing. The first time he was gone overnight she crept out in the morning, past Dorit baking bread in the brick ovens built outside the kitchen, and went into the yard. But the cold blast of air and the heaping snow struck such fear into her that she escaped back into the church and did not venture forth again.

Every Hefensday the folk from the village gathered to hear the gospel. Before, she had never shirked from attending. Now she dreaded it. But the first time she had refused to go, he had slapped her hard and threatened to leave her out with the pigs, so she gave in. He wanted to display her; she understood that well enough. He had hidden her old clothing, forcing her to wear the fine gowns. She was afraid to speak to anyone and, with her silence, feared they all thought her prideful of her new consequence.

At those rare times she was granted solitude, she knelt in the empty chapel, not praying, usually not thinking at all, just resting in the silence of God. Sometimes she dreamed memories of Da.

"Liath, you may let your fancy play with the letters. Treatises have been written about the various schools of calligraphy in old Dariya. But when you learn the old patterns, when you draw the Rose, it must be drawn as exact, each time, as at its creation. There are no elaborations. What you draw with your hand is simply the pattern to which you exercise your mind, until you need no physical link to bring the Rose into your mind. Or, for a sorcerer, to make it manifest at will." He spoke at times with such confidence, such clarity. But now his expression fell and his shoulders hunched, and he looked weary again. "Anne would have taught you better than I can."

Liath rested her hand on Da's white hair, gone white so early. "Don't say so, Da. You said yourself I must learn for the sake of knowing these things, for passing them on, perhaps, but never to expect to have these powers myself."

He sighed. "Do you wish you did?"

She shrugged self-consciously. "I suppose so. I wish you had begun to teach me sooner, Da, about the arts known to the sorcerers, at least. Why did you wait so long?"

"You aren't strong enough yet. It isn't safe, child. It will be a long, long time before I can know we are safe."

Only they hadn't been safe.

"Liath!" The whisper was soft but sharp.

Liath started, banging her knees on the hard floor, then scrambled to her feet and whirled. Stood for a moment, registering this stranger. "H—Hanna?"

"You're so . . . well, not pale, but so gray." Hanna strode forward. She wore a frown on her face. Her energy radiated like heat in the stillness of the cool chapel, warmed only by the brazier of coals which Liath had brought out, for she could no longer bear cold. "Old Johan is passing up through the spheres this time for certain, they say. I saw Hugh ride off. He'll be gone at least 'til evening, so I came over. Mama said I might, and I haven't talked to you since—" She hesitated. Liath simply stared at her. She was having a hard time understanding words spoken by a voice other than Hugh's. "Since that day he struck you outside the inn. Do you remember that man who was there that day? He was traveling through to Freelas. He asked about you, after Hugh took you back to the church. He asked about your Da."

"I don't remember him," said Liath tonelessly. Hanna's words had no real meaning, except perhaps to someone else, someone who was no longer here. "You shouldn't be here."

Hanna stiffened. "Do you want me to go?"

Liath shook her head. That wasn't what she meant, but she hardly knew how to speak anymore, only how to recite aloud words written down by others. "No. but you shouldn't be here." Suddenly nervous, she looked back over her shoulder, toward the archway that led into the nave. "He'll come—"

"He's ridden down to River's Bend. He can't possibly be back until evening."

"He'll know. He'll come back. He'll know I'm seeing someone. He always knows."

"Liath. Sit down. You're shaking all over." Hanna touched her. That touch was like fire sparking up Liath's arm. She could move but only found the strength to do so when Hanna steered her toward a bench and sat down beside her, pressing an arm around her back. Liath gave in to sudden exhaustion and rested her head on Hanna's shoulder. "Lars is gone to visit his old mother, and Dorit is down at the inn gossiping with Mama, so Hugh can't possibly know. Dorit says you're silent as a ghost, slipping around this place. Says you never speak unless the frater speaks to you, and then half the time in some devil's tongue. Or at least, that's what she says." Hanna fell silent and stroked Liath's arm, a rhythmic caress. They sat this way for some time.

Suddenly Liath flung up her head. "What day is it?"

"Ladysday Eve."

"No. what month? What day? What season? Is it still winter?"

Hanna gazed at her, and Liath realized abruptly that Hanna was uneasy, even frightened, but by what, or whom? "It's a month at least to the thaw. Midwinter has come and gone. So has the Feast of St. Herodia. It was a good harvest and there's none in want even at this late season. Most of the rye sown last autumn survived the winter."

"Then Mariansmass, after the thaw," said Liath, struggling to remember something important Da had once told her. Or was it her mother? Yes, it had been her mother. They had been in the garden, on the very day of Mariansmass, pinching off new growth in the garden, thinning, but why were there shoots so early? And her mother, with her pale hair and elegant carriage, a proud woman . . . but even as she recalled the scene, the memory of what her mother had told her fled. "I'll be seventeen," she said, grasping at the only thing she could make sense of.

"Liath. Look at me." With an effort Liath lifted her head and turned it to look at Hanna, whose expression was torn with anguish. "My parents want to betroth me to young Johan. At Mariansmass. I told them I would think about it." Now she sounded bewildered. She was pleading. "What should I do? I don't want to marry him and live out working his land, and bearing his children, every year until I die. I know that is what the Lady has granted us, in our span of years, that I should be proud enough to be a freewoman, but that isn't what I want. Even though I be marked for it. But I don't know what else to do."

Hanna needed her. The shadow door drawn into the great north door in her sealed chamber opened a crack, admitting Hanna past the wilderness, the wasted lands, to her stronghold. "Oh, Hanna." A sudden fire burned in her. "If Da and—if we could only go back to Autun, that's where we lived before we came here, or to Qurtubah and the Kalif's court, or to Darre, where we lived first, then we could take you with us."

"Darre! There are devils in Darre!"

"Devils? Under the eye of the skopos herself?" Liath chuckled. "You mean elves. They aren't truly devils, Hanna. Or even daimones."

"But Deacon Fortensia says they're the product of intercourse between fallen angels and the daughters of men. That's why they're devils."

"That isn't what the blessed Daisan taught. Da always said that elves were born of fire and light, tainted only by the darkness that came into the world in the time of chaos, and that they existed before humankind was ordered by the Holy Word."

Hanna regarded her half in horror, as if Liath had revealed that she herself was a devil, born of unnatural congress between a human woman and an angel who had forsaken the Lady and Lord. "You know so many strange things," she muttered finally.

"It's only because I learned to read, Hanna. You could do so, too, if you wanted to."

"If I was in the church!"

"In Darre. I remember, Hanna!" These memories, born fresh out of the cloud in which she had been wandering, were like a thawing in the frozen northlands. "Da said that it was in Darre that King Henry met the elvish woman who bore him the prince that secured his succession."

Hanna still looked doubtful and a little worried by this ungodly talk, but she squared her jaw and forged forward gamely. "Is it really true that the prince is half elvish? But it must be. Inga says her husband's cousin's wife was in Freelas the day the Dragons rode through, and she saw them. The Dragons, that is. She said there couldn't be any doubt but that he wasn't but half of human kin, he was so terrible and splendid to look upon. He had hair as black as night, skin the color of bronze, and green eyes."

Liath laughed. Stuttered to a halt, having not heard that strange sound for so many months: her own simple laughter. "How could

Inga's husband's cousin's wife have been close enough to the prince, much less the Dragons, that she could see what color eyes he had?''

''He does have green eyes, and he is half elvish, poor bastard. His mother deserted him before he was two months old.''

Liath spun round so quickly she collapsed to the floor, huddling on her knees. Vaguely she realized that, behind her, Hanna rose. Brave Hanna. For there he stood, poised in the archway that led into the church. Of course he had known.

''She never knew Wendish or Varren, only Dariyan and a bit of Aostan, which is like enough to Dariyan that she might understand the one if she knew the other. They say she came out of Alba, which is known as a place where the Lost Ones still walk abroad in secret places and under the moon. But the tongue she spoke most easily was Salian, and it was in Salian she named the child.'' He smiled, as if he was perfectly aware that she knelt rigid, frozen, at Hanna's feet only because of his presence. ''She called herself Alia, which of course means 'other' in Dariyan, though Prince Henry as he was then never seems to have understood the riddle. My old nurse was one of those who attended at the birth, for they had need of many witnesses, since Henry's fertility was proven by this child. This is what my nurse told me: That Alia stared at the afterbirth and the newborn child and the blood that necessarily attends such events and said, 'These are bloody fields I have been brought to. Take it away.' So he was called Sanglant, for that is the name they heard her speak.''

His tone changed, and his eyes, so hard, were riveted on her. ''Liath. From now on you will ride out with me. You can ride, can you not?''

She nodded mutely.

''Then come.''

''But it's so cold out there.''

''You will come. Now.''

She rose and went.

5

WITHOUT even looking up at Hanna, without acknowledging her, Liath stood. She walked down the chapel aisle as stiffly
as if strings moved her limbs for her, walked past Hugh and out
into the church.

In the instant after she passed out of sight, Hugh looked right at
Hanna, really seeing her. He studied her as if trying to decide if she
posed a threat to them. Then, with an unconscious, deprecatory
toss of his fine head, he dismissed her from his mind and turned to
follow Liath out.

"You fool," said Hanna under her breath, watching his form fade
into the unlit gloom of the church. And yet, how could she look
upon *him* and then turn without loathing to meet young Johan,
with his pox-marked face and dirty fingernails and heavy, deliberate speech, on the marriage bed?

"You fool," she said again, just to make sure she understood perfectly well what she was. Satisfied, she knelt on the padded cushion
where Liath had knelt, warmed by the brazier. And she thought,
long and hard, about what she had just seen.

When she left the church, she did not set off for the inn but rather
on the long walk to Count Harl's holding. Possibly, just possibly,
she could talk her way in to see Ivar where his father was holding
him in isolation until the spring journey to Quedlinhame. She knew
a hundred ways to coerce him—however bitter he might be, for
everyone knew now that the southern girl was the frater's concubine—into taking a message with him when he went south.

That man, passing through town three months before, had worn
no clothing, no badge, that might identify him. But late that night
as she stoked the fire, she had watched him writing on parchment.
A letter, perhaps, although he was clearly not a churchman; he had
a beard. What kind of soldier knew how to write?

She had edged closer, trying to get a look, and by chance and luck
had seen him inscribe a symbol at the bottom of the parchment.

She could not read, of course, but an innkeeper's daughter recognized many symbols. This symbol she knew well, although they saw it rarely enough as far north as Heart's Rest.

It was the badge of the King's Eagles.

V
THE INNER HEART

1

"FOR it is said, in the Holy Book," preached Frater Agius, "that our suffering is the penance we endure for our sins."

And it was true, reflected Alain as he stood for the final prayer. He had never been as happy, and yet as utterly miserable, as these last two seasons: autumn passing into winter and now, with the thaw approaching, winter promising to circle round, as all of life passed time and again along the Circle of Unity, into spring. He was learning the craft of the man-at-arms, like the warriors in old tales, just as he had been promised in the vision on Dragonback Ridge and just as he had always hoped he might. Yet, because of the hounds, because he had in his heart turned away from service to the Lord and Lady as he had been sworn by his father to give, he was shunned by every man and woman in the holding except for Lackling.

"Give the blessing," spoke the congregation as one. Agius lifted his hands toward the heavens. He had a strong voice, one suited to the long sermons with which he edified the congregation of Lavas

Holding now that Deacon Waldrada was so sick with the lungfever she could not speak above a whisper.

"May the blessed Daisan, who now resides in the bosom of Our Mother, have mercy upon us and save us. May St. Cecilia, whose day this is, and St. Lavrentius, whose bones sanctify this church, and all of the saints, and our mother among the saints, Clementia, second of that name, skopos in Darre, intercede for us with the Mother and Father of Life, for They are gracious and loveth human-kind. Amen."

Alain waited with the rest of the retainers while Count Lavastine and his kinsfolk left the church. He touched Lackling's elbow, but the boy stared at the great church window, colored red and gold and azure and emerald green, his head skewed oddly to one side so he looked more like a goblin's child than a young man born of a human mother. But he had, always, a fey, misshapen look about him. The rest of the congregation filed out. Alain tugged harder on Lackling's arm, and suddenly the other boy started, glancing wildly around, and fumbled at his belt. He drew out a dirty piece of cloth, unwrapped it to reveal a lump of crumbling cheese and an onion. Eagerly he pressed past Alain and walked with his rolling limp toward the vestibule and the doors.

Alain hurried after him. "Lackling," he called after him, trying to whisper. "You may not. It is forbidden."

"My friend."

Alain turned. Frater Agius regarded him from the altar. Agius' bright gaze made him nervous, and it seemed to Alain that since the episode with the hounds the frater's bright gaze was turned his way far too often. He ducked his head in answer.

"Chatelaine Dhuoda tells me you were destined for the church."

"Yes, Brother." He kept his gaze lowered. "I was meant to enter the monastery at Dragon's Tail."

"A King's monastery, was it not?"

"Yes, Brother."

"Burned to the ground by the Eika, and the monks slaughtered?"

"Yes, Brother."

"Yet you moved swiftly to save the Eika prisoner from further injury, four months ago?"

"Yes, Brother."

"Why is that?"

"The Lady teaches us to be merciful, Brother." He said it quickly, hoping desperately that Frater Agius would end this inquisition so he could get outside before Lackling was discovered.

"You do not hate the Eika prisoner? Though he may have been among those who murdered the men who would have been your brothers? Perhaps, my friend, you were offered to the church against your will?"

Alain flushed, keeping his head down, and did not answer.

"Your parents?" asked Agius, coming down off the dais and walking up the aisle to stand beside Alain. Alain caught the scent of damp wool and the spices of holy water, and a lingering scent of rose oil. Agius' hands were brown and callused, the hands of a man who engaged in manual labor. Yet his accent betrayed him as a man of highest birth.

"I do not know who my mother was, Frater Agius. Henri of Osna, son of Adelheid, fostered me. He is the father I know. My family is from Osna village, my Aunt Bel, who is Henri's sister, and her children, who count me as their cousin. I was raised there."

"Bel and Henri? Named after Henry with a 'y' and Sabella, I suppose, but with a Salian taint. But you are a fosterling?" Agius had sharp eyes, able to cut through to the heart of things. Or so Alain feared.

"Yes, Brother."

"It is said by the people hereabouts that old Count Lavastine, grandfather to the current count, made a pact with devils for those hounds." Alain fidgeted, wishing he was less conspicuous. "It is also said that the bargain drawn up between them demanded blood, and promised blood, and that the hounds would only obey the count or an heir of his blood. I have asked Chatelaine Dhuoda if it is possible that you are the bastard son of Count Lavastine. By my calculations, as I look through the records, he would have sired you just around the time he became betrothed to the woman he later wed. A bastard son sired on a common girl, however pretty, would be an embarrassment, would it not, at such a delicate time? Many such bastard sons are given to the church, to get them out of their family's way."

Some tone in his voice made Alain look up and blurt out: "You? Are you a bastard son given to the church against your will?"

Agius did not smile. "I am not such a one. I entered the church against the wishes of my parents. I was betrothed to a woman I did not want to marry. It would have been a good marriage for my family, but it was not for me, for I had already sworn in my heart to—" He broke off, and after a hesitation went on. "—to devote my life to Our Lady of Blessings." He placed a hand against his chest. "The Lady blessed my suit. I had a brother younger by one year, handsomer and more inclined to such a marriage, and together we convinced my betrothed that he would make a better match. So I took my vows at eighteen, and my brother married soon after. He is dead now, killed in King Henry's wars." He said it calmly, yet Alain thought his eyes flashed with anger and his mouth twisted down with bitterness. "But you look nothing like. Still, strong blood in a child leads it to resemble the mother."

It took Alain a moment to understand. *You look nothing like Count Lavastine.* That was what Brother Agius meant. "What would it matter if I was Count Lavastine's son?" he asked, angry that Henri could be dismissed so easily. "I was fostered out. Even if it was true, he must have meant to be rid of me."

"Surely you don't believe that would be the end of it, do you? Many a noble lord or lady showers favor and even wealth on the bastard sired or born in noble loins. If your heart is indeed devoted to the church, you must think of what you can bring to Our Lady and the blessed Daisan. A noblelady's son might bring wealth or lands, a nobleman's son an endowment to a monastery or, if he is loved enough, his parent might found an institution in which to house him."

"Even if it were true," Alain whispered, "I am only a merchant's son now. I could never prove such a thing." Even if he wished it were true. A child born into the nobility, even as a bastard, might hope for service with the king, might inherit an estate that would allow him to lead his own warband, or if not that, then gain entrance into the king's elite cavalry, the Dragons.

"I have examined the record of births for the year in which you were evidently born. Of the children born in that year, there are only three who, nameless, escape me. The others died as young children and were lifted up to the Chamber of Light, their deaths recorded in the parish register, or else I have tracked them down and seen them, whole and alive, with my own eyes. Of those three, one was noted as a baby girl and born to a legitimately married couple who soon after left these parts. The other two are recorded simply as babes born to unmarried women whose names are not given, though one, at least, received a penance to perform for her sins.

Alas, the deacon who tended the Lavas Church Hearth in those days is now dead, but the cook here has an exceptionally fine memory for these things. She assures me there was no other child born and taken away in that year. Nor has she memory of any foundling left at the church door."

Alain tried to imagine being recognized by Count Lavastine as his bastard son, blood of his blood, invested into a new and exalted rank. But he could only see his father Henri's face, torn by grief as he remembered the woman who had been Alain's mother. A woman Henri had loved.

"You have nothing to say? You are an ambitious boy, are you not?"

"Lord Geoffrey's child, the girl born to Lady Aldegund last autumn, will become Count Lavastine's heir. I heard them speak of it."

"If she lives. If no more suitable candidate can be found. Lady Aldegund comes of Wendish kin. These are borderlands, it is true, but to the people here a child of Varren blood would be preferred. Bastard or not."

"There is no proof," repeated Alain, terribly uncomfortable with Agius and his insistent questioning. Could the frater not let well enough alone? "I have never heard one soul in this holding claim the count got a servingwoman with child. Surely they would gossip about such a thing, if it was known. Count Lavastine had an heir, but the child is dead now, is she not? Surely he will marry again."

"Perhaps. No one speaks of those deaths now, except to say it was a terrible accident. Ah, well. No doubt if Count Lavastine wishes to investigate your birth, he will. Indeed, it is none of my business. He is no kin of mine, and I am in any case sworn to the church now, no longer to the concerns of the world." His voice turned brisk and he looked suddenly preoccupied by other matters. "I will speak to Master Rodlin and Sergeant Fell. I wish you to attend me for one hour each day. I cannot forget you are still sworn to the church. I will tutor you in letters and reading, as is fitting." He turned abruptly to the altar, knelt, and began to pray.

Alain backed down the aisle as silently as he could. Reaching the vestibule, he bolted outside.

Too late! There lay the damning evidence, right next to her. Dressed in sackcloth, her hair streaked with ashes, Withi was huddled, weeping, on her knees on the cold ground next to the church doors. As she had been for ten days now, ever since the captain had caught her fornicating with young Heric in the stables. There had been other witnesses, so he had had no choice but to demand that they confess their faults publicly. Frater Agius had demanded the sinners perform full penance, although the captain had gotten Heric sent home to his own village where his parish deacon might show more mercy.

So Withi wept, her blue eyes no longer pretty but swollen with tears, her face chapped with the cold and her hands red and chafed. Lackling had left the cheese and onion right out in plain sight, as an offering to her, since all he understood was that she was forbidden any food except bread and water. He was hiding at the corner of the church. He darted forward, seeing Alain. His speech sounded more like the grunts and cries of the beasts of the forest than like that of a human man. Withi sobbed out her shame. Some of the men-at-arms paused down the road to look back at her. Alain jumped forward and concealed the dirty cloth with its forbidden treasure under her sackcloth robe.

She gulped down tears. Her hand clutched at the cloth. "You brought that for me?" she whispered. "It is a sin to lighten the burden of a penitent, as if you were a deacon or a frater given leave to lighten the judgment passed on a sinner."

"It's only a lesser sin," said Alain quickly. He could not help but feel sorry for her. Lackling grunted excitedly beside him. "And it wasn't me. It was Lackling—"

She lifted blue eyes to Alain's face. "I won't forget," she said, but to Alain, not to Lackling.

The halfwit screwed his face up and tried to speak. "Wheefoe." She shuddered and backed away from him.

He was only trying to say her name.

Frater Agius appeared at the door. "Friends." He walked over to them. "Compassion is a virtue, but penance cleanses the soul. For pausing here to speak with this penitent, Alain, you will fast next Ladysday and reflect upon the meaning of the lesson I preached today. May the Lady have mercy on your soul. Amen. Now come. I will speak with your masters."

Like everyone else, Agius ignored Lackling. Alain had no choice but to follow. What could he do for Withi, after all? She, along with everyone else, had shunned him after Count Lavastine's return and the incident with the hounds, and yet it hurt him to see her reduced to weeping in the dirt outside the church door. Deacon Waldrada had never been this hard-hearted. The best anyone said of Frater Agius was that he judged all with equal harshness, including himself.

Lackling, after loitering near Withi without getting any kind of a sign that she noticed him, finally lost heart and dashed after Alain. He was as loyal as the hounds but rather worse kept. He did not get meat at all, not even on feast days, such a delicacy being too valuable to waste on a simpleton; besides his odd face, he was scrawny and short and he walked with an odd rolling gait with his bandy legs. Even the dread hounds, who snapped and bit at everyone, treated Lackling with indifference, though of course he could not command them. Alain pitied him and did what he could to protect him from the taunts and cruelties of the other young men and women.

Frater Agius strode so quickly, Alain half running to keep up, that they soon passed the young men-at-arms strolling toward the castle. Had Alain been alone, the soldiers would have called him names or spit at him, but he had learned to endure such treatment because he understood that this, like weeping outside the church doors, was a penance, one he must bear without complaint. But now, because he was under Agius' protection, they only looked at him and muttered.

They found Master Rodlin and Sergeant Fell in the castle yard. All was arranged as Frater Agius wished.

"Huh," grunted Sergeant Fell when Agius took his leave. "You have gathered to yourself strange benefactors, my boy." He exchanged a glance with Master Rodlin, who stood, hands folded, perfectly calm.

Alain wanted desperately to ask if these men, so long in the service of Count Lavastine, thought he was the count's bastard son, but he dared not. He simply obeyed.

When it came time for Sergeant Fell to take the young men training as foot soldiers out into the fields, Alain went along as he had all winter. The snow had been light this year, and though the Mass of St. Herodia had not yet been celebrated, marking the thaw, the fields had been swept clean by the winter winds, leaving a plain, flat ground suitable for war games. And if the other young men hit him harder with their padded spearheads than was necessary, slammed him in the head with their bucklers, if they made him stand at the point in formation more often, where the risk was greatest, he did not mind it. Each bruise only made him stronger. Sergeant Fell nodded gravely and said, only once, that he was taking well to the drill.

Once they got to run ahead as beaters when Count Lavastine and Lord Geoffrey and the other lords went hunting with their falcons, though Alain had to run alongside the hounds to keep them from mischief with the riders. In the forest out past the old ruins the hounds ran a boar to ground, and Lord Geoffrey's young son, born to his first wife, was granted the killing blow.

For one hour each day Alain sat with Frater Agius and laboriously relearned his letters and learned to recite by memory passages from the holy book. In the evenings he sat in the hall and ate and drank. He secretly slipped Lackling bits of fish, and he listened as poets sang, as musicians played, and watched as mimes entertained the count and his kin and guests with their dumb show.

After all that he would slip outside to his pallet in the stockade and huddle under the good wool blanket Aunt Bel had sent to him via a peddler in the autumn. Only in the kennels, alone with the hounds, could he be at peace—with the hounds, and with the Eika prince bound in his cage. The creature had weathered the winter's cold without any sign that it disturbed his equanimity.

The Eika prince fascinated Alain. He was a beast, a savage creature who had almost ripped out the throat of one of the handlers who had come too near him at suppertime that first week of his captivity. The man had not died, but he had lost his ability to speak. The prince seemed to respect only the hounds, whom he surely recognized as like himself in their blunt fury.

It had become Alain's task to feed him, once at noontide, once at evening bell. With the hounds as his snarling escort, Alain would bring a bowl of meat and gruel (the only food the Eika would eat), loosen one of his hands, and step back out of reach while he ate.

That was the curious thing. The prince had the most fastidious habits, both in eating and in caring for his person. He did not tear into his food, although with such small portions as Count Lavastine spared him, he must be hungry all the time. Rather, he ate daintily, with better manners than many of the nobles who sat at Count Lavastine's table. If he must relieve himself (and he did this much less often, Alain judged, than any human person had to), he did so always in the same corner of the cage, as far as he could get in his chains. Alain took pity on him finally and cleaned out that corner every Jedday, since none of the other men would go near the cage. The prince watched him but never, even when a hand was loosened so that he could eat, tried to attack him. Perhaps it *was* only that Alain went everywhere inside the stockade with his retinue of hounds, who were certainly as fearsome and dangerous as the clawed, copper-scaled prince.

Perhaps, as he once overheard Master Rodlin mutter, the Eika devil knew by instinct a child spawned by an inhuman father. But Rodlin treated Alain fairly and never once hit him as he did Lackling or the other boys and young men who served under him if they made a mistake or did not do their chores quickly enough. But how could he be the child born of the mating of a human woman and the shade of an elvish prince at Midsummer's Eve if he was actually the bastard son of Count Lavastine, gotten on a serving girl?

The Eika prince, like a penitent, endured his captivity without complaint through the cold winter and the slow turning of the year.

The Feast of St. Herodia came and passed, and Mariansmass loomed, the first day of spring, the beginning of the new year, which by the reckoning Frater Agius taught him would be the seven hundred and twenty-eighth year since the Proclamation of the Divine Logos, the Holy Word, by the blessed Daisan, also known as the Proclaimer.

A stranger rode into the castle and was escorted to Count Lavastine's private study, emerging two hours later and riding straightaway south, on a fresh horse. The whispers started.

"Is it true? The Lady Sabella will come here?"

"Does the count mean to join her rebellion? To swear himself to her as his liege?"

"Will we go to war against the king?"

"Not *our* king. Henry is not rightfully king of Varre, only of Wendar. His grandfather stole the throne of Varre away for his own children."

Alain worked up his courage, and on St. Rosine's Day, a week before Mariansmass, he asked Frater Agius two questions.

"I beg your pardon, Brother, but am I to return to my village when my year is up?"

"Your year?" Agius was distracted. He was fingering the Holy Book but not looking at its pages.

"My year of service. In a fortnight it will be St. Eusebē's Day."

Agius frowned. "If you wish to return, you must speak with Chatelaine Dhuoda. That is her province, not mine. Certainly such a decision would lie as well in your aunt's hand. But I do not think that Count Lavastine can spare any of his men-at-arms this year."

"I don't wish to go back, not yet," said Alain hastily, fearing he would be misunderstood. He *did* want to stay; he wasn't ready to return to Osna village yet. And yet, was it not disloyal to his father and aunt to stay here so long when they could be using his labor at home? But they would only find some other monastery to send him to. Agius watched him curiously. Alain recalled his other question. "Is it true Lady Sabella is coming here?"

"It is true," said Agius.

"But we haven't prepared—!" He choked back the rest of the sentence. Agius was too preoccupied, taking out his knife and trimming the wick on his lamp, to even have heard Alain's words. And no wonder. Lady's Blood! A princess of the royal house of Wendar and Varre was coming, *here*, to Lavas Castle.

That evening in the hall Count Lavastine rose and addressed his household. His speech was short and direct.

"I have received a message from Her Most Excellent Highness Sabella, daughter of the younger Arnulf, king of Wendar, and of Queen Berengaria of Varre, whose names we remember in our prayers. She bids us greeting and will arrive in Lavas with her husband, Prince Berengar of Varre, and her daughter Tallia, and her retinue, in ten days' time."

Cook was furious, in private. "Ten days! I will have to send you boys out to fetch every pig and sheep from the villages nearby. We'll need at least five hundred. Where shall I get enough wine and ale at this time of year, I ask you? And grain. Chickens! Five wagon loads of turnips, if there are even any left in the cellars. I ask you!"

Chatelaine Dhuoda and her stewards swept the countryside, working frantically for ten days, and brought in all the provender Cook would need as well as additional servingmen and women. Alain worked from dawn to dusk, hauling, fetching, building temporary shelters. There was no time to train at arms; there were no lessons with Frater Agius. Oddly enough, he found he missed the latter as much as the former.

The church bell rang at dawn on Penitire, calling the faithful to the day of penitence. Alain rose, fed the hounds, and allowed himself a handful of fresh rainwater out of the water barrel to wet his throat. From the stockade he could see the road that wound down the valley to Lavas town and the church. Already he saw people, some shuffling forward on their knees, others bent double, the rest with hands clasped across chests, moving toward the church. There Frater Agius would lead the morning service because Deacon Waldrada was still too ill to preach.

Like the stable hands and stock-keepers, he had to care for his charges before he could pray. So had the blessed Daisan wept and prayed and suffered remorse for the sins of the faithful, whose shepherd he was, before he could himself find release from the Earth and pass up through the seven spheres to the heart of the Lord and Lady.

Someone was watching. Alain turned. The Eika prince stared at him. His hair, as white as bone, marked a pale line against the dark slatted walls of the cage. Did he ever sleep? Alain was beginning to believe he did not.

Master Rodlin had left no directions about the prince. All fasted on Penitire. But wasn't the Eika prince pledged to false gods? Alain decided it would be more merciful to feed him. So he brought the portion allocated to the prince, and while the prince ate, Alain spoke in a calm voice—not wanting to startle him—about the blessed Daisan and the Holy Circle of Unity. After all, the light of the faithful could be brought to all creatures. Had not the goblin kin of the Harenz Mountains been brought to the faith by the exertions of St. Martin and his sister, the holy martyr St. Placidana?

"On this day we remember our sins," he said. In the cool, quiet dawn, his voice sounded strange, disembodied, as if someone else was speaking. He heard, like a counterpoint to his speech, the low growls of the hounds as they crunched on bones. The prince ate noiselessly. "And then, for seven days we pray and fast just as the blessed Daisan did at the church Hearth in Saïs, the blessed city. These seven days we call the Ekstasis. In his rapture, as he prayed, seeking redemption for all who might come into the Light of the Circle of Unity drawn by Our Lord and Lady, his soul ascended through the seven spheres until at last, on the morning of the seventh day, it came to the Chamber of Light. And the Lord and Lady in their mercy conveyed him directly to heaven. It is written in the *Acts of St. Thecla*, the Witnesser, that the church was entirely illuminated with the light of God's mercy, so brilliant that she was blinded for seven times seven days thereafter. But the blessed Daisan was gone, taken up unto the Chamber of Light. On that day, which we know as the Translatus, there is feasting and rejoicing, for so may we all find mercy in the grace of Our Lord and Lady."

Like the hounds, the prince seemed to prefer his meat raw, and he ate every bit of it, including the bones. Now he lifted his head and his narrow tongue licked the air. This close, he had the sheen of a snake's skin, a mellow reddish-brown. He smelled not humanlike, sweat and skin, but like a musty cave, entombed, dry stone.

And he spoke. "Halane."

Alain started back two steps, he was so surprised. Then he jumped forward and chained the prince's hand back with the other.

"Halane," said the Eika, slit eyes fixed on Alain. Bound now, he could only move his chin, up and over. His voice had the smooth tone of a flute.

He's trying to point at me, Alain thought. And shuddered. *Halane.*

"My name is Alain," he said, hesitantly, not sure if he was inter-preting the Eika's intent correctly. "I am Alain, son of Henri. Do you have a name?" He copied the gesture the creature had made. "Do you have a name?"

It bared its teeth, but Alain could not tell if, like a hound, the grimace was meant to scare or if it was trying to smile. "Henry. King."

Alain gulped down an exclamation. "King Henry rules in Wendar and Varre. What is your name? Who rules in the lands where you come from?"

"Bloodheart. King of shipmen. I also son. Son of Bloodheart."

Son of the Eika king! Was that truly what the prince was saying? And hard against his astonishment, a wild bubble of laughter tried to escape: The Eika prince thought that he, Alain, was the son of King Henry!

All at once, before Alain could reply, the hounds left off worrying at the bones and ran to the stockade gate. The Eika prince threw his head back and as one with the hounds howled piercingly. Alain clapped his hands over his ears and jumped out of the cage, slam-ming the door shut and chaining it closed. Such noise! The hounds yammered and howled like wild things. He ran to the ladder, climbed it, and from its height saw what the others had smelled and heard.

There, coming down the road, was the most glorious procession he had ever seen. About fifty riders were surrounded by a great mass of servants and other foot attendants. Banners and pennons rose in the breeze, lit by the sun as it flooded the valley with light. Carts and wagons followed behind, most of them painted in bright colors, and at the very end came the stock-handlers and the extra horses and some few beasts of other description, including a great shrouded cage.

Alain flung himself over the stockade, lowered, and dropped to the ground. He ran. In all his life he had never seen or expected to see anything like this: the retinue of a great prince. He made it to the castle gates in time to fall in behind a smaller procession made up of Count Lavastine, who was dressed in a plain tunic and hosen—without ornament—as was fitting for Penitire, and his household. He and his retinue approached, on foot, the great caval-cade of Lady Sabella and met with them before the church, where a crowd had gathered.

Alain gaped at the fine ladies and lords and their splendid horses. All of them wore gold threaded in their tunics and gowns; there was even a biscop among them, her white robes adorned with gold piping and her donkey fitted with a handsome saddle worked with beads and silver. But the most marvelous among them all was Lady Sabella.

Alain recognized her at once since she wore a gold coronet on her brow and a magnificent golden torque around her neck. She wore a tunic thickly threaded with gold, a belt studded with gems, and gold bindings on her legs. At her belt she wore a sword which boasted a hilt inlaid with gold. That she wore a sword was strange but not unheard of for a woman, but Alain shivered, seeing it, wondering what the count's reaction would be. A woman of Lady Sabella's high rank only wore a sword if she meant to lead an army in her own person rather than through the agency of a kinsman. She had a strong face, and she wore her hair plaited back, dressed with gold and silver ribbons but uncovered, like a soldier's. All at once she reminded him of the Lady of Battles, whom he had seen in that vision almost one year ago.

Count Lavastine greeted her in the formal manner, but he did not help her dismount. One of her own vassals did so, holding the stir-rup while she swung down. Then her husband—a paunchy man distinguished only by the gold torque at his neck—dismounted. There were several girls in the party so draped with shawls that

Alain could see no outward sign by which to distinguish Tallia—Sabella's daughter—from the others.

Alain sidled over toward the doors of the church, coming to rest near poor Withi, who had taken up her usual station on her knees by the door.

The biscop, staff in hand, led the company forward to the doors. Frater Agius had come out, and he knelt on the porch in greeting.

"Where is your deacon?" asked the biscop.

"Deacon Waldrada has been ill with the lungfever, Your Grace," said Lavastine. "She is not yet recovered enough to lead the service."

"So do we obey the dictates of Our Lady and Lord. While it is not traditional, nevertheless this brother of the church shall assist me today, together with my clerics and deacons." Almost at the porch, with the lords and ladies following, the biscop caught sight of Withi kneeling in the mud. She lifted her staff and pointed it at the girl. "Who is this penitent with her hair stained with ashes who kneels forward before the others?"

So close behind her, Alain saw Withi's shoulders tremble as the biscop spoke. He wanted to go forward, to comfort Withi, to tell her that surely this biscop, with her kindly face and her gentle but authoritative manner, could not be harsher than Frater Agius. He even took one step forward, only to halt at the sound of Agius' hard voice.

"This sinner has confessed to the sin of fornication, Your Grace. She has repented of her sin and now kneels for the prescribed one hundred days here before the church, so that all may see and hear her cries to Our Lady, who is merciful."

"Poor child," said the biscop. She was an old woman, white-haired but robust, with cheeks rubbed rosy by evident good health. "Shall we not also act mercifully on this day of repentance?" She walked forward and extended a hand to Withi, who merely gaped at her.

All around, the crowd murmured at this sign of compassion from a great biscop, a noblewoman of high rank.

"Come, child," said the biscop gently. "You must enter the house of Our Lady and Lord and be forgiven your sins."

Withi burst into noisy sobs, but at last, under the biscop's kind gaze, she put out a chapped, callused hand and the biscop took it in one of her own white, clean ones and lifted her up. With the girl beside her she led the procession into the church.

Agius remained kneeling to one side. He bowed his head, hiding his expression, so that Alain could not tell if he was furious, or shamed.

2

AS a man-at-arms in training, Alain was allowed to serve at the
high table in the great hall. Dhuoda soon recalled that she had first
noticed him serving at his aunt's table, in Osna.

"Your manners are superior and your bearing is dignified," Dhuoda informed him. "You may help serve wine at the high table."

He did not get to pour the wine directly into the cups of the count
or Lady Sabella or the other high personages, of course. They had
their own servants to do that. But he was assigned the important
duty of standing behind the table in order to make sure the servants' pitchers never ran dry. Because, during Holy Week, it was
customary to eat and drink sparingly—or to fast, as Frater Agius
did—Alain had the luxury of a great deal of standing around and
listening. And listen he did.

"I am a border lord, Your Highness. I have estates lying in both
kingdoms."

"Yet most of your lands are in Varre, are they not? As is this
castle and your most ancient holdings. You are kin to my husband,
Prince Berengar, and thereby a distant kinsman to the crown of
Varre."

"Which resides now in the hands of King Henry." Count Lavastine maintained such a discreet hold on his tongue that Alain could
not tell if he supported Lady Sabella or King Henry. Or, indeed, if he
supported either one.

"Where it does not belong. I and my daughter are the last living
heirs of the royal house of Varre, through my mother, Queen Berengaria. I am the only living child of Arnulf and Berengaria, whose
names I remember in my prayers daily."

"King Henry is also the child of Arnulf."

"Through a woman who was not even a queen in her own right,
but only through her marriage to Arnulf. I am the rightful queen,
Count Lavastine, and when I am restored to my throne through the
efforts of my faithful followers, I will give my daughter Tallia to
the throne of Varre as queen and marry her to a man of noble birth

among those who have supported me. Thus will Varre be restored, separate once again from Wendar and no longer subject to taxes and duties imposed by the reigning monarch in Wendar."

Alain could scarcely catch his breath, hearing Sabella speak so bluntly. Count Lavastine evidently had unplumbed reserves of calm, because not a flicker of emotion escaped him.

"You speak rebellion, Your Highness, against King Henry, who has received the blessing of the skopos in Darre and of the assembly of biscops and presbyters at Autun. Henry was himself named heir by your father, the younger Arnulf. Did you not swear before Biscop Antonia of Mainni seven years ago to reconcile with your brother?"

"So I did reconcile at that time. I was younger, and my daughter not yet healthy. After many years of prayer and with the wise counsel of Biscop Antonia and the considered support of Rodulf, Duke of Varingia and Conrad the Black, Duke of Wayland, I have chosen again to put forward my case. Let us speak plainly, Count Lavastine. I seek your support as well."

Sabella had a bland, almost monotone voice, but the deep furrows of long anger that lined her face gave the lie to her seeming coolness.

"Such a decision cannot be reached lightly," said Lavastine. He glanced toward Alain as if he had known the boy was eavesdropping all along, then smoothly changed the subject to last summer's Eika raids and the prisoner he had captured in the battle at the Vennu River.

Amazed by the count's notice, Alain stood frozen until, mercifully, one of the biscop's clerics signaled to him. Alain jerked himself away and hurried over to refill a fine glass pitcher. For a little while he was busy.

In the kitchens, where he refilled his own ceramic pitcher from barrels brought from the cellar, a different discussion was going on.

"I heard that fifty of those pigs will go to the beast that hides in the cage," said one of Cook's assistants.

"Hush, now," said Cook. "We needn't have your gossip here. Go back to your chopping."

"I heard it, snuffling and clacking its teeth, and one of the handlers is missing a hand. Bitten off, it was, I'd wager."

"It's a monster!"

"Nay, it's only a leopard, that's what one of the servingmen back by the wagons said."

"Had he ever seen it? Why must they shroud that cage, then? Why do they keep it outside the palisade, back by the forest, as if to hide it? It's a basilisk, mark my words. One look and it will turn you to stone."

"I won't have this!" said Cook sternly, then turned her sharp gaze toward Alain. "You, lad, aren't you serving wine?"

He hurried back into the hall, poured, fetched more wine, only to find himself in another lull. A monster in a shrouded cage! He was not quite sure what a *leopard* was, anyway. Was it like a basilisk?

He eased down the dais toward the count but came to a halt somewhat behind the chair of Biscop Antonia. Next to her sat the sallow, quiet girlchild whom Alain had identified as Tallia, daughter of Sabella and Berengar. Alain studied her surreptitiously. No longer truly a girl, she was not yet quite a woman. She had pale features that resembled neither her mother nor father strongly. A fine linen scarf woven with golden lions on a wheat-colored background, whose effect was to render her even paler, concealed her hair. The gold torque around her slender neck was so thick and heavy it appeared to imprison rather than elevate her.

Fish—for of course the noblefolk fasted for Penitire by eating no meat—and vegetables and savories lay untouched on her plate. She ate only bread, although twice he saw her drink watered wine from the cup urged on her by the biscop, who tended to her charge solicitously. Farther down the table, Prince Berengar drank and ate with gusto.

At last, pale Tallia leaned toward the biscop and spoke. "Why can my lord father not observe Holy Week in a Godly manner, Your Grace?"

The biscop patted her kindly on the hand. "You must never mind it, my child. We must each accept the burden that the Lady and Lord have given us to bear."

"My lord father is an idiot," murmured Tallia, and then blushed deeply.

"Nay, child, say not so. He is a simpleton, and is it not said in the Holy Book that 'the simple soul is closest to God'?"

"You are kind to say so," replied Tallia, looking mortified as Prince Berengar called loudly for more wine. Beyond Biscop Antonia, Lady Sabella seemed not to hear her husband's shrill voice.

But the servants hastened to assist him, and soon after Alain noticed Sabella make a hand sign to her steward. Within moments, a pair of burly young men deferentially escorted Prince Berengar, who was now singing the opening stanza of a song Alain usually only heard coming from the barracks, out of the hall.

"Has Frater Agius been with you for long?" asked the biscop, turning to Count Lavastine.

"He came a year or two ago," said the count. "You must ask my chatelaine if you wish more particulars."

"And is he a good man?"

"He is devout. No scandal attaches to his name."

"He is harsh, my lord, in his reading of penance, which is a virtue best left to those exalted brothers who devote their lives to the eradication of their own spiritual deficiencies. But not all souls born onto this earth are granted such vigor in their spiritual pursuits. I would draw your attention to that poor child I found kneeling outside the church this morning. Surely forty days of penance would have sufficed. She is young and pretty and not freeborn, I take it. Would it not have been better for such a young woman to marry the young man in question? So that she might then perform her duty to Our Lord and Lady by producing many fine young daughters and sons while lawfully allowing her body to take part in those earthly pleasures which are also a part of the nature of those of us who are human—for we are all of us, even the blessed Daisan, admixed by darkness, are we not? And then these fine strong children can work your fields, Count Lavastine. If we but aid the Lady and Lord in reaching the hearts of the faithful, in lending aid to all so they may also serve, then so will we all prosper the more."

He inclined his head briefly. "I thank you for your counsel, Your Grace." It was hard for Alain to tell if the count spoke sincerely or sardonically. "Since my men-at-arms do not marry without permission, I must assume that the young man was indeed unmarried. If it is your will, I will speak to my captain and to my chatelaine about the matter. They will resolve it speedily, I trust, and to everyone's satisfaction."

Sabella watched this interaction with a lifted eyebrow, as if waiting. But for what? Biscop Antonia merely nodded, smiling, then turned to make sure that Tallia had eaten all of her bread.

"Your love for Our Lady and Lord is an example to us all, my child, but you must keep up your strength."

"Yes, Your Grace," said the girl dutifully, and she fingered the crusts and then, at last, ate them, washing them down with a sip of wine. Alain's mouth watered. He had drunk only water and eaten only a little bread, as was fitting, and the rest of Holy Week loomed ahead, six days of fasting broken on the seventh day by the Feast of the Translatus. He sighed and went to get more wine.

The next morning at dawn, Alain woke to a knocking on the gate. He climbed the ladder and found himself looking down on Master Rodlin.

"Up quick, now!" said Rodlin sharply. "The count will be bringing Her Highness the Lady Sabella here after morning service, to view the Eika prince. You must make all secure so they may come inside safely. I have five handlers here, and I can send more if need be."

But Alain chose to chain down the hounds himself, and he stood beside them while the count and his guests entered the stockade. Chatelaine Dhuoda, Frater Agius, and the captain walked in attendance as well, so that all together a goodly number crowded into the stockade, pressed toward the side of the enclosure well away from the black hounds. The hounds whined and yipped, calling out to their master, and Count Lavastine came over and acknowledged each in turn: Joy, Terror, Steadfast, Ardent, Bliss, Fear, Good Cheer, Sorrow, and Rage. Old Enmity had died over the winter. Joy had come into heat two weeks before and was believed to be pregnant by Fear. The hounds licked Lavastine's hands and thumped their whipcord tails hard against the wood bar that held them. A few growled at the visitors. Prince Berengar made as if to come over and pet "the sweet dogs," and had to be restrained, but Alain saw that this was all done delicately. Sabella was evidently careful that her husband received no outright insult to his person. Lavastine nodded curtly at Alain and returned to the others.

"Sit," Alain whispered to the hounds, and he edged toward the cage to watch as Sabella, Biscop Antonia, and the others stared at the prisoner. The Eika prince examined them coldly, but he remained utterly still. What an awful fate, to be stared at so, and so helpless in the bargain. The compassion Alain felt for the prince startled him. Shouldn't he hate all Eika for what they had done to Brother Gilles and the other monks at Dragon's Tail Monastery?

"Truly Our Lord and Lady work in strange ways," said Biscop

Antonia. "Such a creature I have never seen before, and yet I know that the creation of all beings on this Earth are the work of God in Unity. But this kind is surely made more out of the things that grow within the earth, of stone and dark metals, than of light and wind."

"You have received no messages, no offer for ransom?" Sabella asked.

"I fear he will be of no use to us except as a hostage," said Count Lavastine. "Truly, he eats as much as two of my hounds and is less useful."

"He does not speak?" asked Sabella. "Perhaps if persuaded he could give information about the ships and movements of his people."

"We have tried. He speaks nothing of our tongue, and no one here speaks anything of his, if indeed these Eika savages speak in words and not just in animal cries."

"Perhaps he could be taught," said Sabella, but even she looked skeptical. "There are marks on the chains, here."

"He tried to gnaw through the metal but could not, even with those sharp teeth. He has since given up trying to escape, or so we suppose."

"Patience is a virtue," said Biscop Antonia. "As is submission to the will of Our Lord and Lady. There may yet be hope that his kin can be brought into the Circle of Unity."

The Eika prince said nothing, made no movement, only watched, surveying his captors as if to memorize their features. Alain wondered how much he *did* understand. He suspected, now, that the prince understood more than he let on. Two days ago he would have said, like the others, that the prince was unable to speak.

"If he is of no use to you," added Biscop Antonia, "then I would gladly take charge of him when we leave here."

Take charge of him? Alain was not sure he trusted anyone but himself to care for the prince. If they discovered the prince could speak, what then? They would torture him; it was the usual way to interrogate prisoners. And why not? The Eika tortured and mutilated innocent villagers and the monks and nuns who haplessly bore the brunt of their merciless attacks. Why should he be merciful toward a creature who would kill him, given the chance?

Blessed are the merciful, for they shall obtain mercy.

"Your Grace is most generous," said Count Lavastine, "but it is not necessary. I consider him surety for the safety of my lands from further attack."

"If indeed," said Sabella, "his kind care enough each for the other that they would forbear to attack you in order to save one of their own. Perhaps, like wild dogs, they would as soon eat their own comrades as their enemies." Lady Sabella moved away, her attendants crowding after her like so many beads pulled along on a string. The hounds, with remarkable restraint, merely growled after them.

As she left, Frater Agius bowed his dark head and clasped his hands together piously. "Little by little is coming to pass that threat spoken by Our Lady through the mouth of Her prophet: 'A scourge out of the North shall spread abroad over the inhabitants of the Earth.'"

Biscop Antonia glanced sharply at the frater. Then she extended a hand. "Stay for one moment, Count Lavastine, if you will."

"As you wish, Your Grace." He waited, his servants clustered behind him.

"What if I can, by interrogation, gain information from this prince? May I trade to you the intelligence so gained in exchange for his person? I have a great interest in those of Our Lord and Lady's creation which are unlike ourselves, which come from elder times and are more memory to us now than familiar sight. Call it a study, if you wish, a catalog done in the style of the Dariyan philosophers, if I may be forgiven a reference to the pagans." She smiled gently and looked questioningly, or perhaps reprovingly, toward Frater Agius. "Yet the blessed Daisan himself rose out of their number to bring to all who lie in darkness the truth found in the light."

"If that is your command." Lavastine looked just barely annoyed, but she *was* a biscop.

"I think it would be best, Count Lavastine." Her gaze shifted, caught on Alain, and stayed there until he wanted to sink into the ground to escape her notice. She glanced beyond him toward the hounds, then all at once moved away to follow Lady Sabella. Count Lavastine escorted her.

Frater Agius, too, was looking at the hounds, who snarled as the biscop walked past, well out of their reach. She did not appear to fear them, as many did. "You tend the prisoner every day, do you not, Alain?" asked Agius suddenly.

Alain bowed his head obediently. "I do, Brother." But he was as aware of the Eika's gaze on him as of Agius'. Staring, both of them. He threaded his fingers together and squeezed them tight, so the pressure might keep him calm.

"You might have seen things others have not."

"Yes, Brother."

"You will speak to me honestly, I trust."

Heat burned his face. He shuffled his feet restlessly but could not answer, either to lie to the frater or to betray the prince. And yet, what duty had he to the Eika prince? Should his loyalty not be given first to Our Lord and Lady and second to the count?

"You will attend me tomorrow," said Agius suddenly. "After morning service. Is that understood?"

"Yes, Brother."

Then, mercifully, he left.

"Halane."

Alain started guiltily and looked round quickly to make sure no one was about, but they had all left, grateful to get out of the stockade. The hounds had settled back on their haunches, waiting patiently for Alain to free them.

"You must not speak," he said, and was aghast to hear himself saying these words. "Only when we are alone. Otherwise they will hurt you."

"No hurt," said the Eika. "No hurt Halane. Go free."

"I can't free you. I must serve the count."

"Name man."

"Count Lavastine is the name of your captor. Surely you know that by now."

"Tre man look. Un, do, tre man. Name man."

What did he want? The name of the people who had come to look at him? Did he think they were all men, males, or did he have no word to differentiate male from female? Alain could not know. But he knew that just as he could not bring himself to betray the captive and helpless prince, neither could he betray the count's trust. What if the prince did escape and then knew by face and name Lady Sabella? If the Eika recognized the word "king," might they not also recognize "queen" or "prince?"

"I can't tell you their names. You must understand that, I beg you."

The prince did not reply. He blinked once, owllike, deliberate. Alain fled. It was too much to understand.

Later that evening, as he served at the table, the talk turned to the reign of the Emperor Taillefer, he who one hundred years ago had united Salia, Varre, the westernmost duchies of Wendar, and most of the southern princedoms into a great confederation blessed and anointed by the skopos in Darre as the rebirth of the Dariyan Empire. Only then did Alain realize that the Eika prince had counted *one, two, three* in a bastardized form of the language spoken in Salia. He knew a bit of it, enough to communicate with those Salian merchants who beached their boats at Osna village. But how had an Eika prince come to learn it? Truly, there was more to him than met the eye.

In the morning, Biscop Antonia led a somber service to celebrate the second day of the Ekstasis. As the congregation left, Alain sidled away to kneel in the chapel. Lackling followed him, and although with signs and whispers Alain tried to make him go away, the half-wit remained stubbornly blind to the hints. Or perhaps he truly did not understand. But the boy knelt quietly, breath sucked in noisily and blown out with a slight whistling through the gaps in his teeth. Lackling had never once broken the silence of church with his grunts, his half-formed exclamations, his snorting chuckles. Alain laid a hand on Lackling's shoulder and in this companionable way they considered the altar, dedicated to St. Lavrentius, who had died before the time of the Emperor Taillefer while bringing the Circle of Unity to the Varrish tribes that lived in this region.

They knelt there so quietly that the mice who nested beneath the altar grew bold enough to venture forth from their safe haven. Lackling held his breath; he loved the tiny creatures. Alain slowly slid a hand along the floor and one of the little brown creatures, dark eyes bright, nose twitching, anxiously darted over to investigate his fingers. Gently he lifted it up and let Lackling stroke its downy coat. Alain did not have the heart to kill them, although they were pests, not when they came so trustingly to his hands.

Suddenly the mouse scrabbled frantically up Lackling's fingers and leaped out of the halfwit's hands. It vanished under the altar and all rustling and scratching ceased.

"My friend."

Even having braced himself, Alain still started when Agius spoke softly behind him. A moment later Agius knelt beside him, although the frater did not allow himself the luxury of kneeling on the pillow laid there for that purpose.

"Is there anything you wish to tell me, Alain?"

Alain gulped down a sudden lump in his throat.

"I swear to you that I will consider this as a private confessional, between you and God."

"A p–private confessional?"

"There are some of us in the church who believe that confession ought to be a private matter between the penitent and Our Mother, in which such as I serve only as an intercessor. I do not believe in public confession, Alain, though some might call me radical for professing such a belief. Each one of us must bend our heart to Our Lady and the Divine Logos, the Holy Word, for it is the inner heart and not the outer seeming which matters to God."

"But, Frater Agius, does not the outer seeming reveal the inner heart?"

"We can never know the inner heart except through Our Mother's grace. It might appear to you that I serve Our Lady faithfully, with a true and single-minded heart, and yet how can you see past this outer seeming to know that my inner heart is riddled with vainglory and pride, in believing that I can serve Our Mother better than any other man? So do I pray each day for the lesson of humility. I beg you, my friend, for the sake of your immortal spirit, tell me the truth of what you know."

"I—I know nothing. The Eika prince spoke a few words to me. That is all." Even clasped before him, his hands shook as he spoke.

"Words in what language?"

"Wendish. I know no other language."

"Many of the people here in Varre also know Salian."

"I know a few words. The prince counted in Salian, or at least, the words sounded something like Salian but not exactly like. But he said almost nothing. He cannot truly speak our language."

"Why did you not tell Count Lavastine?"

Alain felt like a cornered rat. "I—I just think it wouldn't be merciful for him to be tortured, if he can't speak well enough to truly talk to his interrogators." He risked a glance at Agius, afraid that he had revealed disloyalty, but Agius' expression did not change. The frater stared fixedly at the image of St. Lavrentius on the burning wheel.

"You have a compassionate heart, Alain. I will think on this before I act. Is there anything else you have seen or heard that you wish to tell me?"

The Lady of Battles. The vision he had seen in the ruins. The owl that had hunted that night, on Midsummer's Eve. But he dared not speak of these things to Agius or to anyone except his kin. Afraid that he was about to blurt out these secrets, he said the first thing that came to mind.

"Why is Lady Sabella not Queen of Wendar? She is the elder child, isn't she?"

"The sovereign does not chose the heir only because of primacy of age. To rule is a great burden, and the child named as heir must have other qualities. Chief among them is the ability to produce an heir in her own right. A family only stays strong as long as there are strong children to carry on the line. Surely you have heard of the heir's progress?"

Alain shook his head.

"When the heir apparent reaches his or her majority, then she or he is sent out on a progress around the realm, just as King Henry travels constantly on his own progress, seeing to the health of his kingdom. The Lady watches over this progress, and if she grants her favor to the claimant, the woman will get with child, or the man will make a woman pregnant. So is the chosen one marked as heir, for so it is assured that this prince of the realm is fertile."

"But couldn't a man lie about getting a woman pregnant?"

"Both he and the woman whom he has gotten with child must swear before a biscop, in the name of the Unities, that the child is of their conception. And the child must be born healthy, to prove its conception was not tainted with sin."

"What happened to Sabella?"

"She went on her heir's progress and did not get with child."

"But King Henry did?"

"Ah, yes. King Henry did, although in a strange fashion. But that is a tale in and of itself."

"Then why can she rebel now? How can she claim she is the rightful queen?"

"Many years later Lady Sabella married and gave birth to an heir, thus proving her fertility. After the birth of Tallia, Lady Sabella demanded that Henry stand aside in her favor. Of course he refused."

"Oh." Although Agius spoke of the doings of the great nobles, this story had a familiar ring; an Osna family had two years ago gone through an acrimonious dispute over inheritance rights, settled (after one unfortunate death) only by the intercession of the deacon, who had made all the parties involved kneel for five days and four nights at the Hearth in the church while she recited from the Holy Verses. "Do you think her cause is just, Brother?"

"I do not concern myself over such worldly matters, Alain, nor should you." He turned suddenly, skewing round on his knees, and an instant later Alain heard the scrape of the door.

Biscop Antonia, in a white cassock trimmed with gold thread, walked up the aisle to them. She had such a pleasant face that Alain could not help but warm to her. She reminded him of the elderly deacon in his own village, kind Deacon Miria, who treated all children in Osna village as if they were her own grandchildren and whose judgments were firm, compassionate, but always just.

"Frater Agius. I hoped to find you here, at your devotionals."

"I endeavor to serve God, Your Grace, as well as this unworthy flesh can."

She did not reply at once. Alain tucked his head down, trying to efface himself, but he felt her gaze on him. Then it lifted and he glanced up swiftly to see that she regarded Agius once again.

"I have heard from the count that there are old Dariyan ruins nearby. You will attend me tomorrow, and lead me there."

"I am your servant, Your Grace."

"Are you, Brother? I have heard whispers about you, Frater Agius. I have heard you profess a devotion to Our Lady so great that you often, I fear, neglect to pray to Our Lord, the Father of Life. But—" She looked again toward Alain. He ducked his head quickly. "We shall speak of that another time."

Agius merely made, at his chest, the hand sign that denoted submission to his elder's will: fingers curled down and clasped over his thumb.

The biscop moved to the hearth, where she knelt, said a prayer, and drew the Circle at her breast. Then she left the church.

"Go," said Agius. "Meet me here tomorrow, after morning service. I would like you to attend me."

"Me?" Alain squeaked.

Instead of answering, Agius bent double and prostrated himself before the image of St. Lavrentius.

Alain nudged Lackling. "Come," he whispered, afraid to disturb the frater, whose eyes were closed and whose lips moved in rapid prayer. The boy followed him willingly. Outside, Alain had to blink. The sun had come out from behind the morning clouds and now shone brightly. The light stung his eyes.

3

ONLY a small group walked by the isolated forest path to the old ruins: Biscop Antonia and two of her clerics, Frater Agius, Alain, and, of course, Lackling, who attached himself like a loyal hound to Alain and could not be shaken loose. To Alain's surprise, the biscop did not ride her mule but chose to walk with the others, as any humble pilgrim might.

"You, child," she said, indicating Alain. "Walk beside me." Of course he obeyed. "I saw you yesterday in the church with Frater Agius."

"Yes, Your Grace."

"Are you kin to him?"

Surprised to be compared in such a casual way to a man of obviously noble birth, Alain blurted out a denial. "No!" At once he was ashamed of his rudeness. "I am a fosterling, Your Grace. I was raised in Osna village."

"Freeborn?"

"Yes, Your Grace. Or so my father told me, and so was I raised. My father and aunt and cousins are freeborn back to the time of Emperor Taillefer. There is no half-free blood in that family."

"But you are a fostered child." She said it so kindly that although the attention of so great a personage as a biscop rather frightened him, he could not help but want to confide in her. And she was old and therefore worthy of respect. As the saying went: "White hair is earned through good deeds and a good life." And she did so remind him of Deacon Miria at Osna village, a woman to whom all went willingly to confession, knowing the penance imposed would be just, and never too harsh to bear.

He bent his head, flushing, flattered by her interest. "My father is a merchant, Henri of Osna village."

"Your foster father, you mean?"

He hesitated. *Bastard child of a whore.* But Henri had loved Alain's mother. Who was to say Henri was not truly his father? And yet, how could he know? Henri had never spoken of the matter.

When he did not reply, she went on. "I have heard it spoken by the common folk of Lavas Holding that the black hounds are devil's get, and only a person born of the blood of their ancient masters or of the Count Lavastine may handle them without danger. Yet I noticed yesterday that you are left in charge of the kennels and that the hounds obey you as loyally as they do Count Lavastine."

He gulped down a lump in his throat. "Hounds obey those who treat them firmly and without fear, Your Grace. It is nothing more than that."

"Do you fear the Eika prisoner?"

"No, Your Grace. He is bound by chains."

Agius looked back sharply. Alain clamped his mouth shut. He had a sudden feeling that Frater Agius did not want him to speak about the Eika prisoner to the biscop. Agius had his own secrets and, evidently, his own plans. But the Lady smiled on him: Biscop Antonia did not ask any further questions about the prince.

"You are a well-spoken boy also. Quite unlike an untutored country lad."

"I know my letters, Your Grace. Frater Agius has been kind enough to teach me to read, and I knew something of numbers from my aunt, who manages a large household."

"She is a well-bred woman, I take it."

He could not help but smile. "Yes, Your Grace. My Aunt Bel is a very fine woman, and mother of five living children and as many grandchildren born so far." Perhaps more, since he had been gone; with the blanket last winter had come a verbal message that Stancy was pregnant again. Had the child been born yet? Did it live? Was it healthy? Had Stancy survived the birth? He was swept with such a sudden wave of homesickness that he almost faltered. He did not expect to miss them all so very much. Henri would be setting out again after Holy Week, as he did every year. Who would repair the boat this year? Who had tarred it last autumn? No one did as careful a job as Alain did. He hoped Julien was devoting as much time to helping Henri with the boat as he was to courting the young women in the village. And what of the baby? It must be well grown by now, if it had survived the winter. But surely it would have survived the winter; it was a healthy child, and Aunt Bel took good care of her own.

They walked for a time in silence. When they came to the clearing they halted to look out over the ruins, bare stone tumbled in a spring meadow strewn with yellow and white flowers. A broad stream ran along the other side of the clearing: He had not seen it on Midsummer's Eve, but now the running water flashed in the midday sunlight as it flowed swiftly past the grass, bordered by a low rim of white stone, and vanished into the farther edge of forest.

"The Emperor Taillefer is said to have possessed a pack of black hounds," said Biscop Antonia suddenly, her gaze on the ruins but her voice far away, as if she had been thinking about this during the long silence. "But so much is said about the Emperor Taillefer that one can scarcely know which is truth and which a story spun by the court poets for our entertainment." Then, like an owl striking abruptly, she turned her gaze on Frater Agius. "Is that not true, Brother?"

"As you say, Your Grace."

"Surely you have sterner views of truth than that, Frater Agius."

He looked, oddly enough, ashamed. "I follow the Holy Word as well as I can, Your Grace, but I am imperfect and thereby a sinner. It is only through God's unselfish love that I may be redeemed."

"Ah, yes," said the biscop. She smiled sweetly, but Alain suspected she and the frater had just conversed about something else entirely. "Shall we go down?"

They circled the clearing to find the original entrance, where a fallen gatehouse still stood sentry. Crossing into the ruin, Alain was struck by how different it looked now: No glamour gave the stone an unnatural gleam; shadows lay foreshortened on the ground, patches shading grass and overgrown paving. Once fine buildings had stood here. Now this was only a graveyard, the markers of a lost and forgotten time. He followed the biscop as she walked down the roadway, heading into the heart of the complex. She paused now and again to examine the carvings left on the stone: a double spiral, a falcon, its wings feathered with pockmarks, an elaborately dressed woman in a gown of feathers whose head was a hollow-eyed skull.

The clerics murmured, seeing these traces of the pagan builders. Lackling stubbed his toe on a half-buried block of stone and began to cry.

"There, there, child," said the biscop, comforting him, though he was as grimy as only a stableboy could be. Agius stood with his hands folded at his waist and his gaze fixed disapprovingly on the altar house.

"Come along," she said to Lackling. His sobs ended as soon as the pain faded, and he sidled away from her and dogged Alain's heels. They arrived at the altar house. The clerics hung back, but Biscop Antonia crossed the threshold without the least sign of uneasiness. Alain followed her inside. Lackling would not enter.

"You came to these ruins," said the biscop without turning round. She examined the white altar stone. "Or so I have heard the report, from Chatelaine Dhuoda, from Count Lavastine, and from the testimony of the half-free girl, Withi, who is to marry the young soldier. The girl told me she saw black hounds running in the sky but that you did not see them. She said when she first caught sight of you, you were looking toward this building and talking to the thin air, where no person or no thing stood. Did you see a vision?"

Alain had his back to the entrance, but he felt Agius enter, felt the frater's presence behind him. What could he say to her? He could not lie to a biscop! Yet if he confessed, might he not be branded as some kind of ungodly witch? Suddenly being the bastard son of the shade of a long-dead elvish prince did not seem quite so advantageous, not if he could be condemned for it; just as the bastard son of Count Lavastine might become the pawn in a struggle to gain power over the count's holdings if the count had no other direct heirs.

Alain touched his hand to his chest where, under the wooden Circle, his rose rested, warm and somehow bright under cloth. As he shifted, both Agius and Biscop Antonia turned to look at him expectantly, as if they could sense the hidden rose. Suddenly being the child of Merchant Henri and the nephew of Bella Adelheidsdottir, respectable householder of Osna village, seemed a much safer alternative to his other more grandiose dreams.

Yet neither was it right to lie.

"I have had visions, Your Grace," he said reluctantly, lowering his hand, then added, "but I am pledged to the church." Hoping that might explain it.

"It is true," said the biscop calmly, "that many who are sworn to serve Our Lady and Lord are also granted visions, if they serve faithfully, but there is yet a taint of darkness in the world that may bring on false visions and false beliefs." She looked again, pointedly, at Agius.

The frater was beginning to look angry.

"I believe this building is known as the altar house?" She bent to run an age-spotted hand over the marble surface of the altar stone. "This might be the Hearth of Our Lady, might it not? You see, I detect traces of old burning here, in the center." With one finger she flicked dirt out of the runnels carved into the stone. These runnels traced a spiral pattern similar to the pattern carved into the walls outside, but here four spirals led into a fist-sized hollow sunk into the center of the white stone. She smiled, still looking at the altar stone. "It is a terrible burden to carry an inner heart that does not live in harmony with the outer seeming, is it not, Frater Agius? If we each one of us know what we ought to do and act as is fitting, then by our outward seeming Our Lady and Lord will know that we follow the faith gladly and with an honest heart. To profess belief in a heretical doctrine and yet conceal it from all but those who think as you do seems to me to be hypocrisy of the worst sort."

"It is not a heretical doctrine!" cried Frater Agius. His face had gone bright red. "It is the skopos who denies the truth! It was the Council of Addai which denied the redemption and concealed the truth!"

Unshaken by this outburst, Biscop Antonia straightened. She surveyed the circular walls; next to the ground, half concealed by moss and weeds, carvings decorated the white stone, curled snails graven in stone surrounded by delicate rosettes. Counting out her steps, the biscop paced around the altar, measuring it. Then she walked past the frater, who stood as if rooted to the ground by his own passion, and went outside.

Alain hesitated.

Agius threw himself to his knees on the ground. "I will proclaim it," he said, muttering as if to himself or as if to the heavens. "I must speak the truth aloud so those who linger in the twilight of the false belief can come into the true light granted to us all by His sacrifice and redemption."

These were strange and troubling words. Alain sidestepped past the frater, but Agius, forehead resting on clasped hands, did not notice him. Outside, Biscop Antonia was helping Lackling stack loose stones into a pile. She looked up and smiled at Alain.

"He is devout but misguided. I will pray that Our Lady and Lord will bring him back into the Circle of Unity." She turned to her clerics. "There is good stone here. It could be used to improve the wall of Count Lavastine's stronghold, do you not think?"

"The local people refuse to walk up here or indeed to disturb these ruins," said one of the clerics.

"Yet these ruins were surely once greater in extent than they are now. Someone must already have taken stone from here, for these walls to be as low as they are now. There is not enough fallen stone to rebuild them to what I might guess to be their former height. What do you think, Brother Heribert? You have studied masonry and building for the church at Mainni."

"I must agree with you, Your Grace. Unless these were only half walls of stone and the rest built out of timber, but I doubt that. I have seen other ruins from the old Dariyan Empire, and they are without exception buildings of stone with perhaps a timber or thatched roof."

"Let us go, then, and I will ask you to speak of this to the count."

They bowed to her and began to walk back up through the ruins. Alain glanced back toward the altar house.

"Let Frater Agius pray, child. He has need of prayer. Come with me."

So he walked back to Lavas Holding with Biscop Antonia. Lackling trailed three steps behind, shying like a frightened pup at every flutter of the wind through the trees. The biscop sang hymns to the glory of Our Lady as they walked, and although Alain was far too much in awe of her to presume to join his voice to hers, her clerics did so gladly and with vigor.

For the next two days, Alain saw Agius in the same place, as if he did not or could not move: on his knees in the church, head bowed, clasped hands pressed against his forehead, praying in a low murmur that sounded rather like a stream's whisper heard from far off.

Alain served at table. Count Lavastine was polite to Lady Sabella, as of course he must be, but Sabella herself began to grow restive, even to look obviously annoyed . . . as if she was not getting something she wanted.

Twice daily a slaughtered sheep was thrown into the shrouded cage by the scarred and silent man who was its keeper. Once, while out running the hounds, Alain heard the sounds of a creature eating, much like a hound gnawing on bones. But no one dared peek inside, not even the youngest, brashest men-at-arms.

On the evening of the sixth day of the Ekstasis Alain fed the hounds as usual, fed the Eika prisoner, who suddenly lifted his head as if he meant to howl but instead growled low in his throat and shook his chained hands at Alain. The hounds barked and raced to the gate, snarling. Alain quickly ran over to control them, but they milled around him, barking so loudly it was only by chance he heard soft voices from the other side of the gate. He set a hand on the ladder and began to climb, then froze, listening, as the hounds circled and whined below him. Because the stockade was sturdily built of logs lashed together with rope, each log the thickness of a man's leg, they could not see him through it, and he had not gotten high enough that those speaking on the other side of the gate could hear him.

But *he* could hear.

"He has agreed, but reluctantly, and only because I let it be plain that I would not leave until I received the creature as a present in return for our moving on. Now you must win me the other promises I need."

"It is all arranged for tomorrow night, after the Feast of the Translatus, Your Highness. We will remove the prisoner and convey him to the ruins, and there perform the rite. Strong blood will attract the spirits and draw them under my control."

"What of the hounds?"

"You will request tomorrow at the feast that they be tied up before nightfall."

"I see. Ulric brings news to me that the *guivre* is restless. It needs nourishment. We cannot afford for it to break out of its cage as it did two months past when it grew overly hungry."

"We must be patient, Your Highness. If anything remains after the sacrifice, we will transfer it to the cage. But what the *guivre* most needs we cannot procure for it here, as you know. Too many questions would be asked."

"I leave this in your hands, then. Do not fail me."

"I will not, Your Highness. Our Lady and Lord look favorably upon your appeal."

"So you say. But the clerics of the royal schola who walk in attendance on my brother's progress would not agree, I think. They interpret the ruling of the Council of Narvone differently, do they not, my dear biscop?"

"It is true they and I disagree on the use and benefit of sorcery within the church. So do you and I act together, Your Highness, as befits those whose claims have not received a just hearing."

"We leave day after next?"

"Yes, all will be accomplished by then, Your Highness."

The hounds barked halfheartedly a few times as the speakers walked away. Alain felt their absence as much by a cessation of the crawling prickling feeling along his skin as by the lack of their voices speaking out loud. His fingers were wrapped so tightly around one rung of the ladder that they hurt. He uncurled them and shook them free. He barely had time to collect his thoughts before Master Rodlin arrived to call him to evening service.

At the church, Alain knelt with the others, but he fixed his gaze first on the biscop and then on Frater Agius. Had Biscop Antonia truly spoken such strange and awful words? *Strong blood will attract the spirits and draw them under my control.* He could not be sure he had heard them correctly, or understood. She spoke Wendish with an accent; Antonia was a foreign name. Perhaps he should ask Frater Agius, but the frater appeared, as usual, wrapped in an inner tumult of his own. Alain did not know what to do.

He fretted all night, waking at every grunt made by the sleeping hounds, at every gust of spring wind that rattled the door of his lean-to, at every distant shout drawn by the breeze from the kitchens, where the preparations had already begun for the Feast of the Translatus. Once he rose and crept outside to check on the Eika prince, who was, as always, awake.

"Halane," came the whisper, soft on the night air. "Go free."

But Alain fled back to the lean-to and shivered in his blanket the rest of the long, long night. Strong blood. Whose blood? But he knew very well whom they meant.

He could not concentrate at the morning service. At the great feast, begun at midday, he served as always, but his hands and body moved as if separate from his mind. He could not make sense of anything the people around him were saying. He could not follow the play, performed by southern players who marched in Lady Sabella's retinue, depicting the journey and trials of St. Eusebē and the visions she was granted of the great mystery of St. Thecla's witnessing of the Ekstasis and the final miracle of the Translatus: the brilliant light that is the glory of God that rests on the wings of angels, which transformed chapel and Hearth into a vision of the Chamber of Light.

So proclaimed the actor playing the part of St. Eusebē, in rapture. *"And on the wings of angels the mortal body of the blessed Daisan was lifted up to the Chamber of Light where His spirit had already taken up residence with Our Lady and Lord."*

The meal went on for hours. Agius stood by the door and did not eat.

When at last he was free, Alain ran back to the stockade. He had purposefully left the hounds loose, though Rodlin had asked him to chain them. The Eika prisoner still resided, silent, in his cage.

Did she mean to kill him? What was the Council of Narvone? Church business, obviously. Alain knew nothing of church business and ecclesiastic councils, nor anything at all about sorcery except that the deacons warned them all against false sorcerers and the taint of darkness that wandered the land in the guise of handsome men and women, seducers of the spirit and body, who promised much, took more, and gave nothing in return.

Count Lavastine had not promised to join Sabella's revolt; that was all anyone knew. He had remained polite but uncommitted. Just as he had, so many months ago, refused a summons from King Henry, so now he refused the entreaties, or demands, of Lady Sabella. He kept his own counsel and confided his inner thoughts to no one.

Alain sat among the hounds and let their hot breath, their heavy bodies and wet tongues, the friendly lash of their whipcord tails, surround him. Devil's or daimone's get they might be, but he trusted these hounds, for they trusted him.

They growled when Biscop Antonia came from the feast with her clerics to look in on the prisoner.

"We are leaving in the morning," she said sternly to Master Rodlin, "and Count Lavastine has given us leave to take the Eika prisoner into our entourage. All must be ready so we may leave early. Be sure the hounds are chained this night."

She went away again, quickly enough, but right away Master Rodlin berated Alain for not chaining up the hounds. "They'll be taking the Eika monster away in the morning," he said. "And good riddance." He left, looking irritated.

Alain was not sure whom he meant: good riddance to the Eika prince or to Lady Sabella and her entourage, who had pretty much eaten every scrap of food in the stronghold and were in addition commandeering five of the best horses from the stable? But even if

Master Rodlin meant their visitors, it was also true no one would care if the Eika prince was killed or hauled away in a cage. Or if he vanished mysteriously in the night, never to be seen again. Why should they care? He was a savage, was he not?

But did not Our Lady and Lord create all things on this Earth? Was not every living thing beloved in Their eyes? Certainly not all creatures, human or otherwise, lived within the light of the Circle of Unity, and so such ungodly creatures might behave without mercy or in ways that ran against the laws of the church, but was it not then a service to Our Lady and Lord to bring them to the knowledge of the Unities?

What if he was wrong? If he had misunderstood that overheard conversation between Lady Sabella and Biscop Antonia? But it would be worse *not* to be wrong and to fail to act.

He made his decision at dusk. After chaining all but the two most loyal hounds, he took off the wooden Circle of Unity given him by Aunt Bel and hurried over to the cage.

"Sit, Rage. Sit, Sorrow," he commanded. The two hounds sat, obedient to his command. He unlatched the cage. The Eika prince watched him but did not attempt to speak. He slid the Circle on its leather string over the prince's head. Then, with a deep breath caught in for courage, he loosened the chains that bound the creature hand and foot and let him go free.

The hounds remained strangely silent. Nor did they leap forward to attack the prince.

The creature flexed his arms and legs, stretching. Then he turned.

He was fast. Alain didn't see the lunge coming until it was too late. The prince grabbed hold of Alain's left arm. With a powerful, almost careless swipe of one hand, the Eika prince slashed the back of Alain's hand with the white claws that sprouted from his knuckles. Blood spurted out. Alain was too horrified to move, too appalled at his own stupidity: *Now I will die. But surely the Lady and Lord will forgive me, if the error rose from compassion.* The hounds did not stir, did not bolt forward to attack the prince, and that itself was a marvel.

The Eika prince raised Alain's bleeding hand to his mouth and lapped up the blood. Alain was so appalled he felt dizzy. He could only stare as the prince cut his own left hand with his claws and lifted the hand . . . for Alain to do the same, to return the gesture.

"Go free," said the prince. "*Paier sanguis.*" Pay blood.

Sorrow whined. Rage growled deep in her throat, her head turning to look toward the gate.

There was no time to waste. Gagging, Alain took one lick. The blood was staggeringly sweet, like honey. He reeled back. His vision clouded. He heard, distantly, the murmuring of a small group of people as they advanced across the outer court. He heard the soft scrape of metal knives rustling against cloth. He smelled the fetid odor of the latrines, as if the people he heard were downwind from the latrines, although with the wind this night that should have been much too far away from the stockade for him to be able to hear or smell such things.

"Mi nom es fil fifte litiere fifte." Then the prince was gone.

Alain dug his knuckles into his eyes, rubbing hard. The hounds nudged him, and when he opened his eyes, he saw a shadow on the ladder. It climbed, threw itself over the top, and vanished from his sight. He ran.

He got to the top of the ladder in time to see a thin wink of shadow fade into the forest. Gone free. Alain's hand throbbed. He touched the cut to his lips reflexively, tasting the sharp tang of blood.

The forest is alive at night with strange creatures. Bare feet sink into the loam of last autumn's fallen leaves. It is cool, and dark, and leaves skitter in the night breeze in patterns of shadow made plain against darker shadow.

Alain shook himself free. There! He saw a party of six people emerge from the palisade gate beside the latrines. Oddly enough, the taste of honey still lingering on his tongue, he knew at once the figure in the center was Biscop Antonia, although it was too dark to make out more than the suggestion of their presence.

They were coming here.

He scrambled down the ladder and unchained the hounds. He would face Master Rodlin's wrath in the morning and pretend to be asleep tonight. It was the coward's way; he knew that. He ought to confront her . . . but she was a biscop! A great woman of the court. He was nothing, no one, not compared to those of high rank.

He hid in the lean-to while they tapped on the gate. The hounds leaped and barked and growled. After a while, the biscop and her party went away.

"All is prepared," he heard the biscop say with his newly uncanny hearing as she and her clerics walked back toward the palisade. "It is necessary that we act. We must find another to consecrate at the altar. One who will not be missed." The words faded into a sudden vision of running at a steady lope through the night forest.

Mi nom, the Eika prince had said, using the Salian words. My name is Fifth Son of the Fifth Litter. Alain shook his head. He was still dizzy, from fear, from excitement, from guilt, from the taste of blood. He had heard wrong.

"One who will not be missed."

The hounds whined. Sorrow finally nosed loose the latch on the lean-to door and shoved inside, pressing himself up against Alain, licking his face and then, like a healer mending wounds, the fresh cut on his hand.

There was only one person in this stronghold besides the Eika prince who would not be mourned or missed should he vanish. Fear nosed his hand and licked his fingers.

He whistled the hounds to obedience and took Sorrow and Rage with him for protection. But by the time he got to the stables, Lackling was gone.

Stricken, terrified, he took the two hounds up the old path that led by dim and twisting ways into the hills, to the old ruins. He ran, as well as he could, but the path was narrow and the turns sudden and more than once his foot caught on a patch of loose rock or on a root and he slipped, going down hard. The hounds loped along beside him, stopping only to lick and nuzzle him when he fell.

When he came at last to the edge of the clearing and looked out over the old ruins, he thought for an instant that the waning gibbous moon had splintered into two moons and that its other half burned in the ruins, attended by brilliant Seirios, the star known to navigators as the Burning Arrow. But those were lanterns, not moon or star. They stood around the altar house like sentries. A hazy light rose from within, shining up out of the roofless walls.

Lackling screamed.

Rage and Sorrow threw back their heads and howled, as at the moon, a long, frantic yipping howl. He grabbed their collars and jerked them back before they could bolt down into the ruins; they stilled instantly. Ai, Lady, what should he do? What could he do? He heard a thin voice raised—not in song but in a sinuous chant that had no end, rising and falling, curling in on itself and then opening outward. Beneath it he heard mewling, the whimpering of a terrified creature.

He hissed out breath through clenched teeth. He shook, he was so terrified. But he must go forward. The hounds growled suddenly. A shadow appeared at the edge of the forest. Rage and Sorrow stood up, bristling, and tried to drag themselves out of his hands to attack the intruder.

"Halt," he said softly. The shadow moved forward and resolved into Frater Agius. "Sit." The hounds sat.

"Do not go down," said Agius. His face was pale and his eyes shadowed.

The mewling went on, a counterpoint to the eerie chanting. The light from within the altar house walls grew slowly brighter, and within its glow he caught sight of a huge shadow, thrown against the sky, which then vanished. The mewling turned into hiccuping yelps of terror. The hounds jerked forward, dragging Alain with them.

Agius grabbed at Alain's arm to stop him, and Rage spun and snapped at the frater.

"Stop! Sit!" hissed Alain.

Agius took advantage of Alain's hesitation to grab hold of his arm. The frater had a strong grip. "Do not go," he said in that same low, somber voice. He appeared oblivious to the hounds, growling near his feet. "She would only kill you as well, and then what would be the point?"

"Then I must go back to the castle and get help!"

"It is too far. You would be too late."

Held fast, with the awful chanting and those terrible whimpering cries that were all Lackling could manage of words, Alain felt his resolve slipping away. *There is nothing you can do.* How could he act against a biscop?

Below, light flared with an orange heat, as if new wood or some other unknowable element had been thrown on the fire. Lackling sobbed outright, and his piteous half-formed terror cut Alain to the heart.

"I must try to help him!" He pulled away but Agius caught him again. The hounds, dragging him toward the ruins, jumped back and Sorrow sank his teeth into Agius' robe, but still the frater did not let go of Alain or even cry out in pain.

"Let go!" Horrified, Alain cuffed Sorrow and, caught up in pulling Sorrow off the frater and in keeping Rage from bolting down into the ruins or attacking the frater as well, he noticed too late when the wind turned and the hounds stilled abruptly, unnaturally.

The smell of smoke and a whiff of something else, herbs, something unclean, wafted up from the stones. There came suddenly a horrible gurgling scream and with it a thin scent like flesh burning. Agius' hand tightened on Alain's arm. The hounds, ignoring Agius now, closed ranks in front of Alain, pressing him back as if they, too, meant to stop him from running forward.

"Witness," whispered Agius. "As St. Thecla witnessed the Passion of the blessed Daisan, so must you and I witness this suffering." It was obscene to listen to Agius speak so composedly while below, out of Alain's reach, Lackling was being tortured, murdered, sacrificed in place of the Eika prince. And for what?

Wind gusted. Rain spattered down, drumming across the ruins in a sudden slap of cold air; then all was still . . . utterly still, except for a haze of smoke rising from the altar house. Uncannily still, except for the thin reed voice that sounded as if it was buried under rock, and a tiny mewling, like a kitten's, so soft Alain could not understand how he could hear it. But of the normal scuffles and whispers of wind and night birds and the many small animals of forest and glade, there was no sign, as if all had vanished or been struck dumb.

Agius let go of Alain and he knelt, bowing his head. "It is a sign," he whispered, "that I should go out and preach the true word of His Passion, which was His suffering and sacrifice, and of His redemption."

A smell rose out of the ruins like the breath of the forge, hot and stinging. The hairs rose on Alain's arms, on the nape of his neck. Agius lifted his head. The hounds whined and slunk back, cowering, against Alain's legs.

Alain *felt* a presence—many presences—at his back. A shimmer ran through the air like the wind made visible. He heard the biscop speak strong words he did not recognize, only that they must be words of power. Below, in weirdly elegant harmony with her voice, sang the formless, hopeless whimpering that was no longer quite human. Alain wept, but he did not move. He had condemned Lackling and was now powerless to save him.

The stench of burning iron filled the air. Shapes less black than night's darkness filtered past him, shades slipping through the night. They touched him, shuddering out and away, his human body an obstacle to their passage. They wore not human shapes, nor the humanlike shapes of the dead Dariyan princes, the elves who were the elder sisters and brothers of humankind. They wore no shape at all, truly, but that of rushes blown in the breeze that sweeps the lakeshore, bending and swaying and straightening. They seemed otherwise oblivious to him, to the hounds, to the frater, who stared gaping and silent after them.

Down they went, their substance passing through the stones as if the stones were no substance to them. Up they crept from the stream. In they came from all sides.

"*Strong blood will attract the spirits and put them under my control.*"

They pressed in upon the altar house and, with a *whuff* like a candle snuffed out, the lanterns all went out. But the glow still shone from within, brighter, until it, too, was shadowed and veiled by the shades called by blood and magic. Until Alain could see nothing but darkness, swallowing the center of the ruins, and hear nothing but the biscop's voice.

A thin bubbling wail. Then silence. And at last, in the far distance, the faint sound of bells. The hounds collapsed to the ground and lay there, like helpless pups, whimpering.

Alain shook, weeping. The moon came out from behind clouds he had not seen cover the sky, to reveal the silent, empty ruins. The wind began, and at once clouds scudded in to cover the moon and the stars. Rain fell, at first a mist and then harder, until he was soaked and any trace of scent or sound was lost. He stood until he was drenched, seeking, listening, but he saw nothing and no one.

Lackling was dead.

4

AT last the squall passed.

From the altar house there was no sign of movement or life.

"I hope they're all dead!" said Alain with a vehemence that startled him. He had never known he could *hate*.

Agius rose stiffly to his feet. "Come, Brother," he said. "There is nothing we can do now except remember what we have seen, pray it never happens again, and testify where it may do some good."

"Shouldn't we go down, see if Lackling—?"

"If the biscop still stands within, guessing we have witnessed all, do you think she would hesitate to kill us? Martyrdom is an honorable profession, my friend, but not if it is lost and forgotten."

He began to walk up the path, into the forest.

"What were they?" Alain whispered.

Agius stopped and turned to face him. "I do not know."

"Did you know she meant to do this?"

"That she is a sorcerer? It is known within the church that Biscop Antonia and her adherents differ with the skopos on the place of sorcery within the church. That she might herself indulge in the use of sorcerous knowledge is surely to be expected."

"That she meant, tonight, to . . . to . . . ?" He could not form words to describe the horrible thing that had happened.

"The Holy Days are times of great power, Alain. What else is sorcery but the knowledge of the power that lies at rest in the earth and in the heavens, and the means and will to bind and shape it to your own use?"

Water dripped from the trees. All remained silent below.

"Come, Alain," said Agius urgently. "We must start back." Like a halfwit, Alain followed him, and the hounds went with him as though they were sleepwalking. "It is true," continued Agius in that same grotesquely cool voice, "that I did not know at first she meant to sacrifice the Eika prisoner. Your act of unexpected mercy—"

"Led only to a worse crime!" Alain's shout reverberated. Sorrow whined.

"Hush! You may repent your action now, certainly. But the Lady works in mysterious ways. So gave She her only Son to atone for our sins. See this rather as a sign of the infinite mercy of Our Mother, who art in Heaven, who leads this innocent to a more blessed life above, in the holy brightness of the martyrs which illuminates the Chamber of Light."

"A—a sign?" They started down the narrow path, Agius in the lead. As soon as they passed the first sharp bend in the path, the frater lit a lantern.

"From God, of the sacrifice of Her Son on this day which we in our error call the Feast of the Translatus, when it should be known as Redemptio: our salvation from sin through the sacrifice of Our Lord, Daisan. As St. Thecla witnessed the Passion of the blessed Daisan, so must you and I witness this suffering."

"But the blessed Daisan fasted and prayed for seven days! He didn't suffer!"

"So has the church taught falsely for years. So this truth was proclaimed as a heresy at the Great Council of Addai over three hundred years ago. But the truth can never be destroyed. For this is the truth: The blessed Daisan was flayed alive by the order of the Empress Thaissania, she of the mask, as was the custom of those times when a man was accused of being a criminal. And when his heart was cut out of him, his heart's blood bloomed on the Earth as a red rose. But though he suffered and died, he lived again and he ascended to the Chamber of Light, having by his suffering cleansed us of our sin. For it is only through the pity of the Son, the blessed Daisan, through His suffering and His redemption, that we the sinners on this Earth are allowed into heaven."

A heresy. This was truly a heresy, so troubling, so against everything Alain had ever been taught, that for an instant he forgot the altar house, the fate of poor Lackling. Agius was a heretic of the worst kind.

"But the blessed Daisan was a man like any other," protested Alain. "We all attain the Chamber of Light if we strive to cleanse ourselves of the taint of darkness—"

"*That* is the heresy," said Agius softly. "Here is a branch, Alain. Step over it carefully."

Drops of rain spattered down from the trees onto his hands; only then did Alain realize he was still weeping.

"In the beginning were the four pure elements, light, wind, fire, and water. Above them resided the Chamber of Light, and beneath them their enemy, darkness. By chance, the elements transgressed the limits set on them and the darkness availed itself of this to mingle with them." The delicate solemnity of the frater's voice drifted over Alain like a eulogy for the dead, numbing him as he picked his way down the path, following the lantern. The hounds walked behind him, still whimpering, as meek as lambs.

"From this chaos God, the Mother of Life, ordered the world with the Divine Logos, the Holy Word, but there remains in this mixture a quantity of darkness. That is why there is evil in the world. Only the blessed Daisan of all things on this Earth is untainted by darkness. Only through His redemption can we be saved."

Alain gulped down a sob. "I killed him," he gasped, the enormity of what he had seen hitting him with fresh impact.

"Nay, child, you are not at fault. It is truly a terrible thing we witnessed here this night. May our Lady forgive us." He signed the blessing over the boy. "Come now, let us hurry onward and get to our beds before the others discover us here."

The hounds whined, responding to his urgent tone. Rage took Alain's hand into one of her powerful jaws and tugged on him, away, down the path and farther into the forest. Still weeping, Alain went with them.

He dreamed:

A hand, clawed and scaly, dips into a fast-running stream. The water is so cold it stings, but he drinks.

Then, as an afterthought, he touches the wooden Circle that lies against his chest. It remains cold and silent. If there is a god inside, then that god cannot speak. Or at least, not in any language he understands.

He lifts his head, licks the air for a scent. Listens. There! A fox pauses to sniff, then sidles away. Above! An owl glides overhead but sweeps on into the night.

Yet in the night air he scents the coming of morning. He searches for a copse in which to hide himself, to wait again for night, when it is safe to run. North, always north, toward the sea.

VI
THE CITY OF
MEMORY

1

ALTHOUGH the last snow still lay in thin patches in the north lee of trees and along the shaded verge of fields in Heart's Rest, spring was well on its way when Holy Week arrived. Because Holy Week had to begin on Mansday—moon's day—and end on Hefensday—the day the blessed Daisan was transported on the wings of angels up into heaven—the full moon by which the dates of Holy Week were reckoned usually fell *before* the first day of Penitire. But this year the full moon fell on the first day of Penitire, as it had in the year of the Translatus, making *this* year an auspicious one. So were these events recorded in the Holy Verses and the gospels of Matthias, Mark, Johanna, and Lucia.

When Liath rode out to visit outlying hamlets with Hugh—he on the bay gelding, she on the piebald mare—she saw green budding on the trees and delicate green shoots pressing up from the earth. The farmers had begun their tillage, and the sun was warm. She would remain outside, like a groom, holding the horses while Hugh ministered to the country folk who lived too far from a church to attend regular services. These brief hours, alone and outside, were balm to her, although Hugh by this means kept her further isolated from most human contact.

Still, spring brought a kind of infection with it. Dorit, who had treated Liath with indifference bordering on coldness all winter, now attempted at odd moments to exchange pleasantries with her. Lars whistled.

But Hugh was restless. No peddlers had yet come north on the old road that led to the duchy of Saony, the central region of the realm of Wendar; only when the first peddler arrived would Hugh know the roads were clear across the Iels Hills and that the ford at Hammelleft was passable.

On the morning of St. Perpetua's Day, the twelfth day of the month of Yanu, which this year fell two days after the Feast of the Translatus, he rose and dressed early. Often, now, he rode out on his rounds alone so that he might make as much haste as possible. That way, when the road opened, they could ride south at once.

"Liath," he said curtly, "I'm going now. You will inventory our belongings in preparation for our journey to Firsebarg. I will expect to see the list when I return."

"Where are you going today?" she asked, not because she cared but because she could then judge how much blessed solitude she might have that day: a brief morning's respite or a long, quiet, soothing day without him.

But he knew her too well; he knew the small ways she tried to hold herself free of him, and he cut away at them bit by bit. "I am going to minister to my flock," he said with his beautiful smile. He ran a hand from her right shoulder to her left, his fingers tracing the slave's necklace—invisible, insubstantial, but as heavy as any iron collar—his ownership and her capitulation had forged around her neck. "I will return when I return."

So he left.

She decided not to write out the inventory. He might hit her for refusing or he might be amused by such a trivial, passive act of defiance; she never knew which it would be. Out of habit, however, she did go to the schoolroom and with stylus and tablet practiced the curving Jinna script left to right and right to left and back again. Then, more slowly, she copied the Arethousan letters and composed them into the simple words Hugh had taught her. But eventually her mind wandered, unhindered by Hugh's stifling presence. Her thoughts strayed back to the mysteries of the heavens and the passing of days, for this above all else Da had taught to her—the knowledge of the mathematici.

With the first day of the month of Yanu and the passing of Mariansmass, which together marked the spring equinox, they had moved into a new year. It was now the seven hundred and twenty-eighth year since the Proclamation of the Holy Word, the Divine Logos, by the blessed Daisan. She was seventeen years old.

"Da," she whispered, and wiped a tear from her cheek. Da was gone. And yet, was it not also true that everything that Da had taught her remained with her, so that in a way he remained with her, through her memory of him?

"By this ladder the mage ascends." She stiffened suddenly, horrified. What came next? She had forgotten! She did not exercise her memory as she ought, not with Hugh around, watching everything she did. "What do you think of when you sit so still?" he would ask. Better not to sit still. Better not to have him pry. She hated the way he seemed always to be trying to open her up, to get inside, to break the lock both of them knew held the inner door fast against him. She had the book. He did not. It was all that kept her free.

Soon, Hugh would return. But he was not here right now.

She sat back and closed her eyes. She found the city, standing fast in her memory. An avenue paved with white stones led away from the shore to the first gate, and she followed it. The first gate towered before her, admitting her to the first level: The Rose Gate. In her mind she saw each gate clearly, in their proper order: Rose, Sword, Cup, Ring, Throne, Scepter, Crown.

"Sorcery, like any other branch of knowledge, must be learned, used, and mastered. The young apprentice to the blacksmith does not begin by forging a fine sword for the prince. The young apprentice to the weaver does not with her first thread weave the queen's hearth rug. So the rhetor makes her first speech to her mirror, not to the marketplace, and the young man-at-arms fights his first battle against the tilt, not against his liege's mortal enemy. So did the blessed Daisan proclaim the Holy Word for twenty-one years before even He mastered the art of prayer well enough that He might by His own prayer and meditation ascend to the Chamber of Light. Learn these things, Liath. You cannot use them, for you are deaf to magic, but you may think on them, you may practice them as if you were a mage's apprentice, and in time you may have gained a sorcerer's knowledge. To master knowledge is to have power from it."

There, on the gate that rested only in her mind, stood a constellation of jewels like a cluster of stars, tracing the form of a rose. And
on each farther gate, a new constellation, sword, cup, ring, and so
on, as was appropriate. For these constellations also shone above in
the heavens, together with the twelve constellations that made up
the Houses of Night, the world dragon that bound the heavens,
and the many other constellations arrayed as emblems on the
sphere of the fixed stars, set there by the infinite wisdom of Our
Lady and Lord.

Eyes still closed, she drew, in her mind, the form of the rose, but
its shape and airy substance vanished like bird tracks in sand
washed by the tide; she could not keep hold of it. But she could use
the table as a kind of engraving surface. She set her hand lightly
on the polished wood grain and carefully, precisely, traced out the
dimensions of the Rose on the wood. Such a slight task to make her
sweat so; her face flushed with heat, and she felt warm all over.

Hand drawn to the end of the pattern, palm hanging half over
the lip of the table, she paused.

A sudden noise jolted her out of her concentration.

"Liath? Is there a fire in here?"

Liath jumped up so fast she banged her thighs on the table's edge.
Cursing under her breath, she spun around. "Hanna! You startled
me!"

Hanna wrinkled up her nose, sniffing, and cast about, rather like
a dog. "Your brazier must have overheated. It smells like burned
wood. You'd better—" But even as she spoke, the scent dissipated.
Hanna sighed, heartfelt. "At least you have color in your cheeks."
She walked forward and took Liath's hands in hers. "I hate to always see you so pale."

"Does Hugh know you came here?" Liath asked, darting to the
door and looking out. The passageway remained empty. She heard
Lars chopping wood outside.

"Of course not. I saw him riding out—"

"He'll know you're here. He'll come back."

"Liath! Take hold of yourself." Hanna grasped Liath's hands and
chafed them between her own. "How can he know if he's gone from
the village? He didn't see me leave the inn."

"It doesn't matter. He'll *know*." Liath was shaken by a sudden
swell of emotion. "You're all I have left, Hanna," she said in a

hoarse voice, and then, abruptly, hugged her fiercely. "It's all that's kept me safe, knowing I can trust you."

"Of course. Of course you can trust me." But Hanna hesitated and slowly pushed back out of Liath's arms. "Listen. I've spoken to Ivar. He needs servants to go with him, to keep him in proper state at the monastery. He's taking—*me*." Liath, stunned, heard the rest of Hanna's confession through a veil of numbness. "I'm sorry, Liath. But it was the only way I could get out of marrying young Johan. Mother and Father have agreed to it."

With nothing left to hold her up, Liath sank down onto the chair.

"Oh, Liath. I knew—I never meant—" Hanna dropped to her knees. "I don't want to leave you."

I don't want you to leave me. But Liath knew she could not speak so.

"No," she said instead, so softly the words barely took wing in the air. "You must go. You can't marry Johan. If you go with Ivar, then you can find a better marriage or a better position. Quedlinhame is a fine town. Both monastery and convent are ruled over by Mother Scholastica. She is the third child of the younger Arnulf and Queen Mathilda. She is a learned woman. That is why she has the name, Scholastica. She was baptized as Richardis." It was all there, in the city of memory, all the knowledge that Da had taught her neatly lined up in niches, along avenues, under portals and arches, but what good was it if she was utterly alone? She wanted to cry but dared not, for Hanna's sake. So she kept talking. "Queen Mathilda retired to Quedlinhame after King Arnulf the Younger died and their son Henry became king. All of Quedlinhame is under her grant, her special protection, so it is a very fine place, they say. I believe the king holds court at Quedlinhame every year at Holy Week, when he can, to honor his mother. There will be every opportunity for someone as clever as you to advance yourself in service. Perhaps you can even attach yourself to the king's progress, to his household. He has the two daughters, Sapientia and Theophanu, who are old enough now to have their own entourages, their own retainers."

Hanna laid her head on Liath's knees. The weight and warmth were comforting and yet soon to be gone from her forever. "I'm so sorry, Liath. I would never leave you, but Inga will be coming back from Freelas in the summer with her husband and child, so there isn't room for me. It must be marriage or service."

"I know. Of course I know." But hope leached out of Liath like water from a leaking pail. She shut her eyes, as if by being blind she could cause this all not to come to pass by not seeing it happen.

"Liath, you must promise me you won't lose hope. I won't desert you. I'll try every means to secure your release."

"Hugh will never release me."

"How can you be so sure?" Hanna lifted her head. "How can you be so sure?"

She sighed deeply, without opening her eyes. She left the city of memory behind, left the jeweled rose and Da's words. "Because he knows Da had secrets and he thinks I know them all. Because he knows I have the book. He'll never give me up. It doesn't matter, Hanna. Hugh is to be invested as abbot, as Father, at Firsebarg. We will leave as soon as it is possible to travel south." She opened her eyes and leaned down, whispering, although there was no one to hear them. "You must take the book. You must take it away from here. Because he'll get it from me if I have it. *Please*, Hanna. Then if I'm ever free of him, I'll find you."

"Liath—"

But she would never be free of him. He knew. Of course he knew.

She let go of Hanna's hands and stood. Hanna scrambled to her feet and turned just as Hugh opened the door.

"Get out," he said coldly. Hanna glanced once at Liath. "Out!"

He held the door until Hanna left. Then he shut it firmly behind her. "I do not like you having visitors." He crossed to Liath and took her chin in his left hand; his fingers cupped her jaw. He stared down at her. The deep azure dye of his tunic brought out the penetrating blue of his eyes. "You will no longer entertain *any* visitors, Liath."

She wrenched her face out of his grasp. "I'll see whom I wish!"

He slapped her. She slapped him back, hard.

He went white, except where her fingers had left their red imprint on his fine skin. He pinned her back onto the table, pressing her wrists painfully against the hard wood surface, and held her there. He was pale with anger, and his breath came ragged as he glared at her.

"You will not—" he began. His gaze shifted over her shoulder. He caught in a breath. He dragged her off the table and shoved her away. Whatever will had momentarily possessed her was already sapped. She stood numbly and watched as he brushed his palm over the tabletop. He inscribed his hand in a circle, narrowing, spiraling in, to trace the outline of a rose burned lightly into the burnished wood grain. His expression was rapt, avid. Finally he turned.

"What have you done?"

"I've done nothing."

He grabbed one of her hands and tugged her forward, placed her hand over the table where she *had* to see, although the outline was almost invisible. The lines felt like fire along her skin.

"The Rose of Healing," he said. "You have burned its shape into the table. How did you do this?"

She tried to pull her hand out of his, but his grip was too strong. "I don't know. I don't know. I didn't mean to."

He grabbed her by the shoulders, shook her. *"You don't know?"* If anything, he looked more furious than when she had slapped him. "You will tell me!"

"I don't know."

He struck her backhanded. His heavy rings scored her cheek. He struck her again. He was diving into a rare fury. "How many years have I studied to find the key to the Rose of Healing, and you *don't know?* Where is your father's book? What did he teach you?"

"No," she said, while blood trickled down her cheek.

He lifted her up bodily and carried her out of the room and into his own cell. There, he dropped her onto the bed. There she lay, staring up at him. He studied her, and all the while his left hand opened and shut to a rhythm known only to him.

Finally he knelt on the bed beside her. He wiped the thin film of blood off her skin. His touch was gentle.

"Liath." His voice was coaxing, persuasive. "What use is knowledge if it is not shared? Have we not learned well together this past winter? Can we not learn more?" He kissed her cheek, where the rings had cut it open, then her throat, then her mouth, lingering, insistent.

But the fire had woken in her, however damped down it might burn. Ever since she had drawn the rose, a thin edge of sensation burned inside her where before she had felt nothing. Fire melts ice. Each time he kissed her she shuddered away from him.

"No," she said softly, and braced herself for the blow.

"Liath," he sighed. He ran a hand along the curve of her body. His breathing came in unsteady bursts, more ragged even than it had been when he was angry. "I have never treated you ill, in my bed."

"No," she said, compelled to answer with the truth.

"You could have pleasure. But you must *trust* me. I have seen how quickly you learn. How much you *want* to learn. That you want to learn *more*." He laid his full weight on her. Even through their clothing, she felt the heat of his skin, burning off, enveloping her. "You know very well, my beauty, there is no one else you can ask. No one else you can turn to. I am the only one. There were rumors about your Da, dear old Master Bernard, but these villagers let it alone, let him alone, because they liked him. Because the biscop of Freelas has worse things to worry about than one stray sorcerer who sets hex spells to keep foxes out of henhouses."

Trapped in this tiny cell, the walls so thick, the air so still, she was already walled up, lost in a prison of Hugh's making.

"But you would not be so lucky, as young as you are, and the way you look." He stroked her hair in that way he had, running a hand up her neck and catching the hair on the back of his hand, in his fingers, stroking free. "This hair is too fine and too lovely, your skin stays dark through the winter, like the folk from the southern lands, and who in these Lady-forsaken parts has seen such folk, or even believes in them? And your eyes. As blue as the deep fire, or did you know that? I know. I have sought since I was a boy to unlock the secrets of sorcery. There are others like me, others who struggle to learn and to master. Somehow you were born with it in your blood. I know what you are, but I will never betray your secret to anyone else. Do you believe me?"

Even trapped under him, knowing he would say anything to convince her to give him the book, to tell him everything she knew, the horror of it was she *did* believe him. She had a sudden premonition he had spoken those words rashly and without thinking he might be swearing himself to them.

"I believe you," she said, but the words hurt. He knew what she was. A sorcerer makes herself, but two sorcerers must never marry. Her mother had said it once, placing a hand on Liath's brow. Because the child of two sorcerers might inherit a wild streak of magic more dangerous than the king's wrath. Except Liath had inherited a kind of deafness instead. Da taught her, but only so she could protect herself by having that knowledge. *"You cannot use them, for you are deaf to magic."*

Or so she had always thought. But now she had burned the Rose of Healing into the wooden grain of the table.

Hugh would put no barrier in the way of her studying Da's book, other books, as long as she shared everything she knew and learned with him.

"I will be faithful to you, Liath," he said, cupping her face in his hands, a lover's gesture, a lover's sweetness, "as long as you are faithful to me."

Ai, Lady, but it burned, this new fire. It hurt so horribly, running out like lines burned into her flesh, long since dormant. She could no longer cloak herself in lethargy. So it was, so she felt: A momentous decision was about to be made.

He shifted, rolling slightly off of her, and made a low, contented noise in his throat. "Liath," he said, softly, gently, coaxingly, and he tightened his embrace on her.

Hanna was leaving. She herself would leave, to be alone in Firsebarg with Hugh. To go on in this fashion, always resisting him, always frozen, listless, numb. Barely able to acknowledge any human contact but his; forbidden any human contact other than with him, as he strove to isolate her.

Wouldn't it be easier to give in? To give him what he wanted? Mistress Birta had herself said that Liath's position was enviable. She would not be treated badly. She would probably be treated well.

She had burned the Rose of Healing into the table. Lady's Blood, she might even learn enough to see if she truly *was* deaf to magic. Or if Da had truly not known, and she *was* born with a mage's power. Or if Da had known all along, and lied to her.

Why would Da lie to her? Only to protect her.

Hugh ran his hands up her arms. He brushed her throat, tracing an oval there, like a jewel, and she shivered. He sucked in his breath hard and reached to unbuckle his belt. "Stop fighting me, Liath. Why should you not have pleasure? Why?"

Her skin tingled where his lips touched. Why, indeed? It had come time, at last, to choose.

"I will not be your slave," she whispered. She would have wept, it was so hard to say, but she was too terrified to weep. She placed her hands against his chest and pushed him away, locking her elbows and holding them rigid.

He went quite still. "What did you say?"

Having said it once, she knew she must hold to it as strongly as ever she might. She twisted away from him and slipped off the bed to land bruisingly on her knees, huddled on the rug, her gaze on him the way a trapped rabbit stares at a fox. But she raised her voice above a whisper. "I will not be your slave."

He sat up straight. "You *are* my slave."

"Only by the gold you paid."

His mouth pulled to a straight line. "Then it is back out with the pigs." But he smiled as he said it, knowing full well that after a winter of luxury she could never face that again.

Liath thought this over: the dirty straw, Trotter's back, the cold spring nights. "Yes," she said slowly. "Yes. I'll go back out with the pigs." She climbed stiffly to her feet, walked stiffly to the door. None of her limbs worked right.

He was off the bed in an instant. He grabbed her by the shoulders and spun her around and hit her so hard that she staggered. Hit her again. She fell back and hit her head against the wall. She stopped her fall with a hand and shoved herself back up. With a hand shielding her face, she moved to pass him, to get to the door. He struck her. Again. This time, she fell right to her knees and had to huddle there, panting. Pain flamed through her. Her ears rang. He kicked her in the side, and she gasped in pain, gagging.

"Now," he said, his voice taut with fury, "the pigs, or my bed?"

Carefully she rose to her feet. Her balance did not quite work right, and her right eye could not focus. She took an unsteady step, caught a breath, took a second step, and rested her hand on the door latch. Lifted it.

The door opening, and the blow, occurred at the same time. She fell forward into the corridor, onto her hands and knees. Another blow, along the ribs—perhaps it was his boot. She struggled to get to her feet, but each time she rose and showed the slightest movement forward, he hit her again.

Blood hazed her right eye, but it didn't matter, because she couldn't really see out of that eye anyway. She got a hand on the wall and pulled up, and then was flung hard into the other wall. Her head slammed into stone, and she dropped hard. When she tried to stand again, she could not. She lay there, whimpering, trying not to whimper, trying not to make any sound, trying to get her legs to work. His boot nudged her side.

"Now, Liath. Which will it be?"

"The pigs," she said. The words were hard to say, because her mouth was filled with blood. Since she could not rise, she found purchase with her elbows and tried to crawl forward. This time, when he hit her—whether with hands or boot she could no longer tell—a swirl of blackness flooded her. She heard her own labored breathing. She could not see. Her vision grayed, then lightened. She saw the narrow passageway as a hazy pattern of stone and shadow, but that was enough. She heaved herself up on her elbows and drew her body along after her. Forward, toward the pigs.

She heard words, a horrified exclamation, but it was not attached to her.

She hurt everywhere, stinging bruises, sharp deep pain in her bones, a fiery stabbing at her ribs; blood trickled, salty, from her mouth, and yet her mouth was dry. She was so thirsty. She could picture the pigs perfectly in her mind. They lived outside the city of memory, in pleasant comfort: Trotter, who was her favorite, and the old sow Truffling, and the piglets Hib, Nib, Jib, Bib, Gib, Rib, and Tib, some of whom she could tell apart, but she could not now recall which ones had been slaughtered and salted and which ones kept over the winter.

He hit her again, from her blind side, and she collapsed onto the cold floor. Rough stone pressed into her face, but the tiny irritating grains helped her stay conscious; she counted the grains, each one pressing into her cheek, into the open wound, like salt. She just breathed for awhile. Breathing was hard. It hurt to inhale and exhale, but eventually she had to get out with those pigs. She would be safe with the pigs. The book would be safe with the pigs.

Pain like a hot knife stabbed through her abdomen. She screamed out of stark fear. He was going to kill her rather than let her go. Kill her! That hadn't been the choice.

She opened her left eye to see Hugh standing more than a body's length away from her, staring at her, his face as cold and stubborn as the stone. But he had not touched her.

The pain lanced again. Warm liquid trickled down the inside of her thighs. Pain stabbed again. She tried to gasp out words, but she couldn't make them form on her tongue. Ai, Lady! It hurt. She curled up into a ball, and fainted.

Came half conscious when Lars picked her up. Dorit was speaking. Liath caught a glimpse of Hugh and then lost him again. Her thighs were sticky with dampness. The cool afternoon air struck her to shivering as Lars carried her outside. Pain coursed through her abdomen again. She twisted, tossing her head back. Dorit was speaking to *her*, but Liath could not understand.

Lars' jolting walk sent flares of pain up her legs. She fainted.

This time, when she recognized she was awake, she tried not to panic. She was lying on a hard surface. She couldn't open her eyes. Something cold and clammy covered her eyes, like the hand of a dead, decaying corpse. . . .

She jerked, clawed at it, but her hands were captured and held tight in another's strong grip.

"Liath, it's Hanna. Stop that. Stop it. Trust me."

Hanna. She could trust Hanna. She clung to Hanna's hands. What had happened? She was naked from the waist down, legs propped up, lying flat on her back, awash in pain.

Another voice intruded. "Can you sit, Liath? You ought to, if you can."

"Here," said Hanna in that wonderful practical voice she had. "I'll put my arms under you and hold you. Just lean on me, Liath."

Rising up, even to a half sit, made her head throb. The pain in her abdomen came and went in waves. The clammy hand dropped away from her face, but it was only a cold rag. Through her good eye she saw Mistress Birta and, in the background, Dorit. Mistress Birta straightened up from her crouch at Liath's feet. Her hands were blood red.

Dizziness swept Liath. "I have to lie down," she gasped. Even as Hanna lowered her, she fell completely out of consciousness.

Came up again, still lying on the hard surface. Mistress Birta was speaking.

"We'll move her upstairs. I've done all I can."

"I've seen him hit her a few times, now and again," said a new voice which Liath vaguely identified as Dorit's, "but with that temper she has, and her his bonded slave, I've never blamed him. But this." There was a heavy silence, followed by the clucking of tongues. "It's a sin against Our Lady, it is. I couldn't let her lie there, bleeding, when I saw she was losing a child."

Hanna and Birta carried her upstairs. It took that long for Dorit's words to sink in.

Losing a child.

They laid her on Hanna's bed and padded her with moss to absorb the blood still flowing from her. Birta pulled a shift down over her hips, so she might rest modestly.

She choked out the words. "Is it true? Was I pregnant?"

"Well, surely, lass. Do you suppose you can bed with a man all winter and not become pregnant? Hadn't you noticed that your courses had stopped?"

Liath just lay there. She felt Hanna's warm hand come to rest on her hair. So comforting. Dear Hanna. "I'm so tired," she said.

"You sleep, child," said Mistress Birta. "Hanna will sit with you for a while."

"Why did I never think of that?" Liath whispered. "Hugh's child. I could not bear to have Hugh's child."

"Hush, Liath," said Hanna. "I think you ought to sleep now. Lady and Lord, but he beat you. You're all bruises. He must have gone mad."

"I won't be his slave," whispered Liath.

When she woke again, much later, she felt a pleasant lassitude. The little attic room was dim, but some light leaked through the shutters. The old blanket draped over her was scratchy but warm. She was exhausted, but she was at least alone; Hugh was not here.

That counted for something.

Then she heard the pound of footsteps on the back stairs accompanied by raised voices.

"I will not let you wake her, Frater!"

"Let me by, Mistress, and this time I will ignore your impertinence."

"Frater Hugh, it may not be my place to speak so to you, but I will, so help me God, send my husband with a message to the biscop at Freelas about this incident, if you do not listen to me now."

"I am sure, Mistress, that the biscop has greater concerns than my taking a concubine."

"I am sure she does," replied Mistress Birta with astonishing curtness, "but I do not think she will look so mildly on your taking a concubine and then beating the young lass so brutally that she miscarries the child conceived of this illegal union."

"It was no child. It had not yet quickened."

"Nevertheless it would have become one—if the Lady willed—had you not beaten her."

"I remind you that she is my slave, to do with as I please. You forget, or likely you do not know, Mistress, that the biscop of Free-las, though a noblewoman of good character, does not have power-ful kin. But I do. Now *stand aside*."

"But she is still a child of Our Lady and Lord, Frater Hugh. It is Her Will, and not yours, that chooses whether a child be lost before its time. For we women are the chosen vessel of Our Lady, and it is by Her Will that we have been granted the gift of giving birth, a gift accompanied by pain, for how else shall we know the truth of darkness in the world and the promise of the Chamber of Light? I have midwifed many a woman in these parts, and I have seen many a woman miscarry from illness or hunger or by the chance lifting of Her Hand, and I have watched women and their babes die in childbed. But I have never seen a woman beaten so badly that she lost her child, not until now. And I will testify so, before the biscop, if I must."

There was a silence. Liath measured with her eyes the distance from the bed to the shutters, but she knew she hadn't the strength to get there, to open them, to throw herself out in order to escape from him; and anyway, even now, she did not want to die. Light bled into the room and from the yard she heard the cock crow. It must be early morning. The silence made her skin crawl. She waited, shuddering, for the latch to lift.

Finally, Hugh spoke. His voice was stiff with controlled fury. Ai, Lady, she knew him so well, now, that she could see his expression in her mind's eye. "You will return her to me when she can walk. We are leaving for Firsebarg in ten days."

"I will return her to you when she has recovered."

He was furious. She heard it in his voice. "How dare you presume to dictate to me?"

"She may yet die, Frater. Though she is not my kinswoman, I have a certain fondness for her. And she is a woman, and like myself and all women, under the special care of the Lady. For is it not writ-ten in the Holy Verses: 'My Hearth, where burns the fire of wisdom, I grant to women to tend'? You may threaten me if you like. I do not doubt you could easily ruin me, for we all know your mother is a great noblewoman, but I will see Liath well before I let her travel such a difficult road."

"Very well," he said curtly. Then he laughed. "By Our Lord, but you've courage, Mistress. But I will see her before I go today."

Liath shut her eyes and hoped against hope that Mistress Birta would send him away.

"That is your right," said Birta finally, reluctantly. The door opened.

"Alone," said Hugh.

Liath kept her eyes shut.

"I will wait outside," said Birta. "Right out here."

Hugh shut the door behind him and latched it. She heard the sounds he made, the slip of his boots on the plank flooring, his intake of breath, the creak of a loose plank under his weight, the door closing, tugged shut, the snick of the latch, sealing them in together. She did not open her eyes. He said nothing. She was so alive to him that she knew exactly how close he stood to her, how a bare turn would brush his robes against her blanket, how near his hands hovered by her face.

But she knew very well he would not go away just because she kept her eyes shut. Da always said you must face what you feared or otherwise become its victim. Of course, Da had always said it with a derisive smile, since he had been running ever since her mother died.

She tightened her grip on the blanket, took in a deep breath, and looked up at Hugh. He studied her with a curious, intent expression. She stared back at him, suddenly so overwhelmingly tired that fear could take no grip on her.

"Why didn't you just kill me?" she whispered.

Hugh chuckled, smiling. "You are far too precious a treasure to cast away so carelessly." Then his expression changed, so fast, like a black storm rushing in from the sea. "But you must not cross me, Liath. Not ever, not like that, again."

She looked away from him to the coarse wooden slats of the wall. A few stray pieces of straw poked through from the loft beyond.

He settled down comfortably beside her. "You will need some kind of servant while we travel, and I am sure you would feel more comfortable settling in, in Firsebarg, if you had someone you knew with you. There was some talk of the Mistress' daughter marrying one of the freeholders, and also some talk that she was unwilling to. I think it might be well if the girl came with us. Then you would have company, and someone to do the work and perhaps, even, if she proves herself clever, to become chatelaine of our household.

That would be a fair opportunity for someone of her birth. If you would like that, then I will speak with Mistress Birta now."

Our household.

No matter what she did, not matter how strong her will to resist him, no matter how angry he became with her, how cold she remained to him, no matter how well she had locked away her heart or how well she had hidden Da's book and knowledge, Hugh's sheer stubborn persistence would eventually wear her away to nothing. He was utterly determined to possess her. And if she ran away, where would she run to? To death, most likely, or to a life far far worse in degradation and hunger and filth. If she even could run away. No matter how great a head start she gained, Hugh would catch up to her. He always knew where she was and what she was doing. As long as he owned her, as patient as he was, she was helpless against him.

"Count Harl has granted Ivar permission to take Hanna south with his party, to Quedlinhame," Liath said. Her voice was a little hoarse; she didn't know why. She hardly knew she was speaking at all.

"Hanna? Ah, is that the girl's name? Well, I will be abbot, Liath, and in a few more years I will be elevated to the rank of presbyter and gain the ear of the skopos herself. I can offer her better prospects than a common monk can. If you want her, I see no difficulty arranging the matter with her parents. Do you want her?"

Why not give in to the inevitable? If she had only managed Da's affairs better. If she had only insisted he live more frugally. If she had not begged him last spring to let them stay just one more summer in Heart's Rest.

What good did it do to fight this incessant struggle, when she could not possibly hope to win? She could not go on and on and on and on. And if Hanna was with her, surely everything else would not be so bad? She could study, and learn, and divine the secrets of the stars and perhaps far more besides. Perhaps she would discover the mystery of the rose burned into wood. That would be her consolation.

"Yes," she said. Her voice emerged thickly. "I would like Hanna to come with us."

"Where is the book, Liath?" His expression did not alter.

"The book."

"The book," he echoed. "The book, Liath. Tell me where the book is, and I will allow you to bring the girl with us."

She closed her eyes. He touched her, drawing his fingers delicately around her collarbone, tracing her slave's collar—no actual substance, not iron or wood or any element one could touch, but just as binding.

He had won. He knew it, and so did she.

She did not open her eyes. "Under slats, beneath the pigs' trough, in the inn stables."

He bent to kiss her lightly on the forehead. "I will arrange for the girl to accompany us. We leave in ten days."

She heard the latch lift and then Hugh's voice as he spoke to Mistress Birta, drawing her away down the stairs to the common room below. *Ten days.*

She covered her face with her hands and lay there, despairing.

2

THE days dragged by for Liath, one long day after the next. It took her far longer to recover her strength than even Mistress Birta had expected. At first she slept most of the time, an aching, fitful sleep made worse by the uncomfortable straw ticking of Hanna's bed. Even getting up to relieve herself in the bucket by the door exhausted her.

By the time ten days had passed, she could negotiate the stairs once a day. She was sitting slumped on a bench downstairs at midday, waiting for the Mistress to bring her a meal, when Hanna came in from the yard.

Hanna's face was red from the sun, but her eyes were red from tears, and she wiped her nose with the back of a hand, sniffing as if she had caught a cold. She sank down on the bench next to Liath, looking no less dispirited. "Ivar left this morning. I ran down when I heard, but he'd already gone. He didn't even leave a message for me."

Bitter shame wormed its way into Liath's heart. "Mine is the fault. I'm sorry. He needed you. I shouldn't have begged you to stay with me. He never wanted to be forced into the church. He wanted to ride in the Dragons. And he could have, if it wasn't for me."

"Ai, Mother of Life, spare us this!" exclaimed Hanna, letting out an exasperated sigh. "You're as bad as he is. Of course he'll be fine. Count Harl sent two servants with him, so he'll have familiar faces with him at Quedlinhame. And if it's true that King Henry stops there each spring, then he'll be able to see his sister Rosvita, too. She's a cleric in the king's schola. So between her position and the gift Count Harl is making to the monastery, I'm sure Ivar will be treated very well. Probably better than his own father treated him, for there's only the one child younger than him, and she's the apple of her father's eye. With the help of his sister Rosvita, Ivar might even come to King Henry's notice. Don't you think?"

Liath was able to emerge far enough out of her own misery to recognize that underneath Hanna's practical assessment of Ivar's

situation lay a real misery of her own. "Yes," she said, because it
seemed to be the reassurance that Hanna wanted, "I'm sure he will.
They'll educate him." She paused and took one of Hanna's hands in
her own. "Hanna." She glanced around the empty room, listened,
but they were alone. "I know you can tally well enough, but I'll
teach you to read and write. You'll need to know, if you wish to rise
to the position of chatelaine."

Like an echo, Hanna looked around the room also, then toward
the door that led out to the yard and the cookhouse. It sat ajar, and
through it they heard Mistress Birta ordering Karl to run eggs down
to old Johan's cottage to trade for herbs. "But I've no church training. If I know how to read and write, won't people call me a witch
or a sorcerer?"

"No more than they'll call me one." She let go of Hanna's hand
and wrung her own together, suddenly nervous. "Listen, Hanna.
You'd better know now, before we're in Firsebarg. Da—"

"Liath. Everyone knows your Da was a sorcerer. A fallen monastic, too, but one lapse, one child, isn't enough to get a man thrown
out of the monastery. There must have been something else as well,
disobedience, defiance, something more, like studying the forbidden
arts. Deacon Fortensia has told us as many stories as I have fingers
and toes about monks and nuns reading forbidden books in the
scriptorium and falling into love with the dark arts. But your Da
never did anything the least bit harmful, not like old Martha who
tried throwing hexes on people who offended her, after she got
proud about old Frater Robert sleeping with her. But she stopped
that, once it was made plain to her that no one here would tolerate
such things. But your Da was generous. What's the harm in magic
if it's a helpful thing? So says the deacon."

"But Da wasn't really a sorcerer. I mean, he had the knowledge,
but nothing he ever did—"

Hanna looked at her strangely. "Of course he was! That's why
we were all so glad he put roots here and stayed each year, when
we thought he meant to move on. You didn't know? People don't
visit a sorcerer whose spells are useless. What about old Johan's
cow that wouldn't calve until your Da wove a spell to open up its
birth canal? What about that first spring, when the snow wouldn't
melt, and he called up rain? I could tell you twenty other stories.
You really didn't know?"

Liath sat stunned. All she could remember was the butterflies, fluttering and bright and then fading into the warm summer air like the phantoms they were, like the phantom his magic was, which had all faded and vanished after her mother died. "But—but did it ever do any good? A storm can come by itself, you know. The weather can change, even without tempestari to call it up."

Hanna shrugged. "Who's to know if it was prayer or magic or just good fortune? What about that wolf, then, the one that eluded everyone else until your Da trapped it in a cage woven of reeds? That must have been magic, for any wolf could have escaped such a delicate trap."

Liath remembered the wolf. Da had been terrified, hearing reports that a wolf was lurking in the hills but not killing the sheep. He *had* trapped it, though he had let others kill it and had wept for days afterward. It had taken her three weeks of crying and pleading and arguing to get him to agree to stay in Heart's Rest after the wolf.

Hanna was still talking. "Maybe he wasn't a true sorcerer, like the devils who built the old Dariyan Empire, who built the wall south of here that stretches all the way from one sea to the other. It's all fallen over now that there are no more sorcerers of that lineage to keep it standing."

"I don't think Da was *that* kind of sorcerer," Liath said, more talking to herself than to Hanna. "Maybe he pretended to be, even tried to be, even once or twice succeeded. But it was my mother who *was* one. A real one. I remember that, if nothing else. She was murdered for it. I was only eight years old, but I do know that she had true sorcery, and that she worked . . ." Here she paused to glance around the room again, although nothing had changed. Her voice dropped to a whisper. ". . . old Dariyan magic."

Hanna considered this revelation in silence.

"The book—"

"It's gone," said Hanna. "Hugh came and took it. I couldn't stop—"

"Of course you couldn't stop him." Liath was too numb to cry. "It's a sorcerer's book. It has so much knowledge Da collected over the years—" In his own writing. Lady, how she hated herself. She had betrayed Da by losing the book. "You don't have to come. I should have told you sooner, about Da and the book, even before Ivar left. You might not want to stay with me, knowing the truth. You could have gone with Ivar—"

"As if I would have changed my mind! If Frater Hugh is truly going to be abbot, then he must know what he's doing, taking you as his concubine."

This, strangely, was easier ground "He says there are folk in the church who study magic. Da says Lady Sabella shelters heretics as well as sorcerers, to aid her against King Henry."

"Well," said Hanna, thinking it over, "better to be burned than married to young Johan. Lady Above! *You* need someone to shelter you from Frater Hugh. You're still pale, but at least your appetite is good. Mother always says that so long as you're hungry, then you're not sick enough to die."

Liath managed a chuckle.

Behind her, the door that led out front opened. Hanna stood up, lifting her chin defiantly. Liath stiffened. Why did he come every time she was beginning to feel free of him, of that interminable weight he laid on her? Was this his magic, to find and to know, to hunt and to devour? She wanted to crawl under the table, but she forced herself to sit without moving. She felt him, the heat of him, the simple physical presence, as he came up behind her. His hand touched her arm. She flinched.

He grabbed her arm and hoisted her up and she stood, not fighting him. Tucked under his free arm, as if—like Da—he dared never leave it unattended, he carried *The Book of Secrets*.

"You look well enough," he said brusquely. "We're leaving." He glanced disinterestedly at Hanna. "Girl, fetch whatever you mean to take with you and tell the Mistress that my plans have altered. We are leaving now. My wagon is packed and waiting at the church. Go."

Hanna gaped at him, then bolted for the door that led out back.

"We're going," he repeated.

There was a puzzling urgency about him she could not understand. Certainly there was no point in resisting. She had already lost everything. He led her to the door and thence outside. Hanna came running from around the inn.

"I'll just collect my clothes and such," she called, out of breath. "I'll be there. Don't leave without me!"

Hugh gestured impatiently and kept walking. Liath was already too out of breath even to beg him not to leave Hanna behind.

She struggled to keep up, but they had not gotten a quarter of the way to the church before she slumped, dragging on him. "I have to rest."

"You're gray," he said, not with sympathy but as an observation. "I'll carry you."

"I just need time to rest." Lady's Blood! She didn't want to be seen carried by him, like a shameless whore!

"We've no time." He thrust the book into her hands and caught her around the back and under the legs and swung her up. Even with her weight, in his arms, his pace did not slacken. Some other need drove him. She clutched the book against her chest, head swimming, so faint she feared she would drop it.

At the church the wagon did indeed sit outside, heavily laden, covered with a felted wool rug. Three men Liath vaguely recognized as Count Harl's men-at-arms loitered by the church door, armed and outfitted for a long journey. Dorit stood, wringing her hands, by the cart horses, which Lars held by their harness.

Hugh dumped Liath unceremoniously into the back of the wagon, onto the featherbed. A fourth soldier appeared from the stables, leading the piebald mare and the bay gelding. Only the gelding was saddled. Hugh took the gelding's reins and mounted.

"Where is that girl?" he demanded. "We can't wait. If we don't see her by the inn, Dorit, and she comes here, tell her to follow us down the south road. If she hurries, she'll catch us before nightfall."

"But you can't leave her," Liath cried, roused out of her stupor. "You promised me!"

"*We can't wait.*"

"There she is!" called Dorit. Hanna came running along the road, a leather sack thrown over her back.

Hugh urged his gelding forward. A soldier leaped up into the wagon, and Lars jumped back as the cart horses started forward. The wagon jolted under Liath and began to roll. The three other soldiers, one still leading the mare, fell in behind. They eyed Liath and her single possession—the old leather book—surreptitiously but otherwise kept silent. Their path met Hanna's, and she swung in beside the wagon.

"You'll walk," said Hugh from the front. Then added, as if an afterthought, "but you may rest the sack in with the rest."

Hanna tossed her sack into the back beside Liath and trudged alongside.

"What happened?" Hanna asked in an undertone. "He looks in a passion."

"I don't know. But he gave me the book, Hanna."

Hanna said nothing, and by that Liath realized the bitter truth. Hugh let her hold the book because he knew he could take it back any time he wanted. Behind them, the church receded. Dorit and Lars stood by the great front doors, watching the party head away back into the village, to the road that led south. They traveled in silence until, reaching sight of the village and the inn, Hugh cursed suddenly.

Liath raised herself up and looked around.

Four riders—an unusual sight on any day—waited in front of the inn. She recognized Marshal Liudolf. The other three wore the scarlet-trimmed cloaks and brass badges embossed with an eagle that marked riders in service to the king: the King's Eagles. Two were young, one man and one woman. The eldest was a grizzled, weather-beaten man who looked strangely familiar, but she could not place him.

"That's the traveler who rode through last autumn," said Hanna in a whisper. "He asked about you, Liath."

"Keep moving." Hugh's order was sharp.

"Frater Hugh!" Marshal Liudolf raised a hand. "If you will, a word."

Liath could see by the set of Hugh's back that he wanted to ignore this summons. That he wanted to keep riding. But he reined the bay aside. The soldier driving the wagon pulled the horses up. Mistress Birta emerged from the inn and stopped next to the door, watchful, silent.

"As you see, Marshal," said Hugh, "we are just setting out. It is a long journey south, ten or twenty days, depending on the rains, and we have little enough daylight for traveling this early in the year."

"I won't delay you long, Frater. These riders of the King's Eagles approached me yesterday, looking for healthy young persons who might be suitable for service as messengers for the King." Then, oddly, Marshal Liudolf stopped and looked questioningly, almost obediently, at the elder rider.

"I am Wolfhere," said the older man. He had deep-set eyes under silver brows; his hair was almost all silver, with a trace of ancient brown. "You must understand that with the increase in Eika raids, and rumors of trouble in Varre with Lady Sabella, we are in need of young persons suitable to ride messages for the Eagles."

Hugh held the gelding on an uncomfortably tight rein. "I am sure you are. I believe Count Harl has two younger children he might be persuaded to part with."

"We are not looking for children of the nobility," said Wolfhere smoothly, "as you know, Frater Hugh, since you were educated in the king's schola. Indeed, I have always heard it said you were one of their finest students."

"I learned all they had to teach me. You, of course, would not have had the opportunity for such an education. I don't recall your parents' names, or their kin."

Wolfhere merely smiled. "None of the Eagles come from the king's schola. But neither are we looking for landbred children who are unsuitable for this responsibility. I understand that you have recently acquired a young woman who might be of interest to us." He said this without glancing at Liath, although surely he knew she was the young woman he was talking about.

"I paid her father's debt. I am not interested in selling her." Hugh's tone was cold and flat.

"But my dear frater," said Wolfhere, smiling suddenly much like his namesake might bare its teeth in a wolfish grin, "I bear the King's seal. Marshal Liudolf tells me you paid two nomias for her. I have the gold. I want her. You may protest this action, of course, but you must do that in front of King Henry. Until such time as King Henry renders a judgment, it is my right to demand her presence in the king's service."

It was so quiet Liath could hear the soft wind rustling in the trees and the stamp of the old plough horse in the inn stables. Sunlight painted the road the yellow of light clay. The marshal's horse flattened an ear. From out back came the sound of Karl, singing off-key as he worked.

Hugh sat, stiff with fury, on his bay. The old man still did not look at her, but the younger Eagles did. They looked very tall, seated upon their horses, the woman in particular. She had a bold face, and a bolder nose—a hawk's nose, they called it here—and a bright and open gaze. She studied Liath with an interest piqued with skepticism. Her companion looked coolly curious. Their cloaks draped across their horses's backs, revealing a fur lining within. They shifted, glancing at the old man, and their eagle badges winked in the sunlight.

Finally Hugh spoke. "I believe the young person's consent is required."

Unruffled, Wolfhere inclined his head. "That is true."

Hugh dismounted and tossed the reins to a waiting man-at-arms. He walked back to the wagon. Liath wanted to shrink away into nothing, but there was nowhere to run. Hanna hesitated, then moved away to make room for him. He leaned in and pried one of Liath's hands free of the book, clasped it in his, his grasp painfully tight.

"Look at me." Obediently, she looked at him. He lifted her chin with his other hand so she had to look directly into his eyes. Why had she not remembered that his eyes were so complex a blue, not made up of any one shade but a multitude blended together?

"What do you say, Liath?" he asked, so softly but with all his will of iron pressing onto her, all the force of him, all the cold cold winter months. That was what his eyes were like: the pale blue of ice, splintered with cold sunlight, dazzling, but as bleak as the winter winds cutting across fields of ice and snow.

She tried to pull her gaze away, but she could not. He would never give her up. Never. Why even try? She found the city, standing fast in her memory. There, in the treasure-house, she had locked away her heart and her soul.

No. Fire fluttered, banners rising from the seven walls ringing the city. No. But she had no voice. He had taken her voice.

There, like a beacon, she heard the jingle of horse's harness as one of the Eagles' horses shifted, waiting. Waiting for her.

"No," she said, almost a croak, getting the word out.

"You see," said Hugh, not letting go of her, not breaking his hard gaze from her, "that she does not consent to go with you."

There was silence.

Terror seized Liath. They would turn and ride away, leaving her here, forever in Hugh's grip.

"No," she said, louder. And again, "No!" She tried to pull her head out of his grip, but she could not shake it. "No. I don't want to stay with you. Let me go!" But her voice was so weak.

"What did she say?" demanded Wolfhere. A horse moved, hooves clopping, but Liath could not tell whether it moved toward her or away. Please, Lord, not away!

"She says she doesn't want to stay with you, that she wants you to let her go," said Hugh steadily but not without triumph.

"No, she didn't," said Hanna suddenly, her voice carrying clearly across the yard. "She doesn't want to stay with him. He's twisting her words."

"Frater," said Wolfhere in a deceptively gentle voice, "I suggest you let the girl stand alone and speak."

Hugh did not let go of Liath immediately. But slowly his grip slackened and then, his face white with anger, he let her go and took one step back from the wagon.

With no warning, Hanna snatched the book from Liath's grasp.

"Get away!" snapped Hugh, grabbing for her.

Hanna leaped back and bolted to stand in safety between the two younger Eagles "She's been ill," she cried, appealing to Wolfhere. "She's not well enough to travel. I'll have to help her out of the wagon." Yet she hesitated, not knowing what to do with the book.

But hope burned like fire in Liath now, a banked fire come to life, scouring despair out of her. She struggled to her knees, inched over to the side of the wagon. Caught herself on the side, swung over, and staggered, almost falling. But with sheer dogged stubbornness she held herself up. She did not look at Hugh. That was too dangerous by far. She caught her breath, first. Tried to calm the fire. She was burning hot but, slowly, that subsided. At last she looked at Hanna, for strength.

Hanna gazed back at her, clear-eyed, guileless, and smiled, nodding encouragement. In her arms, clasped like a precious child, she held the book. Liath took in a breath and lifted her gaze to meet Wolfhere's squarely. The old man had moved his mount forward and she saw that his eyes were a peculiar, penetrating shade of gray.

"I want to go with you." Her voice gained in strength with each word. "I want to be an Eagle." She ducked her head down, waiting for Hugh to hit her.

But the hawk-faced woman had already dismounted and crossed to stand between Liath and Hugh. She was, indeed, almost as tall as Hugh, and she wore a sword at her hip and a knife at her belt.

"So be it," said Wolfhere. He took two coins from his pouch. They were as yellow as the sun and at this moment twice as welcome. He handed them to the marshal. "Let you witness this transaction, Marshal Liudolf, and pay this gold to Frater Hugh, in recompense for the young person here."

"I witness this transaction," said Liudolf, "and I take these nomias and transfer them into the keeping of Frater Hugh, in recompense for this young person, Liath, daughter of Bernard."

"I won't take it," said Hugh. "I protest this theft. I deny any payment has ever taken place. I tell you now, Wolfhere, that I will bring this matter before King Henry."

"You are welcome to do so," replied Wolfhere. "Nevertheless, the girl comes with me. These are not your men, I believe, to fight this sort of battle, and if any of us are harmed, you yourself would be brought before King Henry to answer for the crime. Whatever benefices you have received, such as the abbacy, would certainly be revoked."

"This is not ended!" said Hugh. And then, in a lower voice, "You are not free of me, Liath."

Liath dared not look at him. She kept her gaze fixed on the fine burnished Eagle's badge that clasped the woman's cloak at her right shoulder: an Eagle, rising on the wind, with an arrow clasped in its beak and a scroll held in one talon.

If she did not look at Hugh then, free of him or not, she was at least for the moment safe from him. If she could ever be safe from him.

"Marshal," said Wolfhere, "I request that you receive this gold and hold it as witness, and witness as well Frater Hugh's refusal of it."

"I so witness," said Marshal Liudolf.

"I so witness," said the younger Eagles.

For a long drawn-out while no one moved, as if the stalemate, having been reached, could not be resolved. Only the song of birds in the trees, and the distant shout of a farmer at plowing, pressing his ox forward, disturbed their silence. The smell of cooking beans wafted out from the cookhouse. The wood of the wagon felt chary under Liath's hand.

"This is not ended," said Hugh finally. He moved and she flinched, but he was walking away, walking to his bay, mounting, giving the signal.

She let go of the wagon just in time to avoid getting a splinter as it jerked forward and, just in time, grabbed Hanna's sack out of the back. Hugh did not even seem to notice. Without another word, without any acknowledgment of what he was leaving behind, he rode south, the wagon and his tiny retinue following.

Liath dropped the bag and slumped to the ground.

"Do you need aid?" asked the hawk-nosed woman curiously.

Da's four books were gone with Hugh, but their texts remained in the city of memory, together with everything else Da had taught her. And Hanna had the other one. "No," she whispered. "No. I just need to rest a moment." She looked up to meet the woman's steady, measuring stare, then broke away from it to look up at Wolfhere. He studied her calmly.

Why? But she could not say it out loud.

"Before you leave, Marshal Liudolf," said Wolfhere into the silence, "I will write a manumission for her. We do not admit the unfree into the Eagles. I need another witness besides yourself."

"I will witness, sir," said Mistress Birta suddenly, stepping forward. "I am a freewoman, born of a freewoman."

"Ah," said Wolfhere. "You are Mistress Birta, if I recollect rightly."

She flushed with surprise and pleasure. "I am, sir."

"And this, I believe," he added, transferring his keen gaze to Hanna, "is your daughter, Hanna."

"Yes, sir, she is."

"Is it your wish that she might be invested into the king's service as well?"

Mistress Birta flushed so deeply, and looked so entirely discomposed, that Liath forgot her own fears and hopes for an instant to wonder about Mistress Birta's secret dreams. "Sir, you must know that for my daughter to become an Eagle would be the greatest honor for my house."

Wolfhere did not smile. Rather, he nodded gravely, acknowledging the truth of her words. "Let us not keep Marshal Liudolf any longer than need be. We will write and seal the manumission now. Then I have business in Freelas. Since I can see that the girl looks exhausted and is too unwell to travel, I propose that I ride north alone, leaving the girl here for a tenday. If that will suit you, Mistress Birta. Manfred and Hathui will stay as well, in case the frater chooses to attempt something rash. Is that well?"

Birta nodded her head. It was the first time Liath had seen her at a loss for words.

Wolfhere dismounted. Manfred swung down and took the reins of the old man's horse, and the reins of Hathui's horse as well, and led the animals away to the stables.

"Hanna," said Mistress Birta, recovering quickly, as any good innkeeper must, "help him with the horses." Hanna nodded and hurried after the young man.

Liath tried to stand but could not. In an instant, Hathui had an arm around her. "I'll help her inside," said the young Eagle.

"Upstairs," said Mistress Birta. "In bed, with a bit of dinner in her. She needs to rest."

"Yes, Mistress," said Wolfhere genially, "I see I can trust you to take best care of her. Marshal Liudolf, shall we finish our business?"

Liudolf's reply was lost to Liath as she entered the warm confines of the inn common room. She barely made it up the stairs, even with Hathui's support, and when she collapsed onto the bed, she simply laid her head down, shut her eyes, and let herself be overcome with the exhaustion of hope fulfilled.

She was free of Hugh. She still had the book. She was an Eagle. All that she needed now was to get her strength back. She could scarcely believe it was true. She slept.

3

LATER Mistress Birta brought her a bowl of bean soup and good dark bread. Hunger brought her fully awake and she wolfed down her food. She hadn't realized she was famished. Mistress Birta retreated as Wolfhere entered the little attic room. He sat on the edge of the pallet and held out a simple brass ring engraved with the seal of the King's Eagles. He smelled of rain and of damp wool. She took the ring gingerly, and while she held it, not sure what to do, she heard the patter of rain on the roof. Cloudy light slanted through the closed shutters. She had slept most of the day.

"This ring represents the seal of our bargain," said Wolfhere mildly, "that you will offer your name and lineage to the Eagles as payment for your service with them."

She was afraid to look at him. "My name is Liath," she said, but her voice sounded false to her own ears. "My father's name was Bernard."

Wolfhere sighed heavily, whether disappointed or sad she could not tell. "Liath, you must either trust me or else it is of no use that I have freed you and brought you into the Eagles. I knew your mother. I have been looking for you and your father for eight years now."

Like a rabbit frozen in the sight of a wolf, she stared at the ring. Outside, the rain slacked off, fading to intermittent drips.

"Had I found you sooner," he added sternly, "then perhaps your father would not now be dead." He lifted a hand, and she flinched away from him. "Ai, Lady!" he swore under his breath. "Now listen you to me, young woman. Listen and heed me well. I will not compel you to enter the king's service as an Eagle. You are free, whatever you choose next, and you may go your own way if you so choose."

"Where else can I go?" she asked bitterly, "but back to Hugh? And I'll never go back to him."

"I will not compel you," he repeated. "But neither will I take you into the Eagles unless you trust me with your full name and lineage. Which will it be?'' He took the ring out of her hand and weighed it, such a light thing as it was, in his palm.''To ride with the Eagles, you must give your trust wholly to your comrades. Otherwise it is worth nothing. If you do not trust me in this small a thing, then you are too dangerous, too weak a link, for us to trust you in our turn.''

"Names are not small things."

"That is true." He bent his head, acknowledging her point. "That is why we ask for them."

"Why did you free me?"

"Because I knew Anne." She started. It was so strange, almost frightening, to hear that name from any voice except her father's. Wolfhere smiled wryly. "I knew you as well, when you were still a babe."

"I don't remember you!"

"Nevertheless," he replied, as calm as ever, "Anne asked me to watch over you, should anything ever happen to her."

She wanted to trust him, but after Hugh she dared not trust anyone. As he studied her, looking more patient than amused, she studied him in return. Advanced in age he certainly was, but vigorous still and with the natural authority that comes to any man who has lived long years and survived hardship. An old scar traced a line down his neck, missing the throat vein by a finger's-breadth. He sat with the steady imperturbability of a man equally used to the councils of kings and the gossip of farmers in a local inn. It would be so easy to just give in to his request, but that was not what he asked of her. What he asked was infinitely harder.

Maybe, just maybe, it was safe to open the first, the lowest, gate in the city of memory. Maybe she could learn to trust him, to trust the other Eagles, as comrades. Her hands shook as she took the ring out of his open palm. "Liathano is my true name," she said, her voice scarcely more than a murmur. "I am the daughter of Anne and Bernard. I know nothing more of my lineage."

So was it done. She was shaking so hard she could barely slip the ring onto her finger, the seal of their bargain. He stood up at once, and though he was not a particularly tall man, he was, without question, imposing. "Welcome, Liath," he said somberly, "into the Eagles. You will find your service hard, but I do not think you will ever regret choosing it. When I return from Freelas, we ride south."

So he left her. "We ride south." This morning, those words had filled her with despair. Now those same words held all the world of possibility in them.

She lay down, but although she was still exhausted, she could not sleep. The straw ticking stuck her in new places every time she shifted on the pallet. The rain had started to pound again, a new shower, and the damp air brought the scent of mold creeping out from the wood. She sneezed.

A scratch came at the door and Hanna peeked in. She, too, wore a ring, symbol of her new status. "I thought you would want to know," she whispered, sitting on the bed next to Liath, "that it's back in the hiding place. You're free, Liath."

Free.

Liath was too tired to reply, so she simply laid her head against Hanna's arm.

Where was Hugh now? Getting farther away with each step, please the Lady. And yet was Wolfhere any better or just another one who wanted to imprison her in a cage of his own making? How had he known her mother? Had he known Anne was a sorcerer? Why had he sought and how had he found Liath over such a long trail, pursued for so many years? Why had Da never spoken of such a man, and why did she herself not remember him, from those old dim memories of the fine cottage and the bright garden?

Yet what was it Da always said? *"No use regretting that you're going to get wet, Liath, once you've closed the door behind you on a rainy day."*

The rain, and Hanna's warmth, lulled her to sleep.

VII
LEAVETAKING

1

ALAIN never found Lackling's body, although for days after, when he got a chance and deemed it safe, he went up and searched through the ruins for any sign of newly turned earth.

But he did not truly expect to find anything. The morning after that horrible night, by design he strayed past Lady Sabella's livestock train out beyond the palisade and took up a station where he might observe the shrouded cage and its mysterious occupant. With his oddly keen hearing, which he still had not grown used to, he overheard the keepers of the shrouded cage speaking among themselves.

"Not much meat left on the carcass but, aye, that will satisfy the beast for now, thank the Lady."

He only stopped looking after Lady Sabella's entourage packed up and left, a grand procession winding its way southwest on the road that led toward the lands controlled by the duke of Varingia. That night, Lavastine called all his people together into the great hall and stood before them. Chatelaine Dhuoda and the clerics waited behind him, but to Alain's eyes they looked as mystified as the rest.

Lavastine looked pale and listless. He stood without moving for a long time, staring into the air as if he saw something there none of the others could see. It was so unlike him, a man made decisive by long habit and a tendency to impatience, that Alain felt a sick sour feeling growing in his stomach—a feeling of dread. The hounds whined, crouching at their master's feet. Rage and Sorrow, as was their wont, sat panting and watching at Alain's heels; they remained, since the night of the sacrifice, remarkably subdued.

This, too, was marked. Most everyone in Lavas Holding now treated Alain with a skittish deference tinged with disgust, like a man who is afraid to spit on a leprous beggar lest he turn out to be a saint in disguise.

"We will leave," said Lavastine suddenly. "We will arm ourselves with weapons and supplies and leave on St. Isidora's Day. We will celebrate the Feast of St. Sormas at the hall of Lady Aldegund, wife to my cousin Lord Geoffrey. There they will be given a choice: join Sabella's rebellion, or lose their lands."

Everyone spoke at once, a rushing murmur.

"But that's barely twenty days!" exclaimed Cook indignantly. "To outfit all that, *and* do the spring sowing? There won't be time to do *either* right."

Others agreed, but Lavastine only stood and stared and eventually all the folk quieted, waiting for him to go on.

"After that," continued Lavastine in that same monotone voice, as if he had heard no objections, "we will ride on and join up with Lady Sabella and her army. We ride against Henry, unlawful king of Wendar and Varre." He lifted a hand imperiously. "So do I speak. Let none question me."

At first Alain could only sit stunned. Cook was right, of course; she usually was. It was a mistake to march out before the spring sowing had been completed. But after a time, like a puppy worrying at his boot, a kind of terrible helpless anger began to gnaw at him. He slipped a hand inside the slit neck of his outer tunic and felt down the leather string until he touched the rose. Its petals brushed his skin, and which was warmer, skin or rose petals, he could not tell.

Lavastine was leading his people to war.

But somehow this didn't seem *right*.

As soon as he could, Alain excused himself from the hall. He made his way to the chapel, ordered Rage and Sorrow to sit, and there he waited by the light of the seven candles that illuminated the Hearth. As he expected, Agius soon arrived to pray. He knelt awkwardly, because Sorrow's bite still hampered his movement.

"Frater," said Alain softly. "Do you think it is sorcery?"

Agius made an impatient gesture. He knelt on the bare stone, but he did not rest forehead on clasped hands as he usually did. For once he was preoccupied by the events of the world. "The count might well have deemed this the wiser course. I cannot say."

"But what do *you* think?" Alain demanded. "He never showed Lady Sabella such favor when she was here. He avoided all her questions. He made no commitments. And we can't just plow half the spring fields and leave the autumn-sown wheat and all of that work to—" He broke off. He had been about to say, "to Lackling and the others who aren't fit for war." But the words choked in his throat.

Startled by Alain's vehemence, Agius looked up at him. The frater was revealed, by candlelight, as a younger man than he usually appeared. The candle flame softened his harsh features, and the lines that scored his face blended with shadow to form a smoother profile. They were the lines, Alain realized, of a man who is never at ease with himself. He was probably not much older than Bel's eldest daughter, Stancy, who had celebrated twenty-five or so Penitires.

"She killed Lackling," Alain managed at last. "She killed him, and she a holy biscop!" This betrayal was perhaps the worst of all. Only imagine what Brother Gilles, that good gentle soul, would have said had he witnessed such a thing! "And now Lavastine says we will march to war when there's work in the fields to be done, and he even speaks of fighting against his own beloved cousin! It isn't natural!"

Agius sighed. "Come, Alain. Kneel beside me. There is much for you to learn about the ways of the world. Perhaps someday you will be allowed to turn your back on the intrigues of the world, as I have sought to turn mine. What the biscop did—" He grimaced as he shifted weight onto his injured leg. Alain crossed hesitantly and knelt beside him. "Be sure that I will report it, if I can. But I may not be believed. She is a holy biscop, ordained by the hand of the skopos herself. Although my word is worth a great deal, there were yet only you and I who witnessed the act. If you were acknowledged, Alain, as Lavastine's bastard, your word would be worth more.''

But at this moment, seeing the pale face and remembering the flat voice of Lavastine as he had announced his allegiance to Sabella in the hall, Alain was not sure he *wished* to be acknowledged as that man's kinsman. Especially if it would bring further notice upon him.

"But nevertheless, Alain, there are many reasons why noble lords and ladies change their allegiances. Many reasons, and few of them good ones. With such games do the great princes while away their days, for they do not turn their hearts and eyes to the Hearth of Our Lady as they ought. They are beguiled by the world and its pleasures. We cannot know that sorcery is the cause of the count's decision.''

"But I know it is!'' Alain burst out. ''I *know!*''

Agius raised an eyebrow. He looked skeptical. "By what means do you know? Are you an adept? Have you received training in the forbidden arts?''

Alain resisted the urge to bring the rose out, to show its bloom, to make Agius smell its fragrance. It was not the season for roses, certainly, but the count had a small garden protected from the winds, open to the sun and often warmed by braziers; roses there bloomed early and late. What if Agius, not believing his tale of the visitation of the Lady of Battles, accused him of stealing it?

Or, worse, what if Agius believed him? What if Agius decided that Alain's destiny was something that he, Agius, must manage?

"No,'' Alain said finally, humbly, bowing his head. "I know nothing of sorcery except the stories any child hears and the tales told by our deacon.''

Agius made a gesture of dismissal, turning the conversation away from this discussion of sorcery. "You must wait and see, Alain. But in any case, these matters no longer touch me. I will remain here at Lavas Holding to continue my preaching.''

"You're not coming with us?'' At once, guiltily, he recalled Sorrow's bite; had he managed the hounds better, Agius would not be injured.

But Agius made no mention of the wound. "I am a frater, bound by my oath to serve Our Lady. Though I have stopped at this holding for a while, I do not serve the count, not as you do. As you must.''

Sorrow, sitting patiently by the door, whined. Alain was reminded of his duties: Master Rodlin would be waiting for him. He rose.

"But, Brother Agius, what if Count Lavastine orders you to follow in his train?"

Agius smiled thinly. "Lavastine cannot order me, Alain. Nor will he try."

Nor, to Alain's surprise, did he try. They marched out on St. Isidora's Day soon after dawn, twenty mounted soldiers and eighty on foot with a train of twenty wagons. Frater Agius did not march with them. Chatelaine Dhuoda also remained behind to tend to Lavas stronghold.

Alain could not be sure whether he was sick at heart or terribly excited. Everything he knew he now left behind. Though he had not seen Osna town for over a year, still, it did not seem in his heart too far away; it was four days' journey in good weather and was part of familiar lands. Now, familiar lands vanished behind him, setting west. They crossed the Vennu River and marched east through unknown fields and strange hills.

He swung back and forth between these two emotions, dread and excitement, all that first day. But by the third day the intermittent drizzle and the slogging pace of the march dampened his spirits and left him with a persistent cough and a constantly dripping nose. His boots were caked in mud, and by the end of each day his feet and hands were chilled through.

Only during the day, if the sun came out while they were marching, did he feel comfortable. He and the hounds slept under a wagon at night, just outside the tent that was always pitched for the count. This way, at least, he stayed dry. Many of the other men-at-arms weren't so lucky, and they grumbled.

On the fourth day of the march, while he was watering the hounds at a stream, someone threw a stone at him from the bushes that grew in profusion along the stream's edge. The stone hit hard enough to bruise his shoulder. He yelped, and there came a snickering from the dense thicket. Then, of course, the hounds surged out of the stream and, growling and yipping, made for the bushes. By the time Alain restrained them, his tormenters had gone, shrieking and scattering away into the wood. He did not see their faces, only their backs; there were three of them.

After that he was mostly left alone, although now and again a dead rat would turn up in his porridge. But because Agius was not there, he had no one to talk to, not really. Master Rodlin treated him politely but coldly, and for the rest, they either avoided him or were too important to notice him. Count Lavastine spoke to no one, except to issue curt orders. Care of the hounds was left to Alain and though the hounds were good companions—and increasingly obedient to his commands—Alain was pretty much miserable through and through by the time they arrived at the stronghold where Lord Geoffrey and Lady Aldegund made their home.

Lord Geoffrey was surprised to see his kinsman, but he came out from the stronghold with the household clerics and his wife's chatelaine and various of her kin to greet Count Lavastine on the last stretch of road. They walked out on foot, as was customary. Lavastine did not dismount to embrace his cousin.

The bluff Lord Geoffrey looked taken aback. "I beg your pardon," he said, struggling for words as he examined Lavastine with alarm. "My dear Aldegund is in bed with a fever, but as all the children have had the affliction and recovered from it we do not fear for her. There is a healer with her." He hesitated on the word *healer*, as if he meant to substitute a different word and had thought better of it, then went on. "But the babe born at Lavas Holding is a fine healthy child, almost six months in age now, and has celebrated her first Penitire. There we anointed her with the holy water and gave her the name Lavrentia, as we promised you. What brings you to this holding, cousin? Have you come to celebrate the Feast of St. Sormas with us? And with such a retinue?"

For no one could overlook Lavastine's entourage. Even Sabella and her great retinue, when Alain had first seen them, had not appeared so obviously battle-ready and intended for war.

"I have come to get your pledge, your person, and your men-at-arms, to join with Sabella."

Lord Geoffrey started visibly. To Alain, this was confirmation of his own belief that Lavastine was ensorcelled. Surely Geoffrey knew his cousin's mind on this matter better than any other person might. "T–to join Lady Sabella?" he stammered.

"So I said," snapped Lavastine.

"But that is treason against King Henry."

"It is treason not to take up Sabella's cause against Henry. She is the elder child, the named heir. Her mother was queen of Varre in her own right."

"But by right of fertility—" protested Geoffrey.

"Sabella has a daughter, born of her womb. By what right does Henry claim the throne? By the right given him by a bastard child born to a creature who cannot even be called a true woman? Is it imagined this creature's oath, before the assembled biscops, is worthy of being called truth? How can we know Henry got the child on her? How can we trust the male line at all? It is only through the female line we can be sure."

Geoffrey appeared staggered by this argument. "B–but, cousin. Your own line, your own father . . . Lavas has for three generations passed its inheritance through the male line."

"Do you stand with me?" asked Lavastine without apparent emotion. "Or against me?" He raised a hand, calling his troops to order. His captain actually hesitated, he was so surprised by this command.

"I—I—I must have time to think!"

"There is no time to think! You must choose!"

Lavastine urged his horse forward and drew his sword. Joy and Fear loped beside him. Geoffrey was too stunned even to shy aside as the count bore down on him, sword aloft. But Geoffrey's clerics and retainers were not so slow-witted. Several threw themselves in front of their lord, so that when Lavastine cut down, it was a man in wool tunic and leggings who took the blow meant for his lord; Geoffrey merely cried out in shock.

It was a cleric in the simple robes of a frater who turned and sprinted for the gate. Perhaps he ran for safety. Perhaps he meant to warn those left inside.

Alain could not know. A crossbowman shot, and the quarrel hit the frater in the back. He went down to his knees, for an instant caught in an attitude of prayer, and then tumbled forward into a puddle. Mud splashed over his robes. The water turned a muddy red.

Lavastine rode on past Geoffrey and the knot of men clustered around him, leaving them to the mercies of his men-at-arms. He passed the dying frater. His captain spurred his own mount forward, calling to the other mounted soldiers to follow, and they galloped after Lavastine. Ahead, at the palisade gateway someone was trying to get the gate shut.

"Hai! Hai!" shouted Sergeant Fell, running forward along the line of foot soldiers. "Form up and drive forward at a trot!"

What happened next happened so quickly that afterward Alain could never entirely make sense of it. He surged forward with the other men-at-arms. He could not help but do so. The hounds barked and nipped at the air, scenting battle. Some he restrained, but three more broke away and these tore after Lavastine.

A struggle had erupted around Lord Geoffrey, though Geoffrey's few retainers could scarcely hope for victory. But they beat about themselves with hands and sticks and their ceremonial spears, even with the lance that held the banner of Lady Aldegund's kin, a white hart running against a background colored the deep blue of the twilight sky.

Lavastine, backed by his mounted soldiers, reached the gates. What resistance they met there was cursory. How could Geoffrey's soldiers have ever imagined their lord's cousin would attack them? But one man had kept his wits about him. One man remained in the lookout tower with crossbow in hand.

Perhaps he meant to shoot Lavastine and his hand wavered. Perhaps he meant exactly what happened. Alain knew of it only because when the crossbow quarrel hit Joy and pierced her heart, the other hounds went wild.

Not even Alain could control them.

Lavastine had vanished into the stronghold. Alain ran. He ran in the wake of the hounds and did not even have to shove his way past Sergeant Fell and through the other men-at-arms; they had scattered when the hounds raged through and began to ravage Lord Geoffrey and his men, the closest targets.

With his spear, Alain beat them back, though in their madness the hounds bit at him. Some of the men he could not save, but he straddled one poor frater with his feet and knocked the hounds away from Lord Geoffrey ten times at least before they growled even at him and then turned and ran toward the stronghold. Their eyes were wild, red-rimmed with the battle madness. Blood and saliva dripped down their muzzles.

What they left behind them was terrible to see, one man with a hand bitten clean off, others with flesh torn to expose bone. One poor lad, the banner bearer, had his throat ripped open. Lord Geoffrey had a number of bites, but he could stand. He swayed; Alain could not tell whether he staggered from the shock of his wounds or from the shock of his cousin's attack.

To be attacked by one's own kinsman was the worst kind of betrayal.

Was this the kind of war the Lady of Battles intended him for?

It could not be. Lavastine had always walked the middle road. Hadn't the count understood that a war between Sabella and Henry would be the worst possible thing that could happen?

At that moment, Alain *knew* that Lavastine no longer moved and thought under his own free will, whatever Agius might say. Even Frater Agius would have been stunned by this unprovoked attack on Lord Geoffrey, whom everyone knew was Lavastine's most favored kinsman. Lackling's blood and Lackling's life had been stolen in order to give Biscop Antonia the power to steal Lavastine's heart and will.

"I will stay with him," Alain murmured to himself, half embarrassed by his own arrogance in stating such a thing. "Someone must protect him." Even if that someone was a common boy, who was nothing, who had nothing—except a rose that never ceased blooming.

Sergeant Fell sent half of his men ahead to the stronghold, but the brief flurry of shouts and cries that had erupted from inside the palisade walls had already faded. With his other men, Fell cleaned up from the skirmish. He appeared profoundly uncomfortable as he placed Lord Geoffrey in custody; a frater known to have healing skills hurried forward from Lavastine's train to attend to the wounded men.

"Hai, you! Lad!" Sergeant Fell caught sight of Alain. "Go on, then. Go on. You must fetch them hounds and tie them up. Think of the children in there."

Several of the men-at-arms quickly, reflexively, drew the circle at their breasts. For who among them could forget that those very hounds had killed Lavastine's wife and child? The full story Alain had never heard, since no person in Lavas Holding would speak of it.

"Go!" ordered Fell.

"My wife!" gasped Lord Geoffrey. "The baby!"

Had Alain waited ten breaths longer he would have been too late. It was easy to follow the path of the hound pack: Alain counted two dead men and eleven wounded ones strewn in a ragged line across the broad courtyard. Servants cowered by the well, protected by five of Lavastine's soldiers.

Lavastine's horse stood outside the great timber hall that was the lord's and lady's residence. At least half of the mounted soldiers had left their horses there and gone on, into the hall, following their count; several terrified stableboys held the horses. Alain ran inside.

The hounds were swarming up the steps that led to the spacious loft above the long hall where the lady and her kinswomen and children and the servants lived. The battle madness was still in their eyes. Alain sprinted and grabbed the last one in the pack by its thin tail, and yanked it backward. It spun, biting.

"Sorrow! Down!"

Of a miracle, it worked. Sorrow sat. Ahead on the steps, hearing his voice, Rage sat as well. But the others flowed upward like water running uphill: impossible to stop unless one is truly a sorcerer, for only by sorcery can such an unnatural act be realized.

Alain took the steps two at a time. He shoved through the hounds and though they nipped at him, they were too intent on their prey to worry about one slender youth in their midst. Lavastine walked forward, sword still raised. He appeared oblivious to the hounds and the threat they posed—not to him, of course, but to the women and children and handful of men who, step by slow step, cowered back toward the far wall of the great hall.

Only two had the courage to step forward. Alain recognized the young Lady Aldegund at once; she was certainly no older than he was, though clearly she was now a woman, no longer a child. Pale and shaking, she took a staff and advanced toward Lavastine, crying: "What is this, cousin? Why have you come in such warlike guise to a hall which greets you in friendship and love?"

She held her six-month-old infant in her arms, the child who it had been suggested might become heir to the childless Lavastine. One older woman, weeping, stepped out beside her, as if to throw herself before her lady, to save her from Lavastine's sword or the hounds' bloody fangs.

Alain grabbed tails and flanks, but still they slipped out and charged. They meant to kill her. They *would* kill her, if no one acted, and likely tear the infant child to pieces.

So he laid about him with the butt of his spear, without thought to the consequences. And he cried out sharply as he beat them back.

"Sit! Down! You will obey me, you beasts! Sit!" Terror had actually reached the lady's skirts before Alain hit the hound so hard alongside the head that the animal was stunned. But the rest, finally, sat, though they growled menacingly, eyes fixed on the huddled mass of Lady Aldegund's household.

Lavastine did not sheathe his sword. "You will pledge your loyalty to Lady Sabella's cause, or you will leave," he said.

Aldegund gasped aloud. She looked about to faint, but when her faithful kinswoman touched her on the elbow, she steadied herself. "That is impossible," she said proudly. "My kin traces its allegiance back to the first King Henry, when Queen Conradina passed over her brother Eberhard in favor of naming Henry, then Duke of Saony, as her heir. Though I married into a Varrish family, I will not betray the faith my kin have held in their hearts for so many generations."

How much it cost her to say this Alain could not imagine. He no longer knew what Lavastine would do. Surely she could not know either and she with a babe in her arms and two young stepchildren to protect. And of course she could not know, not yet, what had happened to her husband.

Lavastine remained unmoved by this brave statement. He said, in that flat voice: "You will give me the children as surety for your good behavior. Then you will leave this place with your retinue and return to your mother's lands."

"These are my mother's lands!" Aldegund protested. "They were given to me upon my marriage! You cannot take them!"

"Can you prevent me? These lands now serve Lady Sabella's cause. I will set a chatelaine over them until such time as you choose the wiser course and support Sabella, or until Sabella herself appoints a new lady to administer them." He gestured, and his men—rather hesitantly but without any appearance of moving to contravene his orders—came forward, rounding up the children.

Alain had finished tying the hounds together on a long leash. They nipped and snarled at each other, but they no longer resisted him. Only Rage and Sorrow did he trust enough to leave off the leash. They sat by the stairs like sentries, watching.

Aldegund clutched the infant against her breast. "This one I will not give up!" she exclaimed. "I am still nursing her. It is an offense against Our Lady to take children unwillingly from their mothers!"

"Leave her the infant at least, Count Lavastine," Alain muttered. He could not know whether the count had heard him.

But Lavastine blinked. His pale hard gaze faltered. He batted at his face, as if to brush away a fly. "Just the elder children," he said, sounding uncertain, almost bewildered. But the moment was brief.

Aldegund's mouth trembled but she did not give way to tears. Lord Geoffrey's two children by his first wife were taken away. Lavastine sheathed his sword and glanced at Alain, marking him with some confusion. Then he shook his head and stiffened, losing all expression. He snapped his fingers and the hounds, swarming together because they were tied to the leash, approached him, licking his fingers and fawning at his boots. He took the leash, turned, and with no further speech to anyone left the great hall.

They celebrated the Feast of St. Sormas at the holding, but it was a somber feast. Only Lavastine and his men-at-arms ate at the banquet tables, served grudgingly but without protest by the servants of Geoffrey and Aldegund. Geoffrey was confined to the tower cell and Aldegund and her retinue to the loft upstairs.

In the morning Lavastine allowed the women to leave with only enough food for the fiveday's journey east into Wendish lands, where lay the estate of Lady Alberga, young Aldegund's mother. It was a pathetic procession that set out—Aldegund, the infant, and her two kinswomen, as well as the wet nurse and only two serving-women. How could anyone be expected to know she was a lady, with such a paltry retinue? Aldegund was not even allowed to keep her own horses but had to ride on the back of a donkey.

Geoffrey was not well enough to travel; the wounds he had sustained from the hounds were bad, although likely not mortal. He was left in the care of frater, with orders that he vacate the holding as soon as he could travel.

Lavastine appointed a chatelain from among his own serving-men, a man born of free parents who had placed himself in the count's service in hopes of gaining something more than the youngest son's share of his parents' farmstead. If Sabella's rebellion turned out to her advantage, this man might well find himself steward of a good holding. If it did not . . .

But as Alain watched wagons of provisions trundling out of the holding—vegetables and legumes taken from the storerooms, shields, good spearheads and strong wooden shafts, a few swords, old helmets and new, cloth for tunics and tabards, milled grain, leather, and five small coffers filled with the silver and gold that constituted both Geoffrey's movable wealth, brought to the marriage as his groom's gift, and Aldegund's portion of her family's wealth—he saw how Sabella improved her chances of winning the throne by this victory.

They marched south through the borderlands that had once separated Wendar and Varre and which were still lands that had as many hands in one pot as the other. At two holdings they found enthusiastic support, and Lavastine took on twenty-four more men as soldiers, though they marched under their own captains.

But over the next ten days they took over three holdings whose noble lords and ladies professed loyalty to King Henry. Not one of these holdings, after they saw Lavastine's retinue and heard his blunt speech, resisted. All of them kept their lives but lost fully half of their movable goods. Lavastine's supply train grew longer and longer, and the five coffers of silver and gold and gems grew to nine.

Soon they reached lands loyal to the duke of Varingia, and they turned westward, back into Varre, to find and join Sabella's army.

"So were Lady Sabella's followers stripped of their lands and wealth after her rebellion failed eight years ago," said Master Rodlin one night when he came back from tending to the horses. He was obviously deeply troubled; otherwise he rarely spoke to Alain and certainly not to confide in him.

Alain had fed and watered the hounds and tied them under a wagon for the night. There they lay, five of the eight who remained—Fear, Bliss, Ardent, Steadfast, and Good Cheer, their eyes open and unwinking, staring at him and at the snapping fire. Now that Joy was dead, old Terror slept in Lavastine's tent, and Alain let Rage and Sorrow run unleashed beside him because he could now trust them to do as he wished and leave people alone.

Alain wanted to speak. He wanted to say, "Is it any fairer when Henry's supporters are divested of lands or riches that have been held in their family for generations?"

But he did not speak. He dared not. They would think *he* sympathized with King Henry.

He did not. He knew nothing of Henry except the name, not truly. Nor did he sympathize with Sabella. How could he, knowing what he did of Biscop Antonia's actions and Sabella's willing complicity in them?

He had a great deal of time to think, and think he did. Of course foremost in his heart was God, Our Lady and Lord, and after them

222   KATE ELLIOTT

his own kin, his father Henri and Aunt Bel and his cousins. But he had left his family far behind, in distance if not in his heart.

It was said often enough in Osna village that Count Lavastine was a godly man, asking fair taxes in exchange for the protection he offered the little port. Because so many merchants lived there, Osna was a target for raiders from all sides, sea and land.

But the protection of the counts of Lavas had served the village well over the years since the emporium there was established in the time of the Emperor Taillefer. No freeholder in Osna village except those who managed their fortunes very badly indeed had ever been forced to indenture themselves in exchange for payment of outrageous rents or taxes. That was the sort of thing the noble lords did in Salia, for they were very greedy there. Not one soul in Osna village had ever had to sell one of their children into slavery in order to meet their debts or taxes; but Salian slaves, children born to free or once-free parents, were brought to Osna every summer and sold to families in the lands nearby or shipped onward, to ports farther east.

So that must be his duty. It was the only thing he could sort out from the impossible confusion of his thoughts. He would stay beside Lavastine, as much as he could, as much as he was allowed to. Was that the sign the Lady had meant for him? Was it Her hand that had brought him friendship with Lavastine's hounds, which in its turn allowed him to remain close to the count?

It must be so. Agius thought he was Lavastine's bastard, but why would a noble lord send his bastard off with a freeborn man and not put the child directly into the monastery, if that was his intent?

Biscop Antonia perhaps thought he was the fruit of a Midsummer's Eve seduction, gotten on a human girl by the shade of an elvish prince. But how could a dead creature, elvish or not, get a living woman pregnant?

And the Eika prince had misunderstood his words completely and thought he was *King* Henry's son!

No. He could just imagine what Aunt Bel would say about such fantasies! *"The Lady and Lord act for a reason,"* she would say. She was a good, practical woman, and to her, as to the deacon of Osna village and the other householders, God worked in practical ways and rewarded those who were faithful, hardworking, and pragmatic. Of course Aunt Bel knew that God worked in the world and that angels might light in modest homes or saints walk abroad to save the weary and forsaken. She would not doubt Alain's rose, or the vision he had seen at the old Dariyan fort.

But she would expect Alain to be made humble by these experiences, not proud.

"Why would these things happen" she would ask, *"if there is not a task for you to accomplish, lad?"*

It was the only answer that made any sense to him: He was the only one who knew *and* believed Lavastine rode to war not because he supported Sabella but because he was ensorcelled.

He did not know what else to do but watch over him. That must be his task.

2

WOLFHERE returned from Freelas after fourteen days. He brought bitter news.

Eika raiders had laid waste to the monastery at Sheep's Head and then sailed eastward to join an army of their kind. Already, as rumor told the story, this very army had besieged the great port city of Gent, gateway to the rich heartland of Wendar and the birthplace of King Henry's great-grandfather, Duke and later King Henry, the first of that name. In Gent's cathedral the first Henry's son, known as the elder Arnulf, had married his seven-year-old daughter Adelheid to Louis, the five-year-old child king of Varre. The elder Arnulf had, of course, made himself their regent. For good measure, he had betrothed Louis' infant sister Berengaria to his heir, Henry's father, the younger Arnulf. That King Louis of Varre had died young, and without leaving an heir, was simply the Lady's and Lord's Grace in granting fortune to Arnulf's house. That Berengaria had died in childbed some years later only sealed the issue. To the Wendish kings, Gent itself symbolized the passage of Varre's noble house and its right to rule Varre into Wendish hands.

"We must ride east," said Wolfhere, "to Gent, to see for ourselves the truth of these rumors. King Henry dares not ride north unless he must, not now. There are too many whispers about the doings of his sister, Lady Sabella. Some even say she is speaking rebellion outright. What a bitter thing it is, that she should cause so much trouble now, when we need our armies so badly here in the north."

He sat in the inn common room, elbows folded on the table, a mug of ale at his left hand. He spoke mostly to Manfred and Hathui, but now and again his eye lit on Liath and Hanna, who sat silent but attentive at the end of the table. It was evening, and many of the locals had come in for a drink, mostly, Hanna knew, to watch the Eagles and listen for scraps of news from the great world beyond. Custom had been up for the last ten days because of their guests, who had gone from being a curiosity to an item of gratifying interest eight days ago when Hathui broke the nose of an importunate, and very drunk, young farmer.

Hanna admired Hathui, a big-boned, strong woman who had, by her own account, grown up in horse country far to the east in the march country of Eastfall, beyond which lay the wild lands and the barbaric Quman peoples, the winged horsemen—so Hathui called them. They lived in darkness, outside the Light of the Circle of Unity, and Hathui's own brother had walked as a missionary into those dark lands and never returned.

"So I dedicated my life to St. Perpetua, Lady of Battles," Hathui had said, *"and swore to fight them instead."*

Until the day she took the ring investing her into the king's service as an Eagle, Hanna had not realized how much she wanted to see the world beyond Heart's Rest before she settled down and, like her mother before her, became chatelaine of her own inn. She had not allowed herself to want it, knowing it was out of her reach; what point was there in reaching for something you could never have? That was why inn work appealed to her, because was it not said that "the innkeeper sees the world through the guests that come in through her door?"

And yet, she could have gone with Ivar to Quedlinhame, where she would have seen the king's court. And yet, she might have gone with Liath to Firsebarg. But it was better not to think about Firsebarg, because that would make her think of Hugh.

"As for you two young ones," Wolfhere added, wrenching Hanna's attention back to the matter at hand, "you will have to learn the ways of the Eagles as we ride. I had hoped to send you—" He broke off, took a deep draught of ale, and sighed, setting the mug down so hard that foam spilled over the side. "That will all have to come later. Are you strong enough, Liath? If not, we can leave you here and—"

"No! I'm strong enough!"

Hanna placed a hand on Liath's arm, to calm her. Liath was stronger, truly, but she was as skittish as a calf and she wore away at herself with her constant fear. And still, even seeing Liath this way, Hanna dreamed of Hugh some nights. Most nights, if truth be told. But there was no other man like him, or none she had ever seen. Better to let go of his memory, to let it fade. Better not to worry at herself dreaming of something she could never have, and most likely was better off not having. Out on the road there would surely be sights to drive him from her mind.

"I secured horses for you in Freelas." Wolfhere blinked guilelessly at Manfred and Hathui. "Do you judge them able to ride well enough?"

"What?" asked Hathui with a sharp smile. "The horses? I haven't seen the horses."

Wolfhere bared his teeth. "Two horses, spirited, and with stamina. No, my child, indulge me in this. The ride to Gent will be hard, and I do not know what we will find there or how quickly we may be forced to leave. They say a king leads this Eika army, and that he is an enchanter. They say he cannot be killed. If these two will hold us back, then we must leave them in Freelas or at our posting in Steleshame."

Here, now, was something to worry over. Hanna was not noble-born, to have been trained young to the saddle. That she had any familiarity with horses at all was only because her parents ran an inn. She held her breath. Liath stared at the fire, obviously distracted.

"Hanna is a serviceable rider but no better than that," said Manfred in his blunt way, "but I judge her will to be strong enough that I trust her to keep up, whatever the hardships."

Wolfhere raised an eyebrow. "Praise from you, Manfred, is praise hard won. And Liath?"

Liath stirred, hearing her name.

"Liath," said Hathui with contempt, "can ride perfectly well, though she claims not to have ridden a horse for over three years. She's still weak. But I believe she will recover as we ride. If she has not by Steleshame, we can leave her there."

"Then it is settled," said Wolfhere, and Hanna stopped holding her breath. "Come, my children, and see your new horses. They were the best I could find on such short notice. We will leave as soon as you have saddled them."

Leave! Hanna felt her feet rooted to the floor, growing into the wood, which would never let her leave her beloved home. To *leave* sounded so wonderful as words. "This soon?" she managed, her voice not quite cracking. "I thought, not until morning—"

Wolfhere's gaze, on her, was softly reproving. A kind man, she saw, until you went against his wishes. "We are Eagles, Hanna. There must be no delay in the king's business. Do you understand?"

She stood obediently. She had dreamed, and she had been given. She refused to let fear get the better of her and especially not after watching Liath be consumed and controlled by her own fear. "Of course, sir."

He chuckled. "And today is St. Eusebē's Day, is it not? The sixth day of Avril. What more auspicious day to begin your apprenticeship as King's Eagles?" He rose. "Hathui, see to provisions. Come, Liath, it is time to move. You and Hanna will come with me to the stables."

Hanna thought his tone softened a little as he looked at Liath. Poor Liath. Hanna knew very well that Liath did not intend to look quite so exotically lovely and quite so pathetically lost. She touched her friend's shoulder, and Liath started and jumped to her feet, banging her thighs against the table, as she always did when startled out of a distraction. But this time she cursed under her breath and rubbed her legs, and everyone, even Liath, laughed.

Out in the stables, Hanna examined the rangy white-stockinged gelding Wolfhere had brought for her before venturing forward with a windfall apple as a greeting. Soon enough she was rubbing its flanks and then saddling it.

Liath's bay mare was more restive, and the other horses were all saddled by the time Liath even considered introducing the bridle. Hathui arrived with the provisions, levied from the villagers as part of their tithe to the king. With the speed of long practice, she loaded the pack mule. Then she and Manfred led the mule and the other horses outside.

"Pack what you wish to bring now," said Wolfhere. "But remember there is little an Eagle can afford to possess, besides the trust of her comrades and her own strength."

"I have nothing but the clothes I'm wearing," said Liath.

It was such an outright lie that Hanna looked at her in surprise, but Liath was looking away, at the wall, not at anything or anyone. If the others noticed, they gave no sign. But they did not know Liath as Hanna did.

"I'll go in and get my sack," said Hanna. "I hope you will grant me leave to say good-bye to my family."

"Of course," said Wolfhere.

There Liath stood, still staring at nothing.

Hanna swallowed, and went on. "My mother would be well pleased if you took formal leave of her as well, sir."

"Ah," said Wolfhere, although the soft exclamation betrayed no obvious emotion. He had seen the book, of course—they all had—but none of the Eagles had made any mention of it. Did he suspect it was important and that Liath was hiding it from him? She could not tell. "Take your horse out to Hathui, then. I will go to your mother. Liath must finish saddling, of course. She can meet us outside."

Hanna let him go out first, as was polite. Liath mouthed the words, "Thank you." Hanna led her gelding outside.

Outside, the midday sunlight lay softly cool over the distant hills and the closer cropped green of the village common. Hanna's entire family had gathered in the stable yard. Amazingly, Karl brought her sack forward—a change of clothes, a pot, a spoon, and a handful of other items—and begged to be allowed to tie it onto her saddlebags. His eyes shone as he gazed up at her, and it occurred to her all at once that he admired her, the bright new Eagle, just as she admired Hathui. It almost made her cry.

"You look like neither fish nor fowl," he said impertinently, spoiling the effect.

But she smiled. She had no fine, practical clothes, no long tunic cut for riding, like the other Eagles wore. She, like Liath, wore a mixture of her old clothes and castoffs from her married brother Thancmar, cut down and patched well enough, and likely to last some time. Birta was never one to stint on cloth, or weaving, or leggings, since she reckoned that if you paid half again as much for cloth that lasted twice as long, then it was a bargain. Hanna felt strange, dressed half as a woman and half as a man, but Liath had herself commented that this was what she had always worn, traveling with her Da.

Birta came up to her and hugged her hard. "Now mind you, Hanna," she said into her ear, "that you look after yourself, and after Liath, too, for she's more fragile than I thought and will need some time to heal."

"I will. I promise it." Then she hugged her father, who was speechless as always, and Karl again. "And a devil will plague you," she added, holding onto his tunic, "if you don't obey Mam and Pap in all things. Do you understand me?"

He gulped out a yes and scurried away to a safe distance. Hanna wiped a tear from her eye with the back of a hand.

Liath came out of the stables, leading her bay mare. If anything new and bulky rested in her saddlebags, anything rectangular, like a book, Hanna could not tell; she must have rearranged and re-weighted the bags in order to hide the book. She did not look at Hanna but made her good-byes to Birta and Hansal and Karl. The locals had come out to gawk, but they remained respectfully back.

At last they mounted and followed Wolfhere down the south road. Of the five of them, only Hanna looked back as they passed around the bend and out of sight of the inn and the common. When the trees veiled the last house of the village and they walked their horses along the quiet road edged by broken fields and the steady march of forest, Liath spoke abruptly.

"I will never come here again."

Hanna shuddered and was suddenly afraid.

"Do you so vow?" asked Wolfhere with a hint of a smile.

Liath started as if she had only now realized she had spoken aloud. "No," she said. "No. I wouldn't do anything so rash. It's just I feel it's true, somehow."

"Anne was given to feelings," said Wolfhere blandly. "Of that sort."

Anne. Liath's mother. Who had been a sorcerer. Who had been killed because of it. *There is much more here than meets the eye.* But Hanna was determined to do whatever needed to be done to protect Liath.

"Come now," said Wolfhere. "We've a long road before us."

So they rode, with little talk and great single-mindedness. Their pace was unslacking—not hard, for the sake of the horses, but constant. By nightfall, Heart's Rest lay far behind them.

PART TWO

THE DEEDS OF THE GREAT PRINCES

VIII
ON THE KING'S PROGRESS

1

ROSVITA of Korvei, the least of the servants of Our Lady and Our Lord, to her most imperial majesty, Queen Mathilda, sends the most humble protestations of her complete devotion and heartfelt greetings in the Name of Our Lady, Whose renowned wisdom and singular glory illumines you, our gracious queen, mother to our most glorious King Henry, second of that name.

The message from her father lay on top of the next page, covering the words she had written yesterday before being interrupted first by a messenger from the north and then by the news of the argument that had erupted among the king's counselors. She slipped the parchment into the pocket sewn in her outer tunic. Her fingers slipped down the smooth silk of her gold vestment, worn by all the king's clerics. It was very fine to the touch. *Like all worldly pleasures*, she reminded herself wryly. The gold vestment, symbol of the king's service, covered the coarse cloth she wore underneath, the black robe that marked her as coming, originally, from Our Lady's Convent of Korvei.

She returned her attention to the book.

At your request I undertake to write of the deeds of the great princes and in addition I have taken pains to write a few words concerning the origin and condition of the Wendish people over whom King Henry, first of that name, was the first to reign, so that in reading of these deeds you may delight your mind, relieve your cares, and relax in pleasant leisure.

Here, yesterday afternoon, she had broken off. It was a relief to return to the quiet of the scriptorium after the uproar last night, which had lasted until King Henry retired from the feast. She consulted her wax tablet, with its worked and reworked sentences, crossed out and scratched over, then set her quill to ink and began writing again.

I confess, however, that I could not encompass all their deeds, but I am writing them briefly and not at length, so that their narration may be clear and not tedious to my readers. Therefore may Your Highness read this little book, being mindful of us and of the piety and devotion with which it was written.

Here ends the Preface to the First Book of the Deeds of the Great Princes.

Rosvita shifted on her stool. Her back was sore already. When she had first come to the King's Chapel as a twenty-year-old fresh from Korvei Convent, she had been able to sit up long into nights broken only by the call to prayer and work by candlelight at the copying and recopying of old texts and, indeed, at texts she had herself composed despite the lack of humility such composition betrayed in one so young. But after twenty years of labor, first in the service of King Arnulf the Younger and now for King Henry, her body was no longer as supple and strong.

But she smiled as she readied a new page. It was as her old Mother Abbess always said: "The pains of age remind us of the wisdom we have won through our trials." Since Mother Otta of Korvei had then been a vigorous old woman past her seventieth year who had never known a day's sickness in her life and who was yet the gentlest, most amiable, and wisest person Rosvita had ever met, the words resonated with a charming and most appropriate humility. Mother Otta yet lived, incredibly approaching her ninetieth year, a sign of Our Lady and Lord's Grace, although she was now frail and almost blind.

For ten years Rosvita had labored, taking notes, speaking with ancient courtiers and biscops, studying old records in the archives of the monasteries and convents through which the King's Court traveled on its endless progress. Now she had begun to write. She hoped she would complete this great project in such good time that Mother Otta might have it read to her before she died.

Here begins the First Book of the Deeds of the Great Princes.

After twenty years of labor in the scriptorium, Rosvita knew well how difficult it would be to make changes once she had begun, the time it would take to recopy an entire page or, worse, a whole chapter. But she had decided at last on the order of chapters, and it was truly time to plan no longer but simply compose.

1. First of all I will set down a few things regarding the origin and condition of the Wendish people, following in this matter only hearsay, since the truth of those times is too thickly obscured in antiquity.

Some hold that the Wendish people lived first in the northlands, from which they were driven south by the incursions of those whom we name the Eika, the dragonmen. Others believe that the Wendish came originally from Arethousa, and that they were the remnant of the great army led by Alexandros, the Son of Thunder, which after its final defeat by the armies of the Dariyan Empress Arku-ak-nia was scattered throughout the world. This opinion I heard in my youth from an old scholar. For the rest, it is commonly accepted that the Wendish were an ancient and noble people, known to the Hessi peoples and written of in their most ancient books, and referred to in Polyxene's History of the Dariya.

We are certain, however, that the Wendish people first came to these lands in ships, and that they landed at the town known as Hathelenga, which lies west of the city of Gent. The natives who lived in those lands at that time, said to be Ostravians, took up arms against them. The Wendish fought valiantly and took the shorelands for their own.

There was a sudden eruption of noise at the entrance to the scriptorium. Clerics and monks, lost in their copying, now started up or turned their heads as old Cleric Monica appeared at the head of a loud and, for the moment, unruly band. But it was not an invasion of the Wendish tribes. It was merely the inconvenient arrival of the youngest members of the king's schola.

Rosvita sighed and set down her pen. She then berated herself for her exasperation and rose to help Cleric Monica herd her charges onto benches at those of the desks which were free. As she sat back down at her own bench, eyeing fresh parchment with the longing of one who knows she will not be able to work any further this hour, a young man slid onto the bench beside her.

"I beg your pardon," he whispered.

It was young Berthold Villam. He smiled winningly at her; he was one of those rare young men who are utterly charming without being the least aware of it. Indeed, of the children and young persons who attended the king's progress, he was her favorite. He had turned fifteen last winter and had, as was customary, been given a retinue of his own. Thus, he was too old for the schoolroom, but he genuinely loved learning or, at least, was desperately curious.

He reached out diffidently and touched the parchment, ink still wet on it, with a forefinger. "This is your *History*?"

Rosvita nodded. Other children, she noted, were sharing benches with the clerics who had been at work in the scriptorium. In the last half year the number of children on the king's progress had doubled. This by itself was a sign there was trouble in the kingdom.

Her gaze settled on the girl who sat, silent and with a mulish expression, on the bench nearest Cleric Monica. This latest arrival was the eldest child of Conrad the Black, Duke of Wayland; though she was only eight years old, she knew she was being held hostage for her father's good behavior.

"Now, children," said Cleric Monica. She was quite bent with arthritis but a formidable presence nevertheless. She glared the children into silence and raised a hand. "Attend. There are enough tablets that you must only share with one another person. Some of you boys need only listen."

Berthold fidgeted, fingers toying with Rosvita's stylus. Like many of the boys and young men who were fated to marry and then spend most of their life riding to war or protecting their wives' lands, he had not been taught how to write, although he could read. He noticed what he was doing and, embarrassed, ducked his chin.

"You may use it," she said. He flashed her a smile and laboriously impressed a "B" into the tablet.

"Attend," said Cleric Monica. "To read the works of the ancients you must know Dariyan, for that is the language in which they wrote and spoke in the old Dariyan Empire. Though there is much knowledge we may gain from those works left to us after the fall of that great empire, there is a greater knowledge yet: that the old Empire, the union of elves and men, was fated to fall because its emperors and empresses would not receive into their hearts the truth of the Unities and the blessing of the Light. That is why, when the great Taillefer restored the empire in the year 600, he called it the *Holy* Dariyan Empire.''

"But no one faults the piety of Taillefer," muttered Berthold, trying to write an "E" that had straight lines, "and yet his empire collapsed and no king or queen has been crowned Holy Dariyan Emperor in Darre since Taillefer. How is *that* explained?"

"A good question," murmured Rosvita, aware suddenly that Cleric Monica's hard gaze had turned their way. It was too bad, really, that the boy must marry. He would have made a fine historian.

Cleric Monica coughed meaningfully and went on with her teaching. Berthold sighed and essayed an "R." Rosvita found her gaze wandering over the assembled children.

The great magnates of the realm were each expected to send a child to attend the king's progress. Some, usually younger siblings, would be educated as clerics and in time join the King's Chapel and Greater Schola. Other children might only pass through for a year or two as part of their education, to get a taste of life in the ever-changing, always moving court as it traveled through the lands ruled over by King Henry.

And a few, whose parents were of suspect loyalty, might stay for a much longer time. Although no one ever spoke the word, these children were hostages, although well-treated ones.

That was not true of Berthold, of course. His father, the margrave Helmut Villam, was King Henry's favored counselor and most trusted companion.

Of the great princes of the realm, the four margraves were usually the most loyal to the king. Of all the princes, the margraves most needed the king's support. As administrators of the marchlands, those lands that bordered the easternmost territories controlled by the Wendish peoples and their allies, they were always at the forefront when the barbarian eastern tribes raided civilized lands for loot and slaves.

From their lands missionaries set out into the wild lands to convert the heathens. Into their lands came the most intrepid settlers, willing to risk the assaults of the heathen tribes in return for good lands to farm clear of obligation to any lord except the king or prince.

For three years the borderlands had been quiet, and because of this the margraves—or their heirs—were able to spend part of every year in attendance on the king. This spring, besides Villam, the king's progress boasted the presence of the illustrious Judith, margrave of Olsatia and Austra.

She had left her marchlands in the capable hands of her eldest daughter and brought her two youngest children to court. One of them, a sallow girl of about fourteen years of age, sat with a slack-jawed expression, staring at Cleric Monica as if the elderly woman had just sprouted horns and wings.

Werinhar, margrave of Westfall, had sent his youngest brother to court. This young man was destined for the church, and like a good cleric-in-training he was at this moment diligently copying down Monica's speech.

As usual it was the dukes—the most powerful princes of the realm—who posed the greatest problem. The three dukes whose lands lay in the old kingdom of Wendar remained loyal: Saony, Fesse, and Avaria. All of them had either children or young siblings here now; Rosvita had seen many young people from those families come and go in the last twenty years.

But the dukedoms of Varingia, Wayland, and Arconia lay in the old kingdom of Varre, and the loyalty of their dukes was less con-stant—and more suspect. So Duke Conrad of Wayland's daughter sat at the front of the class and laboriously copied letters under the strict attention of Cleric Monica. So, half a year ago, Tallia, daugh-ter of Sabella and Berengar, had come of age and left the king's progress to return to Arconia. No one had thought anything of it then; it was a natural progression.

But two months ago Rodulf, Duke of Varingia, had recalled his youngest son Erchanger from Henry's side. And now they heard daily the rumors that Sabella meant to rebel again against Henry's authority.

Berthold snorted under his breath, amused. "Ekkehard's fallen asleep again."

"Ai, Lady," murmured Rosvita. She did not at first have the cour-age to look. When she did, she saw that the only son of King Henry and Queen Sophia was, indeed, asleep, head basketed on an arm, tunic pulled askew to reveal the gold torque around his neck. He was snoring slightly. Ekkehard was a good boy but prone to staying up late at banquets listening to the poets and musicians rather than studying his letters, as he ought.

Monica, blessedly, had not yet noticed the boy was asleep. Most of her attention was reserved for Duke Conrad's daughter, a slender girl who had inherited a full share of her grandmother's blood: She was as black as a Jinna merchant. On her, the gold torque reserved for the direct descendants of kings shone beautifully against black skin.

Berthold, following the line of Rosvita's gaze, muttered slyly: "She'll be very handsome when she grows up."

"So was it said of her grandmother, a great beauty despite that her complexion isn't what we are used to. But the blessed Daisan himself lived in the lands now conquered and ruled by the Jinna, so who is to say he was not himself as dark-complexioned as she?"

" 'For a person is not accused because she is tall or short of stature, because he is white or black, because she has large or small eyes, or because he has some physical defect,' " quoted Berthold.

"Hush," said Rosvita mildly, covering her lips to hide her smile.

"Lord Berthold," said Cleric Monica. "I trust you will attend to my words or absent yourself so the rest may work in peace?"

He bowed his head obediently. Monica lectured for a while more, the words so familiar they sounded a drone in Rosvita's ears. She stretched and rubbed her back, trying to be surreptitious about it, but Berthold, noticing, grinned at her before he finished writing his name.

Abruptly Rosvita became aware of voices from the garden outside, heard through the opened shutters of the window that let light wash over her desk. The others, children and clerics alike, concentrating on their work or on Monica's lesson, seemed oblivious. Rosvita could not be.

Blessed Lady! The king's daughters were quarreling again.

"I *merely* said I think you are unwise to allow such a man so much influence over your councils."

"You're jealous he chose my company over yours!"

"Of course that isn't true. I am only concerned for your reputation. Everyone knows he is a charlatan."

"He's nothing of the kind! They're all envious of his wisdom."

"I thought they were all annoyed by his arrogance and his terrible manners."

Rosvita sighed, laid down her quill, and wiped her fingers quickly on a rag, then rose from her stool, rubbing her aching back. Berthold looked up, startled; she signed to him to stay where he was. Cleric Monica merely nodded curtly at her, acknowledging her leavetaking; no doubt Monica knew and approved what she was about.

Rosvita hastened down the aisle of the scriptorium, cut through the sacristy—startling the aged brother in charge who had fallen asleep by the vestments—and came out into the rose garden in time to see the two sisters in their full glory by the fountain.

They were a strange admixture of their parents. Sapientia was, like her mother, small and dark and neat, but she had in all other ways the look of her father about her, including the unfortunate tendency to flush a bright red when she lost her temper.

Theophanu had the greater height and the finer figure, robust and well-formed, but also her mother's unnatural coolness of temperament; Eastern wiles, the courtiers called it, and had never entirely trusted Queen Sophia, although they had wept as grievously as any when she was laid to rest. No doubt, thought Rosvita uncharitably, because they knew the accepted order of King Henry's court, molded over the sixteen years of Henry and Sophia's rule, would be thrown all into chaos when he married a new queen.

"You're furious because Father wishes to name me as margrave of Eastfall and give me those lands to administer. You want them yourself!" Sapientia's complexion by now rivaled that of the bright pink floribundas twining up the stone wall that bounded the private garden, although the color did not become her as well as it did the roses.

In eighteen years Rosvita had never yet seen Theophanu lose her temper, not even as a small child. Unnatural girl! She had many more effective ways of making her elder sister angry. "I trust that Father will add to my estates when he deems it time. I have never found it worthwhile to beg for duties before he is willing to settle them on me."

Rosvita hurried forward. Poor Sapientia, in the face of this insult that so pointedly must remind her of yesterday's tempest, was about to succumb to one of her famous rages.

"Your Gracious Highnesses," said Rosvita just as Sapientia drew breath, "I have found you at last!" The bright statement had its intended effect: Sapientia, caught in the moment before speaking, lost hold of her thought.

Theophanu arched one eyebrow provocatively. "You bring news?" she asked politely, although Rosvita knew perfectly well the princess was not fooled by this transparent ploy.

Rosvita recalled the message from her father and blessed Our Lady for the inspiration. "It is only a small family matter, nothing important, but with great humility I venture to speak of it before you, Your Highnesses."

"You must confide in us at once," said Sapientia, coming forward to take Rosvita's hands in hers. "We will do all we can."

Theophanu simply lifted a hand in assent.

"I have a brother, named Ivar, who has just been sent into orders. He is to become a monk at the monastery ruled over by Mother Scholastica, at Quedlinhame. I had hoped you might show some favor to me and my family by asking your Aunt Scholastica to watch over him in his early days there. He is very young, perhaps two or three years younger than you, Your Highness." She nodded at Theophanu. "And I believe from the tone of my father's letter that it was not Ivar's intention to enter the church."

"He is a younger son," said Sapientia. "What else might he have wanted?"

"I cannot know his mind. I have only met him twice. He was born at least ten years after I left home to become a novice at Korvei. He is the child of my father's second wife, who is a daughter of the countess of Hesbaye."

"Ah, yes, she had three daughters by her third husband." Sapientia released Rosvita's hands and paced over to the dry fountain. Four stone unicorns, rearing back on their hind legs, regarded her calmly, their stippled surface streaked with old water trails from the spray that had coursed out from their manes and horns. Damaged by winter storms, the fountain had not yet been repaired. Father Bardo had apologized most profusely when the king and his court had arrived at Hersford Monastery to find the garden's charming centerpiece not working.

It was a warm day for spring, going on hot. Without a cooling spray to refresh the courtyard, Rosvita felt the heat radiating up from the mosaic tile that surrounded the broken fountain.

"Her daughter, who is now the wife of Helmut Villam, spoke in my favor last night," Sapientia continued, then laughed. "It will be interesting to see who buries more spouses before they themselves die, Helmut Villam or the countess of Hesbaye. But Villam is on his fifth wife now, is he not? The countess' fourth husband is still alive. She will have to send him away to war as she did with all the others."

"That was a tactless thing to say," said Theophanu. "It is no wonder Father won't send you on your progress."

Sapientia whirled away from her contemplation of the fountain, took two strides to her sister, and slapped her.

"Lady preserve me," Rosvita muttered, hastening forward.

Theophanu neither smiled in triumph nor cried out in pain; her face was as flat as polished wood. "Their loss should not be fodder for your amusement."

"Now, now," said Rosvita, hurriedly placing herself between the two young women. "Let us not argue and strike out when we feel the heat of our passions on us. 'It is well to *speak* first,' as the blessed Daisan said when his disciples asked him what to do when false accusations of sorcery were laid against them."

" 'For the truth shall make us free,' " finished Theophanu.

Sapientia burst into noisy sobs of thwarted anger and fled the garden. From a half-hidden bench a maidservant jumped up and followed her inside.

"I am not sure it is wise to bait your sister in this fashion."

"If she would only think before she speaks—" Theophanu broke off, turned, and took several steps forward to greet the man who emerged at that moment into the courtyard. Like the two young women, he wore a gold torque, braids of solid gold twisted into a three-quarters circle, around his neck. Theophanu knelt. "Father."

He laid a hand on her dark hair.

Rosvita knelt as well. "Your Majesty."

"You must rise, my most valued cleric," said the king. "I have an errand for you, which I am assured only you can accomplish."

Rosvita rose and faced King Henry. As a young man he had been, like his elder daughter, rash at times; now, as always these days, he wore a grave expression that contrasted well with the bright lights of his silvering hair. "I am your servant, Your Majesty." She could not quite restrain a smile. "Your praise honors me."

"No more than it should, my friend. You will indulge me, I hope, by carrying out this errand at once."

"Of course."

"Father Bardo tells me there is a hermit, a holy monk, who lives in a cell in the hills above the monastery. He is old and was once, I am told, a scholar."

Despite herself, Rosvita felt her heart beat faster. An old man, and a scholar as well! Always there were new things to be discovered from the testimony of such people.

"He is known to be well versed in the laws of the Emperor Taillefer, to have knowledge of capitularies of those times that have been lost to us. But he is reluctant to break his contemplation, so says Father Bardo."

"Then ought we to ask him to break his contemplation, Your Majesty?"

"There are some things I need to know about inheritance." His tone, barely, betrayed agitation. Theophanu looked up sharply at her father, but said nothing. "As for you, Rosvita, Father Bardo says this holy monk has heard of your work compiling a history of the Wendish people for my blessed mother and might be willing to speak with you. Perhaps his curiosity outweighs his serenity." He said it with the secular lord's fine disregard for the pursuits of those sworn to the church.

Or his meditations on the Lady's and Lord's Holy Works had not yet quieted his passion for learning. But Rosvita did not voice this thought out loud.

"You are thinking the same thing," said the king, with a smile.

"I am, indeed."

"Then you must speak your mind freely in front of me, or how else will I benefit from your wise counsel?"

Now, Rosvita did smile. She had always liked Henry, as much as one allowed oneself to *like* the heir and later king; in recent years, however, as he had drawn her more tightly into his orbit, she had also come to respect him. "Then I must ask you if there is some certain thing you are hoping to discover from such an interview."

The king lifted his hand from Theophanu's head and glanced around the courtyard. Behind a hedge of cypress, Rosvita saw two courtiers waiting in discreet attendance: One, the elder man, was Helmut Villam, the king's constant companion and most trusted adviser; the other was hidden by the leaves.

"Where is your sister?" Henry said to his daughter. "I was told the two of you walked here together."

"She has gone inside."

"If you will wait, then, with Villam, I would have you come riding with me."

"I will attend you, Father." She rose and retreated obediently to stand with the others. Rosvita caught a glimpse of Berthold Villam. Evidently he had slipped out after her to find out what all the fuss was about. The other person in attendance, now visible, was the formidable Judith, margrave of Olsatia and Austra. Behind the margrave hovered several servants.

The spring sun, glaringly hot in the enclosed garden of stone and hedge and roses, suddenly vanished, cloaked by a cloud.

"You know what is whispered," said Henry. "What none of them will say aloud."

The dukes and margraves, counts and biscops and clerics and courtiers who populated the king's progress spoke freely and volubly of the great concerns of the day: Would Henry's sister Sabella break into open revolt against him? Was this to be a summer of raids along the northern coast, or would the Eika land, as was rumored, with an army? What did the skopos in Darre mean to do about the whispers of heresy taking root inside the church?

But on one subject they were silent, or spoke in circles that surrounded but never touched the heart of the issue. In the terrible arguments that had raged yesterday afternoon and in the tense feast that had followed, where whispers and glances continued the dispute, one name had not been spoken so that it could be heard.

"Sanglant," she said, pronouncing it in the Salian way: *sahn-glawnt*.

"And what is it they say about Sanglant?"

"They speak not of Sanglant but of you. They say your sentiment has overreached your reason. They say it is time to send Sapientia on her progress so she may be judged worthy or unworthy of being named as your heir. And if not Sapientia, then Theophanu."

"Theophanu is not as well liked."

"Not in general, no."

"Yet she is the more capable, Rosvita."

"It is not my place to judge such matters."

"Then whose is it?" He sounded impatient now.

"It is yours, Your Majesty. Such is the burden laid on the sovereign king by Our Lady and Lord."

He arched one eyebrow; for an instant she saw how much Theophanu resembled him, in wit and intelligence if not feature. The church bell began to toll, calling the monks to the service of Sext. She smelled charcoal in the air and the stench of meat being seared over hot coals in preparation for roasting and the night's feast. After a long pause, Henry spoke again. "What do they say about Sanglant?"

Better to tell him the truth he already knew but chose, out of sentiment, to ignore. "That he is a bastard, Your Majesty. That he is not a true man. Whatever other fine qualities he certainly has, and which are fully acknowledged, can never compensate for his birth and his mother's blood." She hesitated, then went on. "Nor ought they to."

He looked annoyed but he did not respond at once. The bell fell into silence; she heard the whisper of monks' robes as the last stragglers made their way to the chapel within the cloister where they would pray.

"I will attend service," he said. "But you will visit the hermit nevertheless, Rosvita. And you will discover whether this holy monk knows of precedent for a child born to a concubine or other unofficial union being named as heir."

His voice dropped even as he said the fateful words. Only she heard them. But surely every man and woman who followed along on the king's progress knew what was in his mind: that his eldest child, the bastard son of an Aoi woman who had emerged from unknown lands to enchant the young Henry on his heir's progress, was and always had been his favorite, though he had three legitimate children by Queen Sophia who were each possessed of a sound mind and body.

She caught a glimpse in his face then of an ancient longing, a passion never extinguished, never fulfilled. But quickly it was covered by the mask of stone worn by the king.

"I will do as you ask, Your Majesty," she said, and bowed her head to the inevitable. Although surely nothing good could come of this obsession.

IX
THE DRAGONS

1

TEN days after leaving Heart's Rest, Liath sat on the old stone wall and enjoyed the spring sun. She was tired, but not overly so; free of Hugh, she had recovered her strength quickly.

This moment of respite she used to study the layout of the holding of Steleshame: the dye vats sheltered under a lean-to; the hen-house; two cauldrons spitting with boiling water attended by three women who stirred wool cloth as it shrank; felters at work in the sun; two of the blacksmith's boys linking tiny iron rings into mail; furs stretched and strung to cure.

Here, within the large courtyard protected by a palisade of wood, lay the remains of an older structure. The Eagles had thrown up an outpost and used the old dressed stone to build a tower for defense. The householder and her relatives lived in a timber longhouse, and the stables were also built of wood. Only the skeleton of the old fort was left, straight lines squared to the equinoxes and the solstices, the map of the sun. She could trace these bones with her eyes, and read, here and there, inscriptions in old Dariyan cut into the stone by the soldiers and craftsman who had inhabited this place long ago.

Lucian loves the red-haired woman.

Estephanos owes Julia eight quiniones.

Let it be known that this outpost has been erected by the order of Arki-kai Tangashuan, under the auspices of the Most Exalted Empress Thaissania, she of the mask.

Liath knelt to wipe dirt from this last inscription, graven into a block of stone half sunk in the ground next to the watering trough. For how many years had it lain here, trampled by horses and cattle, scoured by wind and dust, drenched by rain? She coughed, sucking in a mouthful of dust blown up by a gust of wind. Her fingers, scraping, reached beaten earth; the inscription extended farther yet, buried in the ground.

" 'She of the mask,' " said Wolfhere, behind her. "The heathen empress before whom the blessed Daisan stood without fear and proclaimed the Holy Word and the saving Mercy of the Lady and Lord of Unities."

Surprised, Liath bolted up unsteadily. Wolfhere smiled, a baring of teeth.

"Do not deny you can read it, child. Both your father and mother were church educated, and when you were but six years of age you could read old Dariyan texts with the skill of a scholar bred in the convent."

"Surely not," she blurted out, embarrassed.

His smile now seemed less forced. "Not with the skill of an adult perhaps, but astonishing in one so young. Come, now. There is an armory here, and we must find you weapons that are suitable. Mistress Gisela's niece is sewing borders on new cloaks for you and Hanna."

Hanna was already at the tower, trying the weight of swords. She handled the weapons awkwardly. They had traveled for ten days and during that time Hathui and Manfred had tested Liath and Hanna in swordcraft and found them sorely wanting.

"Eagles are not soldiers," Hathui was saying to Hanna as Liath and Wolfhere paused at the heavy iron-ribbed door that led into the round chamber at the base of the tower. "But you must know how to defend yourself against bandits and the king's enemies. Ai! What *do* you know how to do, woman?"

"I can milk a cow, make butter and cheese," puffed Hanna, "feed twenty travelers a good meal, chop wood, build a fire, salt and smoke meat, ret and spin flax—

Hathui laughed, lowering her sword. She was not winded. "Enough! Enough!" The two women had been sparring, circling while Manfred used a staff to fend off the stray children and dogs and chickens which infested the yard. "The Lady honors those who are chatelaine to a hearth, for is She not Herself Chatelaine to us all? But you're hamfisted with the sword, Hanna. Manfred, give her a spear." He obliged, and Hanna had only time to look longingly toward Liath—as if to say *"I wish you were here and I there at the door"*—before she handed him the sword and took up the spear.

"This is like a staff." Hanna settled her hands into a comfortable grip on the haft. She tried a few whacks at the stout post sunk in the ground in the middle of the yard. To Liath's surprise, Hanna grinned suddenly. "Thancmar and I have crossed staves a few times. When we were younger, we sparred with staves to pass the time while we were out with the sheep."

Hathui did not look impressed. "When you've learned to handle a spear on horseback, you'll be able to boast. But an Eagle unhorsed in bad company is most likely a dead Eagle. What the sheep admired will do you little good here."

Hanna only laughed. "I have ridden hard for ten days and not given up, although the Lady alone knows the blisters I have, and where I have them! I can learn this, too, by Our Lord."

"And you'll still have to learn swordcraft, even so," continued Hathui as if Hanna hadn't spoken. The hawk-nosed woman still looked dour, but there was almost a smile on her face.

"Come inside," said Wolfhere.

Liath ducked under the lintel, built low as an added means of protection, and immediately sneezed. She wiped watering eyes and blinked as Wolfhere lit a brand and searched back into the far shadows of the chamber. Everything was neatly stored away here: sacks of onions and carrots; baskets of beans and peas and apples; jars of oil; wooden barrels of chops packed in lard. Something had gone rancid. Beyond the foodstores of the householder lay five chests closed with hasps of iron. One was inlaid with brass lions. This one Wolfhere opened. The hinges were well oiled, opening without a squeak.

Liath picked her way across to him, once stepping on something that squashed under her boot and sent up the sickly sweet scent of rotting fruit. A fly buzzed in her ear.

"Hathui notes you are adept at knife-fighting, which skill I suppose you picked up from your father Bernard as you traveled. I believe there is an old sword here, still serviceable. It was recovered from the fort."

"Which fort?" she asked, then knew what he meant: This fort, the old Dariyan fort built by order of Arki-kai Tangashuan seven hundred years ago, reckoning by the calendars she knew. Now of course it was known as Steleshame, a small estate under the authority of the freeholder Gisela that was also an official posting stop for the King's Eagles and thus under the king's protection rather than that of the local count.

Wolfhere lifted out a bundle wrapped in cloth and slowly unwrapped it. "It's shorter and blunter than the swords we are used to, but perhaps you will find it a good tool to use as you become accustomed to swordcraft. Hathui mentioned you wield a butcher's knife with great skill."

As he pulled the last layer of oilcloth off, she looked down into the chest and caught her breath. On yellowed linen lay a bowcase, in it rested an unstrung bow. The case was made of red leather. Worked into the leather was a portrait of a griffin, wings outspread. The creature held in its beak the head of a deer, but the tines of this deer's antlers were transformed into the heads of crested eagles, as if, being devoured, the deer was in the act of transforming into the predator that had killed it.

"May I?' she asked.

"What is it you see?" Wolfhere asked, but she had already reached in and drawn out the bowcase. "Ah," he said. "Barbarian work. Look at the shape of the bow."

The unstrung bow curved the wrong way. But Liath knew this kind of bow well enough. She turned the leather case over. No decoration adorned the other side of the bowcase, but there were ten symbols pressed in a circle into the leather, like runes. "Are these letters?" she asked. Wolfhere shrugged. "This is like the bow my father had. He said it came from the east. Da always said this kind of bow had the greatest range and the odd property of being effective from horseback. He taught me to use it, because when we were traveling—" She broke off and looked down at Wolfhere, who still knelt on the dirt floor, a short sword laid on oilcloth at his knees.

"You were traveling?" he asked quietly. "You and Bernard journeyed for a long time, Liath, and never stayed in any one place for too long."

"Until Heart's Rest," she said bitterly. Until she had begged him to stay just one more season, and then another, until what Da rightly feared had happened: His enemies caught up with them. Why not tell Wolfhere the truth? He had not been there when Da was killed. She was in his power now, in any case, if he wished her ill. "We were running. Always running."

"What from?"

His calmness only made her terrible anger—at losing Da, at all the years of fear and hiding that had come to nothing in the end—stand stark in contrast. "Maybe from you."

Wolfhere considered her words for a while, then shrugged his shoulders and rose, lifting the short sword in both hands. "It was said of Bernard that he roved to far and exotic places as a young frater. He was sent out into the dark lands to bring the Holy Word to those who live in night, but I know little of those journeys."

"Da *was* a frater?" Startled, she gaped at him.

"You did not know this, child?"

She shook her head.

"Where do you think he was educated? Do you not know his kin?"

Again, a mute no. She had wondered if Wolfhere knew her father's history, but she dared not ask—in case he asked questions of her in his turn—and she had not expected him to volunteer any information.

"Not a strong lineage but known to be of a family that came east in the time of Taillefer's empire, when the emperor set out to bring Wendar under his authority. That Taillefer failed is not to his discredit, for the Wendish tribes in those days were lawless and had not yet come into the Light of God. Bernard's people built estates in what were then wild lands even as King Henry sends freewomen and men into the lands beyond the River Eldar so he can extend the kingdom eastward, into what are still barbarian lands."

"I have kin living?" She had been alone for so long, first, in faint memories, in the villa with her mother and father and then on the long road with Da, that she could not imagine having kinsmen and women to whom she was bound by ties of blood and obligation.

"Most of that lineage went into the church, so they did not produce many children. In the succession crisis of the elder Arnulf they supported, alas, a claimant against Arnulf and thus lost the royal favor and a not insubstantial portion of their lands. Bernard has a cousin yet living, though the estates she administers are sadly diminished from what they were under their common grandmother. She has a son who rides with the King's Dragons, whom I imagine we shall soon see. Another son is a monk at St. Remigius Cloister. There was also a daughter, who surely is married by now."

"Where is this estate? How do you know all this?" And the question she could not ask: *Why did Da never tell me any of this?*

"Near Bodfeld. It has long been my business to know of your background, Liath." The way he said the words, sternly, almost mercilessly, made her shiver and pull a step back from him. "But I was your mother's sworn comrade in other pursuits, and thus I am bound to her in ways you do not yet understand."

"What ways?" she asked, not wanting to ask but unable not to ask. There was so much she wanted to know about her parents.

"Your mother was one of those who are called magi. And so, in a meager fashion, am I."

"Then—" She barely managed to get the words out through her choked throat. *You are deaf to magic, Liath,* Da always said. But she had burned the Rose into wood, without bearing flame in her hand. "Then why are you in the Eagles?"

"A good question. I was sworn into the Eagles at much the same age you are now, child. Once given the badge of an Eagle, you can never truly leave them. It is the same with those men and few women sworn into the service of the Dragons, where it is said they are more likely to die than retire from that service. So it is said with the king's guard of foot soldiers, the Lions, although it is also said of them that an old Lion is likely to be found at rest in his fields while his wife administers the work."

"Then how did you come to know my mother and father?"

"Our paths crossed. What do you know of magic, Liath?"

"N–n–nothing." But her tongue skipped betrayingly over the word.

"You must trust me, child."

"How can I trust you, or anyone?" Suddenly it poured out. She tightened her grip on the bowcase, felt the smooth wood of the bow pressing against her hip. "Da and I ran all those years, for nothing. I don't know who killed him. It might have been you, or people working for you. It might have been someone else, someone to whom you are opposed. But I can't know! Da only taught me a scholar's knowledge. He taught me little enough of the world. I didn't even know he had a cousin living, a home we might have fled to—" She broke off, seeing Wolfhere's expression, his wry smile, his small shake of the head.

"When Bernard left the church, he was disowned by his kin. He left for a shameful reason, for the love of a woman—your mother, Anne."

She flushed with the heat of her own shame. "Many in the church claim to devote themselves only to Our Lady and Lord and yet do not hold to their vows." She had to look away into the shadows. She began to tremble all over, and her hands went cold. *Hugh.*

"But they rarely leave the church. We all are dependent on the Grace and Mercy of Our Lady and Lord for forgiveness from our sins. A lapse may be forgiven, if one does penance. But Bernard turned his back on the church. As I understand it, he became involved with the Heresy of the Knife, and then he met Anne. To his kin, who count many holy women and men among their ancestors, he may as well have said he denied the teachings of the blessed Daisan and the Circle of Unity altogether."

"That isn't true!"

"It is often whispered of the mathematici, those who observe the heavens and chart their movements and their influence on the plane of this earth, that they worship not Our Lady and Lord but the daimones of the air whose knowledge is greater than ours and whose vision is keener, but who are as ancient as creation, lower than the angels, yet too proud to bow before Our Lady and Lord or to take their place within the Chamber of Light."

"But it isn't true of Da! That he believed any such thing. He was a good man. He prayed, as any other man might."

"I did not say it was true. I only stated what other people often believe of those who are adept in the ancient knowledge of magic. You would do well to remember that, Liath."

"So Da always said," she murmured. "That people believed what they wanted to, whether it was truth or not." She blinked back tears, wiped her nose with the back of a hand. "But I am deaf to magic, Master Wolfhere. So it does not matter what I know."

"Does it not?" he asked softly.

"Are you not finished yet in there?" demanded Hathui from the door, peering in and turning her head to look toward the burning brand which Wolfhere had braced in an iron stand. "Poor Hanna is done for and needs to rest her bruises. Can you bring Liath out for me?"

Wolfhere rose, holding the short sword, and Liath followed him outside. She leaned the bowcase against the stone wall and took the sword, testing its balance. It was heavy, but not so heavy that she could not train herself to hold its weight.

"A good weapon," said Hathui, coming over to examine the sword. "Forged for killing, not to be pretty for some noble lord who has others to do his fighting for him."

"You are not of noble birth, Hathui?" Hanna asked from where she leaned against the wall of the tower. She looked tired but was clearly unwilling to sit down.

Hathui snorted. "Did you think I was? My mother is a freeholder, beholden to no lord. She and her sister and brother traveled east many years ago. That was when the younger Arnulf first offered land to those willing to cross the Eldar and build estates in heathen lands. My aunt is dead now. She was killed by Quman raiders. But my mother and uncle still work those fields. They have gotten more land under cultivation than any of the other freeholders in our valley. What is this?" Distracted, she rubbed at the blade where it was bound into the hilt. The sheen of her sweat on the iron blade made letters stand out for a moment.

" 'This good sword is the friend of Lucian, son of Livia,' " read Liath before she knew she meant to. Had this sword belonged to the same Lucian who had cut into stone his love for a red-haired woman? Then she realized the others were looking at her, surprised, all but Wolfhere. The three children who had been watching crept closer, staring at the strange sight of an exotic-looking young woman not in deacon's gown who could read—and read such ancient words. Liath thought at once of Wolfhere's words: "*I only stated what other people often believe.*"

"I did not know you were church educated," said Manfred, so startled by this revelation that he actually spoke.

Hathui coughed abruptly and moved to chase the children farther back. "Church education won't save your life when the heathen attack you." She beckoned to Liath to step out into the stable yard, which Mistress Gisela kept almost as well swept as Mistress Birta kept her inn yard. "Bear in mind, girl," Hathui added, perhaps sympathetically, "that a cherished weapon is the best kind. Now stand against me. I'll run trials against you."

Hathui was quicker, stronger, taller, and had by far the better reach with her broadsword, but after a few passes she announced herself satisfied that Liath would in time become proficient enough with the short sword to defend herself. Liath was breathing hard, sweating, and had a terrible bruise on her rump from a blow delivered by the flat of Hathui's blade.

"Manfred will cut some wooden staves to the length of the weapons you've chosen," added Hathui as Liath and Hanna exchanged grimaces, "and every day when we stop to rest the horses, we will practice with those."

Liath limped back to the wall, nudging chickens out of her way with her feet, handed the sword to Hanna, and drew the bow out of the bowcase. Hand on the grip, she turned the bow slowly, examining it, then pulled it close. She could discern three layers, a wood core with two strips of horn glued to the belly and sinew layered along the back. The back had been painted crimson; many fine lines and cracks disturbed the sheen of paint. The tips of the bow wore bronze caps, molded into the shape of griffins' heads. These beaks, a thin gash, held either end of the bow string. The bow looked sound.

Nestled in the bowcase she found a silk bowstring. She licked her fingers, then pulled the string through them to smooth down any frayed ends. Finally she braced the bow between right knee and left thigh and, with a grunt, strung it.

She tested the draw by sighting toward the palisade gate. And saw suddenly, on the inside, that the innermost layer of horn was carved all along its length with tiny salamanders twined together like interlinking rings, their eyes flecked with blue paint. Woven into them were ancient letters. She read them falling like the flow of water down the belly of the bow:

I am called Seeker of Hearts.

Hathui had gone over to the water trough to sluice water down her hair and face. Dripping, she returned and motioned Hanna to go do the same, but stopped to examine the bow as Liath lowered it.

"That's a Quman bowcase," said Hathui, not admiringly. "I recognize its type. We took enough of them off dead Quman soldiers. Then we'd scrape them free of the taint of their heathen hands, all that ugly decoration. The bow must be of their make as well. Their bows were shorter than ours and curved backwards. But they were deadly all the same. And their arrows poisoned, like as not. Savages!'' She spit on the ground.

Certainly they resembled old Dariyan letters, but these letters were altered in subtle ways from the letters carved into stone in the old fort or scratched into the hilt of her new sword, from the letters written in old crumbling scrolls she had seen in the scriptoria of monasteries where she and Da had taken shelter as they traveled.

Seeker of Hearts. The words came to Liath's lips, but she could not speak them out loud. No one else seemed to have noticed the strange delicate carvings. The back of the bow was unmarked except for the paint; only on the inner curve, facing the archer, did the bow speak. So did Liath also keep silence. For as Da always said: *"Words spoken rashly can be used as weapons against you,"* and also, many times, *"Keep silence, Liath! To speak out loud your secrets is like to a merchant opening a chest of jewels to every passerby on the road and thereby announcing his wealth to bandits."*

Like *The Book of Secrets.* She did not glance toward the stables, where their riding gear was stowed. Surely Wolfhere suspected she carried the book with her; he had seen Hanna with it. He had never mentioned it, never asked any questions about it, and to Liath, this in itself was suspicious.

"Where did it come from?" she asked, indicating the bow.

"I haven't seen this bow before," said Wolfhere, "but it has been five years since I've ridden through Steleshame."

"I was here two years ago," said Hathui. "I remember nothing like. Manfred?"

He shook his head and extended a hand to take the bow. Liath hesitated an instant, then forced herself to give it to him. He turned it this way and that, examining it, took an arrow from his own quiver, and sent a shot at the palisade. The dull thunk of the arrow burying itself in a log sent the chickens scattering and set the dogs to barking and the children to shrieking.

He grunted, looking satisfied, and gave the bow back to Liath. He said nothing about the carvings.

Mistress Gisela emerged from the longhouse. Her court—the womenfolk of her holding—trailed after her. Liath had seen men and boys and other women at work in the village and fields surrounding Steleshame when they had ridden in that morning. Gisela was a stout woman with the bold gleam of authority in her blue eyes. She was holding a spoon still wet with broth. The smell made Liath's mouth water. Behind her, half grown girls dropped spindles down, then pulled them up again, spinning thread from flax.

"I hope, Master Wolfhere," said Gisela sternly, "that you do not intend to have sport within these walls. Sword practice I do not frown on, but archery belongs outside. My chickens and these children are very valuable to me."

"I beg your pardon, Mistress," said Wolfhere. He gestured toward the bow and case. "Do you recall when this came to Steleshame?"

She frowned. "I haven't seen it before, but you'd best ask the blacksmith. He knows more of which weapons come in and which go out."

That Steleshame had its own blacksmith was a mark of the prestige granted it by the king's protection. But the blacksmith, a short, burly man stained almost as dark as Liath by years of working in fire and ash, did not recognize the bow or the case, nor did he recall when or how the weapon had come to Steleshame. Indeed, no one did, and Gisela soon chased the children back to their chores and the women back to their weaving and spinning.

She presided over the midday meal of roasted chickens, leeks, bread, cheese, honeyed mead, and apples. When the meal was finished and all had toasted St. Bonfilia, whose day this was, Gisela allowed her niece, a handsome young woman with pale blonde hair, to bring forward the two new cloaks.

"Spun last winter," she said, "of Andallan wool from the Pyrani Mountains. The wool from that region is particularly strong and warm. My cousin's husband brought me four bags of it from Medemelacha."

"Medemelacha is a long way from here," said Wolfhere.

"He travels by ship every other year," explained Gisela, not without pride. "We have a prosperous holding, enough to feed the king should his progress ever ride this way!"

"Be careful what you wish for," muttered Hanna. "I can only imagine what it must take to feed all the people who travel with the king."

"It has been six years since the king visited Gent," said Wolfhere calmly, not seeming to scorn Mistress Gisela's boast. "And with the current troubles we have heard of, perhaps you will get your wish."

She nodded briskly. "The Dragons rode through not twelve days ago, as I told you. But they rode in great haste, and I could do no more than give them provisions while the blacksmith checked over their armor and gear. Then they were on their way."

As Gisela spoke, Liath noticed to her surprise that the niece blushed a bright red and lifted the bundled cloaks up to conceal her face.

Mistress Gisela clucked, shaking her head. "Ai, yes, I hope the Dragons can drive the Eika away. Gent is only three days' ride from here, if the rains haven't been bad. It is out through Gent that my cousin's husband travels, down the Veser River and out by the northern sea west along the coast of Wendar and then west and south along the coast of Varre and farther south yet to Salia, to the emporia there. If the Eika continue to raid, or if they invade, as some say they have this spring, then—*well!*" She threw up her hands in distress, but Liath suspected that Mistress Gisela relished having an audience to appreciate her family's importance and far-ranging connections. "How will we trade by sea if the river is in the hands of savages?"

"How indeed. Your hospitality has been most gracious, Mistress." Wolfhere now rose, and Gisela rose with him. "But we must ride."

At this command, the others rose as well, moving away from the table.

"Come forward, child," said Gisela curtly. The niece, hesitant and still blushing, presented the cloaks to Wolfhere. He took them, turned, and handed one to Hanna and one to Liath.

"This is very fine work!" said Hanna, taken quite by surprise.

"I thank you," said Gisela. "You will certainly hear as you travel that Steleshame is renowned for its weaving. I only keep in the weaving room those of the women who are in good health and particularly adept at the craft. The others I sell or put out into the fields with the men. And any of my relatives' daughters who show skill in needlework are fostered here with me until they marry."

Liath merely smiled, stroking the thick gray cloak. It was bordered with a scarlet trim, a length of cloth as deep a red as blood, which had been embroidered with gold eagles from top to bottom. She edged past Wolfhere to stand beside the niece.

"Is this your needlework?" she asked. The pretty girl nodded, flushing again. "It is very fine. I will always think of you when I wear it."

The niece smiled tentatively, then spoke in a voice so muted Liath could barely hear her: "You will see the Dragons?"

"I suppose we will."

"Perhaps you could ask—" She broke off, looked mortified, then finished in a murmur. "No. He won't be thinking of me."

"I beg your pardon?"

But the others had already moved outside, and Liath had to follow them. Boys from the stable had saddled new horses. Hathui was already mounted, looking impatient to be gone.

"I can ride well enough," Hanna was saying. "But I worry that Liath isn't strong enough yet." She glanced toward the door, saw that Liath had emerged. "You know it's true!" she added snappishly.

"I'm strong enough." Liath did *not* want to stay on at Steleshame while the others rode to Gent. She wanted to see the Dragons, to see the soldiers whom Ivar had dreamed of fighting with—not that he ever would now. She wanted to meet Da's cousin's son. *A kinsman*.

And anyway, she couldn't leave Hanna or Wolfhere. They were all that protected her from Hugh. If she stayed in one place, vulnerable, Hugh would catch up with her. He would *know*.

"I think Liath is strong enough," said Wolfhere mildly, "though she has recovered even more quickly than I expected. Now." He crossed to them and, with a sign, showed them that he expected them to stand still. With a bronze clasp he closed the new cloak about Hanna's shoulder, then did the same for Liath. His hands were firm and decisive.

"This cloak marks you as riding under the protection of the Eagles," he said, then gestured to them that they should mount and be ready to ride.

"The Eagles also carry the King's seal as a badge," said Hanna, who like her mother always pointed out these essential details.

"You have not yet earned the right to carry this badge." He touched a hand to the brass badge he wore pinned to his tunic, at his throat. "You must learn the precepts which govern the conduct of an Eagle. And you must swear to abide by them." He paused, glancing toward Hathui and Manfred. Both of them carried the seal, stamped into circular badges. But though they were younger and obviously newer to the service of the Eagles than Wolfhere, the badges they wore did not look newly made, not like Hanna and Liath's new cloaks.

From out in the fields, Liath heard singing. The gate stood open, and now two boys drove two squealing and grunting young pigs in toward the small hut by the far corner of the compound, where they would be slaughtered for the night's feast. Hathui, unable to wait any longer, urged her horse forward, heading out the gate.

"And lastly," Wolfhere said, "no man or woman is given the Eagle's badge until she has seen a comrade die. Death is ever at hand. We do not truly become Eagles until we accept and understand that we are willing to pay that price for our service and our king."

2

TEN days after leaving Steleshame, Liath rode with Wolfhere and the small party of Eagles down into the bottomlands to the west of Gent pushing against a tide of refugees. They came on carts, on foot, leading donkeys and cows or carrying crates that confined chickens and geese. They hauled children and chests and sacks of withered turnips and jars cushioned by baskets of rye and barley. The old road was littered with their cast-off baggage, those who had managed to leave their homes with any of their possessions and not merely their lives. The damp ground was churned to mud by their passage. Where the forest retreated from the road, trails beaten down through grass appeared as the refugees made new paths in their haste to flee.

Wolfhere spotted a lord astride a horse, dressed in a good linen tunic and attended by two wagons, five servants, and ten fine cows. He left the others and drew the lord aside. Their conversation was brief, and the lord and his party left at once, continuing west. When Wolfhere returned, he looked graver than ever.

"Are these the townsfolk of Gent?" Liath asked, staring. There were not hordes of people, but the flow was steady: She had never seen so many people on the move before. Always, she and Da, the occasional merchant who plied his wares between one town and the next, and the fraters, clerics, and messengers about their business for church and king were the only travelers on the roads.

Thinking of fraters she thought of Hugh, shut her eyes against the thought of him. Felt sick, for an instant, and stopped herself from looking behind to see if he was dogging their trail. Somehow, somewhere, he knew where she was; she could feel it.

"Nay, child. These are the farming folk from the estates and villages surrounding the city. Gent has walls." Wolfhere's voice steadied her.

"Then why haven't these people fled inside the city?"

Wolfhere shook his head. "That I can't say. But if they have not, then I fear it bodes ill for those inside Gent."

On they rode, and people walking west called out to them:

"Do you bring word from the King?"

"What of Count Hildegard? Has she come yet? They say she has gathered her kinsmen together and rides to save the city."

"When will the Eika leave? When will it be safe to return to my farm?"

"Is King Henry coming himself with an army?" This from an old woman, her skirts spattered with fresh mud.

"Are the Dragons not here?" Wolfhere called back.

"They are so few, and the Eika so many."

"How many?" he asked, but she dragged her cart onward and her six children ran behind, faces pinched with fear.

After midday there was no one except stragglers. They came finally upon a deacon, walking like any common woman, her white robe and tabard flecked with mud and grit. Her servants led two mules, one laden with the massive silver Circle which had once adorned the Hearth, the other with a hastily folded altar cloth embroidered with gold thread and with the chalice and holy books, all saved from the church she had abandoned.

"Go no farther, honored ones," she said to Wolfhere, signaling her servants to halt. "Turn back while you are still safe. Tell the king that Gent is besieged."

"Why have you not fled into Gent?" Wolfhere asked.

"They are laying waste to the countryside all around." She was, Liath thought, impossibly calm in the face of such disaster. "They are everywhere, good messenger. Gent is surrounded. I minister to the lands and estates west of Gent, so I was able to flee once I saw all my parishioners safely gone. East of the city and the river I cannot say, except that smoke has risen for twenty days, as if many fires are burning."

Hathui inhaled deeply, scenting. "Fresh fires and old," she said. "And dust, as of a great host moving." She swung her head to look west, then back to view the eastern horizon. "You see," she said to Liath and Hanna, "the sky and clouds have a different color. Mark this well, and learn." She inhaled again. "And another smell, like air too long shut within stone walls. Strange."

She made a gesture toward Manfred. The young man rode forward, past the deacon and her servants, and took up a station some fifty strides ahead on a rise, surveying farther toward the east. They could not yet see the cathedral tower above the trees.

Liath could only smell the heavy scent of rain coming from the north, off the distant sea. There, clouds lowered gray-black over the land, though patches of blue still showed through to the south.

"The storm comes from the sea," said the deacon, brushing mud off the sleeve of her robe and then sighing, as if she had just that moment realized it was a pointless endeavor. "I must go, good man. I carry with me a fingerbone of St. Perpetua. Such a holy relic must not fall into the hands of savages."

"Go, then," said Wolfhere.

"And you, with my blessing." The deacon granted each one of them the sign of blessing before she trudged on, her nervous servants glad to be moving again.

Wolfhere's frown was, if possible, deeper than before. They had not ridden more than two hundred strides farther on when Manfred's horse, in the lead, shied suddenly and tried to bolt back. Both Wolfhere and Hathui drew their swords the next instant, while Manfred fought his gelding. The other horses caught the scent and began to sidestep, ears flicking back. Liath braced herself on her stirrups and looped her reins loosely around the pommel. She pulled her bow from the bowcase and nocked an arrow.

The road looped past a knoll of trees which formed part of the eastern horizon, fields half grown with rye lying below within the broad curve of a stream that flowed toward the east and the Veser River.

"That's where they'll be," said Hathui, nodding toward the knoll.

Too calmly, Liath thought.

"Ai, Lady, I'm terrified," whispered Hanna, pressing her horse up beside Liath. She had loosed her spear from its sling and now rested it against the top of her right boot.

"Out into the fields," said Wolfhere. "In the open, we can outrun them."

They turned left and started out across the fields. Green rye grass bent under the hooves of their horses and sprang up behind. Liath kept looking over her shoulder toward the knoll, one hand on her reins, one gripping bow and arrow. A misting rain began to filter down, wetting her hair, but she dared not pull her hood up for fear she would not be able to see as well. At once, as the wind shifted, she caught the scent that had spooked the horses.

It had a dry taste to it, what one might taste in a heat made dry by dust and wind. It smelled like stones heated until they cracked or the musk of a cave inhabited by dragons.

"Hai!" shouted Hathui.

There! Out of the trees came three iron-gray dogs—the biggest, ugliest dogs Liath had ever seen. Five Eika loped after them. The Eika held spears and suddenly as with one thought they threw their weapons. Most skidded harmlessly over the rye, but one spear stuck, quivering, in the ground at the feet of Hanna's horse; the animal bolted back, rearing. Hanna fell from the saddle and hit the ground hard.

Hathui was off her horse in an instant.

"Liath!" shouted Wolfhere. "Ride for the city!"

From out here, with the knoll no longer blocking their view, Liath could now see the distant tower of Gent's cathedral, gray stone rising toward gray clouds and beyond them, eastward, ribbons of darker smoke.

Hanna scrambled to her feet, then cried out, holding her knee. Manfred had already galloped past Hathui, sword held high, heading to cut off the Eika. The creatures had halved the distance between them already. The dogs broke forward, muzzles to the wind.

I can't go.

Liath knew it in that instant, knew that she could not leave until Hanna was safe. Without Hanna . . .

"Without Hanna I might as well be dead," she said aloud. Hanna was the only person she could really trust. "My only protector," she said, and lifted her bow and nocked the arrow and drew.

Sighted on one of the dogs. Staring so, she saw it clearly. Saliva dripped from its jaws and from its long, dangling tongue. It was truly monstrous, with great fangs, a hollow belly, and lean, long flanks.

She shot.

The dog tumbled, yipping with terrible shrieking cries. Its two companions crashed into it and to her horror began to tear into its flesh.

This altercation, slowing the Eika, gave her time to nock and draw again. She caught the Eika who ran out in front in her sight down the length of the arrow, had an instant to register the ice-white glare of its braided hair. And shot.

The Eika dropped like a stone, her arrow buried in its bronze chest. Was it armor, or skin? She stared, horrified, and could not act. Her hands groped blindly toward the quiver for another arrow. A terrible wailing rose as the Eika paused to sniff at their dead comrade, but first one, then the second and last the third leaped up again, charging for Manfred. The fourth Eika laid into the dogs and beat them back from the still-twitching corpse.

Another dozen Eika and perhaps four more dogs emerged from the knoll of the trees. Their keening, their high-pitched barking, hurt her ears, though she could not tell which sound came from which creature. They darted down the hill toward the five Eagles.

"Liath!" Wolfhere pulled up beside her. "Go!" He made a gesture with one hand, something meaningless that she did not understand. For an instant she felt the merest tugging at her heart: *I should go. I am meant to ride to Gent.* Then shrugged it off, found that her hands had grasped an arrow. She nocked it and drew.

This Eika, too, had that startling white hair, bleached like bone. His torso wore a garish pattern of painted colors, blue, yellow, and white, and beneath the paint she caught the suggestion of copper, as if his skin was sheeted by a thin coating of metal. She shot.

The Eika went down, arrow sunk in its chest.

The other three had reached Manfred, who thrust and slashed with his spear. Hathui shoved Hanna up onto her horse and grasped the reins of her own. Thrown spears rained in on them, and Hathui staggered back, her left thigh torn open. Wolfhere pressed forward to aid Manfred. Hanna extended her hand to Hathui, but Hathui gripped her saddle's pommel and threw herself up over the back of her own mount.

Liath nocked an arrow and drew. There! An ax slanted toward Manfred's back. She loosed the arrow.

An Eika staggered back and fell, ax dropping out of its limp hand. Only two were left—except for the dozen racing down on them from the hill, and the murderous dogs. A dog leaped in and nipped at the hindquarters of Manfred's horse; the gelding lashed out, kicking hard. Manfred grabbed at his saddle's pommel, almost losing his grip on his spear.

It was all too quick to register anything except her own fear and their utterly inhuman faces, the long lope, faster than any human man might run, the hands bristling with white claws like sharpened bone, and their strange horrible skin more like scaled metal than flesh.

Too quick to register anything except that there were too many

Eika and not enough Eagles. She nocked and drew and shot, but her hands were shaking so badly the arrow went wild, skidding over the ground twenty paces from the skirmish flurrying around Manfred. There was no time; in twenty more breaths the rest would be on him.

A horn.

It rang clear and steady. As if to herald its sounding, the drizzle let up and the sun broke through the clouds. Liath heard horses.

There! Breaking around the knoll from the east came six riders in mail and heavy iron helmets trimmed with brass, their bright gold tabards marked with a menacing black dragon, black cloaks thrown back over their shoulders. The two Eika harassing Manfred scuttled back and retreated toward their comrades. From the knoll came a shrill, loud whistle. Liath winced and almost dropped her bow. One of the dogs broke away toward the hill. The other hesitated, then rushed the horsemen, who cut it down almost casually.

The Dragons cantered up and pulled in beside Wolfhere, who had ridden ahead to meet them. Liath came up behind him, Hathui and Hanna behind her, Manfred still away in the field, watchful.

"Eagles!" cried the lead rider. He did not remove his helmet; Liath could just make out blue eyes, blond beard, and a grim expression behind the nasal and cheek guards of the helmet. "That whistle will be a signal for reinforcements. We'll escort you into the city."

"There's a deacon," said Wolfhere, gesturing west. "She carries a holy relic and only left her church after all her people were safely gone. She and the relic must be protected."

The Dragon nodded stiffly. "We will escort her west as far as we are able."

"What of Gent?" asked Wolfhere.

"Fifty-two of the Eika ships we have counted already, and more have come since we arrived here. They want Gent's bridges thrown down so they may raid inland at their whim, along the Veser. This, the mayor of Gent refuses."

"Will there be a siege?"

"There already is. Their earthworks line half the eastern shore."

Wolfhere turned. "Hathui, take Hanna and ride with these Dragons. You will follow the good deacon as far as Steleshame and leave her there. Then you will ride south, to deliver this grievous news to King Henry."

Blood wept from the wound on Hathui's leg. Her lips were set thin against the pain, and her reply was curt. "Yes."

That fast, she turned away, and Hanna, with a desperate glance toward Liath, turned after her. Across the field, in the shadow of the knoll, the Eika waited, standing like stone statues and staring toward their foes.

The Dragon lifted up his helmet and set a wood whistle, caught on a silver chain around his neck, to his lips. He blew, hard. Liath heard nothing. The Eika dogs barked wildly and were kicked into silence. The Dragon blew once more, though no sound issued, then tucked the whistle back under his mail and pulled his helmet down to cover his face.

"Ride for Gent," he said to Wolfhere. "Ride hard. There will be more Eika, many more, and soon. And never forget: Their dogs are worse than they are." He reined his horse past Wolfhere and Liath, and with his five comrades behind him headed west, following after Hathui and Hanna. More than half of the waiting Eika broke left, setting off at a comfortable lope, as if they meant to trail the two Eagles and their Dragon escort all the way to the Abyss. Hanna shifted one last time in her saddle, lifting a hand, dropping it when she saw the Eika who pursued them.

Wolfhere spoke gruffly. "Ride! Come, Manfred!"

Liath followed. She could not even risk looking back. Her stomach had clenched into a knot and it felt as heavy as her heart. Not even a chance to say farewell! She blinked back tears.

"No sign," said Manfred, who searched the fields and copses and straggle of burned and ruined outbuildings that separated them from the first distant bridge, the river's edge with its low line of trees, and beyond it the walls of Gent.

They urged their horses into a canter. A hundred questions raced through Liath's mind: Did the Eika have no weapons except spears? No armor? Was their skin their armor? If they were not human, and not of elvish kind, then what were they? And of what breed were their dogs, who looked more like four-legged devils than like dogs? Why did the Eika not pursue them? Ai, Lady, would they catch up with Hanna and the others? Would Hanna win free?

The rain started again. Her horse began to have trouble in the wet ground, and they had to slow down. They cut back toward the road, hoping to find better footing. Her back stayed dry, under the cloak, but already she felt trickles of cold rain dribbling down her

neck and chest. Was Hanna also hampered by the rain? Would the
Eika catch up to them? Or were the savages as reluctant to engage
with the Dragons as they had appeared to be, back by the knoll?

Wolfhere cursed under his breath.

She looked, followed his gaze, and gasped aloud. Striding down
from the north, the heavy gray clouds lowering behind them, came
at least one hundred Eika, hair gleaming that strange, sickly white.
They were armed with spears and axes and with round shields
painted with fearsome red serpents coiled together over yellow or
black or striped backgrounds. Their dogs massed, a restless, low
hedge, before them.

Her horse needed no urging. It found the road, a firmer surface
than the fields, and began to gallop toward the bridge. She looked
back to see Manfred and Wolfhere just coming up onto the packed
earth and rock of the road. Manfred lifted his spear upright and
twisted it to unfurl the banner of the Eagles: an eagle with wings
outspread carrying an arrow in its beak and a scroll in one talon.
But the Eika were closer to the river. Already they ran at a steady
lope that ate up the ground between them and their intended vic-
tims. Even Liath could see that the Eika would reach the bridge before the three Eagles could get there. She reined in her horse,
wheeling around, but behind, back by the now distant knoll, another group of Eika had gathered, more than there had been before.
Manfred passed her and kept riding, seeming oblivious to their inevitable fate.

Wolfhere came up beside her and slapped her horse on the rump.
She started forward again, following him. To what purpose? *At
least*, she thought bitterly, *if Hanna survives she will be invested fully
into the Eagles, a right earned by my death.*

Wolfhere had sheathed his sword; he drew his left arm, hand
clenched, across his chest, and then made a sharp sweeping gesture
outward, toward the advancing Eika.

There came a flash, a glittering of light like a fire's light seen from
inside a dark room. Liath blinked; the horses staggered, whinnying
in terror, and she clung helplessly as her gelding bucked once before
calming. Manfred, a hand flung over his eyes, was almost thrown.

The Eika faltered, but only from a lope to a trot. A moment later,
far away, a rumbling sounded that ended in a sharp clap as loud as
a peal of thunder.

"Lady's Blood," swore Wolfhere, "there's sorcery at work among the Eika. Liath, you must get in to the city, whatever happens to us. Do not hesitate or falter. When you win free, if I am dead, take yourself to the convent of St. Valeria and there throw yourself on the mercy of the Convent Mother. She will give you safekeeping.''

The outrunners of the Eika force had reached the bridge, and they gathered, forming a wall with their shields. She was still too far away to see the walls clearly, to see if anyone moved there, if anyone had noticed their plight. Manfred settled his horse. He and Wolfhere exchanged a glance, and then the young man pressed his horse forward, galloping hard for the line.

"Straight after him!" cried Wolfhere. "And mind you not what you see.''

But she saw nothing, though she felt a tingling on her back and a slap of cold air against her cheeks. Manfred's head and shoulders were abruptly invested with the tiny winkings of a thousand firebugs, but the sight faded against the red serpent shields, the Eika setting their trap and awaiting their prey, raising their spears.

She saw behind the Eika soldiers the stone and timber bridge, the gulf of air beneath, where the steep banks fell away to the river's edge, and beyond, so close now that she *could* see figures standing along the parapet, the walls of Gent.

Without warning, the gates of Gent mawed open with a horrible screeching din.

And out from the city rode Dragons.

They charged at full tilt, lances lowered, teardrop shields as metal-gray as the lowering clouds, all blended together with the steady rain. The only colors were the red serpents and yellow shields of the Eika, the gold tabards of the Dragons as bright as if the sun had emerged, and the brass fittings on their helms like the masks of war.

The Dragons hit with an impact Liath felt as a shuddering in the air. A few broke all the way through and, rather than turning to aid their fellows now struggling with sword and ax against the Eika who had not gone down, they kept coming, heading for the three Eagles. Behind them, the second wave of Dragons hit the disintegrating Eika line. They did not bear lances but rather struck with swords and heavy axes. More Eika swarmed up from the river's banks, and the melee swirled off the bridge and spread out into the fields on either side, a terrible ringing clash. Dogs leaped and ripped at Dragons and horses alike.

Six Dragons pounded up and wheeled round, forming into a loose wedge.

"Behind us," shouted the man who was surely their leader. The broach which clasped his cloak at his right shoulder sparkled with jewels. A golden torque encircled his neck: the mark of a prince of the royal line. His gaze touched on Liath.

She stared, though she could see nothing of his face except his eyes, as green as jade. His helmet was not fitted with brass decoration, like those worn by his soldiers. It was inlaid with gold to form the aspect of a dragon, terrible to look on and yet, together with the other Dragons, all iron and gold and black, beautiful to look on.

Then they were moving back toward the fight. The two soldiers in front of her lowered their lances as Eika sprinted out into the roadway to block them. The weight of their horses drove them through. An Eika sprang up from the roadway and flung itself forward, ax raised high, toward the unarmored Wolfhere. The prince leaned right and cut across Wolfhere's path, swung so strong a blow he cleaved the creature's head from its neck. But more Eika came, and more yet, swarming toward the prince like bees drawn to honey or wild dogs to the hope of a fresh kill. The fighting pressed close all around them, and Liath hunched down, mumbling silent prayers. Manfred stuck one with his spear and then, as another climbed closer and the horses got bogged down in bodies and in the melee, lost it as the Eika fell away off the raised roadway.

They were almost at the bridge, but more and yet more Eika scrambled up, even up and over the stone braces, and formed a thick, living wall.

Dogs poured through their ranks, breaking through the line to spring at the Dragons and the Eagles in the midst. They were horrid beasts, slavering, mad with rage and utterly fearless.

One lunged, barreling against Manfred's horse, then heading straight for *her*. In that instant, she saw its eyes. They were the color of burning yellow.

Too close to shoot. It sprang.

The prince turned halfway round in his saddle and struck it down, across the back, with a single stroke. It crumpled, and her horse jumped to clear its body. That fast. Too fast.

Eika swarmed everywhere, closing, tightening the noose.

With loud cries a new sally of Dragons hit the line of Eika from behind, riding down on them from out of the gates. Eika fell and were trampled or were carried off by the weight of the charge. The Dragons, still in formation, broke ranks, splitting to either side as the Eagles and their escort pounded through. Stone drummed beneath the horses' hooves; then a shift, a slight jarring drop, and they clattered over the metal-trimmed drawbridge. They rode into the shelter of the walls.

The rain stopped, started again as they came out from under the guardhouse into the open space that fronted the gates. The remains of market stalls—some half burned, others in disarray, but all empty—stood in haphazard lines in the great square.

Behind a great keening and wailing arose. Together with the sudden pounding of hooves and a great chorus of shouts, it deafened Liath. She heard no commands, only saw the prince peel away from the escort and ride back out through the gates. Dragons raced through, four abreast, coming back within the walls, and with a winding of gears the gates began to close.

She battled her way through to a vantage point: On the bridge the last dozen Dragons fought a rearguard action to retreat as the Eika hounded them. One soldier had been thrown over a horse. Another lay limp over his mount's neck. But beyond, on the stone and timber span, in the trampled field, she saw no gold tabard, no soldier left lying in the field. The dogs had begun to rip into the Eika dead.

Many of the Dragons were already racing up the stairs to the parapet; the city militiamen rained arrows down onto the bridge from above. The gates swung closed behind the last rider: the prince. He kicked his mount forward just as spears, aimed at his back, darkened the air. The gates slammed shut to a chorus of howls and the peppering smacks of spears hitting harmlessly against the metal-plated gates. A new grinding sounded: the men of Gent were drawing up the drawbridge.

The prince's horse stumbled, dropped, and threw him, stumbled again, and went down, kicking hard, trying to get up. He jumped to his feet, pulled off his helm and tossed it to the ground with an astonishing lack of regard for its rich decoration. He grabbed the horse's bridle and yanked its head down onto the ground. Then, while he cursed loud and long, four of his men ran forward to examine the horse. A spear protruded from its belly, sunk deep. Blood spilled onto the packed earth, mixing with rain. The horse thrashed feebly, then stilled, its side rising and falling in shallow breaths.

From outside, Liath heard the last howls and frustrated wails of the Eika as they finally retreated. The men stationed along the parapet jeered after them.

The prince's hand fell to his belt. He drew a knife and cut the horse's throat. Its blood poured onto his feet, staining his boots red, but still he knelt there, silent now. His black hair was plastered down on his skull from the rain. He had strange smooth skin, bronze-colored, and a striking face that betrayed by its lineaments that his mother was truly not of human kin.

Strangest of all, he had no beard nor any trace of beard.

He looked up, sought, and found with his gaze a man dressed in a rich tunic, head shielded from the rain by a capacious scarlet cloak held like a canopy over him by four servants.

"Butcher it and salt it," the prince said, standing up and turning his back on the dead animal. He had a hoarse tenor; it carried with the authority of a man who expects obedience. "Or so I suggest, my lord mayor."

"Eat *horse* meat?" The man could not seem to find a place to rest his eyes: on the prince, on the dead horse, on the Dragons calmly drawing the spear from the body, on the last gush of blood and entrails.

"It will seem like a delicacy come winter, if the Eika lay in a true siege." The prince saw Wolfhere, gestured to him, and stalked away. A Dragon grabbed the prince's helm from the mud and hurried after him.

Wolfhere quickly handed his horse's reins to Manfred and, without comment, followed.

3

LIATH dismounted and huddled close to Manfred, shaking from the aftermath of battle as the rush of energy left her.

"I've never seen a man without a beard before," she whispered. "I mean, except a churchman, of course."

Manfred ran a finger along his own close-cropped beard. "Eika don't have beards."

She laughed nervously. Her hands trembled and she thought her heart would never stop racing. "I didn't notice. Did Hanna and Hathui escape, do you think?"

He shrugged.

"What do we do now?"

They took the horses to the barracks where the Dragons had stabled their own horses, rubbed them down, and gave them oats; the activity calmed her. She slung her bedroll and saddlebags over her shoulder and followed Manfred up steep stairs that led to the long attic room above the stables where the Dragons had settled in. Fresh straw covered the plank floor, and bedrolls lay neatly lined up along the walls. The smell of horse and stall was pervasive but not overpowering. Men lounged at their ease, dicing, carving wood, oiling or polishing their gear, making small talk. They glanced at the two Eagles, curious, but made no attempt to speak to them.

Was one of these men her kinsman? She tried to examine their faces surreptitiously, looking for some resemblance to Da.

Manfred led her to the far end of the long, low room. There, shutters opened to admit the gloomy light of afternoon. The rain was coming down harder now, but it was already stuffy inside the loft, sticky like summer heat. The prince and Wolfhere sat on bales of hay, facing each other across a table. The prince had a chess set carved of ivory laid out in front of him, eight squares wide, eight across. He toyed with the pieces as he and Wolfhere spoke, picking them up, setting them down in new places: the eight Lions, the Castles, Eagles, and Dragons and—protected by the others—the Biscop and Regnant.

Behind the prince, the only woman besides Liath in the loft sat with the prince's helmet on her lap. She polished the helmet with a rag. She wore the tabard of the Dragons, and her arms were muscular, her jaw scarred by many small white lines, and her nose looked as if it had been broken and healed wrong.

Manfred hunkered down onto his haunches, prepared for a long wait. Liath knelt beside him. Now and again a cooling mist of water touched her face from the rain outside. Straw tickled her hands. Her nose itched.

"I judge the city can withstand a siege. But my Dragons alone cannot lift the siege, not with the numbers of Eika who have invested Gent. We have no news from Count Hildegard, whether she or her brother Lord Dietrich mean to lead an army to aid us. And you say now the king will not bring an army."

"I don't know what King Henry intends, Prince Sanglant. But he may not be able to bring an army here, even if he wishes to."

The prince picked up a Dragon and placed it between two Castles, as if trapping it there. This close, Liath could study the line of his jaw. He had either just shaved or else he did not grow a beard. But then how could he truly be called a man?

"I have heard these rumors, that Lady Sabella means to gather adherents and ride against King Henry. But she swore before the Biscop of Mainni eight years ago never to trouble the king with her false claims again."

"So she did," agreed Wolfhere, "but the Biscop of Mainni is rumored to be among her counselors now. And all three dukes of Varre as well as five counts from Varre have refused to appear before King Henry on his progress."

"This is certainly grave news, but what am I to tell the people of Gent? Given enough time, the Eika army outside will burn and batter down Gent's bridges, and when they have done that, they will have free passage up the Veser whether we will it or no. If they sail far enough up the Veser, then it will scarcely matter what the Lady Sabella demands, since the heart of Wendar itself will be at risk."

"You would counsel your father to consider this the greater threat? But always in other years, Prince Sanglant, the Eika have raided and left, content with whatever gold and slaves they could carry away in their ships."

The prince glanced out the window, although only rain and the timbered roof of the mayor's palace were visible. Distantly, Liath heard drums. "This is not 'other years.' This is not a raid. Already the envoy for the Eika general has refused Mayor Werner's offer of ten chests of gold and one hundred slaves as payment for them to leave."

Wolfhere chuckled suddenly. "I hear two things in your words I can scarcely credit. One is that a man sits as mayor in a city. The other is that the Eika have a general. They are bandits, nothing more, with perhaps a captain to lead each ship, if we can even dignify their packs with such a word. More like the strongest beast who keeps the others obedient by threat of claw and teeth."

Sanglant turned his head to look directly at Liath. She squirmed, horribly uncomfortable; his eyes were so bright and his features so strange and sharp. He examined her with obvious curiosity for so long that she felt the stares of his men, behind her, on her back, as if they, too, wanted to know what interested their captain. For so long that Wolfhere finally glanced over to see what the prince was looking at.

What crossed Wolfhere's expression Liath had never expected to see: He was angry.

Sanglant smiled slowly at her, perhaps with invitation. When he smiled, he had a sudden bright charm, so powerful she felt herself blush. Beside her, Manfred muttered something inaudible under his breath. Sanglant grunted, almost laughing, as if in response. Then, with a shrug and a stretch of his shoulders, he looked back at Wolfhere. The older man's expression was now entirely bland.

"Mayor Werner is an interesting man, overly fond of his family's riches. Is it not said Our Lord judges the worth of his earthly sons by the measure of their generosity to their companions and to the poor? So King Henry would say. Werner's mother was mayor of the town before him, and he was her only surviving son. And, it is said, always her favorite, though certainly the staff of authority should have gone to one of her daughters, his half sisters." He said these words with a trace of bitterness, and yet he also seemed to be laughing at himself. "So far the people of Gent have found no reason to be displeased with his stewardship and thus throw him out in favor of a woman whose authority is, as you say, more likely to receive Our Lady's Blessing. As for the other—" He put out a hand, and the woman handed him his helmet, now bright, the gold face of the dragon like cold fire burning on the hard surface of iron. As he spoke, serious now, he ran his hands over the helmet, tracing the delicate gold work with long, dark fingers.

"There is an intelligence out there which directs these Eika. I have felt it. It knows of me just as I know of it, and we are bent, each of us, on the other's destruction."

"A human man, do you think?"

"I think not. And who better than I to know, my friend. Is that not right?"

Wolfhere bowed his head in acknowledgment.

"But whether it is an Eika unlike in mind and craft to the others, or some different creature entirely, I cannot say. I have fought King Henry's wars for eight years now, since I came of age and was given my Dragons to be captain of. As is my birthright, the child born to prove the man worthy of the throne of Wendar." His tone was as cold as a stinging winter's wind. "But the others were ordinary wars, raids by the Quman horsemen, Duke Conrad's rebellion, Lady Sabella's revolt, which I saw the end of."

"Her *first* revolt," said Wolfhere quietly.

"Rumors do not a revolt make," said Sanglant, equally quietly, then raised a hand to forestall Wolfhere's comment. "But I trust your judgment in these matters, Wolfhere, if you say she is again fomenting rebellion against the king. You have served the throne of Wendar faithfully. Or so I have always heard."

"As have you," said Wolfhere, baring his teeth. "Or so I have always heard."

There was a hiss, an intake of breath, from those of the Dragons close enough to hear the comment. But Sanglant smiled his charming smile, tossed the chess piece carved into the likeness of a King's Dragon up toward the rafters, then grabbed it out of the air as it fell. The movement made the helm roll off his lap, and the scar-jawed woman caught it before it struck the floor.

The prince opened his hand and displayed the chess piece. Its ivory gleam, oiled from much handling, set off the bronze tone of his skin. *Half human*, Liath thought, and then was ashamed of herself: Was she not also different from the rest, with her skin always burned so brown? But at least slaves who worked all day in the fields were burned as brown as she was at summer's end, if they were not burned to blisters. And Da had told her of people living in lands far to the south, where the sun was hotter and brighter, who had skin burned darker even than hers. Was it then better to be fully human but a slave or a heathen, rather than a half-human prince who could never be fully trusted?

I have already been a slave. She wrung her fingers through each other. Her back prickled, as if thinking of those days meant Hugh was watching her. *He is watching me.* Like the *intelligence* that waited, out among the Eika, dueling with Prince Sanglant, so Liath knew Hugh waited, always aware of her no matter how far away she might be from him. He waited only until she came again into his grasp.

I am still a slave, because I fear him. Tears burned her eyes and she ducked her head down so no one would see. But Manfred's hand brushed her leg, as if to reassure her. She swallowed, gathered courage, and looked up. No one seemed to have noticed her lapse.

"Like this chess piece," said Sanglant, "I exist only to be moved by another man's hand."

Wolfhere smiled thinly. He looked very old, suddenly, as he lifted the piece out of the prince's hand. "You are young to be so old in wisdom, Sanglant."

"You flatter me. I am but four and twenty years of age, by the calendars of my *father's* people." This was spoken tartly, almost defiantly.

"In the ruins of the old empire there is another calendar," said Wolfhere, "one that marks its time by the journey of bright Somorhas, who is both evening and morning star, and by the ascension of the seven stars that make up the seven jewels in the Crown of Stars. A child reaches for that Crown. Who knows what will happen when the Crown of Stars crowns the heavens?"

Sanglant stood up stiffly, regally, like a king about to pronounce judgment. "I have never known my mother, Wolfhere. Nor has she appeared to me, in mist or in night or by any enchantment I know of. She abandoned me when I was not yet two months old. If she left me here, if she allowed my father to get me on her, for her own purposes, for some plot spun and set into motion by her people, then I am ignorant of it and of them and of my place in their plans. Indeed, there is little enough trace of the Lost Ones in these lands, though I have heard that in Alba they are more likely to walk abroad in the deep forests. You have said these things to me before, or hinted of them, and I am tired of it and I am tired of your insinuations. I am a soldier. I am captain of the King's Dragons, as is my right, as was the right of those who served as captain before me,

Conrad the Dragon, Charles Wolfskin, and the left-handed Arnulf, all of us bastards of the reigning sovereign. In that service I have left behind me fields covered with blood, so I might prove myself worthy of the name my mother gave me at birth. I have watched my own men die as they fought to protect me and to protect the king's interests. I have killed the king's enemies without mercy and spared none I could find. Hear me now: I serve the king and no one else. Believe in your plots and plans and in the secret workings of the heavens, if you will. But leave me out of them."

He grabbed his helmet, tucked it under his arm, and walked the length of the attic and down the stairs. Only two Dragons followed him: the scar-jawed woman and a blond man who walked with a limp.

When they had gone, it was silent except for the sound of rain and the sloppy clop of ox hooves on the wet street outside. Then there was a rustling, a sigh as of let-out breath, and the men went back to their tasks.

Wolfhere set down the chess piece. Manfred rose, brushed straw from his tunic, and moved to stand beside the old Eagle, who looked out the window for a long time. Then Wolfhere also rose. Liath scrambled up and, keeping her head down, followed Wolfhere and Manfred to the stairs and down to the stables below. She felt as if every man there watched her pass. She wanted desperately to ask about her kinsman, but after the accusations Sanglant had made, she dared not.

She was, for the moment, afraid to ask Wolfhere anything, for fear she would not be able to resist asking him about the ancient calendar he had spoken of. The Crown of Stars she knew; it was a cluster of seven bright stars just outside the grasp of the constellation known as the Child, Second House in the zodiac, the world dragon that bound the heavens. She knew many of the names given by the ancient Dariyan mathematici to the stars, names different from those in common use in these days. But that the old Dariyans had marked time by a calendar markedly different from the one she knew . . . that knowledge Da had never taught her, if indeed he even knew it.

But the stars move in a fixed pattern. Given time and *The Book of Secrets* and paper to make the difficult calculations on, she could work out when next the cluster of stars known as the Crown of Stars would "crown the heavens." She wasn't sure what he meant by the phrase, but surely it had to do with a star reaching the zenith, the point on the sphere of the fixed stars where that star was seen as directly above the observer.

She kept silence as they walked through the stables. How many days had it been since she had been able to observe the heavens? During spring, as Da always said, the Lady clouds the skies so we remember to keep our eyes on the sowing. How many days since Wolfhere had freed her from Hugh? One day short of a month.

She shuddered. It was as if Hugh was speaking, braced outside the walls of the invisible city that protected her heart. Like the Eika who had thrown up earthworks against Gent, he besieged her, only she could see no end.

Thirty days since you were stolen from me.

"Are you well?" asked Wolfhere.

His tone was so gentle she started. They had reached a door. Manfred was about to dash outside; he hung back, looking at her with concern. He had kind blue eyes and a solemn face, not handsome, not ugly, just steady and quiet. A good comrade.

"A little hot." She draped her cloak over one arm and shifted her saddlebags over her shoulder. Manfred darted out into the courtyard, running hard for the doors that led into the mayor's palace. She pulled a corner of her cloak over her hair and started out after him. Wolfhere pulled her back.

"No need," he said, "to bring your gear. We'll be sleeping in the stables."

She had to turn around and go back, of course. She dared not tell him she had the book. *He already knows you are educated as a mathematici*, she told herself as she slunk along, hoping no one would notice her. But it was quiet in the stables. The Dragons were either upstairs, taking their ease, or elsewhere, on guard or out in the city. But what if Wolfhere simply took the book away from her? There would be nothing she could do to stop him or to get it back, once it was out of her hands.

Next to their horses was an empty stall, well padded with straw. Manfred and Wolfhere had left their gear here, neatly stowed, leaving room for them to sleep. She heaped straw up, shoved the saddlebags underneath, frowned. Too obvious. Could not help but reach inside the leather bag and feel the cold smooth grain of the leather binding, the raised letters along the spine. She traced the letters, reading them with her fingers, and felt like the dry wings of a moth the parchment and paper leaves of the three books bound inside the cover.

"What happened to Sturm and his company?" asked a deep voice. "They never came in from patrol."

"You didn't hear that part? They stayed outside the walls to escort the two wounded Eagles and a deacon conveying a holy relic to a place of safety."

"No, I didn't hear." This spoken a bit peevishly. "I was just coming up. Unlike you, I fought a few Eika in this melee and had a bit of cleaning up to do."

The other man snorted. "You mean you let a few get some blows past your guard. I'm as clean as a saint, and the more likely to be blessed by Our Lady with a willing helpmeet for my efforts."

"Hah! These Gentish women are as friendly as wild boars. Do you think he'll pursue the pretty young Eagle?"

It took her a heartbeat to realize that they spoke of her.

"What? After arguing with the old master? I think not."

"How can you say so? He plucked the young Villam heiress unbruised from the vine, and that after she was betrothed and her father had warned him off twice."

She saw, faintly, their shadows drawn on the wall by the weak light shining through the stable doors.

"Nay, lad, you've come from outside the world of the court and don't know its ways yet. What is said and what is done can be two different things. What the heiress and old Villam wanted was marriage to the prince, but King Henry can never allow the prince to marry. It makes the boy look legitimate, does it not? So words were said in public and a betrothal sworn to another family, and the girl got what she wanted and, so they say, a child to boot that was born after her marriage to another man."

"And the prince? Did he get what he wanted?"

"Who can say?" replied the other man, who had the higher voice and the more confidence. "The prince does what his father the king tells him to do. I doubt he minded *that* engagement."

"He *did* look," blustered the first speaker. "At the young Eagle. She's a fetching piece, all bright and warm. Why shouldn't he pursue it? I didn't like the way the old master spoke to him."

"Nor did I. There is no better man than our prince."

The other grunted angry agreement.

"But there is a world outside the Dragons, lad, which is easy

enough to forget as a young hatchling like you. And harder work
it is to know the rules for those battles than for the ones we fight
against King Henry's enemies. So. Listen to what I say. Never anger
an Eagle. Never sleep with a woman if the price, in whatever coin,
is higher than what the pleasure was worth. Now. In payment for
those words of advice you can oil my harness tonight while I go out
hunting wild boars."

"Oil your harness!"

The other man moved. Liath shrank against the wall, tight in a
corner, one hand still on the book, and thought hard of shadows
and silence and invisibility. The two Dragons walked past the stall
without noticing her, the younger man still complaining.

A moment later she heard Wolfhere calling her name. She shoved
the saddlebags under straw and set her saddle and bedroll over
them, then hurried out. Manfred had returned; his cloak was wet
but the rest of him was reasonably dry. He actually smiled, seeing
her. Conscious of his gaze, embarrassed by it, she picked at her hair,
sure there must be straw caught in it. If only Hanna were here with
her. If only she were sure Hanna was still alive.

"There you are," said Wolfhere. "Mayor Werner asks us to sit
down with him at this night's feast. He honors us—or has no new
and better guests to entertain."

"Will the prince be there?"

Wolfhere raised his eyebrows. "I suppose he will. Mayor Werner
would not dare *not* to invite him, even if they do not get along.
Sanglant is too much a lover of good food and drink to stay away."

And it was good food, an astonishing feast for a city under siege:
a side of beef braised with spices Liath had never tasted before; a
pudding; apple tarts; two roasted pigs; white bread; and a great
deal of wine. Liath followed Wolfhere's lead and drank sparingly,
cutting her wine with water. The prince sat at the other end of the
table from her and matched Mayor Werner cup for cup.

Manfred looked disgusted.

"What's wrong?" she whispered to him.

"Come winter townsfolk will starve for want of these scraps."

It was the longest string of words she had ever heard him speak
at one time. "Surely they have their own food stores."

"Enough for a long siege?"

"Do you think the town will be besieged for that long? Surely Count Hildegard will lift the siege."

"If she can."

The eating and drinking went on for what seemed to Liath an interminable time. An old man recited poetry in what he evidently conceived to be the style of the ancient Dariyans; Liath had read a copy of Virgilia's *Heleniad* and cringed to hear him. But there were other poets who sang songs of their own devising that were more pleasing, songs about heroes of days gone by and episodes from the great epic, *The Gold of the Hevelli*. Musicians played on lyres and zithers. There was a juggler, and two girls who balanced and did tricks on a long rope held taut by two men.

But all in all, it was hot, smoky, noisy, and dull.

She excused herself, pleading a need for the privy. After she used it, she did not feel like venturing back inside. It had stopped raining, even cleared partially, so half the sky was stars. Liath clung to the shadows, breathing in the night air, the solitude; it was quiet except for the muted noise of the feast from the great hall and the distant tremor of drums. A quartet of women walked by, laughing merrily, headed for the kitchens, trays resting against their hips.

"A man's a man because he grows a beard," said one.

"But fraters and monks have no beards."

"To make themselves more like women and thus more pleasing to Our Lady! They pledge their bodies and their honor to the church, by cutting off their beards. It is the mark of their service."

"Is that what you say, then? A man's no true man who has no beard and is not a churchman?"

"Well, my dear Fastrada," said one who had been silent up until now, "that may well be true, but I speak truly when I say the prince is a man like any other. Or so it seemed to me."

They all laughed heartily and demanded more details, which she refused to give them.

Liath slunk across the courtyard, praying she would not be noticed, and sneaked into the stables. No one had disturbed the empty stall; all was as she had left it. She went back outside.

The mayor's palace stood on a rise near the eastern bank of the river, itself ringed by a smaller stockade of posts. Climbing the ladder that led to the small parapet, she found herself looking over the city of Gent, the eastern shoreline, and the dark line of the Veser River. The moon was almost at the quarter, waxing; it lent a pale glamour to the night. There were no guards. She supposed those who might once have stood watch here at the palace walls now were out on the city walls. East she saw the fires of the Eika camp stretching both north and south along the river as far as the eye could see. Gent was darker, only a faint gleam of light from the great hall and the distant bobbing torches that marked watchmen on their rounds in the city and guards posted along the city wall. Two dark lines, one east, one west, broke the line of the river: the two bridges that led to the broad island on which lay the city of Gent.

She was alone.

She stared up, thinking of Wolfhere's words. The cluster of stars known as the Crown, toward which the constellation known as the Child reached, had passed out of the sky around the beginning of the year, at the spring equinox. The Lion was fading. Now the Dragon and the Serpent ruled the Houses of Night. The red planet— Jedu, the Angel of War—still shone in the house of the Archer, the bright quester. But soon—within seven days—red Jedu would pass into the house of the Unicorn: ambition joined to will. That foretold a time of advancement, when people with a strong will could take advantage of the power of their will and their clear sense of ambition to get ahead in the world.

Yet Da had always told her to be skeptical of those astrologia who claimed the ability to foretell the future from the movements and positions of the planets along the fixed sphere of the stars. There was a real power to be had in the knowledge of the heavens, but it was not this. She had long since memorized these teachings— though she did not have the ability to use them herself.

"The movement of the wandering stars in the heavens is one of the markers by which the magi and mathematici know the lines through which they can draw down power from the heavens to wield on the earth. By this means they may also distinguish those of the daimones of the upper air who, with their greater knowledge of the universe, are most susceptible at any given alignment of the heavens to coercion or persuasion."

From below she heard low voices, startling her out of her reverie. Footsteps sounded, moving softly up the ladder to the parapet walk. She retreated into shadows, drew her cloak more tightly around her as if it were also a shadow, transforming her into just one more element of night and stillness and darkness.

"It was not a debate of my choosing," said the first as he came up onto the parapet walk and leaned out to look east. It was the prince. She recognized both his voice, which had that odd scrape in it, and his bearing. He was quite tall and had the strong shoulders and confident posture of a man who has trained long and well with weapons.

With him, to her surprise, was Wolfhere. They spoke with apparent cordiality despite their argument in the barracks earlier. "But it affects you nevertheless. I have heard it said more than once that King Henry refuses to let Sapientia leave on her progress, as is her right should he choose her over Theophanu. She is almost twenty years old."

"By which age King Henry had already been named as heir by right of fertility, of which I am the result." Sanglant's tone was flat, almost mocking.

"Then you must speak."

"It is not my place to speak. King Henry has counselors. He has companions, men and women of his own age who have their own birthright, their lands and estates."

"Surely these great magnates cannot counsel the king without some prejudice toward their own advancement."

"Do we not all counsel in such fashion, Lord Wolfhere, not unaware of what would best benefit ourselves? Save for the rare few, who are wise without any selfish intent."

"And who are those, in your opinion, Prince Sanglant?"

"Of them all, I would only trust the cleric, Rosvita of Korvei. She has an elegant bearing that sits well with her affability and benevolence. She is both humble and patient, and she is very learned. All this makes her a wise counselor."

He shifted, turning slightly. Liath pressed back farther into the shadows, round wood posts hard against her back. But there was not enough light from moon and stars for them to see her.

Finally, the prince sighed. "What do you want of me, Wolfhere? Some seek my favor. Others speak ill of me in the hope of turning my father against me. You hint of terrible plots devised by my mother's people and suggest that I conceal from my father and the rest of you my part in those plots. But I am not book-educated like you are. I cannot puzzle such things out from hints and fragments of words and phrases in languages I cannot read. It is said you were invested as an Eagle the year the elder Arnulf died and left Wendar and Varre to the younger Arnulf and Queen Berengaria. But it is also said of you, my friend, that the year Queen Berengaria died in childbed you were taken into the confidence of those who secretly learn the ways of the magi, the forbidden arts. And that it is for this reason, despite your wisdom and experience, that you do not walk among those who name themselves counselors to King Henry."

"An Eagle serves the sovereign by carrying messages and decrees and by observing and reporting back what was seen. Not by giving counsel. We are eyes and ears, Prince Sanglant, nothing more."

"And yet you chance to bring the most beautiful young Eagles into your nest, or so *I* observe." He sounded as if he meant to provoke the older man.

Wolfhere did not reply at once. The drums that beat incessantly in the Eika camp changed rhythm, adding a hiccuping beat in the middle of what had been a straight pattern of four.

Wolfhere spoke so lightly the words resonated like a hammer blow. "Stay away from her, Sanglant. She is not meant for you. Nor are you meant for your father's throne."

Sanglant laughed. "Does anyone expect me to live that long? I am captain of the Dragons, after all. Of all the captains, only Conrad the Dragon served his king for more years than I have so far served mine."

"You can influence King Henry's decision."

"Can I?"

Wolfhere appeared incapable of losing his temper, no matter how annoying Sanglant meant to be. "There is not one soul who moves in the orbit of the king's progress who cannot see he prefers you to his three legitimate children."

"You want me to say I do not want the throne."

"I am not alone in this wish. We must settle the affairs of the kingdom before worse catastrophes befall us because the king and his court are not united."

Sanglant turned his back on Wolfhere and leaned even farther out over the parapet, as if to catch sight of the distant Eika camp or to reach out and grasp the stars in his hands. But he did not look likely to fall. "I refuse, as I always have and as I always mean to do. You must speak to the king on this matter. I am only the King's Dragon, his obedient son and servant. As I always have been."

"That is your only answer?"

"That is my only answer."

Wolfhere bent slightly at the waist, although Sanglant could not see the gesture. "Then I will leave you to your meditations." If he was vexed, he did not show it in his posture or his tone.

"When do you leave?" asked Sanglant.

"My comrade Hathui even now rides to King Henry with news of the siege. We will abide here a while to see what happens, and to see if I can search out this intelligence among the Eika you speak of."

"You trust my instincts?"

"I would be a fool not to."

"That is praise from you, Wolfhere." They seemed, more than anything, like two soldiers sparring.

"As it was meant to be. I bid you good night."

"As I fully plan it to be."

The intent was unmistakable. Wolfhere moved his head as if looking around the parapet walk, the grounds, and the long roof of the palace. Liath stayed as still as ever, sure she had made no sound. Wolfhere did not notice her. He moved down the ladder and soon even the faint noise of his footsteps was lost to her.

There was a long moment of silence, except for the distant drums. She prayed Sanglant would move soon.

Suddenly he said in a low voice, to the empty air: "You've been here all along."

She did not move, dared not breathe.

He pushed back from the edge and walked with perfect confidence in the blackness down the walk to the corner, where she hid. Because she could see so well in the dark, she saw him lift a hand and beckon to her to rise. She dared not disobey.

Standing, coming forward, she halted a safe arm's length from him. "How did you know I was here?"

"I have keen hearing. Don't you know what is said of my mother's people?" His tone was so bitter she suddenly realized that much of what he had said to Wolfhere was born out of a deep resentment she could neither place nor understand. "That they are the spawn of fallen angels, those known as the daimones of the upper air, who mated with human women. That like their unsightly fathers they have the gift of hearing even the unspoken wishes of a man's heart, and then taunting him with them."

"But that isn't what the blessed Daisan taught," she blurted out, and was aghast she spoke so freely.

"What did the blessed Daisan teach?" She could not tell if he spoke with true curiosity or if he was merely humoring her for his own reasons.

The prince is a man like any other," the servingwoman had said. He moved a step forward toward her, and had she been able to, she would have bolted and run away. But she could not.

Not knowing what else to do, she talked fast. "He taught that elves were born of fire and light. For all things arose out of the four elements, fire and light and wind and water. It is only when darkness rose out of the depths that the universe became tainted with evil. So if elves are tainted by the darkness it is only because all things are that exist in this world. Only in the Chamber of Light has all darkness been burned away by the fiery truth of the gaze of Our Lady and Lord."

Because she could see so well in the dark, she saw him blink several times as if at a loss for words. He moved again, coming close enough for her to feel the heat of his body. "So. I am to stay away from you, am I?" He bent, as if to kiss her. Thought better of it and instead touched his own lips with a finger as if seal himself and her to silence. "It's too bad I have always been an obedient son."

He left her there, again alone, walked away and descended into the courtyard, vanishing into the night.

Hugh. Hugh had seen them. Hugh would know.

Ai, Lady. It wasn't Hugh she was thinking of. It was desire. She was bitterly ashamed of what stirred in her own heart. What was wrong with her, that such a feeling could come to life in her breast after the winter she had endured?

Out of a lake has grown an island. The city rises on the island, ringed by seven walls. At the height sits a tower of stone. In that tower are five doors, each locked by the same brass key. But in the door that opens to the north there lies the shade of a secret door that leads to the wilderness. It is bright in the wilderness now, warm and inviting, in those trackless lands where she has thrown away the key. Only she can walk safely there.

But it is never safe.

She sank down onto her knees, head bowed and resting in her hands. She must not be tempted.

The king's son. Sworn to the Dragons, and forbidden. Caught in the intrigues of the court. It was too dangerous to even think of such a man—as if such a man could ever think of her with an honest heart. She must put all such thoughts away.

She must stay hidden in every way she could. She must be careful, because she had no one she could trust, no one but Hanna, who was gone from her now, perhaps not even alive—surely not that—and who had no power in the world in any case.

"Ai, Lady, protect me, your daughter," she whispered. Yet, as bitter as her shame was, she could not stop thinking about the prince. Desire is like a flame, a torch burning in the night. A traveler in darkness cannot help but be drawn toward it.

Liath shut her eyes. She saw torches along the walls in her mind's eye, saw fires burning all along the shore as if they were the temptation that ate away at her heart. Hugh would see them and, seeing, use them to find her.

In her mind's eye she put them out. In the wild lands beyond the city she had built in her mind the sun ceased shining. It was, like a cool spring evening, soothing on her frozen heart. She was still safe; she could make herself safe by not feeling.

On the eastern shore, though she could not see it, fires vanished, snuffed out although there was no onset of rain. Along the walls of Gent a third of the torches blew out, though there was no wind.

X
THE SIN OF PRIDE

1

FIRES burn, thick smoke rancid with the scent of human fear. He stops, licks the air. In the tangled smell of charred wood, dead men, burning thatch, and dust kicked high by the trampling of many feet, he finds the familiar dry musky scent of his own kind—though it is not marked with the peculiar piquancy of his own litter, his own tribe, his home shore.

Beyond, the sea surges below a distant headland, soughing up more softly along the strand where the clean wooden boats lie beached. They smell of seawater and barnacles and the good strong scent of oak flavored with ash and willow.

Shouting and crashing come from the wood beyond. He darts back into a thicket. Some of the soft ones, the humans, are running; their terror and pain are sweet on his tongue, tasted from the air. But he lets them pass. Two are children, carried by a strong mother whose tears smell like the salt of the sea. He senses a new weakness in himself, brought on by his contact with Halane, Son of Henri. He thinks of Old-Mother, who is already beginning the slow trek up the fjall where she will take her place with the WiseMothers. She speaks of the soft moth-

ers with scorn because they cannot bear litters with the strength and numbers of the RockChildren. But Halane had a mother such as this. He lets them run by untouched before he crawls out from the thicket and starts his descent toward his cousins.

Will these cousins greet him with peace in their hearts? Or will they set their dogs on him?

He shrugs off these doubts. OldMother's scent is strong on him. She promised him much before her joints began to stiffen and she passed the knife of decision to the new YoungMother. Even if these warriors are not true cousins, they will not harm one who bears this sign of favor. Nor will any dogs, of any pack, eat one who has been marked by the scent of an OldMother.

Still, though, he carries his new weakness with him as he descends through the forest. The weakness rests within him, but he also conceives of the wooden circle which hangs at his chest as the physical sign of that weakness, a tangible reminder. Other humans flee past, but he avoids them. This new weakness has taught him a lesson: The soft ones are not true people, of course, but they are a kind of people. People can talk. It is the lesson the WiseMothers teach. It is what they whispered to him when he was a half-grown pup and dared venture up the mountainside to the sacred place tended by the SwiftDaughters to see whether the WiseMothers would speak to him or else kill him for his presumption.

"The knife and the tongue are equally strong weapons."

The WiseMothers had spoken twice, and he had always remembered.

"Face your weakness and it can become your strength."

He steps out of the wood and into a landscape torn by wind and sea spray. The soft ones' houses are all burning now. The scent of fire mingles with the pungent smell of sea and sand and shore. The dogs bark, smelling him. Alerted, a Watcher sees him and whistles to question him. He whistles back, sees the sign given for free passage. With new confidence, he strides down to the sea.

Alain woke, cold and shivering, on the ground. He did not stir. The horrible images of his dream swelled in his mind. He still smelled the sea, and the fire burning. He still heard the screams of children and the grunts of men falling beneath the spears and axes of Eika savages. He still saw the monstrous dogs, their hollow bellies and tireless rage, their yellow eyes shooting off sparks. Always they panted, tongues hanging out, saliva—or worse things—dribbling down their fangs.

He shuddered and shifted. Rage and Sorrow pressed against him on either side. Their solid presence made him feel safe.

Unlike the foot soldiers who marched in Lavastine's train, he now had a decent bed to lie on: the carpet that was always thrown down in front of the entrance to Count Lavastine's tent. Every night after watering and feeding the other hounds and sending them in to sleep beside their master, Alain bedded down here. Though it was absurd—he had a spear and a knife and was barely trained in either—he thought of himself as protecting the count despite the fact that two guards stood watch at all times. But no one had demanded he move. Most likely no one dared to, not when he moved with hounds always at his side and Count Lavastine remained oblivious to all but his goal of aiding Lady Sabella.

Rage whimpered and stirred in her sleep. Sorrow was the quieter sleeper, but he would wake instantly if Alain moved. And now, of course, thinking of this, Alain simply had to get up.

Yesterday Count Lavastine and his army had caught up with Lady Sabella. The impressive retinue Alain had first seen at Lavas holding almost two months ago was now a formidable army. Rodulf, Duke of Varingia, and a number of counts and lords had joined with Sabella. Lavastine's arrival with one hundred and twenty more fighting men had been a convenient excuse for celebration. The feasting had lasted long into the night, and Alain had drunk more than he should of the ale passed around to the common soldiers. Indeed, his mouth was dry and sour-tasting, and he had a headache. And he really, really had to urinate.

One of the guards was asleep. The other yawned, disinterested, as Alain got to his feet. Sorrow woke at once as Alain ventured into the sparse cover of wood that lay twenty paces behind the camp. The hound followed, whining softly.

Alain relieved himself. The moon had already set, but a thin line of red rimmed the eastern sky. From the far side of camp he heard the sound, muted by distance, of clerics and fraters singing the service of Lauds, first light. As he turned to move out of the trees, Sorrow closed his jaws over Alain's wrist and tugged. Alain tripped over undergrowth.

"What's that?" A harsh whisper sounded from deeper in the wood.

Sorrow leaned so hard on Alain that the young man fell to hands and knees. Now he was partially screened by low bushes. He peered out through their branches to see two figures carrying between them a bulky weight. They had stopped to rest.

"Hush," said the other.

Alain was silent. Sorrow was silent. The two mysterious men were silent. The clerics and fraters sang, distant voices blending in the chill air as the sky faded from black to gray.

"Nothing," said one of the men. "We'd best hurry before camp wakes." He hoisted the *thing* they carried up higher against his chest and they moved away through the curve of the wood toward the eastern end of camp.

They were carrying a body.

Alain's heart went cold. Sorrow licked his hand. Together they crept after them, Alain keeping one hand on the nape of the hound's neck. To reassure himself, he slipped a hand inside his tunic to touch the rose, still alive, still in bloom. The prick of its thorns gave him courage.

He could not tell if the body was man or woman, alive or dead. They carried it all the way round to the outskirts of Lady Sabella's encampment, where the kitchen tent was set up, and then even past that and past the livestock, to where a shrouded cage rested fifty paces away from any tent or fire. A man, face hooded, arms bound in heavy leather wrappings, met them.

They spoke in low voices. At first Alain could not hear; no *man* would have been able to. But an Eika . . .

Alain strained, stilling himself until he heard Sorrow's soft panting, heard each individual voice, some true, some off, as the clerics sang the final cadences of Lauds. He heard the scraping of claws against wood, the clack of twigs in the dawn breeze, heard even the loam as it crushed down beneath his fingers.

". . . will have no questions being asked."

"Brought him from the estate by Autun. Them are the Biscop of Autun's lands, and so they be the false king's lands. So does Biscop Antonia say, that false king's men are fair game."

The keeper grunted. "As long as we get no trouble of it. You must have walked all day, then, from the lands outlying Autun. Is he still alive?"

"Seems to be breathing. I gave him the drink, just as much as you said. Hasn't woken or eyes fluttered once. What's it for? Make him taste better?"

The keeper's voice radiated his distaste. "No need to make him suffer more."

"You feel mercy for the false king's man?"

"I do my job. Now stand back."

"We can't watch?"

The keeper snorted. "Watch all you wish. You'll regret it."

Some tone in his voice made the other two back away. But Alain knew suddenly he could not stand by, not this time.

He jumped up. Sorrow nipped at his backside but missed, and Alain crashed out of the undergrowth.

"Stop!" he cried.

The two men grabbed him at once and wrenched his arms behind his back. He struggled briefly, but together they were much stronger than he was alone. A thud sounded, inside the cage, as if something had thrown itself against the slats.

"We could throw this one in," said one of the men. "He's fresher and younger."

Sorrow bounded, growling, out of the trees. The two men instantly let go of Alain and backed off, drawing long knives.

"That's one of Count Lavastine's hounds," said the keeper nervously. "Do naught to harm it."

Sorrow sat himself down, leaning against Alain's legs.

"Don't do it," pleaded Alain. "It isn't merciful. It isn't right."

This close, Alain saw the keeper had but a stump of one hand; his face was scored with old deep gashes on forehead and jaw, one of which had torn out his right eye, now healed as a mass of white scar tissue. A bronze Circle of Unity hung at his chest. "It must be fed, boy. Fed with fresh blood. Or do you volunteer to throw yourself in?"

Alain shuddered. But the memory of Lackling's terrified mewling and sobbing was still strong in him. *His* fault. *His* to atone. He thought suddenly of Frater Agius and his dangerous, heretical words: that the blessed Daisan offered himself as a sacrifice in order to redeem us from our sins; that by sacrifice we make ourselves worthy. Driven by this memory, by the intensity which pervaded Agius's speech and prayer, Alain took a step toward the cage.

Sorrow butted Alain so hard from behind he fell onto his knees. Sorrow got a good grip on his arm, tight enough that his teeth pressed painfully into flesh but not so hard that they drew blood. The two men sidled closer, knives up. Sorrow growled but did not let go.

"There's one as disagrees with you," said the keeper with rough amusement. He bent to the body that lay limp at his feet, hooked his elbows underneath the sleeping man's armpits. Despite his lost hand, the keeper was a strong man; he dragged the body easily to the cage, fussed with some kind of attachment, and rolled up a small barred door not more than the breadth of a big man's shoulders in both height and width.

"Let me go!" said Alain fiercely. Heedless of the pain, he wrenched his arm out of Sorrow's grip and flung himself forward. He would stop this murder. He must.

The keeper jerked up his head and then, the movement an extension of his surprise, yanked the shroud half off the cage, revealing—

The two men behind Alain cried out in fear before their exclamations froze in their throats.

The great eye slewed round—for it had only one eye; the other was a mass of putrefaction, worms writhing in infected flesh, maggots crawling out from the pus to wriggle down its beaklike snout. Its gaze struck him like the sword of God.

He could not move.

But he could stare, throat choked with horror. With pity.

It was a sickly creature, however monstrous its appearance. Like a huge bird, it had two taloned feet and two wings, molting now. Feathers and waste littered the cage's floor. Like a dragon, it had a sinuous tail and a featherless head, scaled to an iron gleam, but with a yellowish-green cast beneath, the sign of a creature that is no longer healthy. It heaved its great body awkwardly across the cage toward its meal.

The keeper began to shove the body in, but suddenly the body shuddered and a tiny gasp escaped the unconscious man, the gasp of a man coming awake out of—or into—a nightmare. The huge foot scraped at the body, sunk its talons into flesh, and yanked it inside the cage.

Mercifully, the keeper threw the shroud back over the bars. Alain heard a muffled moan and then the sounds of an animal feeding voraciously. The grip of the *guivre's* eye let him go. He fell forward, shivering convulsively, and began to weep. But he still did not move, though now he could. What he had seen was too horrible.

The keeper closed the tiny door and chained it shut. He peered at Alain with his one good eye. "You'd best go with them, lad. Biscop will want to see you."

Biscop Antonia. It was she, of course, who was behind all this. Frater Agius had refused to confront her in the ruins that night or in Lavas holding on the following day. Now, it seemed, Alain would have no choice but to do so—or else, with Sorrow, fight a foolish skirmish he could not win.

The knowledge left him with a sudden feeling of peace as he was led away, Sorrow padding obediently at his heels.

That feeling of peace, of resignation to God's will, seeped away as he waited in the antechamber of the tent while outside the biscop led the service of Prime, the celebration of sunrise and a new day. All the noble ladies and lords stood in attendance.

But when Biscop Antonia returned, still resplendent in her white vestments trimmed with gold, her biscop's staff held confidently in her right hand, and listened to the whispered explanation of one of her clerics, she merely said:

"This one again? Brother Heribert, take a message to Count Lavastine that the boy will march with my retinue for the time being. Lavastine will make no objection."

The cleric left. Alain knelt outside, miserable and frightened, while the tent came down and was packed into a wagon. Sorrow refused to budge from his side. No one spoke to him, only glanced at him sidelong, but two guards remained at his side.

Just as all was ready, the nobles mounting their fine horses, a commotion eddied through their ranks. A black shape darted free from behind a line of wagons and Rage bounded over to him, taking up her station beside Sorrow. No one tried to stop her. Her presence heartened him as nothing else could.

As the company started forward, two men-at-arms shoved him forward. He walked. What else could he do? Not knowing what to expect was, perhaps, the worst of it. Would he be punished? Executed? Fed to the *guivre*? He could not imagine what Biscop Antonia meant to do with him.

They marched all that day at a steady pace, stopping at midday to water the horses. They marched through hill country, mostly farm and pasture land with stands of forest topping the hilltops and long rides. It was easy country to move through, shallow fords, good grazing for the livestock that traveled with them, not a trace of any force loyal to King Henry.

But in the late afternoon the hills rolled into a long downslope that looked over the valley of the River Rhowne. From here, blurred by afternoon haze, Alain saw the stone tower of the cathedral of Autun, so far away it looked like a mason's tiny model. They had come to the border of the lands controlled by the Duke of Varingia; beyond lay the heart of the old kingdom of Varre, known as the duchy of Arconia. And beyond the duchy of Arconia lay Wendar.

Army and train came to a halt and began to settle in for the night. Alain was directed by his guards to enter the tent. There, at the biscop's order, he sat on a stool. The hounds followed him quietly and draped themselves over his feet.

She put him under the supervision of one of her clerics, a young man with pale blue eyes whom she named as Willibrod. Red lesions encrusted the cleric's hands and neck. While he sat, he shaved wood into holy Circles of Unity and carved letters into the backs of those Circles. Oddly enough, he also bound strands of hair and bits of leaves and some other thing, plucked from what looked like the fletchings for an arrow, onto the backs of these Circles and then strung each one on a leather cord, to make a necklace.

"You are a cleric in training?" asked young Cleric Willibrod. "You are clean-shaven, as befits a churchman."

Alain blushed, easy to see on his fair skin. It still embarrassed him horribly that he could grow nothing more manly than a bit of pale down on his chin. He had not shaved, and yet this cleric, who sat next to him, could not tell whether he was unshaven or clean-shaven.

"I was promised to the monastery," he stammered out finally, "but I serve Count Lavastine now as a man-at-arms."

The cleric shrugged. "It is not unknown for monk or cleric to serve in a lord's army, for is it not sung that while Our Lady tends the Hearth, Our Lord wields the Sword?"

Biscop Antonia came in. Servants surrounded her, bringing a pitcher of water and a fine brass basin and soft white linen so she might refresh her face and hands. Others brushed dust and travel dirt off her vestments while a woman braided Antonia's long silver hair, draping a shawl of white linen over the biscop's head when she was through. Atop the shawl two clerics placed her hat—her mitre—the mark of her rank as biscop. Tall, pointed both at the front and at the back, the mitre was made of a stiff white cloth and trimmed with thickly embroidered gold ribbons. Two white and gold tassels hung from the back of the hat all the way to her feet.

A cleric handed Antonia her crosier and she turned, surveying her retinue with a kindly smile on her face as if to show her gratitude for their service. Her gaze came to rest on Alain. He bowed his head swiftly, mortified he had been caught staring at her and her ablutions. So he did not see her expression, only heard her voice when she spoke.

"There is another I requested be brought to me many days ago. He has not yet arrived?"

"Not yet, Your Grace."

"I hope he can be with us by Compline." She spoke mildly, even hopefully, but Alain now recognized the undercurrent that eddied around her. For all that her aspect was kind and her voice gentle, she did not allow her will to be disobeyed. Clerics scurried away; others took their place, and as a united party they processed out so the biscop could lead the service of Vespers, the evensong.

Cleric Willibrod, left in charge, allowed Alain to kneel and pray as Vespers was sung in another part of the camp. During the final psalm, two soldiers appeared at the open tent entrance. With them, as if he were under arrest, came Frater Agius. His brown robes looked travel-stained and rumpled, and he was limping. Alain was so surprised he jumped to his feet in mid-phrase.

Agius shook free of the guards. He knelt at once to finish the last lines of the psalm, and Alain, shamed by the frater's piety, copied him.

"I thought you had stayed behind at Lavas town," whispered Alain after the last *Alleluia* was sung. "I thought you did not intend to ride with Count Lavastine."

"I did not." Agius rose, glared at the guards, and limped over to wash his face out of the same fine brass basin used by the biscop. Alain was both astounded and entranced by this show of worldly vanity and arrogance on the part of Agius. The frater wiped his face and hands dry with the same soft white linen the biscop had used. "It is not my part in life to involve myself with the worldly disputes that tempt those who have been seduced by the glamour of earthly power and pleasures."

"Then why are you here?" Alain demanded.

"I was summoned against my will."

Agius promptly sat down in the cushioned chair which even an ignorant lad like Alain, unaccustomed to the ways of the nobility, could see was reserved for the biscop. This act of flagrant defiance set Alain shaking. The hounds, catching his mood, stirred restlessly, thumping their tails on the ground and lifting their heads to watch intently.

"I beg your pardon, Brother," said Willibrod nervously. He began picking at the scabs on his skin. "That is Biscop Antonia's chair. It is not fitting for a lowly brother to sit—"

Agius glared the poor cleric into silence.

Through the entryway, Alain saw torches flickering. Biscop Antonia had returned.

2

"IS it fitting," asked Biscop Antonia in her mild voice after the outraged gasps of her servants had quieted, "that a simple frater of the church presume to sit in the seat of one whose elevation was ordained by the hand of the skopos herself?"

"Our Lady has already judged my heart and found it wanting. It is Her mercy and Her forgiveness I strive to be worthy of. Not yours." Certainly Agius was furious, to speak so.

"You are angry, child. Is this the heart you display to Our Lady and Lord?"

The frater did not seem in the least moved by the biscop's soft words. "She knows what is in my heart." He stood up, no longer looking like a lowly churchman brought before a high-ranking biscop but rather like a nobleman made angry by a retainer's presumption. "*You* do not."

A shocked murmuring rose from the crowd of servants; Antonia stilled it with a gesture. "Who speaks now, Frater Agius? The humble frater?" Her voice grew suddenly hard and accusing. "Or the proud son?"

He actually winced, though he did not back down. "I will do penance for my pride. What do you want of me, Your Grace? Why have you had me brought here? I serve the world no longer."

"But you live in the world nevertheless. We cannot escape the world, Frater Agius, though we strive to do so. Even you have not yet learned to submit your will to that of Our Lady and Lord. Some part of your heart still lives in your old station, where you are accustomed to having your own way."

"Our Lady will judge me," he repeated stubbornly. "What do you want of me?"

If there had been any tiny line of harshness in her face, it dissolved now into a sweet smile made the more reassuring by her round, pink-cheeked face and her twinkling blue eyes. "To visit with your niece, of course."

"My *niece!*" He almost roared the word.

"She is being fostered by the Biscop of Autun." Her placid countenance remained unmoved by his anger. "Did you know that?"

"Of course I knew!"

"It was by your suggestion, was it not?"

He glared, refusing to answer.

"You will remain here for the time being."

"Do you mean to make me a hostage?"

She signed. At once her servants and retainers left the tent until
only she, Alain, the hounds, and Agius remained. She glanced once
at the hounds and evidently decided she was safe with them—or
with Alain, who controlled them. "I mean to make you a weapon."

"I am no longer a weapon to be used in worldly pursuits, Biscop
Antonia. When I pledged myself to the church, I pledged myself to
no longer care for the things of this world."

She smiled gently. "We shall see." She nodded serenely at Alain
and left the tent.

Agius followed her, but his way was blocked by guards. For a
moment, Alain thought Agius meant to push past them, to force a
confrontation. Abruptly he dropped to his knees to pray, wincing
when his wounded leg—obviously not yet healed although it had
been almost two months since Sorrow's bite—took his weight. It
took Alain some time to distinguish words out of the mumbled flow
of syllables.

"I am an unworthy son, Oh, Lady, please make me worthy of
Your Mercy. Please judge me not harshly, Lady. Please grant Your
Forgiveness to this sinner. Ai, Lady. Please grant me the serenity to
accept humility and vanquish pride."

He went on in this way without seeming inclined to stop. Hearing
voices raised outside in the short service of Compline, for sunset,
Alain knelt and joined in the prayer.

Biscop Antonia did not return after the service was completed.
Presumably she went to feast. Cleric Willibrod brought bread and
cheese and wine for Alain and Agius; then he, together with several
of the other clerics, went back to making necklaces. The frater
touched nothing although, in the end, Alain got him to swallow a
few sips of wine.

Antonia returned later and went to her bed, her servants and clerics sleeping on pallets around her. Alain slept miserably, huddled on
the ground with the two hounds pressed up against him. Questions
nagged him through his restless sleep. What did Agius' niece have

to do with Lady Sabella's revolt? Agius was, after all, only a simple frater—although a simple frater would never dare seat himself in the chair reserved for a holy biscop.

Every time Alain woke, he heard Agius, still whispering his prayers.

In the morning, Alain was allowed out under guard to let the hounds run. As he returned, he saw a retinue approaching, many finely dressed men and women in rich tunics hung with gold and silver chains. He hurried inside to Agius.

"The biscop and many others are approaching!" he hissed. "Noble folk are with her."

Agius rose, a bit shakily, but he straightened and faced the entrance proudly—not at all like a humble frater. Alain knelt, hounds on either side of him; he could not stand before such noble lords and ladies. *He* was only a simple merchant's son.

The light from outside was dazzling but not as dazzling as the rich clothing of Lady Sabella and the portly man who attended her: Rodulf, Duke of Varingia. Contrasted to their elegant clothing, studded with jewels and trimmed with gold and silver ribbons, and the handsome display of gold in chains and coronets and rings, Biscop Antonia's vestments, merely sewn with gold thread, appeared modest.

Rodulf barked out a laugh and addressed Biscop Antonia. "Blessed Lord! I would not have recognized the child, dressed in such rags, had you not warned me, Your Grace." He stumped forward on thick legs. Broad-shouldered and heavy, he had the red cheeks of a man who eats heartily and never wants for food. Clapping Frater Agius on the shoulder, he shook him with evident good cheer. "What is this, lad? Some disgrace? Ai, I heard your father and mother were in a red rage when you turned your back on marriage to enter the church. But I thought you'd surely be a presbyter, sent down to that damned hot city of Darre to stand attendance on the skopos. What is this?" He grasped a handful of the old robe in one fleshy hand and tugged on it so hard Alain cringed, hoping the cloth would not tear.

"I serve Our Lady," said Agius stiffly. "I never intended otherwise." He made no obeisance toward Rodulf nor toward Lady Sabella, who stood quietly behind, looking stern and thoughtful.

"But you have come to aid our cousin," said Rodulf, indicating Sabella.

"I have not."

Alain dared not stir by one finger's-breadth for fear of the outburst that would certainly come next.

Sabella appeared unflustered. She stepped forward. "You will serve our needs nevertheless, Agius," she said in her flat voice. "I do not have time to spare for a siege of Autun, and Biscop Constance will not give the city over to me willingly, nor can I march forward with Autun's militia and resources—and hostility—at my back. In return for the safe passage of your niece, you will bring me the Biscop of Autun as a hostage by whatever means you must use."

This threat, if threat it was, did not sway Agius. He looked, if anything, more confident now. "If you do not have support enough to march against King Henry, then perhaps you would do better to retire to your own lands and administer them in a manner more fitting than this."

Sabella's thin lips turned up, though she did not really smile. She gestured to one of her servants. At once, a serving woman entered the tent, bringing with her a girlchild of some five or six summers, a well-grown girl with hair as pale and wispy as Agius' was dark and thick. Her face still wore tears, but she shrieked aloud when she saw Agius, tore herself out of the serving woman's grasp, and flung herself on him, crying, "Uncle! Uncle! They killed my nurse!" She burst into tears.

He held her tightly, hushing her with whispered words.

When she quieted, Sabella spoke again. "My outriders came across your niece and her retinue as they rode in toward Autun. There was a skirmish. Some number of her retainers refused to come without a fight."

"What do you mean to do with her?" he demanded. "She is meant for the church, as you must know."

Rodulf fidgeted, playing with the rings on his fingers. He looked as if this interview were distasteful to him. Biscop Antonia beamed sweetly on all concerned. Alain felt her gaze settle on him, and he shuddered as if spiders crawled up his back. Rage growled, and he set a hand gently on her muzzle.

"I mean to do nothing with her," said Sabella. "Unless I am forced to. I want Biscop Constance."

Agius was so pale his dark eyes stood out as if they had been painted black, as a whore might to attract men. The child clung to him, face buried in his robes.

"Constance will not suspect you, Agius," Sabella continued. "You were raised together, and of course, as I recall, there was even talk of a betrothal between you and her before it was settled she should enter the church and you should marry Duchess Liutgard." She touched the gold torque she wore at her neck, then lowered the hand to display her palm, a hand empty to the air. "But that betrothal did not end in *your* marriage to the young duchess but rather in your brother's. A kind and generous man was young Frederic. A good soldier, too. Alas. So many killed in Henry's wars in the east when he ought to have been paying better attention to the lands he claims already to hold. Now." She signed again to the servingwoman, who went forward to take hold of the girl.

The girl began to cry again, clutching at her uncle. He embraced her more tightly at first, a look of utter fury on his face, but in the end, his expression now twisted with self-loathing, he coaxed her into letting go of him. The servingwoman led her away.

"I see we understand each other," said Sabella to Agius. Without further discussion, she left the tent.

"You must see," said Rodulf abruptly, "that I will have no more Wendish kings and biscops set over my lands. You're of Wendish blood on your father's side, so you may have little sympathy for my views, but I hold strongly to them. But still, I do not like *these* methods."

"Many lives will be spared thereby," said Biscop Antonia soothingly, "and the city of Autun will not be devastated by war. Surely we agree that peace is better than war."

"War is at least an honorable profession," mumbled Rodulf under his breath. "Deceit is not, even if approved by a biscop." He went outside.

"We leave tomorrow at midday, then," said Biscop Antonia. "I will escort you." She gestured toward the tent and its furnishings. "Prepare yourselves as you see fit."

When she had left, Alain and Agius were allowed privacy to bathe. Alain poured water from a pitcher into the plain copper basin reserved for the use of the biscop's servants. He stripped off his tunic and washed his chest and arms and face. The water was bitterly cold.

Agius' deep set eyes were red with exhaustion. He knelt and clasped his hands in prayer.

Alain felt a terrible compassion for the frater. Surely Our Lady and Lord did not intend for any one person to so mortify themselves with this agony of self-doubt? Was it not through Their Mercy that people were given the promise of being cleansed of darkness?

Taking the basin, he carried it over to Agius and knelt beside him. "Here is water to cleanse yourself, Brother."

Agius grimaced in pain. "I am tainted forever with the sin of pride," he said between clenched teeth, his eyes tight shut.

For the first time, Alain noticed the frater's feet, half covered by his threadbare robes. They were bare, covered with old, suppurated sores and fresh cuts caked with dried blood and dirt. Every step must hurt. Alain suddenly wished fervently to spare Agius any more pain, for he was so very full of pain, that was apparent by his expression of utter wretchedness. He dabbed cloth in water and gently wiped the other man's face.

"I pray you," said Agius without opening his eyes, "I am not worthy of your compassion."

"Surely every soul is worthy of compassion," replied Alain, surprised. He dabbed more water on the linen cloth and carefully began to wash the frater's feet. "Is kindness not what we are commanded to give freely to our sisters and brothers?" He glanced up. To his horror, Agius was weeping silently. He drew the cloth away at once. It was mottled with blood and pus and dirt. "I beg your pardon. I did not mean to cause you pain."

"I care nothing for my body's pain. It serves to remind me of my sins. Ai, Lady, in my pride I thought I had put aside the threads that bind me to the old ties of blood and earth. But it is not so. I cannot set my affection for my brother behind me. I cannot love him less than I love Our Lady, even though he is dead and in Her care. So now his child is put in harm's way and I am brought forward to be used, forced by that threat of harm, by those who seek power in this world. In my pride I thought I had put my birth behind me. Now I see it is not so. It can never be so, as long as I am bound by old affections. I am not willing to make the true sacrifice, that of unbinding myself from the ties of kin and giving myself entirely to Our Lady."

Not knowing what else to do, Alain went back to washing the frater's feet, dabbing carefully, trying not to break open freshly healed scabs. "Who are you?" he asked, then feared he was being presumptuous.

After a long silence, Agius replied. "I am the eldest son of Burchard, Duke of Avaria, and Ida, daughter of the duc de Provensalle."

In Osna village, it was considered the duty of the eldest daughter to inherit her mother's goods and property and carry on her work and title, and the duty of the eldest son to marry well and thus weave a greater web of connection between households. Only younger children were sent into the church. Surely the great princes of the realm, men and women, expected the same from *their* sons and daughters.

"No wonder your parents were angry," said Alain as the full import of Agius' rebellion hit him.

The frater merely grunted. He sat back abruptly and ran a hand through his hair, tousling it, then fingered his chin to rub at the days'-old beard now growing there.

"What will you do?" asked Alain.

"I will save my brother's daughter, for the love there was between us. So will the number of my sins become greater."

"But you said you would not aid them . . . and she is so young." Alain trailed off. The girlchild was only a little younger than Aunt Bel's youngest daughter, sweet Agnes. "What hold do they truly have over you? Surely they wouldn't—"

"*Kill* her?" Agius smiled sourly. "You are a good boy, Alain. You do not yet understand what we are capable of, we who still pursue the power held before us by the Enemy as a temptation. For the power given us to wield on this earth is an empty power compared to the sacrifice of the blessed Daisan and the promise of the Chamber of Light. But we are tainted by darkness, and so with clouded eyes we grasp at shadows." He clapped his hands once, imperiously. "Cleric! Bring me a knife. I am not worthy to call myself a good churchman with such a beard." His expression was ragged with despair, but he moved with the sure and decided movements of a man who has come to terms with a terrible destiny.

3

AGIUS walked, and Alain walked beside him, trailed by the hounds. Biscop Antonia rode at the front of the procession on her white mule, led by her servants. A cleric carried a green banner on a pole, marked with the badge of her city: a black tower at the confluence of two rivers. The black cloth of the tower was embroidered in gold thread with a biscop's crosier.

"There is so much talk of dukes and lands and biscops and allegiances," Alain confessed. "I can't make sense of it."

Agius smiled thinly. "You cannot make sense of why I am to be used as the snare to trap the white deer?"

"The white deer?"

"That is the name we gave Constance." When Alain nodded, trying to look as if he understood perfectly well what Agius was talking about, the frater gave a sigh of frustration. "Constance is King Henry's sister, his youngest sibling except for Brun."

"But why would Lady Sabella call you cousin? You do not wear—" Alain drew his fingers around the curve of his throat.

"Only those descended from the house of royal kin are permitted to wear the golden torque. It signifies their royal blood. Both Sabella and her husband Berengar may wear the golden torque. Duchess Liutgard is so ornamented. I am not."

"But why would—? And not you—? If you are the son of a duke?" Clouds had come in from the east. It was colder than it had been in the morning. Alain felt the dirt of the road under his boots. If it rained, the road would get muddy; how much rain, how much mud, would it take to prevent this plan from going forward? Yet he marched with Sabella's forces, under the aegis of Count Lavastine. Should he not wish devoutly for her victory?

"As reading and prayer, so the ordering of the world," said Agius with a sigh.

"What?"

"I seem fated to teach you, Alain. I trust to Our Lady's Wisdom that you will take better to the great truth of Her Son's sacrifice and redemption than you have so far to your letters. Now. Attend."

They walked along a deserted road. The farmers and freeholders who owed allegiance to Autun had all fled inside the city walls at the approach of Sabella's army. Though clouds were their roof and the green fields their chamber, Alain felt transported back to the days of lessons with the frater at Lavas Holding. Agius was not an easy teacher, more often ruthless and impatient with mistakes than forgiving of lapses. What he knew he was determined others should know.

"There are ten great princes in the kingdom of Wendar and Varre. Six of these princes we know as dukes. Four we know as margraves, since they administer the marches that lie along the eastern border. The sovereign is first among these princes, not apart from them. It is by their consent and the sovereign's strength that a prince or princess of the royal line comes to be acknowledged as the next ruler of Wendar and Varre."

"But weren't Wendar and Varre once separate kingdoms?"

"I can't imagine what your father was thinking," said Agius with some exasperation, "not to educate you properly."

"My father taught me all the things a merchant's son needs to know," said Alain hotly, stung by this unwarranted criticism. "I can repair a ship. I know a bit about sailing and navigation. I know the worth of coins from many different kingdoms and peoples. I can barter."

"I did not mean your foster father."

Distracted, Alain forgot his anger momentarily. "Surely you don't still believe I might be Count Lavastine's bastard?"

Agius gestured eloquently toward the hounds, which padded faithfully after Alain. They were as meek as puppies—as long as Alain or Count Lavastine was next to them. Agius knew well enough what they would do to anyone else who approached them. "But that is neither here nor there. I will perform the task given me by Our Lady. Attend."

They crested a rise. In the distance, Alain saw the city of Autun, the cathedral tower, the city walls, and the faint glimmer of the River Rhowne as it wound through fields lush with growing grain. Then the road dipped down into forest, and trees obscured the view.

"I will not trouble you with the story of the rise of the house of Saony. It is a long and complicated affair better left to the nuns of

Korvei, who have for many years chronicled the deeds of the great princes of this realm. What you must know is that in the year 679, according to that chronicle, the young King Louis of Varre, known as Louis the Child, died. Two years later the elder Arnulf, king of Wendar, died. Arnulf the younger, his son, became king of both Wendar and Varre. What year is it now, Alain?"

What *year*? It was spring. This particular day was St. Casceil's Day, as had been duly recited in the morning service. Since they had not yet celebrated the Feast of St. Susannah, it must not yet be the month of Sormas, but he could not recall now which day of Avril St. Casceil's Day fell on.

And as for *years*! Alain was not used to the marking of years. He dredged back into his memory, stumbled over a pothole in the road, and remembered.

"It is the year 728 since the Proclamation of the Word."

"That is right. You know of the struggle of Henry and Sabella for the right to sit on the throne of Wendar and Varre." Agius gestured, lips twisted in a frown, toward Biscop Antonia. She had begun to sing and as usual her clerics joined in with great sweetness of tone. Alain could not understand the words, since they sang in Dariyan.

But Agius, distracted, murmured words in time to their singing.

> " 'These four Deacons were treasurers,
> Who held in their integrity,
> The key to the mystery.
> Four doors did they open to us,
> Each one of them with her key.
> To Thee be glory, Who chose them wisely!' "

"Is that what the words mean?" demanded Alain.

"Yes. It is an old song, from the East. But never mind it. We must not be distracted from our purpose. Soon we will come to the walls of Autun and there will be an end to your lesson. Now. What is the name of the king, and who are his siblings?"

"King Henry, of course!" Aware that he had spoken loudly, Alain ducked his head, embarrassed. In Sabella's camp, one did not speak of Henry as king. "And Lady Sabella, who is his elder sister."

"His half sister," Agius corrected. "Queen Berengaria of Varre was her mother. When she died, the younger Arnulf married Mathilda of Karrone, who is Henry's mother. And then?"

"I don't know."

"These are the living children of Arnulf and Mathilda. Henry. Rotrudis. Richardis, known as Scholastica, who is Mother at Quedlinhame Cloister. Benedict. Constance. Brun. Henry also has a half sister who is the child of the younger Arnulf and a concubine. She is Alberada, now Biscop of Handelburg, but that is far to the east in the marchlands, and she has taken no part in the quarrels between Henry and Sabella. Now. Who are the six dukes?"

"I . . . I don't know. Well. Duke Rodulf is one. And isn't Sabella's husband Berengar called a duke?"

"He is indeed. He is Duke of Arconia, although of course Lady Sabella administers his lands, as his wife. Rodulf is Duke of Varingia. The city of Autun lies on the border of those lands administered by Rodulf and his wife, which we call Varingia, and those lands administered by Sabella and Berengar, called Arconia. Perhaps you wonder, then, why the Biscop of Autun is sympathetic to Henry's cause, though her city lies within that region controlled by Lady Sabella?"

Alain nodded dutifully.

"When Sabella first rebelled against her brother's authority eight years ago, the biscop of Autun was one of her principal supporters. So Henry removed the biscop of Autun and made her abbess of a small, isolated convent instead. He then convinced the skopos to install in her place his young sister Constance. The white deer. Of course Constance supports Henry."

"What of the other four dukes?"

"Three of the dukes support Henry. Henry's sister Rotrudis is Duchess of Saony and Attomar. The duchy of Saony is the original seat of power of his family. Before they became kings, they were the dukes of Saony."

"How did they become the kings, then?"

"That you must learn another time, or read for yourself. Now attend." He looked ahead as they came out of the shadow of the trees into sun. A long downslope rolled out from their feet. Soon they would come within an arrow's shot of the city walls. Alain wondered how soon they would be noticed by the people within the city. "Burchard, Duke of Avaria."

"He is your father."

"Yes." Alain wanted to draw him out, but Agius spoke the word so curtly the boy dared ask no more questions. "And third, Liutgard, Duchess of Fesse, who is also of royal kin."

"The one you were betrothed to."

"I see you have listened more closely than I supposed."

"But your brother married her instead."

Agius looked away quickly, hiding his expression. Alain thought of the little girl who had clung to her uncle in Biscop Antonia's tent; clearly Agius's bond to his brother and thus his brother's children was very strong.

With sudden sympathy for Agius' grief and impotent fury in the face of his niece's captivity, Alain asked another question. "Who is the sixth duke?"

A hesitation. At last Agius spoke, although he still looked away, staring at the ground. "Conrad, Duke of Wayland, known as Conrad the Black. Sabella claims he supports her, but he has not brought his forces to march with hers."

"And the margraves?"

Agius had recovered his composure. He lifted his chin—cleanly shaven that morning, as befit a man dedicated to the church—and took in a deep breath of air, as if to fortify himself. "Chief among the margraves is Helmut Villam. Second, and almost as powerful, is Judith, margrave of Olsatia and Austra. Werinhar, margrave of Westfall, is the other."

"You said there were four."

A shadow crossed Agius' expression, the same raw grief. Alain understood at once that this had something to do with his beloved brother. "The margrave of Eastfall and both her sons died three years ago in a battle fought against the Quman."

"Is—is that the battle your brother died in?" A wild guess, but Alain knew he was right by the sharp glance Agius threw him and the frater's sudden grim silence.

They walked for a while. The biscop and her clerics were still singing; the hymn from the East evidently had many verses. He did not want to look at Agius or to ask him any more questions, whether about margraves or verses. Agius held such a store of pain in him that it hurt Alain to see it.

Agius whispered words in Wendish under his breath, in time to the voices of the others.

> " 'Daughters of Nisibia, act as did your mother,
> Who laid a Body within her,
> And it became a Wall without her!

Lay in you a living Body,
That it may be a Wall for your life.
To Thee be glory, Who chose most wisely.' "

As the clerics finished the hymn, the biscop slowed her mule and the entire procession came to a halt. Antonia dismounted.

Autun was built on a hill that rose out of the plain of the Rhowne Valley. Hovels and huts stood outside the walls, but like the fields they were empty of any life except for a stray chicken pecking along the verge of the settlement. Antonia's party was as yet out of arrow shot of the city walls, but at the great palisade gate that marked the main entrance to the city a company had assembled. Two banners flew, and as the company descended the road, coming out to meet Biscop Antonia, Alain made out their devices: One, like the banner of the city of Mainni, showed a tower, this a gray tower surmounted by a black raven. The other banner, so bright a gold it seemed to reflect the sun itself, depicted a white deer.

Agius moved forward to stand beside Biscop Antonia. He was sickly pale. Antonia, looking perfectly at her ease, had a magnanimous smile on her face as she waited for the group from the city to arrive and greet her.

As befit the daughter and sister of kings, the Biscop of Autun had a handsome and impressive retinue. Her clerics wore robes of fine linen dyed a rich burgundy, and each one held a book, a token of their station. Draped over their left shoulders they each wore a long, embroidered linen scarf. There were perhaps thirty clerics in the company; Alain had never seen so many books in one place before. Indeed, it had never occurred to him so many might exist in all the world.

Monks and nuns attended her also, carrying thuribles, round vessels of beaten brass in which incense was burned; the thuribles hung from chains, swinging slowly back and forth to the rhythm of the soft chanting of the company. '"Kyria eleison. Kyrie eleison.'' Lady, have mercy on us. Lord, have mercy on us.

The Biscop of Autun rode a white mule at the center of the procession. Though she wore a biscop's rich vestments and mitre, Alain could see at her neck the golden torque marking her as born of royal kin. She was young, certainly younger than Agius, but she had a grave expression that made her look as steady and wise as a woman twice her years. Her complexion was healthy if pale, and when she dismounted and came forward on foot, hands outstretched to greet her sister biscop, Alain could see she was tall and of good stature, like her elder half sister Sabella. She had a light step and an elegant manner. Alain saw immediately why she had received the name 'the white deer.'

She took Biscop Antonia's hands in hers and at once the soft chanting of her company ceased. There was silence except for the scrape of shifting feet on dirt and the jingling of harness.

"I greet you, sister, and welcome you to my city," said Constance. She had a pleasingly high voice, full and clear. But she did not smile. "I am surprised to find you here, so far from Mainni and the Hearth over which you were ordained to watch."

"I give you greetings in return, sister," said Antonia with rather more sweetness. "I come in the peace of Our Lord and Lady."

"There are others with you." Constance looked back along the road down which Antonia and the others had come.

Of course, the road was empty. Sabella's army was safely encamped several hours' ride into the Duke of Varingia's territory. This was strange, certainly, in itself. The duchy of Arconia remained under the aegis of Berengar and Sabella. Yet a biscop's duties were twofold. She watched over the spiritual well-being of her charges and over the Hearth of the cathedral given unto her by the authority of the skopos. But a biscop must be consulted in worldly matters as well, just as the king or duke had a say in what noblewoman was most deserving of elevation to biscop when a see became empty by reason of death or dishonor. As Biscop of Autun, whose spiritual duty was to watch over the inhabitants of the central portion of the kingdoms of Wendar and Varre—the region known as Arconia— Constance had the right to demand to be consulted on matters pertaining to the administration of the duchy of Arconia. Perhaps Sabella's hold on the loyalty of the populace in her own husband's duchy was not as strong as that populace's love for their new young biscop, Constance.

"I fear there is strife in your family," said Antonia, sounding much stricken at having to be the bearer of bad tidings. "I have come as mediator. I beg of you to come with me to speak of these matters with Sabella and Rodulf."

"It grieves me to hear of such things," replied Constance without any indication this was news to her, "but I fear the ill-will of Sabella, for reasons you must know, and in any case I am loath to leave my people—" Here she gestured toward the city, which lay quiet in the midday sun. "—without my guidance, and without my presence to protect them."

Agius had remained in the background, hidden by the robes of Antonia's clerics. Now he stepped forward. The bleak dark stain of his frater's robes stood out starkly against the brighter clothing of his more worldly brethren.

Constance's expression brightened. She looked delighted. "Agius! You have surprised me." She released Antonia's hands and reached and drew Agius to her as if he were her brother. The show of familiarity astonished Alain. "I did not expect to find *you* in such company."

Just barely Alain caught in Constance's tone a muted disgust for the company Agius was keeping. If Antonia noticed it, she made no sign; she beamed as fondly on them as an elderly kinswoman might approve the reuniting of two feuding siblings.

"I travel where I must," Agius said. He looked torn between his obvious pleasure in seeing Biscop Constance and the dilemma that hung over him as the executioner's sword hangs over the neck of the condemned. "I follow the path which Our Lady has set before my feet."

"And that path led you to Sabella's camp?" asked Constance. If there was sarcasm in her utterance, Alain could not hear it.

"Worldly consideration led me to Sabella's camp, Your Grace."

"I thought you had turned your face away from worldly considerations, Frater Agius, when you refused marriage and took the brown robe of service instead."

He smiled grimly. "The world is not yet done with me, Your Grace. Alas."

"It is ever thus, that the world intrudes when we wish most devoutly only to contemplate God." Constance folded her hands together and bowing her head slightly, as if in submission to God's will. Then she raised her head to look at Agius directly again. "But God in kindness endowed humans with freedom equal to that of the angels. For is it not true that the sun and the moon and indeed even the stars are so fixed that they can only move in the path marked out for them? Yet it is not so with those born of human mothers. Thus must our behavior be reckoned with that of the angels. The praise or blame which a man's conduct deserves is really his own." She turned to Biscop Antonia. "Do you not agree, Your Grace?"

Of course Alain recognized at once that the remark was like a barbed spear: meant to sink in with little hope to ease it out without great pain.

Biscop Antonia had impenetrable armor. She nodded. "It is as you say, Your Grace. Thus do Our Lord and Lady judge our actions, by what we do and by what we leave undone."

Agius made no reply.

This silence Biscop Constance took in stride. "Now that we are met on the road," she continued, "I pray you will return with me to my hall, where my people will entertain you as is fitting with a good feast and a taste of Autun wine."

Agius shifted violently. "I have come to ask," he said quickly, "that you return with us to Sabella's camp, as Biscop Antonia requests of you."

"Surely it would be unwise of me to place myself in Sabella's power, although certainly I hold no personal enmity toward my sister."

"I will hold myself responsible, and none other, if any harm comes to you, Your Grace."

"Are you pledging me safe passage, Agius?"

"I pledge to escort you safely back to your city, Your Grace."

She was startled, though she tried to conceal it. "Then I will agree to go," she said. "Better peace than war, as the blessed Daisan said."

"I will go with you, then," added Agius, "to your hall while you gather anything you need to take to Sabella's camp."

"No need." She shrugged and gestured to her servants to bring her mule. "I am armored with my faith, Frater Agius, as are we all who have given our lives to Our Lord and Lady. And I am made strong by my brother's confidence in me—as he is by mine in him."

"Then it is well we should go." Yet Agius hesitated as both biscops were helped onto their mounts. He came forward and took the reins of Biscop Constance's mule in the place of her servant. "But did not the blessed Daisan say, he who spurns what is offered is all too often in want? It is past midday, and if we ride on now, we and the others of Biscop Antonia's party will have walked all day fasting."

Even Alain did not have to guess at Biscop Constance's reaction to this statement; she was delighted to be able to offer hospitality.

Aunt Bel had said many a time within his hearing: *"So does Our Lady judge us, by our generosity at table."* Aunt Bel was so well-known for feeding folk passing through Osna village that less magnanimous householders sometimes fobbed guests off on her. Never had she turned one away.

"Then certainly we must return to my palace and dine," said Constance with evident pleasure.

They returned, Agius still leading the mule, to Autun. It was the largest city Alain had ever seen, with a stone wall and a stone and timber cathedral and so many buildings all shoved together that he wondered how the folk who lived there did not choke on each other. They passed quickly through the gate and down a wide avenue flanked with timber houses built in a style quite unlike the longhouses of his village. The walls of the biscop's palace rose to the height of three men. He barely had time to catch his breath before they were led inside its imposing timber frame.

There, he was allowed to sit by the great hearth and eat bread so white and soft it was more like a cloud than what he knew as bread, heavy loaves with thick dark crusts. He was given leave to eat as much as he wished of the best cheese he had ever tasted and the leavings of the fowl and fish that made up the biscop's simple midday meal. All this while Rage and Sorrow gnawed on hambones still bristling with meat and fat. Probably poor Lackling had never eaten as much pork in his entire cold and lonely life as the hounds devoured in the course of the next hour. It was a terrible thing to sit and eat with such pleasure while Lackling had not even the peace of a marked grave.

But Alain could not help himself. Even helping to serve at Count Lavastine's table during the visit of Lady Sabella and her entourage he had not seen a meal as casually elegant as this. But then, Biscop Constance was the king's sister, born of the lineage of kings. The dark beams and tapestried walls, the bustling clerics and the fine linen worn by every least servant, served to remind him how small a place Osna village was. Certainly Aunt Bel and his father Henri were respectable and prosperous freeholders. Of this they and their children could always be proud. Bel had lost children to disease but never to starvation, as many did. But sitting in this hall, even in the ashy corner by the hearth, that pride seemed little compared to the great state employed in the service of princes.

What the great ones spoke of he had no idea. He ate too much and then his stomach ached from the rich food, to which he was not accustomed. The long walk back to Sabella's camp seemed to take an eternity. Each step jolted him. He leaned, alternately, on Rage and then on Sorrow, to keep his balance. The two biscops rode side by side, not giving pride of place to the other. Agius, evidently set on maintaining his pose as simple frater rather than duke's son, continued to lead Constance's mule.

Alain hoped he would make it to camp without throwing up by the side of the road.

But after an hour and with the day neither too warm nor too cold and the wind a pleasant touch on his face, he began to feel better. Of them all, only Agius looked steadily worse as they came closer to Sabella's camp.

Scouts had run ahead. As their party crossed the last rye field before the camp began its sprawl through pasture and light woods, soldiers and campfolk appeared to line their path, to stare at the royal biscop. Together, Antonia and Constance made a striking pair: cheerful age and stern youth. To see two biscops in the same cavalcade was a rare sight, and Alain wished suddenly and painfully that Lackling could be alive to see it, for he so loved all that was bright and lovely to look upon—even if only from a distance. But Antonia had brought death to the boy. How could she ride with such a smooth countenance, as if nothing troubled her conscience?

But was it not Agius who spoke of the inner heart? As Aunt Bel said: "*A smooth countenance without reflects a calm soul within.*" So Alain had always believed. Now he wondered. How could any person make dealings with blood and dark shades and by that means bring about the death of an innocent simple boy, and yet show no sign of that terrible sin in her face?

Lady Sabella waited in front of the great tent surmounted by her banner. Her daughter Tallia stood beside her, looking pale and cold in a gown of silk the color of harvested wheat. Duke Rodulf and her other partisans stood at her side or a few steps back; Count Lavastine, in their midst, appeared wooden, drained of life. Sabella did not come forward to greet her half sister but rather waited for Constance to dismount and walk forward in *her* turn.

"Sister," said Constance mildly, "I give you greetings. It is my devout hope we can mend these troubles that have torn our family apart."

Sabella did not offer Constance her hands, the sign of kinship and safekeeping. Instead, she took a step back and signed to her soldiers. They swarmed forward to form a ring around the two women and their retinues. Antonia dismounted and came to stand beside Sabella. Tallia stared somberly at Constance, as if the young biscop were an apparition. Agius sank to one knee, head bowed, still holding the halter of Constance's white mule.

"You are now come to rest in my hands, Constance," said Sabella in the flat voice that disguised her emotions, if indeed she had any. "You are my hostage for Henry's good behavior and for his agreement to give precedence to my rightful claim."

Like a deer, startled by the sudden appearance of the hunter, Biscop Constance threw up her head, eyes wide, looking as if she were about to bolt. But of course she was surrounded. She drew her hands back and folded them in front of her. This gesture allowed her to regain her composure.

"I have been betrayed," she said in a loud, firm voice. She turned to gaze directly at Agius, who rose slowly to face her, his complexion white. "You promised me safe escort, Agius. *Cousin*." The word, said with emphasis and anger, was a weapon, meant to wound.

Agius said nothing.

"He gave you safe escort," interposed Antonia. "He escorted you safely into your city, where we broke our fast. Then we came here, but he had already discharged the obligation. He did not promise you safe passage for a *second* time."

Constance did not even glance toward Antonia. "You have deceived me, Agius. I will not forget it."

"Nor should you," he replied, his voice rough. But he looked beyond Constance to Sabella. Alain was suddenly struck by the age of the two women: Sabella was old enough to be Constance's mother; as indeed she would have been, might have been, had she proven herself fertile on her heir's progress so many years ago, the progress that had resulted in her being passed over for the throne. Tallia, the late fruit of her marriage, looked like a frail reed out of which to create the staff that would grant her the authority of a sovereign queen.

"And so, Lady Sabella," said Agius harshly, "my part in this is finished. Release my niece and let us ride free, as you promised."

"As I promised, I will free your niece into the custody of the biscop of Autun, whom I now restore to the seat taken unlawfully from her by the decree of my brother Henry and with the connivance of my sister Constance." She gestured. An old, frail woman tottered forward, wearing biscop's vestments marked with the badge of the city of Autun.

"You will go against Henry's wishes?" Constance demanded. "*I* am the biscop of Autun."

"And by what right did Henry remove *this* woman from her see?" Sabella's tone was mild but unyielding. "Helvissa was given the biscop's crosier by the authority of the skopos herself twenty years ago. Henry's worldly authority does not outrank the spiritual authority of the skopos in these matters. I merely restore Biscop Helvissa to her rightful place."

But looking at the old woman, whose hands shook with palsy, Alain could not imagine she would be anything except a pawn in Sabella's plans.

"She is Mother to a convent now," Constance said, "not biscop. *I* was invested—"

"You were invested as a deacon in the church, sister. Your election to biscop can, I think, be treated as invalid. It is as a deacon you will remain in my custody."

Constance gasped. Looking furious, she shut her mouth tight.

A servingwoman came forward with the little girl, Agius' niece. The child had the expression of a cornered animal, gone still while waiting for the deathblow. She saw her uncle and leaned toward him as rushes lean in a stiff breeze, but she made no move to run to him. It was as if a leash held her to her captors. Tears trailed down her cheeks, yet she made no sound though her chin trembled. A slender gold torque gleamed at her neck.

"The child will return with the biscop to the city of Autun," said Sabella, sounding satisfied with herself and the fruition of her plan. "But you may not leave me, Frater Agius. I may still have need of you."

"Then my niece remains in your custody." His voice was quiet, too quiet, perhaps. Alain had never heard him so subdued. Agius glanced toward the girl, then tore his gaze away from her. The child hiccuped down a sob in response.

Constance knelt abruptly, extending her hands. "Come, child," she said, more order than request. The child looked to her uncle, got his bare nod, and took hesitant steps forward until Constance's hands rested lightly on her shoulders. "This is Ermengard, daughter of Duchess Liutgard and her husband Frederic of Avaria. She is destined for the church." Only then did Constance look back up at Sabella. "Even our quarrels must not stand in the way of Our Lady's and Lord's will. Let one of my clerics escort her to Autun and put her into the care of my chatelaine, a woman of good birth and education."

Agius stood with hands clenched, gaze fixed on his niece with uncomfortable intensity. The new biscop staggered and had to be supported by a servant.

"I will allow this," said Sabella at last. "Constance, I leave you in the hands of Biscop Antonia. Now." She turned to Duke Rodulf. "We march. Autun will comply with the wishes of her rightful biscop, although we will leave a garrison behind to make sure of their loyalty to us."

Alain caught sight suddenly of Sabella's husband, Berengar, sitting with a servant on the ground in front of Sabella's great tent. The two men—noble and servant—were playing chess. Berengar laughed with great gusto, almost braying with pleasure, knocked over the servant's pieces, and proclaimed himself winner. Tallia flinched. Biscop Antonia set a steadying hand on the young woman's shoulder.

So it was done. The girlchild, Ermengard, was led away in the company of the new biscop of Autun. Constance was led away under guard, though she refused to relinquish her biscop's robes and mitre and scarf, and none there dared take these things from her by force.

"You have deceived me, Sabella," said Agius finally.

"It surprises me to hear you say such a thing," replied Sabella. "For we both promised safe passage and met our obligations. I do not hold it as deceit."

"I do."

"Yet reflect on this, cousin. Were Constance to remain in Autun, there would be war between her people and mine. What better judgment is there than that by which discord is dissolved and peace reestablished?"

"What better judgment? That of Our Lady, who looks within our souls and judges what She sees there."

Sabella lifted an eyebrow, the most expressive gesture Alain had ever seen her use. "I am as you see me, Frater Agius. By this must you judge me. I trust you will submit to the custody of Biscop Antonia."

"I will submit because I have no choice."

"Then he is yours, Your Grace," she said to Antonia.

"And this one as well," said Antonia. To Alain's horror, the white-haired biscop turned her gaze on *him*.

"This one?" Sabella looked first here and then there and finally, with some confusion, found him with the hounds as if she had not truly seen him before. "He is a kennel boy, is he not? I recognize Lavastine's hounds."

"Not just a kennel boy, I believe," said Antonia. "I would be gratified if you would render him into my care."

Sabella shrugged. She did not even consult Lavastine, who in any case no longer spoke except when spoken to and then in that flat monotone which reminded Alain of Sabella's voice. "He is yours." She turned away, leading Duke Rodulf and the others with her. Tallia trailed behind, looking back over her shoulder. Briefly, Alain met her eyes: They were palest gray-blue, like the dawn sky on a cloudless day. Then she followed her mother inside the great tent.

Alain shivered. He dared not look up at Antonia. Sabella's indifference to his fate terrified him. So easily was he abandoned. Outside of Lavastine's camp, none knew or cared what happened to him. What if Antonia suspected, or even knew, he had witnessed Lackling's murder?

"Come," said the biscop in her usual kind voice. "You will serve at the feast tonight, Alain."

He shuddered. She even remembered his name.

"Frater Agius, I hope you are not too proud to serve as well."

"I will serve as I am bid."

But Alain heard the terrible pain welling up underneath the humble words.

Together they were escorted to the river and given some privacy to wash. Agius' expression had taken on such a cast of blankness that Alain feared for him. But the frater said nothing. He knelt on the bank and prayed silently while Alain washed his own face and hands, then, tentatively, peeled off his tunic and washed his chest and back. Finally, not sure when he would have such a chance again, he stripped and waded to the deepest part of the little river, up past his thighs, took a ragged breath, and went under.

He came up, spitting and coughing, into a boiling mass of hounds. They swam round him, their tails whipping against his skin. Rage nipped at him, and Sorrow swam on to the other side of the river and shook himself all over with such power that Alain, in the middle, felt the spray off his coat.

Unexpectedly, Alain felt a swell of simple joy. He laughed. Had not Rage and Sorrow chosen him as their companion? It seemed impossible for Biscop Antonia to harm him as long as the two hounds protected him.

He waded back to shore. Agius was still praying. If his eyes had lifted from his hands even once, Alain saw no sign of it.

"Wash yourself, my friend," said Alain finally. "Is it not what Our Lady would wish, that we appear before her cleansed?"

He was not sure Agius heard the words, so he shook out his clothing as best he could, let himself dry off, and dressed. The guards shifted at their positions, anxious to return their charges to the biscop's custody.

"You are right," said Agius suddenly. He took off his frater's robe. Under it, against his skin, he wore a coarse shirt woven of linen and horsehair. But Alain noticed at once that his leg, where Sorrow had bitten him, was dirty, red, and swollen. Before Alain could utter a word, Agius removed his hair shirt.

Alain could not restrain a gasp. Even the guards murmured in awe and horror.

The stiff cloth had rubbed Agius' skin raw. In places, the open skin was festering.

"Doesn't it hurt?" Alain whispered, feeling the pain like fire on his own back and chest.

Agius threw himself full length on the ground, hands clenched, awful tortured skin exposed. "It is no more than I deserve. I betrayed one for the other, only to find myself betrayed in return. Ai, Lady, I thought only to help the child, for the love I bore Frederic."

"But you saved your niece, surely?"

"Saved her from what? She still remains in Sabella's custody, since Sabella's creature now acts as biscop of Autun in Constance's place. I could not even take the child to safety, back to her mother's castle or to the king's progress. I pray that the king learns of these deeds soon, for they will make him very angry." He spoke more slowly now, almost savoring the words. "The king's anger is a terrible thing to behold." A slight moan escaped him, the sound of a creature mourning. "Ai, Lady, You will judge me harshly, as I deserve. I vowed to leave the world and enter Your service, and yet the world pursues me and grants no mercy from its burdens. Forgive me my sins. Let my belief in the true knowledge of Your Son's sacrifice grant me a measure of peace in my heart."

So on he went, back to his prayers. The guards muttered, listening and watching.

Alain did not know what to do. In an odd way, Agius reminded him of the piteous *guivre*: wounded and suffering in a cage made for it by others. Yet the *guivre* was of itself no pitiful thing; it had a fierce and hideous nobility, separate from human concerns.

After a bit, the hounds ventured closer, then nudged at Agius' prostrate body. The frater did not react to this threat. Perhaps Agius hoped, at that moment, they would tear him to pieces and have done with it. But instead, Sorrow licked at the wound on his leg and Rage licked the sores on his back.

Alain hurried forward to find Agius weeping silently. He knelt and whispered soothing words to him as he might to Aunt Bel's youngest daughter Agnes when she was caught in nighttime fears.

Finally, Agius let Alain help him into the water and wash.

But that night Agius did not eat, nor did he the next day as they marched on, leaving Autun behind. Only in the evening did Alain coax him to take a crust of old bread, scarcely fit for beggars.

Watched as they were, this piece of information was conveyed to Biscop Antonia. She took Alain aside the next morning and thanked him kindly for his care of Frater Agius.

"Although he professes a heresy," she said gently, "I hope to bring him back to his senses and into the church again."

But Alain feared, in Agius' silence and stubborn fixed stare, that the frater had taken into his head some kind of terrible idea, that he meant to do something rash or dangerous. Agius prayed incessantly, even while walking. At every halt in the march he spoke to a growing audience of the curious about the revelation of the Son, the blessed Daisan, through Whose sacrifice our sins are redeemed.

XI
A MOUSE'S HUNGER

1

"LET us rest here," said Rosvita to her escort. She indicated a log
that had, by the grace of Our Lady and Lord, come to rest like a
bench just where the path broke out of the forest atop a ridge. From
this plain but serviceable seat one could see the valley spread out
below, the plaster and timber buildings of Hersford Monastery, the
large estate, and the several villages strung like clusters of grapes
along the Hers River.

She was not sure a magnate of Helmut Villam's stature would
deign to sit on such a humble seat. But she sat down and, after a
moment, handing the reins of his horse over to his son, so did he.

The thin wail of a horn carried to them on the stiff wind that
blew along the ridge top. They watched as out of a copse below
the king and his company emerged, bright banners signaling their
passage.

A white banner marked with a red eagle in profile now flew
among the other—more familiar—pennants. Duchess Liutgard of
Fesse had arrived at Hersford Monastery yesterday. Hersford lay on
the border between the duchies of Saony and Fesse; it was tradi-

tional for the reigning duke to escort the king across into her domain. Liutgard had inherited her position at a very young age—and
perhaps because of her youth she adhered strictly to the old forms.

"I fear you have missed the hunt," said Rosvita. What intrigues
would be planted on today's hunt, their fruit to be harvested many
months from now—for good or for ill?

Villam coughed, flushed from the exertion of toiling up the hill.
A big man, he had spared his horse the last steep climb by leading it
instead of riding. "The hunt is ever on, Sister Rosvita. Only the prey
we hunt differs from chase to chase."

"Do you think King Henry is serious? That he intends to elevate
the illegitimate child over the legitimate ones?"

Villam's smile was slight and self-mocking. "I am not an unprej-
udiced observer in this matter. If King Henry did indeed designate
Sanglant as his heir, against all custom, then can it not be said *I*
have a direct interest in promoting Sanglant's elevation?"

"How would that be so?" she asked, wondering if he would actually state outright what most people believed to be true: that he had
stood by while his eldest daughter, Waltharia, carried on an affair
of some months' duration with the charming Sanglant, an affair
that had ended with her pregnancy by the prince and subsequent
marriage to a sturdy young man of noble birth and pleasant manners.

But for answer, he only smiled knowingly. Behind, his son Berthold, standing close enough to listen in, gave a snort of amusement.
It would be well to remember, thought Rosvita, that the lad had, as
well as undoubted skill at arms, his father's ironical bent and a
seemingly endless store of amiability.

"I think," said Villam suddenly, "the king must make up his
mind to marry again. Queen Sophia has been at peace in the Chamber of Light for almost two years now, and the nuns have sung
prayers in her memory through two Penitires. The king is strong,
but it is always to the benefit of a man to be strengthened by marriage to a woman his equal in courage and wit."

She chanced to glance up at the son, who was obviously trying
to suppress laughter. Since Villam was notorious even among the
great princes of the realm for his weakness for comely young concubines, it was useful to know his children were aware of his fault
and apt to judge him leniently despite it. She sighed. Now that King
Henry had charged her with this errand, she knew she would be

drawn more and more into the intrigues that journeyed along with the cavalcade of physical creatures and goods on the king's progress. The prospect gave her no pleasure. It would only take time away from her *History*.

"He must choose carefully if he marries again," she said, resigning herself to the inevitable.

"*When* he marries again. Henry is too shrewd to remain unmarried, and when a worthy alliance reveals itself, I am sure he will take advantage of it. Henry is a man like any other." Villam stroked his gray beard while he watched hounds and then riders vanish into a stand of wood. He wore his usual affable smile, but there was a certain reticence about his expression, a distance in his eyes as he contemplated the wood below, silent trees which concealed the hunting party within. "A man like any other. Except he has only the one bastard and wishes for no other. None can fault the king's piety."

"Indeed not," she hurriedly agreed. Certainly it was true.

"But it is not piety that stays him from *that* course."

"You are saying, Lord Helmut, that it is memory, not piety, that restrains him from taking a concubine. The events to which you refer occurred while I was still a novice at Korvei. You think he loves the woman still?"

"No *woman*. I am not sure I would call it love. Sorcery, more like. Understand this, Sister Rosvita. She cared nothing for the rest of us." That same self-mocking smile teased his lips and vanished. "And I say that not only because I am a vain man and wished for her to acknowledge my interest in her, and was annoyed that she did not. Certainly, she was beautiful. She had also an arrogance worthy of the Emperor Taillefer himself, were he to descend from the heavens and walk among us as she did then. But we were as nothing to her. Her indifference to the rest of us was as complete as ours is to—" He ran a hand along the smooth surface of the log, long since scoured free of its bark by wind and rain and sun. Picking up a tiny insect, he displayed it, let it crawl across the tips of his fingers, then flicked it casually away. It vanished among the weeds. "—this least of Our Lord's and Lady's creatures. Perhaps it was only a man's vanity, but I always felt she wanted something from Henry, not that she felt affection toward him. But I have never figured out what it was she wanted."

"Not the child?"

"Why leave the child behind if she wanted it? The infant was not more than two months old. No." He shook his head. "Perhaps a sudden madness took her, and that was all. Perhaps, like the beasts of the field, her time came upon her, and Henry happened to be the bull at hand. Perhaps her kind do not think as we do and so we can never hope to fathom her actions and intent. Or perhaps, as some whisper, there are forces at work we are not aware of." He shrugged. "Sanglant is strong and brave, well versed in warfare, generous and loyal and prudent. But he is still a bastard, and a bastard he will always remain."

"So we are brought around again to our purpose here today. I have rested enough, Lord Helmut. Shall we go on?"

He nodded assent. His son handed him the reins to his horse and Rosvita took up her walking staff. She had been offered a donkey to ride, but she preferred to approach a hermit of such holy reputation in the most humble manner possible, as St. Thecla was said to have approached the blessed Daisan when first she came to him begging to become his disciple.

On they went. In fact, she had put off the errand for several days, hoping Henry would change his mind and decide not to send her. But he had not changed his mind. Sympathy for Father Bardo's plight had forced her hand: As long as the king's progress remained at Hersford Monastery, the abbot had to feed them. Hersford was prosperous but not rich enough to host the king's entourage for longer than five or six days.

The broad dirt path soon became a thin weedy track that cut through undergrowth and in and out of stands of trees. Their party had to walk single file and the horses were much bothered by vegetation slapping into them. Rosvita, at the fore, apologized more than once for forgetting and letting a branch spring back directly into the head of Villam's son, but Berthold never complained. It was a still day, a little muggy, suggesting a hot summer to come.

The crown of the hill was not, as she had supposed, the same thick forest through which they had ascended. The path broke suddenly into sunlight and they emerged onto a level field strewn with great fallen stones and the scattered saplings and bushy undergrowth that marked this as a place once inhabited by people but now abandoned, being slowly overtaken by the forest beyond. Four mounds overgrown with lush grass and wildflowers rose in the great clearing.

"I never knew the old Dariyans built on hills as high as this," said Villam, obviously surprised to find ruins here.

Rosvita ventured farther into the clearing. She bumped up against a stone hidden by grass. It was a great block of stone, gray and weathered, with pictures or words carved into it, so worn away by weather, years, and the lichen grown into its curves and grooves that she could not make out what the long-dead builders had chiseled into the stone. She followed the shape of the monolith with her hands, tearing grass away. The block of stone was huge, twice her height though it now lay full length on the ground. At its base she saw the deep hole where it had been sunk into the ground. Now the sinkhole sprouted a thick tangle of nettles.

"This is not a Dariyan ruin, I think," she said when Villam and his son came up beside her. "See. These inscriptions or images here are much worn, and usually we can read those left by the Dariyan peoples. Also, all of the Dariyan forts I have seen were built to square lines. Look."

She turned to survey the clearing. From here the four mounds stood equidistant and at equal angles to the position of the base of the great stone block. The forest surrounded them, tall trees cutting off any view they might have of the lands below.

"It looks as if the other stones are laid in a circle around this one. And all of them contained by the earth mounds. This is not Dariyan work."

"Then whose might it be?" asked Villam. He was still puffing. "Giants must have carried this stone up here. Horses could not have dragged it, not up so steep and high a height as this."

"And with the trees so high," added Berthold, who was clearly intrigued by these ruins, "this serves no purpose as a fort. We can't see anything of the land around us."

Rosvita studied the mounds and the tree line. "I wonder." She used her walking stick to beat the undergrowth aside and made her way across the clearing to one of the mounds. Berthold followed her while Villam remained behind, still catching his breath. The men-at-arms had taken the horses aside to graze. As she walked and became more aware of the old stones around her, Rosvita felt suddenly that the men-at-arms might simply be reluctant to enter the old fallen ring of stones.

Since that certainly was what this was. A giant's ring, some called them; elf crowns, said others. Some said they were the teeth of dragons who had fallen asleep and turned to stone when sunlight struck them. Others said that even before the Aoi, the Lost Ones, had abandoned Dariya under the onslaught of Bwrmen and their human allies from the east, there were other creatures who roamed and built here: giants, or the half-human spawn of dragons, or the descendents of angels. These creatures were said to possess a strength and knowledge now lost to humankind, just as the collapse of the Dariyan Empire some four hundred years ago had left the humans who survived that calamity with but a fraction of the knowledge and wisdom that had grown and flourished in the great union of elves and men known as the old Dariyan Empire.

She used her stick to help her climb up the steep slope of one of the mounds—the westernmost one, she judged by the position of the sun and the shadows. Her robes got in the way, and she yanked them free of her feet and of grasping bushes with a grunt of irritation. Berthold did not follow her up. Rather, he ranged around the base of the mound, knocking at slabs of stone and shoving aside shrubby stumps of plants with the butt of his knife.

Breathing hard, cheeks flushed, she scrambled up to the uneven top of the mound and stared out with great satisfaction. Indeed, as she had suspected, from the mounds one could see out over the trees, although the lines of sight did not bring her eye down into the valley but rather to the summits of other hills and to the heavens themselves. From where she stood she had a good view of the clearing, the footprints of fallen stones in the tangled undergrowth; as far as she could tell, they had been aligned in a circle.

"Look here!" Berthold sang out with sudden excitement. He stood below her at the base of the mound on the side that faced away from the stone circle. She made her way carefully down to him, arriving at the same time as his father.

He was pink with excitement. "I've seen old mounds like this before. There was a cluster of them out by the river at my blessed mother's estate on the Auras River. Always there is some kind of opening, a passageway. And see. *Here.*" He had found a sturdy stick and wedged open a fallen slab of stone. Rosvita knelt and peered in. A dark opening yawed there, black as pitch and with the scent of air and objects long uncovered to the light. She shuddered and drew back. Berthold, with all the enthusiasm of youth, took her place, shoving the opening a little wider.

"Do you think that wise?" asked Villam suddenly.

"We crawled into the other one." Berthold shoved his shoulders into the gap so far his voice was muffled. "There was nothing but a dry chamber deep inside. Some old bones and broken pots. And dirt."

Villam drew the Circle of Unity at his breast. "Is that the way to respect the remains of the dead?" he demanded. "Or at the least, to be prudent when dealing with—" He broke off.

"Ai!" said Berthold with disgust, backing out. "It's too dark and we have no torch. Even if I could move this slab, there's a bend in the passage ahead, and there'd be no light to see by. But I could come back up tomorrow or the next day, with some of my men and torches." He glanced up over his shoulder, grinning sweetly. "With your leave, Father."

"And disturb what manner of creature?" asked Villam, looking appalled.

Rosvita could not help but nod in agreement. The old tomb, if tomb it was, was better left undisturbed. But Berthold had all the blithe enthusiasm of youth. He looked delighted.

"Do you suppose?" he asked. "No. If old sorceries were at work here, then certainly they have long since gone to sleep. There might be treasure!"

"Surely, Sister Rosvita," said Villam, appealing to her in the face of his son's excitement, "you believe, as I do, that it is better to leave the dead asleep and not to disturb them unless they themselves invite you in."

"I know little of sorcery, Lord Helmut. The sisters of St. Valeria are better known for their studies of the forbidden arts while we at Korvei have long labored over our chronicles. But any suggestion of sorcery is not to be taken lightly. Whether living or long dead."

She spoke sternly, hoping to make some impression on the young man, but Berthold merely nodded his head obediently and then went to investigate the other mounds.

Villam sighed. "He is a fine boy. But too curious, and lacking prudence."

"We will be riding on from Hersford Monastery soon, Lord Helmut. I will attempt to keep an eye on him until that time."

"I thank you."

Watching the young man pressing through the grass, her gaze traveled along the forest's edge. And there, she saw a track. It was no more than an opening among trees, but it corresponded to the vague directions given her by Father Bardo. *"Beyond the height of the hill follow the trail of the animals, or so I have been told."* Father Bardo had not, evidently, seen fit to visit the most famous holy member of his own cloister. But then, Father Bardo enjoyed his comforts and did not like to leave the pleasant luxuries of the monastery.

Be not too proud, Rosvita, she chided herself, *lest you be judged as harshly as you judge others in your turn.*

"That is our trail," she said, turning full to face the forest.

At once, her back to the mound and the thin black opening that yawned from it, she felt something watching her.

She spun back. Immediately that sense of an unseen presence vanished. It was only an overgrown mound with a passageway blocked by stone slabs.

But Villam had a strange expression on his face. "I had a sudden feeling," he said, and shook himself. "As if something clutched at me, trying to find out what I was, just as a blind man might grope at what is before him because he can only see and recognize it with his fingers."

"Let us move away from here," said Rosvita.

"I will fetch my son," he said, "and meet you at the path."

He hurried away. Cautiously, she turned her back to the mound. Again, she felt the unseen presence, but more muted, as if it was keeping its distance. It took a great deal of resolve for her to walk away from the mound toward the trail without looking back over her shoulder.

Villam and Berthold and the men-at-arms met her at the trail, which was scarcely more than a parting of branches. It led into the trees. But she took not more than one hundred steps, sloping down, before she found herself at a rocky outcropping. There rose a spring from a defile. Set back against tree and rock was a tiny hut. It had fresh plaster on the outside walls. Moss grew on the roof, giving the thatch a coat of green.

She became aware of the wind soughing through the trees and the clack of branches against rock, of the chitter of small creatures, hushing as the horses stamped, and the singing of birds in the boughs above.

It had been completely, unnaturally, silent in the clearing of fallen stones. There had been no sound but what they had brought with them or made by their own efforts.

Here it was quiet but not silent. Villam and his men stood respectfully back while she approached the hut. A bench hewn from a log sat in front of the door, which was built of many branches lashed together. This crude door had no latch. A small opening, about the length and breadth of her arm from hand to elbow, was cut into the bottom of the door.

She knelt and spoke in a soft voice.

"Brother Fidelis. I am Rosvita of Korvei. I am come to beg speech of you."

Nothing. No reply, no sound from within the hut. It was so miserably proportioned that Rosvita could not imagine that a man would ever truly be comfortable in there, never able to stand completely upright nor to lay down at full extension.

"Brother Fidelis?"

Nothing.

She had a horrible sudden fear he was dead. But that would be no terrible thing if the old hermit had died peacefully as he meditated and was then borne up to the Chamber of Light by angels. It would certainly be disappointing, for there was much she had hoped to learn from him. She smiled ruefully, aware her desire for learning caused her heart to be restless and thus not always able to single-mindedly contemplate the mercy of Our Lady's and Lord's Grace, as she ought.

Still, no sound. But what if the *thing* from the mound had taken him? What if some *thing* did live here on the height of the hill, an old *thing*, unused to company and jealous of its privacy, hating all things that still walked with confidence in the light of day?

But then, faintly, she heard a rustling.

"Brother Fidelis?"

His voice was like the whisper of leaves stirred along the forest floor by a searching wind. "Recite to me something from your new work, this history of the Wendish people that you labor over, Sister Rosvita."

"I have not brought it with me," she said, startled by this request.

"I am humbled for my curiosity." She heard amusement in that dry, quiet voice and a trace of a Salian accent in the way he pronounced the Wendish words. "But it is ever thus, my friend, that my heart seeks peace while my mind is yet restless." She smiled, and as if he had seen that smile, he continued. "So is it with you, I believe, Sister. But you did not come here to receive my confession."

This surprised her even more. "Are you wishing to give a confession, Brother? Of course I will hear you, if you are driven to speak."

"I am full of sin, as are we all who live on this earth. I have been a faithful son of the church, but alas, my heart has not always been faithful to Our Lady and Lord. Devils have appeared to tempt me."

The door of lashed branches stared at her, revealing nothing except the smooth coat of wood worn clean by time. Of course at this moment she wanted nothing more than to know in what guise devils had appeared to tempt Brother Fidelis. He was as old as Mother Otta, of a great age, having passed nine or even ten decades, or so it was said in Hersford Monastery. But it was not usual for a woman to hear the confession of a monk; that was done by a male cleric or one of the fraters. Most monks turned away explicitly from the world and that included the ministrations of deacons, who were of course all women.

Behind the blank screen of the hut, Brother Fidelis coughed, a scraping sound made worse because he seemed to have so little strength to manage it. "We are like, you and I," he said finally when he had recovered his breath. "I know what you are thinking, for I would be wondering the same thing, were I out there, and you in here. I have taken a vow of silence for many years now and shut myself in this hut so I would not be distracted by the world, but I feel that my time on this earth is coming to an end. So I will speak to you now, and answer your questions."

She settled back onto her heels and set her hands on her thighs, letting him catch his breath. "I have come at the order of King Henry. He wishes to know if you have any knowledge of the laws during the reign of the Emperor Taillefer."

"I was given as an infant to the cloister founded and ruled over by St. Radegundis, she who was the eighth and last wife and then widow of Taillefer. I served at that cloister among the brothers in the monastic quarters until her death, which occurred some fifty years after the death of Taillefer." Here his voice quavered and she had to bend until her ear touched the wood in order to hear him. His labored breathing was louder than his words. "That was a time of trial, and I did succumb, to my everlasting sorrow." He took in a deep shuddering breath.

There was a long silence. Rosvita waited patiently. Behind, horses stamped. A bird trilled. The men-at-arms talked in low voices between themselves. Not even Villam dared approach the hut though Berthold was wandering restlessly along the outcropping, testing the rock for handholds.

"After that time I left the cloister to wander the world. With my voice I said that I sought more evidence of the miracles wrought by St. Radegundis, who in her merciful kindness and open-hearted generosity was the best and most pious among us. But in my heart I sought knowledge. I was curious. I could not find in me that detachment which we seek, those of us who are dedicated to the church. Knowledge tempted me too much. In the end I came here, when I became too weak to walk many miles at a stretch. At last I left even the monastery behind and was carried to this hill, to seek and find detachment. But I have failed in that also." His voice was gentle, a little slurred. "It is well that Our Lady and Lord are merciful, for I pray they will forgive me these weaknesses."

"I am sure they will, Brother," she said, much touched by this *vita*, this brief history of his life.

"So I have some knowledge of the laws of Taillefer," he finished. "Ask what you will."

Here, she hesitated. But the king himself had charged her with this errand, and though she served the church, she also served the king. "King Henry wishes to know about the laws of succession among the Salians, during the time of Taillefer."

"Taillefer's influence once extended as far as these lands. But he died without naming an heir, as you must know, Sister, for you, like your sisters at Korvei, study the old chronicles. And without an heir, his great empire soon fell to strife between warring claimants for his throne."

"He had living daughters."

"Legitimate daughters, of whom three were in the church. But in the Salian tradition only men are allowed to be sovereign, and their women queen consort, not more than that."

"Yet Our Lady and Lord reign together in the Chamber of Light."

His breath whistled out, and she listened to him breathe for a bit, gathering strength again. "Did the blessed Daisan himself not say that 'people have established laws in each country by that liberty given them by God?' People do not lead their lives in the same manner. So is it with the Salians and the Wendish peoples."

"So did the blessed Daisan remind us that we are not slaves to our physical nature."

He wheezed out a soft laugh and then, again, she had to wait while he regained his breath.

"Some chronicles say," Rosvita added, "that Queen Radegundis was pregnant when her husband died, and that it was this child—had it been a boy—whom Taillefer would have named as his heir. But no one knows what became of the child, whether it was still-born, murdered, or not brought to term."

"Radegundis never spoke of the child. Of all those who were at Taillefer's court at that time, only one servingwoman by the name of Clothilde remained by St. Radegundis' side throughout her years in the cloister. Perhaps she knew the answer to the mystery, but she kept silence also. It is that silence which brought about the end of Taillefer's great empire. If a boychild had been born and acknowl-edged, that boy would indeed have reigned after him. If Queen Ra-degundis could have found support among the Salian and Varren nobility, for enough years, to raise the child to manhood."

Rosvita reflected gravely on Sabella, raising revolt against a king as strong as Henry. Imagine how much more likely the nobles would be to fight over a throne held by a child. No infant was safe from the intrigues of the great princes, all of whom sought power. According to the histories, Radegundis had been very young when she had married Taillefer, more pretty than wellborn, for by his sixty-fifth year Taillefer could choose his wives as he pleased. No young queen without strong family connections could hope to guide her child safely through such a world, with so many dukes and counts set against her.

"In Varre or Wendar," continued Fidelis, "the one daughter who was not pledged to the church would have inherited and held the throne, if she was strong enough. But the Salians preferred a bas-tard boy to a legitimate girl. With my own eyes, when I still lived at St. Radegundis Cloister, I read a capitulary from that time, stat-ing that an illegitimate son could inherit a father's portion. This is why the dukes and counts of Salia and the bastard sons of Taille-fer—for he had as many concubines as wives—fought over the em-pire and brought it to ruin."

This, thought Rosvita sadly, was the message King Henry wanted to hear: *"A capitulary stating that an illegitimate son could inherit."*

Yet she hesitated, for Brother Fidelis also spoke of ruin. "Then a bastard son *could* inherit throne and crown in Salia?"

"One did. He ruled for four years before he was murdered by the duc de Rossalia under the flag of truce. And for his perfidy, the duc de Rossalia was punished by the fitting justice of Our Lady and Lord: His lands were purged and plundered for twenty years by the raids of the Eika savages until no house was left unburned and all his people fled. But the throne passed to distant cousins of Taillefer, not his own seed, legitimate or otherwise, and his lineage vanished from the Earth."

Rosvita allowed herself a deep sigh. Four years. Not an auspicious or stable reign.

"This is not what you wished to hear?" asked Brother Fidelis. She felt that he could see her expression, indeed, practically see into her very soul.

"It is not what I wish that matters. But perhaps, Brother, it is this message—of ruin and the downfall of bastard sons—that needs to be spoken to King Henry."

"Even I, in my hut, have heard whispers of the bastard son Henry got with an Aoi woman. The birds sing of this child, and at night when I am at my meditations the daimones of the upper air whisper to each other of the child's progress from infant to youth to man, so that I cannot help but hear them."

Was he jesting or serious? She could not tell. Nor did he elaborate. His breath whistled, a thin sound in the quiet afternoon, as fragile as the desiccated straw that had fallen from the thatch to the cold earth below. Rosvita felt the hard pressure of dirt on her knees. One of her feet was falling asleep.

"Speak to me of your work," he said.

And she heard in his voice the same yearning that ate away at her; a constant curiosity, like a mouse's hunger, insistent and gnawing.

"I am writing a history of the Wendish people, which will be presented to King Henry's mother, Queen Mathilda. She now resides at the convent at Quedlinhame where she has found peace, I trust, and where she watches over her son and her other children. Much of the history will deal with the reigns of the first Henry and the two Arnulfs, for it is by their efforts that the Wendish people rose to the power they now have."

She thought. He breathed, patient. The task of writing this history rose before her in her mind's eye, daunting and yet attractive exactly because it was a challenge. And this man, certainly, would understand what drove her, her curiosities, her fears, the need to investigate and discover. " I have worked as one who walks in a wide forest where every path lies covered deep in snow. I have had no one to guide me while I made my way forward, sometimes wandering devious paths, sometimes hitting the trail. There is so much you might tell me, Brother Fidelis. So much you must know! So much you must have seen with your own eyes or heard from those who did see!"

"I have little breath left to me." So weak was this utterance that she thought for a moment she had only imagined it. "Indulge me, Sister. As a child confesses to its mother, may I confess to you now?"

She was aware of bitter disappointment. But she could not refuse him. "I have taken orders as a deacon. I can hear confessions."

He spoke very slowly now, a few labored words with each wheezing breath. "I have sinned once, and greatly, for lying with a woman. That was many years ago, though I think of her still with affection. I have tried to be content. I have tried to still the anger that eats away at my heart. And so at last I have found peace of a kind. I have looked away from the world and seen that its temptations mean nothing compared to the promise of the Chamber of Light." He had such a kind voice, that of a man who sees his own faults and forgives himself for them—not arrogantly or leniently but with wisdom—knowing that he, as are all humans, is hopelessly flawed. "But still devils visit me. Not in the guise of women, as they so afflict some of my brothers. Not even in the guise of she whom I recall so clearly." Now he paused. To hear him breathe, harsh rasps torn out of a weak and failing chest, was painful. "But in the guise of scholars and magi, tempting me with knowledge, if only . . . if only I would . . . "

His voice failed. She could hear his breath, so faint the flapping of a butterfly's wings might have drowned it out. All at once she became aware of the world beyond her. The birds still sang. Were they singing of the deeds of Sanglant? But she could not understand their language. Berthold had clambered to the top of the outcropping and was surveying the lands below with evident pleasure. The vitality of youth sang out from his figure where he stood—never completely still—at the edge of a sheer drop-off. Villam had stationed himself at the base of the outcropping and was clearly annoyed, or worried, but unwilling to raise his voice and thus disturb the holy man.

It was hot, though the sun was hidden behind clouds. Sweat had broken out under her wool robe, trickling down her spine. She restrained herself from wiping her neck. Any movement on her part might cover Brother Fidelis' next words.

She heard him shift within the tiny hut. "If only I would tell them what I knew of the secrets of the Seven Sleepers. But I swore never again to speak of these things. And yet . . . "

She waited. He did not continue.

From inside the hut she heard the sound of something being dragged, not something as heavy as a body, something light but solid. A shadow crossed the slit cut into the door, then a dark shape slowly emerged. Heart beating suddenly fast, Rosvita took hold of it and drew it out.

It was a book.

Laboriously bound, stitched out of parchment leaves, it was a book written in a clear, elegant hand.

"On this I have labored many years when I should have been meditating on the Holy Word of God in Unity. I pass it on to you, so that it will hold my spirit on this earth no longer. Godspeed, Sister. May Our Lady and Lord watch over your labors. Do not forget what you have learned here. Fare you well."

She stared at the book. Inscribed on the cover were these words: *The Vita of St. Radegundis.*

Then, finally, his last words registered: *Fare you well.*

"Brother Fidelis?"

The sun came out from behind the clouds, blinding her momentarily, its light was so unexpectedly bright.

"Go, then," his voice said, sounding in her ears. Spoken like a command, strong and firm, it was utterly unlike the frail voice with which she had conversed through the screen of branches.

She rose, keeping a tight hold on the book. "Fare you well, Brother. I thank you. I will keep your words locked in my heart."

Did she hear him smile? It was only her fancy. The hut stood in front of her, small and ragged, as poor a hovel as any beggar might build for himself to keep the rain off his back. She backed away, not wanting to turn her back on the old man, for fear of seeming disrespectful. Stumbled over the ground.

Villam caught her arm. "The interview is ended?"

"It is over." She looked back. No sign of life came from the hut.

"I heard nothing, and saw nothing," said Villam. "Except my son, climbing like a young squirrel trying to dash its brains out on the cliffs below."

"Let us go," said Rosvita. She did not have the heart to speak of their conversation.

Villam accepted her reticence. He signed to his men. Together they made their way back along the trail, this time skirting the clearing of fallen stones. Rosvita was too sunk in thought to observe the clearing or even think much of it, though Berthold tried to detour over to one of the mounds and was stopped by his father.

King Henry would not like what Brother Fidelis had said, not if Henry wished to name Sanglant as his heir. It was all very well to say a bastard might inherit the throne in Salia. But not when the price was death, civil war, and the extinction of a noble lineage. Perhaps Henry would see reason. He was a good man and a good king, and he had three strong legitimate children.

But that was not what ate at her. Like a hand scratching at a door, the question nagged at her. Who were the Seven Sleepers?

In all her reading and study, preparing to write her work of history, she had come across a few references to the Seven Sleepers. It was an innocuous story, one of many set among the tales of the early martyrs; even Eusebē mentioned it, in passing, in her *Ecclesiastical History*.

In the time of the persecution of Daisanites by the Dariyan Emperor Tianathano, seven young persons in the holy city of Saïs took refuge in a cave to gain strength before they presented themselves for martyrdom; the cave miraculously sealed over them and there they were left to sleep until . . .

Until when? That Rosvita had never learned, or even thought to ask. As she had learned over twenty years of studying the chronicles and interviewing eyewitnesses to events fifty years ago, not all tales were necessarily true.

But something in the way Brother Fidelis had said the words, his hesitation, his suggestion that creatures who were not human worried at him in his solitude, plaguing him to make him speak of these "seven sleepers," made her think this was more than just a legend.

"You are solemn, Sister Rosvita," said Villam, understandably trying to draw her out.

"I have much to think about," she said. He was too well mannered to press her.

2

THAT night they celebrated the Feast of St. Susannah, saint beloved by cobblers and goldsmiths and jewelers. The king's retinue filled up the old monastery's guest houses and half the villages within an hour's walk of the cloister, in addition to those who stayed in tents pitched in the surrounding pastures. The brother cellarer, in charge of provisioning the monastery, was actually heard to mutter that the king's retainers were too many and too fond of their food and wine.

Henry presented a sober face to the assembly. Only Rosvita and Villam knew why she had spoken to the old hermit. Only Rosvita knew the content of that interview and Henry's reaction to it when she had told him the whole.

He had thought for a long time while she stood, patient and silent, beside him. Although Father Bardo had offered his own study to Henry, to use as bedchamber and receiving room, Henry chose the upstairs room in the chief guest house. The room was spacious but boasted no ornamentation.

Here, with both shutters open to the spring air, she and King Henry were alone for a brief time.

Except on formal occasions, Henry always dressed in the style of his people, if more richly than most: knee-length tunic trimmed with gold braid; leggings and; at this time of year, soft leather boots worked with eagles and lions and dragons, the three pillars on which his power was built. The Eagles were his messengers, the Lions his faithful foot soldiers, and the Dragons his heavy cavalry, the pride of his army. But these were only his personal weapons.

His power as king of all Wendar and Varre rested on the submission of the great princes of the realm to his overlordship.

His black leather belt was embossed with the sigils of the six dukedoms, painted in gold: a dragon for Saony, a lion for Avaria, an eagle for Fesse, a *guivre* for Arconia, a stallion for Varingia, where horses were bred, and a hawk for Wayland.

He wore four gold rings, one for each of the marchlords: Helmut

Villam, Judith of Olsatia and Austra, and Werinhar of Westfall. The margrave of Eastfall was dead now and the ring she had received in her turn from Henry lost on the battlefield or stolen away by looters to adorn some Quman lord out on the grasslands.

A fifth ring, bearing the seal of his sovereignty, he wore on a golden chain around his neck.

He wore no crown. It traveled, along with his robe of state, his scepter, and the Holy Lance of St. Perpetua, Lady of Battles, in an oak chest carved with griffins and dragons grappling in eternal war.

He listened to Rosvita's account of her interview with Brother Fidelis. He considered it while she waited. In his youth he had been more impetuous, blurting out his first thoughts. Now, eighteen years after his election to the throne of Wendar and Varre, he had mastered the skill of sitting still.

"But Taillefer did not himself designate one of those illegitimate sons as his heir," he had said finally. "I need only look at my own family. Sabella was found unfit to rule, just as I would have been, had I not proven myself capable. In that case my father would have designated one of my sisters, or my brother Benedict, as heir. But he chose to present me to the dukes and margraves for their affirmation after my heir's progress. Taillefer did not single out any child, bastard or otherwise. If he had, events might have fallen out differently."

Rosvita was left none the wiser, for though she asked circumspectly, he offered no more insight into what he meant to do. His daughters Sapientia and Theophanu sat on either side of him at the great feast that night. His young son Ekkehard was prevailed upon to sing, accompanying himself on the lute; the child truly did have a sweet voice. If Henry chose to put Ekkehard in the church, his would be a fine voice raised in prayer to heaven.

At midmorning the next day two Eagles rode in, covered with dust, travel-worn and weary. They brought grave news.

"Gent is besieged," said the senior of the two women, a grim woman who favored her left leg. She was not reticent in addressing King Henry. "We were five Eagles, riding to Gent to see the truth of these rumors for ourselves. Within sight of the city but outside the walls, we were set upon by Eika. I was wounded in the attack. So my comrade—" Here she indicated the other woman, who was young, perhaps the age of Berthold or Theophanu. "—and I fled west to carry this news to you, Your Majesty. We rode part of the way with a company of Dragons. They escorted a deacon and a holy relic to safety. The rest of the Dragons, including Prince Sanglant, remain besieged within Gent.''

''You say it is a raiding party?'' asked Henry quietly.

She shook her head. ''Not according to the Dragons who escorted us, Your Majesty. At last count there were fifty-two Eika ships.''

Henry was sitting on a bench in the unicorn courtyard, attended by his companions and courtiers. This information sent up a murmur, quickly stilled when Henry lifted a hand to quiet them. ''Do you think they mean to invade?''

''According to Sturm—he was the commander of the company we rode with—the Eika want the bridges that connect Gent to the east and west shore of the river thrown down. That way they can raid upriver at their leisure.''

''And this Commander Sturm, where is he now?''

''He returned to the vicinity of Gent. He and his men hope to harry the Eika outside the walls, to aid their brethren trapped within.''

Henry glanced to his right, where Helmut Villam stood. ''Gent lies within the lands administered by Count Hildegard, does it not?'' Villam nodded.

''What of her forces?'' the king asked.

''I do not know,'' admitted the Eagle. ''They are not within the city. Certainly she must have news of the siege by now.''

The king gestured, and a servant brought him a cup of wine. He sipped at it thoughtfully. ''You said there were five Eagles?''

The woman nodded. Her companion, already pale, began to look quite white, the look of a person who has spent many sleepless hours in fruitless worrying; she had the light complexion that betrayed northern blood, light blue eyes and coarse wheat-blonde hair twisted into braids. The older woman betrayed neither anger nor grief. ''The others rode on. I don't know if they got into the city safely, but I believe they did.''

''You did not see them enter within the walls?''

''I did not. But the man I rode with, Wolfhere, bound my comrade Manfred and I to him with various small devices. Had he died, I believe I would know of it.''

''Ah,'' said Henry, one eyebrow arching. ''Wolfhere.''

To Rosvita, mostly, one Eagle was much like another. Nobleborn

boys and girls were given their own retainers when they came of
age or, if circumstances warranted, they served with the Dragons.
Service as a king's messenger or in the king's infantry was relegated
to the children of freeholders, not those of noble birth. But every
cleric in the king's chapel and *schola* knew Wolfhere by sight or at
least by reputation. There was no Eagle senior to him, and it was
sometimes whispered—though not so often these days—that he
knew many things beyond the ken of human knowledge. He had
been in favor during the reign of the younger Arnulf; some claimed
he had too much influence over Arnulf, especially for a man not
born into a noble family. That favor had ended within a year of
Henry's ascent to the throne. Wolfhere had been banished from the
king's presence. Rosvita did not know why.

"Yes, Your Majesty." The woman had a strong gaze, and she was
not afraid to look King Henry in the face. "I am proud to call him
praeceptor." Instructor and guide. She used the Dariyan word deliberately. Rosvita guessed she knew something, at least, of Wolfhere's
reputation at court.

Henry's lips turned up. Rosvita knew him well enough, after all
this time, to see he admired the young Eagle's forthright manner.
"How long have you served in my Eagles, and what is your name
and lineage?"

"For seven years I have served in the Eagles, mostly in the marchlands. I joined as soon as I came of age. I am named Hathui, daughter of Elseva, a freeholder in Eastfall."

"And your father?"

"My father was called Volusianus. He was also born of free parents. But alas, Your Majesty, he was killed while in the service of
King Arnulf, fighting the Redari."

The king glanced toward Villam, who gazed benignly at the
young woman. Rosvita remembered well the last war against the
Redari; it had taken place in the final year of Arnulf's reign and was
mostly fought in the March of the Villams. Indeed, the lands over
which the Villams held authority had greatly expanded after the
capitulation of the Redari tribesmen and their conversion to the
faith of the Unities.

"After his death, my mother and her sister and brother were
among those who traveled east of the Eldar River with grants given
them by King Arnulf, to take lands for themselves, under the authority of no lord or lady."

"Except that of the king."

She bent her head slightly, acknowledging the truth of his words. "Except that of the king," she repeated.

Henry lifted his left hand, signing her to rise. "You will travel with my court, Hathui, daughter of Elseva, and serve me." This signal honor was not lost on the gathered assembly, who were no doubt wondering how much the king intended to favor this commoner. Rosvita examined the courtiers. Who would be first to attempt to befriend the Eagle and who first to attempt to bring about her downfall?

Hathui seemed untroubled by this sign of favor. "And my comrade, Hanna, daughter of Birtha and Hanal? She is new to the Eagles and has little experience, less training, and no kin nearby."

"She may join us as well. You may act as her praeceptor."

It occurred to Rosvita suddenly that Henry was rewarding the two Eagles for another reason: for bringing him news of his son.

"We must consider an army," he said, turning to Villam. "How soon can we ride to Gent?"

3

AFTER her initial shock wore off, Hanna found herself more frustrated than honored by her elevation to one of those exalted Eagles who waited in personal attendance upon King Henry.

Not because of Henry, of course. He was everything she had ever dreamed a king would be: stern but with the capacity for laughter; elegant in appearance and yet without the kind of vanity that leads men to wear fine clothes and jewels for the sake of showing off their riches; gracious without being friendly; unwilling to tolerate incompetence and delay.

But there was only so much a king could do when it came time to attempt to move his vast entourage—the king's progress—quickly, or when it came time to raise an army from lands as far apart as the northwesternmost reaches of the duchy of Saony, the highlands far to the south of Avaria, and the distant marchlands to the east.

Raised by a briskly efficient innkeeper, Hanna was amazed at how slow everything moved and how many arguments there were between chatelaines and stewards and lordlings over fine points of status and honor that would make not one whit of difference to the people trapped in Gent if the Eika broke through the city's walls.

"At this rate they'll be dead before we leave this monastery," she muttered to Hathui that evening as she watched yet another noble lord—a young woman in this case—making excuses before the king as to why it would take her some unreasonable number of days to raise levies and then yet again longer beyond that to march those levies as far north as Gent. Lady bless! Beyond being maddening, it was also boring. She stifled a yawn and felt Hathui shift her weight. "How is your leg?"

"It will do," said Hathui. "Attend to your duties. Who is that?"

"What?"

"Who is that speaking before the king?"

Hanna stared, but she could not tell one noble lordling from another; they all ran together in her mind in their handsome embroidered gowns or tunics and gold-braided leggings and fine necklaces and rings.

"That is part of your duty, Hanna," said Hathui sternly, sounding much like Wolfhere. "You must memorize all the great houses of Wendar and Varre and learn the names of the lords and ladies of those lineages and their alliances by marriage and kinship and oaths, and which dislike whom and who wishes to marry for advantage where, and what estates have lost their lady and thus are being willed to the church or given to the king to reward to some family who has done him a signal service."

"Ai, Lady," swore Hanna under her breath. "All that?"

"And more besides." But Hathui grinned, taking the threat out of the words. "*That* is Liutgard, duchess of Fesse. Because Fesse lies in the center of the kingdom, it is a long ride from there to Gent, which lies to the northeast. Also, the duchy of Fesse lies next to the duchy of Arconia, which is the duchy administered by Henry's half sister Sabella. Surely you have heard the rumors that Sabella plans to rebel against the king?"

Hanna had heard so many rumors just in the eight hours since she and Hathui had arrived at Hersford Monastery that she had given up trying to sort one out from the next. "And? What difference does that make to Duchess Liutgard?"

"This difference: that Liutgard does not want to send away troops to Gent, which lies many days' march north and east, when her own lands might be threatened by Sabella. Henry must balance the threat to Gent against the threat to Fesse."

Hanna sighed. "How do you keep this all straight?"

"That is only the beginning."

But Hanna could see Hathui was laughing at her, not without sympathy. "Was it difficult for you, when you first came into the Eagles? Did it all seem like so many names that had no meaning attached to them?"

Hathui shrugged. "When Wolfhere is your praeceptor, you never admit you are struggling. But, in truth, it did seem difficult. After a time, though, I began to sort them all out. You must know the name of every villager in Heart's Rest, do you not? And in the neighboring farms and hamlets?"

"Of course!"

"Well, then, think of the noble lords and ladies who move on the king's progress as a village. Some remain in the village all the time;

others come and go according to what duties they have on their family's estates. Truly, Hanna, they are no different from common men and women. I have observed they have their feuds and their secret lovers, their alliances and their disagreements, just as any folk do. They sleep and eat and pray and use the privies. I am not convinced that, if you were to put one of them in a simple freehold-er's smock and any hardworking freeholder into an elegant tunic, you could tell who was the noble lord and who the farmer."

"Hathui!"

But Hathui only smiled her proud marchlander's smile and signed that Hanna should attend to the proceedings again.

Attend Hanna did. For some odd reason, Hathui's shocking opin-ions made it easier for her to sort out one noble from the other. That thin glaze of intimidation had worn off, shorn away forever by Hathui's blunt observations. She noticed the old counsellor—the margrave Helmut Villam—yawning as Duchess Liutgard promised she would ride out at dawn the next day with her retinue. But it would still take some weeks before a levy could be raised, and longer still to march that force across the kingdom.

The very young man standing beside Villam—his son, that was it, though Hanna could not remember what the boy's name was or if she had even heard it yet—fidgeted and looked very much as if he wished to be somewhere else. Hanna's milk brother Ivar had that look sometimes when he was thinking about another prank to play or some expedition into the forest he wanted Hanna to come along for; Ivar was the sort of person who was either full of a manic energy or gloomily downcast.

How was Ivar faring now? Had he reached Quedlinhame Cloister yet, to begin his life as a monk? Hanna was a bit unclear on dis-tances within the kingdom and where all the different cities and cloisters were. But one thing Hanna did know: Ivar would not take well to cloister walls. He was bound to get into some kind of mis-chief.

She sighed. Ai, Lady. There was nothing she could do for Ivar, not now. She had chosen Liath over Ivar and now, as if to punish her for her choice, the Lady had granted she be separated from both of them.

Duchess Liutgard finished her business with the king and moved back to make room for a noblewoman who appeared to be about the same age as Henry. This woman wore her years proudly. Her hair was coiled into long braids and pinned back; though it was gray now, Hanna could see it had once been a rich brown.

Hathui leaned to whisper in Hanna's ear. "Judith, margrave of Olsatia and Austra."

The margrave informed Henry that she would ride immediately to her estates in Austra and raise at least two hundred men to ride to Gent.

"And do not forget that my son Hugh is abbot at Firsebarg now. If you will send word to him, I know he can send a contingent to reinforce yours, Your Majesty."

Hugh! Hanna did not breathe for a moment. She had almost forgotten Hugh, but staring at this imposing woman she was struck anew by memory of him. Judith was a woman of mature years, broad in girth and dignified of manner. She had delicate features not yet obscured by old age, and Hanna could see Hugh's features there: the sharp planes of his handsome face, the bright, deep-set eyes, the haughty expression. But the margrave's hair had obviously been dark, quite unlike Hugh's light hair. Was it true that Hugh's father had been a slave from Alba, whose men were renowned for their golden-haired beauty?

"Don't be a fool, Hanna," she whispered to herself. Instantly she wondered how Liath fared. Had they gotten into Gent safely? Was Liath well? Injured? Dead? Did Hugh think of Liath still? Of course he never thought of people like Hanna at all. What if he led a contingent of soldiers to Gent? Could Wolfhere protect Liath from Hugh when he did not understand what had taken place over that winter at Heart's Rest?

Hathui's fingers grazed her elbow, a reassuring touch, though surely Hathui couldn't guess what she'd been thinking. And Hanna had no desire to betray such feelings to anyone else, not when she was herself ashamed of them, knowing how viciously Hugh had treated Liath. This was no time for such nonsense, as her mother would say. She shook herself and attended to the business at hand.

Later, after the audiences were over, Hathui was sent to the king's physician and Hanna was sent to the guest house where the king's children made their residence.

Hanna paused inside the door while the two guards posted there—by their gold tabards sewn with a black lion members of Henry's Lion infantry—examined her curiously.

Hanna was more curious about the king's children. Ekkehard

was young, still in the schola, not yet old enough to be given a retinue of his own and sent out into the world as an adult. Right now he sat beside one of his sisters, who accompanied him on a lute. He had a beautiful voice.

> *"When the ships came down from the north*
> *And he saw the gleam of gold in their belly,*
> *Then he plunged into the waters*
> *Though they were as cold as his mother's heart,*
> *Then he plunged into the waters*
> *And swam until he reached them.*
> *With his sword he killed the watchmen*
> *With his knife he killed the steersman*
> *And the oar slaves bowed before him*
> *And begged for him to tell his tale.*
> *When he captured the ships,*
> *This was his song."*

That was Theophanu, accompanying him. Though the king's court was in a constant hum, and had been since morning, she sat calmly and strummed a lute in time to her brother's sweet singing.

The other sister, small and dark and neat, was Sapientia. She paced back and forth, back and forth, like a caged animal. Hanna took a hesitant step forward. Sapientia saw her, began to rush toward her, then stopped short, recalling her position. She beckoned.

"Do you have a message for me, Eagle?" she demanded.

Without losing track of the song, Theophanu raised her eyes briefly to take in the scene and went back to her playing. Ekkehard sang on, oblivious.

Hanna dropped to touch a knee to the floor. "Yes. King Henry charges you to go now to the smith's quarters."

"Hai!" said Sapientia under her breath, exultant. She turned and gestured to her servingwomen, who sat sewing near the fire. "Come!" she said, and strode out so quickly they had to drop their sewing work on the bench and had not even time to grab cloaks before running out after her.

Hanna hesitated. Ekkehard was well into the song by now, a song within a song, really, wherein the hero Sigisfrid relates to the hapless oar slaves his many great deeds as well as revealing for the first time his forbidden love for his cousin Waltharia, the love that would doom them both. Ekkehard had, in fact, an astonishing command of the epic. Hanna had heard old master bards sing from the great epic while taking a night's lodging at the inn, and while Ekkehard's rendition was clearly immature, it was still compelling.

Theophanu glanced up again to study Hanna. The princess' gaze was clear and completely unreadable. Suddenly self-conscious, Hanna backed away and ran right into one of the Lions.

He steadied her with a grin. "Begging your pardon, my friend," he said. "You rode in from Gent with the other Eagle, this morning."

"Yes."

"You're new to the Eagles?"

She nodded. She didn't quite trust him: He was a good-looking young man, and the few good-looking men in Heart's Rest—like her brother Thancmar—were, in her experience, full of themselves.

He opened the door, grinned at his companion guard, and followed her outside. "Where are you barracked tonight?" he asked. He did have a pleasant smile, and a pleasing face, and very nice shoulders, but Hanna loathed men who were full of their own self-importance. *All, except Hugh.* She shoved that thought away.

"With the Eagles, I expect," she said coldly. "Wherever they sleep."

He considered. In the torch-lit entryway, he did not appear downcast or offended by her rejection. In fact, she was not entirely sure he had taken her words as rejection. "Well, if we'll not be barracked together," he said quickly, glancing behind him. "I'm on duty, so I haven't time to talk. You were at Gent. Did you see the Dragons there?"

"We saw one company of them, but I never got inside the city. We turned back, Hathui and I."

"Was there a woman with them, do you know?"

"A woman? With the Dragons? Not that I noticed."

"Ai." He grimaced, disappointed. Had he a sweetheart among the Dragons? Having misjudged him, she suddenly found him rather attractive. "My sister rides with the Dragons."

"Your *sister?*"

He laughed outright. "You're thinking a common born lad like me has no business having a sister in the Dragons."

Since she was thinking so, she did not deny it.

"It's true most of them are nobleborn, bastards usually, or

younger sons without a bequest to get them into the church. But
my sister never wanted anything except to fight. She dedicated herself to St. Andrea very young, before even her first bleeding, and
couldn't be swayed. She joined the Lions, bludgeoned her way into
them, more like. I followed after her."

Hanna remembered how her young brother Karl had looked at
her the day she rode away from Heart's Rest as a newly-hatched
Eagle. Had this young man watched his sister ride away so? Had he
followed her, years later, because of that admiration?

"She distinguished herself," the Lion continued, eager to talk
about his sister in front of a new audience. "Saved the Dragon banner, she did. Some say she saved the prince's life, although others
say no man or woman can do that. That he's under a geas, spoken
on him when he was an infant by his mother, that he can't be killed
by mortal hands or some such kind of thing. Ai, well. I say she
saved his life."

"I didn't see her," repeated Hanna, sorry she hadn't. "What's her
name?"

"Adela." He touched a hand to his chest and gave a little bow, a
courtly gesture no doubt picked up from watching the noble lords.
When he smiled, he had a dimple. "And I'm called Karl."

She laughed. "Why, so is my brother called Karl. I'm Hanna."

"Ai, Lady. That's a bad omen—that you might think of me as a
brother." And, that suddenly, he had remembered it was night, and
he was young, and she was—well, pretty, perhaps, but at the least
desirable and a new face among so many familiar old ones. She
flushed and was angry at herself for doing so.

"And what does your sister say? About the prince?" she said, to
say something.

He grunted. "Nothing but praise, which is tiresome in a woman
when she's speaking of a man. She's as loyal as a dog to him. They
all are, the Dragons. I don't see it myself." He ran two fingers down
to a point at his chin, along his fine light beard, musingly. "How
can you call him truly a man when he can't grow a beard?"

Since Hanna did not know the answer to this question, she wisely
said nothing.

The door into the guest house opened. "Hai! Karl! You've had
enough time." His companion blinked into the night, saw their
figures, and beckoned. "Come on. Back inside. You'll get nothing
from an Eagle, you know how they are."

Karl blew her a kiss and went back to his post.

"Lord, have mercy," she muttered and hurried back to the chamber where the king held court. But Henry had gone to bed, or so Hathui told her.

"Where do we sleep?"

"You haven't been propositioned yet?" asked Hathui and laughed when Hanna betrayed herself by blushing. But the older woman sobered quickly enough. "Attend to my words, Hanna. There is one thing that will get a woman thrown out of the Eagles, and that is if she can no longer ride because she carries a child. 'Make no marriage unless to another Eagle who has sworn the same oaths as you.' "

"That's a harsh precept."

"Our service is harsh. Many of us die serving the king. I'm not saying you must never love a man, or bed one, even, but do not make that choice lightly and never when it is only for a night's pleasure. There are those—old men and women mostly—who know the use of certain herbs and oils—"

"But that's magic," Hanna whispered. "And heathen magic, at that."

Hathui shrugged. "I've seen a deacon use herbs and chants from the Holy Book to heal wounds, so if that's magic, I suppose some in the church don't frown on its use. I'm just saying, Hanna, that if the desire is strong enough, there are ways to prevent conception, though they don't always work. But every gift from the Lady is both burden and treasure. That is the lesson She teaches: Just as fire can both warm and kill, so can that feeling we call sweet passion bring as its fruit death or a blessing in the form of a healthy child." She smiled wryly. "Sometimes it is easier to devote yourself to a saint, as I did. I had no virginity to pledge to St. Perpetua when I became an Eagle, so I offered my chastity instead."

"You were married before you became an Eagle?"

Hathui shook her head, one side of her mouth quirking down and an eye ticking shut as if she was trying to close up an old memory. "No. It was taken from me by a Quman raider. And if I ever meet up with him or his people, he will pay for what he stole."

Hanna felt her mouth drop open.

"You'll catch flies," said Hathui, who had already recovered.

"I—I'm sorry."

Hathui snorted. "What do you expect, from barbarians? I had no lasting harm of it, not like my aunt, who was killed in that raid."

"But—but does this mean I can never have a child?" Hanna considered this prospect without pleasure. It was not something she had ever thought about before. She was a woman, and not in the church. Of course she would have children.

"Of course not, if you wish for children. But you must either leave the Eagles or marry within them. A child born to a woman who is married to another Eagle is accepted. I have seen three such children."

"Have you seen a woman cast out of the Eagles for—well, for bearing a child?"

"I have." Hathui touched her brass badge, her long fingers tracing the eagle embossed there. "This is her badge. She died of the birthing, alas, and the child, too."

Hanna made the sign of the circle at her breast. Death or a blessing. Those words seemed apt enough. It was the kind of thing her mother would say.

"Come, Hanna. Let's sleep. There's bound to be more and much more running to do tomorrow." Hathui kissed Hanna affectionately on the forehead and took her by the arm. "We'll get our blankets. We can bed down here, at the foot of the king's chair."

"At the foot of the king's chair!" This was such a signal honor that Hanna wondered if her parents would ever believe it had actually been granted to their very own daughter.

"Indeed, he said so himself. He's a fine lord, is our king, and I am proud to serve him."

In the morning, just after the office of Terce—the third hour of the day—was sung, another Eagle rode in. He came from the west. He was faint with exhaustion; his horse had foundered.

Grooms took his horse. Hathui took him in hand and with Hanna following at her heels led him in to where the king held audience with Helmut Villam, the margrave, Judith, and others of the nobles in attendance, discussing the final plans for their dispersal to collect armies that could ride to Gent. Henry broke off their conversation and rose.

The Eagle threw himself on his knees before the king. "Your Majesty." He could barely speak, his voice was so hoarse.

"Bring him mead," said the king, and mead was brought.

The man gulped down a cup of the honey-flavored wine, and it soothed his coughing. He apologized. "I beg pardon, Your Majesty."

"Your news?"

"It is terrible news, Your Majesty." Almost, the man wept. "I am come from Autun. I have ridden four days and five nights, stopping only to change horses." He shut his eyes.

The tension in the chamber became unbearable as everyone present waited for him to continue. Hanna tried desperately to remember where Autun was, and what its significance might be. Wasn't it the seat of a biscophric? Yes! That was it: Henry's younger sister Constance was biscop of Autun.

As she remembered this, the Eagle took hold of himself and continued speaking. "I was able to escape Autun because of the aid of Biscop Constance's chatelaine. Autun is now in the hands of Lady Sabella."

Several of the courtiers spoke at once, then fell silent when Henry raised a hand. The king looked grave, as well he might. "The city has fallen?"

The Eagle spoke on a sigh. "By treachery, Your Majesty. Biscop Constance is a prisoner in the hands of Lady Sabella and her retainers. Sabella has installed Helvissa as biscop of Autun."

"Helvissa, whom I removed eight years ago with the consent of the other biscops of the realm?"

"Indeed, the same one, Your Majesty. Autun surrendered without a fight out of respect for the safety of Biscop Constance. Not one soul in Autun considers Helvissa their rightful lord. But that is not all. Sabella has an army, and Duke Rodulf of Varingia marches with her."

None moved or spoke, waiting for the king's reaction.

All Hanna could think of were those awful words: *"Sabella has an army."*

"What of Duke Conrad of Wayland?" Henry asked quietly.

Hanna did not recall how Duke Conrad of Wayland fit into the convoluted kinship surrounding the king's court and that of the great princes, but to everyone else, the question seemed fraught with meaning. All waited. Villam wiped his lips with a knuckle. Duchess Liutgard—who had not yet left, though she was dressed for riding—clasped and unclasped her hands nervously.

But the Eagle only shook his head. He looked utterly exhausted. "I do not know if he marches with her or if he does not. I had to escape in the middle of the night. I have no information beyond that—only that Sabella marches east."

East. Even Hanna knew what that meant. East, to Wendar.

"She swore me an oath," said Henry even more softly. He looked furious and his movements, as he turned to beckon to those closest to him, were as taut as those of a lion's, waiting to pounce. But he did not rage out loud. "Wendar itself is in danger. Sabella rebels against my authority and that rebellion we cannot tolerate. We cannot ride to Gent."

These words struck Hanna like a hammer's blow.

"Ai, Lady," she murmured, her heart leaden in her chest. What was going to happen to Liath?

4

"WE cannot ride to Gent."

What cost to Henry to utter those words?

Rosvita glanced at Villam, saw him looking at her in that same instant, as though they shared a thought. Three legitimate children Henry had. For the sake of the kingdom, he must risk the loss of the fourth.

Henry's hands were clenched. He stared for a long while at the fine Arethousan carpet under his boots, a geometric pattern of imperial purple and pale ivory, floral circles encasing eight-pointed stars. The rug had come as part of Queen Sophia's morning gift to Henry, for only she, daughter of an emperor and niece of the reigning Arethousan emperor, would dare to walk on purple. Some few of her possessions, as she had wished, had been sent back to Arethousa upon her death. Henry had kept this rug, perhaps against her wishes, for was it not also said of Henry that he believed he alone of all the reigning kings had the power to wear the mantle of the Holy Dariyan Emperor? Others had attempted to take on the title worn first by the great Taillefer. None had succeeded. The "new" empire, restored by Taillefer, had lasted a scant twenty-four years and had died with Taillefer. No king facing civil war could hope to make himself emperor, even with the support of the skopos herself.

"Make ready to ride," King Henry said at last. "We leave at dawn."

The Eagle, though he had ridden hard and through great danger, received no sign of the king's favor. He was dismissed to get food, drink, and rest. The king retired to his bedchamber. The others went out to their own retainers, and soon the king's retinue was in a great uproar as they prepared to march. Those nobles, like Liutgard and Judith, who had been ready to return to their estates were now—with whatever soldiers they had—turned into Henry's army. There was no longer time for raising levies from far-off estates.

Eagles were dispatched to Rotrudis, Duchess of Saony and Atto-

mar, and to Burchard, Duke of Avaria. Also, Eagles rode to the estates of lesser counts and lords. A great stock of grain and
vegetables vanished from the monastery's cellars into the king's
wagons, and chickens and geese were caged and the cages thrown
on top of heaps of turnips and beans and baskets of wheat and
barley and rye. Given the terrible news of Sabella's revolt, not even
the cellarer complained when every cask of ale left in the monastery's wine cellar was rolled up the earth ramp and into wagons.

Just after Vespers, Villam came to Rosvita where she labored in
the scriptorium, packing her notes and stylus and parchment, her
quills and ink, into a chest for the journey. He appeared so close to
panic that she immediately set aside her book and came to him.

"My son is missing," he said. "Have you seen him today?"

Guilt struck at her heart. So much had happened she had forgotten about her promise to keep an eye on the boy. At once she suspected where he had gone. "I have not seen him. His retainers?"

"Six are also missing, young men of his own age, none of the
older ones. The others will say nothing." Clearly, Villam suspected
the worst.

"Bring them to me."

With grim satisfaction, Villam left. She finished packing and left
the chest in the care of one of her servants. She met them before the
Hearth, the only place with any semblance of peace in the entire
valley. Villam brought two men: a white-haired man with the look
of a faithful, battle-hardened retainer and a much younger man,
not above sixteen or eighteen years, who was flushed and had obviously been crying.

Rosvita studied them both. The old man she gave up on at once.
He looked like the old praeceptor, the man who had been assigned
many years back to train the boy at arms and whose loyalty would
be fixed to the young lad he had half raised; he could not be swayed
by fear. But the younger man could.

"You do not mean to lie to me?" she demanded of the young one.
"Who are you, child? Who are your parents?"

Stammering, he told her his name and lineage.

"Where is Lord Berthold?"

He betrayed himself by glancing at the old man. The old retainer
glared stubbornly ahead. The young one began to fidget, twisting
his hands together, biting at his lower lip.

"Look in my eyes, child, and swear to me by the name of Our Lady and Lord that you do not know."

He began to cry again.

That quickly, as if to spare the young man the shame of lying or of betraying his master, the old armsmaster spoke. "He knew nothing of the expedition. I advised against it, but, once determined, Lord Berthold would not be swayed."

"Yet you did not go with him!" Villam lifted a fist as if to bring it down, hard, on the Hearth, and only at the last instant remembered where he was. He slapped the fist against an open palm instead. It was getting dark. Her ability to read the subtleties of their expressions was already lost to her. Two monks entered the chapel, brands burning in each hand; they began to light the sconces. Soon the office of Compline would be sung and the monks would take themselves to their beds for the night.

"So did he order me, my lord. I am his obedient servant. And in truth, I feared no mischief. They are only old ruins. I have seen such with my own eyes and feared nothing from them. I made sure he took six of his best men-at-arms with him when he left this morning after Prime."

"Yet he has not returned."

The old armsmaster hung his head. Even in the inconstant light of torches she could now read clearly his guilt, his recognition of his own bad judgment, written as plainly as if he had spoken aloud.

"Take torches, picks and shovels, whatever you need, and ten of my men-at-arms and the rest of my son's retainers. Go now."

They did as Villam ordered.

Rosvita joined the prayers at Compline. It was crowded, for not only the king but every noble who could command room crowded into the monastery's church. But when the others filed out, Villam remained, and he knelt on the cold ground, hands clasped in prayer, for the rest of the night.

The monks sang Nocturns, then, at first light, Lauds. King Henry arrived for the office of Prime fully arrayed for riding, wearing a coat of mail. Sapientia walked behind him, also fitted for riding; she carried her father's helm under one arm and she wore the badge of St. Perpetua, Lady of Battles, on her right shoulder. Theophanu would remain in the train, behind the main army, with those like Rosvita who did not fight.

As soon as Prime was sung and the last prayer spoken over the

Hearth, Henry left the church and crossed to where his horse waited, already saddled. It was just dawn. No men had returned from the night expedition to the old ruins.

"We must ride," said King Henry.

Villam bowed his head, for of course he knew the king spoke truthfully. He splashed water on his face to refresh himself and then, with the others, set forth.

That morning the army did not range out ahead of the cavalcade of wagons and animals that constituted the people and goods of the king's progress. At midday, a party from the monastery caught up to them.

Rosvita hastened forward from her place in the train in order to hear the news. Berthold was a good boy, full of promise. She felt herself responsible. She had not watched over him as she had said she would.

But she read no hope on the face of the old armsmaster, who came forward as spokesman for the others.

"It is a grievous tale I have to tell, my lord." His voice was even, but his eyes betrayed the depth of his distress.

"My son is dead," said Villam, as if voicing the words would cause the worst of the pain, of a father's loss of his favored son, to be over with quickly, to fade that fast into the dull ache of a loss suffered years before. Better that than the raw grief that cut to the heart.

The armsmaster bowed his head. "No, my lord." But his tone was not encouraging. He caught breath and could not for a moment go on.

Rosvita slipped into the crowd. Folk made way for her as she came up beside Villam. He saw her and set an arm on the sleeve of her robe, steadying himself. King Henry, now, had come from his place at the front of the army. People made way for him so he could stand beside Villam.

"I have seen strange things I cannot explain. This is what happened."

This, St. Ambrose's Day, the second day after the Feast of St. Susannah and the third day of the month of Sormas, had dawned clear and fine and the weather looked to continue that way. Surely this was an omen that the Lord and Lady favored their expedition. And Rosvita noted, as the man told his story, that the weather did not shift, nor did the fine down of clouds that lined the northern horizon spread to engulf the sky. The sky remained clear; the sun remained warm. What this meant she could not be sure. If sorcery was awake, it was not at this moment directed at them.

"It took us many hours to climb the slope," said the armsmaster. "Even with the moon's light and though we followed the path, it twisted and turned in such a confusing fashion that we lost our way several times. We came to a stand of wood, tall northern pines, which none of us had seen from below. At first light we came to a rocky outcropping which we had not known was above us, though one of your men-at-arms, my lord, recognized it as that place where the holy man had retired to meditate.

"To our amazement, as the light rose and we could see more than an arm's length in front of us, we saw two lions resting at the height of the rock. When they saw us, they sprang away into the rocks and we lost sight of them. Fearing for the life of the holy man, we hastened to his hut."

Now he drew the Circle of Unity at his breast and then touched knuckles to lips softly, as if giving a kiss to the Lady.

"When I touched the door, it fell easily aside, revealing what lay within." He blinked several times as at a sudden blinding light. "A miracle! There sat the holy man, upright in that tiny space yet not touching the side of the hut. He smelled as fresh as if fields of flowers had bloomed there inside with him, but there was nothing except him, the thin white loincloth in which he was dressed, and the dirt floor. And when we ventured to touch him, to wake him, for he appeared to be asleep, he was cold as stone. He was dead." His voice shook.

Rosvita bowed her head and said a silent prayer for the dead man. His name would be added to the prayer lists which were sung in full every Penitire. Yet she could not mourn Brother Fidelis; he had ascended to the Chamber of Light. And she had something of him with her still, the book he had given to her.

"Ten of the men I sent ahead to search for the ruins you spoke of, my lord," continued the armsmaster, "While I remained behind with the others to give a proper burial to the holy man. I cannot explain . . . some other force watched over us, for as we dug the grave in the hard ground the lions appeared again on the outcropping above. But they made no move to approach us. Indeed, they appeared to watch over us, that is all, and when the holy man was decently laid to rest, they vanished.

"Then we found the track and soon after dawn we came out into the ruins at the height of the hill. But what a strange sight met our eyes! You said they were ruins, but they were nothing of the kind! There lay before us a circle of standing stones with a huge stone placed at their center."

"Upright?" demanded Villam, jerking forward as if he had been yanked.

"Upright and perfectly placed, with lintels across. I have seen such ruins in my years, which were surely the work of giants, but never one as perfectly preserved as this."

"Impossible!" cried Villam. "They were fallen to pieces just three days past."

The armsmaster bowed his head until his forehead touched his clasped hands. He remained in that position for some time while King Henry drew Villam back and spoke soothingly to him.

"We marveled," said the armsmaster finally, in a whisper. "The mounds were open. Each one had an entrance framed by stone slabs. We lit our torches and walked inside, somewhat hunched over, it is true, but the walls were so cunningly laid together with flat stone that they were more like the corridors of a stronghold than of a tomb. But each mound was the same. We entered by a passageway which led in a straight line to a round chamber that lay at the center of the mound, buried under dirt. And in that chamber, nothing. No other passages. No sign of graves or of the bones of giants or sacrifices. No sign of treasure. Nothing. Except a single footprint, caught in the dust. And this."

He extended his right hand and unfolded it, like a petal opening to the sun. In his hand lay a gold ring.

Villam groaned out loud and snatched the ring out of the old man's hand. He turned it over, and over again, but there was no doubting the look on his face. "His mother's ring," he whispered, "which she willed to him on her deathbed."

After that he wept, and the others wept with him, the armsmaster and young Berthold's retainers. By not protecting him, they had failed their young lord. Henry, quick to tears, wept as well, as befit a king showing sympathy for the pain felt by others and so—as was a kingly virtue—by himself on their behalf.

Rosvita could find no tears. The tale had overset her. It had astonished her, and yet set her mind racing. Strange forces were at work. How could stones of such size be lifted and returned to their places?

From where had come the lions which the men had seen? Why had Brother Fidelis given her the book at just that time, as a man might dispense of his possessions when he knew death was upon him? What had he meant by his reference to the Seven Sleepers?

What had prompted Berthold to go exploring with *six* young companions?

Rosvita did not believe in coincidence.

At last, Villam mastered his grief, though surely it would haunt him in the months to come. He had, after all, a duty to his king, and a war to fight.

With somber faces and heavy hearts, they rode west to meet Sabella's army.

XII
BLOODHEART

1

THE streets of Gent were chaos and only the misting slant of rain over rooftops and roadways kept them from boiling with clouds of dust in the pandemonium. Mud and dirt were everywhere; no one dared use precious water to clean. The wells continued to supply water and with the river on both sides were unlikely to run dry, but no one cared to take that chance. It was still possible to wash by the river's bank on the island's shore, but the Eika had primitive bows and even stone-tipped arrows could kill.

Liath had seen many places in her life; she had lived in the skopos' city of Darre, visited villages built on the ruins of the magnificent ancient cities of Sirraqusae and Kartiako, resided near the Kalif's palace in the fine clean Jinna city of Qurtubah, passed through the seat of the Salian kings, Pairri, taken ship at the emporium called Medemelacha along the coast, and walked among the proud, bustling townsfolk of the cathedral city of Autun. She and Da had passed through villages recovering from famine, avoided towns flying the red banner that warned of plague; she had prayed at churches small and vast, including the great basilica dedicated to St.

Thecla the Witnesser in Darre. In eight years she and Da had traveled as much as a thousand people might in an entire lifetime.

But she had never seen anything like Gent: a prosperous cathedral city crammed with twice or three times its usual population, the refugees fled within the walls from the countryside, and living constantly on the edge of terror. Siege was an ugly business.

Now she walked through this chaos every day.

Mayor Werner was a vain man, spoiled by his mother and accustomed to getting his own way. He was overjoyed at the opportunity to have a King's Eagle at his beck and call. In the evenings, Werner expected Wolfhere to attend him at the feasts he held every night. Werner was—reasonably enough—terribly impressed by Wolfhere's age and knowledge and reputation as a man who had once been King Arnulf the Younger's most favored counsellor. So in the evenings Wolfhere could not question Liath about the life she and Da had led for the last eight years.

Liath made sure she came to Werner's attention, and so during the day she waited on Werner and ran messages here and there within the walls of Gent. Most of the messages were pointless, but it gave her something to do—and it kept her out of Wolfhere's way. She had many questions she wanted to ask Wolfhere, but as Da said, *"Always measure the ground before you jump the stream."* She was not fool enough to think she could outwit Wolfhere and she did not yet feel confident enough to face him. So she avoided him.

But, running messages for Werner, she could not avoid the city. This day she felt an undercurrent of madness running like ground lightning through the streets. On her way to the armory to get the daily count of swords forged and spears readied and to find out how their fuel was holding out, she had to shove her way along the plank walkways despite that she wore the red-lined cloak of a King's Eagle. Folk crammed the streets, some of them carrying their earthly belongings on their backs as if they had no place to rest them. Others spoke, gesticulating, shouting, in pockets at corners or under the shelter of overhanging houses or bursting out of alehouses.

"Make way!" she said, trying to force her way through a knot of men gathered at the corner of the marketplace. "I am an Eagle."

"Cursed Eagle!" shouted one of them, lifting a staff threateningly. "You're well fed enough, up there at the palace!" He was ragged and thin, stooped by hunger, but anger is its own food. And

Liath became aware at once that his many companions, at his back, stared at her with hostile expressions. One fingered a knife.

"Come now, my friend." Another man stepped forward, a stout artisan with smudged hands and a grim face. "This Eagle is but the King's messenger. She is not responsible for the mayor's faults. Let her by."

Grudgingly the other man stepped back, his comrades with him, muttering.

"I thank you," she said to the artisan.

"I think you will find it better to avoid the marketplace," said the artisan, "for there are many angry folk gathered there. "There is an alleyway back by here. Go, and when you return to the palace tell the mayor from me, a good citizen of Gent, that he should beware the inner beast as much as the outer one, if he will not feed it properly."

"I will," she said, puzzled by this reference. She took the side route gladly but even here she had to make her way through refugees huddled with all their belongings—what they could carry—against wooden walls, some of them without even a bit of cloth to cover their heads against the rain. Babies cried. Children whimpered. An old woman sat wrapped in a filthy shawl whose fancy embroidered edge peeked out beneath a caking of mud. She tried to bake flour and water mixed to a muddy paste into flatcakes over a steaming fire placed hard up against the back of a house.

Ai, Lady, thought Liath. How easily a fire could start, in drier weather. Maybe it was for the best that it rained. But then, she had a roof over her head.

"I pray you! Eagle!" The man's voice was soft, thickened with the congestion of a grippe.

Surprised, she halted in the shadow of a pile of garbage. It stank. The bones and skin of rats lay littered at the base of the pile; the flesh had been gnawed from their small remains. She smelled urine and feces. A man wearing the heavy tunic of a farmer emerged from the shadows; he had a thin, desperate face and mucus running from his nose. She stepped back, startled, away from him.

"I pray you," he repeated. "Take me to the mayor."

"I cannot. I only run errands."

"Please," he begged. Then he tried to grasp her hand, to pull her. She bolted back and yet something in his manner stayed her from running away. "Please. There must be something you can do. My daughter."

"Your *daughter*?"

"She's ill and she hasn't enough to eat. Here. See."

His daughter. Her grief at Da's death choked her anew and tears flooded her eyes. Numb, she followed the man into the tiny garbage-strewn alley, a fetid corner where he had made shelter for them. The girl was perhaps eight or ten years old; it was hard to tell. She coughed incessantly, half in sleep, but when she heard her father's footsteps she raised her arms piteously toward him.

"Da?" she whispered. "Da, I feel such a pain in my chest. I'm sorry, Da, I meant to be stronger." Then she saw Liath. Her eyes widened and she went into a spasm of coughing.

The man knelt beside her and petted her, soothed her, until she calmed and quieted. Then, with an agonized expression, he looked up at Liath. "We are not poor folk, Eagle. I was a good farmer and paid my rents faithfully to Count Hildegard. I lost my wife two winters ago to the lungfever, and the babe she'd just born died with her. This child, my Miriam, is all I have left. But we have nothing here and no kin, no one to help us and I can find no work. Please, can you help us, Eagle. They say in the marketplace the mayor feasts every night, but out here we have nothing. I am feared she will—" He broke off and buried his face in the girl's hair.

Liath gulped down a sob. It hit her, then, again and so sudden, so unexpected: Da was dead. He was dead and he was never coming back, never going to walk beside her again or comfort her again or teach her again. No matter what his flaws were, for they were many, he struggled with the darkness as do all of humankind, yet he did his best and he was a good man and he had always, always, taken care of her. Tears and rain mixed on her face. The girl gazed at her in awe, the man in desperate hope.

"Can you not go to the cathedral?" she asked. "The biscop has allowed many of the refugees to camp in the nave and I believe she tries to feed them as well."

"I have tried," he said, hope dying in his eyes, "But there are so many. We were turned away even before we could reach the steps. The mayor's guard beat us back."

She took her Eagle's ring off her finger and held it out. "Take this," she said, trembling, "to the palace and ask for entry to the stables. Tell the Dragons there that I mean for you to have employment from them. You can care for horses, can you not?"

He swallowed. "I had sheep and goats and chickens, but never a horse."

"Chickens, then," she said recklessly. "Take your daughter. This will gain you entrance. You must do it, for I need the ring back and so I will fetch it from you there."

"Da!" whispered the girl, and then coughed.

The man began to thank her so profusely she was afraid he would draw attention to them, even here behind the midden. She could not save them all.

"I must go," she said. "I have an errand." She fled gratefully into the rain and cried the whole way to the armory and back.

Werner kept her busy for the rest of the day, and that night, to assauge his fretting, he called for a lavish feast which she had no appetite for. Afterward she took a turn on watch late into the night and then lay down to sleep just before dawn only to sleep fitfully and then be woken mid-morning by a distressed servant. He begged her to come to the hall at once.

"Eagle!" Werner paced in his hall, frantic. "Have you heard? Have you seen?"

"I beg your pardon, Mayor Werner," she said. "I have just woken. I was on watch last—"

"Lady and Lord! What have we come to!" He threw up his hand and called for a tray, popped a sweetmeat into his mouth as if that could comfort him in his distress. "I have already sent Wolfhere and the other Eagle down to the tannery, so now what shall I do? What shall I do?"

She waited as he snapped at a passing servant. That seemed to calm his nerves enough for him to speak coherently. "A crowd of people has gathered outside the gates. Outside these gates, as if *I* were their enemy! What a calamity this is!"

"Have they said what their purpose is, Mayor Werner?"

"Bread and beans!" he snorted. "Bread and beans! The good citizens of Gent would never act this way if these country people were not acting as a bad influence upon them. There is at least one deacon who—imagine this!—has inflamed them with tales of feasting here in my own hall going on while their children starve! No child starves within the walls of Gent. The biscop sees to that. They are calling me a glutton and say I feast while their children starve! Imagine! Can you imagine?"

She waited, but unfortunately he appeared to expect an answer. Carefully she said, "I am here to serve you, Mayor Werner."

"Someone must go out and placate them," said Werner, eyeing her with a mixture of craftiness and doubt.

"They are asking for *you*, my lord," said the steward cautiously.

Werner smoothed down his fine wool tunic nervously, twining his fingers into the soft leather belt. Its gold buckle was studded ostentatiously with lapis lazuli. "I can't—it would be too dangerous—" His distracted gaze caught again on Liath and his expression brightened. "Eagle, fetch Prince Sanglant. He will attend me. After all—" He began twisting the rings on his fingers, a habit Liath had seen him indulge in before. They were stunningly beautiful rings, one set with tiny rubies, one with an amethyst, one with an engraved stone of lapis lazuli of a particularly intense blue; the fourth was a thin circle of cunningly-worked cloisonńe so delicately done Liath could not imagine how human fingers could have wrought it. "After all he is here to protect Gent, and if the crowd were to grow angry or vengeful, or to threaten me . . . "

She nodded obediently and withdrew from the hall. Outside, the sun shone. From the safety of the great courtyard, bounded by the palace and great hall on one side, the kitchens and outbuildings on the second, the barracks and stables on the third, and the palisade gates on the fourth, she could hear the crowd that had gathered on the other side of the palace compound gates. They spoke in many voices, but their murmuring was edged with fury and with that kind of desperation past which there is nothing left to lose.

Werner could not afford to have riot within and siege without; abruptly she realized what the artisan in the marketplace had meant by the inner beast. She straightened her tunic and twisted the end of her braid in a hand, then cursed herself for caring what she looked like. Perhaps it was true Prince Sanglant looked at her now and again, but he looked at every remotely attractive woman he came within sight of. Liath only noticed because she would watch him, and try not to watch him, when they were in the hall at the same time or passing in the courtyard or around the stables.

But this was not time to reflect on such trivial concerns. As Da always said, *"No point in worrying at a loose thread while the sheep are being eaten by wolves."*

She steadied herself and strode to the stables and then down the long dim passage. She saw no sign of the man and child she had tried to help. Beyond the actual stables, but within the palace stockade, was a stableyard with its own gate. In this yard the Dragons took their ease in the fine spring sun or—most often—practiced with sword and spear. So did they now.

She paused at the doors, brushing straw dust off her nose and trying not to sneeze. Two men sparred with staves. Several of the younger men pounded dutifully on a sturdy wooden pole set upright in the ground. An older man sat on a bench, repairing a pair of boiled leather greaves that had been oiled to a fine brown sheen. Sanglant laughed.

His laughter was so sharp and bright that it rang on the air. She found him half hidden behind a line of laundry hung out to dry in the warm morning sunlight. He came out from the shadow of the laundry, head flung back. Sweat beaded on his forehead. He held a sword wrapped in cloth in one hand and his teardrop shield painted with the black dragon device in the other. He wore not his mail but only the padded gambeson that went underneath armor. After him came two others—the woman and a young man with light hair and a yellow beard—similarly armed; they had obviously been at sword practice.

Sanglant wiped the sweat from his face and turned to look directly at Liath, across the stableyard. He lifted a hand. All activity ceased and every Dragon there turned to look at her. She bit down a sudden impulse to flee, lifted her chin, and walked across the yard to the prince.

"Mayor Werner wishes you to attend him," she said boldly and clearly. "There is a crowd—"

"Ah, yes," said the prince interrupting her. "I was wondering when Mayor Werner would send someone to fetch me. They've been gaining in numbers since dawn." He seemed more amused than angry or worried. He handed sword and shield to the woman, got a spear in exchange, and gestured for Liath to precede him. No one else came, only him. As they walked back through the stables, she felt his gaze on her back.

He said, "I've never seen you use that bow. It's of Quman make, is it not?"

"It is."

"It's a strange pattern, the deer who is vanquished and yet whose antlers are giving birth to griffins."

The observation startled her, but she dared not slacken her pace or turn around.

"You have such brilliantly blue eyes," he added, as if it was an afterthought. "Like the heart of fire. Or that fine lapis lazuli stone on Mayor Werner's finger."

Her cheeks burned. She did not know what to say.

They passed out through the stable doors into the courtyard to find Mayor Werner and a number of palace stewards and serving-folk huddled together in an anxious band.

"Open the gates," said Sanglant, striding past Liath.

"But—!"

"Open the gates!"

Werner could not bring himself to give the order until he had been helped to the safety of the palisade wall, out of reach of the ravening hordes should they decide to swarm inside. But once on the parapet, he could be seen by the crowd beyond. Liath climbed up after him and saw the people below. They were, indeed, country folk and poor people, frightened, thin, and desperate—the same sort of people she had pressed through yesterday. Seeing the mayor above they began to call out, some with anger, some pleading, some cursing. One man lifted a tiny child above his head as if willing the mayor—whose round red face clearly betrayed that he never wanted for food—to see the hunger on the child's face. A few had staves or scythes, and these shook them angrily while Werner tried to shout out a few conciliatory phrases but got nowhere; nor could he be heard above their noise.

The gates opened. Sanglant walked out, spear in his left hand, right hand raised, open, and empty. He had no escort. Suddenly nervous, Liath got out her bow, nocked an arrow, and drew down on the prince so she could get the first shot in if anyone assaulted him.

He glanced up as if he had heard the creak of the string rubbing against the bronze caps as she drew it back. He smiled—his charming smile—up at her, as if her protection amused or flattered him, and for an instant she forgot where she was and what she was doing there. Then he looked away, out into the crowd, and lifted his spear. The people moved restlessly, their attention shifting suddenly from the mayor to Sanglant. He waded out into their midst, obviously unafraid; he was easy to follow because he was half a head taller than the tallest person there. They parted to let him through, and at some point he found a box or a block of stone to stand on and with this platform he held the spear up over his head and with his right hand gestured for silence.

To Liath's amazement, the crowd quieted.

"Oh dear, oh dear," murmured Werner, and then, suddenly, realizing Sanglant was not about to be set upon and rent limb from body by the mob, he stopped muttering.

"You must pick three of your number," said Sanglant without preamble, "and they will be brought before the mayor to speak your grievances. Choose them quickly and do not argue. The rest of you must go to your homes or to wherever you are staying. I will request that the biscop mediate." He paused.

His voice sounded so hoarse Liath was astonished it carried so well, but his voice always sounded like that. He shifted, and the sunlight caught on his gold torque, winking. Liath lowered her bow. She could not concentrate, not looking at him. Did not the ancients write that desire was a curse? She found that her hands were shaking, and she let the arrow go slack. The prince was in no danger.

Although perhaps she was.

"Let me tell you," he went on, "that Gent is a city under siege. The enemy who waits outside the walls is more implacable than your hunger, for there are stores enough in this city if they are rationed fairly but there is no mercy in his heart, if he even has one. We cannot fight among ourselves, for that way lies death for everyone. You are within your rights to demand food if your children are hungry, but none can expect feasts—"

"The mayor feasts every night!" cried a woman in a shrill but carrying voice. She wore deacon's robes.

"Then you, good deacon, may come before him and tell him what you think of that. You are the first. Let two more be chosen."

His brisk command stilled the crowd. Already the people on the fringes were drifting away. After a brief flurry of talk, two men came forward with the deacon, and they followed Sanglant inside. Liath recognized one as the artisan who had aided her in the marketplace. The gates closed behind them; only then did Werner venture down from the parapet. Once brought inside the great hall, the three commoners appeared subdued, perhaps cowed by the mayor or—more likely—by Sanglant's imposing presence.

"Eagle," said Werner, "you will find and bring the biscop to me. Beg her to attend me, that is."

Sanglant moved, and almost Liath thought he was going to offer to escort her. But he did not. Instead, with a sigh, he went to sit in the chair beside Werner.

Ai, fool! She cursed herself as she hurried away. The gates were opened to let her out, and this time the folk dispersing from the square parted to let her through as she jogged from palace to cathedral. Maybe Da had been right; he usually was. *"Are you so vain?"* he had asked her. But he had been speaking of Hugh, and she had been right about Hugh. Da had not understood what Hugh truly wanted.

But she did not want to think of Hugh now. She never wanted to think of Hugh again.

Gent's biscop was a woman who wasted little time; Liath was sent back with a message that Werner could expect her within the hour and that a solution to this difficulty would be found before nightfall or else she would impose one.

When Liath returned to the hall, the deacon and artisan had, evidently, spoken already. Now the third representative, an elderly man in the good linen tunic of a person of wealth, regaled the mayor at length about the positions of the stars in the heavens and the fate they foretold for Gent in general and the mayor in particular. Werner listened with such rapt attention that he did not acknowledge—or perhaps he did not notice—Liath's return.

"For in the writings of the church mothers, and in the calculations of the Babaharshan mathematici," intoned the man in that sonorous voice only the truly self-important can manage, "it is written that the passage of Mok into the sign of the Healer, the eleventh House in the lesser Circle, the world dragon that binds the heavens, betokens a period of healing and hope whose emanative rays are only intensified by the passage of Jedu, the fierce, the Angel of War, into the same sign, as will happen very soon, very soon indeed, for fierce Jedu soon will move out of the Unicorn and into the Healer. So should you take heart that the heavens grant us hope at this dark hour, and you should be generous in relieving the burdens of those of us trapped inside your fair city."

"Oh, spare us this nonsense," muttered Liath under her breath.

She regretted saying it at once. She had forgotten how well San-glant could hear.

Sanglant glanced at her but said nothing.

"Say on," said Werner to the man, who continued, oblivious to everything except Werner's rapt attention.

"Yes, the heavens give us hope. You must not expect disaster for no comet has flamed in the sky and only such glowing swords por-tend ruin. Therefore, we may all feast and celebrate for our rescue is at hand—" Werner was, indeed, beginning to look more cheerful. "—and if gold is laid out in a pattern known only to me, then I can read by various diverse and secret means the exact hour and day of our liberation!"

"Ah," sighed Werner ecstatically.

Ai, Lady! This man would do more harm than good. But Eagles had no opinions. Princes might, however. She had to risk it. "He's a fraud," she muttered under her breath.

At once, Sanglant lifted a hand for silence. "Where did you learn this knowledge of the heavens?" he asked the old man. "How can you assure us this is true?"

The man clapped hand to chest. "Noble prince, you honor me with your notice. I was trained at the Academy of Diotima in Darre, under the shadow of the skopos' palace itself. In the Academy we learned the secrets of the heavens from the writings of the ancients and also how to foretell the fates of man and the world from the movements of the stars."

"For a price," said Liath. "Usually in *gold.*"

Then was aghast she had spoken out loud. But how could she help it? In all their wandering, Da had never passed himself off as an astrologus or haruspex—one of those men or women who claimed to be able to divine the fate of "kings and other folk." Frauds, all of them, Da claimed, though he was learned enough that he could have made a decent living for them both had he been will-ing to do so. But Da respected the knowledge he had and, perhaps, feared it as well. It was nothing to trifle with. It burned in her heart that the knowledge he had paid for so dearly should be treated as merely another form of commerce—a lucrative trade visited upon the ignorant and gullible—by such people as this charlatan.

The old man frowned imperiously at her. "Mine is a proud trade, and though some in the church have frowned upon it, it has not been condemned—"

The deacon interrupted him. "At the Council of Narvone, the casting of horoscopes was outlawed. Only God and the angels may have foreknowledge of our fate."

"Well, I—" he spluttered. "I do not cast individual horoscopes, of course, but I have great knowledge and none dare scorn me, for I know the ways of the heavens. I have studied the very *Astronomicon* of Virgilia and—"

Liath snorted. "Virgilia wrote the *Heleniad*. It is Manilius who wrote the five books called the *Astronomicon* that I suppose you speak of. And the Academy founded by Diotima of Mantinea rested in the city of Kellai, not in Darre."

Sanglant coughed, but he was only stifling a laugh.

She faltered. Every person in the hall stared at her as if she had suddenly begun speaking in a foreign tongue, like the disciples at the Pentekoste, touched by the Holy Word.

Ai, Lady. She had let her impatience with fools and that old slow-burning anger at Da's death get the better of her. She had betrayed herself to them all.

"What—?" said the mayor, mouth popped open with the look of a fish on a platter. "What—? I don't—"

"I am outraged!" said the man who claimed to be an astrologus, and the deacon, too, stepped forward, staring with interest—or was it surprise? or was it suspicion?—at Liath.

"Mayor Werner," said Sanglant, cutting into this so sharply that all of them drew back from Werner's chair. "I have need of this Eagle, messages to be run to those of my men who are posted along the walls. You have this business in hand, I believe, and the biscop will arrive soon."

Werner opened his mouth.

"Good," said Sanglant. And to Liath: "Come."

She followed him outside. Her heart hammered hard in her chest. But for some strange reason she was not afraid but instead relieved—and even elated.

He halted in the great courtyard, full in the sun, and stretched shoulders and neck like a great beast settling itself after a triumphant struggle. Then he studied her, and because she had already betrayed herself, she was not afraid to look directly at him in return.

"I have heard the *Heleniad*, of course," he said, "or parts of it at any rate. In the king's progress many poets have sung the epic to entertain the court, and of course you have heard the poet who resides in Werner's palace recite it over these past ten nights."

"Mangle it, more like."

He smiled. "Perhaps you would render it more pleasingly."

She shook her head sharply. "I am not poet or bard, to sing in public."

"No, you are not. You are something altogether different, I think. Is there truly such a book as this . . . *Astronomicon*?"

"I have heard of such a book, but never seen it. There is a reference to it in the *Etymologies* of Isidora of Seviya where she comments on—" She broke off. Lord in Heaven! Was she trying to *impress* him?

"You are truly Wolfhere's *discipla*, are you not?"

"I don't know what you mean by that."

"I don't know what I mean either," he said sharply, and frowned and looked abruptly away from her. It was almost painful to have him look away; she had not realized how much his gaze warmed her, or at least how much she wanted his attention. Like bread given to a hungry child.

She winced, for was it not a true enough comparison? She was alone and he was here—

He was like no one she had ever laid eyes on.

Sanglant lifted a hand, and she tensed, but only because half of her willed him to touch her while at the same time the other half feared what his touch—the tangible and irrevocable sign of his interest in her—would unleash. How could she even feel this way after what had happened with Hugh?

But Sanglant was not trying to touch her; he opened his hand to reveal her Eagle's ring. "A man brought this to me yesterday. I believe it is yours?"

He waited. Finally, as carefully as one might pluck a jewel from the coils of a snake, she picked it up off his palm. "It is mine. What happened to the man—?"

"We gave him shelter and employment of sorts." His eyes glinted. She could not read his expression. "His daughter I sent to our healer. She may yet live."

"I thank you," she said softly. The ring was still warm from his skin.

"Let me," he said, and he took her hand and slipped the ring onto her finger. He glanced up over her shoulder, released her abruptly

and stepped back. "Here is your praeceptor." Acknowledging Wolfhere, he allowed himself a brief, self-mocking smile. "She is yours,"
he said to Wolfhere. "Though perhaps you should watch her more
closely." He spun and left them.

Wolfhere crossed his arms over his chest and frowned at her. She
twisted the ring and, blushing, said nothing. The stench of the tannery clung to his clothes. "Prince Sanglant is right," he said finally.
"I should indeed be watching over you more closely." He gestured.
"Come."

She dared not disobey.

2

WERNER detained them again, but in the end Liath found herself seated opposite Wolfhere in the empty stall that had become both bedchamber and storage room for her and Wolfhere and Manfred.

"Now," said Wolfhere in the quiet tone of a man who intends to brook no disagreement, "for twenty-five days we have bided here in Gent and you have avoided me except when I have demanded your time to teach you about the duties of an Eagle."

"Mayor Werner has need of my services as a messenger."

"Mayor Werner thinks too much of his own consequence and is perfectly willing to enhance it by having a King's Eagle to carry his messages for him on trivial errands. You would be more useful running errands for the Dragons . . . and their captain."

She flushed.

"He is a king's son, Liath. What is commonplace for him would be disastrous for you." She flushed more deeply, mortified. "Remember the precepts I have taught you, and understand that you must hold to them once you are fully an Eagle." She tried to nod but could only manage a slight jerk of the head. Mercifully, he changed the subject. "In any case, this evening I have excused myself from the feast, which apparently will be much reduced now that the biscop has stepped in to set up rations for the city. Manfred will attend Mayor Werner. *You* will attend me. It is time for you to witness the workings of the magi, even one as weak in the craft as I am."

"Da said I was deaf to it," she blurted out. Anything to delay.

"Deaf to what?"

"To magic." There, it was spoken out loud.

"So he *did* teach you magic. You must trust me, Liath. You cannot conceal the truth from me. I know your background too well."

Better, it appeared, than she herself knew it. She shrugged, trying to appear nonchalant, but Wolfhere's gaze was too keen. She could not fool him. And yet . . .

Wolfhere lifted an eyebrow, waiting for her to speak.

She brushed a piece of straw off her leggings and shifted her seat. She was by now thoroughly sick of straw; it poked through everything and tickled her nose all night. Behind her, her saddle provided reasonable support. But she felt the presence of the book, hidden beneath the saddle and within the leather saddlebags. Could Wolfhere feel the book's presence as well? Was he only biding his time?

"What do you mean to do?" she asked.

"I mean to seek a vision of this intelligence Prince Sanglant speaks of, whatever creature it is that directs the Eika siege." He rose. Because she no longer had a choice, she rose with him and followed him out of doors.

It was dusk in Gent. Clouds had come in after that glorious morning sunlight and now it was again a dreary, overcast, damp spring evening. St. Melania's Day, Liath thought, named for the saint who had admonished the patriarchs of Kellai when they refused to accept the supremacy of the Lady and Lord of Unities. It was also the seventeenth day of the month of Sormas. Because cloud covered the sky, she could not orient herself by the stars. And dared not. It was bad enough Wolfhere knew her father and mother had studied the forbidden arts. She had only made it worse by speaking so rashly in Mayor Werner's hall.

This night the streets were mostly empty. Perhaps the morning's excitement had exhausted everyone. Their footsteps were swallowed in the greater hush of a city turning over from day to night, from activity to restless sleep, haunted always by the presence of the Eika outside the walls. A thin sheen of moisture from the afternoon's shower covered the plank walkways that kept them above the muck of the streets. The drums that always pounded in the Eika camp were, thank the Lady, muted this night, though still audible. Even so, she found her footsteps falling into beat with them; she skip-hopped, trying to walk off the rhythm.

Wolfhere smiled and they turned past the old marketplace and skirted the edge of the royal mint, which was heavily guarded. The wind shifted, bringing the stink of the tanning works up from the western bank of the river. There, work went on into the night at adjacent warehouses where armor and weapons were being turned out from iron and wood and leather that had been carted in from the countryside by the refugees.

He led her across the central square of Gent and up the steps of the cathedral. Built all of stone, its massive front stood like the shield of faith in Gent's center. They slipped inside easily, since the doors had no locks.

And in any case, some of the refugees from the countryside had taken up residence in the nave. Liath hesitated in the entryway, hearing the shuffle of bodies within, coughs and whispers. No light was allowed after sunset, even in a stone building, for fear of fire, but she could see blocks of shadows, awnings and blankets thrown up as walls between the benches to separate one family from the next. Everyone had settled down to sleep. Wolfhere touched her on the arm and she followed him silently to the stairs that led down to the crypt.

Liath had never been afraid of the dead or the darkness. As Da always said: *"Those who rest in the Chamber of Light are at peace; the others have no power to harm us."* Even so, it soon became so dark as they descended stairs made first of stone and then, as they descended still deeper, of bare earth, that even she with her salamander eyes could not make out the walls but had to feel her way by touch.

Wolfhere, ahead of her, stopped, and she steadied herself, one hand on his shoulder. It was utterly black. The crypt smelled of clay and lime. It was damp. At the edge of her hearing came the sound of the slow drip of water.

It nagged at her, that uneven sound, a droplet of water shattering to pieces on stone, then, finally, another. It reminded her of the water in the crypt of the church where Marshal Liudolf had locked her up after Da's murder. It had been dark there, as well, and she had been imprisoned. Until Hugh came.

Her chest was tight with fear and she clutched convulsively at Wolfhere's shoulder, suddenly terrified. *What if Hugh lurked in these shadows?*

"Call light, Liath," said Wolfhere.

"I can't."

"Seek in your mind for the memory of light, and call it forth."

She shook her head. She was sweating now, although it was cool in the vaults. Strange noises caught in the air. She knew Hugh was far away and yet felt him as if he was just about to touch her.

Wolfhere continued, as calm as ever. "If I remember, there is a torch here. Think of flames, then, and call fire to it."

"I was not taught these things!"

Air stirred behind her neck. Light! She shut her eyes, though it was hard to find the courage to do so, even when she couldn't see. She formed a picture of light, the chamber illuminated, sunlight streaming in through the windows of her memory tower to limn the four doors of her tower that led to nowhere and to everywhere, to cover as with a gold wash the fifth door, set impossibly in the center of the room. *Light.*

But nothing came. In the frozen tower, the light was as cold as midwinter's kiss and though it illuminated, its touch did not bring life. A tendril, like a spiderweb come loose from its moorings, brushed the nape of her neck. She flinched and batted it away, but there was nothing there. And yet there was something behind her, always stalking her.

She could stand it no more. *"Better to go forward,"* Da always said, *"than to look behind at what's creeping up on you."* She shoved past Wolfhere, stumbled on level flagstone floor, and groped along the wall. Her hand came to rest on the stem of a torch. She wrenched it free and spun, holding it out like a weapon, but it touched nothing. There was nothing, except her own fear.

And that sparked anger. What right had Hugh to plague her like this? Would she never be free of him? His was the dark presence always at her back, and yet there was another, which she could not name, whatever had stalked her father and herself for all those years.

"Leave me be!" she cried. The stone walls of the crypt sucked her voice away, muffling it.

"Now, Liath—" Wolfhere began.

Ah, but she was furious by now, a raw anger that throbbed through her like fire. The torch in her hand caught flame and burned with a strong, uncanny light. She started back, blinking away tears. Wolfhere looked sickly pale, but then her eyes adjusted and she saw he was smiling wryly.

"That's better," he said.

Liath was horrified. She had called fire, by what means she did not know. Now Wolfhere thought she knew the arts of sorcery.

And yet, if she could call fire, why should she *not* learn the arts of sorcery? Why should she not become magus and mathematicus? Was it not her birthright?

Wolfhere made no more mention of the blazing torch, nor did he ask her how she had accomplished the deed. He crossed the crypt floor and because she did not want to be alone in this buried chamber, she followed. Under the broad stone arches that held up the crypt he paused to study the famous tomb of Biscop Mariana, predecessor of the current biscop. Nestled between her grave and the heavy stone wall of the crypt lay another tomb. Carved of less imposing granite, it nevertheless displayed a more elaborate epitaph.

Here lies Flodoard, presbyter of the Holy Church, servant of Our Lord and Lady, guide and instructor to Louis, king of Varre. Devout in practice and humble in spirit, he was the best among us. So does he rest in the light of truth above.

Liath became aware all at once of the space opening behind her, the vast womb of the cathedral, and the monuments that marked the graves of the women and men who had served within these precincts. *Best among us.* She felt at peace, here among the holy dead. She might not be safe with Wolfhere, or any other mortal man or woman, but surely these holy ones remained her guardians as they guarded all who kept faith.

"I have heard it said a saint's tomb lies hidden in the crypt of Gent Cathedral." Wolfhere surveyed the dark cavern. The hush was profound. She could hear not even the least sound from above, though several hundred refugees crowded the church and beyond the doors the city of Gent certainly lay restless in its uneasy sleep, one eye always open toward its besiegers. Tombs faded into the darkness, marking distance by their shade of gray in the torchlight. Liath could not see the far walls or even the opening that led to the stairs. Gent was an old cathedral, its foundations laid, some said, in the last years of the old empire by a half-elvish prince who had converted to the faith of the Unities as the empire collapsed around him.

Wolfhere walked farther into the crypt, into dark chambers and down a short flight of steps, and Liath followed him. The deeper they went, the fresher the air smelled, tinged with the dry sweetness of some kind of grain. She sneezed.

"But it is also said," added Wolfhere, "that only those of great holiness, great innocence, or great need ever find that grave."

"Whose grave is it?" Liath asked, casting about, looking for any least gleam of silver light or hidden corner of stone concealed in the shadows, but she saw nothing besides the tombs of biscops and presbyters, holy deacons and robed mayors, and one count of Gent whose effigy showed her holding a scroll in one hand and a knife in the other.

"St. Kristine of the Knives, she who endured unspeakable torments in the last days of the old empire rather than yield her place to the invaders. It is said of her that though an empire might fall from grace, she could and would not fall because of her great strength."

But they found no saint's tomb.

They returned to the half-flight of stairs and passed into a dim corridor and thence into a side chapel that contained two tombs so ancient their inscriptions were almost rubbed away, as well as a single slab of black stone that glinted when she brought the torch up beside it.

She knelt and ran a hand along its surface. It was smoother than glass. "This is obsidian," she said. "Though some say that this is not stone at all but the remains of dragon bones that have been exposed to sunlight."

Wolfhere knelt opposite. "By this means, I will view. Did Bernard teach you the art of vision?"

She shook her head. She had never seen Da "vision" anything, although she had read it was possible to look long distances through certain media: water, fire, and certain kinds of stone. "Is it—is it *right* to practice the forbidden arts on holy ground? In a church?"

He glanced up. His gaze was mild but direct. "It is needful, and Our Lord and Lady do not prohibit what is needful. Or so agree the church elders at the Council of Kellai. The church did not condemn sorcery, Liath, though at the Council of Narvone it imposed a penance on those who practice it outside the supervision of the church."

What had Hugh said to her? *"I am sure there are those in the church who have made it their task to learn the forbidden arts of sorcery, but I have not found them so far."* "But they are called the forbidden arts," she whispered.

"It is true the church looks with disfavor on those who seek the elder arts, those practiced by the ancient heathens which have come down to us in their writings. Those which can be used by the unscrupulous to gain power. But it would be more than foolish to deny that such arts and powers are within our grasp, or to attempt to condemn them as heresy is condemned. It would be impossible, as well as dangerous. So in her wisdom Skopos Mary Jehanna, who presided over the Council of Kellai, was first to pronounce some of the forbidden arts as lying within the provenance of the church, and that ruling was confirmed by the Council of Navrone a hundred years ago. Indeed, in these days the Convent of St. Valeria is known for its study of the forbidden arts."

"But you are not in the church."

"I received some part of my training at a monastery in Aosta, at a schola there. I was never pledged to the church. Now. Attend."

He opened the leather pouch that hung from his belt and took out a flask. Then he took dagger and sword from their sheaths and laid them to one side. He unstoppered the flask and offered it to her. She shook her head, and he took a drink himself and set the flask down.

She waited. It seemed safe, now, to betray her intense curiosity. He knew what her parents were, after all. And had she not called fire?

He placed both hands, palms down and his shoulders' width apart, on the glassy black stone surface. For a long while he simply stared at the rock face. It was so quiet in the crypt she felt she heard the sound of dust settling on the tombs and the slow creak of stone shifting against the bones of the earth. The darkness beyond the flickering torchlight no longer scared her; it was merely shadow and silence and the physical remains of the dead, their spirits long since risen up through the seven spheres.

"Liath."

She started up. Wolfhere glanced at her, surprised.

He had not spoken.

His look was a question. She shook her head and settled back. "I beg your pardon," she said.

"What is it?" he asked. Either he had not heard the voice or he was more subtle than she feared.

"Nothing." She settled back into place, her grip tight on the torch. It blazed with undiminished strength. "A spider crawled up my hand."

Whether he believed this excuse or not, he accepted it. He turned his left hand palm up, the back of the hand still lying on the stone, fingers curled up slightly as if he was about to cup a sphere. "Sorcery is a mental discipline, not a physical one. It is the manipulation of the unseen forces that surround us, that are always active, though they are invisible to our five senses. There are those who profess knowledge of the forbidden arts who use physical means, incantations, chants, and objects, to focus their minds and reveal knowledge beyond what is common. These we know by many names, depending on what elements they seek to manipulate. The tempestari try to control the weather; the haroli seek to call down the daimones of the upper air, who are almost as knowledgeable as the angels. The sortelegi cast lots and make predictions, and old wisemen and women who may yet remember the old gods and have not yet turned their hearts entirely to Our Lady and Lord make predictions by means of the flights and cries of birds. These we call augures. Even unlearned folk have among them those who by diverse means and complicated misunderstandings have some simple skill in magic."

He paused and seemed to be waiting for her to comment.

The marble tomb at her left hand was engraved with the likeness of a woman wearing a biscop's mitre and robes: *Caesaria, deacon and biscop.* In the carving, the biscop held a shield depicting a saint, a woman with arms outstretched holding a knife in each hand; she also wore, as the sign of her martyrdom, a knife buried hilt-deep in her breast—St. Kristine.

"But the church condemns some magi," said Liath, "and watches with suspicion over any who are not sworn to its service."

"True enough. The church does not approve of those who seek such powers without its guidance. There will always be people who use the arts only for their own gain or to harm others. These we call malefici. The worst among them are those who consort with devils by means of blood and sacrifice. But others also remain suspect, chief among them those we know as the mathematici, for the study of the heavens is derived from the arts of the Babaharshan magi and the church looks with disfavor upon arts known to be heathen in origin."

And what of those who can speak a name and have it resonate across a great distance? This was not the first time she had heard that voice, calling her name, but obviously it must be the voice either of a magus or of some creature not of human birth, an angel or a daimone. Or a devil in service to the Enemy. She shuddered.

Wolfhere lifted a hand to touch her, briefly and reassuringly, on the knee. "You are safe with me, Liath."

She said nothing. She did not believe him. He regarded her silently. Suddenly calm, she examined him: his grave expression; the stern light in his eyes which was, nevertheless, touched with kindness; the marks of age on his skin; and in his hair and beard, where only a trace of the younger man remained, a few strands of brown hair nestled among the silver.

It was not that Wolfhere might personally wish her harm; she did not believe that. But she suspected his ultimate ends. She suspected him of wanting her for some other purpose, one which he chose not to reveal to her. *"Trust no one."* Even if he meant well by her, how could he protect her from the fate that had stalked Da? How could he protect her against a power that could strike death onto a man without unlocking door or window and without leaving a mark on the body? How could she protect herself?

Wolfhere laid his hand back on the stone. "But if the mind is properly trained, none of these other ways are necessary or even preferable. By what means do the magi focus and train their minds?"

"The ladder."

He nodded. " 'The ladder by which the magi ascend.' Can you recite it?"

She had tried so hard not to think of these things while she had been Hugh's slave that it took her some little time to walk back through the city of memory, to mark the gates, the levels of the great city in which all her knowledge was stored. "There are seven rungs on the ladder, which correspond to the seven spheres of the heavens. First is the rose of healing. Then the sword of strength. The cup of boundless waters. The ring of fire, which is known to us also as the Circle of Unity, the symbol of our Lady and Lord who together form the God of Unities. The throne of virtue. The scepter of wisdom. And the Crown of Light, which we also know as truth."

Wolfhere nodded. "These are the tools the magi use. Follow with me, in your mind's eye. Through the ring of fire we may see a vision of another place." He drew his hands farther apart and stared fixedly at the black stone.

Liath felt his silence reach a new and deeper level, as if he were drawing away from her, although of course he did not actually move. But she had never learned to build the ring of fire in her own mind; Da hadn't taught her the mental exercises beyond the sword of strength. She stared at the expanse of stone that lay between Wolfhere's hands, one palm down, the other palm up. Her grip tightened on the torch. The air itself seemed to grow taut. Wolfhere sucked breath in between his teeth. His pupils widened, then shrank to pinpricks as at a sudden bright light.

She saw nothing except black stone.

"What do you see?" he whispered, as if the words took effort.

"Nothing."

He shook his head suddenly and his pupils expanded. He seemed to be searching. "I, too, see nothing," he murmured. "Campfires, tents, their ships, and a kind of darkness that shades the center of their camp." He shut his eyes, then lifted his hands off the stone and, rather like a dog letting itself off guard, shook himself slightly all over. He looked at Liath. "This enchanter shields himself against my sight. That bodes ill, I fear. My powers are not strong, but as an Eagle I am adept at certain things. Seeing is one of them. You saw nothing as well?"

"I saw nothing." But her nothing was not, she realized, the same nothing as he had seen. She had truly seen *nothing*. Da had been right all along; she was deaf to magic.

But then how had she managed to cause the torch to catch flame?

Wolfhere frowned. "I have never heard Eika were accomplished magi, or that they had any skill at the forbidden arts, or even knowledge of them. They are savages, after all. But I no longer doubt Prince Sanglant. There is a presence among them who controls great power. That must explain—" He ran a hand over the slab of obsidian. "Strange."

"Explain what?"

But now an edge came to his voice. "Sit still," he ordered. He traced a ring on the stone and then rested his hands, one palm up, the other palm down, a shoulder's width apart. He stared at the black surface, intent, concentrating. She saw nothing, but she felt a breath like wings brushing her cheek.

"An eagle!" he breathed sharply, starting back. "An eagle in flight, plummeting to earth." He jumped up. "Come, Liath. We must go back. I don't know what this portends." Hastily, he collected his weapons from the floor, and they hurried back to the stairs that led out of the crypt. When Liath stuck the torch back in a sconce, it snuffed out as soon as it left her hand, plunging them in darkness. Wolfhere grunted, sounding surprised, but he said nothing. They climbed the stairs by feel and hastened out of the cathedral.

It was dark and still overcast, but after the blackness of the crypt, the night did not seem heavy. The Eika drums sounded louder now; they usually reached their peak at midnight.

As they walked swiftly back toward the mayor's palace Liath recalled Wolfhere's broken sentence. "You said the presence of an enchanter might explain something."

"Ah." For the space of twelve steps, clipped and hard and rapid on the plank walkway, he considered. "When we rode into Gent, I cast a spell to attempt to delay the advance of that group of Eika who were coming after us. Nothing more than an illusion. My skills are not great, and I am only adept at certain arts of seeing. I warned you to ignore what you saw."

The flight to Gent was still graven in her mind with the vivid colors of a freshly painted mural. What he spoke now made her suddenly understand that which she had almost forgotten, because it had made no sense at the time.

A flash, a glittering of light like a fire's light seen from inside a dark room. Her horse had almost thrown her, and Manfred had flung a hand up to cover his eyes, as if to protect himself from a much fiercer vision.

A tingling on her back. The tiny winkings of fireflies.

But that was all she had seen. Either Wolfhere's magics were indeed very small, or else . . .

"I knew there must be some kind of sorcery at work," he continued. "Now I know it is more powerful than I feared. To dissipate my illusions is one thing. To cloud my seeing is entirely another."

Or else she had seen only the faint edge of his magic—or not *his* magic at all, but the barest trace of the enchantment that had protected the Eika against it.

"You've thought of something," Wolfhere said.

"No. Nothing." Until she understood it herself, she would not confess this mystery to him. It would give him power over her, more power than he already had. "Only what Da said: 'To master knowledge is to have power from it.' "

"True words," commented Wolfhere.

The palisade marking the inner fortress, the mayor's palace, rose before them in the gloom. She heard the distant buzz of many voices speaking at once.

Were they true words? When Da said, *"trust no one,"* had he meant her to include *himself*? She was deaf to magic, yet he had begun to teach her the arts of the magi. She was deaf to magic, yet she had some kind of power; she had seen it manifested twice, once when she had burned the Rose of Healing into the table in Hugh's study and this night in the crypt, when she had caused the torch to light.

"Is that all you have thought of?" he asked.

She remained mutely silent.

"Have I made any attempt to harm you, Liath?" he asked gently, if a little accusingly. "To bring you to harm?"

"You brought me to Gent!" But she said it with a wry smile, hoping to distract him.

They came through the wooden gateway into the courtyard of the mayor's palace. The stone-paved courtyard was awash in torchlight, smoke and flames setting a yellow haze over the people gathered like so many bees swarming. This was a new crowd, smaller than the one this morning, and agitated in a completely different way.

"Alas that I did," he murmured. Then he grabbed her by an elbow and with a grim expression pulled her through the crowd, shoving Dragons and rich merchants and the mayor's retainers ruthlessly aside so that he and Liath could get to the center.

There, they found the mayor, Manfred, and Prince Sanglant— and an Eagle, battered beyond belief, his cloak torn, his head wrapped in a bloody, dirty cloth, one arm hanging useless at his side, and his horse dying at his feet.

He looked up, saw Wolfhere emerge out of the crowd, and tried to get to his feet, but staggered. Manfred steadied him.

"Find a healer," Prince Sanglant ordered, signing to his Dragons. "Bring a stretcher, and wine." His closest attendants, the scarred-face woman and the man with the limp, hurried off.

Mayor Werner's complexion had a ghastly white cast under torchlight. But it was not only the light but also his expression. He looked like a man who has seen his own grave.

"Lie down, my son." Wolfhere knelt beside the Eagle and lowered him onto Manfred's bundled cloak. "What is your news?"

Liath crept closer. Blood soaked the Eagle's tunic, and he breathed in ragged bursts. The broken end of an arrow protruded from his chest. She caught in a gasp and took an involuntary step closer. The next instant, a hand caught her by the shoulder.

She knew before she looked, felt in her whole being, that she had come up beside the prince and that it was he who had stopped her from going forward. His hand seemed to burn her shoulder even through the cloth, though she knew it was only the shame of her desire that made her feel his presence so keenly. She risked looking up at him because it would be cowardly to do otherwise. But when their eyes met, he was the one who looked away. He let go of her and even took a half step away. She had a sudden uncomfortable notion that her presence troubled him.

The Eagle coughed, spitting blood. Ai, Lord, the arrow had caught him in the lung. It was only a matter of time.

"Bad news." His breath came in bursts now. His skin flushed a deep red as he struggled to speak. "Count Hildegard. Riding to Gent. Many troops. We were ambushed. I escaped to—"

"He came to the east gate less than an hour ago," said Sanglant. "These folk brought him here." He gestured toward the crowd, which by dint of glares and simple force from the prince's ever-present escort of Dragons, had finally moved back, giving the rest of them air. "Though he would have gotten through the streets more quickly had they stayed in their beds and not swarmed out into the streets to get in his way."

"What of Count Hildegard?" Wolfhere asked.

The man coughed again, this time clots of blood, and when he spoke, Liath had to bend forward to hear him. "I don't know. Perhaps she won free. Our Lord—"

He went into convulsions. Liath threw herself forward and helped hold his shoulder down, Manfred opposite her, while Wolfhere leaned on a leg and Sanglant grasped the other. As if from a distance she heard Mayor Werner wailing and the cries and sobbing of the crowd.

The Eagle went lax. Liath sat back, looked up to find Sanglant staring at her, his hands resting on the man's left leg. The prince stayed there, poised like that, for a long breath. Wolfhere muttered a curse and hunched over, ear to the injured man's chest.

"No need," said Sanglant, not taking his gaze off Liath. "He's stopped breathing. There is no pulse of blood. He's dead." That strange hoarse scrape in his voice lent a verisimilitude of grief to his words that she did not see in his expression; not that he was pleased, either, just that death no longer grieved or surprised him.

She looked away in time to see Manfred cover his eyes with a hand. Wolfhere remained bent over the body for a long while, his face hidden. Finally, he straightened.

"He is dead." He sat on his heels while beyond Mayor Werner wept copious tears, although not, Liath suspected for the dead man but rather for the loss of hope.

Sanglant lifted a hand. The Dragons drove the onlookers out of the courtyard. "This is no time to weep," the prince said, rising and turning to Mayor Werner. "He was a brave man, and he deserves this honor: that we not lose heart because of the news he paid his life to bring us. Count Hildegard may yet win through."

"If she does not?"

"If she does not," replied the prince, "if her force is utterly broken, then we will ration food more strictly and settle ourselves in for a long siege. We have good water supplies here. There is yet hope that Wolfhere's companions will reach King Henry. Some of my own men still reside outside the walls, and they will harass the Eika until we can either break out or another force comes to break in."

Finally Wolfhere moved, but only to unpin the brass badge the dead Eagle wore at his throat. It was wet with blood and drying spume. He wiped it off on the tatters of the dead man's cloak. Then he rose, and Manfred and Liath rose with him. Wolfhere extended a hand, open, the badge lying on it, winking in the torchlight.

"What are the precepts which govern the conduct of an Eagle, Liath?"

They were simple enough. She had memorized them easily. "Serve the king and no other. Speak only the truth of what you see and hear, but speak not at all to the king's enemies. Let no obstacle stand in the way of your duty to the king, not weather, not battle, not pleasure, not plague. Let your duty to your kin come second, and make no marriage unless to another Eagle who has sworn the same oaths as you."

She could not help it. She glanced toward Sanglant, who had turned back to watch her, or to watch Wolfhere, she could not tell which. His gaze was steady and a bit imposing, but he made no sign or sound.

Yet as she took a breath, to finish, she saw that Manfred also watched her, but with an odd expression, as if he was watching to see what she would do or how she would react. Had she been blind? Was his affection for her something more than that of comrades?

She dismissed the thought quickly and with impatience; to believe so was vanity, nothing more. Just because Hugh had desired her and no other woman in Heart's Rest did not mean every man desired her.

Manfred smiled sadly at her. She smiled back and continued.

"Aid any Eagle who is in need, and protect your comrades from any who might harm them. And, last, abide by your faith in Our Lady and Lord."

"Do you swear to abide by these?" Wolfhere asked.

It was quiet now that most of the crowd had been chased away. The mayor had stopped wailing. He huddled behind Sanglant, his servants clustered round him with solemn faces and hands clasped in prayer. Torches flared, and as the wind shifted it blew smoke into her nostrils, stinging and bitter. From the east, stronger now, she heard the Eika drums.

"I do so swear," she said quietly understanding now what was going on.

Manfred knelt and pulled the remains of the dead Eagle's cloak across his slack and bloody face, concealing it. Wolfhere leaned forward across the body, lifting the badge. But Sanglant stepped in and set a hand between them.

"As the king's representative, it is my right," he said.

Wolfhere hesitated only a moment. What choice did he have? He relinquished the Eagle's badge to the prince. And Sanglant fastened it to Liath's tunic, his fingers at her throat. His lips were turned up slightly, but Liath could not be certain if the expression was meant to be a smile. She only knew that she was flushed. He kept his gaze where it belonged: on the sharp pin as he fastened it through the cloth of her tunic. But when he had finished, he did not immediately drop his hands away. He met her gaze and mouthed three words which, with his back to Wolfhere and Manfred and all the others drawn back or gone, only he and she knew:

" *'Make no marriage.' "*

Then he turned and walked away and soon was lost in the darkness beyond the torch-lit haze. She watched him go, then, self-consciously, dropped her gaze away. But it came to rest on the dead Eagle. She touched the badge at her throat. The metal was cold and still slick with the effluvia of his dying.

"Now you are truly an Eagle," said Wolfhere softly, not without triumph.

3

LIATH woke at dawn, stiff and shivering. It was colder than it had been the night before, and as she slipped her wool tunic on over her shift she noticed the light was of a different quality as well. Throwing her cloak over her shoulders, she went outside.

The clouds had blown off, and from the parapet she saw the glittering cold disk of the sun, bright but with the breath of old winter on it, a last reminder of snow and ice and the grip of cold weather. She stamped her feet and rubbed her arms. She refused to let memories of Hugh spoil this day, her first as a true Eagle. She touched the brass badge at her throat. Surely this badge protected her from him. Surely not even a noblewoman's bastard like Hugh would attempt to make her break her oath that had now been given to the king's service. Or at least she told herself that. It was too clear and fine a morning to taint with fear.

The eastern shore was shrouded with fog that the sun had not yet burned off. She could not see the Eika camp and only the suggestion of earthworks, dark forms shouldering through the white blanket of fog. To the west she saw clouds. Licking a finger, she held it up. The wind was coming from the east; those western clouds, then, were those that had covered Gent last night. She smiled, slightly; Hathui would merely snort at this profound observation and point out that a child could have made it.

But thinking of Hathui made her think of Hanna. Where was Hanna now? Had she escaped the Eika? Had she found safety? Had they reached the king, and was he even now marching to raise the siege? She missed Hanna so badly. The bite of cold made it worse because cold wrenched her mind back to Hugh, to that night when she had chosen not to die, when the light had bobbed an erratic course out to her where she huddled in the pig shed only to reveal itself as Hugh, with a lantern. Hugh, who had taken her back inside—

But there was no point dwelling on that. *"No point thinking only of what troubles you,"* Da always said. But Da had been a master at

ignoring the trouble that stalked him, whether it be debt or whatever had finally caught and killed him. She wiped away a tear with
the back of a hand, then clapped her hands together, rubbed them
briskly, trying to warm them.

"Liath!"

She turned. Below, in the courtyard, Wolfhere waved at her. She
climbed down the ladder and jogged over to him.

"I must prepare the body for burial," he said. "But in my surprise
and haste last night I forgot my flask in the cathedral crypt."

She nodded. "I'll fetch it for you."

"Come back here after," he said. "We'll bury our comrade after
Terce."

The city was more restless than usual, this day, this early. People
wandered the streets as if looking for lost relatives. The hammering
of blacksmiths sounded a steady din from the armory, and a constant stream of men and women carried loads on their backs—
metals, leather, anything that could possibly be made into weapon
or armor—down to the warehouses where the armories had been
set up. There were, Liath noted, no children on the streets at all.

When she reached the cathedral, she heard the final psalm of the
office of Prime.

" 'God, Our Lady and Lord, have spoken and have summoned the
world from the rising to the setting sun.' "

She hurried up the steps and through the open doors. The cathedral was packed: with refugees, with townspeople, with the Mayor
and his entourage. At the front, in the place of honor, knelt Prince
Sanglant, his blue-black hair and the wink of gold at his neck a
beacon for her gaze. He wore mail and his fighting tunic, and fifty
Dragons knelt with him, all arrayed for battle, helmets tucked
under their arms. The biscop stood before her gold biscop's chair,
set behind the Hearth; she raised her arms as she led the congregation in the final verses of the psalm.

> " 'Our Lord is coming and will not keep silence:
> fire runs before him and wreathes him closely round.
> Our Lady summons heaven on high and Earth
> to the judgment of the people.
> Think well on this, you who forget God,
> or you will be torn in pieces
> and no one shall save you.' "

All were kneeling. Liath knelt in the side aisle, at the very back of the crowd, and spoke the final Kyria with the congregation.

Lord, have mercy. Lady, have mercy.

Then, in the hesitation as the final prayer died into the air and the congregation waited for the biscop to dismiss them, Liath stood and slipped along the wall to the shadowed corner of the vestibule where a heavy wooden door barred passage to the crypt. It creaked as she opened it. She glanced back, but the hum of the crowd, rising, stretching, waiting perhaps for a word from biscop or mayor about last night's message, covered the noise. She left the door ajar behind her.

A thin line of light marked the door as she descended, and at the first sharp corner it glanced off stone and illuminated a bead of water caught on a delicate spiderweb. Turning the corner, she lost sight of the door, though the suggestion of daylight still trailed after her. She went as silently as she could, not wishing to disturb the peace of the dead. She reached the bottom, foot slamming into level floor where she thought there was another step down, and paused to let her jolted shoulders recover.

Strange, that the light from above still gave a steady if faint radiance, just enough that she could see the shape of her hand if she held it up in front of her face. Last night—but of course, last night it had already been dark when she and Wolfhere had descended; that was why it had been pitch-black. Abruptly, she heard a noise above, from the stairs. She froze, listening.

Footsteps descending. They were heavy and accompanied by a fine rattling and shaking, many small chains muffled in cloth. The pale ghosts of tombs watched from the gloom. She was, she discovered with surprise, not afraid at all. Indeed, without knowing why, she was expecting him.

"Liath," he said. She could only see his shape, bulky in armor, only feel the air shifting as he stopped five steps above, his body blocking the narrow passage.

"You heard the door creak," she said, "even above the noise of the congregation."

"Below the noise of the congregation," he corrected. She felt that he smiled or perhaps only wished that he did. In any case, he walked down the rest of the stairs. He stumbled on the floor, not expecting it so soon, and swore. "Damn, it's dark down here. How can you see anything? What are you doing here?"

"Fetching something left behind."

"An answer worthy of Wolfhere. I am not your enemy, Liath."

"No," she said. Her voice shook. "I never thought you were."

Seeking, his hand found her shoulder; he was like a blind creature groping by sound. The crypt echoed strangely, and even the faint harmonics of his mail, rippling and clicking with his every least movement, got caught and distorted among the tombs and the vast breathless cavern, all air and stone.

"Who are you?" he asked. "Who are your kin?"

"I am the daughter of Anne and Bernard. I know nothing of my mother's lineage, save that she is of free birth. Wolfhere knew her. It's likely he knows things about her he has not chosen to tell me."

He chuckled, a soft sound on an exhalation of breath. "Wolfhere is not a man for sharing confidences. Or so my father claims. But I did not expect you would be given the same treatment as the rest of us."

His hand on her shoulder was terribly distracting, but neither did she want to move away from him. "Why? Why do you say that?"

"He favors you. Or I should say, he seems to be protecting you."

"Perhaps he is. I don't truly know."

"Ah. And your father's kin?"

"I know little about them, save that they came west and settled in Wendar during the reign of Taillefer. There is still a cousin who holds lands near Bodfeld, but I have never met her. One of her sons rides with the Dragons."

He removed his hand from her shoulder, and she was sorry to lose the contact. He shifted, restless, and she glimpsed in the half-darkness the shape of his head, tilted back, then cocked to one side, as if he was listening. She could only hear the weight of the stone above her, a heaviness more sound than feeling.

"Bodfeld," he murmured. "That would be Sturm. But he is trapped outside."

"I met him!" She thought back, recalling the Dragon who had led the company which had saved them from the first attack of the Eika. But all she had seen of that man were blue eyes, blond beard, and a grim expression. Much the same expression, she supposed by the tone of his voice, which Sanglant wore on his face right now.

"He is a good soldier.,"

This praise for her kinsman warmed her, though it was delivered bluntly and without any suggestion he meant it as flattery toward her.

"Why did you follow me?" she asked boldly.

Rather than answer, he sat on the last stair but one. It was an unexpected gesture and oddly moving; now, instead of towering above her, his head was level with her chest. He appeared less imposing. Perhaps that was his intent.

"A good lineage, if not of the first rank," he said. "Which may account for your lack of deference."

Stung and embarrassed, she flushed. "I beg your pardon, *my lord*. My Da always told me we came of a proud lineage and need bend our knee to none but the king."

He laughed softly. Obviously he was not offended.

"You didn't answer my question. Why did you follow me?"

He shook his head, refusing to answer. Perhaps he did not truly know.

But she knew. She was not afraid of Sanglant. His reticence piqued her, irritated her. Surely the darkness, the stone, and the earth hid them from the sight of any who might be watching. Only the cold tombs gleamed with a faint phosphorescence, but the holy sisters and brothers of the church were used to sin, were they not? Did they not preach forgiveness? Was it not allowed, even once, to give in to the urging of your heart?

Liath had forgotten she had a heart. It hurt, like a wound salved with salt, to rediscover it now. Sanglant did not move. She could not make out his expression. Gold gleamed softly at his neck, the twisted braid of gold that was the emblem of his royal kinship. She could make out the outlines of the black dragon on his tabard, as if it had been stitched with thread spun of moonlight and dew-laden spider's silk.

Was it true he had no beard at all, like a woman? Impulsively, she raised a hand to touch his face. She almost flinched away, thinking of Hugh's unshaven face, but Sanglant's skin was nothing like: his was toughened by exposure to the weather, chafed by the chinstrap of his helmet, and cool.

And beardless. He might have shaved an hour ago, his skin was so smooth.

Her heart was beating hard. Hugh's shade was furious, but he was far away at this moment, very far away.

"Sanglant," she whispered, wondering if she would have the courage to—

To what?

He took her hand in his—though his were encased in gloves sewn of soft leather—and drew it away from his face. "Down that road I dare not walk," he said quietly but firmly. He let her hand go.

Numb, she let it fall to her side.

"I beg your pardon," he added, as if he meant it.

Ai, Lady. She was annoyed and embarrassed and such a jumble of other emotions she could not disentangle them one from the other. Sanglant was a notorious womanizer; everyone said so. Why was he rejecting *her*?

Sanglant shifted restlessly. This was her punishment. She could almost hear Hugh laughing, that soft arrogant sound. *You are mine, Liath. You aren't meant for anyone else.* Tears stung her eyes. This was her lesson: that she must remain locked within her tower. She must not—could not—succumb to temptation. It would never be allowed. She was already hopelessly stained.

"I must go," he said abruptly. The hoarseness in his voice made her think, for a wild moment, that he was sorry to be leaving; but his voice always sounded like that. He stood, mail shifting. "We're preparing for a sally out of the walls if we see any sign of Count Hildegard or her people."

"Why did you say that, last night?" Anger helped her fight against tears, anger at Sanglant's rejection of her, at Hugh for his unrelenting grip on her, at Wolfhere for his half-truths, at Da for dying. "Why?"

"What did I say?"

"You haven't forgotten."

He made a sharp gesture, and she understood abruptly that he had *not* forgotten and that he spoke as much with his physical being as he did with words. "Make no marriage, Liath," he said harshly. "Be bound, as I am, by the fate others have determined for you. That way you will remain safe." But he mocked himself as much as he spoke to her.

"*Will* I remain safe? And from what? What are you safe from, Sanglant?"

He smiled derisively.

How could she see him smile? It was far too dark.

But it was not dark, not entirely. His face and front were illuminated by a soft white light, like muted starlight. The black dragon winked and stirred in that light as Sanglant moved, looking beyond her into the vaults. His eyes widened in shock. He lifted a hand, stood there, poised, frozen, and utterly astonished.

Liath turned. Just behind her, so close she felt the displacement of air, Sanglant knelt.

She stood beside the tombs as if she had just stepped out of the earth itself. She wore a long linen shift of a cut Liath had never seen except in mausoleums and reliefs carved into stone. Her face was as pale as the moon, marked by eyes as blue as the depths of fire. Her long hair, gilded with that same touch of unearthly light, looked like spun gold, hanging to her knees. Her feet were bare. They did not quite touch the floor of the crypt. In each hand she held a knife, and those knives shone as if their blades were made of burning glass.

And she bled, from her hands, from her feet, from her chest where a knife stood out, its blade thrust deep to take her heart's blood. Blood slipped in trails like the runnels of tears down her shift from that wound, and she wept tears of blood.

But she gazed on Liath and Sanglant with the calm serenity of one who is past pain and suffering. And she beckoned to them.

Hesitant, hand clutching through cloth and wood the Circle of Unity she wore as a necklace, Liath took slow steps forward. Sanglant followed. She heard him murmuring a prayer under his breath.

She spoke no word, merely retreated farther into the night vault of the crypt, into the warren of chambers where the deacons and lay-brothers and sisters, servants of the biscop, were buried, least known and least honored.

There lay a plain gravestone, flat against the earth. It bore no markings, no inscription; a gray-flecked fungus obscured half its face, grown in a pattern that might have revealed a new mystery had there been better light. But the light that limned the saint—for how could she be anything but a saint?—was enough to see the hollow that opened up behind the simple gravestone, a sinkhole that transmuted into stairs, leading down and farther down yet into total blackness.

Sanglant knelt beside the grave. Liath ventured forward, following the saint, who descended the stairs. *Her* light receded away from them and was lost around a bend in the catacomb. Liath set foot on the first stair.

"Go no farther," said Sanglant abruptly. "The air smells fresh here, and it carries the scent of oats."

She halted, looking back over her shoulder. Already the unearthly light dimmed, as a candle gutters.

He added, impatiently: "The soil in the river valley and east of Gent is rich enough to grow wheat and rye. Only in the western hills do the folk hereabouts grow oats. This tunnel must lead miles from the city."

"But she called to us—"

Voices sounded from above, accompanied by the ring of mail and the stamp of heavy feet. Torchlight streamed into the chamber, sending streaks of light glaring over stone and tomb and earth. Liath shaded her eyes.

"My lord! Prince Sanglant!"

He rose and turned as the first of his Dragons found him.

"My lord Sanglant!" It was the scarred-face woman. She looked first at him, then at Liath, who still stood half in the sinkhole, then back at the prince.

He said quickly and loudly, as the others crowded in, "We have followed a vision of St. Kristine. This is where it brought us."

A few drew the circle at their breasts. None seemed inclined to laugh or make jokes, even finding the prince alone in such a place with an attractive and young woman.

"The fog has lifted from the eastern shore, my lord," continued the woman. She, too, wore armor and, with her exceptional height and broad shoulders, looked as ready for hard battle as any of her comrades. "The watch has spotted Count Hildegard's banner among a mob of horsemen. They are fleeing just ahead of an Eika horde. They are coming to Gent."

Sanglant looked once, and sharply, toward Liath. He was not a man who betrayed emotion easily through the expression of his face; she could read nothing there now. But he lifted a hand and touched his cheek with a finger, an unconscious echo of the moment she had touched him so. Realizing what he was about, he jerked his hands down. Then he swept out at the head of his Dragons. Their heavy steps and the weight and clink of their mail rang through the crypt like thunder, hurting her ears. None waited for her.

She waited, but the light died, torchlight and the pale fluorescence of saint's light, both together, leaving her in a gloom relieved only by that faint trail of plain good sunlight filtered through dust and darkness. Air touched her face, as soft as a feather, rising softly from the catacomb at her feet. She smelled fresh earth and growing things, although she could not have sorted oats out from that distant aroma of earth and hills and open air.

The saint had vanished down the stair into the black mystery beyond. Liath dared not follow her, however desperately she wished to. Perhaps, for a moment, she understood Sanglant. *Down that road I dare not walk.* But that did not lessen the ache.

She shook herself and stepped out of the sinkhole. Groping, she made her way back to the large vault, found the obsidian slab and the little flask tucked forlorn and forgotten up against Biscop Caesaria's tombstone. Liath unstoppered the flask and took a draught. It was bitter enough to make her eyes sting, but bracing. Thus fortified, she climbed back to the living world above.

Like Sanglant, she did not doubt that St. Kristine of the Knives had appeared to them. But she could not answer the most pressing question: Why to them? And why now?

She reached the steps of the cathedral in time to see Sanglant mount his horse. He received his helmet from the woman, but before he settled it over his head, he glanced up toward the open doors. Their gazes met across the mob that had gathered. The noise in the streets was that of people hysterical with fear and hope.

He did not smile at her, only looked. Then someone spoke, and his attention was pulled away. He settled his helmet on his head and by that means was transformed; he was Prince Sanglant no longer, but captain of the King's Dragons.

Their gold tabards were as bright as sunlight and his most of all, the black dragon sigil stitched onto gold cloth with veins of silver thread. They looked, indeed, as terrible as their reputation, fierce and unforgiving in iron helms faced with brass; that his helm with its delicate gold dragon was also beautiful only made the contrast between the fine ornamentation and the grandeur of their stark and forbidding strength the more striking.

The prince hefted his teardrop shield on an arm, touched his sword's hilt, and led the way. The rest clattered behind him, over one hundred, headed down the main avenue to the eastern gate where they would meet the rest of their fellows, those who were already on duty and those still arming.

She ran back to the mayor's palace. The people on the streets, seeing her scarlet-trimmed cloak and her Eagle's badge, parted to let her through.

Wolfhere waited, pacing impatiently back and forth in the Lady Chapel where the dead Eagle had been laid out. The corpse was now clad in a white linen shift, face decently covered by a square of white cloth; it lay, as was appropriate, at the foot of the Hearth.

"Liath!"

She handed Wolfhere the flask. He took it reflexively, without really noting it, and thrust it between belt and tunic. "I sent Manfred ahead to the eastern gate, to be our eyes with the Dragons. Go there now. If they must ride out, you will watch and report back to me. A horse has been saddled."

Everything was happening so fast. She checked herself for bow, quiver, and sword; all were there. Then she hurried outside to the courtyard where a horse was indeed waiting, one of Mayor Werner's geldings, a big handsome bay. His size helped her more than her Eagle's badge now. The streets were thronged and more and more people spilled out of their crowded homes as word spread through the city of Count Hildegard's approach.

But the closer she came to the eastern gate the more the crowd thinned; in a besieged town, even with as daunting a force as the Dragons within their walls, the townsfolk chose the path of prudence. A street ran parallel to the river wall. Here she found a group of boys, old enough to be useful and young enough to be fearless and, thus, enamored of the Dragons. She handed her reins over to one, a gangling weed of a boy with a thin face and quick eyes. From this vantage point she could see the ranks of the Dragons, ten abreast, about two hundred of them, lined up in the open space that fronted the gate.

The boys, city-bred and city-wise, showed her a ladder that led up the wall and to the wall-walk. She clambered up, surprising the men of the city's militia who stood watch there, looking out anxiously to the eastern shore.

The fog had lifted, or most of it, in any case. Out on what had once been rich cropland the land boiled with movement like flies swarming over a carcass. The Eika were out in force. The level

ground gave a clear view. After a few minutes of confusion, she
began to sort out the picture displayed there like a shifting mosaic.

The Eika were out in force, truly; they infested the ground. She
had never seen so many bodies in one place, and all of them mobile.
The green and white banner that marked the remains of Count Hildegard and her retainers bobbed unsteadily in a tight mass of horsemen supported by a straggling line of running infantry. Those who
could not keep up were enveloped in the mass of Eika that came
close behind, swallowed and consumed. The Eika closed in around
the count's force, slowly cutting them off, encircling them. Only
one narrow strip of unclaimed ground remained: the road to the
river and the eastern bridge to Gent.

It was a race. Liath could not imagine how the count and her
remaining soldiers could reach the bridge in time—unless the Dragons sallied out into the very jaws of the Eika army.

This thought hit her with the force of a bracing flood of cold
water on a hot day. It cleared her mind. Clearing, her vision
clouded, and she closed her eyes and rubbed them with her knuckles. Opened them.

Now, as she stared with horror, the view of the fields beyond the
river looked utterly different.

There was a banner, green and white, bearing the blazon that
was, probably, the badge of Count Hildegard's lands and kin. But
no human retainers surrounded it. No horsemen rallied to it, no
infantry fought desperately at the rear. It was surrounded instead
by the ice-white glare of a thousand Eika warriors jogging at a brisk
pace along the thin strip of road that led to the stone and timber
bridge. That led into Gent.

What she had seen before was illusion.

What she had seen before was what everyone else saw, all the
watchers along the wall, the Dragons who had left their horses and
gone to the posts above the gate to call down their report to the
prince, to judge to the instant the best moment to sally out. What
they saw was a vision brought by a terrible and powerful enchantment, brought into being by what skills she could not imagine, only
that she was the only one who saw past the enchantment to the
truth.

"You are deaf to magic," Da always said.

Or else guarded against it.

The thought hit her with such force that for one awful moment she simply could not move or think.

But she had to think. What had happened to Count Hildegard and her soldiers she did not know, but she could guess. The count's army had been utterly destroyed, and the banner wrested from the dying hands of her last loyal retainer to be used now as the lure to draw the Dragons to their death.

And she was the only one who could stop them.

4

LIATH practically slid down the ladder, she moved so fast. Splinters sliced into her left hand, but the pain was only another goad. The boys who held her horse stared after her as she sprinted toward the Dragons, whose attention was entirely on the men who stood watch above the gate.

"Let me through!" she cried. "I must speak with the prince."

They let her by without demur. Sanglant sat his horse at the front of the line, in conference with others: an elderly militia man, a dismounted Dragon, and his chief attendant, the scarred woman.

Sanglant caught sight of Liath; perhaps he had heard her voice. He lifted a hand to silence the militia man, who was speaking.

"But my lord Sanglant!" the man protested, misunderstanding the prince's intent. "There are too many of them! It would be foolish to sally out into such numbers. If Count Hildegard can win through, we will open the gates to receive her." Then he saw Liath and stuttered to a halt.

"You can't!" Liath cried. She took the reins of Sanglant's horse out of the hands of a Dragon, as if by holding his mount's harness she could control the prince's decision. "Count Hildegard isn't out there at all. It's an illusion. There's magic—"

Sanglant was off his horse at once. Without waiting for her or anyone, he ran to the wall and took the steep steps three at a time to the lookout over the gate. She scrambled after him. Manfred stood here with two Dragons and a cluster of city militiamen. He motioned the others aside so the prince could come forward. Liath pressed up beside Manfred; surely he would believe her, if the others could not see. There, on the parapet, protected by a timber wall covered by animal skins soaked in water, they stared out at the far shore.

She saw so clearly now. There must be more than a thousand Eika, two thousand perhaps, a vastly greater number than those who defended Gent. The barbarians jogged forward at a steady trot, the banner swaying in their midst, a prize of war. Their enormous dogs loped beside them, muzzles lifted to the wind. There was rank after rank of blue and yellow shields with their menacing red serpent blazon, the dark line of their weapons, held at the ready; their bone white hair gleamed in the new sunlight as the fog dissipated along the shore of the river. How could anyone see this as the remnants of Count Hildegard's army? The Eika called out, too, in words she could not understand, only that they sounded like taunts in her ears. The dogs ran silently which was, perhaps, worse. The river streamed on, oblivious. Drums beat to the time of running feet.

They came closer, and closer. Liath could make out the details in the green and white banner: a boar on a white field. She could see the long flanks of the dogs, saw their tongues lolling out. The Eika had come so close, first rank almost on the bridge itself, that the prince had possibly twenty breaths to make a choice.

"Don't you see?" she cried.

Sanglant narrowed his eyes.

"Manfred!" She grabbed Manfred's arm and shook him, hard. "It isn't Count Hildegard at all! It's only Eika! Look harder. You're an Eagle. You must be able to see with true sight."

"There!" called Sanglant. "In the fourth rank. There is Count Hildegard and her brother!" He pushed away from the wall.

The banner and the first of the Eika troops hit the bridge. Their footsteps sounded like the hollow tramp of doom on the stone and timber structure. A shrill keening rose from the front ranks of the Eika, as if they had caught the scent of their quarry. As if they had seen Sanglant's dragon helm on the walkway above and knew he was waiting for them.

"The Eika are almost upon them!" cried Manfred, jerking his arm out of Liath's grip. He shot her a single glance, as if to say he was sorry.

Sanglant looked then, piercingly, at Liath. He wavered. Clearly he did. He wanted to trust her that much. But then he looked back. Howls rang from the bridge, a chorus of them, dogs and Eika joining in strength until they deafened her. The faces of those watching, those whose faces she could see, went white with horror. Liath could no longer imagine what they saw, or what they thought they saw. She could only see the Eika army almost upon them.

"Open the gates!" Sanglant commanded.

As he pushed past her, she grabbed his arm. The Dragons nearest him swore and lunged for her. The great wheels that controlled the gate began to creak and roll, and the doors swung outward.

"Close the gates!" she yelled, but no one listened. Below, the Dragons parted, half to each side, making room for the flight of the count and her retainers into the city. "It's an illusion. It's a trick."

All she could see of Sanglant's face was his eyes, jade green, staring hard at her. He shook his head. Then he was gone, down the steps.

The gates creaked farther open, gaining speed. Mirroring them, the Eika in the front ranks broke into a dead run.

"Manfred!" she screamed, grabbing his cloak, shaking him. "Can't you *see*? Manfred! Trust me!"

But it was too late.

The gates opened. Count Hildegard's banner passed the last pylon, crossed over the transition from bridge to land. And Eika poured through the open gate into Gent. Sanglant, caught on the ladder, could not reach his horse or his men.

The square below boiled into chaos. Their howling reached a peak, so sharp and high it hurt her ears. Manfred gasped aloud and then he shoved her along the walkway.

"Run! Run along the wall until it's safe. Find Wolfhere!"

She stumbled and went to her knees just as an arrow thudded into the militia man standing, still in shock, behind her. He grunted, more surprised than pained, and tumbled slowly to his knees. Gripping the arrow as if to his chest, the man fell forward to the edge of the walkway and over as she grabbed for and missed him. He landed atop two Eika warriors just as they hacked at a Dragon cut off from the others. They went down under his weight, but more came behind them, many more, like the unstoppable waters coming up the river at floodtide. Then the dogs found him; some ran on, but others began to feed. Liath gagged, bile rising in her throat.

A mailed hand yanked her to her feet. She came up hard, jolted against a tabard—a black dragon sewn with silver.

It was Sanglant. He did not speak. He pulled her along the walkway behind him so fast her feet barely touched the ground. She could not even look back to see what had become of Manfred. She was too numb even to feel fear; she felt completely paralyzed.

Two arrows stuck out of Sanglant's back, quivering, points embedded in mail. One shook loose and fell harmlessly away. Militia men knelt, shooting with their bows, aiming out over the wall

toward the bridge where Eika crowded in from the eastern shore. It
was too confused in the square fronting the gate to hope to shoot
Eika safely without chancing to hit Gent's defenders.

The defenders were hopelessly outnumbered. Already the Dragons had been borne back by the force of the unexpected assault and
the sheer weight of numbers and ferocity. The Eika gave no quarter.
Beyond that, she could make out no pattern to the battle swirling
at the gate except that of iron-helmed Dragons fighting desperately
to form back into ranks.

She heard, distantly, the creak of the wheels that moved the
gates. Then screams. She smelled smoke.

In a staccato pattern arrows thunked into the wood just behind
her, like a sudden spatter of drum beats, sharp and final. Sanglant
grunted and swore and stopped. She turned her head. An arrow
stuck out from his left leg, just above the knee. As she watched—as
if time obeyed different laws here—a drop of blood welled up
through leather and leaked out, following by a second and then a
third, sending a trail of red down the curve of the knee. Red blood,
just like her own, like any human's blood.

She could not get any breath in to her lungs. She was going to
choke.

"Break it off." Sanglant let go of her.

Obedient, she gripped the arrow, one hand braced against his leg,
the other clamping down over the fletching. Blue, she noted idly;
the feathers were stiff as metal, digging into her skin. The shaft was
strong. Somehow, she snapped it in two and tossed the end away.

He grabbed her and tugged her on.

"My lord prince!" A militia man called to them from the safety
of a lookout post built into the wall. Sanglant pulled her inside,
where the white-bearded militia man threw back a hatch to show a
trapdoor beneath.

"This way, my lord," he said. Liath was unable to catch her
breath. She stared at the man's brown cloak, strangely fascinated
with its plain weave and ordinary texture. It had been patched on
one shoulder with a piece of material that did not match in color,
as if taken from a different batch of dye.

Sanglant leaned against the closed door, panting, for this moment safe from arrow fire. Liath heard the sounds of the battle,
swords chopping at mail, at iron-rimmed shields; the alarm, a thin
horn rising like a clarion again and again, alerted the people of Gent.

Sanglant pushed away from the door and crossed to an embrasure. He had not let go of Liath, so she perforce had to follow. The archer standing there moved aside instantly. Together, she and Sanglant stared out the thin slit of a window toward the eastern shore of the river.

The angle of the lookout post was such that the embrasure's line of sight took in the river's bank where the bridge touched the eastern shoreline. Eika poured onto the bridge, but even as they watched the tide slowed, stemmed by the half-closed gates, by the resistance from within the city, by the narrow path itself, the roadway and bridge, that forced the Eika warriors close together.

But although they slowed down, they still moved inexorably forward, howling and keening like wild beasts.

On the eastern shore, swathes of fog concealed patches of field. A shadow lay over the land, wreathed with mist, there on the far shore.

Neither fog nor mist. Something about it: a pattern, a shifting, the way her eye wanted to slide away from it. It was an enchantment. She forced herself to look hard at it, to *not* believe it was shadow and fog but rather concealment.

It dissolved, or not dissolved as much as faded from her sight and resolved into four figures. Two of them were Eika warriors painted and outfitted like the rest of their kind, red serpent round shields resting casually against their legs, two-bladed axes cradled like infants in the crooks of their arms. Between the two warriors stood an Eika remarkable for his scrawny stature and his apparent nakedness: He wore only a ragged loincloth and a gold belt. In his hands, he held a small wooden chest. A leather pouch hung from the belt.

But beside these three stood one other, one unlike the rest by stature alone, by some indefinable quality Liath could not name, yet recognized. She could not tear her gaze away; he was a huge Eika whose face and arms and chest had the scaly sheen of a creature clothed in living bronze. He had no tunic, nothing covering his chest—not even the garish painted patterns sported by his warriors—only layers of necklaces, beads, shells, and bones strung together and mixed in with chains of gold and what looked like gold and silver coins, holes drilled in their centers and strung on thin ropes of metal. His stiff trousers were sewn of cloth dyed a brilliant blue, belted by a mesh of gleaming gold that draped in delicate folds to his knees. He wore gold armbands, like twining serpents, around each thick arm. His hair glinted bone white in the sunlight, braided into a single braid that hung to his knees.

Beside her, Sanglant sucked his breath in between his teeth.

"There!" said Liath. "Do you see him?"

"I see him." He shook his head as if to shake away an annoying insect. "He is the one whom I felt all along. His is the power."

"He is the enchanter." She felt the power, just as Sanglant did.

Sanglant leaned forward into the embrasure, suddenly intent, staring hard toward the distant Eika. His lips parted. "Tell me your name," he whispered.

The Eika enchanter shifted, head turning so abruptly that Liath shuddered. It was as if he had heard. He looked around and focused that fast, looking *toward* them although certainly he could not see them, concealed as they were by the timbered walls and the narrow confines of the lookout post. Certainly he could not know the prince watched him from there.

And yet, why not, if he was truly so powerful an enchanter?

She thought, then, that he spoke a word in reply, but she could not see him clearly to guess at the syllables he spoke, and she certainly could not hear above the clash of battle raging in the city beyond.

"Bloodheart," said Sanglant in a low voice, staring out as if the two of them watched each other, tested each other. "We will meet, you and I."

Beyond, on the shore of the river, the Eika tide swelled. The knot shoving forward on the bridge broke loose and Liath tore her gaze away from the Eika enchanter to see the gates shoved open and more Eika flood in to Gent.

Jerking back from the embrasure, Sanglant turned to Liath. "Go to the cathedral. Save those you can." The militia man waited, nervous, taut, at the trapdoor.

"Where are you going?"

But it was a stupid question. She knew the answer before Sanglant said the words, although he said them anyway.

"My Dragons need me. We will hold them as long as we are able." He lifted a hand and touched her cheek with his mailed hand—as she had touched his, in the silence of the crypt.

Then he hefted his shield, raised his sword, and was out the door before she could say anything more. She started after him, back to

the wall-walk, only to see him descending an outside ladder. Then
he was gone, running into the chaos that raged around the gates as
the battle moved steadily outward, farther into the streets of Gent.
A cry went up, a piercing shout, his name called over and over.
Before the militia man grabbed her she saw the overwhelmed Dragons rallying, fighting on horse or by foot toward the lone figure of
their prince who seemed to be intent on running alone full into the
force of the Eika assault.

A hand clapped onto her shoulder and dragged her back away
from the door just as an arrow thunked into it. A burning arrow.
Smoke make her eyes sting. It guttered against the wood; the
bearded man slammed the door shut, but she heard more arrows
thud into it, an echo of the drums that pounded relentlessly in the
Eika camp.

"This way!" he said urgently. "Down two levels to a tunnel beneath. It runs all the way from this lookout post to the mayor's
palace. You will meet up with a larger tunnel, which runs straight.
Take no side tunnels, they only lead to other posts. I pray that the
Eika have not yet taken the other posts and gotten into the tunnels."

She descended the ladder, not looking back. The man did not follow. The first ladder gave out on dirt, a tiny space within the wall,
banks of sod and timber, so tight she could hardly breathe. She
found the other ladder and climbed still farther down, twelve rungs,
to a tunnel lined with fired bricks. The space was barely wider than
her shoulders. She hesitated, touched her bow, then drew her short
sword instead. Her fingers brushed the words graven in the hilt:
"This good sword is the friend of Lucian."

"I pray you," she whispered, "be my good friend as well."

She walked cautiously, for it was dark and she could hear the
distorted echoing noises of battle not far above her, crossing and
crossing back like a complicated tapestry being woven. Pray God
that this tapestry was not to be the fall of the city of Gent.

The narrow side tunnel debouched into a larger passageway, one
that might support two men walking abreast but not more. Behind,
where she judged the wall stood, she caught the flickering glare of
fire and smelled the stinging scent of smoke. Her eyes had already
adjusted to the dark. Ahead, it was darker and more silent.

Behind, she heard a grunt and the hard thunk of a person landing on dirt. She whirled. Saw the betraying gleam of white hair. What else to do?

She had the advantage. She ran forward, and just as the Eika whipped round, she stabbed it in the gut. Felt the resistance of its skin, as if it was alloyed with metal. But Lucian's was a good sword indeed. Perhaps the Dariyans had known secrets of metallurgy lost to the blacksmiths of today. Perhaps Eika skin was not as tough as it looked. The blade sank in and pierced the creature through.

It howled and sliced at her. She yanked backward and cut at its face; it went down. The stink was horrible. Above, fire flared and she heard a man screaming over and over and over again, Ai! Ai! Ai! and more distantly, heard through smoke and pounding feet and shouting and the whole chaotic cacophony of a battle being slowly and brutally lost, a sharper call: "To the prince! To the prince!"

She jumped back from the Eika's body. It twitched and she fled away down the tunnel. If any followed, she did not notice them. She was too busy running. Too busy remembering.

He had touched her cheek. Did he care for her? Surely he would be killed. And what did it matter, now? There were not enough defenders in Gent now that the Eika had breached the gate. Not enough in any case, if the Eika had, as their leader, an enchanter— even if his only gifts were for illusion. Illusion was a powerful weapon in the hands of one who dared use it any way he wished.

"*Save those you can.*" So Sanglant had said. Surely that was why the saint had appeared to them. Saints, like angels, like the daimones of the upper air, were not bound to the world of time: They could see the future.

She passed side tunnels and all she heard was fighting and screaming, all she smelled was blood and smoke.

The tunnel led to the barracks. She climbed up a narrow ladder into the tackroom, head butting into a trapdoor which, with main force, she shoved open from underneath, scraping knuckles on the iron bands that bound the trapdoor together.

The barracks were entirely empty now; there was only the distant sound of drums and the clarion call of the horn. And, drifting ever closer, the aroma and music of battle. All the Dragons were gone. *Gone.* Dead, soon enough. She had no energy to cry. She had to warn Wolfhere. She had to lead as many people out through the catacomb as possible before the city fell. She no longer doubted Gent was doomed.

But at the door of the barracks, she stopped dead. Hesitated and turned back, staring at the empty ranks of stalls, smelling the straw, some of it dry, some of it damp with urine or manure. The barracks would burn very well.

She ran back to the stall where she and Manfred and Wolfhere had slept. Manfred's saddle sat against a post, just where it had always sat this past month. Its presence was like an accusation. What had happened to him? Was he still alive? Had she thought of him once since the breaching of the gate? But she did not have time; she should not even be here. Every moment meant another life saved, or lost.

But she had to get the book. She heaved her saddle up and over, grabbed the saddle bags and slung them over her shoulder. Then she sprinted back, outside, crossing the deserted courtyard. It was far too quiet, here in the mayor's palace.

"Liath!"

Wolfhere stood on the palisade. He practically jumped down the ladder, he was in such haste to get to her.

"No hope!" she cried. "The Eika have breached the gate. Everyone must arm and fight, or go to the cathedral."

"How—?"

"An enchanter." She remembered, suddenly, that strange exchange. Someday it might be important that more people than she and Sanglant knew that name. "He calls himself Bloodheart."

Wolfhere nodded once, sharply. "Then go, Liath. Go. If you win free, you must get word to the king."

She did not wait to ask him what he meant to do. She did not have time. Already smoke rose in thick clouds, heavy, black, and forbidding, from the eastern part of the city, and flames licked the roofs of houses near enough to see. Perhaps the mayor's guard had already run to the eastern gate.

But when she crossed out through the arch and started down the main thoroughfare of Gent, she found utter confusion. The street was packed, every soul there wild with fear. Half of them seemed to be headed to the western gate. Some few, armed with butcher knives and staves and shovels and hatchets and any object that might be used as a weapon, shoved their way toward the east. But not as many ran east. Mostly, the people of Gent had forgotten everything and completely panicked.

Liath pushed and elbowed her way through the crowd. At first she tried to yell, every third step, "To the cathedral!" but there was no point to it. Her voice simply could not be heard above the roar of shouting, donkeys braying, chickens squawking, children wailing, fire snapping, and untold feet slapping down on plank and stone roadway—all headed every direction and none.

But she needn't have worried. Pushing her way along the length of the palace palisade, crossing the square, and reaching the broad steps and inviting facade of Gent Cathedral proved the easiest part of her journey.

The cathedral was packed.

People were shoved together on the steps, crowding in, crying and pleading, lifting their children high over their heads so the infants might be granted sanctuary inside if not their own selves.

"Make way!" Liath cried, although their noise drowned out her words. She drew her sword and used its hilt to knock hard into the people. When they turned, angry or sobbing, they gave way before her Eagle's badge.

In this fashion, though slowly, she got up the steps. If possible, it was more crowded inside. All of them had shoved inside until she could not understand how anyone could breathe pressed up toward the Hearth, the haven, the holy space. Surely not even savages like the Eika would profane the holy space of the God of Unities.

They stank of fear and sweat. It was impossible, absolutely impossible, to imagine getting through this crowd to the Hearth where she might hope to find the biscop. She sheathed her sword.

And then, amazingly, she heard a shift in the tone of the crowd. Like a muting blanket drawn bit by bit across the congregation, the wordless mutter and yelling and weeping took on form and flow. Creeping back from the front, a hymn slowly took hold.

"Lift me up!" Liath commanded.

Half to her surprise, two men did so, grabbing her by the legs and hoisting her up. There, at the Hearth, the biscop presided, arms lifted toward the heavens as she led the congregation in a psalm.

> " 'You that live in the shelter of Light,
> you who say, 'The Lord is my safe retreat,
> the Lady the fastness in which I trust.'

He will cover you with His pinions.
She will grant you safety beneath Her wings.
You shall not fear the arrow that flies at night
or the spear that stalks by day.
A thousand may fall at your side,
ten thousand close at hand,
but you it shall not touch.' "

Liath sang with them. When the psalm finished in a somber *Kyria*, the biscop turned her hands, palms outward, and the mass of people quieted so all were listening. Only the hiccuping sobs of terrified children broke the silence.

"Pray, let us have silence," cried the biscop.

In that moment, while silence trembled and the roar of fire and battle and distant drums leaked in through the walls and the open doors, before the panic of the people outside could overset this tenuous peace found here, Liath raised her voice. She called attention to herself in the very way Da had warned her against.

"Never be noticed. Never stand out. Never raise your voice."

"Biscop, I pray you, listen to my words. I am a King's Eagle!"

The men holding her shifted, and she had to steady herself, one hand on each of their shoulders. Every head in the cathedral skewed round, faces bleached white with fear. The biscop lowered her hands and signed to her to continue.

"Your Grace, please believe my words. I have seen a sign. St. Kristine appeared to me—" Liath faltered. She could see she was losing their attention, their belief. "St. Kristine of the Knives appeared to Prince Sanglant! It was a true vision. There is a catacomb beneath the cathedral, a tunnel, leading west. By this way—"

That was all she had time for.

A shout rose from the gathered crowd outside.

"The Dragons! The Dragons have broken!"

Liath clapped her hands over her ears just as the two men lost their grip on her. She fell but could not land hard because the people were packed so tightly in the cathedral. Even shoving, panicking, trying to move one way or the other, no one could shift more than half a step to right or left.

The next instant a horn call blasted through the space, echoing off stone, deafening her and every other soul inside. But it silenced the crowd long enough, just long enough, that the biscop could be heard.

"This I say!" she cried in her powerful voice. "This I say to you, my people, that I will not stir from this Hearth until all have reached safety or the Eika have been repulsed. So must all who are fit take up any weapon you can find and fight to save this, our city. In the name of Our Lady and Lord, in the name of St. Kristine who, though she suffered and died in this holy place, did not forsake us."

She drew breath, but such was the power of her voice and the tense expectation that none spoke or filled the void with clamor.

"So has St. Kristine appeared to the prince, he who even now fights with his own body to spare ours pain and desecration. This is my word, and you my people shall obey it. Let those who are children or who are nursing children follow this Eagle into the crypt, in an orderly fashion. Gather the children, for they and the holy relics of this Hearth are the treasures of our city. We must save them, if it is so willed by Our Lady and Lord and the saint who watched over us. Let the elder children shepherd the younger, and let the infirm wait with me at the Hearth. Let us put our trust in God. Lord, have mercy. Lady, have mercy upon us."

Her deacons brought torches. With the crowd parting before her, Liath took a torch and led the way down into the crypt. As she descended the steps, all the din and tumult was lost to the muffling encasement of stone and earth, to the cloak of death and the pale tombs of the holy dead. The torch burned steadily, heat blowing in her face, stinging her eyes.

She stood while deacons carrying the holy relics of St. Kristine crowded behind her and the stairs filled with softly weeping children, pressing, waiting. She felt them at her back like a weight: on her all depended.

"*Save all you can*," Sanglant had said. And others, crying out: "*The Dragons have broken.*"

She had no idea where the saint's tomb was. Everything looked changed. The crypt opened out before her in silent mystery, taciturn, unwilling to give up its secrets.

Then, on a whim, she knelt where her footsteps and Sanglant's, so short a time before, had scuffed the earth. She cast about, and— *there!*

On the dirt perhaps two strides away she saw the flecking of dried blood.

She followed this trail left by the bleeding saint. It led her to the sinkhole and the stairs that yawned into the black earth beneath.

The crypt quickly filled behind her. Deacons whispered, frightened. An infant sobbed and was muffled.

Of the battle in Gent, she could hear nothing. She did not know whether Sanglant yet lived; she had no idea what had happened to Wolfhere and Manfred.

She could at least hope that Hanna had made it away from Gent alive. It seemed ironic now that Hanna, forced to flee, had been granted the safer path, though it had not seemed so at the time.

She could not delay. What lay there in the dark earth could not be worse than the fate awaiting those who faced the Eika onslaught. She took in a deep breath and started down the steps.

She counted as she went, aware always of the press of refugees at her back though she never turned to see them, to help them, to make sure they did not stumble. She had to walk the unknown path. She counted eighty-seven steps, because counting gave her the courage to go on, speaking the numbers aloud so she couldn't hear, so the blackness didn't seem so utterly enveloping. The air was close, smelling of mildew and earth. Once, or twice, hand brushing the wall, she thought her fingers touched worms or other moist creatures that live only in the night. But she did not have time to flinch. She had to press forward.

The steps ended and the floor leveled out and turned sharply. It widened to the width of her outstretched arms. She paused then, but only that one time. The torch illuminated rough stone walls and a low ceiling hewn out of rock. The floor here was also rock, strewn with small stones and pebbles that rustled under her boots. But it was fairly smooth, as if water had once streamed through here or many feet marched back and forth, grinding it down under the weight of years and passage.

She could not see far ahead of her, but she felt the air had a flavor untouched by burning and war and death. She smelled oats, a touch caught on a bare wisp of a breeze borne down from distant hills. That gave her heart. The deacons pressed up behind her, the wooden chest which contained the saint's relics jutting into her back. A child said, in a high, wavering voice: "But it's so dark. Where is my momma?"

She walked on into the darkness. She led them, counting until it became ridiculous to count, past one thousand and two thousand and beyond that. The tunnel ran straight, like an arrow toward its intended victim.

She wept as she walked, plain good tears, quiet ones. She could not afford to sob. She could not afford to be blinded by grief. Behind, she heard those who followed, the thin wails of infants and the helpless weeping of children who could not understand what was happening to them. The deacons murmured in soft voices to the rhythm of their step, the words of the psalm they had sung in the cathedral:

> " 'For She has charged Her angels
> to guard you wherever you go,
> to lift you on their hands.' "

On she walked, leading them. On and on, away from the fall of Gent. So few would be saved.

"We will hold them as long as we are able." His last words.

He was not meant for her, of course. It was foolish, an infatuation, not love, surely, for love is built on ties of blood or of shared work and companionship, not on a glance or the stray wanderings of stubborn and insistent desire. Never meant for her, even if he had lived. It was not only the difference in their births, for she believed what Da had told her, that she need only bend her knee before the king. They were freeborn, of an old lineage, so Da always said, though he had never given her more information than that. Of a lineage that had gained lands in return for lordship over themselves, beholden to no count or duke but only to the king. As Hathui's people had, in these times, in the eastern marches.

No, it was more than that, and utterly different.

"Be bound, as I am, by the fate others have determined for you." So Sanglant had said. Was it not the duty of the captain of the King's Dragons to die in the service of his king? And hers to live, if she was able?

Was she not bound by that other mystery, of Da's death, of her mother's death eight years before, of the treasure-house, the secret, that she both carried in her saddlebags and even perhaps in her own person? *Of her own person?* She had been made a slave because of another man's desire to possess what was hidden within her. She was now always and ever marked by that slavery, just as she was marked by Da's murder and by the mystery of the white feather she had found next to his dead body. Deaf to magic—or guarded against it. But bound to it, whichever was true.

Some destinies cannot be escaped.

So she walked and left Gent behind. She felt nothing in her body, not truly. She could not afford to be crippled with grief, and during those long months with Hugh she had learned how to put strong emotion away from her, locking it away behind a sturdy door.

But she allowed herself tears. She wept for Sanglant and for what could never be. She wept for Da, for her mother, for Wolfhere and Manfred, for the dead Eagle whose badge she had inherited. For all the souls, the brave biscop and her people, who would die. Liath had seen the Eika enchanter who named himself Bloodheart. She did not believe he would show mercy or respect the sanctity of the Hearth. Why should he? He had not been brought within the Circle of Unity. He had slaughtered Count Hildegard and then used her banner as part of an unscrupulous trick. He wanted Sanglant for reasons she could not fathom. But he and Sanglant were engaged in a duel set in motion before they had ever set eyes on one another.

Her torch burned steadily and did not go out or expend its substance. She held it in front of her as a beacon; it was the only light left to her.

Not the only light. She had to believe Hanna was alive. She would find Hanna again.

She reached up without thinking and touched her badge, felt the eagle embossed on brass. Hanna was all, except for the Eagles. She truly was one of them now. And that, perhaps, gave her a place where she might find safety.

So she walked. The tunnel ran on and on and on. If those behind her faltered, she did not know. She led them and did not look back.

5

THE Eika had breached the eastern gates just after dawn. It was midday by the time Liath emerged, blinking, half-blinded, and exhausted, from a narrow cave mouth into the glaring light of a fine spring day.

Behind her, the refugees from Gent staggered out, stumbling after a steep climb up several hundred steps. The tunnel itself had been long and made arduous because of fear. But Liath feared the final climb, up steps carved into rock, would prove too much for the smallest and weakest of the refugees, thus holding up those who tried to escape behind them.

They came so slowly. First the anxious deacons emerged, carrying the holy relics from the cathedral. Then came a long line of children, younger carried by elder, infants in the arms of their mothers. There were women in all stages of pregnancy, including one who had gone into labor. Here and there, other folk appeared—a blacksmith with his hammer and tongs, his skills too precious to waste in a hopeless fight, the two lanky girls who had performed as acrobats in Mayor Werner's palace, the elderly bard who had mangled the *Heleniad* and produced his own atrocious imitations of old Dariyan verse at the many feasts in the great hall.

Too slowly. A clump of a dozen would stream out, and then there would be a pause, so long Liath would catch her breath and pray this was not the end of the line. Then more would emerge, stumbling, halt and lame, or a child collapsed and no longer able to walk on its own. The trickle would as suddenly turn again into a steady stream as those held back behind the knot hurried out and dispersed onto the hillside.

Liath could not bear their grief. Hers was heavy enough. She walked out away from the cave, which lay half hidden by shrubs and trees in a great jutting ridge of hill.

It was just as Sanglant had said. There was a field of oats here, straggling along the hillside.

Stumps of trees edged the ripening oats, and beyond them the forest climbed back into wilder lands. Two huts sat in the shadow of the trees. As she watched, a man came out from behind the closer of the huts to stare. Then, waving his arms, he ran over to the deacons. They began to talk all at once. Liath edged closer, then recalled that as King's Eagle she had every right to listen to their conversation.

"—but . . . but it is a miracle!" the man was crying, hands clapped over his cheeks. "The cave narrows and ends in a rock wall one hundred paces back. We have hidden in there, now and again, when Eika scouts rode too close by. A company of Dragons sheltered there five nights ago. But never have I seen steps or a tunnel leading east!"

Though the sky was clear, they heard a low rumbling like distant thunder. Liath hurried back and scrambled up the ridge that sheltered the cave. From its height the hill dropped away precipitously to the river plain below, stretching eastward, green and gold patched with earth, to a stark horizon. From here she could see the river winding like a dark thread through the plain. The sky was so clear the sun's light had leached away the most intense blue at the zenith, washing the land in brightness. Distant Gent looked like a child's toy, tiny carved blocks fashioned in the model of a city.

Arnulf's city, some called it, where King Arnulf the Elder had joined his children in marriage to the last heirs of Varre.

The city was on fire. Liath stared for a long time. Smoke stained the horizon, reaching in streaks toward the heavens. There was so little wind this day that the smoke rose straight up in thick columns, obscuring her view. The city lay too far away for her to identify buildings, but she could not even pick out the cathedral tower.

On the plain, ants crawled. The Eika had come to feast on the leavings. She shook her head. She felt by turns numb and then suddenly engulfed with a crushing grief. No matter how she tried she could not push it away any longer.

She abandoned her position to three boys who came scrambling up behind her. They stared and pointed at the view, and one gaped at her. His thin face appeared familiar, but she could not place him. Perhaps he had been a servant at the mayor's palace.

He said, "I lost the horse," and then burst into tears.

She fled. She had nothing to say to him, or to any of them. As she climbed back down, careful to find good footing among the loose scree and wiry roots, she watched the refugees emerge from the cave mouth. Children and yet more children, a dark-haired plump child of indeterminate sex carried in the arms of a thin pale-haired girl who did not look strong enough for such a burden, a few older people now, some of them carrying bundles on their backs, a few precious possessions, or else nothing at all, only themselves. Some fell to their knees to praise God for this deliverance. Others merely sank onto the ground and had to be helped away, to clear the path that led out from the cave's mouth.

But they were coming out too slowly. So few would escape. Surely by now the Dragons had been utterly overwhelmed. At any moment she expected the stream of refugees to end, or Eika to spring forth, hacking right and left with their axes and deadly spears.

"Ai! Wagons!" cried one of the boys at the ridgetop.

And another: "They bear the mayor's colors!"

Liath ran with the farmer to where a road—such as it was—cut up near his farmstead. A few brave deacons followed, but the rest remained by the field as if the cave and the reminder of the saint's mercy would grant them safety. Liath took out her bow and gave herself cover behind a tree. The farmer hefted a pitchfork.

But they needed no weapons, not this time. The wagons did indeed belong to Mayor Werner. They lurched and careened over the two ruts that served as road. The mayor himself, red-faced and flushed with weeping, sat in the front of a wagon driven by—

"Wolfhere!" Liath leaped out and ran forward, jogging—almost dancing—beside the wagon as it pitched and jolted the rest of the way up the hill, coming to rest at last beside the two poor huts of the oat farmer.

Wolfhere swung down, looked her over carefully, then beckoned to the farmer. "Show these servants where they can build a fire. Somewhere out of the way."

"And alert the Eika?" the man protested.

Wolfhere made an impatient gesture with a hand. "They have found better prey today than the poor pickings they could scavenge here." The farmer retreated obediently.

"I saw Gent," said Liath. She could not take her eyes off Wolfhere. She could not believe he was alive. "It's burning."

"So it was when we left."

"How did you get out?" She stared back, hoping to see—

But there were no Dragons in attendance, only servants from the palace, about thirty of them walking alongside the ten wagons. A pale, pretty woman drove in the last of the wagons and, dry-eyed and grim, began to rub down the horses. Liath recognized her: She was the servingwoman who had, everyone knew, been carrying on an affair with the prince. Would she weep for her lover? Or was she only glad to be alive?

A man came up beside her to aid her; in the wagon's bed a girl-child raised her head weakly to look around. It was the pair she had saved from the streets, father and daughter.

Refugees from the tunnel swarmed forward, surrounding Mayor Werner, drowning him in questions and pleas and demands. "Where is my husband? Do you know what happened to my mother? Has my brother been seen? What of the mint? My father guarded there. Does the biscop yet live?"

And on, and on. Like a coward, she thought bitterly, the mayor had saved himself rather than die in the defense of his city. That duty he had left to Prince Sanglant and the Dragons.

"My good people," he cried, wiping tears from his cheeks. How she had come to hate his voice, filled with self-importance and a trace of the whiny, indulged son he had been. "Pray, grant me silence. There is no time to waste. We must begin to march. It will take many days to reach Steleshame, and most among us are weak or young. We have emptied the stores from the palace. This must serve us on our journey. Listen to my words!" Now, finally, the ragged band of refugees had quieted and drawn closer while yet others still emerged, in ones and twos, from the cave mouth.

"Let the elder children shepherd the younger, and let the children be divided into groups so there will be no confusion and none left behind. Let those who are strong enough carry food on their backs, so there may be room in the wagons for those whose legs grow weak. We will pass out bread now. In one hour we begin our journey. We dare not wait longer than that."

With that he turned and began directing his servants. The pretty servingwoman pulled back the heavy cloth that had been draped over the foodstuffs in her wagon, and she began distributing bread with the efficiency of long practice, aided again by the father. Deacons began to organize the children into groups of ten, each under the command of an adolescent. A woman, sobbing quietly, nursed her infant while another child clung to her skirts. One of the slender acrobats came up cautiously to the woman and offered her and the child bread. At the cave's mouth, more refugees stumbled out into the noontide glare. Now, however, there were servants to guide them to food and a place to rest until the next stage of the journey began. Now, one in five of the refugees were adults with wounds or singed clothing; there were, perhaps, eight hundred people in the oat field. She judged, by measuring the height of the sun with her fingers, that she had emerged an hour or so ago. Would the Dragons never come?

But of course they would not. Prince Sanglant would not leave the city until every last soul was safe or dead.

"Liath." Wolfhere beckoned. She followed him back behind the hut where the farmer had built a fire in an outdoor hearth. It blazed merrily, a lattice of sticks that collapsed as those at the lowest rung burned to ash. The farmer set more logs on the fire and, at a sign from Wolfhere, retreated, leaving them alone.

"We must look," said Wolfhere.

"How did you get free?" she asked. "Did any others—? Where is Manfred?"

He shook his head. For the first time she saw his mouth tighten, concealing heart's pain. "We loaded the stores into the wagons and made our way to the western gate. Others fled the city by that gate as well, though many died at the hands of Eika. Some may have escaped. But we came later. By that time the battle that started at the eastern gate had grown until it engulfed half the city. So we were able to get away with less trouble. We lost only one wagon, and that because its axle broke. And we met Dragons—"

"Dragons!"

He lifted a hand sharply, silencing her. "You will remember them. They were the ones who saved us when we first rode into Gent a month ago."

"Sturm," she murmured. Her cousin, if report was true.

"They cut through a company of Eika, freeing us."

"And then?" she demanded.

He frowned, almost wincing, as if the memory did not bear recalling. "Then they rode into the city by the west gate, to join with their fellows."

Liath shut her eyes.

"Attend," said Wolfhere. "We have no luxury for grief, Liath. We must see with Eagle's sight. That is our duty."

"Through fire and stone?" she whispered.

"Not every Eagle has such skills, it is true. Now. Attend." He shut his eyes and raised his hands, shoulder width apart, palms facing in toward the fire.

"But it's true," she said, interrupting him. He had to understand. "I can't see that way. In the crypt I saw nothing, not because there was a shadow, but because I saw only the stone. And the Eika— There *is* an enchanter, and he is Eika, not any other kind of creature." This memory hurt, it was still so raw. Remembering how Sanglant had seen and named the Eika chieftain. "That is how the gates were breached. He wove an illusion. It wasn't Count Hildegard's forces at all."

Wolfhere opened his eyes and stared at her. "Go on."

"It was an illusion. Everyone saw the banner and the count and her people. Everyone. Except me. *I could see through the illusion.*"

"What are you saying?"

'I am saying that I am deaf to it, as Da said. Or else guarded against it. I don't know which." Immediately she cursed herself inwardly for confessing to him. But she had been so happy to see him. Surely that joy meant he could be trusted, or trusted in part. He had saved her from Hugh. He had treated her with unrelenting kindness and good will. And she had, she realized, come to care for him. Reflexively she rested a hand on the warm leather of her saddlebags, feeling the book hidden within. She waited.

Wolfhere looked truly startled. "Bloodheart," he said. "Illusion. I understand now. I did not before. I wondered why I had seen nothing of Count Hildegard's soldiers within the city, even the last survivors of that force. I wondered how the gate had been breached. For I saw it, too, Liath. I saw her banner, and her retainers, pursued by Eika. From the palisade at the mayor's palace I saw them reach the bridge, and then I saw no more. And yet you say *you* saw through the illusion."

"I did."

"I cannot explain it, either to you or to myself. Attend me, Liath. Tell me what you see." He lifted hands again and shut his eyes, then, after a moment, opened them, staring into the fire.

Yellow-orange flame licked the air. Liath stared hard at it. She envisioned in her minds' eye a circle branded into the air—the Ring of fire, fourth step on the ladder of the mages. Through this she viewed the flame.

She saw nothing but the lick and spit of fire. And yet, had she not once seen salamanders, their blue eyes winking in the coals of the hearth? Had she not once seen butterflies called up by her father in the summer garden? Once, years ago, before her mother died, she had seen magic. *Before her mother died.* Then everything had changed.

Da was protecting me.

He had given his life to protect her. To hide her.

There are spirits burning in the air with wings of flame and eyes as brilliant as knives. At their backs a wall of fire roars up into black night, but there is nothing to fear. Pass through, and a new world lies beyond. In the distance a drum sounds like a heartbeat and the whistle of a flute, borne up on the wind like a bird, takes wing.

Wings, settling on the eaves. A sudden gust of snow through the smokehole. Bells, heard as if on the wind.

"Where is she?" said the voice of bells.

"Nowhere you can find her," said Da.

The fire blazed higher, growing, engulfing the logs until it burned like a storm. And in the flames she saw battle, the steps of the cathedral, the Dragons in a last ragged line, so few of them now, the last, their horses and their comrades strewn like so much refuse along the course of their retreat. Dogs—those who were not raging in the thick of battle—fed voraciously. She shuddered, convulsed by nausea.

A last knot of city militia fought desperately by the mint and then finally were overwhelmed. Behind them, the palisade of the mayor's palace and the timber roof of the great hall burned in sheets of flame, a terrible bright backdrop to the last killing field.

The Eika pounded at the Dragons, axes chopped down again and again on the teardrop shields, red serpents pressed against dragons, shoving them by sheer weight of numbers back and back up the steps to the doors.

There! Sanglant, limping and bloody, striking at either hand as he retreated step by step, the last man in the wedge, taking the brunt of the onslaught. At his right hand, the scarred-face woman, ragged Dragon's banner draped around her shoulders, her spear working, jabbing, wrenching free; at his left, Sturm, blue eyes grim as he cut down first one Eika then, when that one fell, the next. Manfred stood half inside the cathedral doors, staring; *seeing*, as was his duty.

But one by one, Dragons fell. Gent burned, and the streets were deserted except for Eika, prowling and sniffing in doorways and looting. Except for the dead. Except for the feeding dogs.

A wagon had been brought into the square fronting the cathedral and from atop this, surrounded by his howling troops and by a pack of slavering dogs, Bloodheart surveyed the ruins and the last stand of the Dragons. He leaped down and hefted a spear in his huge hands, ran with it to the steps and took them two at a time. Behind him came his soldiers, their mouths open in shrieks and howls Liath could only see, not hear. Only the naked old Eika male remained behind in the wagon, but even he grinned, jewel-studded teeth winking in the reflected glare of flame.

Bloodheart's charge hit the last Dragons like a hammer. So few, and already wounded and exhausted, half of them went down, crushed beneath the assault. Sturm vanished in a hail of ax blows. The scarred-face woman was torn away, the weight of huge dogs bearing her down. Dragons shouted their prince's name, but they were all separated now, a few at the door, a few swarmed and surrounded and harried down to the base of the steps, and Sanglant in the center—the eye of the storm—striking on either side like a madman as he hacked his way toward Bloodheart.

The blow that took him came from behind.

Surrounded, flanked, engulfed. A screaming Eika had leaped into the gap that opened behind the prince. The creature swung. Sanglant jerked and then collapsed, that fast, like a rock let drop. His body landed hard, sprawling, at the feet of Bloodheart.

The Dragons were gone, vanished, as if they had never existed. Bloodheart stared down at the prince. He bent and wrenched the helmet from Sanglant's head to reveal the lax face. He twisted a hand under the gold torque and yanked it off, his white claws cutting the prince's face and neck. Blood seeped, slowed, stopped.

Bloodheart raised the gold torque up like a trophy, threw back his head, and howled with triumph.

Liath shuddered. She could not hear it, yet she could—as if borne miles on the wind, as if carried through the ranks of the refugees who fled through the tunnel, as if cutting straight to her heart.

But she could not look away.

Bloodheart lowered the torque but only because he had to beat back the dogs. He hit hard around himself, using both haft and head of his spear, and he growled and cursed at the dogs, driving them back from his prize: Sanglant. The dogs cowered finally and sat back on their haunches, eyes burning yellow with rage, tongues hanging out, muzzles rimed with saliva and blood. The biggest of them snarled, baring its fangs at the Eika chieftain, and he struck it hard on the head with his bare hand; his own claws—a bristling growth at his knuckles—sliced its cheek open. It whined and groveled before him. The others slewed their ugly heads round and stared hungrily at the prince's body, but they didn't move in. Yet.

Soon. Soon he would be theirs.

Liath leaned in toward the fire as if she could reach and drag the corpse to safety, spare it this desecration. The heat burned away her tears, but it could not burn away her pain. It could not change what she saw and so witnessed.

Bloodheart shook himself and whirled once, spinning as if he felt the breath of an enemy on his spine. His gaze lifted to the middle distance. Everything shifted; the fire flared before her. She blinked, and he was looking at *her.*

"Who are you?" Bloodheart demanded, gaze impossibly fixed on her through the fire. "You trouble me with your spying. Be gone!"

He spit. She flinched back and was staring at fire, roaring and crackling and consuming, burning, buildings of stone consumed by the dull red of heat and the white-blue searing of flame, smoke thick and oily in her nostrils. She heard the pound of horses galloping past, a haze of distant shouting, a faint horn caught on the wind. But these were no buildings she had ever seen before. These were not the buildings of Gent.

A figure turned, staring, a male figure, armed with a bronze breastplate and silver-tipped lance. "Liathano," he said.

But through him a gateway, his shade itself is the gateway, like stars seen through a gauze of fine linen. A drum sounds like a heartbeat, and a flute draw its music over the air like the rising and falling of waves. She sees through flames, staring out through a fire but a different fire, not her own.

There on a flat stone sits a man—not a man, perhaps, for his features are exotic and unlike those of any man Liath has seen except there is a passing resemblance to Sanglant, that bronze-tinged skin, the high, broad cheekbones, the beardless face. He is dressed strangely in a long, beaded loincloth so cunningly worked that the pattern of beads describes birds and leaves woven into a tight embrace. Leather sheaths encase his forearms and his calves, covered with gold and green feathers

and tiny shells and gold beads and polished stones strung together. A
cloak trimmed with white shells and clasped with a jade brooch at his
right shoulder drapes to his waist. He twists lengths of fiber—flax,
perhaps—along his bare thigh, binding them into rope.

He looks up, startled, and stares at her but without truly marking
her. Behind him, a figure moves, too far away to be plainly seen.

"Liath."

She jumped back and found herself, face singed from heat, staring at the hearth fire and at Wolfhere, across from her. Tears stood
on his cheeks, but only a few. He stared into the flames and finally
drew his gaze away as if from down a long distance and murmured,
so soft she barely heard him:

"Aoi."

She blinked, bewildered. Who had spoken her name, there at the
end, wrenching her out of that final vision?

"Those were the Lost Ones, Liath."

"Who were?" But she could not make sense of the world, of her
fingers on her hands, of the snap of fire or the brush of wind on her
face.

Ai, Lady. Sanglant was dead.

Wolfhere shook himself all over, like a dog—or a wolf—and stood
abruptly. "This mystery must be solved later," he said. "Come,
Liath. Our first duty is to the king, and he must have word of this."

"Word of what?" To form the question was difficult enough. She
could not move. She could not even remember what it was to move.

"Of the fall of Gent. Of the death of his son."

The death of his son.

"Fed to the dogs," murmured Wolfhere. He grimaced like a man
enduring an arrow's barbed head being dug out of his thigh.

Liath fell forward onto her knees and clasped her hands before
her. "Ai, Lady," she whispered. "Hear my pledge. I will never love
any man but him."

"Reckless words," said Wolfhere, his tone sharp. "Come, Liath."

"Safe words," she replied bitterly, "since he is now dead. And I
will follow the fate others have determined for me."

"So do we all," he said quietly.

They left the fire still burning and returned back around the huts
to find the field crowded with refugees forming into staggered lines,
making ready to leave.

"Has so long a time passed?" Liath asked, amazed. She judged that another hundred or so refugees filled the oat field, and a few more trickled from the tunnel, scarred, shaking, and weeping. But these had left Gent hours ago. They could not know what had just transpired, what she and Wolfhere had seen. "How long did we look into the fire?"

Wolfhere did not answer. He had gone to confront Mayor Werner, to demand that the Eagles be given two horses. Liath did not listen to the argument; she stared at the cave's mouth, where people still emerged into daylight, blinking, weeping, frightened, relieved. How many more would arrive? Was Manfred among them, or had he been killed? Did the biscop survive?

"Liath!" Wolfhere called to her, impatient, tense, and angry. "Come!"

Horses were brought. Werner sputtered and looked furious, but could not refuse. Liath took the reins of a gelding and mounted.

"What about Manfred?" Liath asked, looking back over her shoulder past the line of wagons and the tidy groups of refugees as they got into place, ready to begin their long march. She stared hopefully, hopelessly, toward the cave's mouth.

"We can't wait," said Wolfhere. He urged his horse forward, angling up to the old road.

The first of the wagons jerked forward, heading west for Steleshame and safe haven. The refugees, with murmurings and sighs and one voice that could not stop sobbing out its grief, began to walk. But Liath hesitated, staring back.

Perhaps it was a trick of the eye. She thought she saw a faint figure standing on the rocky ridge above the mouth of the cave: the form of a woman draped in a gown of ancient design, herself wounded yet standing, unbroken by those wounds. The patron saint of Gent still watched over her flock.

Perhaps it was a trick of the breeze. She thought she heard a shout from the last figure to clamber out of the cave's mouth. "The tunnel is closed! It's sealed shut as if it never existed!"

"Liath!" Wolfhere was already into the trees. Wagons trundled up the road behind him.

Liath followed Wolfhere onto the old path that led into the forest and away from Gent. They soon left the ragged column of refugees far behind.

XIII
THE SHADOW OF THE *GUIVRE*

1

SABELLA'S army pitched camp in the Elmark Valley, at the eastern edge of the lands inherited by her husband. Here, fifty years ago, the kingdom of Varre had given way to the lands ruled by the kings and queens of Wendar. In the highlands beyond the valley lay the outermost villages sworn to the duke of Fesse, whose loyalty to the Wendish royal house was absolute.

News came at dusk that an army commanded by Henry himself had arrived at the town of Kassel, within a day's march of the border and their position. That evening Biscop Antonia's clerics moved through camp, passing out amulets—one to each soldier. Alain walked with the clerics, by now accustomed to their presence; he slept, ate, walked, and prayed within sight of either Willibrod or Heribert.

Agius, too, of course. But Agius' company was rather like the hairshirt the frater wore: Alain supposed that its constant rasping harsh presence was good for the soul and thus its elevation toward a more holy cast of thought, but for himself he preferred not to be always rubbed raw.

No doubt this failing on his part revealed how lacking he was in true holiness. But then, he had only to watch Agius each day to observe a man who wished for nothing except union with God. Alain admired the ferocity of Agius' devotion. For himself, and despite his circumstances, Alain was amazed and heartened to be seeing something of the world at long last. He supposed, and prayed, that Our Lord and Lady would forgive him for wishing to experience the world before trothing himself entirely to Their service.

"What is this?" Agius asked when Alain and the clerics returned, late, to Biscop Antonia's tent. Agius preferred to pray under guard rather than roam through camp in the company of Antonia's clerics, whom he despised. Also, perhaps, he wanted to remain obviously caged, a hostage, rather than let anyone believe in the fiction of his willing complicity to Sabella's cause. "Is this an amulet?"

Cleric Willibrod stammered something incomprehensible and scratched at his lesions.

Heribert, who never appeared cowed by Agius' high station, held out the amulet impatiently. "It is for protection. Take it."

Agius raised a haughty eyebrow. "Magic? Does Biscop Antonia dabble in magic now as well as treason?"

Willibrod giggled nervously.

Heribert dropped the amulet into Agius' hand and turned away. "It is late, brother," he said to Willibrod. "We must pray and then go to our sleep."

Biscop Antonia's camp bed remained empty: She was still in conference with Sabella and the other lords. Outside, a guard yawned. Rage and Sorrow found their favorite corner and turned several times, in the way of dogs chasing their own tails, then settled down. Agius stared at the amulet, fingering it, turning it this way and that.

Alain sat on his haunches beside the frater. "Do you think it is magic?" he whispered.

Agius shrugged. "I know nothing of magic, or nothing more than you might, I suppose."

Alain wore one of the amulets around his own neck, tied there with a bit of string. He held it out, comparing it to the one Agius had. It was a small circle of wood, innocent enough, for it appeared to be a Circle of Unity, the very ornament any person would wish to wear at his breast. But carved on the back were tiny letters Alain did not recognize, and bound in with the string were a strand of hair, a thin delicate quill that appeared to be from a feather, and a single withered elder leaf.

"There is an old woman in our village who can understand the language of the birds," said Alain. "Once a man traveled through Osna village claiming he could read our fortunes by reading the map of the heavens on the saint's day on which we were born. But he charged coin for this prophesying, so Deacon Miria said he was a fraud and drove him out of the village."

Agius frowned at the letters burned into the back of the wooden circle. "I do not know this script or these words," he said. "Nor do I intend to ask our brother clerics what the words mean, if they even know." He looked up, meeting Alain's gaze. His expression was forbidding. Alain knew at once what he was recalling: the night when Antonia sacrificed Lackling, when the spirits came, drawn by the scent of blood. After that night, Count Lavastine had changed from a decisive, clever man to a puppet dancing to strings controlled by someone else's hands.

"Biscop Antonia must mean to use magic," Alain whispered, glancing back at the clerics. They were praying and did not seem to be attending to their captives' conversation. "She has used it before."

"But for what purpose?" Agius murmured. "And how? There were a few among those in the schola, when I attended the king's progress as a boy, who might know or guess. Margrave Judith's bastard son, for one. He was always interested in what the clerics never wanted to teach him. But the forbidden arts never interested me. I had already discovered the lost words of the blessed Daisan and the suppressed testimony of his holy disciple St. Thecla—"

He broke off and stood. Sorrow raised his head and growled, low in his throat. Alain sprang up just as the biscop swept in with her retainers. Her robes bore a sheen of raindrops, glittering in the torchlight. The air that swelled into the tent on her heels was laden with moisture. Distantly, Alain heard drunken singing, something bawdy. Sabella had recently dismissed her latest concubine in favor of a younger, handsomer man, a freeborn soldier in Duke Rodulf's guard. There had been a bitter if brief confrontation between the two men five nights ago, in which the abandoned man had come off poorly. The cast-off lover was now the object of ridicule and of a great deal of bad verse.

"Cleric Heribert," said the biscop. The young cleric came at once and knelt before her. "See that a bed is set here, in the corner with our other guests." By this euphemism she always referred to Alain and Agius. "Then go and bring her here. We must make room. More have come to join Sabella's army. 'So shall all the people gather in the house of righteousness.' "

" 'Do not invite all comers into your home,' " retorted Agius. " 'Dishonesty has many disguises.' "

Antonia spared the frater a pitying glance, as one might to a boy who, old enough to herd the goats, still wets himself. Then she turned her kindly gaze on Alain. Sorrow growled. Alain set a hand on the hound's muzzle, silencing him. "Come, child," said the biscop, ignoring the hound's hostility. "We will speak while I am readied for bed."

Willibrod brought a stool for Alain and hovered anxiously behind him while the biscop's other servants helped her with her mitre and vestments, lifting them off and folding them carefully into the elaborately carved and painted chest that sat at the foot of her camp bed. The biscop wore a robe of fine white silk beneath. She sat and one of her servingwomen unbraided and rebraided her hair while Antonia toyed with a gold Circle of Unity studded with gems. Alain watched, by turns, his hands and then hers.

"You are continuing your lessons in the evenings?" she asked.

"I am, Your Grace."

"Read to me." She took from the bed a book so beautifully bound in a carved ivory case that when she opened it and handed it to him, he was at first afraid to touch it. She nodded that he was to take it from her.

Gingerly, he took the book out of her hands. At first he just gaped at the pages. The facing page was beautifully illuminated with an image of the seven disciples raising their hands toward the heavens, celebrating the miracle of the Pentekoste. The scrollwork was traced in gold ink, and the large initial letter that initiated the text held within its heavy black outline countless tiny owls perched on a narrow Tree of Wisdom, each clutching in one claw a tinier scroll or pen, all of which had been executed in cunning and meticulous detail. He had never touched anything this rich before.

"Read, child," she repeated.

Haltingly, he began to read. " 'So it happened that when seven times seven days had passed after the Translatus, Thecla heard the voice of the blessed Daisan and her vision was restored. He showed himself to her and her companions and gave proof that he was alive. He spoke to them for seven hours, teaching them about the God of Unities and the Chamber of Light.' "

Heart pounding, he stopped and took a few gasping breaths. It was bad enough to read when Agius stood over him, but Antonia's watchful gaze made him terribly nervous. Agius had knelt, as he always did when anyone read from the book of Holy Verses.

"You have improved," said Antonia. "But you are still far from fluent. Go on."

He sent a silent prayer of thanks to the Lady and Lord above. He could puzzle out the language of the church, Dariyan, but the truth was that any book but this would have been impossible. He had heard this story so many times in Osna church, when Deacon Miria read aloud from the Holy Verses or told the story in loving detail from memory, that if he did not recognize a word, he still knew what ought to come next.

" 'And the blessed Daisan told them, "You will receive power when an angel bearing the Divine Logos, the Holy Word of God, comes upon you. You will bear witness for me in Saïs, and all over Dariya and even into Arbahia, and away to the ends of the earth."

" 'When he had said this, as they watched, he was lifted up and a cloud removed him from their sight.

" 'Then they returned to Saïs from the hill called Olivassia, which is near Saïs, no farther than a Hefensday journey. Entering the city they went to the house where they were lodging: Thecla, Peter and Matthias and Thomas, Lucia and Marian and Johanna. All these were constantly in prayer together.

" 'This was then the day called Pentekoste, the fiftieth day after the Ekstasis and the blessed Daisan's Translatus into the heavens. On this day while they were all together, there came suddenly from the sky a noise like that of a strong driving wind, which filled the house where they were sitting. And there appeared to them tongues like flames of fire.' "

Antonia sighed and nodded her head, as if the tale affected her deeply. "So did the disciples speak in every tongue of every nation," she said, "even in those languages which they did not know. So did the Blessed Daisan reveal that the Holy Word and message of Light was meant for all peoples, of every kind."

"Even the Eika?" Alain asked. "Or the Lost Ones? Or the goblins who live in the Harenz Mountains?"

"Even they," she replied solemnly. "For it is not our part to judge which kind may enter the Chamber of Light and which may not."

Alain thought of Fifth Brother. He thought of how he had told the Eika prince the story of the Ekstasis and Daisan's Translatus up into the heavens. But the prince could not understand Wendish. And yet . . . that story had caused the prince to speak his first word to Alain, to betray both that he could speak and that he had an intelligence that understood and sought speech. It had caused the prince, savage that he was, to attempt friendship, of a kind.

A servant brought a pitcher filled with steaming water. Pouring it into the fine ceramic basin, the servingwoman wet a cloth and carefully bathed the biscop's face, then patted her skin with oils perfumed with the scent of lavendar.

"Go on," said Antonia, her eyes shut as the servingwoman drew the cloth away from her face. "Read on, child."

He swallowed and glanced at Agius, but the frater had placed his forehead on his clasped hands and was staring at the carpet. Licking his lips nervously, Alain went on.

" 'Now there were living in Saïs peoples of every nation under heaven, and because of this miracle a crowd gathered, and they were all amazed and perplexed.

" 'Thecla stood up with the Six and addressed them: "This is what the prophet spoke of. So say the God of Unities: 'This will happen in the last days: we will pour out upon everyone a portion of our Holy Word. Your women shall see visions and your men shall dream dreams. Yes, even the slaves shall be given a portion of Our word, and they shall prophesy. And We will show portents in the sky above and signs on the earth below—blood and fire and storm. The sun shall be turned to darkness, and the moon to blood. Call upon the Lady by Her name, the Mother of Life, and call upon the Lord by His name, the Father of Life, and ye shall be saved and lifted in glory to the Chamber of Light." And the other disciples clasped their hands and raised their voices in loving prayer, as affirmation to her words.' "

A cleric entered and leaned to whisper in Antonia's ear. She smiled kindly and made a gesture, then rose herself. "We have a new guest in our tent tonight," she said. As she turned, the entrance was pushed aside and Cleric Heribert, accompanied by two guards, led

Constance into the tent. Behind him came servants carrying a wooden pallet and feather bed.

In the intervening days Constance had lost her biscop's vestments. Alain did not know if she had given them up or if they had been taken from her. Her face, at least, was unmarked by signs of physical coercion.

"My blessed sister," said Antonia, coming forward. Constance extended a hand, as if she meant Antonia to kiss it, but Antonia merely clasped it fondly, as she might the hand of a kinswoman. If this impertinence irritated Constance, she did not let it show. After all, Sabella had taken her biscophric away from her and by that standard Biscop Antonia now stood above her in the church's hierarchy, if not in that of the world. Even in her biscop's vestments Constance had worn the gold torque that marked her as born of royal kin; in simple deacon's robes she wore it still.

"I am so sorry," Antonia continued, "at this loss of comforts. But you were alone with your servants in the other tent, and now it appears that Duke Conrad's cousin, the son of his father's sister, has joined us with twenty mounted men and fifty infantry."

"And what of Conrad?" asked Constance coolly. "He has not come to join Sabella? Perhaps he has thought better of lending his aid to an unlawful rebellion." One of her servants brought forward a stool, and she sat. She had not acknowledged Agius' presence, not even with a glance, nor had he looked up from his prayer. But there was a tautness in the frater's shoulders, as if his body betrayed what his eyes and lips resisted: any comment on the presence of the woman he had betrayed.

"Duke Conrad has not arrived. It is said his wife Eadgifu is within a sevenday of her time."

"Their fourth child, this will be," said Constance. If she was nervous or angry, she only betrayed it by the slow movement of her right hand, stroking the fingers of her left. "But that is only an excuse, Your Grace. Eadgifu has kinswomen with her; there would be no need for her husband to stay with her at such a time. Do not deceive yourself. If Duke Conrad has not come to Sabella's side yet, then he does not mean to do so."

"Nor has he gone to Henry's side."

Constance smiled faintly. "Conrad is not without ambition on his own behalf. Besides my family, he is the only other surviving descendant of the first Henry. Should the children of Arnulf the

Younger waste themselves on a war over their right to the throne, his will become the surviving claim."

"Do you forget the claim that might be put forward by Duchess Liutgard?"

"It is true she is of royal kin, being the great-grandniece of Queen Conradina. But when her grandfather gave up his claim to the throne and supported Henry instead, he gave up his claim in perpetuity. No. Liutgard's loyalty is assured." Here, as if despite herself, she glanced at Agius, and he, looking up briefly, met her gaze and winced away from it.

"Then what is it you counsel?" Antonia asked. She did not use the honorific granted to a biscop—'your grace'—and the omission was clearly deliberate; Constance was no longer Biscop of Autun as long as Sabella controlled the city.

"I counsel peace," said Constance. "As ought we all who have given our service to Our Lady and Lord."

Antonia signed to her servants, and they brought pillows and a feather quilt to the pallet. "It is late," said the biscop. "We march in the morning."

"Once you cross into Wendar you will have signaled outright your defiance of my brother's reign," said Constance, "beyond all else that has occurred in these last months."

"So will it be," replied Antonia with one of her kindly smiles, as if patient with a student who is slow to learn. "Henry waits at Kassel, so our scouts inform us. That is where we will meet. Now, let us pray, and then rest."

She knelt, and her servants and cleric knelt with her. Constance hesitated, but then, proudly and with the noble air of a woman who will not let adversity beat her down, she knelt as well and joined in the prayer.

That night, Alain dreamed.

The pitch of the boat rocks him, but he does not sleep. There are twenty prisoners, taken to be slaves, huddled in the belly of the boat. They weep or moan or sleep the sleep of those who have given up hope. His cousins took only the strong ones, the young ones, who will give service for a hand of years or longer before they succumb to the winter ice or the predations of the dogs. Some might even breed, but the soft ones' infants are weak and fragile, not suited to survive. How they have grown to spread themselves across the southern lands is a mystery he cannot answer, nor dare he ask the WiseMothers, for they do not care to hear of the fate of infidels. But did Halane Henrisson not speak of a god and of faith? He touches the Circle that hangs at his chest. It is cold.

Waves slap against the hull and oars creak with a steady beat in the oarlocks as the longship pierces forward through the seas. This music he has heard for all of his life and its cadences are like breath to him. It is a good night for travel on the northern sea.

He stands at the prow, watching mist stream off the waters. He studies the stars, the eyes of the most ancient Mothers, those whose bodies were at last worn away by wind and borne up into the vale of black ice, the fjall of the heavens. The moon, the heart of OldMan, spreads light over the waters.

Once he, too, took his place at the oars. But that was before his father stole the secret of the enchanter's power and, binding that power into his own body, lifted his tribe and his litter of pups out of the endless pack struggles and made them supreme.

Once he toiled with the others, but that was before his father drilled holes in his teeth and studded them with jewels to mark his primacy. Now, together with his nestbrothers, he leads.

This ship does not belong to his home tribe, but he is marked by the wisdom of the WiseMothers, and his father is a great enchanter and chief of the tribes of the western shore. So these cousins have accepted him as their leader. Of course, he had to kill their First Brother and the dogs' pack leader, but that is the way of each litter and each tribe: Only one male can lead. The others must bare their throats or die.

Do the soft ones pick their leaders in this fashion? Are they weak because they do not? He does not understand them, nor does he understand why Halane set him free. Compassion is not part of the cruel north. As OldMother once said, the RockChildren would have died out long ago had they succumbed to compassion.

The wind brings the scent of shore to his nostrils. One of the slaves sobs on and on, a whining cry that grates on his nerves. Before, he would have set the dogs on her or cut her throat with his own claws. Now, the memory of Halane stays his hand. He will abide. He will suffer the complaints of the weak.

For now.

The smell of freshwater touches his lips. He licks them, suddenly thirsty, but he will not give in to this need yet. To give in quickly is to build weakness. Behind him, as if catching his thought, the dogs growl.

He turns his head and growls back at them. They subside, accepting his primacy.

For now.

He smells a grove of ash and the still, wise scent of oak. They pass forest here as they voyage east. East, to where his father hunts.

The oars beat the sea, sunk steady and deep. The wind whips at his face, and salt spray rimes his lips. From the shore, he smells a hint of charcoal, and he casts back his head and scents, touching his tongue to the air.

Alain woke. He was completely awake, uncannily so, eyes open and already adjusted to the blackness. Rage slept. Sorrow whined softly but did not stir. Beyond Sorrow, the blankets where Agius slept lay empty.

By the light of the coals in the brazier, Alain saw a dark shape kneeling by the pallet on which Constance slept. His heart pounded. Was someone about to murder her?

Almost, he sprang up. But his hearing was keen, this night. He heard their breathing, heard the dry slide of skin against skin as they touched hand to hand, heard them whisper in voices as low as the murmur of daimones on the night air.

"Frederic was involved with Sabella's first revolt. Why should I trust you now, after what you have done, knowing what I do about your brother?" But her words were entirely at odds with her tone and with the sense Alain had that she held tightly to Agius' hands, more like a lover than a stern biscop.

"He was discontent. He was very young. He came of age, and my father gave him a retinue but no other duties. His was a rash soul, and it wanted action. You know that is true. So when the rebellion failed, he was disciplined and married off to Liutgard."

"Do you consider that punishment? Marriage to Liutgard?" Almost, she laughed.

"Ai, Lady. It would have been for me." Here he choked on the words, they came forth laden with much emotion.

"Hush, Agius." She stirred on her pallet, and Alain thought she lifted a finger to the frater's lips, touching him most intimately there.

Alain flushed and looked away. For some reason he thought of Withi, of her shoulders and the white expanse of bosom she had let him glimpse, that day before he followed her up to the ruins at Midsummer's Eve. He had never touched a woman so.

"You must love God, Agius," murmured Constance. "Not the world and those who live in it. Biscop Antonia tells me you are involved in heresy. I have no reason to trust her, so I will let you defend yourself to me against such a base accusation."

"I cannot. I will not. After you were promised to the church instead of to—" He faltered. "—instead of to marriage, I swore I would not rest—"

"You swore you would avenge yourself on your father and my brother. But you must not, Agius. You must let this anger go. There was nothing you could do. There was nothing I could do."

"My father *swore* before the Hearth. As did your brother. But Lord and Lady did not strike them down when they went back on their vow. So I knew by this sign that their pledge was empty, for it was sworn to the shadow of the truth. They had listened to the false words of those who presided at the Council of Addai, those who suppressed the truth. So did St. Thecla speak the truth of the end that came to the blessed Daisan. I have seen the scroll that records her words."

"Where have you seen such a scroll?"

"It is hidden, lest the church burn it and destroy her true speaking, which is shamefully forgotten. 'Then came the blessed Daisan before the judgment of the Empress Thaisannia, she of the mask. And when he would not bow before her but spoke the truth of the Mother of Life and the Divine Logos, the Holy Word, then she pronounced the sentence of death. This he met joyfully, for he embraced the promise of the Chamber of Light. But his disciples with him wept bitterly. So was he taken away and put to the flaying knife and his heart was cut out of his breast.' "

The hush was so deep, and Agius' voice so low, that Alain thought he could hear the sifting of the coals, red ash burning and cooling to gray.

" 'A darkness fell over the whole land, and then the blessed Daisan gave a loud cry and died. His heart's blood fell to the earth and it bloomed as roses. There came a light onto the land and to the ends of the Earth, and it was as bright as the garments of angels. By this light Thecla and the other disciples were blinded. And they lived seven times seven days in darkness, for they were afraid.'

"But I am not afraid, Constance. I am not afraid to proclaim the truth. Did the blessed Daisan not say: 'Be assured I am with you always, to the end of time?' Did the Mother of Life not give her only Son for the forgiveness of our sins?''

Constance sighed. "Ai, Agius, this is heresy indeed. How can you speak these words? It is a serious charge, to be brought before the presbyter who watches over the order of fraters. Is this what you want? To be condemned as a heretic?''

"It is better to speak the truth and die than to keep silence and live.''

"You are bitter, Agius. You were not like this before.''

With an abrupt movement, he buried his head against her chest. He spoke, his voice muffled further by the cloth of her robes. "Forgive me, Constance. I did it to save the life of my niece, for the love that lived between her father and myself.''

"You have always loved too deeply, Agius.'' She sighed, her breath catching in her throat. "You know I forgive you. How can I not? You are first in my heart, after my pledge to Our Lady and Lord.''

"Yet you did not protest. You did not rebel, when your brother gave you to the church.''

"I know my duty,'' she said softly, stroking his hair.

Agius was, Alain realized, weeping quietly. Constance wept as well, and Alain felt that by licking his tongue into the air he could taste the amalgamation of their tears, each into the other. Perhaps Agius did love too deeply. But was it not written that the blessed Daisan loved the world and all the people on it? Was love not the chief blessing granted to human beings by the mercy and grace of Our Lady and Lord?

Alain could feel their closeness, could taste the heat of their bodies, pressed against each other—and he felt envy. What would it be like to love a woman that much? So much that, if those hints Agius gave were true, he had turned away from the world when it came about that he could not marry her and instead devoted himself to the church as a humble frater, far below his rightful station in life? Would any woman ever weep for Alain? Press herself close against him?

Ai, it was true, that old saying. Envy is the shadow of the *guivre*, the wings of death. Alain knew shame, for he desired what was not his to have. He had been marked twice, once by the church and once by the Lady of Battles, whose rose he bore.

But he could not help but think of nights in the longhouse when as a child he lay awake, listening, hearing the soft sounds from other beds, Stancy and her husband, Aunt Bel and Uncle Ado, before Ado died. Of all the adults Alain knew, only his father Henri and those pledged to the church did not engage in such congress. Agius and Constance engaged in nothing now more intimate than an embrace, and yet there was so much more between them that it flared like a bright light, like the heat of coals in the brazier.

There was another brazier in the tent, this one placed beside the bed where Antonia slept. Alain glanced that way reflexively, trying not to move or betray that he was awake. But he gasped, more of a grunt, then bit his lip. He did not breathe for the space of five heartbeats.

Antonia's eyes were open. He caught the glint of dim light against them, eyes glittering in night. Constance and Agius were too caught up in themselves to notice. But he did.

She watched, silent. She appeared to him like a huge yawning maw, sucking in life and air. She watched, he felt, not because she had her own yearnings or because she wanted to spy and thus gain information, but because she was greedy, because like a cat laps up cream or a griffin suckles the blood of its mother, she wanted as much as she could take from them. As if she intended to gather to herself and hoard all that intensity of emotion.

It made him sick, the feeling of her watchfulness.

He shut his eyes and turned his face against the safe, warm flank of Sorrow.

Later, when there was no more whispering, he slept.

2

THEY held council at dawn outside Antonia's tent.

"I still say the battle comes too soon," protested Duke Rodulf. Obviously this argument had been raging for many days, and he was not quite yet resigned to losing it. "We risk everything by meeting Henry now."

"Meeting Henry now is exactly what I planned for and wish for," said Sabella. The odd thing about her voice, as monotone as it was, was the way its lack of emotion lent her an air of stubborn decisiveness. She was not a bright light or a leader of great radiance; she did not even have that brusque impatient authority by which Lavastine had (once) ruled his lands. Like a boulder rolling down a slope, she made no great claims, sparked no great fire, but simply crushed any obstacle in her path. "He has rushed to meet me. He has no great force with him today."

"Yet according to our scouts he has a greater army than what we have gathered here." Rodulf frowned and shook his head.

"Not as great a force as the one he will gather, given time to raise levies. Given time for his supporters to raise levies from their lands and march them across Wendar to Henry's side. No, this is as small a force as Henry will ever wield in defense of his crown. And this time it will not be enough."

"You are sure of this," said Rodulf. Of all the various nobles and petty lords in attendance on Sabella, he was by now the only one who still questioned her. She endured his questioning, as she must: He was a duke, her equal in rank in all things except for the gold torque. But Rodulf's mother's mother had been a princess of Salia, so in this way he, too, came of noble lineage.

Alain stood behind Biscop Antonia, hiding among her clerics, and watched the council. By now Cleric Willibrod was not alone among the clerics in having a rash and unsightly sores on hands and lips, though he remained the only one who picked nervously at them. Only Heribert, as fastidious as any man Alain had ever met, maintained his clean, unstained skin. But as chief among Antonia's clerics, he kept himself above the actual work; he only *supervised* the care of the vestments, the making of amulets, the care for the sick in Antonia's train, and the rest of the multitude of small tasks that accompanied attendance on a biscop.

"I am sure of this," said Sabella. "Now is the time to act. Now is the time to fight." She looked at Biscop Antonia; the biscop nodded, answering an unspoken question. Sometimes Alain wondered if Antonia controlled Sabella the way she controlled Lavastine, but even now he saw no sign of such a thing. Sabella and Antonia worked in concert. What grievances, in their inner hearts, drove them to these deeds he could not tell, though he wondered mightily. Sabella's complaint was the more obvious. She believed she had been deprived of a throne which was rightfully hers. But had not God spoken, by default, when Sabella had ridden out on her heir's progress and returned without having conceived a child? Henry, on his heir's progress, *had* conceived a child, even if it was with as strange a mate as an Aoi woman. Why could Sabella not accept what fate—and God—had decreed for her?

No more than could I, he thought ruefully. Fate—and the God of Unities—had decreed he must enter the church as a novice, and yet here he was, marching to war, seeing more of the world than he had ever expected to, though this was exactly what he had dreamed about.

So did they all ready themselves. Duke Rodulf took himself off to his own troops, and Sabella waited for her horse to be brought to her. The army formed a great cavalcade as it rode east, crossing the El River at a shallow ford and marching up into the highlands. They now moved through the lands that owed allegiance to the duke of Fesse. They were in Wendar.

By bringing armed troops into lands outside Arconia, Sabella had now crossed the line past which there was no going back. Alain could not help but feel a thrill of excitement. The men he marched beside, the guards and clerics who protected Biscop Antonia and her "guests,"—Constance and Agius—felt it, too. They laughed and sang boisterously and made jokes among themselves, boasting about what they would do with the riches they intended to loot from the bodies of Henry's soldiers: a spearhead, a good dagger, any kind of armor, shield or metal helmet or leather surcoat or, for a truly lucky man, a mail shirt or a sword.

No matter who won this battle, Alain realized, a great deal of wealth was about to change hands.

At midday the two armies met as if by design. They arrayed themselves on a broad field. Henry's force took the better position. The field sloped gently upward toward steeper heights beyond, and Henry had ordered his forces so Sabella would have to attack up the hill at him.

But she seemed unperturbed.

"Hai!" she said fiercely and triumphantly to Duke Rodulf, who had dropped back from his mounted soldiers to consult with her. "Look you, at the banners of Henry's forces, and tell me what you see."

From his place in Antonia's retinue, which marched always at the side of Sabella, Alain surveyed Henry's army. It seemed vast, unnumberable; he had never seen so many people gathered into one place at one time. He could not even count that high, though he heard Cleric Heribert whisper to Antonia:

"Something less than eight hundred men, and perhaps a third of them mounted."

Alain recognized the dragon of Saony, but the men assembled under the banner of Saony's duke were no more in number than those who rode in Count Lavastine's retinue. The eagle of Fesse flew over a more formidable band of soldiers, many of these mounted. One group of these mounted soldiers was massed tightly around a figure wearing a surcoat of white and gold, royal colors; this person must be Duchess Liutgard. A banner also flew for Avaria, and though Alain glanced to where Agius stood meekly beside Constance, he did not think Agius was paying any particular attention to the banner of his father's dukedom *or* to that of the woman his brother had married in his stead. Agius was praying. Constance stood calmly, hand raised almost to her throat but resting lightly on her chest, and her lips moved as she spoke—seemingly to herself—the names of the lords and counts and dukes who rode in Henry's host.

In the center a huge bold banner of red silk fluttered in the stiff spring breeze. Three animals, stitched in gold thread, were displayed in a column on the banner: an eagle, a dragon, and a lion, the signs of Henry's authority. Even from this distance Alain thought he recognized the king himself, surrounded by a richly arrayed group of retainers.

The king wore a crested iron helm and mail sleeves, and his chest was protected by a metal breastplate over a mail shirt. He wore also, on his legs, mail to protect his thighs and iron greaves on his calves; indeed, many of the mounted soldiers in his retinue wore such greaves, a sign of their wealth and station. In his left hand the king held a lance, in his right hand nothing, so that he might better grasp his sword when it was needed. The shield hanging from his saddle was of iron, without device or color.

Like the other common soldiers, Alain did not even have a metal helmet much less armor this elaborate. He could only imagine how many sceattas such equipment would cost. Not even Duke Rodulf wore such impressive armor, though certainly he was heavily protected.

It was a formidable army. Only two ducal banners waved in Sabella's forces: the *guivre* of Arconia and the stallion of Varingia, but both she and Rodulf had fielded many men, though not as many were mounted or armed as well as Henry's men.

It seemed a desperate gamble.

"Conrad the Black has not chosen to appear on the field," said Rodulf to Sabella, squinting at the line of banners and soldiers on the slope above them.

"Conrad plays his own game," said Sabella. "If he will not support me, then I am just as happy that he chooses not to support Henry either. But don't you see, Rodulf? Don't you see what is lacking, there?" She gestured broadly, her arm taking in the entire line of Henry's army and the banners displayed. "There is no Dragon banner. The red dragon of Saony I see, but there is no black dragon. Henry's best fighters are not with him on the field!"

Rodulf whistled breath out between his lips. "So are they not. I no longer despair, Sabella."

"Nor should you ever have despaired. Do you wear your amulet, Rodulf?"

"I do, but—"

"That is all that matters. Return to your men."

"Where *are* the Dragons, then? Surely Prince Sanglant has not turned against his father? I never heard before that the boy had the least drop of rebellious blood in him." He laughed, a little nervous still but obviously resolved to see this fight through to the end. "I often wish my own children were so obedient."

"Surely you heard me mention that my informants said the

Dragons had ridden north, well out of the way, to fight Eika raiders?''

''Ah, of course. Strike at the sheep while the watchdog is out hunting the wolf, eh?'' He grimaced, more by way of a grin than a frown. ''If the Dragons stood beside Henry on this day, I would judge it wiser to ask forgiveness than to fight. But—''

''But they do not. And now you do not need to make that choice. Go, then.'' She made a sign to one of her men-at-arms. He had been expecting the signal, because he turned and rode back toward the train.

Rodulf reined his horse away and with his attendants rode back to his soldiers, who held the right flank opposite the banner of Fesse. Lavastine and a motley assortment of lordlings as well as levies taken from monastery lands made up the left flank, facing the lion of Avaria and the small contingent that had marched long days from Saony—or perhaps, Alain supposed, there had not been time for a contingent to come all the way from Saony. Perhaps the banner of Saony rode over those folk who had been in attendance on Henry already. Perhaps they flew the banner more to show Saony's loyalty than to boast of their force of numbers.

''They mean to parley,'' said Constance suddenly and clearly as several figures carrying a blue banner marked with a silver tree detached themselves from Henry's retinue and rode into the open space that separated the two armies. ''That is Villam's device.''

''Of course,'' said Sabella.

Abruptly, the figure in white and gold rode out under the banner of Fesse to join Villam.

Sabella nodded toward Biscop Antonia. ''You know what to say.''

The biscop was already mounted on her white mule. She signed to her clerics and all but Heribert dropped back away from her.

''Tallia,'' said Sabella curtly. Her daughter came forward reluctantly. ''Attend Biscop Antonia. It is time for you to be seen.'' The girl nodded obediently, but she did not look happy; she looked, in truth, more like a mouse caught in the clutches of an owl.

Antonia measured the number in Villam's party: Villam, Duchess Liutgard, and two others. She considered the company around Sabella, but her gaze fell finally on Alain. ''Come, child,'' she said. ''You will lead my mule.''

Sabella raised an eyebrow. ''A kennel boy?''

''Something more than that, I think. These two hounds that accompany the boy are Lavastine's hounds. Villam will recognize them and by that know Lavastine willingly marches with us."

Sabella snorted. "So we will send Lavastine's hounds as proxy? I am amused, although my brother will not be. That serves my purpose also. Go, then."

Given no choice, Alain took the mule's reins and led the animal forward, up the slope. Sorrow and Rage padded at his heels. Cleric Heribert followed suit, taking the reins of Tallia's horse and walking alongside Alain, so the biscop and the girl rode side by side, granting them equal status.

As he walked, he studied the four figures they had been sent to meet. Two were Eagles; he recognized them by their cloaks trimmed with scarlet. Both were women, one of them surely no older than he was himself. It was this younger one who held Villam's banner in her left hand.

The hale older man had to be Villam. He was armed in a fine mail shirt; over it, he wore a handsome tabard marked with the device of the silver tree.

But Alain's gaze kept snapping to the fourth member of their party. *Duchess Liutgard.* This, then, was the woman Agius had refused to marry. She was tall and rather younger than he expected. She had a cleanly arrogant face and a steady gaze, and a hint of temper in her eyes.

She held her own banner, an odd affectation, and rode a beautiful white gelding outfitted with harness worked with gold ornamentation. Her armor was richer than Villam's, more elaborate even than the king's. Indeed, it surprised Alain to see a woman of this rank, in the prime of her childbearing years, riding to war and thus putting herself at risk. But her expression, the very set of her jaw, suggested that Duchess Liutgard had a strong will that was not easily overridden.

She noticed his gaze and, curious in her turn, looked him over; much could be said at a parley simply by the choice of people sent forward to conduct it. He could hear Aunt Bel's voice: *"Keep your hair tidy and your hands washed, lad. And meet new folk with a face that is neither too sullen nor too smiling, for they will trust neither one."* He tried to school his face to an expression of indifferent humility.

Now his gaze slid to Tallia. He had never been quite this close to the young princess before. She had fine clean skin, brushed with freckles, and in the sun her wheat-blonde hair had a touch of fire's gold in it. Her lower lip trembled. He risked a glance back at Antonia, but the biscop wore her usual expression of kindly solicitude.

Villam, with some show of reluctance, dismounted and kissed the biscop's ringed hand as a mark of respect for her office. After a deliberate pause, and after handing her banner over to the other Eagle, Duchess Liutgard followed suit. The two Eagles were not important enough to be allowed this honor; like Alain and Heribert, they hung back and observed.

"Lady Tallia," said Villam, nodding toward the girl, "it is a pleasure to see you again."

She nodded in return but did not speak. At this moment, she looked incapable of speech.

"Is there no one else who comes forward with you to parley?" Villam continued. "Duke Rodulf does not grace us with his presence."

"I think you know his opinions well enough."

"It is true," said Villam, not quite hiding a smile, "that Rodulf is refreshingly frank. But I see other banners here which surprise me. Count Lavastine is known to me, and to the king, and yet he does not come forward with you to speak his mind."

Barely, Antonia's lips quirked. She gestured toward the hounds. Villam looked that way. His reaction was twofold, and rather strange. At first he looked annoyed. Antonia was suggesting, of course, that Lavastine was either a dog running at Sabella's heels or else that the count himself meant to insult the king by sending the two hounds as his representatives. But then Villam registered Alain. He looked at the boy, studied him for one awkward moment; something in his face betrayed him, and he had to look away to hide it—a grief he could not share. Oddly, Duchess Liutgard touched him on the elbow, the way one steadies a man who has stumbled.

"I would have speech," continued Villam after a moment, "with Sabella."

"Of course," said Antonia smoothly, "any words which you speak here will reach her. I am merely the vessel through which they travel. Indeed, Sabella has words for her brother as well."

"No doubt," said Villam dryly. "But I fear we speak of deeds, not words, now. Why has Sabella marched with this army out of Arconia, the territory she administers for her husband Berengar?"

The mule shifted, and Alain tightened his grip on the reins to still it. Antonia opened one hand and gestured eloquently toward Henry's red silk banner. "She is grieved by her brother's usurpation of her rightful place as queen of Wendar."

Villam shook his head. His eyes were dark and heavy, as if he had recently endured many sleepless nights. "That dispute was settled eight years ago. Sabella vowed on your ring, Biscop Antonia, to hold no more grievance against King Henry and to retire to her own holdings and be a faithful supporter of his rule. Has she broken that vow?"

"She swore that vow under duress, as you yourself witnessed. Only those who have sworn themselves to wear martyr's garments are expected to choose death over life, no matter what the charge. So does Our Lady forgive us for our attachment to life, as long as our hearts remain pure and our bearing dignified. As long as we do not forsake our duty to God."

"Is that how you interpret the scripture?" asked Liutgard sharply, suddenly coming to life.

"I do not intend," replied Antonia with a patient smile, "to debate scripture here, my lady." She turned back to Villam. He was a tall, broad man, and though she still sat on her mule, she did not loom over him as she would have a smaller man or woman.

"Sabella is a reasonable woman. Henry may keep his title as duke of Saony, giving the county of Attomar to his sister Rotrudis. Sabella will take the crown and throne of Wendar, and Varre will go to Tallia. She will show her favor toward Henry by allowing his young son Ekkehard to marry Tallia and become king of Varre as Tallia's consort."

Villam was too old and wily—and too burdened by that other, nameless grief—to get angry. "I would laugh if only the suggestion were not so offensive. As well as ridiculous. To Sabella, King Henry sends these words: She may keep her dukedom if she turns and quits the field now."

"It is not her dukedom to quit, Villam. Berengar is Duke of Arconia."

Villam grunted, finally sounding irritated. "Your Grace, please do not treat me as if I were a fool. Berengar is a fine and noble man, I am sure, but he does not—shall we say—carry a full kettle of wits with him. Sabella rules that dukedom as both man and woman." Then he quickly nodded toward Tallia, who had flushed a bright pink and was staring so hard at her hands that first Alain, and then

Heribert, and then the two silent Eagles, and finally the other three—who knew better—also looked at the girl's hands to see if something was growing there. "Begging your pardon, Lady Tallia."

She murmured something indistinguishable, but its tone sounded like apology.

Antonia spoke. "If we cannot agree, Lord Villam, there is no point in discussion, is there?"

"You wish to fight?" He looked genuinely puzzled. As well he might: Henry's force was clearly larger and, more importantly, had more mounted soldiers. Their weight and overbearing force alone assured Henry victory.

"Of course we do not wish to fight," said Antonia with a heartfelt sigh. "Of course we wish for peace, Lord Villam. Duchess Liutgard. All souls wish for peace, for is that not the devout wish of Our Lord and Lady? But is it right for Sabella to allow Henry to continue on a throne that is rightfully hers?"

"She did not—"

"She has a child. Here is Tallia, before you. Henry has only the word of a heathen woman, if you can even trust the word of an Aoi. Is it not said that elves are children gotten by fallen angels on human women?"

"In fact," began Liutgard, breaking in as Antonia took breath, "if one studies the *Dialogue on Fate*, one reads that the blessed Diasan said that elves were—"

"I do not mean to discuss church matters here." Antonia made a sharp sign with her right hand, as if she was lopping off her left hand at the wrist. *Silence.*

Duchess Liutgard whitened; she looked mightily annoyed, and her mouth tightened. Villam made a soft noise, and with an obvious effort the duchess kept silent.

"How can we know Henry earned his heir's right?" Antonia continued. "How can we know Sanglant is his son at all? Sabella was Arnulf's first choice as heir. Not Henry. Men may swear all they wish that any child is of their begetting and their blood, but only a woman giving birth before witnesses can *prove* a child is hers. No man can do that, for even if he locks a woman up, there are creatures not of human blood and earthly make known to have other methods of entry."

"You are saying," said Villam quietly but with real growing anger, "that Henry lied about Sanglant and his heir's progress."

"I say nothing about Henry. I say Henry can never know, and thus we can never know. Why do you think the church encourages inheritance to pass through the mother's line, Lord Villam? Duchess Liutgard? The old Dariyans practiced adoption, bringing any kind of person into their houses, but the church outlawed that practice for inheritance purposes over three hundred years ago at the Council of Nisibia. So do some of us work today to ban inheritance through the male line." Antonia had by now worked up real fervor. Always, she presented a benign facade. Alain had never before seen her so impassioned. "If Henry continues his reign, who will become sovereign after him? The children of Sophia and Arethousa? Will the taint of the East infiltrate our kingdom? Does this new heresy that has spread its tendrils into our fine pure faith not come from the lands ruled by the Arethousan emperors? Will our rulers be Arethousan, and not of Wendish blood?"

"They will be Henry's children," said Villam firmly. "And strong rulers, despite what you say, Biscop Antonia."

"Beware Arethousans bearing gifts," she replied, darkly. "Had Henry married a good Wendish woman of noble birth, I would not be so adamant in my cause. But he did not. Two women he is known to have consorted with, both of them foreigners and one not even of human blood." She had finally and entirely lost that placid grandmother's face. Beneath it, she was hard and cold. "I cannot trust such a man. Nor will I trust his offspring. Sanglant! His pet! A bastard child who isn't even human and probably isn't even his, since we have only the mother's worthless word that she did not act the whore. And Henry makes a fool of himself—everyone knows; it is common knowledge throughout Wendish lands—because he favors such a child! I do not call this a kingly virtue. I do not think this shows strong judgment. Sabella married, as was her duty, a man of her own people. But Henry cannot be content with that, can he? He has his eye on greater things, does he not? He has his eye on the chair of the emperor, in Darre. He wants to follow in the wake of Taillefer. Well! Let Henry nurse his own lands before he sets off to heal others. Let him mate with a woman of his own people before he breeds with the whores of strangers." Antonia was by now quite red and quite furious. Alain was both impressed and horrified.

Liutgard made as if to stride forward and confront the biscop physically, but Villam stayed her with a gesture. "I have heard enough insults," he said. "There is no more to be said. Let this battle be on your head, then, Biscop Antonia. Let it be said, from this hour forward in all the chronicles that record this day, that Sabella rejected King Henry's leniency when it was offered and chose to face his rage." He mounted, reined his horse around, and set off up the hill.

Liutgard tossed her head, like a spirited horse, and met Antonia's gaze with one no less hard. "You are like a sweet water well that has been poisoned by the venom of a *guivre*." She turned and followed Villam, the Eagle bearing her banner trailing in her wake.

One of the Eagles hung back. Alain stared at the younger one. She had the palest hair—a coarse white-blonde—he had ever seen, except for the hair of the Eika prince. Her gaze caught his, and, for a moment, they simply looked at each other; she appeared more curious than hostile. And she had astonishingly pale blue eyes.

"Hanna!" said her companion sharply, calling back over her shoulder. The young Eagle wrenched her gaze away from Alain, glanced quickly at the hounds, then followed her companion up the hill after the two nobles.

"Is it true, Your Grace?" asked Tallia.

"Is what true?" Antonia had recovered her outer calm. "Come, child, we must ride back behind the lines. The battle will soon begin."

"T–those things you said. About Henry."

"Of course it is true. Why would I say such things if they were not true?"

"Oh," said Tallia, and that was all.

Meekly, she let Cleric Heribert lead her back to her mother. When they arrived at Sabella's banner, Willibrod took the mule's reins away from Alain. Tallia was taken back behind the lines to the safety of the supply train, where the noncombatants awaited the outcome of the battle. One wagon had been brought forward from the train. This was unusual enough but made more so because Alain recognized it as the shrouded cage that concealed the *guivre*.

"You saw no sign of the Dragons?" Sabella asked.

"None. And I have never heard it said the Dragons hide themselves. Always they ride in the vanguard."

"Bastard and whore's child he may be," said Sabella grudgingly, "but Sanglant is known for being brave. What of the others?"

"I saw none."

"None of Henry's children?"

"None."

Sabella frowned. "That is unfortunate. I was hoping I might catch one or all of them for hostages. It would serve me well to have them in my hands."

Antonia's reply was so soft only Alain—and perhaps Heribert—heard it. "It would serve you better if they were dead."

Sabella's captain rode up with the message that Rodulf's people were ready. "You must go back behind the lines, Your Grace," said Sabella to Antonia. She settled her helmet over her mail coif and tightened the strap. The banner of Arconia flapped beside her, held by one of her men-at-arms: a green *guivre* with wings unfolded and a red tower gripped in its left talon, set against a gold silk background. "You I cannot afford to lose."

"What of our guests?" The biscop looked, and smiled, at Constance and Agius.

"Take them with you. They are too valuable to risk here where the battle will be fought."

Antonia signed, and Constance and Agius were led away under guard. "Come," she said to her attendants. They began to move back. Alain hesitated. "Come, child," said Antonia, beckoning to him. "You will attend me as well."

Sabella noticed his hesitation. "This is one of Lavastine's men-at-arms, is it not? It is time he returned to the count's levy."

"But—"

"Do as I say," snapped Sabella with the expression of a woman who has no time to argue.

Antonia paused. Her face became a mask of stillness. Then, as the sun comes out from behind clouds, she smiled in her usual benevolent fashion. "As you wish, my lady." She did not bow, but she gave in. So. Sabella danced to no puppet strings. Antonia might control Lavastine, but she did not control the daughter of Arnulf.

Once Antonia was gone, no one paid the least attention to Alain though several rough men-at-arms pushed him back and told him sharply to find his place, only to apologize when the hounds growled at them. But they made the sign of the Circle at their breasts, as if he was some evil thing.

He retreated to the back of the line. Sabella had in her own company over one hundred well-armed mounted soldiers and perhaps twice as many skirmishers and infantry; all together (according to Heribert's count) she had six hundred or so soldiers. But Henry's army was bigger, and Henry commanded more of the heavily armored cavalry that was the backbone of any lord's army. Of the infantry Lions, there was one century, but by all reports most of the Lions manned the eastern frontier against the raids of the Quman horsemen and other barbarians.

Alain trotted along the back of the line. He heard leather creaking as men shifted, waiting, anticipating the first step. On the hill above, none of Henry's soldiers moved. Alain could see the red silk banner flapping against blue sky and trailing white clouds, but the heads—some helmeted, some with hard leather caps, some with no covering at all—of Sabella's soldiers blocked most of his view.

Was this how a battle was fought? Was there a strategy involved, or did the two sides merely wait until one commander lost patience or nerve and sent his side forward—or into retreat?

A gap opened between Sabella's leftmost company of infantry and the rightmost company of those men under Lavastine's command. The men stood with their arms tight against their sides so they could rest the weight of their shields on their hips. Most of these men carried spears; few common men had the wherewithal to purchase a sword.

As Alain sprinted past the open ground, dashing for safety among Lavastine's men, he looked up toward Henry's army. Movement coursed along the ranks. Then, suddenly, the sky darkened with arrows. Most of them fell harmlessly in front of the line of Sabella's army; some overshot. A few found their mark. But even as men cursed and one shrieked in pain, the archers among Sabella's army took aim and shot.

They had to arc their arrows higher, to gain the height, but, if anything, this volley had more effect. A ripple passed down the line of Henry's army as if many arrows had hit their mark. And the line moved.

Horses started forward at intervals. Henry had sent out his skirmishers, mounted men armed with spear and shield or even spear alone. They raced forward, flung their spears, and turned back to gallop out of range, only to turn again—

Alain dashed along the rear of the line and saw Lavastine's back and the black coats of his hounds just as a great cry went up from the crowd of soldiers around Sabella's banner. A rank of infantry trotted forward into the empty field that lay between the two armies. They pulled the shrouded cage along with them.

"Hai! For Henry!" the host above them shouted.

Alain shoved his way through to Lavastine's side. The count did not even notice the boy, he was so intent on the battle. At his leftmost flank, about twenty of his own skirmishers had raced out to meet the skirmishers opposite them. One group of horsemen broke away from the banner of Saony and began to sweep wide, disappearing into the forest.

Lavastine sought and found his captain. "Send a company after them," he said.

Another cry rent the air from Henry's army. The king rode a few paces forward and lifted his lance.

"The Holy Lance of St. Perpetua," murmured Lavastine, but to whom, Alain could not tell.

St. Perpetua. Lady of Battles.

Alain groped at his neck, found the rose. King Henry carried the Lance of St. Perpetua, a relic of the greatest antiquity and holiness. Was it not the Lady of Battles herself who had come to him, a simple merchant's son, on that stormy day above Osna Sound? Was it not the Lady of Battles who had changed his destiny?

He could not imagine for what purpose he had been led here, to this day and this hour and this moment.

Henry's army began to move down the hill, picking up speed so their weight could smash through Sabella's line. And first, in their way, was that knot of infantrymen, dragging the shrouded cage up the slope.

The cage jutted and bounced and lurched. Stuck. One of the wheels had gotten stuck. Henry's soldiers picked up speed and force. Sabella's captain shouted a shrill command and lifted a white banner, waving it. The line of her army lurched forward in its turn.

Lavastine lifted an arm. And Alain found himself lost as the two armies lumbered forward to their inevitable meeting. Rage and Sorrow whined. He faltered, unsure where to march, how to fall into place, or what to do. He was not even armed, except with his eating knife. What was he meant to do?

He fell behind and from this vantage point could see nothing except banners and pennants and the chaotic blur of movement on the hill above.

But he knew instantly when the first ranks met. It was a clamor unlike anything he had ever heard, made the more terrible because of the unforgiving clash of sword and spear set against the sudden harrowing screams of mortal men.

He thought of Rodulf's warnings and Sabella's answer: *"This time it will not be enough."* How could she hope to win against a better armed and larger force?

He could not know whether the cage was opened deliberately or knocked over accidentally in the charge. He only knew it had happened because at that moment there came from the center of the milling battle a shriek from a hundred throats as from one throat that froze his heart in his chest. He could not breathe for so long a span of time that he coughed and gulped air when Rage butted him from behind, jarring him out of his stupor.

On the slope above, half seen through the chaos of soldiers scattering, through horses rearing and screaming, through the press of bodies and of many men intent on moving forward or on running away, he saw it rise into the spring day as a bird flies toward the heavens and freedom.

Only to be yanked hard, almost to plunge to earth again, because of the great iron collar that bound its leg to a heavy iron chain, the shackle that tied it to the earth and captivity. It screamed its rage and righted itself, still in the air, the downdraft of its great wings toppling men from their horses.

Still shrieking that harsh eaglelike cry, the *guivre* swept its gaze across the battlefield. And everywhere that men by design or accident met its eye, those men froze, unable to move. Everywhere, except among the soldiers of Sabella's army, who wore the amulets so painstakingly wrought by Antonia's clerics.

The slaughter began.

3

KING Henry was the kind of man who left nothing to chance.

In a strange way, he reminded Hanna of her mother, Mistress Birta. He had a hard, pragmatic side and yet was as likely as any other person to give full expression to his feelings. But to Hanna the most important thing about Henry was what Hathui had said of him that same evening after they had reached Henry's court at the monastery of Hersford and been taken in as members of the king's personal household: "He's a fine lord, is our king, and I am proud to serve him."

Hathui, with her fierce marchlander's independence, was loath to serve anyone. That Henry had captured Hathui's loyalty so quickly was to Hanna's way of thinking a mark of his kingliness. *He* was the true heart of the kingdom, not any city, not any holy site, not any palace or stronghold.

Now, sitting astride her horse as Villam conferred with Henry after the disastrous parley, Hanna worried. She was not, by nature, a worrier, but she had come to be one these past weeks ever since she and Hathui had been forced to leave Liath behind. It was all very well for Hathui to proclaim that she would know if something had happened to Wolfhere and Manfred. A constant nagging anxiety ate away at Hanna. What if something terrible happened to Liath? Hanna had sworn in her heart to protect Liath, and now she had broken that promise.

Through no fault of your own. Isn't that what Birta would say? Isn't that what Liath herself would say?

But Hanna could only think of broken promises as she stared down the slope toward Sabella's army, drawn up in a strong line below them. She had sworn to protect Liath, and now she rode far from her side. Sabella had, by all reports, sworn an oath to Henry and now she had broken it. *By my deeds*, Hanna thought, *I belong on Sabella's side.*

Then, angry at herself for this ridiculous musing, she let out an exasperated sigh. There was no use blaming herself. She was not the Eika chieftain who had beseiged Gent. She had not asked those Eika to attack the five Eagles. She *had* fallen off her horse and sprained her ankle, but the truth was, she was still not that experienced a rider. She and Hathui had brought the message of the seige to Henry as quickly as they could. She had done her best and now must live with what came after. It was not her fault but rather Sabella's that Henry could not ride immediately to Gent.

Liath was the one who worried incessantly and to no purpose, wondering what she had done wrong rather than accepting that sometimes one did nothing and still had ill luck. That was the way of the world, though perhaps Deacon Fortensia might say it was a heathen way of looking at things.

But Hanna and the rest of her family still laid flowers at the foot of certain trees in the forest and offered garlands where the spring rose from rock along the south ridge. Of course she believed in Our Lord and Lady and in the Circle of Unity. But that did not mean the old spirits had ceased to live in the world. They had only gone into hiding.

The old spirits—like that boy who had held the reins of the biscop's white mule and stared at her so strangely. He had an odd, fey look about him. And those hounds! They weren't ugly, like the Eika dogs she had seen, but they looked as deadly; yet they sat next to the boy like sweet puppies. Ai, well, there were a great many strange things that walked abroad in the world, if only one had the eyes to see them.

"—the young Eagle—"

She shook her head and attended to what Henry was saying.

"—will attend Sapientia. She knows what to do. I will have Constance back before Sabella can retreat and take her away as a prisoner."

Henry was surrounded by his century of Lions. Hanna searched and found Karl's broad back among the ranks; if she craned her neck just right, she could see his profile. He did not notice her. With his fellows, he stared intently down the slope toward the restless mass of Sabella's army. The Lions were ready for battle.

Henry and Villam finished their consultation. Hathui rode away with a message intended for Theophanu, who had been left in charge of their supply train. Henry, ever cautious, had left the train and his noncombatants behind in the fortified town of Kassel.

Hanna was sent back behind the lines to the wood beyond. Henry had chosen this field to stand and fight because of the lay of the land. Guessing that Sabella would bring her supply train with her rather than leave it behind in Arconia, he had hidden some eighty mounted soldiers in the woods and put Sapientia—with a veteran captain at her side for good measure—at their head. Concealed by the trees and by the skirmishing that prefaced any battle, they would sweep wide round Sabella's right flank and hit all the way back to the supply train, thus freeing Constance.

Or causing her to get killed, thought Hanna, but she supposed Henry would rather see his sister die than remain a hostage. After all, as long as Constance remained—alive—in Sabella's hands, she was a weapon to be used against the king.

That was how Hathui had explained it, at any rate. But Hathui had been raised in the harsh cauldron of the borderlands, which were in a state of constant war. There, as the hawk-nosed Eagle had said more than once, one killed one's children rather than let them fall into the hands of Quman raiders.

Sapientia looked like a greyhound being held on a tight leash: eager to run. She was small enough that Hanna was surprised Henry let her fight.

Of course every adult fought in the right circumstances, under conditions of siege or a raider's attack on a village; it would be foolish to waste any strong arm. But women—blessed by the Lady with the gift of bearing life—did not often join the ranks of armed soldiers. Some, who dedicated their lives to St. Perpetua or St. Andrea—both soldiers for God—turned their hearts away from marriage and childbearing, as Hathui had done. Others by reason of unusual size or strength served a year or two in a lord's levy before returning to their holding and taking up their old lives.

But it was no shame for a noble lady to excuse herself from battle: that was what she had a husband and brothers for. Her first duties were to administer her lands and bear children to carry on her lineage. And Sapientia was particularly small, so that Hanna—running messages to her retinue from Henry—had been aware of the trouble the king and his smiths had gone to, to outfit her in decent armor.

But Sapientia wanted to fight, to lead her own unit. And Henry allowed her to, because—Hanna suspected—he had something to prove thereby. Something for her to prove to him, most likely. No person could become sovereign if he, or she, could not lead the great princes and their levies into battle.

"When will we go?" demanded Sapientia, and the old captain spoke to her soothingly, calming her down.

From the direction of the field, Hanna heard the soldiers raise their voices in a great shout: "Hai! For Henry!" That was the signal.

Sapientia lifted a hand and at the head of her troop of soldiers began to ride, circling through the trees. Hanna kept tight hold on her spear. She rode toward the back of the ranks, protected by them; no one expected an Eagle to fight unless they were overwhelmed. But she was still nervous. She stared through the trees, half starting every time new trees sprang into view. Luckily the soldiers next to her were too intent on what lay ahead to notice how jumpy she was. Possibly they were jumpy themselves, but she doubted it. For her first command Henry had given Sapientia experienced soldiers who had, most of them, spent time fighting in the east. After all, if this raid went well, they could fold up Sabella's right flank or even overtake and engulf her rear, thus preventing her from retreating.

Distantly, through the trees, Hanna heard a change in the echoing noise from the field. One of the soldiers beside her grunted: "They've engaged," he said to the man beside him.

They rode on, curving back to the right. A horrible shriek rose above the distant thunder of battle.

"What was that?" muttered one of the soldiers.

But then, at the fore of the company, the riders broke into a gallop. They had sighted their quarry. Their pennants whipped behind, streamers of red and gold.

Hanna saw the line of wagons ahead, drawn up in twos to make a wall and a gap between where the noncombatants could take shelter. Amazingly, Sabella had left only a token force to guard her supply train. A few arrows cut through the sky, their whirring like a warning come too late.

Sapientia raised her voice in a shrill cry: "Haililililili!" and, with her soldiers fanning out, they hit the line of wagons and broke into a dozen small swirls of fighting, soon stilled.

Hanna hung back, watching. Hathui had drilled this into her over the last ten days as they had ridden west to meet Sabella.

"You are the king's eyes and ears. You watch and mark all that occurs. You are not meant for heroics. You are meant to live and bear witness."

But there were no heroics here. Sapientia's troops took over the supply train easily and began to herd their new prisoners together, searching for Biscop Constance. A cry came from the woods on the opposite side of the line of wagons. Hanna rode closer, to investigate.

There! Among the trees she saw riders, but she could not identify them. Sapientia's captain took twenty soldiers and rode into the wood to head them off.

And at that moment, someone grabbed her reins and jerked down hard on them. She started and swung her spear around to point at—

A frater.

She stared. He had a harsh face. One of his lips was bleeding.

"Give me your horse!" he demanded. This was no humble churchman. After almost twenty days in the king's progress, Hanna recognized a great lord's arrogance when she saw it.

But she hesitated. He was dressed as a simple frater, after all.

"Ai, Lady, grant me patience!" he said aloud. "Eagle! Dismount and give me this horse!"

"For what purpose?" she demanded in her turn. "You are in Sabella's train—"

"I am Sabella's prisoner, not her ally."

"How can I know—?"

Distantly, that awful shriek rose again on the wind, followed by a strange muttering, like calls of triumph and moans of defeat melded together, like a battle gone to rout.

The frater grunted in anger, grabbed her arm, and yanked her bodily off the horse. She hit the ground hard enough to jolt her and scatter her wits. The animal shied, but he jerked down on the reins and, while Hanna was trying to pick herself up, threw himself over the saddle and swung his leg over. Kicked the horse, hard, and with robes flapping up around his thighs, he rode at a gallop off toward the battle. Lady! He was barefoot!

Panting, Hanna heaved herself to her feet. In the woods, two forces had met and blended together: she caught sight of the red dragon of Saony. Friends, then, but as soon as she thought it, she heard shouting.

"Lavastine's riders are coming! Turn round! Turn round and face them!"

Ai, Lady! What had Hathui said? An unhorsed Eagle is a dead Eagle. The frater, and her horse, were long gone. Still clutching her spear, Hanna ran for the shelter of the wagons.

4

THIS is what it had all meant, of course. Alain saw that now with a clarity obscured only by the screaming of men and the milling of soldiers lost, frightened, and running, or caught up in the brutal and numbing work of slaughter.

Henry's soldiers—those caught by the *guivre*'s glare—were like so many trussed pigs, throats slashed while they squealed. This was not battle of the kind sanctified by the Lord of Hosts, who did not falter when He was called upon to wield the Sword of Judgment. This was a massacre.

Alain knew it was wrong, knew it in his heart. The *guivre* screamed in rage, trying to break free, beating its wings frantically. Sabella's first rank of horsemen moved steadily up the hill, their progress slowed because it was so easy to kill Henry's soldiers, because they had to scramble over the dead and dying and over horses collapsed onto the grass. On the far right flank, a melee swirled, back and forth, but the standard of Fesse wavered and began to move backward.

Above, about half of the century of Lions had begun to march forward to meet Sabella's army. The rest either could not or would not march. And behind them Henry sat on his horse, unmoving. Was he waiting and watching? Or was he already caught in the *guivre*'s eye?

The mounted soldiers opposite Lavastine's forces were trying to turn Lavastine's soldiers back so they could punch in to aid Henry's center. Alain ran, fought his way through the back ranks of archers and spearmen who had fallen back after the first skirmishing. He shoved, and Rage and Sorrow nipped and bit to make a passage for him, toward their sisters and brothers, the black hounds who attended Count Lavastine.

Alain reached the count, who was sitting back from the front lines, waiting and watching the progress of the battle. Alain grabbed his stirrup and pulled hard. Lavastine stared down at him. There was no sign in his eyes that he recognized Alain.

Desperate measures for desperate times. He prayed for strength to the Blessed Lady. Then he grabbed Lavastine's mail coat and tugged as hard as he could.

Because the count was not expecting it, he lost his seat. Alain shifted his grip to the count's arm and pulled him right out of the saddle. Lavastine fell hard and lay still.

And a spear pinched Alain between the shoulder blades. He dropped to his knees and fumbled at his neck as he turned his head to look up and behind.

It was Sergeant Fell. "You know me, Sergeant!" Alain cried. "You know the count is acting strangely. This is wrong! We shouldn't be here!"

Fell hesitated. Lavastine's captain fell back from the front lines, seeing the count unhorsed. All at once the hounds surrounded Alain, growling and driving everyone back. No one dared strike them. Alain found the rose and drew it out.

"I pray you, Lady of Battles, come to my aid," he breathed. And he brushed the petals of the rose over Lavastine's pale lips, just below the nasal of his helmet.

Beyond, he heard the clash of battle. Here he was protected, caught in an eddy, surrounded by a black wall of hounds. Sorrow licked Lavastine's face, and the count opened his eyes. He blinked and passed a hand over his helmet as if feeling it there for the first time. Then he sat up. Alain grabbed him under the arms and the hounds parted to let Sergeant Fell through. Together, Alain and the sergeant pulled Lavastine to his feet.

"What is this?" demanded Lavastine, staring at the chaos around them, his front rank of fighters pressing against the fighters from Saony. Fesse's banner was retreating. In the center, Sabella's banner moved up and farther up and came against the banner of the Lions. The *guivre* shrieked. The Lion banner toppled and disappeared from view. Henry, surrounded now only by his personal guard, did not move.

The captain pressed his horse through the knot of hounds and men, who parted to let him through. Sergeant Fell let go of the count and grabbed his horse's reins before it could bolt. The *guivre* made all the horses nervous, and they shied at every harsh call and scream.

"We are marching with Sabella, against Henry," said the captain.

"We are not!" cried Lavastine. "All of my men, withdraw from the battle."

This command raced through the ranks like wildfire. Lavastine mounted his horse and pulled back, and step by embattled step his soldiers withdrew from the battle until the captains of Saony's line realized what was occurring and, at last, let them go.

But Henry's center was broken. Sabella was halfway through the Lions and still Henry had not moved. As Lavastine's soldiers cleared the field, Alain stood his ground and their retreat eddied around him and ebbed until he stood among the dead and watched Saony's cavalry wheel and turn to aid their king. He watched the *guivre* twist and turn, still battering against the wind and against its shackles, watched its baleful glare sweep across the ranks of Saony's soldiers. Watched as half of Sabella's company split off to strike at this new threat.

A few arrows and spears cut through the air from the ranks of Fesse's troops to slide harmlessly off the *guivre*'s scaly hide and fall to the ground. The grass was empty around the *guivre*; Sabella's soldiers, though protected against its gaze, gave it a wide berth. Not one soul had come within reach of its claws, circumscribed by the length of the chain that fettered it to the iron cage.

Slowly, Henry's soldiers were cut down or retreated up the hill toward the king—for their final stand.

The rose fell from Alain's suddenly nerveless fingers. He could not stand by and watch any more. He could not judge the rightness of Sabella's grievance against Henry. But he knew it was not right that she win by these means, as horrible as they were. Lackling had been murdered to gain Lavastine's support. Henry's soldiers could not fight, so as to pit honest strength against honest strength, but were scythed down like wheat.

He ran across the field, stumbling on corpses, jumping over men who writhed or struggled to drag themselves to safety. He ran toward the *guivre*, and paused only once, long enough to take a sword from a noble lord's slack and bloody body. He did not even register the man's face.

But another figure reached the *guivre* before he could. Someone else, riding a dun-colored horse. The man flung himself off the horse and slapped it on the flank. The horse bolted away.

And the frater—for it was Frater Agius, Alain saw that now as he ran, knowing suddenly that he would come too late—walked without fear into the circle of the *guivre*'s talons.

Its cry was as much delirium as fury, but it stooped and plunged. Half-starved and long since driven wild by captivity and the torment of its wasted and suffering body, it took the food offered it.

Agius vanished under a flurry of metal-hard wings and sharp talons. The *guivre* lowered its head to feed.

Henry's army—what was left of it—and Henry himself came to life. With cries of rage, driven almost to a frenzy by what they had witnessed and been helpless to prevent, they charged and hit Sabella's line, which had fallen out of formation as they took the hill and killed their easy prey. The soldiers from Fesse and Avaria regrouped and slammed into Duke Rodulf's stretched-thin line. Saony's troops fell back, reformed, and drove for Sabella's faltering center.

Alain ran for the *guivre*. Already the first of Sabella's men, shocked and not yet recovered from this reversal, stumbled backward past him. He ignored them, though Sorrow and Rage nipped and barked, protecting him so no man tried to stop him.

Why would any man try to stop him? The *guivre* loomed huge, this close, a stooped shape that was yet as high as two men, one standing on the other's shoulders. Sun glinted off its scales, and it fed with the rapacity of a creature who has been denied pleasure for too long. Alain came up behind it, thought of striking but did not. It remained oblivious to him. He heard the crunch of bone and—Ai, Lady!—a horrible moan that pitched up into a strangled wail and was abruptly cut off.

He circled the great beast. Worms fell from its diseased eye to slither away on the ground. From this side it could not see his approach. And anyway, it was too busy feasting.

He raised the sword just as he heard a warning cry behind him and then a cry from farther away: "Hailililili!" and the thunder of hooves and shouts of dismay, carrying Rodulf's name on the wind, and again and again the cry of "Henry! For King Henry!"

He brought it down with all his strength on the creature's neck. It screamed aloud, deafening him, and lifted its great and ugly head from what remained of Agius. Lifting, casting first to its sighted side and then slewing round the other way, it beat its wings, sending him tumbling forward underneath it. It was an ungainly thing, not meant for the ground; it had only the one set of talons and wings.

It clawed for him, missed, because it could not see him, tottered, because it was so ill and could barely find its balance. Alain stumbled back and righted the sword, turning it so the blade pointed up. His heel met resistance and he fell to one knee. Glanced behind himself.

The *guivre* had opened Agius at the belly, to feed on the soft entrails. Horribly, the frater's eyes caught on and tracked Alain; he was still alive.

The *guivre* screamed its fury and found its footing. Its shadow covered them, Alain and the dying Agius.

But, of course, as the old tales told, every great beast has its weak spot. Alain did not hesitate but plunged the sword deep into its unprotected breast.

Blood fountained, pouring over him like the wash of fire. He let go of the sword's hilt and jumped back, grabbing Agius and tugging him as the *guivre* writhed in its death throes. Spitting and coughing, blinded by the stinging, hot blood, he stumbled backward, dragging Agius. The *guivre* fell and the impact jarred Alain off his feet. He collapsed on top of the frater. The *guivre* shuddered, a great convulsion, and was still.

Agius breathed something, a rattling word and then another. Alain bent, eyes streaming, his hands smarting. A body slammed up against him, and then Rage was licking his face and hands. He tried to chase her away. He could not chase her away and concentrate on Agius.

"Free the white deer," whispered Agius. "Ai, Lady, let this sacrifice make me worthy of Your Son's example." His eyes glazed over and he shuddered once, like the *guivre*, and died.

Sorrow nudged up against Alain. The hound had something in his mouth. Rage licked Alain's eyes clean of the *guivre*'s blood and Alain blinked into sudden brightness and made sense first of all of the field lying washed by the sun's light and the chaos ranging there: Sabella's banner fell back and farther back yet. All the weight of victory had shifted. With the death of the *guivre*, their standard, Sabella's soldiers had lost heart and now they turned and fled.

A thorn cut Alain's cheek, a thin prick. He started back to see Sorrow carrying the rose in his mouth, brought from the other side of the battlefield. Its petals had darkened to a deep blood-red, as red as Agius' blood that yet leaked onto the ground.

Alain dropped his face to his hands and wept.

XIV
THE PROMISE
OF POWER

1

ROSVITA could not concentrate when she was waiting. She paced up and down in the feasting hall that adorned the palace built by the first duke of Fesse some eighty years ago. Now and again she walked over to the great doors that opened onto a beautiful vista of the town of Kassel, lying at the foot of the hill on which the palace had been erected. A huge gray-blue stone capped the lintel of this monumental doorway. When Rosvita stared up, she saw tiny figures and patterns carved into the stone, their outlines blurred by age.

In the town below, a few bedraggled streamers still decorated the streets. When Henry and his army had marched in, the town of Kassel had been recovering from the raucous Feast of St. Mikhel, celebrated four nights before. Though the biscop dutifully spoke out against several of the local customs, even she could not prevent the usual festival which involved a young woman riding through the streets of Kassel clothed only in her hair—or in this case, in a gauzy linen undershift, some attention being shown to modesty— while the townsfolk closed their shutters and pretended not to watch her go by. After this procession everyone trooped out of doors and drank themselves sick. Rosvita was not sure exactly what had happened in the original story to force the poor woman to ride out in such a humiliating way, only that St. Mikhel was by a miracle supposed to have clothed the hapless virgin in a light so blinding it protected her from the stares of the heathen and the ungodly.

"It is said," said Princess Theophanu, coming up beside Rosvita to stand in a splash of sunlight, "that this stronghold was built on the ruins of a Dariyan fortress which was itself built on the ruins of an older palace whose great stones were set in place by the daimones of the upper air." She indicated the huge lintel.

"Like the stone circles," said Rosvita, thinking of young Berthold. "Though some say they were set there by giants." That was what Helmut Villam had said, that day when they had explored the old fallen stone circle and Berthold had still walked alive in the light of day. Ai, Lady, this sorrow she must bear with her. But she could not allow it to drag her down. "Come," she said, turning to Theophanu. "We will read from the book I was given by the hermit, Brother Fidelis. In this way we may reflect upon the life of a holy woman while we wait to hear from King Henry."

She turned back into the hall, where light and shadow played among the thick wood pillars and in the eaves far above. No fire burned in the hearth this day; it was warm enough that only cooking fires in the kitchen house needed to be lit. Servants dressed in tabards sewn with the gold lion of Fesse lingered nervously beside the side doors. One brought wine forward, but she gestured for him to take it away. She was not thirsty.

Young Ekkehard had fallen asleep on a bench. His gentle face and sweet profile reminded her bitterly of Berthold Villam, who was lost to them now. Ekkehard was a good boy, if a little too fond of carousing late into the night and singing with the bards who traveled from one great court to the next.

"It is just as well," said Theophanu, coming up beside Rosvita.

"What is just as well?"

Theophanu nodded toward her younger brother. Of all Henry's children, Ekkehard looked the most like his father: golden-brown hair, round face, and a slightly arched, strong nose. At thirteen, he was lanky and tall and a bit clumsy except when he was playing the lute, but so—it was said—had Henry been at that age before he grew into the broad and powerful stature of his adult years. "It is just as well," said Theophanu, "that Ekkehard loves music and the pleasures of the feast more than he does the promise of power."

Rosvita did not quite know what to make of this bald statement.

Theophanu turned her dark eyes on Rosvita. "Is that not the source of Sabella's rebellion? That she is not content administering her husband's dukedom? That she wants more?"

"Is greed not the source of many sins?" asked Rosvita.

Theophanu smiled innocently. "So does the church teach, good sister."

Theophanu was old enough to have her own retinue, and yet her father kept her close by his side, just as he kept Sapientia beside him rather than giving her a title and lands to administer. Did Theophanu chafe at this treatment? Rosvita could not tell. Was she angry that her sister had been allowed to accompany Henry to meet Sabella on the field and been given her own command? That she had been left behind when truly she was larger and stronger and more fit physically for the exertions of battle? Theophanu's expression and her inner thoughts on these matters remained unreadable.

Rosvita unwrapped the old parchment codex from the linen cover in which she had swaddled it and turned carefully to the first page. Brother Fidelis' calligraphy was delicate yet firm, betraying the lines of an older age in the loops and swirls of the occasional fillips of ornamentation he had allowed himself as he wrote. A Salian hand, Rosvita thought; she had examined many manuscripts and books over the years and come to recognize various quirks and telltale signs of specific scribes or of habits learned in certain monastic schools.

She touched the yellowing page with reverence, feeling the lines of ink beneath her fingers like the whisper of Fidelis' voice, coming to her as from down a long tunnel, through the veil of years.

Theophanu sat beside her and waited, hands clasped patiently in her lap. Rosvita read aloud.

" 'The Lord and Lady confer glory and greatness on women through strength of mind. Faith makes them strong, and in these earthly vessels, heavenly treasure is hid. One of this company is Radegundis, she whose earthly life I, Fidelis, humblest and least worthy, now attempt to celebrate so that all may hear of her deeds and sing praise in her glorious memory. The world divides those whom no space parted once. So ends the Prologue.' "

Rosvita sighed, hearing Fidelis in these words as if his voice echoed through the ink to touch her ears. She went on. " 'So begins the Life. The most blessed Radegundis was of the highest earthly rank—' "

Ekkehard snorted and woke up suddenly, tumbling off the bench onto carpets carefully laid there by his servants. At that same moment, one of Theophanu's servingwomen appeared in the doorway.

"An Eagle!" she cried. "An Eagle comes."

Rosvita closed the book with trembling hands and wrapped it in linen. Then she clutched it to her breast and rose, hands still shaking, and hurried over to the great doors. Theophanu came with her, but the king's daughter was completely calm. Ekkehard was talking excitedly behind them, and his servants swarmed around him, helping him up. The chatelaine and other servants of the duchess of Fesse crowded behind Rosvita and the princess.

The Eagle was Hathui, the young woman Henry had honored by taking her into his personal retinue. She handed off her horse to a groom and walked forward to kneel before Theophanu.

"Your Highness, Princess Theophanu," she said, lifting her eyes to look upon Theophanu's face. She had the rare ability to be proud without being impudent. "King Henry sends word that his sister Sabella refuses any terms of parley, and that battle will be joined."

"What of the course of that battle?" asked Theophanu.

"I do not know. I rode quickly, and without looking back, as is my duty."

"Bring her mead," said Theophanu. She stared off across the town. Kassel was laid out as a square with two broad avenues set perpendicular to each other, dividing it into four even quarters. An old wall surrounded it, the last obvious remains besides the baths that this had once been a Dariyan town in the days of the old empire. The town had probably been larger then, and certainly more densely populated. There was room now within the old walls for a few fields—mostly vegetables and one impressive stand of fruit trees as well as some common pasture for cows—between the last line of houses and the town gates. Outside the wall lay fields, rye and barley because of the soil of this country, the red clay of the highlands.

Where had all those people gone, and what had become of their descendants? Had they fled back to Aosta, to the city of Darre out of which the empire had grown? Had they died in the wars and plagues and famines that had devastated and ultimately destroyed the old empire? Had they simply vanished and never returned, like poor Berthold?

Rosvita could not help but wonder. *"Knowledge tempted me too much,"* Brother Fidelis had said. At times like this, she knew she also was too curious. Henry might be dead and all he had worked for overthrown. Or he might have committed the terrible crime of slaying his own kin, the very crime that—some chroniclers wrote—had brought about the fall of the Dariyan Empire. And here she stood, wondering about the history of the town of Kassel when the peace and stability of the kingdom was at stake!

"Come," she said to Theophanu, "let us sit down again and wait."

Theophanu, barely, shook her head. "It is time to saddle our horses," she said quietly. "And to gather together healers. Either we will ride to the battle to give aid to the wounded, or we will ride away."

"Away?"

Theophanu turned now, her dark lashes framing eyes as startlingly large as those of queens in ancient mosaics. She looked entirely too composed. "If Sabella wins, then Ekkehard and I must remain out of her hands at any cost. We must be prepared to ride to my Aunt Scholastica at Quedlinhame."

Rosvita placed a hand on her chest and bowed slightly, showing her respect for the young princess. Of course Theophanu was right. She had learned politics at her mother's knee, and her mother Sophia had learned politics in the court of Arethousa, where intrigue ran in webs as convoluted and dangerous as those in any court in the world of humankind.

This, then, was the choice Henry had to make, because it was long past time for him to send one of his daughters on her heir's progress. He had to choose between Sapientia, the daughter who was bold and open and yet too often did not show good judgment, and the cool, inscrutable Theophanu, who had fine political instincts but none of that vital charismatic charm that marked a sovereign as the chosen of God. One was too trusting; the other, no one trusted. No wonder Henry dreamed of placing his bastard son Sanglant on the throne.

2

FROM frater to deacon.

"Get me a horse!"

The woman who made this demand of Hanna had the imperious tone of a noblewoman though she wore simple deacon's robes and her braided hair had not even a shawl to cover it. But there was nothing Hanna could do. She had no horse, having lost it to the desperate frater.

"Begging your pardon, Deacon," she said, hefting her spear just in case the woman meant to attempt an escape while Princess Sapientia's soldiers fought off the new attack, "but all who are in this train are now in the custody of King Henry."

To her surprise, the deacon laughed. "Of course, child. Do you not know me?"

Hanna could only shake her head while she stared into the woods, hoping to catch sight of the princess' troops. A few soldiers lingered. Most of the people in the supply train were down, wounded or dead, or else they milled around aimlessly with that lost look on their faces of men and women totally out of their element. Some ten paces behind the deacon lay two guards in Sabella's colors; both were dead. About five wagons beyond their bodies, Hanna suddenly saw a woman in biscop's vestments being helped onto a wagon.

"Ai, Lady!" she breathed. "That is Biscop Antonia."

"She must not escape," said the deacon in a hard voice. "Find me a horse, or find my niece and bring her back from the woods."

My niece. Hanna had a horrible thought. She risked a close look at the woman's face and decided it could well be true, that the resemblance could be marked in the cast of the woman's features, in her nose and jawline and piercing gaze.

She bent to one knee, swiftly, and bowed her head. "Begging your pardon, Your Grace," she said quickly.

"Never mind that!" snapped the woman. "I do not want Antonia to get away. And I have no weapon that can stop her."

Hanna obeyed her. She ran toward the woods, sure that she would get run through at any moment. But Sapientia's troops came riding back, flanked by the red dragon soldiers of Saony. The other troop of soldiers, Lavastine's skirmishers, had evidently retreated. Hanna hailed her, and the princess pulled up at once.

"Your aunt, Biscop Constance, waits for your protection," Hanna cried, grabbing hold of the reins as Sapientia's horse shied away. Hanna knew horses well enough to see that this one had, besides a nervous disposition, a heavy-handed rider, and far too much excitement to cope with. "She begs of you to stop Biscop Antonia from making her escape."

Sapientia's expressive face lit up. "Captain!" she cried, "you must find and protect Constance. Follow, you who are with me!" She urged her mount forward so quickly she tore the reins out of Hanna's hands. Perhaps thirty of her troops went with her; the rest hung back, confused or waiting for confirmation of this order from the old captain. He muttered something under his breath, then raised his voice so all the soldiers could hear him.

"You ten, you return to the wagons and protect Biscop Constance. We have more than enough soldiers here. The rest, and you soldiers from Saony, will return with me to the field where Henry fights." They began to form up. He looked down at Hanna. "Eagle! You remain with Biscop Constance."

She nodded, happy at this moment to be subject to an authority that knew what it was doing. They rode back toward the battle, whose outcome none of them knew.

So it was that, despite everything and despite several flurries of disorder caused by Sapientia's enthusiasm, Biscop Antonia was taken prisoner together with her host of clerics. Duke Berengar was found, huddling underneath a wagon with only one loyal servingman at his side; he was so frightened he had pissed in his leggings. Hanna actually felt sorry for him when he was brought before a stern Biscop Constance who, having taken command of Sapientia's forty soldiers, now controlled the supply train. But Constance showed him—not pity, but indifference. Hanna quickly understood why: she had seen that slack-jawed gaping and sudden bursts of inappropriate laughter before. Berengar was a simpleton, and therefore a simple pawn—a mere Lion in the game of chess. He did not matter.

The person who mattered here was Biscop Antonia, who looked

to Hanna's eyes rather cheered at the thought of being in Constance's power. Antonia was a kind-looking woman who did not bear herself with the haughtiness of most of the nobly-born but rather with a smiling modesty. And yet in the parley, faced with Helmut Villam, she had raged with a passion that did not appear to be part of her now.

And there was one other prize, hidden among the clerics.

"Ah," said Constance. "Come forward, Tallia. I will not hurt you, child."

The girl was led forward. She was crying, and it made her nose red. She had nothing to say for herself except to throw herself on Constance's mercy. But Hanna kept looking past her toward Antonia's clerics. They were the most unsightly mass of churchmen Hanna had ever seen; they all looked as if they had some form of pox, with red sores on their faces and hands and rashes along their chins. Several of them were coughing feebly, and one—the most sickly of the lot—had a thin stain of blood on his hand when he lowered it from his mouth.

Ai, Lady! thought Hanna. *What if they have the plague?*

"Separate them from the others," said Constance to Sapientia, as if she had the same thought. "But I will keep Tallia and Berengar beside me."

"Are they sick?" demanded Sapientia, who had finally dismounted after riding around in the trees for a while, looking for someone else to fight. She had returned from the woods to declare she would ride back to the battle, but Constance had forestalled that with a direct order, aunt to niece, and even the brash Sapientia dared not go against a biscop's command. Constance could not be more than four or five years older than Sapientia, but her authority far outweighed that of her brother's daughter.

"I do not know if they are sick," she said now, "but we must be cautious. I have heard many tales of the plague in Autun, which was hard hit by a sickness some twenty years ago. Take them aside and guard them, but let none touch them."

Biscop Antonia showed no sign of the disease, nor did the one young cleric who stood closest to her. But Constance did not look likely to let the biscop out of her sight, sickness or no.

"You will answer for what you did, Antonia," said Constance.

"We all answer to God," said Antonia reasonably.

A thunder of hooves alerted them. Sapientia's captain had returned with the rest of her troops but without the skirmishers from Saony. His expression was chilling.

"What is wrong?" cried Sapientia.

Antonia smiled knowingly.

"Good captain," said Constance in a firm but calm voice. "What news do you bring?"

He appeared stricken. "The Lord has blessed us with victory, Your Grace, but a terrible prize it is this day."

For one instant, Antonia's triumphant expression was wiped clean to show something nastier, cunning and brittle, beneath. Hanna glanced toward Constance, who looked grave—as well she might. When she looked back at Antonia, the old biscop had regained her usual expression, as placid as a saint's, as smooth as cream, and Hanna had to shake her head, wondering if she had imagined that other face.

"Give us your report," said Constance. Sapientia looked likely to grab her horse and gallop away, but—after one sharp look from Constance—she stayed where she was.

The captain dismounted and knelt before her. "Victory belongs to King Henry, but at high cost. Many lie dead on the field, for Sabella used—" Here he faltered. "—she brought a creature on the field, a terrible thing that truly must have sprung from an evil sire, and by its magic her army slew fully half or more of Henry's army—aye, indeed, almost all of his Lions—while they stood frozen on the field, held in the grip of some misbegotten enchantment."

Sapientia gasped aloud. Soldiers muttered in disbelief and horror. *Almost all of his Lions.* Hanna gulped back a sob of foreboding.

Constance raised a hand for silence, and it was granted her.

"How then did Henry win the day? If all transpired as you report?"

"I do not know. Only that a man—a frater—threw himself on the beast and somehow it was distracted from its sorcery and killed."

Antonia said something under her breath, but Hanna could not hear. Her face remained pleasant, but her eyes had grown hard.

Constance paled. "A frater?" she asked. "What do you know of this?"

"Some say it is the son of Burchard, Duke of Avaria, but I can scarcely believe that—" Constance lifted a hand sharply and he fell silent.

One tear rolled down Constance's cheek, and then the wind blew it away and it vanished as if it had never existed. "Take her away, out of my sight," she said, pointing at Biscop Antonia, "but guard her closely." The captain, startled, jumped to his feet and did as he was told.

"What about Sabella?" Sapientia called after the captain. "Did she escape?"

"No," said the captain as his men surrounded Biscop Antonia and led her away to one of the wagons. "Villam captured her himself, though he was sorely wounded. Some fear he will not live. She is in Henry's custody now."

Constance shut her eyes and remained that way for a long while as Antonia was taken away and lodged in a wagon under heavy guard, as Sapientia finally lost patience and called for her horse.

"Come, Eagle," called the princess. "You will ride with me."

"No," said Constance suddenly, opening her eyes. "Go if you wish, Sapientia, but I will have an Eagle by me, as is my right." She touched the gold torque at her neck.

"It is true," said Sapientia thoughtfully, tossing her head, "that your loyal Eagle reached us from Autun, and that was how Father knew to ride here." Then, strangely, she smiled. "But without an army, how can Father ride to Gent?"

"Ride to Gent?" asked Constance. "Why would Henry wish to ride to Gent?"

Sapientia reined her horse aside and rode away without answering the question, back to the battlefield to meet her victorious father.

"Ai, Lady," murmured Hanna. For it was true. Henry had marched with a large army, fully eight hundred or more soldiers. He could raise more, it was true, but it would take months to raise levies from the far-flung lands of Wendar and Varre and the marchlands and more time after that to march them all the way to Gent. Sabella had lost many soldiers as well, this day; how was Henry in any case to trust the lords of Varre, who had risen against him? They might well refuse to give him an army, to save the son none of them had any love for.

They would not think about the people of Gent and what they might be suffering. They would not think about Liath and the danger she faced. What did kings and princes care for the lives of Eagles? Like swords, they were only a tool to be used for the nobles' own gain.

3

KING Henry was in a foul mood. He was, indeed, in as rare a fury as Rosvita had ever seen him.

At Kassel they had received news of the victory and ridden out at once, only to arrive to find Henry pacing back and forth, back and forth, outside the hastily erected tent in which Helmut Villam lay. It was rumored Villam was dying. All of Henry's servants and the various lords and ladies in attendance on his progress looked terrified, cowering at least twenty steps from him. Henry was perfectly capable of delivering a stinging and unprovoked rebuke to any persons who placed themselves in his line of sight.

Theophanu, sizing up the matter in one glance, drew Ekkehard aside and led him away to where shelters had been set up for the wounded, to give succor there. The Eagle Hathui, adept at being anonymous, walked over and took up her post beside the tent's entrance, close to the king and yet so still, so effaced against the plain cloth siding, that he seemed not to notice her.

Rosvita found herself beseiged by courtiers begging her to bring the king to his senses. She calmly distracted them and sent them off on various useful errands and finally found a person who might give her information: Margrave Judith.

The margrave sat in a camp chair and surveyed the scene from a safe distance. Her servants kept importunate courtiers away from her, and so she sipped wine in a semblance of solitude and watched Henry pace. Servants fluttered close to the king and were chased off.

Beyond, Rosvita saw carnage. The field was littered with corpses. Most of the wounded had been moved, but there were far far too many to bury so quickly. Possibly the field would simply have to be abandoned; it had happened before. Men and women—common soldiers and people from neighboring farms—walked among the dead, looting the corpses for valuables. Rosvita supposed the best booty had already been taken by the king's servants or by the noble lords.

Strangest of all, and worst to behold, a creature lay in the center of the field of slaughter, a great beast so ugly in death that she shuddered to look on it, even at this distance. Its head was as big around as a cart's wheel, resembling more than anything a grotesque rooster's head, but it had the sinuous body and tail of a reptile and the talons of a giant eagle.

"That is the *guivre*," said Judith with the detached interest of one who has taken no harm in the midst of disaster.

"A *guivre!*" Rosvita stared. "I have read of such monsters but never hoped to see one."

The creature lay with one huge eye open to the sky, staring blankly at the blue heavens above. Its wings wore a sheen like metal, feathered with copper, and—most gruesomely—the shape of a man's body was half covered by its carcass. Some rash looter had stolen the dead man's shoes—or else he had been barefoot. Small white things, like maggots, crawled over the *guivre*'s body. Rosvita looked away quickly.

"What has happened?" she asked Judith.

"A great beast has met its death, as you can see," said the margrave. She had blood on her tabard, a rent torn in her mail shirt, and a purpling bruise on her right cheek. Her helmet, somewhat dented, sat at her feet. "Ai, Lord. I'm too old for this. No more children, no more fighting, or so the healers say. A man can fight long after his hair has gone silver, if he lives so long. I hurt to the very bones. After this, my daughters' husbands ride out, as is proper, or if a woman must attend the battle, then one of them can go!"

Rosvita did not know quite what to say. She had seen death many times, of course, but never on such a scale as this. Up, among the Lions, an Eagle knelt weeping over the body of an infantryman.

"It was a hard-fought battle," Rosvita said finally.

"Which? The one on the field, or the one we witnessed just before your party rode in?"

"Which one was that?"

"Henry's argument with Duchess Liutgard."

Rosvita did not know Duchess Liutgard well—the young duchess came to court rarely—but she did know that Liutgard possessed the fabled temper that had, so the chroniclers wrote, marred the reign of her great-great-aunt, Queen Conradina, a woman fabled for having as many arguments as lovers and both in abundance. "Why should the king argue with Liutgard?"

Judith found a stain of blood under one fingernail and beckoned to a servant. The serving woman hastened over and washed the margrave's hands while she talked. "Liutgard rode beside Villam when Sabella's guard was overtaken. They fought loyally—"

"Liutgard and Villam?"

Judith smiled, but there was a hint of derision in her expression. "That is not what I meant. Sabella's retinue fought loyally and many were slain before the fight was given up. Rodulf died there."

"Duke Rodulf? That is grievous news."

"He fought for Varre, as he has always done. More for Varre I would suppose than for Sabella. Alas, he could not bring himself to accept a Wendish king."

"Perhaps his heirs will be more reasonable."

"Perhaps," echoed Judith with a quirk of the lips that expressed doubt more than hope.

"Villam was wounded?" Rosvita asked. She was beginning to wonder if Judith was toying with her for her own amusement.

"Badly, yes." If this distressed the margrave, she did not show it. Rosvita had never much liked Judith, but the margrave had been loyal to Arnulf and then to Henry, never wavering in her support. She was not an easy woman to like, yet neither could she be dismissed. She was far too powerful for that. "Because Villam was wounded, Liutgard was able to take Sabella into *her* custody."

"Ah." This explained much. "I suppose that did not sit well with Henry."

"It did not. That was what they argued about. Henry demanded that Liutgard surrender Sabella into his custody. Liutgard told him she would not until Henry was calmer and more able to think clearly."

"Ai, Lady," murmured Rosvita. "That was rashly spoken of her. She might have found more diplomatic words."

"Diplomacy is for courtiers and counselors, my dear cleric, not for princes. I have never found Liutgard possessed of subtlety in any case. You know Burchard's son is dead?"

"Burchard's son?" What had the Duke of Avaria and his children to do with this? The subject changed so quickly, and before Rosvita was done understanding the last one, that she did not follow the leap. Liutgard had married the duke of Avaria's second son, Frederic, but he had died several years ago.

Judith sighed ostentatiously, examined her fingernails for traces of blood or other detritus of armed struggle, and allowed the servant to dry her hands on a clean linen cloth. Then with a gesture she dismissed the servant. "Sabella seems determined to take the men of that line with her in her defeats, though she cares not one whit for them. I speak of Burchard's elder son, Agius, the one who went into the church."

Judith related a rather confused tale of the *guivre*, the frater, and a boy who had led Count Lavastine's hounds to the kill.

"You are going too quickly for me," said Rosvita. "I do not know what part Count Lavastine has in this battle. The last I heard of him, he had refused Henry's command to attend him on his progress. That was almost a year ago."

"He turned up at the battle on Sabella's side." Judith paused and brushed a finger along her upper lip where a fine down of hair grew, the mark of her impending passage from fertility to wisdom. "But that is the strange thing: he withdrew his forces from the battle halfway through."

"After the *guivre* was killed, when he saw which way the wind was blowing?"

"No. Before that, when it appeared all was lost for Henry and that Sabella would win. No one can explain it, since Lavastine and his men have fled."

At long last, Rosvita was beginning to see where all this led. "What of Henry and Sabella?"

"We are at a stalemate there, it appears. Liutgard refuses to turn Sabella over to Henry, and Henry rages, as you can see."

"Have you attempted to intervene, my lady?"

"I?" Judith smiled.

That smile. It was that particular smile, one Judith was famous for, that made Rosvita not like her, although she had no other good reason. The margrave of Olsatia and Austra was loyal to the house of Saony, had pledged her loyalty first to the younger Arnulf and then after his death to Henry. But Rosvita did not believe any affection or deep bond held her to them. Rosvita believed Judith remained loyal to Henry because she needed him and what he could bring her: his military support. The position of prince in the marchlands, the unstable border country, was a precarious one, and Judith had called on—and received—aid from Henry more than once.

Like many other noblewomen of the highest rank, Judith had given birth before her first marriage to a child gotten on her by a concubine or at any rate some handsome young man not of noble birth whose looks had caught her youthful fancy. That first marriage, as such marriages were, had been arranged for her by her kin to the mutual advantage of both houses. The concubine had long since disappeared. But the child had lived and thrived.

Lady bless, but Judith had petted and cosseted that boy; perhaps he would not have turned out so insufferable had he not been so handsome—those who had been at court longer than Rosvita said the boy resembled his father, in looks, at least; some said in charm as well. He had been a brilliant student, one of the most brilliant to pass through the king's schola in Rosvita's time there, but she had not been unhappy to see him leave. How unlike Berthold he had been in all ways except the one for which *she* of all people could not condemn him: curiosity.

But Hugh was gone now, into the church, and no doubt caught up in church concerns and his new position as abbot of Firsebarg. Without question his mother hoped to elevate him to the rank of presbyter, and with that honor he would leave Wendar to live in the skopos' palace in Darre. He would have no reason to trouble the king's progress with his presence. Thank the Lady.

"I have sent my personal physician to attend Villam," said Judith. She shrugged her shoulders, settling the mail shirt down more comfortably over her torso. "But no, I have not attempted to intervene. That duty is for his counselors."

Rosvita smiled wryly and humbly. By such means did God remind her not to pass judgment on others. She nodded to the margrave and excused herself. It was time to take the bull by the horns.

"What have you to say for yourself," demanded Henry as soon as he caught sight of her. "Why have you not brought Sabella to me? Ai, Lady! That idiot daughter of mine has made a fool of herself, according to report, right in front of everyone and not even knowing she was doing so. Ai, Lord, what did I do to deserve such children?"

"I am here now, Your Majesty," she said, trying to remain calm. Henry was so red in the face that his veins stood out and he looked likely to burst. "And though my lineage is a proud one, you must know I cannot give orders to such as Duchess Liutgard."

He considered this for at least two breaths, which gave her time to put her hand on his elbow. The touch startled him. It was not her place, of course, to touch the king without his permission, but the gesture served to make him think of something other than his grievances.

"You are angry, Your Majesty," she added while he was gathering his wits.

"Of *course* I am angry! Liutgard denies me the very person whose treason may yet cost me the only child—"

"King Henry!" She said it loudly and sharply. She knew with bitter instinct that he had been about to say something he would later regret. Something about Sanglant. "Let us go inside and see to Villam."

Had no one thought to calm him by appealing to his genuine affection for his old friend and companion? Rosvita could not believe they were so nervous of him as that. She gestured toward the tent. He frowned at her, but he hesitated. Then, abruptly, he went inside, leaving her to follow. The Eagle—Hathui—nodded as Rosvita ducked inside. Approvingly? Rosvita shook her head. Surely no common-born Eagle, not even one as proud as that one was, would think of approving or disapproving the actions of the nobly born.

Villam had lost his left arm just above the elbow. Rosvita dared not ask how he had taken the wound. The old man seemed half asleep, and she feared even whispers would wake him.

But Henry pushed the physician aside and laid a hand—gently, despite the fury that still radiated from him—on Villam's forehead.

"He is strong," he murmured, as if to make it true. The physician nodded, concurring.

"There is no infection?" asked Rosvita softly.

"It is too early to tell," said the physician. He had a light, rather high voice, marred by a strong accent. "He is, as His Majesty say, a strong man. If no infection set in, then he recover. If one do, then he die."

Henry knelt beside the pallet. The physician dropped to his knees at once, as if he dared not remain standing while the king knelt. Henry looked up and gestured to Rosvita. She knelt beside the king and murmured a prayer, which Henry mouthed in time to her words, right hand clutching the gold Circle of Unity hanging at his breast.

When she had finished, the king looked over at the physician. "What do you recommend?"

Rosvita studied the man. She did not trust physicians. They seemed to her like those astrologi who wandered from town to town promising to tell people's fates by reading the positions of the stars—for a substantial fee, of course: They catered to the credulous and the frightened. But this man was beardless, so he was either a churchman or, just possibly, a eunuch from the East. She wondered where Judith had found him and what trade the margrave might be carrying on with Arethousa.

His voice, when he spoke again, confirmed his status. It was too high for a true man. "I learn by the writings of the Dariyan physician Galenē, she of old days but great learning. This I follow. A man with such a wound must rest many weeks in a dry, warm place. The wound must keep clean. The man must—" He broke off and made eating gestures with a hand. "—ah—take broth and other food good in the stomach. His body will heal, or it will not heal. We aid. God choose." He drew the Circle at his chest and bowed his head to show his submission to God's will.

Villam's right arm lay folded across his chest. Henry took it now, and the old man's eyes fluttered open and focused, but he did not speak. Henry brushed away tears.

"You must go to Kassel, Helmut, and there recover your health," said Henry softly. "I march on Autun to restore my sister to her biscophric." He leaned forward and kissed the old man gently on either cheek, the kiss of peace, and rose.

This interlude had calmed him outwardly. The king nodded to the physician, who in the Eastern way touched his forehead to the ground.

Outside, Henry turned to Rosvita. "Let Sabella wait," he said in a low, intense voice that betrayed the rage still boiling within him. "Let her wonder, while we ride to Autun and I refuse to see her."

Rosvita smiled slightly. Henry had indeed returned to his senses. How quickly he turned the tables. Now, rather than Liutgard keeping Sabella from him, everyone would speak of Henry's anger being so great that he could not bring himself to look his sister in the face. That was, of course, much more effective.

But there was one question she had to ask, though she dreaded it. "You will not ride to Gent?"

His jaw tightened. He clasped his hands behind his back, as if holding them there was the only way to control himself. "Two-thirds of this army is dead or wounded. I will restore Constance, and more besides, and then we will have the summer to raise an army. Gent must hold firm until autumn." His eyes flashed with anger. "And Sabella will learn what it means to raise her hand against me a second time."

4

HENRY and his retinue camped outside Autun for three days before Biscop Helvissa worked up enough courage to open the gates and let them in.

Alain watched from a vantage point above Autun as the great gates swung open and the people of Autun swept out with wild rejoicing to welcome Constance back to the city.

"Henry will not leave Helvissa as biscop for long," said Lavastine. He stood beside Alain, a strange enough occurrence in itself, and together they stared down at what remained of Henry's army and of Sabella's rebellion. For the last many days, as they had marched west to Autun and then camped here, out of sight, Alain had seen groups of men fleeing westward, the remains of the men-at-arms levied from the lands controlled by Sabella, Duke Rodulf, and the other lords who had come under their sway. Fleeing westward; fleeing back to their homes. They had work to do, after all, in the fields. The time for spring sowing was long past. Now they must hope that summer would be long and the harvest delayed and that their families had been able to plant something against winter's hunger. Now they must hope for a good crop of winter wheat and rye for next year.

Besides Henry's army, and the retinues of the great lords who remained in Henry's custody, only Lavastine's company remained intact. He had sent Sergeant Fell on ahead with the infantry, for the count and his people also had fields to tend and next winter to survive. Miraculously, none in his company had taken any serious wounds. All would return to their families.

But Lavastine had remained behind with his twenty mounted soldiers, and he had shadowed Henry's progress to Autun and now waited here. Alain did not know why Lavastine waited or what he meant to do. All Alain knew was that something had changed radically. Now he slept *in* Lavastine's tent, on a decent pallet, and he was fed the same food that the count ate; he had been given a fine linen tunic to wear instead of his old ragged wool tunic, now much worn and patched.

"Come," said Lavastine, turning away as Henry's banner vanished into the city. "We will return to my tent."

They went, the hounds leaping around them, in fine good spirits this beautiful day. Alain was troubled. He still had nightmares about Agius. If only he had saved the frater. But he had not. Agius had sacrificed himself—and for what? Agius did not love King Henry. He had acted *against* Sabella and Antonia, not *for* Henry, though his action had saved the king.

Ai, Lady. If only he had the courage, but he did not. He had stood by while Lackling was murdered, because he had feared Antonia's power. He had said nothing after he had witnessed the feeding of some poor innocent to the *guivre.* He had accused no one—though surely the word of a freeholder's boy would never be listened to by the nobly born. He had not even thought to throw himself in front of the *guivre* at the battle; that he had managed to kill it was only because of Agius' willingness to sacrifice himself for the good of others.

Or for his own revenge on Sabella.

Alain sighed. It was all too deep and convoluted for him to make sense of.

"Come inside," said Lavastine, as much order as request, and yet Lavastine's attention toward him was perhaps the greatest mystery of all. Alain followed the count inside. He was half a head taller than Lavastine but never felt he towered above him, so intense was Lavastine's presence. Truly, the sorcery Antonia had laid upon Lavastine had been powerful in order to overcome that commanding disposition.

Lavastine sat in a camp chair that one of his servants brought to him. "Sit," he commanded Alain, sounding irritated that Alain had not sat down immediately.

"But, my lord—" began Alain, while around them the count's captain and servants stared. They were just as amazed as he was that the count wished a common boy to be seated beside him as though they were kin.

"Sit!"

Alain sat.

Lavastine called for wine, two cups, and then dismissed everyone but Alain. When the flap closed behind the last retreating servant, a gloom pervaded the tent chamber. Thin shafts of light lanced through gaps in the tent walls, illuminating a line of carpet, the hilt of a sword, the ear of a hound. The hounds panted merrily. Sorrow rolled onto his back and scratched himself along the spine of the carpet. Rage growled and snapped at Fear, who had crept too close to Alain.

"Alain Henrisson," said the count. "That is what you call yourself?"

"Yes, my lord."

"You saved my life and my honor on the field of battle."

Alain did not know what to say, so he merely bowed his head.

"I did not intend to support Sabella. Nor, for that matter, did I intend to support King Henry. My lands are my concern, as are the safety and well-being of the people who live there. That is all. I never wanted to be dragged into these conspiracies. But you could not have known this. Why did you act as you did?"

"B–because . . . I . . ."

"Go on! You must have had a reason."

Seeing that even in this friendly mood Lavastine was irritated by delay, Alain spoke as quickly as he could, hoping it made sense. "I—I saw that Biscop Antonia wasn't—she had Lackling murdered. She was going to murder the Eika prince you took prisoner, but he—he got away. Then she killed Lackling and I couldn't trust her—"

"Hold, hold, boy. Who is this Lackling?"

"One of the stableboys, my lord."

Lavastine shook his head slightly. The name meant nothing to him. "She had him murdered? Why was this not brought to my attention?"

"She brought strange creatures, my lord, to the ruins, and then you changed. You were—"

"Under a compulsion, yes." He made what was almost a spitting motion, as if the word, passing his lips, was distasteful to him. "I suppose Biscop Antonia would have denied everything and set her word against yours. Go on."

"Well, then, my lord, it just seemed wrong. The battle seemed wrong, that Sabella should win by treachery and sorcery and that poor imprisoned creature—"

"The Eika prince? But he escaped."

"No. I meant the *guivre*."

"The *guivre!*" Lavastine barked a laugh. "I have no compassion for such a beast as that." He set a hand on the head of the hound that sat at his feet; actually, the hound sat half on his boots. This one had white in its muzzle, a sign of age, and Alain recognized it as Terror. The hound lifted its head to get a scratch from Lavastine's fingers.

"No, my lord," replied Alain, because it seemed expected of him. But he had compassion for the beast, horrible though it was; it had suffered, too, and he had killed it as much to put it out of its misery as to save Agius. "And Frater Agius—"

"Yes," said Lavastine curtly. "Frater Agius saved the king at the cost of his own life. And you, what reward would you have for saving my life?"

"I?"

"Since there is no one else here, I would suppose I mean you! When I ask a question, I wish for an answer."

"B–but I wish for no reward, my lord. I did what was right. That is reward enough in the eyes of Our Lord and Lady, is it not? But something for my family, perhaps—"

"Ah, yes. Your family. This Henri, he is—?"

"A merchant, my lord. His sister Bel is a freeholder of some distinction in Osna village."

"Yes. Near where the monastery was burned last year. What does Henri the merchant say about your parentage, Alain?"

Alain squirmed in the chair and took a sip of wine to cover his discomfiture. The wine was fine and smooth; he had never tasted anything as good before. Wine such as this did not come to the lips of common folk, not even the freeborn.

"He says—" *He says.* Alain thought, briefly, about lying. But Henri and Aunt Bel had not taught him to lie. They had treated him as kin, and it would dishonor them to twist their words now, even if the truth disgraced him before Count Lavastine. "My mother was a servant woman at your holding, my lord. My father Henri . . . had an affection for her. She was known to—" He bit at his lip. Ai, Lady, he could not simply call his mother a whore. "—to have consorted with men. She died three days after giving birth to me. The deacon gave me into Henri's care in return for his promise to offer me to the church when I turned sixteen."

"You are older than sixteen, are you not?"

"Seventeen now, my lord. I would have entered the church last year, but the monastery at Dragon's Tail—"

"—was burned. Yes. That is the whole of the story?"

"Yes, my lord."

Lavastine sat in the gloom and toyed with his cup, turning it around and around until Alain feared he would spill it. From outside, Alain heard Lavastine's captain speaking, something about Henry and Autun and the king's mercy, but even with his sharpened hearing, he could not string the phrases together into intelligible sentences. Sorrow yawned a dog's yawn, full of teeth, and threw himself against Alain's legs, leaning there until Alain was practically tipped over. He adjusted the chair, and this movement stirred the count to a decision.

"Attend, child," he said in his brisk, impatient way. "I must now tell you a tale and you must listen carefully, for this story I have never before confessed the whole of, and I will not speak it aloud again while I live."

Alain nodded and then, realizing the light was dim, managed to whisper, "Yes." The hounds snuffled and whined and grunted, eight fine black hounds, beautiful creatures, if vicious.

"I married once," said Lavastine softly. "But as all know, my wife and daughter were killed by my hounds."

"But how could that be?" asked Alain, curiosity overcoming good sense. "Or the child, at least—"

"Listen!" snapped Lavastine. "Do not interrupt." Fear, thwarted of a place at Alain's side, had gone to the entrance and nosed aside the canvas flap. By this new stream of light, Alain saw Lavastine smile grimly. "How can that be? Even I don't know the true story of how my grandfather got the hounds, whether he received them in exchange for some kind of pact—with whom, I don't know—or whether they came to him as part of his birthright. But my father— the only surviving child—inherited them in his turn, and I—also the only child who survived to adulthood—in mine. So my father arranged a marriage for me at the appropriate time so I could beget children—more than one, it was hoped—to carry on the line."

He drained the cup of wine suddenly and set the empty cup down on the carpet. "I was young, then, and I had taken a lover, a pretty girl from among the servingwomen. We often met up among the ruins, because I wanted to keep our meetings secret. But in time, as happens, she became pregnant and begged me to acknowledge the child so that she would not be branded as a common whore. But my bride was proud and covetous, and when she came to Lavas she told me she wanted no bastard child running about the hall. So I put aside the other woman and denied any knowledge of the child, and confessed my sin to the deacon, may her memory be blessed. The deacon promised to take care of the child and assured me I need trouble myself no longer. She was not even a freeborn girl." He picked up the winecup, tested it as if he had forgotten he had drunk it all, and set it down again with some annoyance. "I was not, perhaps, without fault in this matter."

Alain gulped air. He had forgotten to breathe. "Did she die? Giving birth, I mean."

Lavastine jumped up and strode to the entrance. He slapped Fear lightly on the flank and the hound retreated; the flap fell shut. "You will remain silent while I speak, Alain."

Alain nodded but Lavastine's back was to him.

"No more wine," muttered Lavastine. "Yes, she died in childbed." He turned and spoke crisply and rapidly, as if to hurry the story to its ghastly conclusion. "My bride was young, strong-willed, impatient, and argumentative. Since I was of the same disposition, we did not suit. She rarely allowed me into her bed. I refrained from taking a concubine, but I soon suspected that *she* had taken a lover. I could prove nothing because her servingwomen were loyal and helped her hide this fact. When our first child was born, I did not trust her. I did not believe the infant was my child, and yet—" He made a sharp gesture and strode back to the chair, but did not sit. "Yet it might have been. She raised the child to distrust me, though I tried to befriend it. The child was often a sweet girl, or so I could see from a distance. And with a daughter to assure the succession, my wife gave up the pretense. She forbade me her bed completely and began to flaunt a lover openly, a common man. She might as well have slapped me publicly in the face. But she said, 'what you had, a commoner in your bed, I may have as well.' She became pregnant again and I *knew* that this child was not—could not have been—mine. I demanded she put our daughter to the test, to face the hounds."

Alain gasped, then clapped a hand over his mouth. Of course, he could now see what was coming.

"She tried to run away with the child. The hounds broke loose that night."

Even the hounds were silent, as if listening. Sorrow and Rage were young, not more than three years old. Ardent and Terror were the eldest of the hounds. Had they been there that night? Had they pursued the fleeing pregnant woman and her bastard child? Had one of them been the first to catch up to the fugitives?

Lavastine spoke so softly Alain had to strain to hear him. "On her dying breath she cursed me. 'You will have no heir of your own body. Any woman you marry will die a horrible death. I swear this by the old gods who still walk abroad and whose spawn these hounds are.' The next year I did my duty and became betrothed to a young woman of good family. One week before the wedding she was drowned when her horse inexplicably collapsed while she was fording a river, on her way to our wedding feast. The year after, I married a young widow. She sickened at the feast itself and died of the flux two days later.

"I have not tried to marry again. I want no more deaths on my conscience. But now . . ."

Now? Alain said nothing, but he waited.

Lavastine crossed the carpet to stand in front of Alain's chair. The dim light made him loom above, more shadow than living man. "I began to wonder last autumn, after I returned from the campaign against the Eika raiders, but I forgot everything under the compulsion. Now, isn't it as obvious to you as it is to me?"

At first Alain did not understand what the count was trying to say. But then he realized the hounds were lying every which way about the tent, some by Alain, some by Lavastine's chair, some shifting as Lavastine moved. Alain touched the hem of his new, fine tunic, sewn with embroidered ribbon so rich even as prosperous a householder as Aunt Bel would have to trade a child in exchange for an arm's length of such an exquisite piece of fabric.

Lavastine took one of Alain's hands in his and lifted him to his feet. His mouth was set in a thin, determined line, and when he spoke, his tone allowed for no argument.

"You are my son."

5

LIATH had nightmares. Every night, the dogs came and tore at her flesh, ripping her, tearing her limb from limb. Every night she would wake, sweating, heart pounding, and bolt upright in her blanket until the cool night air washed the stain of fear from her. But it could not wash away her grief.

Then she would weep.

Always Wolfhere slept through these episodes, or pretended to be asleep. She could not tell which. She did not want to know which it was. He was deeply preoccupied, spoke only when spoken to or when it was absolutely necessary to get supplies or new mounts. Only once, in an unguarded moment, did she hear him whisper a name.

"Manfred."

They rode many days. Liath did not keep track of them. Though the skies were clear and perfect for viewing, she did not follow the course of the moon through the Houses of the Night, the world dragon that bound the heavens. She did not trace the courses of the planets through those same constellations. She did not repeat the lessons Da had taught her over and over again. She did not walk in the city of memory, so laboriously built, so carefully maintained for so many years.

She mourned and she dreamed.

Sometimes, if she chanced to stare into a hearth fire or campfire, she would get a sudden feeling she was peering through a keyhole, watching a scene that unfolded on the other side of a locked door.

There are spirits burning in the air with wings of flame and eyes as brilliant as knives. They move on the winds of aether that blow above the sphere of the Moon, and now and again their gaze falls like a blazing arrow, like the strike of lightning, to the Earth below, and there it sears anything it touches, for they cannot comprehend the frailty of Earthly life. They are of an elder race and are not so fragile. Their voices have the snap of fire and their bodies are not bodies as we know them, but the conjoining of fire and wind, the breath of the fiery Sun coalesced into mind and will.

"But are we not their cousins, then? Were we not born of fire and light? Is our place not here out beyond the sphere of the Moon, as theirs is?"

The first speaker shifts, studying the flames, for he too stares into the fire and across some doorway impossible to touch he watches Liath. He seems to know she is listening, that she can see him. But he speaks to the woman who stands out of sight in the shadows behind him.

"We are not as old as that, my child. We were not born of the very elements themselves, though they wove themselves into our shaping. We are the children of angels, but we can no longer live cast out from the Earth which gave us birth."

He lifts a hand. Liath recognizes him; he has come to be familiar to her, but he frightens her, not because he looks threatening but because he is so utterly inhuman, so unlike Da or any of the other people she knows, those few she has come to care for, even unlike Hugh, who is an abomination but a fully human one. He is Aoi, one of the Lost Ones, old, surely—such is the authority of his bearing—although he looks neither young nor old by any sign she knows how to read. He has the look of Sanglant about him. That frightens her, too, that seeing this strangely clad male reminds her bitterly of Sanglant, whom she wishes only to forget. Never to forget.

"Who are you?" he asks with simple curiosity, neither angry nor frightened, not like her. "Who are you who watches through the fire? Where have you found this gateway? How have you brought it to life?" Across his bare thighs rest the strands of flax he is twining into rope, a longer length each time she sees him through the fire. But the rope grows slowly, a finger's-breadth, a hands-breadth, while days pass for her as she and Wolfhere ride south and west, seeking King Henry.

She cannot answer him. She cannot speak through flame. She fears her voice will echo down unknown passageways and through vast hidden halls, that wind and fire will carry it to the ears of those who are listening for her, seeking her.

The sorcerer—for he must be such, to have knowledge and vision together—plucks a gold feather from the sheath that encases his right forearm and tosses it into the flames.

Liath started up, scrambling back as the fire flared up and then, abruptly, died down. She blinked back tears, streaming from smoke, and wiped her nose. Her face was hot. Behind her, the door slammed open and Wolfhere walked in from dark night outside.

She sat in the middle of a small guest house—such as the abbot granted to Eagles, not the best of his accommodations but not the worst either—at the Monastery of Hersford. The fire snapped and burned merrily, innocent of any sorcery. She might have dreamed . . . but it was no dream. When she dreamed, she dreamed of the Eika dogs.

"What did you find out?" she asked.

Wolfhere coughed and wiped his hands together, dusting something off them. "Henry and the court celebrated the Feast of St. Susannah here, but they were called away west. According to Father Bardo, Sabella raised an army and Henry had to ride west to meet her, before she entered Wendar. She removed Biscop Constance from the biscop's chair at Autun and set another woman there as biscop in her place. And took Constance prisoner, as well."

Liath set her elbow on her knee and her head on a hand. She was very tired, now, and did not much care for the troubles and intrigues of the noble lords. "Sabella would have done better to send her army against Bloodheart," she muttered.

"Well," said Wolfhere, "the great princes most often think of their own advantage, not that of others. Father Bardo does not know what happened to the king, or if it came to battle. Come now, we'll sleep and ride out at dawn."

She dreaded sleeping, but in the end her exhaustion drew her down, and down, and down . . .

. . . into the crypt at Gent, where corpses lay strewn among the pale tombs of the holy dead and the dogs fed so voraciously she could hear the cracking of bones . . .

She started awake in a cold sweat, heart racing. Ai, Lady! How much more of this must she suffer? Wolfhere slept on the other side of the fire, which lay in cold ashes, as cold as her heart. Only one wink of heat remained, a flash of gold among the gray.

Without thinking, she reached—and plucked from the dead ashes of the fire a gold feather.

6

HENRY held court in the great hall of the biscop's palace in Autun, his three children sitting on his right side, his sister Constance and other trusted counselors on his left. Earlier, in the cathedral, Biscop Constance—restored to her position—had celebrated Luciasmass, one of the four-quarters masses of the year. Rosvita knew that the mathematici gave these other names, the spring and fall equinoxes and the summer and winter solstices, but she preferred to think of them as the masses celebrating the blessed Daisan's four missionary disciples, those who carried the Holy Word to the four quarters of the Earth: Marian, Lucia, Matthias, and Candlemass, known to the old pagans as Dhearc, the dark night of the sun. This last was the feast of St. Peter the Disciple, burned alive as a sacrifice to the fire god of the Jinna when he would not recant his faith in the God of Unities.

After mass, Henry and his court had returned to the great hall where feasting would continue late into the night, for this was midsummer and the sun stayed long in the sky, celebrating the triumph of the Divine Logos, the Holy Word, and the promise it offered of the Chamber of Light.

But Henry had business to conduct. He sat beside his sister and gathered his folk together. They waited in orderly lines, crowding in from outside, more even than the people who had marched with him, for many of the more prosperous natives of Autun had also come to see the king and pledge their loyalty.

On this occasion, Henry wore his cloth-of-gold robes of state, and in his left hand he held his scepter, symbol of the king's justice, and on his right hand he wore the gold ring of sovereignty. On his silvering hair rested the heavy crown, studded with jewels. Biscop Constance blessed him and anointed him with oil blessed by the skopos herself and scented with attar of roses.

Thus was he confirmed in the eyes of his court and of the people of Autun as their king, chosen and approved by the divine wisdom of Our Lord and Lady.

"Let justice be served," said Henry to the multitudes. He called before him the heirs of Duke Rodulf.

Rosvita felt some sympathy for the young man who came forward, his retainers cowering like frightened dogs at his heels. He had none of Rodulf's bluff authority and was in any case barely past his majority. The duke had probably brought the boy along to get his first taste of war, only to have the poor child be forced to witness his father's death.

"Who are you?" Henry demanded, although he knew perfectly well who the young man was.

"I am Rodulf, son of Rodulf and Ida." The boy's color was high, and his hands trembled, but he did not disgrace himself.

"Do you speak for the heir of Varingia?"

"I—I speak for my elder sister, Yolande, who was named heir by my father five years ago."

"And where is she now?"

"A–at Arlanda Holding, the fortress built by my father." Young Rodulf bit his lip and waited. The penalty for treason was, of course, death.

"Let her present herself to me before Matthiasmass," said Henry. He extended a hand, as if beckoning, and the young man practically flung himself forward onto his knees before the king. "If she does so, I will demand these things from her in return for clemency. Fifty of Varingia's finest horses, for my stables. Gold vessels and vestments to adorn the cathedral in Autun, as recompense for the insult given Biscop Constance. A convent founded in the name of my mother, Queen Mathilda. And you, young Rodulf, with ten young noblemen of good character, to join my Dragons and protect my kingdom."

The boy began to weep. The crowd murmured, impressed by the king's justice—and his mercy. Rodulf's family was no kin of his, so he could easily have taken their lives in payment for their treachery. Rosvita nodded. This was the wiser course.

"I shall carry the message, Your Majesty," said the boy. "We shall abide loyally by your side from now on. I swear it." Constance brought forward a reliquary which contained the thighbone and a scrap of the robe once worn by St. Thomas the Apostle, and young Rodulf kissed the jeweled box and then the king's ring, to seal his oath.

"Let Biscop Antonia be brought before me," said the king.

Under heavy guard, Biscop Antonia was brought before Henry. She had her hands clasped in front of her, and she beamed as fondly on him as she might on a favored nephew.

Henry sighed. "You are under the protection of the church, Your Grace, so although you have conspired against me, I am forced to send you to Darre and let you plead your cause to the skopos herself. Let her judge your treachery."

"I have not forsworn my oath to the church, Your Majesty," said Antonia sweetly. "I doubt not the skopos will pass judgment in my favor." She was attended by only one cleric, the one known as Heribert.

Constance moved forward, looking grim. "What of your other attendants, Biscop Antonia? Half of them are dead and the rest soon to die of a disease which strikes none but them, not even the holy nuns who have ministered to them as they lay dying."

"I grieve," said Antonia, "but even I cannot interfere with the hand of Our Lord, when with His sword He cuts the thread that binds us to life."

"There are some who have accused you of sorcery," continued Constance, determined to have this out now. She did not look at Henry for permission, nor did he attempt to stop her. She was the only other person here whose spiritual rank was equal to Antonia's, and no secular power could intervene. "There are some who speak of amulets fashioned by your clerics at your order, and that their suffering is the mark of this cruel sorcery, the same sorcery that brought a *guivre* to the battleground and let Sabella's soldiers walk free of harm from its gaze while Henry's soldiers were stricken to stone."

Antonia unclasped her hands and raised them, palms up, in a gesture of innocence. "If their suffering is a mark of sorcery, and I the sorcerer who devised such amulets, then how is it I stand untouched by disease? How is it that Heribert—" Here she signed toward the young cleric who stood, as always, one step behind her. "—remains unstained as well? Many things cause disease, including evil spirits. I am sorry they are suffering, and I do what I am allowed to ease their pain, for it grieves me sorely, but what has stricken them comes from other hands than mine."

"Enough," said Henry suddenly, interrupting just as Constance took a breath to speak again. "We have gone over this a hundred times, and I no longer wish to speak of it. Biscop Antonia will be taken under guard to the skopos in Darre, there to stand trial accused of certain sorceries condemned by the church at the Council of Narvone."

Antonia was led away with her retinue of one. But even from her vantage point to the left of the king's throne, Rosvita could see no sign of fear or regret or repentance in the old biscop's expression. She looked, indeed, as angelic as an ancient faultless grandmother who has seen all her children and grandchildren grow to adulthood.

Henry sat for a long while in silence. The crowd did not grow restless; indeed, they scarcely stirred. They knew that next, surely, he would call his sister Sabella before him.

Finally, he made a sign, and young Duchess Liutgard came forward. "I will now agree to speak to the woman you hold in your custody," he said.

Liutgard gave a curt assent and glanced once up at Rosvita, as if to thank her for her part in saving Henry from rash action.

When Sabella was brought into the hall the hush was so profound that Rosvita thought she heard the barking of hounds in the distance. Perhaps she was hearing things, or perhaps some lord kept kennels nearby.

Sabella refused to kneel before her brother. Henry did not rise and go forward to greet her, nor did he extend his hand for her to kiss. Rosvita did not think Sabella would have granted him that honor, that homage, in any case.

"What do you have to say?" he asked instead, gaze jumping past her for a moment to linger on her entourage, whose expressions were certainly more contrite and fearful than hers was. A servant wiped spittle off Duke Berengar's lips. Young Tallia stood pallid in a green silk gown, looking more like a captured fawn than the princess she was.

Rosvita glanced toward the other princesses, Henry's daughters. Sapientia was, of a mercy, behaving circumspectly today, holding her temper, her tongue, and her enthusiasm in check. She sat as still as she was able and watched the proceedings with a dark and avid gaze, as if soaking it in, as if playing herself in the role of queen. The pool of stillness that surrounded Theophanu was of a colder kind; she had no expression on her face, nor did she react when each judgment was passed. Even young Ekkehard, who half the time looked as if he was about to fall asleep, had jumped and murmured in surprise at the clemency Henry had shown to Duke Rodulf's heirs. Next to these three handsome and robust children, Tallia was a colorless bloom, lost in the glare of her mother's ambitions.

"I have nothing to say," said Sabella.

Henry's wrath was evident though he did not lose himself now to his anger. "You have conspired against the rightful king of Wendar and Varre, anointed by the hand of the skopos, named by our father, Arnulf, as his heir, confirmed as such by the great princes of the realm. This is treason, and the punishment for treason is death."

A gasp from the multitudes, quickly stifled. Every soul crowded into the hall strained forward. The air itself seemed not to breathe or to allow for any breath, for even the rise and fall of a single chest might stain the clarity of sight and hearing that reigned within the hall.

"But we are kin, and you wear the gold torque of the royal house." Henry did not touch the one he wore at his neck, but Sabella—as if involuntarily—reached up to touch hers. "I will not stain my hands, nor the hands of my children, with the blood of my kin. But this I will do. This judgment I will pass."

He rose.

"Your child, Tallia, I take as my ward and remove to my custody. Your husband, Berengar, duke of Arconia, I judge unfit to rule, and I strip from him his rank as duke. He will retire to Hersford Monastery, where the holy brothers will care for him as is fitting. And you, Sabella—"

No one moved. No one spoke.

"From you also I strip the title of duchess, and from your heir I take this title, for all time. The duchy of Arconia is without a duke, and so it comes to me to dispose of this title and the authority it grants. I give it now into the hands of my sister, Constance, Biscop of Autun, and you I give into her custody, as you once held her unwillingly in yours."

The crowd could no longer restrain its astonishment. They burst into a haze of noise so loud Rosvita could scarcely hear herself think. Sapientia, echoing the crowd, leaped to her feet and a moment later, sheepishly, with her brother tugging on her sleeve, seated herself. Theophanu had not stirred, but she had a thin smile on her face.

Sabella said nothing, showed nothing except a deadly and bitter anger, but there was nothing she could do. She had gambled and she had lost. Duke—no longer duke!—Berengar was blowing his nose onto his sleeve, and at once his servingmen led him away. Poor man. He would be better taken care of in the monastery, Rosvita supposed. Tallia was crying. Tears made her fair skin blotchy and her nose red. Sabella turned and snapped angry words at her daughter, but it was too noisy for Rosvita to make them out.

What a great roar of sound there was in the hall, shouts of "Henry! King Henry!" and others, acclaiming Constance as duke and biscop—an unprecedented act, to combine the two titles in one person. But Constance was being rewarded, of course, for her constancy. And the people of Autun were clearly happy about it; they loved their biscop.

Except Rosvita could not understand why she heard the sound of hounds barking so loudly and a sudden edge to the ovation of the crowd.

"Clear the way!" someone cried.

"Out of the way!" shrieked a woman.

"Lord protect us! Devil's spawn!"

Quickly, guards hustled Sabella and her retinue aside.

Into the hall came a most astounding procession, the last fugitive, the only one unaccounted for after the battle: Count Lavastine and his famous black hounds. With him walked his captain and a finely-dressed youth caught in that twilight between boy and man.

King Henry blinked several times, but that was the only sign he gave of his astonishment. The count walked boldly forward and stopped below the king's dais. He did not kneel.

"Last year," said Lavastine, "you sent an Eagle to request my presence on your progress. I have come."

This was so brash that Henry almost laughed. But the situation was too grave for laughter.

"It is late, and the summons was long ago," said Henry, "and you rode all this way in strange company, Count Lavastine."

"So I did, Your Majesty, but not of my own will. I have witnesses to prove that another's hand controlled me and that I did not march with Lady Sabella because I wished to, but because I was compelled to."

"It is a good excuse, Count Lavastine. Indeed, an elaborate and cunning one, now that Biscop Antonia has already been accused of other condemned acts of sorcery."

These words were spoken so harshly that Rosvita expected Lavastine to respond in kind, but for once he restrained his famous irritability. "I will give sworn testimony before your clerics," said the count. "I have others who will bear witness in my favor including, I hope, my kinsman Lord Geoffrey, whom I treated very badly while under this compulsion."

"Your testimony will be sent south with the party who accompanies Biscop Antonia to the skopos," said Henry. "But I will tell you truly, Count Lavastine, that I know you withdrew your forces from the field of battle while the tide still flowed in Sabella's favor. This will tell in your favor, when I come to pass judgment on you. But tell me, we all thought you had escaped. Why do you come before us now? I know you have no love for me."

"I am not a conspirator, Your Majesty, and I intend to clear myself of these charges. I have nothing to hide. But I do have a boon to ask of you."

"Ah," said Henry.

"Ah," whispered Theophanu, her mouth parting slightly as she leaned forward, intent now.

"He wants something," murmured Sapientia wisely to Ekkehard. "That is why he has come here now when he could have escaped back to his own lands."

"Hush," said Constance.

The crowd quieted. There was a great rustling of cloth as people shifted position. The hounds that sat in attendance on Lavastine— the only retinue he needed—growled. One rose up and bared its teeth at an importunate lord who inched too close.

That was when the strange thing happened. Count Lavastine did not move. His captain, of course, got a brief sick look on his face. It was well known that Lavastine must be a fine and generous lord to command the loyalty of so many good servants and soldiers, since they were any of them at any time likely to be rended limb from body by the black hounds.

But the *youth* spoke a quiet word, and the hounds subsided.

"Kneel before the king," said Lavastine, and the boy came forward obediently and knelt. He was tall, lanky, with black hair and amazingly clear eyes; he was not precisely handsome or elegant, but Rosvita found that it cheered her heart in some inexplicable way to look upon him.

"You know I am twice widowed and without an heir," said Lavastine, "and unlikely to get one now, for reasons I have long since confessed and done penance for. So I come before you, Your Majesty, to ask this of you. That this youth, my bastard child Alain, be recognized as my heir so he may inherit my title and my lands when I am dead.''

Lady above! Rosvita's knees almost gave out from under her. She turned her gaze to study Henry's expression. Indeed, by the crawling feeling she had on her shoulders and her back, everyone looked at Henry. His children—his three legitimate children—stared fiercely at him. Constance had laid the back of a hand against her cheek, and her eyes were closed.

In the silent hall, a laugh rang out.

"What will you do?" cried Sabella mockingly. "What will you do, brother? Make one bastard a count, and the other one a king?"

Henry made a sharp and angry sign with his right hand. The guards escorted Sabella out of the hall and back to the tower where she was being held prisoner.

Henry took one step down from the dais and laid his ringed hand on the boy's head. He met Lavastine's gaze, and the two men remained locked that way for some moments.

"Many a lord might claim a bastard so as not to lose their lands to an unloved kinsman. How can you prove this?"

"My deacons keep careful records of all the births and deaths at Lavas Holding, but I believe you need no better proof than this." Lavastine whistled.

The hounds swarmed forward, and even Henry stepped quickly back up onto the dais. The youth started up, eyes wide, and called the hounds to order. Like so many meek retainers, they obeyed him instantly and threw themselves at his feet. When Henry took a step forward, they growled.

The boy snapped his fingers and chased them back to a safe distance away from the king.

"What of you, child?" the king said, looking finally at the youth. "What is your name?"

"I am called Alain, Your Majesty." He had a clear voice, and he did not falter in his words, nor did he speak coarsely, as a low-born boy would have.

"Is it true?"

He bowed his head modestly. "Count Lavastine has acknowledged me as his son."

"What do you know of your birth?"

"I was born in Lavas Holding to an unmarried woman who died three days after I was born. I was raised by freeholders in Osna village and promised to the church. But—" He related quickly a story of Eika and a burned monastery. "So I came to Lavas Holding to serve for a year."

"And saved my life," interrupted Lavastine, who had been tapping his feet impatiently throughout this recital, "and freed me from the compulsion laid on me by sorcery. I was not the first to suggest the connection, indeed, Your Majesty. Frater Agius, who served at my holding, mentioned the matter to me some months ago, but I was hesitant to believe him."

Constance lowered her hand from her face.

Henry blinked several more times and raised a hand to his lips. "This is the youth who killed the *guivre*, then!" he exclaimed. "Many stories were told of what happened that day, but we searched and none could find the man who saved my kingdom. Come, child, kiss my hand."

Alain glanced back at Lavastine—at his father—and then knelt before the king and was granted the signal honor of being allowed to kiss his hand.

"This cannot go unrewarded," said Henry. He had gained in spirits since the bitter confrontation with his sister. Indeed, he appeared almost elated.

Rosvita had a sudden feeling that Henry was about to commit an act whose repercussions would haunt him for a long, long time. She stepped forward, raised a hand to gain the king's attention—but it was too late.

"By my power as king of Wendar and Varre and by the right of law recorded in a capitulary from the time of Emperor Taillefer, I grant you, Lavastine, Count of Lavas, the right to name this youth as the heir of your blood, though he is not born of a legitimate union. He may succeed to your title and to the authority vested in that title over your lands. Let my words become law. Let them be recorded in writing."

Ai, Lady. Everyone knew what this meant, why Henry's expression was so triumphant. He had made his choice. Now it remained only to see it through. Sapientia started to her feet so suddenly her chair tipped over; she began to speak, stopped herself, and bolted from the hall instead. Ekkehard gaped. Theophanu raised one expressive eyebrow but made no other sign.

"Henry," muttered Constance softly enough that no one but Rosvita and the handful of others crowded onto the dais could hear her, "do you know what you are doing?"

"I know what I am doing," said Henry. "And it is past time I did it. Long past time. *He* is the only one I can trust to take my place as sovereign king when I take my leave of this Earth and pass up through the spheres to the Chamber of Light."

Constance drew the Circle at her breast to avert ill omen.

"No one," proclaimed Henry, louder now, "and no argument, can sway me from this course."

From the doors came a shout.

"Eagles! Make way for Eagles!"

They came in haste, two of them, travel-worn and weary. One was young and startlingly dark, as if a summer's sun had burned her so brown her skin had stayed that way. She bore a touch of summer's brightness with her still, so much that the eye lingered on her.

The other was Wolfhere, who had been banned from Henry's presence and Henry's court many years ago. But he strode forward with no sign that he remembered—or chose to obey—that ban. The young woman looked riven by sorrow, the strong lines of her face set in a mask of wretchedness and hopeless longing. Wolfhere looked grim. Behind her, Rosvita heard the two Eagles, Hathui and her young companion, gasp out loud.

"No," murmured Hathui to the younger one. "Do not go forward. We must wait our turn."

"She's wearing an Eagle's badge," whispered the younger one. She sounded ready to burst into tears.

"Ai, Lady," swore Hathui. "Look at their faces." And was silent.

The two new Eagles paused before the dais.

"Why have you come before me," demanded the king, "when you know you are forbidden my presence?"

"We come from Gent," said Wolfhere, "and we bear grievous news. Gent has fallen to an Eika assault, and the Dragons have been wiped out, every one. Prince Sanglant is dead."

"Lady," breathed Henry, clapping a hand to his chest. He spoke no other word. He could not speak.

Rosvita saw at once he was paralyzed by this terrible, terrible news. And because someone must act, she did so, though she felt as if someone else was acting, not her. She went to him and took his arm. Almost collapsed herself, because his whole weight fell on her and he appeared so close to fainting that it was only with the aid of the Eagle, Hathui, that she got him out of the hall and into the private chapel that opened onto a garden behind it.

There, he threw himself onto the stone floor in front of the Hearth, in his gold robes, heedless of the crown tumbling to the floor, heedless of his scepter, which slipped from nerveless fingers. He groped at his chest and drew from next to his skin an old scrap of cloth stained a rusty red.

He could not weep—not as the king must weep, easily and to show his sympathy for those of his people who suffer. This pain was far too deep for tears.

"My heart," he murmured into the unyielding stone, "my heart is torn from me." He pressed the cloth to his lips.

Hathui wept to see him.

Rosvita drew the Circle at her breast and then she knelt before the Hearth, beside the prostrate king, and began to chant the prayer for dead souls.

7

AFTER the hall was cleared and she and Wolfhere given bread and mead, after some hushed consultation between various noble lords and ladies whose names she did not know and whose faces all blurred into a single unrecognizable one, Liath was escorted to a small chapel.

Wolfhere did not come with her. Indeed, she saw they prevented him and led him away by another hall. A fine proud woman in biscop's vestments brought her before the king, who sat on a bench, no longer in his fine robes and regalia. He was held upright by a cleric and several other attendants, one of whom wiped his face repeatedly with a damp cloth. Liath knelt before him. His right hand clutched an old bloodstained rag.

"Tell me," he said hoarsely.

She wanted to beg him not to make her tell, not to relive the fall of Gent. Not again, Lady, please. But she could not. She was an Eagle, the king's eyes, and it was her duty to tell him everything.

Not everything. Some things she could not—and would not—tell anyone: Sanglant's face close to hers, the light in his eyes, the grim set of his mouth, the bitter irony in his voice when he told her, "*Make no marriage.*" The feel of his skin when she had touched him, unbidden, on the cheek. No, not that. Those were her memories and not to be shared with anyone else. No one need know she loved him. No one would ever know, not even Sanglant. Especially not Sanglant.

Telling the story would be like living through it again. But she had no choice. They all watched her, waiting. Among the crowd stood Hathui, and the Eagle nodded, once, briskly, at her. That gesture gave her courage. She cleared her throat and began.

Barely, barely she managed to get the words out. Terrible it was to be the bringer of this baleful news, and worse still to relate the story with the king staring at her as if he hated her, for whom else could he hate?

She did not blame him. She would have hated herself too, did hate herself in a way for living when so many had died. At last she stumbled to a halt, having spoken the last and most damning part of the tale, the vision seen through fire. She expected them to question her closely, perhaps to lead her away in chains as a sorcerer. The king lifted a hand weakly, half a gesture. It was all he could manage.

"Come," said the biscop. She led Liath away. Outside, she stopped with her under the arched loggia that opened out into a pretty garden, lilies and roses and brash marigolds. "You are Wolfhere's discipla?" she asked, using the Dariyan word.

"I—? No. I don't know. I am newly come to the Eagles, just after Mariansmass."

"Yet you already wear the Eagle's badge."

Liath covered her eyes with a hand, briefly, stifling tears.

"What you saw in the fire," said the biscop, going on in what she perhaps meant to be a gentler voice, "is known to us as one of the arts by which certain Eagles can see. Do not fear, child. Not all sorcery is condemned by the church. Only that which is harmful."

Liath risked raising her head. The biscop was quite a young woman, really, pale and elegant in her fine vestments and tasseled biscop's mitre.

"You are Constance!" exclaimed Liath, remembering the lineages Da had taught her. "Biscop of Autun."

"So I am," said Biscop Constance. "And I am evidently now Duchess of Arconia, too." She said this with a hint of irony, or perhaps sadness. "Where were you educated, child?"

"My Da taught me," said Liath, now cursing the fate that had separated her from Wolfhere. She did not have the strength to fend off pointed questioning of her past and her gifts, and certainly not from a noblewoman of Constance's education and high rank. "Begging your pardon, Your Grace. I am very tired. We have ridden so far, and so quickly, and—" Almost the sob got out, but she choked it back.

"And you have lost someone who is dear to you," said the biscop, and in her own face Liath saw a sudden and surprising compassion. "One of my clerics will show you to the barracks, where the Eagles take their rest."

A cleric led her to the stables. There she found herself alone in a loft above the stalls. Shutters had been thrown open, admitting the last of the daylight. She flung herself down on the hay, then rose again, wiping her nose, and paced. It was as if, reciting the awful tale, she had passed some of her numbing grief off onto King Henry. Now she was too restless to rest. Grooms murmured below. She was utterly alone.

For the first time in months, for the first time since Hugh had taught her the rudiments of Arethousan—all those damned impossible verbs!—she was alone.

Carefully, she lifted *The Book of Secrets* out of her saddlebags and unwrapped it. She opened it to the central text, that ancient, fragile papyrus, dry under her skin as she ran a finger along the line of text, written in a language she did not recognize but glossed here and there in Arethousan. The Arethousan letters were still strange to her, but as she concentrated, opening doors in her city of memory, finding the hall where she had stored her memory of the Arethousan alphabet, she could transpose them in her mind into the more familiar Dariyan letters and thus form words, some of which she had learned from Hugh, most of which were meaningless to her.

At the very top of the page, above the actual text, was written a single word in Arethousan: *krypte*.

"Hide this," she whispered and felt a sudden, sharp pain in her chest. *Hide this*.

She put a hand over her mouth, breathed in, calming herself, and then studied the text beneath. The letters that made up the text were totally foreign to her, unlike Arethousan letters, unlike the more common Dariyan letters; perhaps, faintly, they resembled the curling grace of Jinna letters although these had a squarer profile. She could not read them nor even imagine what language this was.

But a different hand had glossed the first long sentence with Arethousan words beneath, translating it; only that first sentence had been glossed completely. On the other pages brief glosses appeared here and there, a commentary on the text. But this sentence, at least, she could read part of. Perhaps it gave a clue as to the subject of the text. Perhaps that had been the scribe's intent in translating that entire first sentence.

Painstakingly, pausing now and again to listen for the movements of the grooms below, she sounded out the first sentence.

Polloi epekheirēsan anataxafthai diēgesink peri tōn peplērophorēmenōn en hēmin teratōn, edoxe kamoi parēkolouthēkoti anōthen pasin ak-

ribōs kathexēs, soi grapsai, kratista Theophile, hina epignōis peri hōn
katēkhēthēs logōn tēn asphaleian.

The light was getting dim, too dim for anyone to read—except
someone who had salamander eyes.

"Many people . . ." she whispered, knowing the first word, and
then skipped words until she found another word she knew and
here she stopped short, heart pounding, breath tight in her throat.
". . . about magical omens . . ." She skipped back to the pluperfect
verb, such an odd form that Hugh had taken pains to point out the
form to her. ". . . magical omens which have been fulfilled among
us. It seemed good to me . . ." Here again followed words she did
not know, and then, again and suddenly, one she did. ". . . all the
things from the heavens . . . to you to write about . . ." She shut
her eyes, so filled with commingled horror and stark excitement
that for a moment she thought her emotions would rend her in two
like the Eika dogs. "Theophilus." That was a man's name. ". . . so
that you may know about these—these words? These *spells?*"
Could it be spells? ". . . in which you have been instructed by word
of mouth . . ." The last word she did not know.

Her hands shook. Her breath came in gasps. *All the things from
the heavens.*

She heard voices below. Hastily she bundled up the book and
stuck it away into her saddlebags just as people came up the ladder.
It was Wolfhere and Hathui.

Hanna was with them. All the excitement, all the grief, all the
days of longing and hope and sorrow, overwhelmed Liath. She
threw herself into Hanna's arms and both of them burst into
wrenching sobs, the release of so many weeks of tension and fear.

"We must pray for Manfred's soul," Wolfhere said. He wiped a
tear from his seamed face. They knelt together and prayed.

Afterward Wolfhere rose and paced. "I would give you Manfred's
badge, if I could, Hanna," he said. "Though you did not see him die,
you rode with him, and that counts for the same. You have in any
case earned it twice over." He sighed. "But it is now beyond recov-
ery. Will you wait? I will commission a new one to be made."

Hanna held tightly to Liath and Hathui, still holding their hands,
and she nodded gravely.

"So will it be done," said Wolfhere.

"I must return to the king," said Hathui. She left.

"It is late, and we have ridden far and all suffered much," said Wolfhere to the other two. "Let us rest."

Liath found herself a pallet on which to sleep, a richer bed than any she had lain in since—

Hugh.

No. She was safe now. She need fear him no longer.

She set her sword, her good friend, beside her. Reached into the bowcase to touch the wood and horn of her bow, *Seeker of Hearts.* Last, she settled her saddlebags next to her body. She felt the book like balm against her soul and, nestled against it, hidden as well, the gold feather; she had hope now that she might in time puzzle out the secret of the inner text.

For the first instant she feared sleeping, but she was so very very tired she could no longer fight it off.

Hanna lay down beside her and put her arms around her. "I thought you were dead," she whispered. "Oh, Liath, I am so glad you are alive."

Liath kissed her on the cheek and wiped the last tear from her face. There was nothing more she could do, not now, except to rest and pray that her path would seem clearer in the morning. There was so much she had to learn and so much she must discover about herself, about the book, all the things Da had hidden from her for all these years.

krypte. "Hide this."

"*Trust no one.*" Da had not meant to leave her alone. He had meant to protect her, for as long as he could.

"I love you, Da," she whispered.

Sleeping in her friend's embrace, she did not dream.

8

HENRY would not leave the chapel, or perhaps he simply could not. At last, with the efforts of several servants, he was taken to the bedchamber set aside for his use. There he lay silent and un-moving on the bed, not because he slept but because he did not have the strength to stand or to kneel or—even—to mourn. His children came in, Theophanu shepherding a trembling Ekkehard. No tears stained Theophanu's face, but she was pale. Sapientia was sobbing noisily. As a girl, Rosvita recalled, Sapientia had idolized Sanglant, had followed him like a puppy even to the point of being annoying, but Sanglant had never lost his temper with her—not that he had had much of a temper, being in all things a tractable child. It might be that Sapientia truly mourned him, despite her jealousy at her father's preference for the bastard over the eldest legitimate child. Rosvita had never observed that Sapientia was capable of duplicity.

Margrave Judith appeared in the doorway, spoke to a servant, and was ushered inside. She walked over to Rosvita. "News from Kassel," Judith murmured, eyeing the king with interest and—perhaps—pity. "Helmut Villam has taken a turn for the better. It appears he will live."

Roused by this whispering, Henry pushed himself up, though it was clearly exhausting for him to move at all. His face was graven with sorrow; he had aged ten years in one hour.

"Is it Villam you speak of?" he said. "What news?"

"He will live," said Rosvita in a calm voice, which was surely what the king needed at this deperate time rather than more hys-teria.

Sapientia caught in a sob and let it out, bursting into a new stream of tears.

Henry shut his eyes. Slowly, he lifted a hand, the cloth, to his face. He murmured something, a word. No, it was a name: "Alia."

The touch of the old rag appeared to give him strength. "I want him gone!" he said. "Gone! Out of my sight. Send him south to Darre with the escort for Biscop Antonia."

"Whom, Your Majesty?"

"Wolfhere! But keep the other one here, the one who also witnessed. Where is Hathui?"

She stepped out from the shadow by the doorway. "I am here, Your Majesty."

"You will stay by my side," he ordered.

"Yes, Your Majesty."

"It is time," he continued. His voice broke on the words, and yet none there would have mistaken him for anyone but the king. "Sapientia." Startled, the young woman flung herself to her knees and clutched at the bedcovers, bowing her head. Henry reached out but did not quite touch her hair. This mark of affection he could not quite—not now, not ever, perhaps—bring himself to show for her. "You will ride out in the morning on your heir's progress."

Her sobs ceased. She began to speak.

He turned his back on her. "Go," he said, the word muffled by the cloth in which he buried his face.

Rosvita began to move forward, to lead Sapientia away before she did something foolish, but Judith forestalled her. "Let me," said the margrave. "I will see she is outfitted and sent properly on her way."

"Thank you," murmured Rosvita.

The margrave led Sapientia from the room. The servants hovered nervously, but Henry did not move. He had done what was necessary. He had done what should have been done months ago, but she was not about to tell him that now. Sanglant was a brave man and a good soul—half human though it was—but he was not meant to be king. She sighed, heartfelt. The servants brought water and cloth to bathe the king's face.

Theophanu glanced toward Rosvita and asked a question with her expression. Rosvita shook her head. Better to take the living children away so as not to remind him of the dead one. With a slight nod, Theophanu led Ekkehard out of the chamber.

Henry did not respond, not when his servants offered him wine, not when they bathed his face. He was as stone, lost to the world. Together with the Eagle, Rosvita stood vigil beside him long into the dark night.

9

ALAIN could not sleep. The bed he had been given was too soft and too warm and too comfortable. He just could not sleep. The hounds snored softly. Count Lavastine snored, too, in a hushed counterpoint to the hounds. Unlike most noblemen, Lavastine did not sleep in a room with his servants; no one dared sleep within range of the unchained hounds. Perhaps it was the very lack of bodies that made Alain keep starting awake. He had never slept so *privately* before. In Aunt Bel's longhouse there were full thirty people sleeping at night, and in the stables—

Not my Aunt Bel any longer.

He sat bolt upright for perhaps the tenth time, and Sorrow woke and whined softly, seeking his hand and licking it.

Lavastine's heir. This in his wildest dreams he had never imagined. He knew at that moment he would sleep no more this night, so he rose and dressed quietly and slipped outside, Sorrow at his heels. Rage slept peacefully and did not stir.

Outside, a servant woke instantly. "My lord, may I escort you?"

How quickly they changed their treatment of him. But he was Lavastine's heir now, sealed by the king's own words. He would control their fates and their families in ten or twenty years. He knew better, from serving in a lord's household, than to try to go anywhere alone. It would never be allowed.

"Is there a chapel nearby?" he asked. "I wish to pray."

One of the biscop's clerics was found and Alain was escorted to a tiny chapel whose Hearth bore a fine jeweled reliquary box sitting in muted splendor on the polished wood of the altar. The chapel was not empty. A servant girl knelt on the stone before the Hearth, polishing the pavement with her own skirts.

In the next instant, just before she looked up, like a mouse caught in the act of nibbling at the cheese, he recognized her.

"My lady!" he said, aghast to find Tallia on her knees on the stone wiping the flagstone with her fine silk skirts. Her hands were red, rubbed almost raw by the unaccustomed work.

She stared at him, eyes wide and frightened. "I pray you," she said in a whisper, "do not send me away. Let me unburden myself before Our Lady in this fashion, by the work of my hands, though it is unworthy of Her regard."

"But surely you do not wish to ruin that fine cloth?" Alain could just imagine what Aunt Bel would say if she saw silk of that quality being used to sweep floors, however holy.

"The riches of Earth are as dust to the glory of the heavens and the Chamber of Light. So did Frater Agius preach."

"You heard Agius preach?"

"Did you not hear him as well?" she asked timidly. She came forward, still on her knees, and clasped Alain's hands in hers, almost in supplication. "You were his companion. He saw that you were of noble birth before any other did, is that not true? Was his vision not a gift to him from the Lady Herself? Did he not preach the true Word of the blessed Daisan's sacrifice and redemption?"

"That is heresy," Alain whispered, glancing around, but they remained alone in the chapel. Sorrow sat panting by the door, and no man dared enter because of him.

"It is not heresy," she finished, her pale face taking color as she took heart from whatever memory she had of Agius' preaching. "You must acknowledge it. You heard him. You must know it is the truth."

"I—" It made him deeply uncomfortable to have a princess who wore the gold torque marking her royal kinship kneeling in front of him—and speaking of heresy, in a biscop's palace. "You must rise, Princess." He tried to tug her to her feet, but she was either stronger than she looked or holding fast to her purpose. Her hands were warm on his, warming his, and he looked into her face and did not understand what he saw there.

"I pray King Henry will put me in the church," she said, staring up at Alain.

Or marry her to me. The thought popped unbidden into Alain's mind. He was so stricken by it that he let go of her hands and sat down on the nearest bench. Ai, blessed Lord and Lady. He was a lord, now, heir to the count of Lavas. He could think about marriage.

"Then, when I am made deacon, I will preach," she said in a fierce whisper. "I will preach the Holy Word Agius taught me, though the skopos calls it heresy. If they condemn me for it, then I will be a martyr, as he was, and ascend to the Chamber of Light where the saints and the martyrs live in the blazing light of Our Lady's gaze and Her Son's sweet glory."

Alain almost laughed, not at her but at the strange path that had brought him here to this chapel on this night.

Serve me, the Lady of Battles had said, and she had given to him a blood-red rose as her token, as the sign of her favor. He had served, as well as he was able. He had ridden to war. He had broken the compulsion laid by sorcery on Lavastine, and he had killed the *guivre*, though only because of Agius' sacrifice. He had tried always to do what was right, though sometimes he had failed. He had not saved Lackling, but he had saved the Eika prince, although perhaps the life of the savage had not been worth the life of the poor simple boy. But it was not his place to judge the worth of their souls.

And Alain knew that although he had been raised from freeholder's son to count's heir, a huge leap in the world of men, such fortune could only have come about because of the presence of divine favor.

"Come, Tallia," he said, bold enough to use her name and hoping he would not be judged proud and insolent for doing so. "It is not fitting that you kneel. Sit beside me, I pray you." He gave her his hand and helped her up and, after a hesitation, she deigned to sit beside him on the bench.

She glanced past him toward the door and shuddered.

"What is wrong?"

"The hound. It scares me."

"I won't let it hurt you." He snapped his fingers. "Sorrow, come, boy." Sorrow padded dutifully over to him, and as if pulled along behind it on a string, his distraught servant crept into the chapel where he could observe safely, from a distance. Tallia shrank back from the hound's massive presence, but he bade the hound sit and then he took her hand in his and, whispering softly, let her touch the hound's head. "You see," he said, "they are like any soul that wishes only to be touched with compassion and not with hatred or fear."

"You are very wise," said Tallia, but after a moment she withdrew her hand from Sorrow, though the hound made no move to snap or growl at her, obedient to Alain's command.

Alain smiled wryly. "I'm not wise. I'm only repeating what my fa—" But Henri was not his father. Lavastine was his father. Yet at this moment it did not truly matter. Henri had raised him as well as he was able. "I'm only repeating what others have taught me."

There was a sudden flurry of movement by the door. Rage bounded in, followed by Lavastine. Tallia shrank away, but Rage sat down firmly on Alain's slippered feet, as if to make sure he did not run, and ignored the girl.

Lavastine ran a hand through rumpled hair and glared at Alain. "What do you mean by this?" he demanded.

"I—my lord—I—"

"Well! Out with it!"

"I couldn't sleep. I just came here—" He gestured, half terrified that he had offended Lavastine, half confused by the expression on Lavastine's face, which he could not interpret.

Lavastine caught himself and made a simple bow. "Princess Tallia. I beg your pardon." He called to a servant. "Escort the princess back to her chamber."

Given no choice, Tallia left, but she cast one look—pleading or grateful, Alain could not tell—back at Alain before she was led away.

"She's in disgrace now," said Lavastine, sitting down on the bench beside Alain and absently letting Sorrow chew on his hand. "And her mother certainly is." He rubbed his beard, then fingered the silver Circle that hung at his chest on a gold chain. "Henry might be willing to marry her off, if the right bargain was offered. Any lineage is strengthened by royal blood." He stared at the Hearth for some moments longer, though he was obviously not viewing the fine reliquary or meditating on its holy contents. Then he shook himself, this stillness as much as he could muster in the course of one day. "Come, lad. It is almost dawn, did you not know?"

Alain had not noticed, but now through the glass he saw the faint glamour of light. He shook his head.

"I had a terrible fright when I woke and you weren't in the room. I thought I'd dreamed it all, the Eika prince, Sabella, the campaign, and you, my son." Lavastine stood and beckoned to the servants. "Go on, then! I see no reason to wait. Henry has pardoned us and I for one do not intend to wait in this dark palace and intrude on his grief. Nor remind him of what I have gained that he has lost." He took hold of Alain, his hand closing over Alain's wrist as if he meant never to let go of him.

"Come, *son*," he said, relishing the sound of the word on his tongue.

"Where are we going?" asked Alain. Beyond, through the glass windows of the chapel, he saw now the enclosed garden, its flowers and hedges rising from the gloom into the light of a new and fine day. Distantly, he heard a woman's voice intoning the mass for the dead.

Lavastine smiled. "We're riding home."

EPILOGUE

AT first he did not realize he was still alive. Caught in the middle of a waking sleep, his mind awake but his limbs as leaden as a corpse's, he became aware he rested half on cold flagstone and half on another body. His spine was aflame with agonizing pain, but even as it flared through him it began to dull down into a throbbing ache.

He could not quite manage to open his eyes. But he knew he was surrounded by bodies, strewn about him like so much refuse. Some few were still alive. He heard the muffled thunder of their heartbeats, felt their shallow breathing on the air, though he did not touch them. The body he lay on was, certainly, dead, but only recently so. Warmth pooled out from it, turning cold as he fought into full wakefulness.

It was so hard to wake up. And perhaps better not to.

No. Never let it be said that he did not fight until his last breath.

He heard the snuffling of the dogs. He began, then, to be consumed by dread: that the dogs would reach him before he could move and defend himself against them. There were few worse fates than being torn to pieces by dogs, like some dumb passive beast caught outside the stable.

He heard their growls and the way they shoved their muzzles against cloth and skin and metal, smelling for the ones who still lived. He heard the low rumble of voices, farther away, speaking words he did not know but in a guttural language he recognized— that of the Eika savages. Now and again these unseen speakers laughed. Now and again the dogs barked in triumph, and then he would hear a man's grunt or a scream, cut off, and then he would hear—and now he cursed his keen hearing—the flow of blood and the rending of flesh from bone. Once he recognized, however briefly, the voice of one of his own men.

Still he could not move.

A nose nudged his slack left hand and a hard fang traced up the sleeve of his mail shirt. The dog growled. Its hot breath, rank with fresh blood, touched his cheek.

He struck.

Miraculously, he twitched. His right hand moved. And then, throwing himself on his side, he slammed his mailed glove into the dog's muzzle. It staggered back, and he shoved himself up. He had gotten to his knees when two more dogs hit him, snarling and biting, from behind. He threw one of them bodily over his head and jabbed his elbow into the ribs of the other, groped at his belt for his knife but found no weapon.

His left hand had lost its glove. One of the dogs caught it and sank teeth into flesh. He hammered the creature's jaw down onto the stone floor. Stabs of pain lanced up his left arm, but he pried the beast's mouth off his hand, heaved up its stunned body, and threw it at the other two.

Now more came and more yet. They closed in, circling. He waited, panting, and licked the blood from his mangled hand.

One jumped in and snapped at his mail shirt. He swung and struck it, and it leaped back, but now behind him another broke in and nipped at his heel. He kicked. It yelped and bolted back.

He spun, staring them down. But they were only waiting, only testing him, to see how quick, how strong, how determined he was.

Beyond the dogs he caught sight of other shapes, but this fight—with the dogs—was to the death, and he did not have time to look. He had no helmet, no tabard, no protection on his bleeding and torn left hand, but he still had a mail glove on his right hand and the good mail shirt covering his torso and upper arms. He still had the dogs themselves, and though they were terrible to look upon—eyes sparking fire and tongues hanging out, saliva dripping from their fangs—they were yet mindless rage-filled beasts and he was smarter than they were.

He backed up, stepping and stumbling over the dead, found a wall at last, and with this at his back he stared them down. A few sat down on their haunches and growled, unsure now. He singled out the biggest and ugliest one and darted out before any of the dogs could leap in upon him, grabbed the beast with a hand on each side of its thick neck, and with every ounce of strength he possessed swung it round and smashed it against the wall. It fell, limp, to the ground.

They erupted into a deafening chorus of howls and swarmed him, all leaping in at once. Their weight carried him down until he was trapped under their bodies, his arms and legs pinned. He was helpless. He was, at last, going to die.

One—the biggest yet—fought through the pack to stand over his chest. Its head loomed over his face, its great muzzle yawning wide as it howled its triumph before the death strike.

And he saw his chance.

It bit down—he slammed his head up under its jaw and lunged for the creature's throat. Clamped down.

Ai, Lady. He could not rip its throat out, but, by the Lord, he could crush its windpipe until it suffocated. The big dog thrashed above him as he bit down. Its iron-gray hide tasted like metal. Blood leaked down his own throat. Its paws scrabbled at him, slowed, and then went lax. He felt the windpipe crack and, finally, jaw aching, he dared let go.

The beast collapsed on top of him.

The other dogs, worrying at his arms and legs, backed away. They snarled at him as he struggled to his feet. He spit out hair from his mouth and wiped his teeth. He ached everywhere. But he had killed it.

Movement coursed through the lofty space, and just before the Eika came, he finally realized that he stood in the great cathedral of Gent. Had they dragged every one of his Dragons in here? He did not even know how much time had passed since the fall of Gent. It could have been an hour or a day, or perhaps the enchanter had other spells surpassing even his illusions by which he could change the course of the stars.

"What have we here?" A huge Eika moved into his line of sight, shoving dogs aside, striking them back with his clawed hands.

"Bloodheart," he whispered, because he had long since learned to mark his enemy by name.

The Eika enchanter laughed, a rasping sound like a file sharpening iron. "A prince among the dogs! This is a fine prize to have in my pack. Better even than this—" And Bloodheart tapped his left arm. There, wrapped around his upper arm like an armlet, Bloodheart had fixed the gold torque that signified royal kinship.

Sanglant could not help himself. He growled, low in his throat, to see his father's gift to him made mock of in this way. He sprang forward and flung himself on the Eika chieftain.

Bloodheart was strong, but Sanglant was faster, and he had already marked with his gaze the sheath that held Bloodheart's dagger. He found the hilt, wrenched it free, and with Bloodheart reeling backward, plunged the dagger into that hard skin, through it, up to the gold and jeweled hilt, right into the Eika's heart.

Bloodheart threw back his head and howled in pain. Then he grabbed Sanglant by the neck and shook him free and threw him hard to the floor. The dogs swarmed forward, but Sanglant struck wildly around with his fists and his hopeless fury drove them back. That fury was a companion when all his other companions were dead or dying. The dogs sat again—except for two more who lay still—and with saliva rolling down their tongues they stared at him, ringing him so he could not move without coming within range of their teeth.

With a grunt, Bloodheart yanked the dagger out of his chest. He cursed and spit toward Sanglant, then laughed, that awful rasping sound. He handed the dagger to a small Eika who was naked except for a dirty cloth tied over his loins, a wizened creature made grotesque by the strange patterns painted on his body, by the sight of his body, so like a man's body except for the sheen of scales that was his skin. The small Eika spit on the blade and licked it clean. The blood hissed and bubbled, and then the small Eika pressed the blade against the wound on Bloodheart's chest and with some unseen sorcery burned the gash closed.

Sanglant winced at the acrid scent, but that wince sent a dog nipping forward toward his legs. He cuffed it hard, almost absently, and it whined and slunk back. He stared as the knife was lifted to reveal a thin white scar on the bronze sheen of the enchanter's hide.

"You'll have to do better than that," Bloodheart said, taking in a deep breath and puffing his chest up. The girdle of tiny gold links, interlaced into a skirt of surpassing beauty and delicacy, shifted around his hips and thighs as he moved, a dainty sound quite at odds with his bone-white hair and the blood that spattered his arms and knees and the one last streak of blood that trailed down his bare chest.

He grunted, grabbed the biggest of the dead dogs, and dragged it backward. Then, looking again at Sanglant, he bared his teeth; jewels winked there, tiny emeralds and rubies and sapphires. "You'll not kill me that way, prince of dogs. I do not keep my heart in my body."

Sanglant felt a warm trickle running past his right eye. Only now did he feel the gash, whether opened by Bloodheart's claws or one of the dogs he could not know; he did not remember getting it. He only hoped it would not bleed too profusely and obscure his vision.

Several of the Eika warriors came forward now, grunting and pointing, rasping out words in their harsh language. He could guess what they said: "Shall we kill him now? May I have the honor?"

He braced himself. He would go down hard and take at least one with him, in payment for what the Eika had done to his beloved Dragons. There was nothing else he could do for them now. Under the voices of the muttering Eika he heard no faint breathing, no catch of air in a throat, no gasp of a loved one's name. He risked one look, then, swept his eyes across the vast nave of the cathedral. Light shone in through the huge glass windows, cutting light into a hundred shafts that splintered out across the carnage within.

There was Sturm, his company heaped around him in death as they had been in life. There was Adela, a woman as fierce in her own way as the Eika were in theirs, but she was dead and—he had to look away—ravaged by the dogs. There, where he had come to his senses, lay the Eagle, poor brave soul, who had stood with them to the bitter end. Dead now, every single one of them. Why did he still live?

With his other senses he remained painfully aware of each least shifting of the pack of dogs as they twitched their shoulders or shifted their flanks or closed their mouths and then opened them again to bare teeth, a threatening smile much like Bloodheart's. Better to go down fighting against men, even if they were Eika, than to be thrown to the dogs. There was no honor among the dogs.

"Shall we kill him?" the Eika warriors demanded, or so he supposed by the way they pointed at him and hefted their axes and spears, eager to swarm him and bring him down, the last, the prize of the battle.

"Nay, nay," said Bloodheart in the tongue of Wendish men. "It is our own way, is it not? See how the dogs obey him. See how they wait, knowing he is stronger and smarter than they are. He is First Brother among the pack, now, our prince. He has earned that right." He leaned down and unfastened from around the neck of the dead dog its iron collar. Rising, he barked out words in his own language.

The Eika soldiers laughed uproariously, their harsh voices echoing in the nave as hymns once had. Then they threw down their weapons and swarmed Sanglant. Because they were smarter than the dogs and stronger than he was, they pinned him finally, though he did some damage to them before he went down.

They fixed the iron collar around his neck, dragged him along the nave, and fettered him by a long chain to the Hearth, so massive and heavy an altar that though he strained he could not move it. The dogs loped over to him. A few worried at his feet but in a curious way, not precisely hostile. One bit at him, and he slapped it hard across the muzzle. It whined and backed away, and it was at once jumped by another; they fought for a moment until one turned its throat up to the victor.

"Stop!" snapped Sanglant, and there was, this time, no killing.

The strange old Eika man was chanting in a soft voice, hunkered down and rocking back and forth on his heels. He had a little leather cup and he shook it and rolled white objects out: dice or bones. Then he passed a hand over these objects, studied them, chanted again, and scooped them up. The cup he tucked away into the pouch he wore at his belt. A small wooden chest sat beside his feet.

More Eika swarmed into the cathedral, and they began dragging corpses down into the crypt. Others carried a great throne carved out of a single piece of wood. The huge chair was painted gold and red and black and ornamented with cunning interlock, dogs and dragons biting each other, mouths to tails, in endless circles. They set this chair beside the Hearth, in mockery of the biscop's seat.

On this throne Bloodheart sat and he surveyed his new domain with satisfaction. Possessively, he rubbed the gold torque on his arm. Sanglant could not help himself: He reached up and touched the iron collar that now circled his neck where once he had worn gold.

The movement drew Bloodheart's eye. He learned toward Sanglant—but not too close. No closer, really, than he would have gotten to his own dogs.

"Why are you still alive," Bloodheart asked, "when all the others are dead?"

"Let me fight," said Sanglant, and suddenly feared he sounded like he was pleading. Ai, Lady, he did not want to die such a dishonorable death. He would not have wished this on his worst enemy, to die like a dog, among the dogs. "Give me an honorable death,

Bloodheart. Let your boldest warrior choose weapons and we will have it out, he and I."

"Nay, nay." Bloodheart bared his teeth in a grin. Jewels glinted, a rich treasure studding his teeth. "Am I not king among the Eika of the western shore? Have I not fought down all the other tribes until they all bared their throats before me? Do I not boast a king's son in my pack of dogs?" He laughed, pleased with his triumph. "I think not, my prince. You are the prize in my pack, a fine lord with his handsome retinue. For my dogs are like to the kingdom of Wendar, are they not? Led by *you*." His grin turned into a snarl. "Lead them for as long as you can. For you will weaken, and when you do, they will kill you."

Beyond, the Eika methodically looted the corpses before they dragged them into the crypt. One, rifling the Eagle's body, ripped his Eagle's badge from his cloak and tossed it. It landed at the feet of Bloodheart, who picked it up, bit it, and spat.

"Brass! Pah!" He tossed it down and Sanglant swatted dogs aside and grabbed it up from the floor. But that turmoil set the dogs to snapping and snarling again. He made good use of the badge; it had a clean, rounded edge and was good for jabbing. The dogs backed off and settled down again. One of the big ones growled at him, but he made a sharp gesture, and it lifted its head to expose its throat to him in submission.

He wiped hair from his lips, trying to clean the horrible taste out of his mouth. His left hand throbbed. Blood leaked, slowed, stopped—as had the gash on his head, which had already stopped bleeding. That was the secret of his mother's geas, of course, the one she had set on him when he was an infant, the day she vanished from human lands. That was what her blood had given him: keen hearing and unnatural powers of healing.

An Eika grabbed the dead Eagle by the heels and dragged the body away toward the crypt. Sanglant pressed the Eagle's badge against his cheek.

He was hit so hard by the memory of the young Eagle—*Liath*—touching him on his cheek in the silence and intimacy of the crypt that he was dizzy for a moment. The dogs, alert to any least weakness, stirred and growled. He tensed; they quieted.

By the Lady, he would not, he must not, let Bloodheart win. This at least he could believe, that Liath was still alive, for the last report he had been given before he and his Dragons were utterly over-whelmed was that the children of Gent had been led to safety.

"You are speechless, Prince," said Bloodheart. "Are you half dog already? Have you lost the power to talk?"

"I am like you, Bloodheart," he said, his voice hoarse; but his voice always was hoarse now, for he had survived worse injuries than these. The iron collar, and his chains, weighed heavily on his neck. "My heart rests not within me but with another, and she is far away from here. That is why you will never defeat me."

But the dogs, ever watchful, growled softly. They were willing to wait.

APPENDIX

The Months of the Year:
Yanu
Avril
Sormas
Quadrii
Cintre
Aogoste
Setentre
Octumbre
Novarian
Decial
Askulavre
Fevrua

The Days of the Week:
Mansday
Secunday
Ladysday
Sonsday
Jedday
Lordsday
Hefensday

The Canonical Hours:
Vigils (circa 3:00 a.m.)
Lauds (first light)
Prime (sunrise)
Terce (3rd hour, circa 9:00 a.m.)
Sext (6th hour, circa noon)
Nones (9th hour, circa 3:00 p.m.)
Vespers (evening song)
Compline (sunset)

The Houses of Night (the zodiac):
the Falcon
the Child
the Sisters
the Hound
the Lion
the Dragon
the Scales
the Serpent
the Archer
the Unicorn
the Healer
the Penitent

THE GREAT PRINCES OF THE REALM OF WENDAR AND VARRE:

Dukes of Wendar:
Saony
Fesse
Avaria

Dukes of Varre:
Arconia
Varingia
Wayland

Margraves of the Eastern Territories:
the March of the Villams
Olsatia and Austra
Westfall
Eastfall